CHRONICLES OF THE FALLEN

To Katelyn Goertzen
Ayer Lancaster
7|09|2012

CHRONICLES OF THE FALLEN

Rebellion

AYA LANCASTER

authorHOUSE®

AuthorHouse™
1663 Liberty Drive
Bloomington, IN 47403
www.authorhouse.com
Phone: 1-800-839-8640

Published by AuthorHouse   03/29/2012

ISBN: 978-1-4567-7949-8 (sc)
ISBN: 978-1-4567-7948-1 (e)

"That's the thing about fate. You can't do anything to stop it. If you try, it will alter the paths to the future, the ones Rave's foreseen. These paths must unfold and join without fail. Disturb them even for a bit, and we all die for real. No coming back from hell."

Lenora

Acknowledgements

For my parents, who supported me with their hearts, thoughts, and prayers. I can't thank the two of you enough.

For my brothers, Kamil, whose insights on the demonic world were the best I could hope for, and Alam, who was always listening to my story. Thanks a lot, you guys.

For my sisters-in-law, Tami and Miranti, I'm so thrilled to hear your opinions and laughs. Have fun with the babies, Sorayya and Aliyaa.

For my dearest uncles and aunties, my cousins, Ellen, Tya, Gita, Turzi, Bowo, Gani, Adit, and the rest of my really big family, I'm absolutely glad to have you all by my side with your criticisms, frowns, laughs, giggles, and so much more.

For my best friends from college, Fendy Safitri, who was kind enough to design the cover for this book, and Nora Natalia, who was always with us, thank you both for being around me with spirit and laughs. Your opinions meant so much to me. Also, lots of thanks to Fendy's mother and her sisters, Ira and Wendy. You always made me feel at home whenever I came over, and you're the best cooks I've ever met. Thank you for the enthusiasm you showed about this book. I'm so grateful to have known you all. These last few years have been so great. I hope we can have a lot more to come.

For Miss Lilia, who was always there for me whenever I needed her in the more than three years we've known each other, your opinions, advice, jokes, and insights on 'the other world' department are the best companions I've ever had. Not to mention your information about the others too.

For my teachers, I'm forever grateful, for without them, I wouldn't have the courage to follow my heart and make the decisions that led to where I am now. Thank you.

For my old friends from sixth grade, Yasha guys and many others from eighth to ninth grade who knew about the very first idea for this book, added a few bases, and laughed about it together, thanks a lot. I won't forget all the crazy things we did.

For my friends Wikan, Dhiany, Gena, Vita, Wanda, Iko, Donny, Meita, Astrid, Aulia, and all the others who first suggested finishing these chronicles and publishing them, thank you so much for your full faith in me and for everything we've shared. I hope we can get together a lot more often.

For Jerzy Rendon, my first contact at AuthorHouse, whose responses were so quick that I almost couldn't believe it, especially when I got her first call, thank you. It was a really big deal for me. For Jennifer Weideman, my coordinator, thank you so much for your guidance and patience. It meant so much. For Joven Morales, thank you for keep contacting me, it must have been quite a trouble to adjust the time to call me. For Jessie Klinger, and the Gambia design team, Rod Stark, my editor and the editorial department, this book wouldn't have been turned from mere fantasy to reality without your hard work. Thank you for everything.

Lastly, for the readers who are curious enough to read the first page and hopefully go through until the very last word, this book wouldn't mean anything without you.

You guys rock!

Prologue

He was engulfed in flames.

Floundering, his tormented screams echoed throughout the void. He caught glimpses of the lifeless sky around him as he fell onto the earth at blinding speed.

His black wings wrapped him, and his black robe whipped hard against his thick armour as he wound through the cold wind of the night. He couldn't risk damaging his wings by using them to alleviate himself. If he transformed them into their true form and it got burned by the holy flame, he would turn mortal.

And that was the last thing he wished for himself.

The ground swiftly grew closer to him. He began to draw out his powers to make sure he'd fall right where he intended, but the flame suddenly burst even bigger. He cried out and ceased his attempt. He had no choice but to place his entire being in the hands of hope.

To his surprise, his prayers were answered, though by whom he didn't want to know as he crashed into the cold, blue water of a massive lake somewhere at the feet of mountains.

The holy fire burning him slowly perished. He closed his eyes in tremendous relief as he held fast to a small pouch within his grasp. It contained the one item that saved his unholy life from being obliterated into nothing. It was only thing amongst the very few that possessed the ability to negate the flame's eternal nature. It prevented the holy fire from claiming his life, and his visage was spared from the irreversible damage it should have done.

The flame burned a quite significant part of his midnight blue armour along with his flesh. Raw pain gnawed him mercilessly from his right chest all the way to his wrist. Nevertheless, he was no longer on the verge of death.

The pain began to cease as his body started to heal itself, but it was too soon for him to let out a relieved breath, for he gazed upward and saw through the water that the heavens had sent forth another of their fierce punishments. A massive sphere of blazing holy flame descended from the heavens directly upon him.

Cursing inwardly, he willed himself ashore and ran for his life. He had managed to make a short distance when the sphere landed and set ablaze the entire lake, causing a violent gust of hot wind that sent him flying.

It was no longer than five seconds before the cold water completely vaporized, leaving nothing but vast wastelands.

The unholy landed hard and rolled a few feet away. Sharp pebbles tore his skin and his blackened wound, but he didn't dare to seize the chance to stop even for a second.

He sprang to his feet and began to run. As he sprinted, he held out his hand with the pouch resting on his palm. He conjured an image of the one imprisoned deep within the earth, with whom he'd struck a bargain before he began his deadly mission.

He managed to complete his task, but unbeknownst to his higher Echelons from whom he received his mission, he did something else. Both deeds had caused all of Heaven to unleash their wrath, and now he ran with all his might to avoid it.

As he mentally hurled curses to his Echelons and all of Heaven, he felt a surge of power course through his body, sending the charred pouch to the one he intended.

He ran deeper into the woods as fast as his feet could take him. After a while, he finally stopped under a big oak tree and sought to take a bit of rest to let his wound heal.

Lifting his gaze upward, worry stretched on every inch of his ruggedly chiselled face. He exhaled. "The fire fest stopped," he said, with a frown directed to the sky.

Heaven never ceased when they seek to deliver punishment, why had they stopped now?

"Either they didn't see me get out of the damn lake or they're planning something else," he mused, a bit suspicious, but he decided to let it go, for he had other priorities. "At least, the thing's safe, and now I gotta meet him. *He* needs to know this," he muttered to himself as he panted.

He glanced around, and a hint of smile played on the curve of his lips as his mind went to the one unholy other than himself. One who usually occupied this part of the forest, but currently not present–the she-devil he secretly held dear in his heart.

After nearly being burned to death, he'd made up his mind. He'd find her and tell her what he needed to say. Unfortunately, his train of thought was ended abruptly by a lethal presence that manifested near him.

Turning to his left, he saw the true bringer of death smiled evilly at him.

He blanched at the sight that screamed terror. He'd predicted that this particular being would try to corner him since thousands of years ago, but he still didn't like the prospect of facing him, especially when he had just decided on the very thing that mattered to him more than his own life.

What was worse, this being could easily overpower him in his prime. There was no telling what he could do to him now that he was severely wounded.

"My Lord," he greeted him as he straightened himself, all the while trying to suppress the lump of fear before it surfaced under the cold gaze of the unholiest of them all.

Most revered him as the Morningstar, while others called him the Son of Dawn–Lucifer.

"Well, Ezryan, still alive, I see," The Devil Lord said as he eyed Ezryan from head to toe, as if sizing him up. "Although just about." His voice turned icy cold, making the wounded devil triple his caution.

"My Lord, please forgive my insolence. I'm honoured that you came all the way out here," Ezryan said, keeping his voice calm, "but may I inquire as to why you would endanger yourself by doing so, especially with all Heaven after my life?"

Lucifer maintained his cold gaze without so much as an answer. Instead of saying a word, a huge trident forged of black steel and reeked with demonic essence materialized with its base planted on the ground next to him.

Ezryan mentally rolled his eyes. *"No wonder those glowed-ass punks stopped. I should've known the reason wouldn't be because they wanted to be the most generous people of the friggin' year,"* he thought bitterly as he readied himself.

Lucifer grasped the trident and levelled the sharp tip at him. "People up there won't do anything since they will see what I'm about to do. It's not that I'm doing them a favour, because that would be revolting, but, alas, your time to leave this living realm has come. And I have to say, I shall deliver your demise with relish." His beautiful face was marred by a twisted, sickening smile in anticipation.

Ezryan swallowed hard as a dreadful thought clenched his chest.

Did his master realize what he did? There was no doubt that his master knew what he'd done that day, but was that the sole reason he cornered him now?

Grinding his teeth, Ezryan kept his stoic face. "My Lord, what exactly have I done?"

His master spat. "You don't possibly think I would not notice who denied me my prey, now do you? Please do not insult me, Commander."

Ezryan gulped. *"He knew all right, but it looks like he doesn't know what I just did."*

With his hand upon his wound, Ezryan's features hardened. "I have no say then, for it is clear to me that you have acknowledged the truth," he admitted, realizing that it was futile to deny his master's accusation. "Truth is, I've been waiting for you to come and finish me off," he said, feigning surrender but with different thought in his mind. *"But if you think I'm gonna let you kill me, you're dead wrong. Not a chance, jerkass. Not before I do what matters most."*

Lucifer shot him a glare full of the promise of death. "Showing your true colours with that impudent manner of talking? No matter, but really though, I would go as far as to say that I'd never have guessed my own Hieldhar, commander of the First Legion, knew of their existence. And as you've surmised, I've been dying to kill you ever since. Your keeping the soldiers in line is the only thing that spares your life, but no more," he said with apparent disgust both in his voice and on his face.

A tic worked in Ezryan's jaw, both from the immense pain of his wounds and from the prospect of imminent death that stared straight at him. "I would never deny that I too am surprised to have known the despicable deeds you've done to your own soldiers, those who vowed to give their allegiance to you, those who lay their faith solely upon you. Instead of returning the favour, you slowly bring true death to our door and sacrifice every soul you deem would threaten your throne."

"Silence!" Lucifer's retort echoed. Without warning, he threw the trident straight at the commander.

Instincts kicking in, Ezryan manifested a sword and grasped it with his uninjured left hand. He deflected the trident, but the wounds had affected even his reflexes, for he was unable to intercept his master's next move.

As he tossed the trident away, another one materialized in Lucifer's grasp. He charged towards Ezryan and stabbed him. The trident went through the blackened flesh of the devil's right chest, pinning him to the tree.

Ezryan gasped as excruciating agony choked him. His sword fell and disappeared. He felt the cold hand of Death slowly grasping him, followed by flashes of every face of his companions. And the last was that of the she-devil who had claimed his heart.

Seeing her image, new-found courage and strength burst through him. He forced himself to level a grudging stare at Lucifer.

Lucifer motioned to Ezryan's ear. "Before you die, there's another thing I want you to know, Hieldhar," he said evilly.

In spite of the bile that nearly strangled him at the malice in his master's voice, the devil still glared at his master. It was then that the Devil Lord whispered something that made the blood leave his beating core–his worst nightmare.

He shook his head frantically. "No! Don't! You can't!" he bellowed to Lucifer, who ignored him and stepped back with a malevolent smile on his face.

In that single moment, the fear left in Ezryan shattered, leaving him raw with hatred. "Don't you fucking dare!" he roared. But he could do nothing to stop him.

Laughing at Ezryan's terrified gaze, Lucifer pulled a silver pendant from under his black robes, a triangle-shaped pendant with a single grey eye eerily fixed on the devil before him. It was his ultimate weapon. Rygavon, the Dark Light that would banish everything in its path.

At the sight of the seemingly harmless pendant which housed horrible powers, Ezryan knew there was no chance for him to remain alive if he stayed here any longer–not when his master was all out to kill him.

He braced himself for the only chance he had to save his life, but he needed to wait until the moment was ripe, for he wouldn't–*couldn't*–risk allowing his master to pursue him.

"Farewell, Commander," Lucifer said idly as he raised the pendant as it began emitting pitch-black light. In an instant, all hell broke loose. Black flame exploded throughout the forest and burned everything that stood in its way. The commander raised his left hand and manifested a shield as he discreetly gathered his powers, but it took only moments before his shield started to break under the merciless wrath of the Dark Light.

As his shield began to falter, he could hear his master laugh at him in cruel derision. "Just give in, Hieldhar. It's no use to fight the inevitable," the Devil Lord taunted. "And then I will make my words true after I'm done with you," he added with mocking laugh.

The devil had to ground his teeth to keep his focus from splitting as the Dark Light slowly engulfed him. He knew he had no other choice but to leave. He needed to, both in order to survive and to protect his companions. Above all, to protect *her*.

He had to make the Devil Lord who was killing him think that she knew nothing of his deeds, that she was oblivious to what he'd done two hundred years ago and the existence of his secret haven.

The only thing that still left him uncertain was the promise his master had just now whispered to him. Would he actually do it?

Mentally shaking his head in denial, he continued to maintain his shield, but it was only a matter of moments before he was completely swallowed. Right before his shield shattered, he summoned the powers at his disposal and willed himself to where his other companions resided, knowing the Dark Light would eradicate every trail of him leaving, but he wasn't fast enough.

The Dark Light managed to savagely burn his entire right side, making the burn wounds he got from the Heavenly Flame worse. Unimaginable pain tore through him as he began to fade. He screamed until his throat was torn and bleeding. He fought to stay conscious, but his wounds were far too severe. Still, he managed to keep his eyes open, for all that agony biting his body paled in comparison to the deep sorrow and regret that swelled within him.

"I am not gonna die! Not before I tell her!"

He roared that thought in his mind as he entered the portal leading to his destination. The threshold closed itself behind him, and what little heat the Dark Light emanated immediately ceased.

Falling face down on the grass, the familiar scent of his haven welcomed him, along with glints of moonlight that his eyes captured as a male and a female materialized somewhere near him.

"Brother!" The male knelt next to him, and he felt the soft touch of a pair of dainty hands that belonged to the female. "His wounds are too severe. He won't be able to survive them," she said with a sad voice.

The commander barely heard the male's response to the female. He didn't even have the strength to gaze upon them. His only thought was fixed on someone other than the two, the one he just left behind for who knew how long. That was, if he managed to stay alive.

"No! I will survive! No matter what . . . they have to know what's coming . . . she has to know! I have to protect her!"

His mind conjured one memory from the faraway past in his attempt to stay conscious, but even that was washed away as the pain brought him down slowly like poison, leaving only a distant thought.

"From that day forth, I vowed to protect her . . . she's the only one . . . she always has been . . ."

But all that thought had to perish in the end, for he finally lapsed into the cold darkness of death. With one last breath, he closed his sapphire eyes and whispered her name as if it were his lifeline. "Yve."

Chapter 1

Seven hundred years later...

I found myself gazing upon vast wastelands with no signs of life for as far as my eyes could see and my ears could hear.

The sun was astoundingly near with mesmerizing, yet threatening flame that steadily burst forth without mercy.

I was perplexed at the sight. "Where exactly am I?" I directed the question to myself or whoever had the knowledge I sought.

As if whoever had control of this bizarre situation wanted to confuse me further, the lifeless earth under my feet began to quake violently. I planted my heels as I once again observed the barren surface of the land.

It was then I saw multiple figures jutting out of the ground not far from where I stood.

Upon seeing this astonishing, yet somewhat horrifying scene, a surge of fear I'd never known coursed through me with terrorizing speed, driving my agitation out of my mind until it was no more.

The quake ceased abruptly, and the newcomers too had come to a halt. An unknown force was radiating from them, calling out to me to come closer.

I was about to succumb to its tantalizing voice, when a faint whisper warned me of terrible danger. The force overpowered the fading whisper, and my feet started to carry me forward without even realizing what I was doing. A dread that I couldn't identify voiced their plea throughout my soul.

They begged me to stop, but with each step I took, their plea was to no avail.

When I reached them, a lump of terror laden with amazement rendered me breathless as I gazed upon the sight.

Each of them was bound to a huge black wooden cross. They were battered, and they writhed in excruciating pain. My unholy self *should have rejoiced at the violence, yet for many reasons I couldn't comprehend, potent despair began to devour me as I saw that nails locked their arms and ankles to the cross, combined with countless deep, brutally jagged wounds that scarred their flesh.*

"Who are they? Who did this to them?" I let slip those thoughts as I attempted to keep the crushing, unfathomable despair at bay.

Suppressing the bile that was rising to my throat, I tried to further scrutinize them out of fear that I would find the familiar faces of my companions under their gruesomely deformed faces. I soon realized I was at a loss, for not only were they no companions of mine, they were, to my utter disbelief, the revolting, two-legged animals known as humans.

Every single one of them was just a mere human on the brink of death.

Yet, for some reason I couldn't understand, in the back of my mind a peculiar recognition of their bloodied visages consumed me.

"Why do I feel like I'm familiar with the likes of them?" The question echoed within me, along with humiliation mingled with bafflement.

I searched my mind for the slightest hint to help me better understand the situation. "Who tortured them? Why were they victimized in the first place? And why, for reasons which certainly did not involve my best interest, was I cornered by these repulsive feelings towards humans?" I inquired over and over.

Without warning, all of them simultaneously burst into flames.

My core was dangerously close to ceasing in utter disbelief, which was defeated by an incredibly profound guilt and a bottomless well of overwhelming grief. My feet could support me no more, and I dropped to my knees. I wept tears of blood and screamed in helplessness and sorrow far more torturous than anything imaginable.

I jolted awake as I let out a loud gasp.

Beads of sweat trailed down my temple as I struggled to steady my breath. Fighting the shivers as I observed my surroundings, I soon came to realize that I was high above the clouds and wrapped within my black wings.

I was still floating at the spot where I usually slept for the last seven hundred years. I winced as I released a breath of relief and ran one hand over my temple. In growing agitation, I raked my long, black hair with one hand. Yet again I awoke and got bombarded by frustration caused by my sheer cluelessness.

It had been happening for the last three centuries. Whenever I slept under the cover of my black wings amongst the dark velvet sky, I'd see these incredibly preposterous nightmares.

Not to mention they were seriously dull.

I didn't even know why I kept experiencing these dreams, because it sure as hell was not my nature. Seers might have dreams, not a soldier like me. For who-knew-what reasons, inconceivable guilt burned me from the inside out each and every time I had these dreams.

Yeah, like I didn't have enough fire all around me back in the Aryad . . .

The worst part of it was the object of my nonsensical guilt. They were the disgusting, easily manipulated, two-legged animals packed with traits that belonged to their lack of knowledge, the infamous seven (supposed) sins–God's favourite creatures: the humans. If any lesser soldiers or the Echelons were to hear about this, I would be totally humiliated. I wouldn't be able to get my hands on my enemies, I couldn't get involved with our wars any more, or worse, I'd be ditched just like an unworthy third-class devil.

Thinking of confiding this weird problem to somebody, my thoughts drifted to my sister, Vrathien, the Master of War. She was the only one who knew about it.

I rubbed my temple in frustration as my thought went back to my stupid problem. Damn, at times like these, I really wished Ry was still around to annoy me or something. Well, definitely something.

He went by the name of Ezryan. He was the thirteenth Hieldhar of the First Legion where Vrae and I belonged, a total bad-ass when it came to violence, massacre, and chaos. Not to mention that in all his glory and with the formidable aura radiating through his wickedly delectable features, he was definitely the stuff of legends. Not that I would ever spill this thought to any soul in existence.

Vrae and I were two of the very few soldiers he had trusted most back in the day, but unfortunately, when the Heavenly Flame obliterated his ass, which was the finest I'd ever seen and I'd seen much, I was assigned to do a job alone . . . as usual.

At the forever-emerging thought of his death, I felt a familiar wave of pain strike me hard in the gut.

I was told that he was killed when he was ordered to overhear upstairs' secret, one the Echelons said would help us gain the upper hand for millennia of human existence. He was the one assigned to the job, not the ordinary Alvadors, because of the importance of the secret, but since he failed, no one would ever know what it was.

If he was still alive and kicking, would he jest and mock me for having those stupid nightmares? Or he would he not do anything because he didn't have a damn clue like me?

My thoughts then drifted to the time when he was still alive. As the commander, he usually had his gig alone, much like me. But sometimes, he went along with me, my sister, and other comrades of ours. We would jump into human wars and make them a whole lot gory as we revelled in the bloodbath of mass slaughter.

We really had a good time whenever we were at it. We'd throw mockeries at Azrael, the Angel of Death himself, every time we ran into the guy. And he was, by far, the only one who'd deliver a strange retort in our direction, instead of exploding his temper like a balloon pinched with a needle. Well, his reaper underlings weren't as fun as he was, though, since the only thing they had was a ghastly appearance like that of a corpse, and they all had no kind of emotion, one package deal with their job description as the reapers. They picked souls of the dead, and there was no talking along the way. Sometimes, it kinda made me want to slap one of them in face just to see their reaction.

Azrael was one of the few of the fluff-ass kind that never took a side. That was one of the few things I ever liked about any of them. They always spat at us with a full display of disdain, when they didn't even have the juice required to scratch me.

Well, it was time to leave those thoughts aside. It was still dark, and I was high in the sky, hanging around like a boring human with absolutely nothing to do. Not that humans flew, but what-the-hell-ever!

Those angels, bright-for-nothing God's creation, didn't come down here for some time either. Not that I wanted to pick a fight. It would be stupid and wouldn't do me any good, but sometimes boredom did almost kill me. It made me eager to take some mundane lives.

Up to this point, there was no ambush as far as I could tell. There was definitely none directed at me, but I didn't know how it was with my other comrades.

Heaving a long breath, I decided that nothing big was going down, either from upstairs or the middle. I hadn't seen Vrae for weeks either. It'd be fun if I ran into her and made some killings. However, far from finding any angel's life to take, I couldn't even track her whereabouts.

Abruptly, my senses began to kick me back from my long contemplation as I realized something was wrong. You see, being a soldier had many perks that I certainly wouldn't mind to take on any day, except for this one–being followed by three parts of a golem whose purpose was to keep a close eye on us. We all had one designated golem whose parts were on our tail.

And note the key word "close". Each and every one of them *was*, in fact, a freakish, bulging, mind-boggling, *eye*. They were parts of a magically constructed five-eyed golem, infused with bits of *our* life force.

Wait, made that *six*.

The fourth, fifth, and sixth, however, weren't part of the peeping group in the field. The fourth and fifth were placed in the Aryad. They were set to tail us whenever we went inside. As for the last one, it was connected to the other five and stored whatever they'd seen, in case the soldiers suddenly died or crossed the line. Not that it would be of any help in the latter matter, since those who'd determined to do so, would either "trick" those things or, if they had balls enough, destroy them.

And there was this: to ensure those things served their purpose to spy on us and annoy us, each one was provided with a pair of wings like those of a bat. Imagine my unrelenting desire to stomp on all of them whenever I heard the constant flapping of their wings . . . which would mean each and every second I spent not sleeping.

Most of the time, I could force myself to tolerate the not-so-far distance at which they placed themselves, but today, I noticed, they were floating much closer than they should be.

With my heightened hearing, which was so-not-helpful in times like these, combined with them getting nearer, things definitely didn't get anywhere near better in the "ignoring boredom" department.

Cursing inwardly at the one responsible for controlling these things, I struggled to rein myself in before I accidentally blasted them in mounting anger. It was then that an idea popped in my mind.

I should go pay the guy a little visit which might involve violence.

Deciding that was the better thing to do, I went through the clouds, which were freezing like –well, I was gonna say hell, but that was ridiculous as it was.

I flew past endless forests below, all the while pondering how unusually quiet the sea of green trees were. Moments later, I stopped above the Croatoan woods. This place was named after one of Pestilence's favourite entourage, who once marked the area as his domain. I didn't know why, but he was determined to turn the humans who set foot here rabid and drive them into frenzy. Unfortunately for him, no living human got this close to the edge of the earth.

At least not yet.

Now the guy, just like his boss who went riding with his three siblings to who-knew-where, had been MIA. Or maybe he was out there spreading his germ warfare. Who knew?

I just hoped he wasn't around the place I had to go to, because it would be hell to get in touch with him. Me and contagious people–well, it was definitely a disgusting thought. Not that they'd have any effect on me, but still, it was disgusting.

Anyway, deep within the thick, green canopy of this forest, there was one of our many gates to go downstairs.

Humans had to go up first, to be *judged* before going south. So much privilege to be animals, although most of them ended up down there in the end–for lower grades too. Sometimes, I couldn't help laughing whenever I thought about them. Everyone from upstairs always told those vermin we were evil.

Sure, we *were* evil, but most of the time all we did was just a little bit of whispering here and enticing the right people there as we were supposed to according to the red tape set on us. But guess what? They'd often carry out the rest of the job far beyond our expectations. Talk about asinine!

And *we* were the ones who always got the credit for what *they* did. I really couldn't understand whose logic was at work here.

Proceeding towards the heart of the forest, I then halted as I sensed a familiar tingling down my spine, indicating that I'd found what I was looking for–a protective shield that was erected around the gate.

I looked around to make sure no one was on my tail–well, at least no one that was attacking. After I was certain nothing was out of the ordinary aside from those too-damn-close mongrels, I dove straight into the shield.

I landed and my wings turned into a black silk robe that wrapped across my shoulder and fell all the way to my ankle. My gaze fell on the two devils standing in front of a fairly massive boulder covering the entrance: Zoran and Gevirash, guardians of this place. Both of them carried a spear and wore brown soil-coloured robes that covered dark red armour with a gate crossed with spears embedded on their left chest. It was the emblem of Valthors, Guardian of Hell Gate. As guardians, each of them possessed deadly powers and could be more lethal than a battalion of soldiers.

But that wasn't what I sensed from them right now.

Zoran, with his light grey eyes encircled with red and shoulder-length dark brown hair pulled into a ponytail, always tried to joke and often failed miserably, but at least he still could lighten the air no matter how tense the situation.

Gevirash, on the other hand, was a bit more serious than his partner, but with the same amount of stupidity nonetheless. His eerie red eyes could give people goose bumps just by looking at them, and his long wavy brown hair fell freely just over his shoulders.

I sauntered towards them, and Zoran waved at me in greeting. "Hi Yve, you got a call?"

"Nope, just want to visit you guys," I said with a nod.

Both of them stared blankly, making me let loose a grin. "Nah, I wanna stop by Amon's."

Gevirash feigned a shocked look. "Having an initiative mood swing? It's not like you to go in without being summoned first. What's up? You slaughtered somebody by mistake and wanna clean it up before the Echelons come banging on your door?" He grinned.

I screwed up my face at him when he mentioned the Echelons. Those would be the guys whom I called the revolting bunch. "That's very funny, G. Though as appealing as it sounds, why in the hell would I do that? I'm happy enough with the humans I get to play with, and there are plenty of them. Besides, with Amon's stupid toys on my tail, obviously I'm so not in the mood to do things I'm not supposed to."

Stretching out, I then stared at them both. "Actually, I'm here to pay him a visit, because, well, perhaps you should sense it for yourself," I said, and I tilted my head upward.

Their always-tuned-to-the-ether senses caught my meaning and grimaced in horror.

I crossed my arms in vexation. "See? Here I am trapped in the boredomland and *he* decided to put those things a whole lot closer!" I snapped my fingers, pointing at the eyes floating above us. "I swear if some upstairs' fluffs decide to pick a fight, they'll be dead for bugging me when I'm in a really *bad* mood," I exclaimed in anger.

Zoran raised his hands. "Whoa, whoa, hold it over there, lady. We don't want any fight here; we're just here to guard this Gate, like we always do."

"And I know what you're saying. We're lucky enough not having those since we won't be going anywhere. Hell, having those around me definitely would piss me off too." Gevirash inclined his head.

"Thanks for being sympathetic," I yawned. "And who said I wanna pick up a fight with you two? Then again, maybe I'll just borrow your spear in case some light-assed bastard comes down. It might be real fun if I get to play poke-the-nose with theirs." I pointed heavenward.

Zoran snorted. "Talking about poking noses, we heard there were twenty of those guys ambushed you few weeks ago and you did more than just poking, you *kicked* their asses. You sure are scary, Yve." He laughed good-naturedly.

My lips curved in a sadistic smile as I recalled the battle with relish. "Hell yeah, those twenty good-for-nothing garbage were down in no time. Hell, they didn't even put a scratch on my hair, especially with the red tape regarding *their* asses. That's why I've been bored almost to death if I were to put it. By the way, before I go in and start ransacking his den, have you two heard anything?" I asked them in an almost hopeful tone.

Zoran grimaced at my threat, but his partner paid no heed. "Heard about what? Really, Yve, you can fly here and there, having fun with that trash, while both of us are stuck down here." Gevirash broke to a yawn as well and poked the ground with his spear.

My gaze fell to where his spear pointed, and I saw scrambles of obscene symbols, mockeries, footprints, and traces of the ground being dug with the tip of the spear. Damn, they *were* bored to hell . . .

"Yeah, pretty much for being the honourable guardians of this Gate. And what are you rambling about? Nothing's coming down here lately, like you said. What, are you waiting for something or did you hear words that something might happen? Don't tell me the reason for this whole rambling of yours is really boredom." Zoran started to inspect the surroundings, as if expecting myriads of angels would jump at us from the woods.

"Too damn good to be true, my friend," I mused.

I raised a brow at Zoran's useless action scanning the woods and cast an insulted look at him. "Dude, you think I'm a no-brainer? No one's tailing me here like usual, well, no one that's killing anyway, and yes, like I said, I'm bored to death."

They both stared at me, as if saying *"You wanna talk to us about boredom? Seriously?"*

Struggling to force myself not to laugh considering the fact that they *did* have far too many experience in the "boredom" department, I cleared my throat. "All I'm saying is just that I don't like this irritating situation. Either it turns out to be a quiet day before the storm hits us all–this stupid silence–or it's just another timeout before some fun pops up again. Hell, I don't know. Maybe I'll just have a little chat with you two and prolong Amon's leisure time before he gets the inevitable kick in the ass. How's that sound guys?" I grinned.

They looked at each other and then replied my words with a big smile on their faces. I did chat with them as I said I would. Apparently, they only heard minor things from the very few regular passers. Well, you couldn't expect more from people that were going straight to the basement, no matter what their business was. Another reason was that this Gate wasn't the one most people would use.

I didn't come here on purpose in the first place. It just happened to be the closest Gate to where I slept, and the guards here were the only ones who didn't have the words "Hello, I'm a statue and I'm boring" branded on their foreheads.

Exhaling in aggravation, I joined my hands behind my head. "Really though, I'm surprised none of the shiny bunch comes down here to spread their holy crap all over the place. Hell, I could use their fluff to make nice chicken wings," I snapped.

Before either of them responded, I suddenly sensed someone was coming, followed by the sound of clapping wings. We lifted our gaze up just in time to see Vrae landing before us.

"Talk about wings," I muttered, and the two snorted.

She folded her wings around her body as I did; only they turned into blood-red robes. She strode towards us. "Yve," she called as she nodded her greeting at both guards who returned it with their own.

"Hey, it's a damn good time for you to show up. Is something up?" I asked her.

Before she could answer, she was interrupted with a groan coming from Zoran. "Gee, and here I thought the two of us had lessened your irritating situations a bit. That's an insult you know." He screwed his face as if I really had insulted him.

I rolled my eyes at him. "Please, you're breaking my heart. I'm just asking her." I turned from him and faced Vrae again. "Is there anything?"

She cleared her throat. "Don't get your hopes too high 'cause I don't think anything big's going down. I only heard some rumours. Some say there will be a minor ambush from upstairs' meddling imbeciles as usual, while the others saying a big time war's gonna start, either between those primates or between us and vermin from up there. Hell, beats me. I have no freakin' clue. I don't even know which one's reliable. And there's this one saying there are MIAs, but he's a little vague on who they are and from what rank."

I gave her a blank look at that.

"I'm not saying we ought to check though. The others might already be on it," she said rather quickly.

I averted my gaze elsewhere and absently frowned as a train of thoughts went through my mind. There were MIAs? I was sure as hell hadn't heard of *that* one.

"What is it? You think we got to check it out?" she asked, pulling me from my deep thoughts.

I shrugged. "I don't know. Don't jump to conclusions yet. You've been hearing these words for how long?" I crossed my arms over my chest.

"It's been for a couple of weeks now. Why?" She inclined her head, and her waist-length hair fell over her shoulders.

"For a couple of weeks, huh?" I left her hanging there and immediately fell into deep thought.

After a while, I decided it might be better to check it out after all, well, to kill off bits of the boredom that was biting at me. "Yeah, I think we gotta go and see what's what. Besides, this bothersome silence is really pissing me off. Anyway, it could be anything; it could also be bull crap. Who knows? Well, maybe Amon does, and talking about him, I just remember I need to have a word with him," I said with an evil smile curved my lips to tell her my point, noting that her surveillance party also put themselves a helluva lot closer.

After she saw my face when I said it, her eyes suddenly gleamed in understanding. "Oh, yeah, you remind me there. I think I also gonna have a word with him–perhaps, more than a word." We gave each other a wicked smile as if we'd offed the guy.

"Oh, great, just leave us here, again, thank you very much you two." Gevirash's mouth formed a pout. But then he flashed us a wide grin. "Easy ladies, I'm kidding. I know you gotta check this out, and we can't possibly go anywhere."

I snickered. "That's right, Gev. You know your job and so does Zoran. I'll stop by again later when we're out. And I thought I did tell you that my intention was only to buy Amon a bit more time?"

"Speaking of Amon, you're not really gonna kill him, now are you?" He continued with a made-up frightened look on his face.

I shrugged. "I don't know. After having a little word with him, we just might," I replied with an upset look, but then I saw them blanch instantly when they heard me.

Rolling my eyes at their gullibility, I then gave them a "duh" stare. "It's a joke, guys, a joke. J-o-k-e. Regardless how irritating he can be, even I realize he's the only master of golem sorcery we have," I said lazily as I waved up and down. *"For now,"* I thought in wicked delight, but I didn't say it in case it made them go antsy on me.

Vrae stifled a laugh. "Gee, guys, I didn't know you liked him that much," she inserted, and they gave her a you-know-why-but-whatever look.

"At any rate, thanks for putting an end to my annoyingly tedious hours. If there's anything, I'll tell you right away. How's that sound?" I ended up giving them that promise, taking into consideration them talking with me minutes ago.

The two of them exchanged a droll stare and then turned to me and Vrae with a big smile on their faces. "That's a promise, don't forget. We wanna be the ones getting the latest news. That'll be a refreshing change. Anyway, you two will get the chance to relax for a minute once you're inside since they will be back to their owners. The other two wouldn't be able to follow you once you enter the Lasinth," Zoran said, with that wide smile still hanging on his face.

I scoffed. "Yeah, right. At least they won't be this annoying." Even though they were able to follow us everywhere else, they couldn't get into a certain area like Amon's–talk about a smart mistake! "Well, luckily, nothing's gonna piss me off any more today. Then the deal's a deal."

"Give our regards to him, would ya?" Gevirash added.

"Will do, see you boys later." Vrae and I said our goodbyes to those guards and walked past them towards the huge boulder. We went through it and felt something like thin silk brushing us. We appeared on the other side of the Gate, which was deep within the earth. The first thing we saw, as it should be, was that we were standing on the edge of a cliff, about a thousand feet above a path made of soil and rock which led to many tunnels and holes. Magma calmly gulped around them, constantly flowing throughout the earth.

Flames burst in every corner, and the agonized screams of many humans faintly echoed somewhere far away. Their voices sounded almost like dying whispers from the distance.

Well, no surprise there, because the punishment blocks were quite far from here, but that wasn't where the both of us were headed.

We jumped down and landed smoothly on the hard soil. As I had surmised earlier, familiar flappings, though distant and subtle, could be heard immediately as we strolled down the straight path in the middle, ignoring many forks splitting from the road, and in that time we traded all information we'd obtained. We also discussed the rumours she had heard when the two of us didn't see each other.

Truth be told, in contrast to what the Echelons always did with me, they always assigned her to do her job in groups. So when she didn't get to go with me, she'd be with the others, whereas I mostly got to do my job alone.

Besides, I often did things better that way. That didn't mean I was restrained from having partners though, which was why every now and then she or the others would go with me to wreak as much havoc as we could. These past weeks, however, I hadn't got to meet anyone who was resourceful enough to know even a little update.

And I wouldn't possibly ask Amon through his stupid toys.

Indeed, it was true that among the five that were set to tail us, there were two whose purpose was to relay messages from the Head Intel himself to us and vice versa, aside from surveying us in the field. Each one was for inside and out of the Aryad. However, it wasn't as if it had the ability to talk by any means.

Well, if you could put mimicking Amon's voice and ours in an annoyingly-deep-and-made-you-wanna-puke kinda way under the category of talking, then yes, they all *had* the ability to talk. But the main reason why I so didn't wanna get anywhere close to those things was that I didn't wanna blow them to oblivion by mistake.

That would open a whole can of worms I really had no interest in.

After quite a long walk, we finally reached the deepest part of the area. Before us now stood a ten-foot high sturdy door with carvings and torches of blue flame attached to it. Behind this door was a long, massive hallway divided into several department areas. The hallway led all the way to Amon's den which located at the very end of it. We called this door "entrance to the Lasinth."

Humans and the lower class of devils wouldn't have a slightest chance to go through this door. Even standing in front of it at a gap of several feet wouldn't save them from feeling the extreme heat spread by those flames. They couldn't flash themselves inside either, for there were various protective spells set in place.

Only the devils that were directly below us, called the Machordaen, those who were of the same level as Vrae and myself, and those above us could go through it–somewhat like a special clearance.

Other than us, no one would be able to enter if they weren't in the presence of those with clearance.

Abruptly, I felt the pair of winged eyes move themselves to a further distance, which made me gleefully rejoice. I raised a hand, and the blue flames simultaneously died. The door then opened slowly on its own.

We went through and entered a vast, much darker hall. As we walked in, the door closed behind us. The hall was lit only by few torches of blue flame like the ones outside. Along the walls, there were carvings, shows of brutality by our kind in any way imaginable.

We passed through some devils huddled in wide spaces along the way, divided by thick, rectangular stone jutting out of the surrounding walls. They seemed to be doing experiments with magick, which we didn't have a clue about, because that wasn't exactly our area of expertise.

We entered an area that belonged to pact makers, yet another long stretching hallway. Judging by their combined chatter of delight and their grim murmurs, along with bundles of scrolls that were being tossed around, it seemed as though they were busy working on a deadline or something. Either they were listing those humans who had made pacts with them, or they were watching out so the humans couldn't weasel their way out of the pact, or they were preparing themselves to collect. Hell, maybe they were doing all three.

What I mean about the pact-makers is it wasn't that *they* were the ones who needed to make the pact with those human imbeciles. It was they who needed those makers. They were doing all these dealings with humans because it was their job to gather souls through this angle.

I talked with those makers once in a while, and I couldn't help laughing every time I heard things those animals wanted; they didn't care even if the price for their insignificant stupidity was going down to the basement for eternity after they got what they wanted and enjoying it for a mere ten years of their crippled lives.

Ignoring the furore, Vrae and I walked past them straight to a lone door in the far end, behind which the guy we were about to meet was working.

He was the one named Amon, the one I, Vrae, Zoran, and Gevirash had talked about earlier. If you thought he was Amon as in one of Astaroth's entourages, you'd missed the bull's eye, because the one we were about to talk to was a completely different guy. And no, Astaroth wasn't the inventor of the Tarot card either. He was one of dukes of Hell who governed forty infernal legions and had no business at all with the soldiers under the Echelons.

Amon had firm knowledge of many things, but that wasn't because he had some divine ability like a fortune teller who tells past and future. He knew things because as our Head Intel, he had most sources he needed.

Well, humans weren't exactly the race that came to mind when talking about the "Intelligence" Division.

Vrae raised her hand this time, lifting the seven layers of spells that covered the door, and entered. I followed suit and closed the door once we were inside. Judging by the faint tingle brushing my skin, I knew that the barrier had been formed again the second the door closed with a distinct click.

No sooner had I shut the door than we saw him in all his glory. Yeah, right . . .

We often forgot his six-foot-five height since we had seldom seen him arise from his big grotesque armchair with thorns and spikes on its sides, just like the sight before us. He had in one hand a scroll which, by the look of it, was a cross reference of sorts to the other one in his other hand. Two horns jutted out of his head, and his straight, blond hair fell just over his shoulders. His lean body was covered with thick dark-green robes.

This chamber, his den as some of us called it, was no larger than the two cubicles outside combined, but there were two more doors behind him, leading to two chambers. One of them, perhaps, was more massive than the entire Aryad and a whole lot more revolting, whereas the other was his private room.

Taking his green eyes off the scrolls, he put them on his similarly grotesque-looking desk, and his lips curved into a greeting smile. "Well, well, well, if it isn't the famous Sisters of Mayhem. What's up, ladies?" He addressed us as a pair of similar armchairs leaned against the far wall glided on their own and stopped in front of his desk.

Vrae and I each sat on one. "Nothing. We just heard some rumours. It's been quiet for a while, and that part really gets on my nerves. So we thought to ask you whether you know anything," I explained.

"And there's this rumour regarding a few MIAs," Vrae added.

Amon let out a scoff as if he had been offended. "You thought to ask *me* whether *I* know anything? Ladies, you just love to throw insults at people, don't you? I wouldn't be in this part of our home sweet home if I didn't know anything," he retorted.

He gathered the scrolls and put them aside. "And I also know this silence has been nagging on you both. No surprise on that part. And thanks for the threats, I humbly appreciate it," he said with a laugh, reacting to our angry tirade rather gleefully. At a glance, it would appear as though he was unaffected by those threats, and usually he was, but my ears caught something else underneath his good-natured laugh.

It sounded as though he was nervous and was bracing himself for getting a good kick in the ass.

My eyes glinted maliciously at the thought. Well, if my presumption of what I heard in his voice was correct, and I had no doubt it was, this guy before me was indeed hiding something. But then it might be wise if I just waited, and that was what I did.

"Very funny, Amon. You know what, you just remind me there. The thing is, dude, I wanted to tell you this: if both of us get out of here and see those stupid toys of yours still winding that close on our backs, I swear I'll blow those things off on sight. It is *already* an insult if you think either of us would do anything stupid like not following orders from the Echelons, let alone putting us under further scrutiny. Now that, *Iverand*, is almost equal to a death wish in my book," I remarked calmly, and I gave him a maybe-I'll-just-kill-you-right-now glare.

He cringed as if I'd struck the right chord. "Whoa, whoa, slow down, lady. I did intend to tell you earlier but got distracted. I'm just doing my job, okay? Recent events required me to increase all means of surveillance. That was an order. It's not like it was only you two who got my sweet little creations on your tail. Hell, I'd rather have all of them back inside there,"–he pointed at the door to the massive chamber–"having to stick in the corner like this, but as you both know they couldn't go anywhere in here except to remerge with their rightful owners. Come on, cut me some slack here. You know the Echelons have enforced their use as spies since the Stone Age. And yeah, I prefer to have all of them alive and sound rather than find them in pieces, putting them on scary ladies like you two." He laid down his defence.

I could almost see a glowing sign above his head, saying *"Please save us poor golems, from further abuse."* Well, that went for us all.

Vrae rolled her eyes. "Whatever, back to business. Anyway, Yve's right. Those golems you called "sweet little friends" *are* getting to my nerve today. Since you said there was a reason for that, why don't you just cut to the chase and tell us already? Or I'll be really happy to blow those things off instead of her," she snapped.

He finally conceded. It was, after all, his fault that he hadn't informed us sooner. "You two really don't have a sense of humour, do you? Okay, so you really wanna know?" he asked in a truth-is-out-there tone.

"Just fill us in with whatever you got, okay?" I tapped his desk and gave him a your-time-is-ticking glare.

He acted as if he were thinking pretty hard before telling us everything. In the end, he agreed. "Fine ladies, because I'm such a nice moon god Amon, I'll fill you girls in. I don't wanna have to pick my friends in pieces anyway," he mumbled.

I let out a scoffing laugh. "You know what? That's pretty good–the moon god Amon thing. And thanks for appreciating our words this time." I cast a meaningful look at him.

He cleared his throat. "As you know, there are rumours here and there, and your sweet sister Vrae here got them right. Good for you, pretty ladies. My sources ain't just rumours which most of the time are unreliable. See, the Veil of Sights has been spouting some weird omens recently." He tilted his head towards a pitch-black hole gaping from top to bottom in the far wall.

That bottomless darkness was a natural cave, but it wasn't hollow as it supposed to be. There were layers of a blackish substance that felt like air turned half solid and appeared like water in zero gravity. It honed in on the ether, catching disturbances caused by nature, human sorcerers, devils, or, hell, spirits. No one knew how the Veil first came to be, but since it had its use, the Echelons decided to utilize it until now.

He then turned his attention back to us both. "Well, at first I didn't find anything within a few miles radius, so I checked in a wider scope. It was a couple of weeks ago, like Vrae said she heard about the MIAs, when the Veil suddenly spewed "unknown peril, D'arksin," followed by seven golems raising red flags and then melted. They belonged to Levarchon scouts out on patrol in the area."

Before he continued, I cut him off, "Wait, wait. Levarchons? Are you sure it wasn't soldiers under them? 'Cause Levarchons aren't supposed to be that weak–well yeah, if they try to confront us."

He rolled his eyes. "Yes, all seven were Levarchons. Now let me finish this, will ya?" he said with a scowl, so I raised my hands and let him continue. "I quickly checked each of the sixth eyes of their golems and saw all of them projecting the same thing. They entered the D'arksin forest and not long after, there was this violent commotion, and then, poof, nothing. Not a sight of whoever or whatever caused it," he said in a rather theatrical tone.

When none of us said anything, his light green eyes gleamed with a half relieved, half musing look. "Okay, I know you both are aware of their level of power, and that's not even within a mile of yours, since fifty of them would be dead in no time should they pick a fight with either of you. But still, you know full well that they can't be easily defeated if they're battling something or someone outside the chain of command, right? Only higher ranks of angels could overpower them, so the question becomes who or what could've done that?"

I gave him a blank look at his question.

He let out a short breath. "That day, the energy of those seven sky-rocketed and then collided with something before it completely vanished," he said grimly.

I frowned. "After that, what? Surely you sent people straight there to check on them?" I asked with mounting curiosity, along with a whole herd of questions that were swarming in my head.

He answered me with a curt nod. "Yes, five Alvadors were sent to look for them," he said as he tapped his fingers on his desk.

"D'arksin, huh? A few months ago there was a tremendous earthquake around there, right?" I asked Vrae, who answered with a short, "Yeah."

"That's right, but anyhow, let's get back to the matter at hand. Another event," he went on, "occurred just a week ago. This time it was those Alvadors whom I sent before. They got themselves another order straight from the Echelons, since they hadn't been able to obtain anything useful in regard of those Levarchons, except for few tracks of blood, their shields, but not the Levarchons themselves," he said in the same low grim tone.

He paused to let that fact hang in our heads before he continued. "In short, those Alvadors were, well, sent up there, close enough to hear anything serious. Unfortunately, whatever word the Echelons wished to hear will remain a mystery; for they were also gone missing in a very similar manner before they even got the chance to reach the distance required to accomplice their mission.

"Well, something or some people definitely offed them. Either they were all killed by somebody upstairs, someone who we've never known before, or something else did it and then dragged them out of your sight," I said.

He nodded in agreement. "I still haven't figured it out–well, not yet anyway."

We fell silent for a moment, and suddenly a thought occurred to me. "So, you're telling me nobody's checking those trails further? Has an Imirae wielder been sent to examine the shields?" I asked him.

He sadly shook his head. "All of those are still in the area, because I'm currently a bit short on Machordaens. The Echelons sent most of them out on patrol because of these MIAs. Hell, even the Imirae wielders are being put on alert, but I still haven't got the chance to get one of them to check it out yet."

"And you didn't even bother to let us into the loop, even after the Varkonians had been alerted. Why?" I asked in impassive voice, but he obviously noted the peril headed his way.

Bracing himself, he gave me an apologetic smile. "Well, I'm sorry, but the priorities from the Echelons are to find the culprit and protect all Imirae wielders in the area because, well you know, they're all touchy subjects. Since each Cherxanain has his or her respective duties, the Echelons ordered that you all not be alerted unless the circumstances turn grim."

Exasperated, I laughed bitterly. "So, what is it? Were they were worried about our jobs, or are we just expendable compared to the Varkonians? Damn, they're lucky I'm tolerant to a certain extent. Otherwise, I might've made them eat all of those golems they're so keen to force on us until *they're* the ones to turn grim," I retorted in indignation.

He cringed at my threat on the golems, but I could see in his gaze that he realized my boiling anger was aimed mostly towards the Echelons and not them. Well, mostly it wasn't.

I glanced askance at Vrae and was a bit surprised to see a flash of searing red in her eyes for a split second. Even though I could feel her faint aggravation through her mental shield, I wasn't sure at whom she was directing that glint of malice, so I raised a questioning brow at her. *"What?"* I passed the thought to her.

"Nothing," she replied, and her face returned to that emotionless look it had worn throughout Amon's long explanation.

"Look, guys, I'll be honest with you," he started, and we looked straight at him. "Truth is, there was no order to increase the surveillance on Cherxanains today, well, yet, seeing the fact that there's been no progress in finding the culprit."

I arched a brow and recalled his earlier words that we were not to be alerted unless the situation was getting worse.

"So why did you do it with us?" Vrae voiced the question I wanted to say.

He heaved a heavy sigh. "Well, what else could I do to get you two down here? I know there are only two things that could make you come and see me on short notice–either to get you upset or to give you a job. Since I don't have the latter, it would be all-out risky if I used the eye to tell you I had one. When I learned that Vrae caught wind of the disappearance, I thought that was my chance, so I kinda rolled the dice and hoped to hell you wouldn't kill me before I get to tell you that something is killing the soldiers." He forced a grin.

I winced at his statement. "Buddy, that's one helluva gamble," I remarked, and Vrae nodded her agreement.

He blinked in surprise and responded to my words with a nod. I could see that he looked more at ease now compared to seconds ago when we both threatened him. Abruptly, he tilted his head as if he had just remembered something. "Oh yeah, I almost forgot. Actually, there's another top secret I wanted to tell you. Luckily, none of the bunch asked me to swear not to tell anybody."

I exchanged a puzzled look with Vrae who shrugged her cluelessness, and then we turned our attention back to him.

"Listen to this. Around four days ago, I heard that he–well, you know of whom I'm speaking." He gave us a meaningful look.

I crossed my arms over my chest. *"Damn, this can't be good,"* I cursed inwardly as I exchanged a knowing look with Vrae, who evidently shared my thought.

"Yeah, we know," we said in unison.

He cleared his throat. "So, his guards told me that he's been telling something weird, starting at exactly midnight. He kept saying these lines over and over. The Great War between heaven and hell will erupt, and the wheel of destiny of the human world will be set in motion. The damned shall be vanquished and thrown to another realm. They will become nothing but spirits and apparitions. Eons after the war, the once destroyed world will arise from the ashes with all its glory. It will be marked by the union of the essence that belongs to both worlds, and thus unfold the omens of resurrection. The destroyed world will arise once more."

I winced at that . . . prophecy, or whatever that was. Vrae suddenly made a noise which I assumed to be a snort. "Hell, Amon, that sounds like bull crap to me. I know that he does say something useful every once in a while, but gee, that's a prophecy, isn't it? You're saying, I mean, he's saying that we're gonna be destroyed by armies from upstairs? Puh-lease, now *that* is an insult," she interjected.

"Well, I don't know if the one he meant was our world," Amon said hastily, when he looked at our faces, which definitely scared the bejeezus out of him.

"And there's one I don't get. We're gonna fight those ass-glowing bastards from upstairs, right? So why in hell are the ones whose fates are gonna be decided those two-legged monkeys? Could this mean upstairs' bastards are willing to destroy them in order to put us down?" Vrae asked him in a wondering tone.

Amon grinned at her insulting those angels. "Hell, beats me. I was wondering about that part as well, but I think it's unlikely though, not with their Holy Dad being that overly fond of them.

And there's the merging part. I mean, if, to put it crudely, we're really gonna turn into some sort of ghosts, how in the hell do we, as revolting as it sounds, "unite the essence" with humans? Possessing them isn't exactly what I'd call "uniting". Above all else, I don't think, whoever it turns out to be, they would be happy if they learned about this, ehm, prophecy of his, let alone the Echelons." His voice was filled with anxiety as he looked at us.

After that, I was only half paying attention to whatever they were saying. As for me, I was thinking mostly about the fourth lines, the merging, and suddenly I remembered about my nightmares.

The ones about humans.

Was this the thing Cain was babbling about? Did he somehow know about it? How did he manage to know in the first place? Could it really be possible that I'd end up merging with those wretched human vermin?

Furthermore, he said devils and humans. This could only mean that I wasn't the only one, right? But who were the others? Should I try to find out who they might possibly be, or leave things as they were?

Really, this was nowhere near funny, but even though he'd been locked up all those thousands of years and had not even originally been one of the devils as well, as the first son of Adam, Cain had proved that he was useful after all, especially about his former kind.

When I was in the middle of all those mind-boggling questions, suddenly Vrae patted my back. "Is something wrong?" she asked.

I quickly shook my head. "It's nothing." I abruptly turned to Amon. "Okay, Amon, is there anything else you got?" I asked him casually, but I still felt Vrae's wondering gaze on my back. Since she didn't say a thing, I silently felt a surge of relief and hoped Amon didn't notice anything between us.

Amon let out a short breath. "Nothing for now, I guess. Tell ya girls what, I'll send both of you the latest word. It's my job anyway. If anything goes weird, either a minor ambush or any other crap that might happen, I'll tell you right away. How's that? Just promise me you two won't blow my friends to oblivion, okay? It takes days to create one, and I don't want to be bugging you with mandatory from the Echelons to take your blood again," he remarked, practically begged.

I cringed. *"That does sound revolting."* Lowering my voice to a purr, I looked him straight in the eye. "Amon, you're reading our minds. Thanks, that's a promise. And if you do keep it, and also keep your word that you will order those things to keep their distance as far away as possible, I give you *my* word that you'll see your, ehm, friends in one piece. I don't know what Vrae thinks though. Vrae?" I gleefully asked her.

"Fine by me, but it's like she said–as long as you *do* keep your promises, okay?" Vrae grinned.

"Ladies, you two have broken my heart, questioning my word like that, let alone the extra you demanded, but what the hell, I know I *am* the devil saint and putting my ass on the line by giving you your space. Just don't let anybody except the three of us, Zoran, and Gevirash know about this, yeah?" He lifted the edge of his lips in a wickedly devastating smile.

I shrugged. "No problem, just no more closeness for your little friends. A deal's a deal. Keep your word and we keep ours," I said.

He let out a suffering sigh. "Gee, right until the end you're still threatening me. You really are unbelievable all right. Anyhow, you two have finished your business, right? Now can you ladies please leave me in peace and quiet? You know–life without death threats?" he asked, feigning annoyance.

I shrugged off his tone. "Right, whatever. Thanks again anyway. Glad to know you're still having some fear of a death sentence." I started to rise from my seat when a thought occurred to me. "Oh, and I almost forgot, Zoran and Gevirash said hey."

He started and arose as well. "Give them my regards," was all he said in return. His trepidation was evident only in his eyes while his voice and expression remained calm.

I nodded, not wanting to press him further on the private matter between him and those guards. "Catch you on the flip side. C'mon Vrae, it's time for us to roll." I turned to my sister and started to leave Amon alone like he wanted.

She arose but pulled me to a stop and then turned to him. "Amon, those Levarchons and Alvadors that were supposed to look for them haven't been found yet, have they?"

"Well, hell, no, I didn't say anything except them went AWOL, now did I? What? Is there something you wanna say?" he asked in return.

Vrae raised a hand so he would wait, and then she turned her attention to me. "Yve, seeing that this silence has been getting to our nerves, what d'ya say we check things out ourselves? You think you're pissed enough with this silence to come along?" She asked with her back to the Head Intel and flashed a wicked smile to me.

"Hell, count me in. Okay with that, Amon?" I glanced at him.

He fell silent for a minute and then gave us his answer, "Sure, I'll keep digging on my part while you two are at it. I'll know if you find anything. I'll send you the word if I run into something."

She *tsked*. "Yeah, your buddies sure will start squeaking if we run into anything, but whatever, let's go, Yve. Bye." She dragged me out, leaving him without any chance to say more, and then we went through the area we'd passed on our way to Amon's chamber.

Without wasting any more time, we made our way out to where Zoran and Gevirash were standing. When we met them again, we quickly got engaged in a swift discussion about everything we'd learned from Amon, and we left them afterwards.

We jumped to the sky, leaving the Croatoan woods behind us seconds after we flew. Minutes later, we finally reached D'arksin woods, the very place those seven Levarchons were last detected.

The second we both arrived at the spot, we immediately checked the area. For a while we didn't find anything. Zip. Zero. Nada. No animals, no track of battle, no nothing.

Then, just a few yards from the spot where we started our search, we found several tracks of blood, devil's blood, along with the Levarchons' armour and other things all over the ground.

"These must be what those Alvadors found. What do you think, Vrae?" I held up a piece of armour that was embedded with a two-headed gargoyle that belonged to the Levarchons in front of her face.

She shoved away my hand as she threw an annoyed look at me. "No idea. I mean, hell, like Amon said, even fifty of them will be wasted in no time against either of us, let alone just seven," she snapped.

"And like he also said, no one can beat them that easily unless the opponent was an outsider or a higher rank of those guys from above. So what happened here? It's not like they just freakin' melted like a golem!" I retorted in frustration as I threw the armour to the ground.

"Yeah, trying to guess who our enemies are is pissing me off more than fighting a whole herd of them," she said in a voice laden with repugnance while she continued to wander off and checked her surroundings.

She stopped dead in her tracks and looked at me. "Yve, if we had to take a shot in the dark here, who do you suggest the enemies were? Some gangs upstairs never made one single move against us, and now, whoever they are, they are making trouble out of the blue? Or not one of them, but a whole new kind of enemy, because you and I know full well our kind will never mess with special forces like them," she said as she pointed at the remains.

I snorted. "Unless they've gone rogue." She narrowed her gaze at my response, and I raised my hands in surrender.

"Anyhow, why, whoever they were, should they be looking for trouble now? Did those Levarchons get themselves into something that they weren't supposed to?" She raised a host of questions for me.

I looked around. "Well, no matter what, I prefer to think it was a new kind of enemy than the alternative: someone upstairs wiping out our subordinates. Just thinking of it makes me sick to my stomach. None of the frequent visitors from above ever humoured me when I needed to have a bit of fun. But then again, if someone among them does have what it takes, it'll make it much better, no matter how sick I am," I rebuked her.

"Uh-huh," she said with a subtle nod.

"But," I went on as I smiled evilly. "If there *were* some people here, maybe in the deep slumber and they woke up all of the sudden, and if by stupid luck, the ones who woke them up were those Levarchons, well, that would've made their Christmas, 'cause I don't know about you, but if someone wakes me up in the middle of my sleep, I'd blow the guy on sight."

She arched a brow. "I'm with you there, but for argument's sake, if there were people or who knows what out here, why the hell did those golems, not to mention the Veil, never pick up anything all this time. Hell, not even we ever found anything weird in this area, which is a usual patrolling spot for those soldiers." She pointed out that trivial piece of information.

"Yeah, and the timing with Cain starting to babble that shit was, well, too damn good if you ask me," I remarked, half checking the surroundings, half thinking about the fourth line of that so-called prophecy we heard from Amon.

"You're thinking about the fourth line, aren't you?" Vrae asked me in a low voice, barely a whisper.

"Bull's eye, Vrae", I thought, but I kept it quiet. I realized that those revolting eyes were still around, and I made a gesture to warn her. When she looked at my expression, she caught what I meant and fell silent.

Minutes afterwards, we finally found something near the edge of the D'arksin woods, roughly eight hundred meters to the north from the spot where we found the emblem, their blood and everything else. There we saw a lot more than just set of tracks.

It was those seven Levarchons, shredded and torn to pieces. Their blood was all over the trees, as well as their weapons and everything. Their bodies and all other remains were covered by some kind of protective shield.

"Well, this explains few things." I raised my brows when we first spotted the covered remains.

As I approached the shield, an unmistakable feeling like a tickle brushed my skin. I shook my head. "No wonder those Alvadors couldn't find them. The level of this spell is several levels above theirs–in other words, level with ours. The same goes for those stupid golems. They can't see through this, not with the current magick they have. It only contains a moderate amount of power. Unless he did something to up the magick, they won't see a damned rat," I spat.

Vrae nodded. "He should've done it the moment something like this occurs. We better remind him next time to use everything he's got in case something happens." Vrae touched the shield and curled her lips.

"Hell, that's Amon for ya. Never uses his full power until disaster mocks him right under his nose. It's also beyond me why in the world he hasn't tried to up them to the level. We don't need to have those on our tail." I went on a tirade as I also examined the shield in front of our faces.

"Yeah, once again that guy didn't fail to amuse us. But at any rate, this is confusing, I mean, why the hell did whoever tore these guys to pieces bother to cover the remains?" she asked with a questioning stare directed at me.

I winced. "To pay them last respects?" I asked innocently, but I could barely stop myself from laughing outright.

Upset with my unhelpful answer, she threw a dry gaze at me, to which I replied with a sorry-couldn't-stop-myself grin.

"Unless they're entirely different beings like we've guessed, they should've known that anyone on the same level or, for the sake of argument, above it can see through this shield easily and cast the counter-spell to undo it, right?" she asked.

I nodded, getting her meaning. "Right."

She indicated the scene again. "So, why did they do it? Don't tell me they just didn't want to be found in order to continue their deep sleep. That'll made me seriously angry–putting us through all these problems just because someone out here had been disturbed and thought maybe it'd be funny if they blew our subordinates to pieces to make us think they'd just gone MIA, "she said in that typical upset tone of hers.

I scoffed. "Gee, looks like they've successfully upset you. That'll make their day."

She rolled her eyes and turned her gaze elsewhere. "Well, I don't know about you, but seeing these makes me wonder whatever happened to those Alvadors," she said quietly. "Do you think there's a chance that whoever they ran into when they were about to report whatever they supposed to were the same people?"

I bit my lip as I considered her. "There might be a chance. If they did run into whoever that is, then there's a possibility that all of them, dead or alive, would be confined around here," I said with my eyes scanning the gruesome scene.

"All right, I'll look for them. I'll leave these guys to you," she said, and she started to get ready for take-off.

It was then I noticed something outrageous about the scene.

"Wait, Vrae." I stopped her just as she spread her wings.

She strode towards me. "What, you noticed something?"

"What's wrong with this picture?" I indicated the entire scene.

She gave me a stare that said *"Are you blind or just wanna piss me off?"* as an answer. "Well, I don't know what could be more

34

wrong than the fact that some bastards shredded them so dead. That's just crazy, don't ya think?" she asked acerbically.

Crossing my arms, I chuckled at her retort. "Not that, grandma. Well, I'll give you two hints, then. First, take a look at these guys." I indicated the limbs of the soldiers scattered on the ground.

"I've looked enough, and no, they didn't say a damn thing nor did they blink."

I mentally rolled my eyes. I would've laughed at her face and made a stupid expression had the situation been not so ridiculously impossible. "Fine, then let me ask you this. How many do you think these guys fought?"

She opened her mouth, no doubt wanting to give me another caustic retort, but she closed it when my question started to sink in her head. She turned her blood-red eyes from me to the pieces of limbs scattered on the ground, then to the blood all over the trees. The more she observed them, the more I saw her eyes widen. "There's only . . ."

I raised the edge of my lips. "One?" I finished her question.

She shook her head in denial. "No fucking way! There's no way that could happen! If it were angels, the Veil should've shown it!"

I shrugged. "It should, but it didn't," I said calmly.

"Wait a sec. The Alvadors, you reckon they ran into whoever offed these guys?" she asked in disbelief.

"Highly possible, but if that's the case, can you check the surroundings? Use your widest scope while you're at it. I'm gonna get rid of this stupid shield and see things thoroughly. If we're lucky, we'll find something significant." I pointed at the remains.

She nodded. "If I run into anything, I'll send my doppelganger to you. It'll lead you straight to me." She moved away, transformed her robes into wings, and spread them.

"Fine, I'll finish this in a blink. Now go." I jerked my head.

"Okay, catch you later." Flapping her wings, she jumped to the sky and flew off to the west.

Seconds later, I lost her track of energy completely and started to cast the counter-spell. Fortunately, this type of spell was easy enough to break without wasting too much energy. If everything went as usual, I should be able to sense even the slightest bit of energy print belonging to the caster when I had almost finished the incantation. That would allow me to decide whether the caster was either a devil or vermin from upstairs. On occasion though, both Vrae and I encountered humans whose energy was strong enough among their race to cast low-level protective shield, even though its power wouldn't get close to the ones cast either by devils or angels.

After a few moments, I realized there was something weird.

I finished the counter-spell, and then the shield wore off, but I didn't catch even a glimpse of energy print as I should. No dark trace of energy belonging to devils, or set of holy crap left by angels. There was nothing.

What was this?

At any rate, whatever in the hell it meant, I had better inform Vrae immediately before she did something that led to annoying troubles.

All of the sudden, I heard something in the bushes a few feet to my left. I took my stand and prepared to attack whoever it was.

Chapter 2

"Stop! It's me!" Vrae's voice yelled from the bushes, and now she stood before me. Only she wasn't Vrae.

I recognized the scent of doppelganger all over her.

"Gee, do that again and you might as well consider yourself lucky if I don't blow you before you can say "stop". And why the hell did you come out from the bushes? You have wings, for Ezryan's sake! You could just land in front of me!" I snapped at her, and then I pulled back the energy I had drawn to blow her up on sight.

"Forgive me, Shakra Yverna. Shakra Vrathien told me that you were dispelling the protective shield which covered the remains of the Levarchon soldiers, so I simply didn't want to disturb you while you were at it," the doppelganger said, looking as if she were ready to blow herself up as a punishment.

"Okay, that's fine. Just don't do it again. Next time, my concentration won't break that easily. If you have to land near me, you land near me. Remember that."

"Yes, Shakra, I will remember that." The doppelganger looked a bit relieved but still showed regret on her face.

I frowned as I noticed something odd about her. At first I couldn't put my finger on it, but after a few seconds, I realized she didn't have half the powers Vrae usually gave her doppelgangers.

"Explains why I didn't pick a damn thing from her earlier," I thought.

"If she sent you here, then she already found something, did she not?" I asked her while I started to examine the remains of the Levarchons.

"Yes, indeed she did. After she flew away to the west from you a moment ago, she did not change course for a few miles, and then it was not long afterwards when she encountered the same protective shield as this one, the difference being that the one she encountered was covering the remains of the Alvadors you both were looking

37

for. Unfortunately, they also suffered the same fate as these soldiers. So she summoned me and told me to go to you, and she also summoned the others to check the surroundings like you asked of her here. She began to mutter the counter-spell as we spoke." She stayed still, watching me checking whatever was left behind by the Levarchons.

"So the Alvadors were dead as well. Amon's not gonna like it one bit. This only gives us more reason to really remind him to use his full power with the golems next time. Anyhow, screw that. Did she find anything aside from the remains and the shield?" I asked, while holding a piece of arm belonging to one of them.

I sensed a little trace of energy remaining on the soldier's palm.

"I don't know if there was anything else. I flew straight here right after she elaborated on the situations and told me to go to you," she answered with a wondering gaze on her eyes, looking at the piece of arm I held.

"Is that so? Well, I guess we'll be able to see everything ourselves when I've finished checking these guys." I spun the arm I held and looked at it closely.

"Do you sense anything wrong in that arm?"

I ran my fingers on the gruesomely jagged cut on it. "By the look of things, this one was blown to pieces just a second before he launched his energy to attack the assailant. Either it was a quick move from their assailant, whoever that was, doing that with all seven of them and moving in for the kill, or this guy was the only one left standing at the time he was about to attack," I said, and then I sent my own energy into the arm, trying to sense the nature of the energy the assailant might have left in it.

After a moment of concentration, I found only the same trace of energy I had sensed in the shield: plain energy with nothing else left in it to guess who the owner was.

"Stupid bastard! At least you could just leave your energy print for me to guess just who the fuck you were, attacking our subordinates like this and then covering it just for your fucking convenience!" I snapped in fury.

I spun the arm again, slower this time, hoping I'd find anything, no matter trivial it might be, that would help me to determine who the attacker was.

Seconds later, I finally had to force myself to realize that it was useless to continue looking for evidence when the bitches that tore these guys and hid them were so good in covering their tracks.

When I was about to put the arm back where I found it in the first place, I suddenly couldn't feel my right arm which I was using to hold the Levarchon's, and the piece of limb I was holding just fell to the ground.

What the hell?

Startled, I put my left arm on my right, and a ghostly pale blue colour appeared on the tip of my fingers, and then it spread all the way to my elbow as it started to shake.

"Is something wrong?" The doppelganger approached.

"Well, that's one way to put it, yeah. It seems the bastards left something behind for whoever found their victims," I said grudgingly as I started to draw my healing power and concentrate it on my right hand.

I hung on to whatever luck I had and hoped I could get rid of whatever penetrated it. *"Why didn't the bitch just leave some plain bombs or whatever rather than this kind of thing? My body could've healed* that *kind of injury,"* I mused indignantly.

"It's not some kind of poison, is it? Do you need help with that?" she asked cautiously.

"Nah, I don't think this poison would kill me, if it *is* some kind of poison. It looks like it's just a side-effect of mixing my own energy with the energy that belongs to the bastard. I just hope this won't cause any more trouble. Otherwise, we gotta go to Vrae and warn her ASAP before anything happen," I said, all the while trying to concentrate on my right hand.

"Any more trouble? Like what?" she sounded more alert now than a minute ago.

I was about to look at her when suddenly everything went dark.

"What the fuck?" I snarled, following with a series of curses that rolled off my tongue as I realized I couldn't see a damn thing, never mind my own hand. I could still hear the doppelganger next to me though.

"Well, obviously no one pulled pranks and turned off the light," I thought sarcastically. Last I looked, that stupid blue colour in my arm didn't go anywhere, so what the hell was happening here?

"What is it!? Is something wrong, Shakra?!" The doppelganger said in alarm, realizing that there *was* something weird going on.

"Well, it seems I do need your help on this one. But first, tell me, is my arm's colour back to normal yet, or is the blue thing still trying to invade my whole hand and make its way to my body?" I moved in the direction from where her voice came.

"It's almost gone. Now the only parts of your arm that are blue are your fingers, Shakra. But can't you see it?" she asked, definitely sounding worried as if I were about to collapse seconds later.

"Nope, I wouldn't be asking you if my eyesight was intact, would I? No, my eyesight has gone south. Hopefully, this just temporary–the effect that only happens when you have almost finished getting rid of whatever it is. We definitely have to warn Vrae before she touches any of the Alvadors' body parts. We don't have a freakin' clue what might happen to her if *she* uses her energy," I said, trying to finish this as fast as I could.

After that, I sensed the doppelganger's healing energy approach. I cautiously stepped away from her. "Whoa, wait. I changed my mind. If the colour is wearing off, it might be better to let me finish the job. We don't know what would happen if you added your energy to the mixture. Thanks for trying to help, though. Just hope that my speculation's right and this will end in no time, okay?" I asked her quickly.

"As you wish, Shakra," she said warily.

Fortunately, my hunch didn't disappoint me. The doppelganger said the colour was worn off completely, and a moment later my sight was coming back to where it belonged.

"Well, that's that. Now, let me cover these guys first so they'll stay intact for the Machordaen to find," I said, and then I quickly cast the Machordaen-level protective shield.

The doppelganger didn't say anything but kept her silence, with a wary look on her face still hanging there.

After I was finished, without warning, my body was paralyzed and everything went black. The last thing I heard was the doppelganger shouting "Shakra!" at me.

I opened my eyes with a start.

"What the . . . ?" was the first thing I said when I opened my eyes. I found Vrae on her knees beside me, and the doppelganger sat right behind her.

"Welcome back," Vrae said, and then she indicated her doppelganger. "She carried you here after you passed out. Fortunately she was just in time to stop me touching the Alvadors' body parts." She extended one hand, helping me to sit.

"Gee, thanks." I turned to the doppelganger, who flashed Vrae's smile at me, and then she faced her master. "Is there anything else you need, Shakra? If there's nothing else, I will be going back."

"No, I think that will be all. Thanks again for carrying her here and stopping me from getting blue filth." She smiled and gave her permission to the doppelganger.

"It's my pleasure, Shakra. Farewell then," she said to both of us.

When she started to fade, I stopped her. "Wait a sec. I need to ask you something."

"What is it, Shakra?"

"When I was out, was there anything unusual, anything, either on me or the bodies I covered?" I asked, hoping she'd sensed or seen something while I was out.

"If I recall it correctly, Shakra, there was nothing else happening. Then again, I did not notice anything because I was in a hurry to carry you here after you'd fallen unconscious, Shakra, and I was able to stop Shakra Vrathien just in time before she touched any of them," she explained, her voice laden with regret.

"I see. Well, that's fine. I doubt anything else would happen anyway, just checking. Thanks. See you again some other time."

"You're most welcome, Shakra Yverna. Farewell, and be careful." and then she was gone from both Vrae's and my sight.

My gaze fell on Vrae who gave me a weird stare. "What?" I asked.

She raked her blood-red hair with her fingers. "Care to elaborate what the hell happened back there? I've no doubt Amon will annoy us with a lot of questions when he knows you passed out. Your golem should have raised a red flag when you did. Not to mention, he too found out that the Alvadors were butchered as well as the Levarchons. But lucky for them, they keep their distance. I imagine they'd suffer pretty severe damage if they flew nearer like before." She grinned.

"Oh, great, just fucking great, those things are the last living beings in existence I wanted to see I was going under, let alone

Amon. Why didn't you just blow up those damned things?" I sighed heavily, knowing it was all too late.

"Tough luck, Yve. Suck it up. We promised him to let those things alone as long as they keep their distance. And they *did* keep their distance," she said, trying to stifle a laugh this time, but then her expression turned back to dead serious.

"Well, laugh all you want . . . Anyhow, let's get back to business. But before I go through the details, let me say this to you. The assailants are going to pieces when I get my hands on them. They're really, totally, *absolutely* pissing me off," I said with cold fury in every word.

For a moment neither of us said anything. I was back on my feet and walked to the Alvadors that were shredded behind Vrae.

"So these guys weren't lucky as well, huh?" I knelt near a piece of leg.

"Yeah, their state was almost the same as the Levarchons we found back there." Vrae jerked her head to those dead soldiers and stared at the remains as well.

I turned to her. "How many doppelgangers did you summon, aside from the one you sent to me?"

"Well, as I recall, I sent four in other directions. It shouldn't be long before at least one of them comes back here. And just what the hell happened back there? You haven't filled me in with anything since you woke up, and my dop just babbled about some side-effect or something. Was it the energy which the bastard left behind, or was it something else got you?" She asked in a demanding voice.

I raised my hands at her rain of questions. "Slow down. I'll explain one step at a time."

She glared at me. "You're joking, right? What is this, baby combat tutorial? Just fill me in, will ya?" she demanded.

I gave her a droll look in return. "Fine! Fine! Gee, I just woke up, welcomed by another pack of meat, and my own sister can't restrain herself for just another ten seconds."

"Get over it. Now cut to the chase."

"Okay, first I wanna ask you something. Did you get any kind of print in the shield when you were dispelling it? Was there any dark trace, blood scent, holy crap, anything?" I asked her quietly, taking a pretty good guess that she encountered the same thing I did.

Vrae was aghast at my question. "You felt it too then? There was nothing left to ID the owner. I thought it was me who getting weird vibes," she said in a wondering tone.

I scoffed at her words. "You may be weird sometimes, but not that weird. So either the asshole was really *that good* in covering his tracks, or he was something else. One thing for sure, the bastard who wasted the Alvadors is the same as the one who tore up the Levarchons."

"Indeed. I think there's a much higher possibility that this guy is something else entirely, and not normal to boot. I mean, no matter how strong an entity can be and no matter how capable it is in covering its own tracks, it's bound to leave its own unique energy print in any shape," she explained with a confused look on her face.

"Well, that is the known theory. Then again, whether this guy's not a *normal* entity or his energy print is no energy print, how the hell can we know who or what this guy is, let alone get our hands on the bastard? It wouldn't be funny either if his print was no print," I snapped furiously and kicked the nearest piece of leg.

"Okay, leave that question for later. Just how exactly did the bastard's leftovers manage to drag you under?" Her wariness was tangible in her eyes.

I ground my teeth and told her everything up to the point I was getting the weird blue thing in my arm. I paused to reign myself in as I felt my fury mounting.

She urged me to continue, and I cleared my throat. "Well, your doppelganger should've told you the rest, ending with me passing out. That's all. Happy now?" I fumed, still a little bit pissed at the fact something unknown had managed to drag me into unconsciousness.

When I finished telling her what she wanted to know, she just kept her silence.

"Okay, since we could find nothing on this guy, and it's dangerous to touch the remains, we'd better play it safe here and avoid touching anything. I'm thinking to ask Amon to summon a Varkonian, preferably Zade if he could manage it, to check the remains later. Now we just go back and tell him directly about all of this mess. Might as well we remind him about his golem spell while we're at it," I said with a sigh.

"No touching anything, gotcha. But first, I gotta cover these guys up, and second, you forgot about the doppelgangers I've sent out there. Should we be waiting for them here or call them when we've reach Croatoan?"

I winced when she reminded me about the doppelgangers, and she rolled her eyes in return. Grinning with apologies, I jerked my head towards the forest where we came from. "Well, just call them now. I wanna kick Amon's ass over this mess."

She sneered. "I'm with you on that. I gotta raise a shield, and then I'll call them." She approached the piles of limbs and began muttering the spell to form the Machordaen-level shield, the same as the one I had put over the Levarchons.

After she'd done the job, she summoned the rest of her doppelgangers. Moments later, they approached from four different directions. They landed right in front of us, and Vrae immediately asked them questions with me standing behind her.

It seemed the first three of the doppelgangers didn't come across anything weird, except for the one who went northeast from her spot. Nothing special though, just tracks of battle that looked like the exact spot where those Alvadors fought whoever the bastard was who had ended their lives.

Vrae finally finished questioning the last doppelganger, and after asking few more details, she dispelled them all. Turning to me, she nodded. "It's all a big bunch of bullshit. Nothing but Alvadors all over again."

I raked my hair and let out a short breath. "Yeah, I hear ya. By the way, Vrae, what happened with you? You didn't get to tell me anything before."

She winced. "All right, but there's not much to tell. I didn't exactly find anything until I found these guys here," she said with one hand indicating the scattered limbs of the Alvadors.

"Fuck," I cursed under my breath. "Nothing else?"

"No, I just dispelled the shield, and before I got to check any of them, my dop carried you to me, thus stopping me from getting any weird shit like she had told you."

I *tsked*. "Fine, let's get the hell outta here then."

She nodded and we jumped to the sky, putting D'arksin woods in our rear. Seconds later we entered the Croatoan once again.

Chapter 3

Amon was resuming his work with the scrolls when he caught a slight disturbance on the Veil. He rose from his seat and strode across the room to the Veil. Its surface went quiet, and then a wave broke it, making Amon hold his breath in anticipation.

The wave finally formed several lines. Amon cursed upon reading it.

Seven Fallen Levarchons
Five Fallen Alvadors
One Wounded Cherxanain
One Wounded Varkonian
Forest of D'arksin

"Damn, those soldiers are dead after all. But who's wounded?" he muttered in horror, yet concerned for the well-being of the two female soldiers, despite the fact that they really enjoyed threatening his life, both playfully and literally.

As the Veil's surface turned into smooth pitch-black substance, he quickly strode towards the Hall of Golem, and once inside he flew to where the two golems designated for the female soldiers were sitting in their shallow cave-like, holes.

Amon's eyes scanned both golems closely, and he heard the eerie, hollow whispers coming out from one of them. It was the one he created for Yverna.

Amon pointed at the golem's right hand that it rested palm down on its bent knee. The golem held out its hand and turned its palm face-forward. On it, a lid opened, revealing a small hole fitted for one of the eyes that spied on the Cherxanain.

Amon stepped aside, and from within the hole silver light burst forth. The light gathered in front of the golem and formed a sphere.

It projected whatever was happening with the female soldier who supposedly somewhere in the D'arksin forest.

What he saw in there didn't make him any happier. It showed him Yverna who lay still on the ground. He cursed at the sight. "She'd better be fine, or somebody's gonna be gutted so dead," he remarked with gritted teeth. He turned his gaze to someone else who was kneeling by her side. He recognized the devil as Yverna's sister, but she was doing something that made him frown. She was shouting at her supposed sister in panic. *"Shakra Yverna! Please, wake up!"* Her frantic voice reached his ears.

"That's Vrae's doppelganger," he mumbled. "Where the hell is she?"

He turned his gaze to another part of the scene and saw the aftermath of a massacre. "The Levarchons! Fucking prick!" He shook his head in indignation.

Amon snapped his fingers and the sphere vanished. The golem moved its hand to assume its previous position and settled back into silence.

He landed and went back to wards his den. Sighing in frustration, he sank into his chair with questions swarmed in his head. "Just who or what killed them?"

$$* \quad * \quad *$$

Vrae and I touched down just a few steps from the guards.

"Well, this must be one hell of a day for the two of us, meeting you three times in a row." Gevirash waved at us excitedly.

"Pal, you have no idea what happened while we were in those stupid woods," I sighed. Vrae said nothing and just gave me a weird gaze.

"Then fill us in," Zoran said, and Gevirash nodded vigorously.

"Yeah, what exactly happened out there?" Gevirash jerked his head at the woods.

"Well," Vrae started. "Nothing much. Yve here got the worst of it."

I directed a peeved glare at her. "Yeah, I got the worst of it, thank you so much for your tremendous help."

"You're welcome," Vrae retorted.

Gevirash grimaced at the obviously sour exchange, but Zoran obviously didn't notice any of it. "Hello, there are two people here waiting for explanation. Would you mind letting us into the loop?" He waved his hand and distracted me from my thoughts.

I cast another upset look at Vrae before I turned to them. "Okay, fine. Sorry about that. So, where were we?" I gave them a sorry-I-forgot-about–you-two look.

"Well, how about you start from the point you and Vrae found the Levarchons and the Alvadors?" Gevirash asked with a childish expression on his face as if he were hoping I'd give him a candy bar.

"We didn't exactly find them at the same spot. We found the Levarchons first, and then I headed elsewhere to search for the Alvadors. She stayed behind to examine the bodies," Vrae said with a nod at me. "Once I found those Alvadors, I called forth five of my doppelgangers," she said before I could stop her.

I grimaced as the Valthors started rambling on asking many we fought. They went on and on until I raised both hands. "People, stop!" I snapped. Both of them shut their mouths immediately.

Turning to my sister, I cast a next-time-think-before-you-say-anything look at her and she replied with a sorry-my-bad shrug. Grumbling curses under my breath, I shifted my gaze back to the guards. "We didn't exactly fight anything, 'cause not even a damned rat showed its face."

"Yeah, I didn't even give them half of my powers, just a quarter. One I sent to Yve to lead her to me, and I had the other four go in different directions."

Zoran and Gevirash simultaneously rubbed their chests in relief. It was actually funny if I wasn't too damn annoyed by whatever it was that had dragged me under.

"Got past the 'holy shit, five dops!' hour?" I feigned a shocked look with raised hands.

The Valthors grinned and nodded. I immediately explained everything to the point where I told them that the Levarchons were put inside a protective shield.

"They were all torn up and they were put inside a protective shield of your level? Well, I've no doubt the Machordaens will be able to find them in another hundred years." Zoran shook his head.

47

"I'm with you on that one, but I don't get it. I get that Machordaens are not that much of a high level, but shouldn't those golems be able to get past that level and see, well, almost anything? Not to mention the Veil," Gevirash mused in bafflement.

Vrae nodded. "You got that right. Just so you know, Amon's not exactly real big on doing anything useful."

I scoffed. "What she meant was he'd never use that much power until Azrael went stripteasing right in front of his face," I remarked in vexation.

Vrae winced at me. *"Really? So I meant it like that? How hilarious. I didn't know I had such a revolting imagination,"* she said innocently in my head, and I pretended to look elsewhere while swallowing my laughter.

Both guards burst out laughing. "You know what? I'd be enjoying myself if that guy would do it here. Sometimes humour would feel good for the both of us." Gevirash grinned broadly, and from the look on his face, I had no doubt whatsoever that he was thinking of something that was even more outrageous than what I had just said.

I arched a brow. "I didn't know you ever dug into that kind of crap. If it was me, I'd be puking all over the place if Azrael should ever do something as disgusting as that. Anyhow, we're off the subject."

Taking a deep breath, I continued up to the part where whatever-that-damn-thing-was managed to render me unconscious. Both the guards' jaws dropped when they heard it.

"You okay?" Gevirash asked carefully, half concerned, half afraid to see what I might do to him for asking me that, because he knew very well where my upset limit was, as well as Zoran who stood really still and silent.

Feeling myself walking on dangerously thin ice, I drew a breath to rein myself in before I would accidentally strangle him. "Fine, thanks for asking. Just let me finish with it," I said abruptly. "Anyway, when I woke up, I was already near Vrae because the doppelganger carried me to her while I was out, and apparently she was just in time to stop her from getting dirt like I did. As for the rest, well, there's nothing much, seeing the fact that it might be dangerous if we don't have any clue about what'll happen if Vrae uses her power on the bodies and if there is nothing that could help us decide who the jerk was. So she covered the Alvadors as well, and we came back here," I ended quietly.

"Right," Gevirash said, and then he turned to Vrae. "What happened with you before then?"

Vrae shrugged. "Nothing. I found the Alvadors, but my doppelganger dropped her on me before I could do or get anything."

"So, after all that you guys came back here, huh?" Gevirash asked.

"Any idea yet what did all that?" Zoran added the question.

Vrae shook her head. "No clue. That's why we're here to get Amon to call Zade."

Their faces lit up at the name. "It's been a long time since we saw him," Gevirash said vigorously. "Say hi to him for us."

I nodded. "Will do. In the meantime, tell us. You guys meet anyone or hear anything peculiar while we were gone?"

They shook their heads at the same time. "Just your colleagues, Cedram, Lokya, and Kirana walked past here after you left. They each brought human orbs. Reckon they were about to report and then give those souls over to Malik," Gevirash said.

"They didn't look like they've heard about the slaughtered soldiers, nor did they say anything," Zoran added.

I exchanged a relieved look with Vrae and shifted my gaze back to them. "All right, keep your eyes and ears open, guys. We're off to Amon's."

"Okay," they said in unison.

We walked past them and talked about our next-to-nothing discovery along the way. Either they were dragged after they were dead, or the fight was so immense that it ended far away from where it began, which was even more confusing, because if the killer dragged them from the spot, why the hell did he even bother to do so? Or if, for argument's sake, the fight really grew *that* immense, why didn't we find any tracks leading to the remains? Hell, when we found them, it looked like they had died right on the spot.

Aside from that, we talked a bit about meeting Zade. The guy was a little bit out of the ordinary. He was of Varkonian rank, devils who had special abilities called Imirae. This meant he was able to see everything that had happened to any dead soldiers right through their own eyes in case the circumstances of their death were unusual–for instance, if they got slaughtered by their fellow soldiers for no reason.

In other words, devils gone rogue.

Devils with his ability were usually sent in when any of the warriors in the area came across anything that was out of ordinary, just like the situation we had got ourselves into. He could help identify who was doing the slaying and send out a warning. On several occasions, I saw him do lots of wicked tricks in regard to manipulating memories. Each of the Varkonian had different core powers aside from their Imirae, and as far as I knew, they were forbidden to talk about it outside their own bunch and, of course, the Echelons.

We once again arrived before Amon's den's door. Vrae lifted the incantations, and we entered his room. The moment he saw us, he hurriedly assailed us with questions. To my utter disgust, the first thing he asked was very wrong.

He strode towards me, and his eyes went from my head to my armoured shoes. "Yve, are you all right? I couldn't believe it when I saw you went under!" he blurted without thinking about the repercussions.

Vrae gave me a suck-it-up look. I didn't do anything aside from replying to her with a glare that said *"Why don't you try sucking it with a straw and see how that turns out?"*

I almost couldn't stop myself from fuming. I then turned to Amon. "Thanks for your concern. I just don't think it's necessary to talk about it," I remarked calmly, but I could feel my eyes searing in malignant pitch-black.

Obviously, Amon noticed that too. "Sorry, didn't mean to embarrass you and all. Just don't kick my ass," he said hastily.

My lips curved in a smile I didn't feel. "No, it's okay. Thanks for asking anyway." Abruptly, Vrae patted my back, and I turned to her. The expression on her face was clear, as if she were attempting to tell me something.

"Let me do the talking this time, before you go berserk and accidentally snap his neck."

I just gazed at her in silence as I concealed my laughter at the wishful thought. She then distracted Amon's attention from me and quickly explained everything.

In the end, as both of us intended, she reminded Amon about his spell, to which he replied with a helpless, sorry-I-didn't-know-it'd-turned-out-this-way grin on his face.

She rolled her eyes and kicked his ass a bit, which made him yelp. She then continued with the request to dispatch one Machordaen team to take care of the remains. But when she asked him to call Zade into the scene, he was aghast.

"Do we really need to summon him? I mean, is it really necessary?"

Vrae looked as though she was ready to throw more than just a tantrum at him. "Dammit, Amon, what's gotten into you this time? I've already made it clear to you how bad the whole circumstances are, and the way we see it, there's nothing we can do to ID the bastard without getting stupid filth, which you already know by now isn't really a fun-and-games situation, and so we're not in the fucking mood to waste our time with those things!"

Amon glanced askance at me, and I replied to him with a don't-even-start glare. He wisely shifted his eyes from me and returned to his previous position, which was on the receiving end of Vrae's tirade.

"The only option available for us is to call Zade and ask him to use his Imirae! Why are you acting this way all of the sudden, anyway?" Vrae snarled and gave him a do-you-really-want-to-feel-my-feet-on-your-throat look.

Yanking his ass to a safe distance in case Vrae decided to throw another kick, he then raised his hands so we'd listen. "Down, girl! I just wanted to make sure we really need him, that's all, because last I looked, he was summoned by the Echelons to do whatever it is he's gotta do. Those Echelons could be inane and ludicrous at times. Like I couldn't get around them and find out myself. I didn't get this job by boosting my ego like an idiot," he ranted in one breath.

Vrae crossed her arms. "Finished?" she asked acerbically.

He winced and sighed heavily. "Yeah, the point is, I don't know if he'll be able to lend a hand in this. I just hope he's finished whatever order he's got, so he'll be able to aid us without me getting my ass kicked by the Echelons for distracting him from doing his job," he said defensively.

I mulled over their argument. Making sure my anger was no longer in the dangerously combustible area, I cleared my throat to interrupt them. "Why don't you check it out and see? You can summon one of the Machordaen commanders. When he or she gets here, we'll say you gave us permission and pass them the order while you zero in on Zade. How's that?" I asked him lazily.

"Look who's finally back in business!" Amon beamed. He then fell silent, seeming like he was truly considering my suggestion.

While he was deep within his thoughts, Vrae acted as if she were watching a human game, her eyes moving back and forth between Amon and me. In the end, she settled her gaze on Amon.

Finally, after a full minute, he decided to accept my suggestion. "Okay, that's fine by me. You just wait here. And you might want to make sure the commander won't spill anything. It's your call though."

We nodded at his advice. "Will do," I said.

"See ya." He sauntered to the door few steps behind his armchair, opened the door and vanished into the massive chamber in which golems of all the soldiers resided. He'd track the Varkonian's whereabouts using his.

After Amon left, Vrae and I looked at each other.

I chuckled. "I liked it when you kicked his ass, but I wish you'd kick him a whole lot harder than that."

"Yeah, and he'll never quit sulking about it, and worse, he would've keep us out from anything that happens."

"No doubt about that. Anyway, let's just wait and see until one of them gets here," I said idly as I stretched out in the armchair and absently let my eyes wander around until they stopped at the Veil.

As the one who was given full responsibility to control the flow of information concerning all soldiers and put us under constant surveillance, Amon had had the sole privilege to use the Veil. Only those who'd mastered the golem sorcery and other black arts were given this position, and over the last thirty thousand years, no one else had mastered enough ability in golem sorcery as Amon did, thus firming his grasp on the position. He had sat here for far too long, making even the Veil of Sights unofficially known as his.

Vrae broke into a yawn. "Yve, I think I'll take a nap," she said as she glanced at the Veil that had caught my interest.

I nodded without looking at her and studied the Veil for a minute before deciding that a moment to close my eyes was in order. Careful not to stab my thighs that were protected only by a pair of thin pieces of metal with jutting spikes, I lifted my legs and let them dangle from the armrest. I closed my eyes as I leaned on the backrest and sighed.

It was a short moment after when I heard footsteps growing nearer and stopping outside. I bristled with that familiar tingle that was coming from the door. Vrae and I straightened ourselves just in time as one of Machordaen commanders opened the door.

He entered and shut the door. As the barriers formed themselves, he addressed us. "Hail Lucifer, may the Dark Light of his Rygavon burn the heart of mankind for all eternity and protect you both, Cherxanains." He bowed with his fist upon his chest.

"Hail Lucifer, and the same goes to you," we both replied to him in the same manner, aside from the bow.

"State your name and team," I said sternly.

He straightened himself. "I am Teghari, commander of the fourth squad," he replied firmly. He then gathered his courage to speak. "May I ask your permission to speak?" he asked carefully.

I nodded. "Permission granted."

He bowed his gratitude. "I thank you for your generosity. If you don't mind me asking, I wish to know where Iverand Amon is."

I indicated the room at the back. "He's inside the Hall of Golem at this moment, attending to a certain matter. He will return soon enough, don't worry," I said.

He showed his understanding with a nod and then he straightened himself again.

"Iverand Amon told you that you would be receiving the order from us, did he not?" Vrae began.

"Yes, he did."

"Good. First of all, we must ask you to keep this a secret. Only you and your team shall have knowledge about this. Do you understand what I'm asking you?" Vrae smoothly delivered the question while maintaining her poise.

Perplexed by her request, Teghari averted his alert gaze towards me, his expression asked for further explanation.

I arched a brow at his bafflement. "Do not draw false conclusions, because we are not seeking to cross the line or anything similar. We merely wish to prevent a riot. We have yet to procure any lead as to the exact nature of the recent events. Even Iverand Amon has advised both of us to ensure none of this reaches the ears of the public. So, let me ask you the same thing she did: do we have your word that our requests will remain within your team?" I asked him calmly.

He stopped dead at my demand for his word. He kept silent for a moment, and so did Vrae and I. Suddenly, he firmed his stance.

"Forgive my forwardness, but is it true that Iverand Amon advised you in the first place, Cherxanain Yverna?" he asked carefully.

I hastily restrained myself from glowering at him, because the guy had the right to know, especially when it concerned anything about his direct superior.

"Yes, he did. I did not speak lies. So, again, do we have your word, Teghari?" My gaze began to darken at him as I felt nearly at the end of my tether.

"Why is it so damn difficult to get a simple order for discreetness outside the playing field?" I mused while a tidal wave of anger threatened to drag me back down.

He fell into silence once again, but this time, it seemed he was considering everything I'd told him . . . along with the hint of malevolence he should've seen in my eyes, which perhaps would be just the incentive he needed to leap to the right decision.

Fortunately, a moment later he did agree to our request. "Very well, Cherxanains, I swear on the name of Hieldhar Ezryan and Rygavon that I shall keep this to myself, and I assure you both that my squad will do so as well."

"Good. Now we shall give you the knowledge of the recent events," I said. Before I could go on any further, I felt Vrae's warning gaze fall on me. I telepathically calmed her. *"Don't worry; I will only give him all the info about the Levarchons, the Alvadors, and the bastard. I'm not so stupid that I'll feed him with Cain's BS as well. Relax."*

"Good, just reminding you, that's all, since we want to prevent any riot here, don't we?" she retorted sardonically.

I ignored her comment and debriefed Teghari on the need-to-know basis. After that, I asked him to move out with his team immediately and bring the remains for Zade to check on them later. I ended our requests with an order to mark where the remains were.

"I thank you for enlightening me on the recent events. Now I understand why even Iverand Amon advised you both to keep them quiet. Please forgive my lack of vigilance. I will have my team en route as soon as possible."

"That's what we'd like to hear. And do not concern yourself, for you have the right to ensure the Iverand truly asked that of us. Just send us word immediately when you have accomplished your task or if you stumble across anything peculiar out there. Do I make myself clear?" I asked him.

He nodded, and then he bowed to us. "Crystal, Cherxanain. I shall do as you wish. I take my leave then. May the Dark Light of Rygavon be with you always. I'll get this done and report to you immediately."

"Thank you, and may the Dark Light be with you as well. Tread with extreme caution, Teghari, as you carry out your order in regard to the slaughtered Levarchons and Alvadors. We do not wish for that fate to fall upon you or your team. Now go," Vrae added, and Teghari left the chamber immediately.

"Gee, I'll never fit in with all that formality crap," I sighed as I went to the chair and once again relaxed.

"Me neither." Vrae shook her head and followed suit. "But it does good having someone to show that much respect to us once in a while, don't you think?" she snickered.

"Yeah, tell me about it. Although I still don't get it why those Machordaens respect Amon that much," I said as I stifled a laugh and moved to Amon's desk.

"You don't say. Anyway, do you think Amon will be able to get Zade and drag his ass into this mess?" she wondered.

"Well, he might if Zade has already been dragged out from whatever it was our merry band of Echelons wanted him to do," I replied quietly, and then I resumed my previous position.

We both fell silent for a while. I couldn't pick up what she was thinking or feeling since she sealed herself off completely like I did with myself. As for me, I was caught once again in those stupid dreams and Cain's bull crap.

I had no idea what these recent events held for us all, let alone the so-called prophecy Cain was babbling out.

"You okay?" I bristled all over when Vrae suddenly pulled me back from my thoughts.

"Yeah, just wondering what the hell those guys are doing so damn long," I hastily answered. I didn't want her to realize what I was thinking, or feeling for that matter. Then again, from the look on her face, I had no doubt whatsoever that she'd figured it out. As usual, she was one of the extremely few who most of the time could read me like a damned open book, while I looked like a sternly closed one to others.

"I definitely have to work on my shield. Just how the hell does she do that anyway?" I pondered with disbelief and some exasperation. Luckily, she didn't bring any of it up. Instead, she silently turned her gaze to the ceiling.

Abruptly, the door that led to the Hall of Golem behind Amon's desk was jerked open, and the Head Intel came through. I caught glimpses of what lingered behind it and a bile rose to my throat. Even a mere glimpse could make me sick with repugnance.

Roughly slamming the door shut, Amon strode to his chair and sank in. I exchanged a baffled look with Vrae and turned to him. "Dude, what happened? You look like the Echelons barbecued your dog."

He winced in bafflement before my remark registered. Feigning annoyance, he scowled at me, but his eyes betrayed him by shining brightly with glee. "Nice, like I ever get to bring one in here," he replied in amusement. Yet there was a tangible trail of scathing anger in his voice.

"So, you made it?" I asked him carefully.

He closed his topaz eyes as he rubbed one of his perfect brows. "Yeah, he'll be here any minute," he answered quietly, and then he opened his eyes to look at us. That was when he blinked as if he'd just noticed something. "Looks like you're enjoying yourselves," he remarked with a smirk, indicating our so-not-appropriate positions in our chairs.

We didn't even bother to put our legs down. Hell, I even raised both arms and bent them behind my head with fingers entwined. "Well, we know you won't be bothered, and nobody else is here, and we don't care." I gave a nonchalant remark, to which he replied with a snort.

"What is it then? You look pissed." Vrae urged him.

He sighed. "The Echelons demanded explanations for my request to summon Zade," he began curtly, definitely displeased.

"That doesn't sound good," I thought with various creative curses directed towards the incredulously asinine Echelons.

Catching the cue, Vrae and I straightened ourselves. "After you did, what'd they say?" Vrae asked.

"They, with all their gloriously inane minds, didn't approve it at first, even after I told them that he doesn't necessarily have to be on site. Even if he does, you both will be there with him," he said, his anger mounting.

I rolled my eyes as I realized where this was heading. "They still didn't approve you?" My own temper began to rise.

He cleared his throat. "Well, fortunately, there were some of them who came through in the end, and the others followed them like the cattle they are," he said with fair amount of disdain in his voice.

Perplexed, but had a good idea of who they were, I leaned forward. "Let me guess. They were Bynethar and Xamian or Kathiera and Faemirad."

He balked at my remark. "Well, it was the former pair. How can you tell?"

"All these thousands of years you've worked under their command, don't tell me you still have no decent idea as to who has brains for brains and who has shit for brains?" I asked sardonically.

He suppressed the urge to laugh and turned it to short coughs. "That's a really good point. It's a pity though, that the latter pair only has the brains for their own interests."

Abruptly, the barriers disappeared, and the door opened once again. We stood up and turned, just in time to see a stunningly handsome devil come into view.

Almost seven feet in height, Zaderion (we called him Zade) wore silver armour with three eyes that formed a triangle embossed on its chest–the crest of Varkonian ranks. The armour hugged his well-muscled body, and a pair of leather pants cupped his long legs. A pair of horns jutted out of his head, and his wavy gold-blond hair fell over his broad shoulders. His blue eyes had shades of green that gleamed with amusement, quite a contrast to his sharp features.

But despite the friendly look on his handsome face, I knew the savageness that dwelled beneath it. Unlike the rest of the Varkonian who didn't hang around us too often, he could unleash almost as much violence as both of us could if need be in battle. And our kind of violence was just too damned gory, which indicated how bad an influence he'd gotten from us both.

"Ladies, long time no see," he greeted us. "It's damn good to see you both, although here in this kinda place, but whatever, good to see you two."

Amon, after hearing his words, pouted. "What the hell did you mean with "this kinda place"? Gee, is there any of you that have even a freakin' bit of respect?" He curled his lips.

Vrae and I sneered. "Fortunately for you Amon, yes indeed we have it, but then again it's unfortunate that neither one of us, well, have as much as you expect us to. And yes, it's good to see you too, Zade. How have you been?" I asked, giving him a broad grin, and so did Vrae.

Zade burst out laughing. "I've always liked that about you, girls. Thanks for asking. I've never been better, and sorry, dude, but I'm with them on that one."

Amon was still pouting at first, but then, as if to regain his honour, he cleared his throat and wiped the ugly pout off his face. "Whatever! Back to business. You had Teghari's team out there?"

I nodded at his question. "Yeah, they're on their way."

"We also had his word that our request won't be going anywhere, although in the process he had to piss us off a little bit," Vrae interjected.

"How so?" Amon asked, aghast, while Zade was listening with curiosity gleaming bright in his eyes.

"Well, not much. He just asked us whether you truly had us keep these circumstances a secret. It seemed he wouldn't be convinced before we *really* confirmed it or he hear it directly from you," I explained.

He winced. "Wow, I had no idea he'd do that. I mean, even though technically the one who has the power to give them orders regarding intel business is me, nevertheless Cherxanains all the way to Hieldhar have power over them in the battlefield. I didn't tell him to keep it secret through the eye, because it's too conspicuous. I thought he'd go without question anyway," he said, looking a bit befuddled.

I felt as if something had stabbed my core when he mentioned "Hieldhar", but I ignored it. "He'd apologized in the end though for behaving like that, but really, just what exactly did you treat them with that he gets fussy like that?" I crossed my arms over my chest.

When he didn't say anything but simply stood stunned, I chuckled. "Just kidding! At least some of us really show you some of the respect you need, and believe me, you do need it." I said nonchalantly, while Zade seemed to struggle to hold himself from bursting out laughing.

"Gee, right, fine, mock me all you want, you're lucky, like I said before, that I'm a devil saint." Amon rubbed his brows.

The three of us rolled our eyes at his compliment-for-myself comment and ignored it. "And I didn't know what to say when I heard what you said to Zoran and Gevirash–that I'll never use my magick's full power until Azrael's stripteasing right in front of my face." He said with his eyebrows arched.

Zade's laughter filled the room again, louder this time, and between his laughter, he turned to me. "You really said that? Why did I never think of that before? Thanks for the idea, 'cause that's really funny." All of us laughed at his comment, even Amon.

I sobered up and cleared my throat. "Okay, enough with the stupid jokes. Zade, has he elaborated to you everything we've encountered up to this point?" I asked him with a firm expression to show I was back to business.

The Imirae wielder nodded subtly as an answer. "Yep, he told me everything on our way here, and to be honest, damn, I've never thought in a million years that he would ever have the guts to spill rotten beans like that. I wonder what our bosses might do to him right now, or at least what they might order his guards to do."

"Beats me, although he does have a brain when it is about his ex-race. It seems he still can't shut his hole up on certain things." Vrae let out a slow breath.

"Yeah, either we must be grateful for the warning in it or we must rip him to pieces for the humiliation it offered." I snapped.

Zade cleared his throat. "Guys, I don't know about you, but, when Amon told me about that BS, my thoughts jumped to Ry." His intense gaze fell on us.

Amon, Vrae, and I were immediately alarmed at his words.

"You're saying there's a chance that this crap of Cain had anything to do with whatever it was Ry was supposed to find out?" I asked with immense curiosity in my voice, while Vrae just lowered her gaze to the floor.

"Well, it's only a guess. I didn't think of him on purpose anyway," he added quickly.

Vrae lifted her gaze from the floor. "But then again, if it does have anything to do with Ry's last order, it's surely worth checking everything we know, don't you think?" she asked. I caught something in her voice that told me she was hiding something.

"Let's roll to the archive then," Amon said as he started for the door.

I shook my head. "What the hell for? I've been there for ages, and nothing mentioned a damned prophecy or even any nonsense that resembles one. Well, if you count them making Ry one of the Echelons' favourite boys as nonsense, then I guess there is one. As if," I said sarcastically.

Amon screwed his face at me. "I was thinking that it probably ain't safe to talk about it here, but whatever, fine, no archive." He strode back to his chair.

Scoffing at him, my thought drifted to the Archive, where Amon intended to take us. It was a massive dome with countless shelves that filled the room almost all the way to the ceiling. The shelves were positioned like a circular maze that followed the shape of the chamber. The deepest area was where all information regarding Hieldhars who fell in the line of duty was stored. All of us had our own respective area there, starting with commanders at the centre of the archive, followed with us Cherxanains and Varkonians, Machordaens, Alvadors, Levarchons, all the way to lesser soldiers.

I remembered the Hieldhars area quite well, because, as I said, for a while after I received news of Ry's death, I'd spent time in there, trying to dig as much information as I could. I did all this because I believed–no, I knew that there were more sinister reasons than just the significance of whatever secret they wanted from up there. One of those reasons would be because they wanted to get rid of him without causing any uproar. It was something that was kept tight between me and him, but I had a hunch why those fucking Echelons sent him on that suicide run. I knew, because he had been used as target practice by them for a long time before he received that order. After months of looking, I didn't find anything, and the Echelons just scrutinized me further. In the end, I gave up digging centuries ago.

Amon sank into his chair and manifested another one for Zade. "Fine then, Yve, what if you tell us about his last job? Did he ever say anything to you?"

"Hell, I have no idea, and you knew very well that I was doing my own gig when he got his ass burned down. I don't know why you're asking me first. At any rate, even though I've tried to dig anything I could centuries ago, I didn't find anything that held that much importance. I might as well have asked you first." I tilted my head at him.

"Damn, it might be as well if I didn't ask you at all," he sighed, while I grinned towards him, giving him that it's-your-rotten-luck-man look and all. He then turned to Zade and came up with no luck there either.

But when he asked Vrae, who had just kept her silence as Amon asked Zade and myself, suddenly she made a firm gesture as if she were determined to tell us something. It seemed that she was waiting for the right moment to spill whatever it was.

"Okay guys, I think the time has come for me to let the three of you know about this. I'll explain to you all everything I know about Ry's last job."

Chapter 4

Amon made a choking noise. "Come again?" he asked.

"What is it, Vrae? What aren't you telling me? You know something about what exactly his job was?" I rocked her.

She nodded, and slowly she put away my hands. "Yes, bits of it, but let's just chill, okay?" She then turned to the Iverand. "Amon, can you make sure that no ears of the Echelons are around?"

Amon froze at her question. He eyed her for a moment and then raised one hand to the ceiling. In an instant, I felt other barriers engulf the chamber. It almost rendered me breathless with the pressure.

"I'm sorry for the inconvenience, but this way even the Echelons won't have a chance to sneak a peek." he explained. "Which is why I'd rather we all go to the archive," he said, looking meaningfully at me.

I shrugged off his comment. "No matter," I said, and our attentions were fixed on Vrae once again.

She let out a long breath. "First of all, I must tell you that on the night right before he departed to carry out the order he was burdened with, he was looking for you, Yve," she said, her voice filled with evident turmoil.

"He what?" the three of us were stunned at her words; even Amon couldn't shut his jaw.

She cast a miserable look at me. "Yes, indeed he was. But because he wasn't able to find you back then and ran into me instead, which was when I told him that you'd been given another gig by the Echelons, he changed his mind. So instead of you, he gave me a bit of inside information on what he was about to do, and it was much more than what the Echelons told most of us seven hundred years ago," she said bitterly.

My body shook as potent anger coursed throughout my body like poison. "He told you something about his last order? The very order that got him killed? Why the hell didn't you tell me, Vrae!? You knew I was looking for every fucking bit of information ever since the moment I received the news that he was burned down in the line of duty! A damned duty that none of those fucking Echelons ever mentioned specifically to any of us–except for the crap that he was sent to overhear the shit of upstairs! You'd better convince me with your next words, Vrae . . ." I ended my tirade with a cold warning while the other two just stared at us both.

She held both hands up in surrender. "I know you're angry. You have every right to be, but please, just listen. I'm not keeping you from this on purpose. I couldn't tell you because he entrusted me with this secret, and he specifically requested me not to. Not before the right moment arrived," she said, and then she took a deep breath before she continued.

I winced and inhaled a bit to calm myself down. "Okay, I'm listening. So, you're saying that Ry told you not to tell us anything before the time was right?" I asked her quietly as I looked at her eyes. What I saw there made me realize that she was telling the truth. It wasn't her fault or her choice. Snapping at her wouldn't change the fact that Ry really did specifically ask her not to give this piece of information to anyone including me, not until the right moment.

She nodded. "He did. At first I didn't know why he changed his mind and kept me in the loop instead of you and, furthermore, why he strictly forbade me from telling you everything until the right moment."

"I take it that you did ask him why the hell he forbade me to know whatever it was he told you?" I stared at her, demanding damned good answers.

She sighed wearily at my hostile tone. "Well, you could be a little happier about me now, knowing that I did ask him." She folded her arms over her chest.

"And? What was the cause? It'll be a whole lot better if we keep the true nature of his damned job for last, because I won't let you to be going anywhere until I get the answers I need," I pressed.

"Don't worry, I will. Like I said, the time is right, and as I vowed to him, I will tell you everything. Right now, it means you guys are included," she said, and she turned to the other two, whom I had almost forgotten were there in light of what Vrae had told me.

"You even vowed on it?!" I asked her sharply, and looking at her gaze made me realize how difficult the situation was for her and for Ry, which made my anger lessen a little bit at a time.

Hearing what she said about letting them in the loop, Amon tried to lighten the situation at hand. He turned to Zade as he screwed his face up. "Oh, good, so a certain someone didn't forget about us after all, Zade."

Unfortunately for him, Zade was doing it a whole lot better than he did. "Really? I don't think they were forgetting about me, but I do have this feeling that the one who was being forgotten is you, mate," he said calmly. The three of us started laughing and Amon started to pout yet again.

"Thanks for the joke, boys. Now let's get back to business, shall we?" I said firmly.

"Fine, you were asking why he forbade me to let even you in the loop. Well, that was because he said that if something should happen to him concerning this job, the Echelons would be watching over you closely in case you received any info from him, whatever that means. He said he didn't want to cause you troubles like that." I gaped for a second when I heard that, and I just raised my eyebrows without saying anything.

Then, as if she were taking advantage of the three of us falling into complete silence, she went on, "Yes, I know that it was a bit weird for someone like Ry to ever say something as sentimental as that, but all and all, he just didn't want to make the Echelons grow suspicious on you."

I was about to say something, but she raised her hands to stop me. "Don't cut me off just yet. There's more. He also asked me to gather any intel no matter how insignificant in silence and to wait for the next time Cain told us anything weird about war between us and the vermin from upstairs, and more specifically, humans. He also mentioned that some unusual events would occur around the same time he did it. Only then could I pass this information on to you and to any people the both of us trusted most, on condition that we had to keep the number small."

Amon suddenly spoke up after hearing what she said about Cain. "No kidding? Ry told you that Cain would spill out some shit, and the Levarchons and the Alvadors as well? He knew about those all along?"

"It seems to be the case," she said sadly.

"In the name of Rygavon, Ry, what did you get yourself into?" Amon said in disbelief as he sank into his chair, while Zade just stared at the floor with his face turned pale.

Vrae's face turned ghostly pale, and there was a glint of despair in her blood-red eyes. "How I regret it to this day that if only I hadn't agreed to vow to him to keep this secret from everyone including you, Yve, then maybe he would still be alive or maybe we would be able to rescue him in time. The warriors were suffering so much, lost, scattered, and leaderless after he was gone," Vrae answered him with evident anguish in her voice.

After I'd managed to pull myself together, I patted her shoulder. "It's okay. He would never have asked you any of that and even made you vow on it if he didn't know the circumstances. He must've known whatever danger it brought upon you before asking you to do so. It's I who must say sorry to you. He put the burden on you all these centuries just because he didn't want to trouble me, which was a very silly reason, I might add." I forced a grin.

She shook her head and smiled half-heartedly. "You don't have to apologize."

"But I do. And you shouldn't have hoped you had unmade your vow. It'd kill you, you know," I said seriously.

She stared blankly at me and didn't say anything.

"She's right. You did the right thing, Vrae. You should just get over it," Zade remarked quietly, and he lifted his gaze from the floor.

"Thanks, Zade, and apologies accepted." She grinned at me. "Now . . ."

"Let's kick the sentimental things out of the way." I finished her words.

She nodded, but before she could continue any further, I cut her off. "Wait! Tell me, why didn't you tell us all of this earlier? I mean, before we checked on the Levarchons and those Alvadors. Amon already let us in the loop by telling us what happened to them and especially what Cain had said."

Amon and Zade stared at me and then at her. "Well, to tell you the truth, I wasn't sure about it. Was that the right time that Ry meant in the first place? Is the disappearance of those soldiers the unusual event he mentioned? Hell, I wasn't even sure that Cain's crap was the one he meant, since the bastard tends to spill shit every now and then. Sorry," she said with a helpless look.

I waved her words in dismissal. "That's understandable. You should play it safe anyway. But at any rate, we finally found something important about these recent events and the real reason behind his assignment," I said, intending to wait for a moment so she would have time to recuperate from saying what she had told us up to this point.

Vrae seemed to realize my intention for the moment, so she changed the subject. "But really, it was fortunate that your hunch was working in the right direction in the first place, Zade." She smiled at him.

"Well, maybe it's your lucky day, looking for me instead of Darvahl or the others to check out those Levarchons and the Alvadors, just when I've already had my back off of any job." He grinned back.

"Gee, and what makes you think either of us would call Darvahl? Not that we have anything against the guy, but let's just say neither of us like that nosy guy enough to let him hang around us." I grinned.

"I know what you mean. I don't like him most of the time myself. And really, I wish I could've hung around you a little more often, 'cause your jokes really got me. Talking to you is a whole lot more useful for me than chatting with other wielders. Most of them are too full of themselves and make me nauseous. I wouldn't mind if it were you girls, but them? Yuck," he said as he shivered.

"Well, thanks for the compliment. We'll make a note not to do anything that'll make you nauseous." I winked at him and then turned to Amon. "And by the way, Amon?"

"Yeah?"

"Something just occurred to me. Did you put your golems on Ry when he went to do his last gig? I mean, if you did and he was attacked, you could've sent out a warning, and yet none of us got any. And also when he talked about all of this to Vrae, you did put them on Vrae, right? So why didn't you know anything?"

Amon grimaced at my words. "Oh, that. Ehm, actually, when Ry was making his way up there, my, uhm, pals bailed when he'd reached a certain range. They couldn't stand getting too close."

I rolled my eyes. "Right, I'd expect nothing less from your *pals*." He grinned sheepishly at my comment.

"And as for why Amon didn't know anything about this, well, I'll explain that," Vrae interjected.

We all turned to her.

"Actually, Amon did watch us as usual, but when Ry told me all this, we were using a blocked channel."

I raised my brow, and Zade just stared blankly at her. So they had communicated mentally. That made sense, since it allowed us to communicate safely without the risk of being overheard.

Amon scowled. "So that's why! If I recall it correctly, right around the time you said when you met Ry, I'd wondered why you two were just floating around not saying zap, just making expressions like a mute film."

Vrae gave him a droll stare.

"Okay, whatever, let's get the obvious stuff out of the way. You ready to tell us the rest of it?" I cut him off and turned to Vrae.

She regained her composure before she continued. "Okay, I'll begin with the moment after he made me vow not to tell you guys. First, as I've told you, Yve, I asked him why you couldn't be told about this as well, and you already heard the answer. Then afterwards, he started to tell me all of it, at least, what he did know at that time."

"What's that mean, 'what he did know at that time'? Didn't he know all about whatever it was already?" My wondering gaze fell on her.

She shrugged. "Hell, how would I know? He was the one who said it. Anyhow, he started to babble out things, which, I admit, sounded more like crap at first. But when I heard the whole thing, hell, I'd say that was the first time my body literally shook in fear. I even wished that I've never heard any of it in the first place." Her face turned pale, as if remembering something really hideous, while the three of us watched her, feeling curious even more about what Ry had told her.

"Brace yourself, sister. Now let's hear what you've stored in the box for us. We need to hear it. *I* need to hear it." I levelled a stare at her, all the while trying to ignore her shivering in apparent fear of talking.

She drew her breath. "You're the one who needs to brace yourself. Listen to this. Ry told me that the Secret of Heaven which he needed to overhear was about the Omen of Resurrection. The part about Cain blabbering shit? Well, he said that he knew Cain would eventually get at least a bit of the secret, and he also said that if we were lucky, Cain would get his hands on the part of it which will help us avoid permanent destruction."

"What did he mean, 'permanent destruction'? And I thought that Cain's prophecy was just BS. You're saying that the crap he spilled out was a part of the Secret of Heaven? How in the hell was he able to get one of those without going anywhere?" Zade asked anxiously.

She indicated Amon with a nod. "Amon told us about Cain's BS, right? 'The Great War between heaven and hell will erupt, and the wheel of destiny of the human world will be set in motion. The damned shall be vanquished and thrown to another realm, become nothing but spirits and apparitions. Eons after the war, the once-destroyed world will arise from the ashes with all its glory. It will be marked with the union of the essence that belongs to both worlds. Thus unfolds the omens of resurrection. The destroyed world will arise once more,'" she quoted Amon's words from hours earlier.

"Yeah, what of it?" the Iverand asked slowly, while I just stared at her.

"Well, from what Ry told me, our bosses already have a small piece of information about our coming doom, which, as the prophecy declared, is the big war between hell and heaven, but when the exact time is, they still hadn't figured out until now."

"What! They all knew?" I was enraged at her statement.

"Yes, that was why he was sent up there. He was the one they chose because this little piece of information was considered to be vital. It seems that our bosses decided that sending ordinary Alvadors wouldn't be enough. They thought that ordinary angels or even Arcs would try apprehending whoever it was that might try to overhear. If it was Ry, it'd be a piece of cake dealing with them all. What they didn't count on was maybe the part where God Himself would kill anybody they sent."

"Yeah, and we lost him because of them. Not even a scrap of his robe was ever found after that! Maybe that's why they never revealed what exactly happened to Ry in the first place. They don't want anyone to smell their fucking stinks!" I snarled.

She concurred. "I know. Every time I think about it, I can't help but feel a burning anger stir in me. But the bottom line is that the Echelons thought that if Ry was able to get this secret, we might be able to completely destroy the upstairs army before they start pulling weird stunts on us. Thus, we gain complete control over the upstairs army."

I arched a brow at that. "Did he say for how long?"

She nodded. "He said we'd have the upper hand for at least four millennia, which would allow our subordinates to drag more humans to our side, and hell, maybe the Xarchons would be able to butcher the humans freely without them getting in the way," she said quietly.

"That's something indeed," I mused at her mentioning Xarchons. They were the most violent of beasts that we'd unleash at the humans every now and then when we were assigned to wipe out a kingdom and its people, and they sure could slaughter people in pretty messy and gory kinds of ways. The only ones who'd bother to stop them were people from up there–which was really a buzz kill.

"Just a second. This permanent destruction thing you mentioned earlier. Were you talking about the dumb war or the one Cain mentioned? And how the hell, as Zade asked you before, did Cain manage to get his ears on those?" Amon asked in disbelief.

"I'll explain one at a time, okay? I also asked Ry that, so just listen. First, the merging part." I was alarmed immediately when she mentioned that. She wasn't about to tell the guys about those shit dreams I'd been having, was she? I shot a warning gaze at her, to which she replied with a chilling expression that told me not to say a damn thing.

"Ry told me that if we are to arise after that war which *will* destroy us . . . I know it sucks, just hear me out," she said hastily, when I opened my mouth to argue. "I'll say it again. If we are to arise after this war, the ones amongst us who have been experiencing dreams or visions regarding humans must not be harmed." She glanced at me for a split second. Obviously she wanted to see my reaction. I just stared blankly at her as she continued. "Because if Cain was able to apprehend the knowledge of it and tell it to us, it will confirm that these particular devils will be our ticket to resurrect our world once more and to be even more able to roam than during all these millennia of our lives. And the Omen of Resurrection Cain mentioned was indeed about our world."

After that the three of us just stared at her. We didn't know what to say. And then after a brief moment, she went on, "I asked him how Cain knew about this while he was locked up in that hole of his. Ry just said that he went to Cain's cell and discussed everything. He also mentioned that he would give something to Cain on his way back from up there that would enable him to obtain that bit of prophecy. I asked him what it was of course, but he wouldn't tell me, not even through a channel. He was afraid someone might find out." She took a deep breath again and fell silent for a second as if she were thinking about what she would tell us.

She then inclined her head. "At any rate, he mostly feared that our bosses won't believe whatever Cain says and they would just look for these devils and then exterminate them by whatever means necessary. He said that there's high possibility that they would go on a rampage out of fear that these so-called half breeds are the ones that will ultimately lead us to our permanent destruction, not preventing it."

Amon suddenly raised a hand, stopping her before she said anything else. "One quick question. Did he ever mention to you how in the hell he was able to get hold of such information? Not even I know about any of this. Don't tell me he gave you his my-special-inside-guy crap like he used to do, or the I-did-my-homework BS," he snapped.

I was wondering about the same thing we were thinking, and the three of us stared at her.

She just shrugged. "Well, this is your lucky day Amon, 'cause you're right. The precise crap he gave me would be, 'I asked my special inside man who was doing some research while I was off doing my part of homework on it.' So basically, he said both of the things you've suggested." She grinned helplessly.

"Shit, I knew it. Dammit, Ry," he murmured.

"Hey, don't kill the messenger, all right? Anyhow, he also said that . . ." she hesitated.

"What? He said what?" I shook her.

She looked straight at me, and I saw her blood-red eyes gleaming with guilt. "He said–before he continued telling me the rest of it–that he probably wouldn't get a chance to meet you, me, and the rest of us, Yve. I was outraged when he said that, but when I looked at his face, I came to realize that that mission will claim his life one way or the other," she said, and she slowly pulled herself away from me.

The three of us were speechless after hearing what she said. After seconds of silence, I broke it. "You're saying that he knew he would be leaving us all for real? That he knew Big Guy Himself would kill him?"

"If you had looked at his face when he was saying all this, you would think the same. He seemed certain. You know that he wouldn't act like that if he was only dealing with vermin."

"You bet he wouldn't," Zade said bitterly, and he cast a blank look at me. I returned his blank stare with my own as I wondered what he was thinking.

I had no idea what he was thinking at that time, and he also didn't say zilch, so I looked away from him and faced Vrae once again. "So, those stupid bosses didn't let loose any intel on him. Hell, not even you knew any of this, did you, Amon?" I asked him without averting my gaze from my sister.

"Nope," Amon said flatly. For a second I could've sworn I saw a glint of fear as if he were hiding something in his eyes, but I decided not to press it.

I turned to Zade. "I take it you didn't know squat either," I remarked. At my words, he just gave me an expression so blank that I couldn't even put my finger on what was on his mind.

After a second, his lips formed a thin smile. "Hell, no, I didn't know shit about shit in this. And do I look like a suicidal? I wouldn't want to be killed by you two, especially not by you, Yve. Not when I still wanna hang out with the two coolest girls among the devils. You know that I'd tell you ASAP if I had any sort of clue in this, now don't you?" He made a face as if he were really begging us.

I stifled a laugh. "Whatever, weeping boy. Just don't start crying on me. If you do, I'll show you why they call us the coolest girls among the devils, you dig?" I grinned at him.

He winked and held his hands up to feign surrender.

"Basically, we're screwed, huh?" Amon asked Vrae, who fell silent.

Abruptly, she looked straight at me. "Not just yet. We may not be able to apprehend the secret now, but we can try to find a way to make sure Cain's prophecy about our world's resurrection comes true. That way, we can bitch-slap those smart-ass bosses right when they don't even know it's coming at them."

"Now, that's the best thing I heard from you for the last several hours. Any idea how do we start it?" I asked her, without knowing what was in her mind.

And then I heard her saying something in my head that made me almost kill everyone on sight. *"Yve, I'm really sorry. You're not gonna like this. I'm telling everyone, if we're lucky, one of them shares your fate as well."*

I shot a warning gaze at her. *"What are you, numbnuts? Don't you even dare . . ."*

A tic worked in her jaw. *"Now isn't the time, dammit! Are you saying that you'd rather keep all of this quiet while Ry had his life ended by God Himself for our sakes, including, oh yeah,* yours?*"*

I stopped dead at her harsh question. Finally, Ry won, and I had no choice but let her tell everyone. Besides, like she said, if we're lucky one of them also would be in on this mess.

"Fine, you win. Just make it damn fast."

"That's more like it. So here goes nothing. Brace yourself. I don't have a clue what they will say."

Amon and Zade just stared blankly at us both, knowing that we were communing telepathically.

Vrae shifted her position. She seemed even more uncomfortable than before. "My first bet would be the so-called Votzadirs." The term meant half-breeds in our language, and it made my stomach churn.

"You mean those who've been experiencing nightmares about humans? Hell, I wonder when you'd bring that one up," Zade said.

Vrae and I just stared at each other. I didn't know why he was so interested in this. "Why is that? You have something in mind, buddy?" I asked him with obvious curiosity in my own voice.

"Not just something. I have a confession to make. Hell, all this time I didn't have a friggin' clue about what's been happening to me all these past centuries. I thought I was having lunatic episodes," he said, partly relieved and partly embarrassed.

I arched a brow at that. Could it possibly be?

"You've been having those as well?" I asked, before I realized what the repercussions would be, and I regretted it, for Zade and Amon both stared at me.

After a few brief moments my worst thoughts proved mistaken, for Zade beamed instead of scorning me. "You too? Gee, thank Hell for this," he laughed.

I frowned. "Would you mind explaining what's funny in all this?"

He started at my tone and grinned apologetically. "Nothing, it's just that I thought somebody as lousy as Darvahl would be in on this, which, by the way, will make me really, really nauseous."

Before I could say anything, he seemed to realize my anger. "I'm sorry, I know this isn't funny for you, but look at the bright side here. We and maybe the others will determine our resurrection. Well, yeah not so much for the bosses, I'd say, because we all know that they won't be that generous. Hell, they didn't even think much of Ry."

"He's right. There's no way they would protect us, especially you two. Hell, we might as well watch our backs a whole lot closer from now." Amon looked at each one of us.

"Yeah, we've thought about that as well, which is why only she gets to know the problems I've had with humans in my head all these centuries." I jerked my head at Vrae.

She didn't say anything but made a firm gesture at the three of us. "Okay, then it's settled, although this will leave us one more problem to fix." I realized what she meant almost immediately, whereas the two males just stared blankly at each other, evidently confused.

"Yeah, she's right about that," I interjected without hesitation.

When the two of us didn't spill nada, Zade threw a puzzled look at me. "And that would be what?"

The two of us turned our gaze on Amon. "Him," we said in unison.

Right after we indicated the Iverand, they too realized what the problem was. "Bloody hell, they're right. You're in tight spot in this. We can't expect the Echelons to sit tight if the worst case scenario should happen and all of us, including you, had to save our asses and get the hell outta here pronto."

Amon fell silent for a second after he heard Zade's words.

I nodded. "Exactly! That's our problem. Although I do have this feeling that they won't dare touch you as long as they don't slip anybody in to steal your golem sorcery, or worse, the Echelons force you to take an apprentice." I jerked my head at the door leading to the Hall of Golem. "But as soon as they do, and they know you're with us, just get your ass out of their sight."

He pouted playfully. "Now you're telling me you that you acknowledge me?" I narrowed my gaze at him and he raised his hand in surrender. "Just kidding, but you do have a point there. Anyhow, I don't think they'll zero in on us in this matter any time soon. I'm not even sure they know that we know–well, not yet anyway."

"Yeah, you're saved for a couple minutes. Now, before we're way too much off the subject, we better get back at it." I glanced at Vrae, who winced. "Right, you meant the thing Ry told me, correct?"

"Yeah, the one you said scared you shitless."

She snorted. "Har, har, very funny, but yeah, it did scare the shit outta me. So, ready?"

"Ready when you are," the three of us said in unison.

"Fine, I don't think it will hold that many surprises now that Cain has spilled out the most rotten bean of the century. I'll just make it quick. Yve, about the bastard we intended for Zade to check out earlier?"

"What about him? I have a bone to pick with him for knocking me out with leftovers."

"Now, hold on a minute. We're not talking about how that bloody bastard managed to drag you into going under. Back then, Ry said something. He didn't exactly mention any particular description, but when I went through a bit of thinking about it, I think this is the thing he was babbling about. He mentioned that someone or something would appear around the time Cain started muttering shit."

"What the hell did he mean by that?" Amon blurted, unable to hold himself.

Vrae shrugged at his question. "He wasn't sure either. All I know was that he told me this newcomer would slaughter everything and everyone in silence, and that no one would ever acknowledge its existence until it was too late. He wasn't sure whose side this entity is on either."

"Could he be more vague?" I pondered sarcastically.

"The whole point is that this guy, hell, whatever it turns out, will either be our big help in the upcoming war with upstairs or our worst enemy, even worse than God's Right Hand, that Michael guy–well not that he's really that badass or anything. But the worst possibility is that the guy would exterminate everything in his way and thus destroy the balance, along with our last card to resurface as the prophecy predicted we would."

"Did he at least tell you that he had a wild guess about who the fuck that is? 'Cause I absolutely have no friggin' idea," I snapped.

Vrae shrugged. "You don't say. Anyhow, now that you mention it, he did say something. The thing is, this is the part where I got scared shitless like you said. He thought that this guy was Big Boss's oldest creation, older than anything we've ever known, that is. He told me a bit of inside intel he's got."

"What do you mean the bitch was His oldest creation? You're saying we were right then, when we thought those Levarchons and Alvadors ran into something that's been in a dreamland? If that's the case, either they woke it up by accident or it was the time for the bitch to come back to reality," I said as I tapped my fingers on Amon's desk.

"I suspect so. But the thing is, I've never heard of something that was way older than Lucifer or those wretched Arcs from up there, and I know you haven't either, Yve."

I shrugged. "Hell, no. Don't know squat about whatever that is."

She turned to Amon and Zade. "You two got anything on this? What about you, Amon? Ever stumble across anything before? Any weird intel would suffice."

"I don't know. I've never heard of any of this before, have you?" he turned to Zade.

"You're asking me? What are you? Blind? I'm just an Imirae wielder. I know nothing about everything, you ken?"

"Okay, okay. So the bottom line is, we gotta gather intel on what we can and watch our backs in the process. And hell, we gotta dig up anything on this old coot. Maybe that's why we couldn't ID the guy in the ordinary ways," Vrae said.

"Yeah, this is why we need you even more to check those remnants, Zade," I added as I averted my gaze to the Varkonian.

"Sweet! Always the fun job. I got it," he winked.

"Now, this is all I got for now. By the way, do you think we should tell Zoran and Gevirash about this? They already know a bit of it, and we can count on them to put their ears closely to the ground. What do you guys say?" Vrae asked.

"Maybe we should, and not just them. We should pay Cain a visit too and get our hands on whatever it was Ry gave him. If we're lucky, Ry might've told him something he didn't tell you." My gaze turned to Vrae.

"One question," Amon said, and we all turned to him. "Are we even sure Ry managed to send Cain whatever it was?"

"Look, I know that Big Boss upstairs even wiped out an entire lake just to fry his ass, but I don't know how he did it. He just told me he wouldn't fail, even if it was the last thing he'd do," Vrae remarked in grim voice.

Amon nodded slowly, and I cleared my throat to set them back on track, even though combustible rage threatened to explode in me any minute over what Vrae had just told us. "And after the seven of us, including Cain, start zeroing in on this matter, I take it Cain won't be doing the intel gathering himself, which leaves six of us. We should take precautions and start to think about means to communicate with each other in case the worst should happen."

"As for Cain, he was the one who spilled the rotten beans which turned out to be the key to this problem, so we can't ditch him, although frankly, I don't have any idea of how to drag him out from the bosses," Vrae added.

"Well, we can think about that one bit at a time. Now, time's against us today. We should be off, or someone might notice that the three of us have been down here for too friggin' long. And the last thing we need right now is someone poking his nose into our business," Vrae said as she pointed to the door.

When I saw Amon was about to say something, I cut him off. "But that doesn't mean you can get those things of yours too close," I remarked calmly as I gave him a hard stare.

Amon sighed and *tsked* at me. "Mean to me right until the end!" He sighed helplessly. "Fine, use doppelgangers then. By the way, are you guys going to check those soldiers and Alvadors?" he asked.

I nodded. "Yep, what about you?" I asked him, while Vrae and Zade just stood waiting. "I'm gonna check the archive. Maybe it did record something, but I missed it. Hell, maybe there's something happened before my day," Amon said.

"I don't think I'm coming though," Vrae said abruptly, and we all turned to her. "I think I'll just tell Zoran and Gevirash. If we're lucky, they'll hear anything from the passers, if there are any. About Cain, I think we should wait."

I nodded. "Okay, can't agree more than that. So, see you guys on the flip side."

Amon nodded. "Fine, we're done for now." He then undid the barriers he had placed on top of the original ones, and then we left him to go to our separate ways.

Chapter 5

Amon stared at the door after the three soldiers left his den. Slowly, he turned around and made his way to his chamber, which lay behind the door on the far corner of the room. His face grim, he opened the door and went inside. As he closed the door, his gaze was fixated on the large, gruesome painting that hung on the wall at the right side of his bed that occupied the centre of the chamber, aside from two shelves that stood on either side of the wall with full with scrolls of golem magick and other forms of sorcery, including records of his own experiments.

Without paying any heed to the shelves, he walked across the room straight to the painting and stopped dead before it as his mind wandered to what lay hidden behind it. For seven hundred years, the scene of brutal slaughter had concealed his secret, something that not even the Echelons knew about.

It was another golem he had created.

It was the one golem that none had knowledge of, aside from him and possibly the one it was assigned to. It had stayed there ever since Amon saw its last horrific vision, the last sign of existence of the one it watched over.

No, not the last sign of existence. The last sign of the devil's *presence* in this realm.

He'd kept his promise not to breathe a word to anyone regarding what he might see in this golem's sixth eye, but not even in his wildest dreams had he thought he'd ever see something like this come to pass.

"I could never understand why this one remains with no apparent presence of life force. It was supposed to self-destruct the moment he *went down at Bahyrdanam. The only thing I could come up with is that* he *survived. But is that even possible?"* he wondered, and an uneasy feeling went through him.

Those words that appeared on the Veil were by far the most disturbing ones he'd ever seen. They left him with mounting suspicions and curiosity that made him restless.

And just now, this story had just kicked him over the edge. The golem itself, which should have been destroyed on its own the moment the devil it watched upon had ceased to exist, still lingered with all six eyes in their places. Not only that, it also changed its color immediately into the dark brown of soil, the golem's true color before it was infused with the devil's life force.

It had stayed that way since the devil's disappearance. At least, that was what he saw two nights ago.

But now . . . now he had to make sure. Would it still be the same as he'd last seen it?

With his core thundering violently in his chest, he raised his hand towards the painting. Using his powers, he moved it slowly outward, revealing the hole where the golem was supposed to be sitting motionless. But what he saw there almost made his knees buckle.

At first glance, nothing seemed to have changed, except for one thing. The golem's hands had changed color. It had turned back to the way it was supposed to be: skin of a light brown color, indicating that the presence of the life force that was tied to a devil still lingered within it. Furthermore, its skin gleamed sapphire, the devil's energy print. Aside from that, nothing had changed. All six eyes still remained in their places all over the golem.

Amon swallowed audibly and quickly closed the hole with the painting. Bile rose in his throat. He strolled towards his bed and sank in it.

"How could this possibly be?" he mused. Immeasurable disbelief and fear for the devil in the matter swelled within him. He rose up and headed back to the door that led to his den. He reached the knob, but he stopped before opening it.

"What kind of Iverand have I been, not able to foresee the lengths to which Lucifer would go in order to make sure no one challenged him?" He clenched his fist with an anger he hadn't felt for a long time—anger for having been betrayed, and he hadn't even known about it in time to save the one devil that was considered to be the true leader of them all, rather than their own master, the master who,

judging by what he'd seen from the golem's eye, had attempted to annihilate that devil himself.

Despite the fact that he knew full well that betrayal was one of major games played among his kind, not even he would've thought that their master and the Echelons would ever have done something so outrageously low–and far too risky a gamble.

No matter how inane they might be, even they should realize what the repercussions would be if they were to betray the entire legions who had sworn their allegiance to them, especially to betray those born with tremendous powers and to whom they had given theirs.

Above all else, the Echelons and their master should've known the position that was held by that particular devil amongst the legions. The only thing that kept them from rebelling against the Echelons was the false story of the devil who had been sent falling for their sake by the Heavenly Flame of God.

Had they known that it was their master who had actually attempted to exterminate him, both he and the Echelons would have all hell broke loose on their hands. The planet would be roasted alive faster than Michael could blink.

But now, new hope stirred in him. If it was true, then the supposedly dead devil would return soon, if he hadn't already.

A faint smile curved his lips and he said the devil's name. "Ezryan."

*   *   *

I walked with Zade after the four of us got out from the den, and Amon's merry couple of toys came at us as soon as we got out from the Lasinth.

"That sure was faster than Amon could say cheese." I sneered mentally.

Well, I hoped the Iverand would be able to find something while Vrae let those guardians in the loop. She might as well get herself something useful in this mess.

"What's on your mind?" Zade suddenly pulled me from my thoughts.

"Uh, nothing." I hurriedly answered him.

"Okay, I know that this crap of Cain's must've really pissed you off, but maybe there's a bright side to it," he said trying to cheer me up with that devastating smile of his.

"I wouldn't say that, but anyhow, if in the end being in this mess could get me one step closer to the truth of what happen to Ry, then so be it," I said sternly.

Weirdly enough, I saw a glimpse of sadness in his gaze when I said it, like back then at the Aryad. He didn't say zilch once again, so I didn't ask him about it.

"Okay, but anyway, before we go check those remains at the Devorcae, I have something to take care of at my base," he said.

I nodded. "No problem, let's get going." I jerked my head at the path leading to his base.

After a few moments, we reached a small door. The word "Varkonian" was written on it. He opened the door and turned to me. "Wait here for a sec." He started to walk away.

"Just hurry." I smiled at him, and he went inside.

Rubbing my brow, I recalled the last time I was at the Devorcae. Let's see, it was, uh, okay, two thousand years ago. I was there when Zade and two other Varkonians examined the victims who turned out to be the handiwork of a devil witch.

Well, the said witch died a pretty gruesome death in the end. By my hand.

Anyhow, aside from examining weird dead bodies, the place was also used to check any unusual items that were found. Teghari and his team were supposed to take the remains there.

A few minutes later, instead of him, one of Amon's toys descended and stopped just a few feet above me. Its centre slit open into a mouth.

I rolled my eyes and braced myself, knowing what kind of voice would come out of it. *"Here goes."* I sighed.

"Yve," the eye said, relaying Amon's words in its revolting voice as I'd expected. "Teghari's golem just contacted me."

"What did he say?" I prompted, half cringing at the thought of what would it sound like at Amon's side, and yet I almost couldn't stop from snickering at this little fact.

"If I'm lucky, this time he might be pissed enough with his toys' voices and try to fix them." I mused, but reality kicked me back to earth, because there was no way he'd do that.

"He and his team can't bring the remains to the Devorcae. There's no choice. Zade's gotta go there to check them, so I need you and Vrae to guard him. I have them waiting for you guys over there."

I winced at that, and gave the eye a scathing glare when its words registered. "Dude, I don't know if your golem got it right, or if it got drunk, or if Teghari is pulling pranks on you, but your golem said the Machordaen couldn't get them here?" I asked slowly.

There was silence for a few moments before the mouth opened again. "Very cute, Yve. I'm laughing my ass off here, or so you want me to say. Sorry to disappoint you, but no, they're not drunk. Do you think they even could be? And Teghari is not a five-year-old human either. I've checked his golem and confirmed his report," the eye said.

I almost burst out laughing at the eye's epic failure in attempting to impersonate Amon's offended rambling. Sometimes I couldn't tell whether I should vomit or laugh about it to his face.

"Okay, what's happened then?" I asked, suppressing the urge to laugh.

"Apparently, when they tried to bring it to the Aryad, the remains emitted some kind of energy, and the soldiers were blasted back. The same thing happened when they tried to flash to the Gate."

Now that was one sure way to light the fuse on my combustible temper. That urge to laugh instantly turned into a cold fury. "Could this get any more abhorrent?" I mumbled and *tsked*. "Fine, whatever, tell 'em we'll get there ASAP," I said as I waved my hand, dismissing the eye.

"Okay," the eye, or rather Amon, replied through it. The mouth closed and re-joined the other one several feet above.

"If it gets any more annoying than this, I might take a page from the white fluff's book and call whoever that is an abomination." I thought with my anger spiking.

Seconds later, Zade came out from his base. I jerked my head at him. "Well, you're a bit late, Varkonian."

He gave me a confused look. "Huh? What are you talking about?"

I let out a weary breath. "Well, Amon just relayed Teghari's report through his toy. It seems that we have no choice but to go to D'arksin."

A deep frown lined his brows. "What did he say?" he asked.

"Whoever the bitch was, they really did a number on us. Aside from the energy which knocked me out, they also left something else in the remnants."

"And the effect was . . . ?" He asked curiously.

"The Machordaen failed to bring them to Devorcae. Each time they tried to move them, they were all knocked back," I drawled furiously.

"You have got to be kidding me," he expelled a tired breath.

"Come on, we don't have another minute to waste. I really need to know who the bastard was, leaving something like that," I mumbled through clenched teeth.

"Okay, chill. Don't kill me out of anger here." He raised his hands as if to surrender.

The two of us quickly walked towards the Gate which Zoran and Gevirash were supposed to be guarding. Vrae would probably still be there as well if we were lucky.

Several minutes afterwards, we reached the end of the path. He let me jump upward to the cliff first, and he pulled up the rear. We went through the boulder's mirage and ended up at the entrance where the three we'd expected to meet were standing.

Zoran, Gevirash, and Vrae greeted us. "What's wrong? You two seem a bit tense. And shouldn't you be at the Devorcae?" Vrae asked, arching a brow at us.

"That's one way to put it, yeah. In fact, you should join us. Amon told me that." I jerked my head in the forest's direction and exchanged a look with Zade, who turned to her. "Yeah, he said he wants you to join us, Vrae."

She looked at the guards who shrugged, indicating their cluelessness, and then she turned to us. "Okay, but first, please, can one of you tell us what the hell happened?"

I let out a short breath and explained to them what Amon had told me. After I'd finished, Vrae just frowned at us. "So, we're heading to the D'arksin. Is that it?"

"Yeah, we have no other choice except to have Zade check the remains on site. C'mon, are you coming or what?" I tilted my head.

She nodded. "Yeah, I wanna see it for myself anyway. Can I ask you guys to keep an eye on the passers? We might as well keep an ear open," Vrae asked the guards, who looked rather delighted at her request.

Gevirash cocked his head. "Okay, we understand, seeing that things have gotten serious. Just go, and don't forget to fill us in with whatever you find out later."

Zoran nodded. "Yeah, and be careful."

"No sweat. Come on," I said to Zade and Vrae. The three of us then jumped to the sky and headed straight to D'arksin.

Moments later, we arrived at the spot where I had left the Levarchons, and as Amon told me, Teghari and his soldiers stood near the protective shield that covered the remains.

The moment he saw us, he immediately gave us his salute. I asked him if there was anything new, but unfortunately there was nothing, so I dismissed him.

After he'd gone, I asked Vrae to go to the Alvadors, where some of the Machordaens were supposed to be waiting for us. She left us and I turned to Zade, who stood and started dispelling the protective shield.

Right after that, he knelt beside a piece of hand that had belonged to one of the Levarchons. He grabbed it, and his hand began emitting a deep, silver light. I could feel his energy, which I recognized as the Imirae.

A moment later I looked at his face and frowned. He was sweating and looked so tense that I didn't even dare to ask him what he felt in that piece of arm. Point taken. I'd never seen him like this whenever he'd been using his Imirae. Usually, he could "see" whoever the enemy was almost instantly.

All of a sudden, he cringed as if something had hurt him.

I immediately put my hand on his shoulder, but the moment I touched him, an electro-shock jolted through me for a split second and he screamed.

He pushed my hand away, and his whole body was engulfed in a bright gold light that lifted him to the air as he kept screaming over and over.

"Zade!" I yelled as I flew up to reach him. When I couldn't even touch him without making him roar in pain, I mentally called Vrae, and she came immediately.

She looked aghast at the sight and tried to reach him as well. After a minute that felt like all eternity with his never-ending screams, the light suddenly disappeared and he fell.

We grabbed him as he went limp and laid him slowly on the ground.

"Zade, wake up!" Vrae snapped as we rocked him, and yet he wasn't responding.

He laid there with both his eyes open with the eerie look of a corpse. Vrae cast a terrified look at me. "What the hell is this, Yve? What the hell happened to him?"

I stared back at her and frowned. "Do I look like I know what got him? All I know is that a minute after he started using his Imirae, he began sweating, and he looked as if he was using every ounce of his energy to ID the caster, which is unheard of, because you know as much as I do that Imirae wielders are seldom required to use so much energy to ID, well, anything. After that, that light thing appeared, and you know the rest."

Vrae shook her head. "Well, apparently 'anything' has become 'almost anything' I'd say, looking at his current situation."

"You got that right. Anyway, you have any idea how we can restore him?" I asked her, and I stared down at the Imirae wielder who lay limp on the ground.

"I might have a wild guess," she replied, staring at him in wonder.

"And that would be what?" I asked as I narrowed my gaze at her. *"Somehow I have a vague idea where she's going with this."*

"How did you manage to get rid of that blue filth that invaded your body?" she asked.

I almost couldn't stop myself from rolling my eyes at her for asking me that. Why couldn't I be wrong sometimes?

"You know full well that I only used my healing power to get rid of that. I've told you."

"Yeah, you have, but really, did you just use your healing power, or was there anything else beside that? A bit of your Avordaen perhaps?"

This time, I did roll my eyes at her mentioning our particular power that we used to blow our enemies on sight. "And for what? To cut off my own arm? No thanks, I have lots of other useful things to do, more useful than blowing my arm to oblivion, I should say."

"Okay, whatever. Thanks so much for that useful explanation," she shot back rather sarcastically, which I ignored. "All right, this isn't getting us anywhere, but it does leave us with one fact," she continued.

I scoffed. "And that is? I don't see anything that's exactly useful."

She curled her lips at my response. "You have to use your healing power on him." She glanced down at Zade.

I shot an acidic look at her. "What are you, a whack job? Perhaps you didn't notice. Using my healing power against the bitch's energy was enough to drag me under, and may I remind you that I didn't go through all that screaming in agony like he did? Who knows what will happen if I used that on *him*? I might end up killing him, and he's no good to anybody dead!" I snarled at her.

She hastily shook her head to stop my tirade. "Might, Yve, might! Who knows, you might end up saving his ass."

I fell silent as I considered her. "C'mon, he's no good to any of us withering like . . ." she was cut off in mid-sentence, because all of a sudden Zade shook tremendously as the same blue color that invaded my body from earlier started to spread on him.

"Withering like this, you mean?" I clenched my teeth.

"C'mon, I know it's gambling with danger, but we don't know what will happen if we just let it go like this. I'm sure Zade would want you to take your chances," she remarked.

"Easy for you to say," I mumbled, but decided to heed her advice as I saw the blue color spread rather faster than it had on me.

"Dammit, buddy, I'd better not end up killing you. So, here goes nothing." I settled myself next to him and used both hands to start channelling my healing power.

Moments later, the blue filth was beginning to withdraw. Gee, I was sure I was about to kill him.

When the blue filth was just a hair's width from disappearing from his fingertips, I suddenly felt a vicious pain as if something were burning my blood stream. The second that blue thing completely left Zade's body, I felt another brutal pain stabbing my body.

Before I could react, my chest felt as if a whole herd of bulls were stomping brutally on it, and blood flowed out of my mouth. Everything went black this time, with the real Vrae calling out to me, "Yve!"

Minutes later, or so I thought, I woke up. The first thing I saw was Vrae's face, similar to when I had woken up several hours earlier.

"This will be the second time I've said 'welcome back' to you in the last few hours," she said to me with a grin.

"Yippee," I said as I broke into a yawn. I felt something wet around my mouth and wiped it just to find my own blood.

"It's been a long time since I last spurted a mouthful of my own blood. Luckily it wasn't from fighting some damned Arcs," I thought as I licked a bit of it and dissolved the rest.

She snorted at my response. "Anyhow, this ain't funny. You were supposed to heal him, not vomit blood right in front of my face. Just what the hell was that all about? Did you get any vibes when you used your healing power on him?" She asked, folding her arms over her chest.

I shook my head and looked at Zade, who was sleeping right next to me. I sat up and cast a dry look at her. "No sign of him waking up any time soon, I see."

She *tsked.* "Come now, don't you start on me. At least you managed to get rid of that blue filth just as we expected."

"We? What we? That expectation was expected by you and you alone. If he's not waking up . . ." I narrowed my gaze angrily at her.

"Fine, fine! Dump it all on me." When she was about to continue her words, we suddenly heard a groan. I looked down and saw Zade moving, and a second later, he opened his eyes.

Damn, the guy almost made me have a heart attack. Thank Rygavon I didn't kill him. "Look who's joined us on planet Earth. How are you holding up, Varkonian?" I grinned at him.

"I feel superb, Cherxanain. Thanks for asking." He grinned back weakly as he sat up.

Suddenly he gasped as his eyes caught something on my face.

"What?" I asked, arching my brow at him.

He frowned. "Just what the hell did you do that made you cough up your blood? Don't tell me it isn't yours, 'cause I know the smell. It's still all over your mouth."

I glanced at Vrae, who shrugged. "Well, first, I'm sorry. This was caused by me almost killing you."

Vrae raised her hand to shut me up. "She's exaggerating. She vomited blood after she healed you from whatever it was that got you earlier. She was sure she would kill you, but I told her to take her chances. You could've died for all we know if she hadn't tried."

I curled my lips at her, but when I looked at Zade, I saw him smile widely at the both of us. "Thanks, really, I appreciate it."

I shrugged. "Don't mention it."

"Well, then it's settled." Vrae flashed a grin at us.

"Okay, enough with the sentimental hour. Zade, just what the hell happened to you?" I asked him.

He slowly averted his gaze and stared at the ground. "The thing was . . . well, I don't even know how to begin. The only thing obvious is that now I know why Ry had suspected the bastard was way older than anything God had created," he said with a shiver.

"And why the hell is that? You saw something weird? Because if you did, hell, fill us in. Neither of us was able to detect shit in those things," I interjected.

He swallowed. "Okay, here goes. When you try to identify someone's energy print, usually the things you feel would be dark traces, holy craps, or maybe human stench, right? That is, assuming you weren't using Imirae. But you can't see whoever it was."

"Yeah, so what of it? If you were using the Imirae, you should've sensed and seen a lot more than that, something more than meets the eye," Vrae said with a frown.

"We already know that. The question is, is there anything particular you sensed or saw in that?" I asked, pointing at the piece of arm on which he had used his Imirae.

"You ladies sure can't slow down," he muttered.

"Yeah, tough luck. We don't have another bleeding minute to waste either," I snapped.

"You make a bleeding point," Vrae interjected as she held her laughter.

I threw an annoyed stare at her. Damn, could she be any less obvious with the bleeding on my part?

Luckily, her so-bad-timing joke made an impression on him, because he abruptly cleared his throat. "Okay, I get it. Well, like you know, usually when we use the Imirae, aside from the energy print, we get a real vivid look on whoever the caster was. But, in this case . . ." his voice faded.

"Yes?" we both prompted.

He sighed wearily. "I saw not only a glimpse, but millions of images." Right there he fell silent yet again.

Vrae cast a puzzled look at me and turned her gaze back to him. "It's not a problem then. You saw *lots* of glimpses of that bastard," Vrae remarked in a rather sarcastic tone.

I studied Zade's expression as I searched for something that might give me a hint as to why he was so damn full of trepidation.

Seconds later, I found it among his words. "Wait a sec, if that's true, why in the hell did you have to use that much, unless . . ." I stopped dead as I realized what those glimpses indicated.

My mind conjured the face of one of my enemies, one that was pretty difficult, even for me, to waste–Farsanzi, a rogue devil witch.

For unknown reasons, she dragged lesser devils to fight each other by implanting images in their heads. She even went as far as to make the Xarchons break off their killing spree and massacre the soldiers. In the end, she made her biggest mistake and tried that move against me, intending to make me go on a rampage against the other Cherxanains, but her low tricks only sent a vicious headache to my head, so I blew her to oblivion, because what she was doing to my head seriously pissed me off.

As for what happened to Zade, if I guessed it right, the Varkonian wasn't just getting stupid migraines, but rather something far worse–hence the golden light and that electro-shock. But then again, there was something. I'd better ask him.

Before I could open my mouth to ask him, Vrae cut me off, "Mind telling me what you've got? You seem like you've realized something." At her remark, Zade turned his attention to me.

I cleared my throat. "Okay, sorry about that. I'll explain it as simply as I can."

"So?" she asked.

"You guys still remember Farsanzi?"

She frowned at my out-of-the-blue question. "The rogue bitch you blasted to oblivion two thousand years ago? Yeah, barely. Why?"

"You remember her specialty then?" I went on–and, thank Rygavon, again both of them still remembered that bitch. I saw an understanding expression on their faces.

"You mean, whatever got him wasn't so different from her powers? But as far as I remember, her powers . . ."

"Didn't include making anybody from our level scream in agony and engulf them in golden light. I know that. It's just the same principle, okay? Images inside our heads," I interjected.

When neither of them said anything, I went on, "I'm taking a shot in the dark here about why you had to use that much energy. It was because those images you saw didn't exactly show you who the bastard was, wasn't it?"

Vrae looked at me and then at Zade, who confirmed it. "Yes, you're right. The images weren't urging me to attack someone either. Contrary to what it should be, I saw those images through the culprit's eyes. They were images of places, races, and slaughter unlike anything I've ever seen. And I don't know why, the pain of those victims was reaching out to me–hence the agony I felt. Hell, I don't even know if those places I saw were on earth at all," he said as he once again stared at the ground.

I raised my brows at his remark. "Races? You mean human races or some new kind of races?"

"And these places. Are you sure they weren't places on earth? And I meant to ask, was it unlike the earth as in other planets, or unlike the earth as in a different plane?" Vrae added with a deep frown.

Zade gulped. "I'd say it was more like the latter, though I'm not entirely sure what plane that would be. It was all black–the grass, the trees. I don't even know if I got it right or if the massacre I saw was in the middle of the night over there, well, wherever that was. As for the races," he went on as he looked at me. "It did look like humans, but their eye colours were way too beautiful compared to humans', and they had these long, pointy ears like elves in humans' stupid fairy tales. There were a few others who had small horns, but they were not devils. As far as I can remember, none had wings like us or those angels up there," he explained.

I sighed. "Okay, they were a different kind of beings, and hence you called them 'races'. I've never heard of that kind of existence though. Were they the victims? The bastard killed them or what?" I asked him.

His brows knitted into one hard line as if he were struggling to remember it, or trying to shove whatever he saw about them out of his head. "Yeah, you got that right. Those beings were more like the butchered. Even that isn't enough to describe what that whatever-it-was had done to them," he remarked in repugnance.

Vrae cocked her head. "Well, the bitch sounds like a charmer. Gotta meet him sometime. Might as well invite him to have dinner," she said sarcastically.

I snorted. "That's very thoughtful of you."

She curled her lips. "Yeah, whatever, I was just trying to joke with myself. So, what do we do now? We haven't the slightest idea of where the bastard could've gone to or what the guy looks like."

"Maybe we can try to dig up some info back in the archive, using those images you've seen, Zade," I said.

He nodded. "That would be a start."

"And what about these guys?" Vrae asked as she pointed her finger at the remains.

I thought about it for a second. "We can't do anything, so we're left with three options. One, we just leave them covered like this; two, we send all of them off; or three, we ask Amon to call their head team and let them decide what must be done with these guys."

The two of them exchanged look. "I think we'd better take the third option. All the same, we better get back to the Aryad. There's nothing else we can do here." Vrae shook her head.

"Wait a sec," Zade interrupted, and we turned to him. "What is it?"

Abruptly, he stood up, followed by Vrae and myself. "How's this idea? We try to bring these guys in ourselves."

I sighed in exasperation at his question. "Well, good luck trying that. If there's another light got you, I'm definitely outta here. Send me a card if you manage to stay alive."

He stopped dead at my rather sarcastic answer, but quickly regained his composure.

"Hey, I don't have to use even the slightest amount of energy, now do I? Maybe if we just do it . . ."

I rolled my eyes at his obstinacy and shrugged. "All right, fine, be my guest. Try flashing yourself to the Devorcae then."

"Okay, I'll try bringing that piece of arm first." He went and took the arm while Vrae and I just stood there watching.

"Here goes nothing." With that he vanished, but just a second later there was a sudden loud boom, followed by him blasting back out and falling right in front of us.

"Ouch! Ouch! That hurt, dammit!" He swore under his breath. He quickly stood up and levelled his gaze at us. I just lifted the edge of my lips as he sighed heavily. "Fine, you win. The third option then."

"That's more like it. We'd better cast that protective shield again." I turned to Vrae and frowned at her. "What about you? Shouldn't you go back to the Alvadors?"

She shook her head. "When I was about to cast the counter-spell, you called me back here," she said as she tilted her head at me.

"Either we should be grateful that we don't have to waste another minute, or that was just another piece of sheer luck behind stupid disaster," I thought sarcastically. "Well then, would you mind if I asked you to place the protective shield? I'm kinda low on magick here."

She was startled by my request, and then she turned to Zade who shook his head. She then nodded, knowing that both of us were better not using any energy for now. After she'd finished, the three of us went back to Croatoan.

"Gee, this will be what, Yve? The second time we go back there from here?" Vrae asked sardonically, as the three of us flew.

"Yeah, we might as well ask Zoran and Gevirash to get a jackpot for us if we have to go back and forth for the third time." I shook my head as Zade laughed when he heard my sarcastic retort.

Suddenly a pale, bluish ball of light appeared a few meters ahead, and it came right at us, causing the three of us to stop dead in the mid air and roll sideways to avoid it.

As we looked at the direction from where it was coming, we saw more of them fly straight at us.

Chapter 6

We deflected those lights at once. "What the hell was that?" Zade shouted.

"The hell if I know!" I yelled back.

"C'mon, get down there!" Vrae pointed at the sea of trees right below us.

We landed and quickly separated to hide ourselves behind the trees as we looked at the direction from which those blue lights came.

"Just perfect timing for us to have company," I muttered grudgingly under my breath.

"Not a good time for having sarcastics now, Yve," Vrae said as she stared in the blue lights' direction.

"Psst!" suddenly Zade called us. "You two saw anything?" he whispered.

"Guys, I think it safer to talk this way," I said.

Both of them nodded, and all of us stared in the blue light's direction once again. After minutes that felt like eternity, suddenly other trains of blue light were shot at us.

Gee, I really hated being cornered like this. I'd better try to topple the blue light. If I was lucky, I could even get a glimpse at whoever the caster was. Judging by those stupid bluish balls earlier, they wouldn't be devils or better yet, Arcs.

"I'm meeting them head on," I told them.

Vrae threw an indignant look at me. *"What, are you crazy? You don't have enough juice to do that!"* she snapped.

"She's right, Yve. Just stay low for a sec. They might reveal themselves, or better yet, leave us," Zade interjected.

I cursed under my breath. *"You really wanna believe that? By then those bastards will either have us surrounded or will call for backups! We don't have any more minutes to waste here, not with you just recovering from that gold-whatever light, and I've wasted pretty* much all of the healing energy on my end as well. Vrae could handle them of course, but if by stupid luck this battle draws the attention of the bastard who wasted the Levarchons and the Alvadors, and neither of us knows the nature of the bitch, who knows what can happen? And if they manage to wound you somehow, Vrae, I won't be able to heal you just yet," I snarled.

She breathed heavily as the blue lights kept on coming at us. *"Fine, but do you have enough energy to attack them? Do you have enough power to do some damage?"*

"Don't worry. I still have enough to burn these woods to the ground, but my healing power's almost MIA. When I jump, those bastards will change target. Blast them when you get a clear shot."

I saw her nod. *"Okay, I'll back you up."*

"Me too," Zade added.

I braced myself for my attack as I saw both of them ready themselves. I jumped to the sky, and seconds later, as I expected, multiple blue spheres were coming at me.

I deflected twenty of them and blasted the rest. Damn, I still couldn't see the bastards. Where the hell were they?

"Anyone see?" I cautiously searched for the enemies from above them both.

"Nope, not yet. We still can't get a clear shot," Zade replied.

"Wait, I see one. Looks like there are more of them," Vrae interjected.

"Well, hurry up! What the hell are you waiting for?" I snapped as I kept on blasting the blue lights that were coming at me.

"Show yourself, you piece of shit!" I shouted in the lights' direction. These bastards were beginning to piss me off!

Glancing down, I saw Vrae aim at the small gaps along the trees all the way to the north, and then shoot multiple bolts through it. Seconds later, I heard screams ring out from that direction.

"You got 'em!" I yelled as I immediately flew to where Vrae launched her bolt. When I arrived, I saw that six of them had disappeared. Aside from those six, there were four of them circling another one who was withering on the ground. He was definitely the victim of Vrae's attack. I immediately approached them, and those four began to fade, leaving that fifth one.

Or should I say, they *were* trying to leave him.

"Not so fast!" I yelled as I raised my hand, directed my palm at them, and launched my powers to keep them from escaping. As the four of them were locked where they were standing, Vrae and Zade arrived.

"So, you locked them up," Vrae said as they landed.

"Yeah, great job on blasting this one," I smiled wickedly as I pointed at the one who was withering and bleeding profusely on the ground.

"I can't believe just five of them could make us go through all that trouble." Zade shook his head in disbelief.

"No, before you came here, there were six others that disappeared." I glanced at our captives, and one of them hissed and glared at us. "You got a problem?" I glared back at the bastard.

Vrae raised her hand to stop me, and then she knelt beside her victim. "Who sent you all here?" she asked.

"Fuck you!" he growled at her.

I kicked his head, and he growled in pain. Vrae cast a dry look at me, which I answered with a smirk. She rolled her eyes and then faced our hostage. "No thanks, I have a much higher standard," Vrae retorted.

Zade laughed at her comment. "Damn, I should definitely hang around more often with you girls."

Vrae snickered at his remark. "Well, thanks. By the way, why don't you two check those four?" She jerked her head at the four attackers.

"Got it." Zade and I moved to the rest of our captives.

"Okay," I said to the first of the four. "So, tell us, just who's the bitch that sent you all to attack us?"

"Don't you dare address the Irgovaen like that! The likes of you will never lay eyes on him and his queen!" He snarled and spat at me. Without even flinching, I deflected it. It stopped dead in the air and went right back at him.

I directed a puzzled look at Zade. "'Irgovaen and his queen'? I thought we agreed that there was only one assailant?"

He shrugged. "Maybe the only assailant was this Irgovaen trying to protect his high queenie?"

I rolled my eyes at his response. "Very revoltingly romantic. I'm not wasting my time for an old horny couple," I rebuked him as I curled my lips.

Zade laughed. "Thought you might say something like that. So what are we going to do with these guys?" He folded his arms and grinned at me.

I turned to the one who tried to spit at me earlier. "Really, what the hell did this couple feed you with that you all have to be that loyal to them?" I smiled disdainfully at them.

"Torment us all you want, but you won't get shit!"

I frowned at him. "Of course I won't get shit. All I want is to get my hands on their heads, good and proper," I said with mocking venom in my voice.

Zade snorted at my sarcasm. I pretended not to hear him and focused on my prey while trying to put aside an urge to grin. "You sure you won't spill any beans on this guy?"

"Never! You'll have to rip me limb from limb, and not even that would make me give you shit!" he yelled as he put that I'd-rather-be-tortured-to-death expression on his face.

I sighed as I turned to Zade. "This will take a while. Would you like to watch or would you rather play with the other pack of meat?" I jerked my head at the other three captives.

"I wouldn't mind watching," he shrugged.

"Suit yourself." I shrugged. Folding my arms, I faced that brick-wall bastard once again. "Once your own doom is being unraveled, there's no turning back." My voice turned eerily heavy as I thought of a way to . . . *persuade* him.

"You know nothing about doom," the bastard said as he looked at me disdainfully.

Oh, man, he'd done it. No living being in existence could give me that look and die in peace the next second. As I glanced askance at Zade and he saw the look on my face, he realized what was coming. I started to draw on my energy, and then I unleashed it slowly onto the moron's body. The second I started doing so to the lowlife, never-ending screams thundered in the woods. All creatures that resided there were running for their lives as despair echoed throughout their home.

Vrae suddenly patted my back and I stopped. The bastard was withering as he fell to the ground, and it seemed he was only one step from death.

"What?" I asked as I faced her.

"The bitch's screams are torturing my eardrums." She curled her lips at me while Zade just stood there and watched us.

I curled my lips back at her. "Here, I thought you'd enjoy hearing them. And you know, if you were not too uptight for your own good, we could have fun paying them back a bit. Just play with your own toy."

She sighed and lifted the edge of her lips. "Fine, you made a point. Just try to make the screams lessen a bit, and get your hands on just a bit of info, if possible, that is. And my toy's dead, I think the screams killed him."

I sneered. "Aww, that's a shame, but anyhow, I hear ya. Just let me deal with this goon."

With that she left me with my new toy once again, a toy that was almost dead though. "So, ready to spill it, moron?"

The devil that now withered on the ground at my mercy rolled around weakly. "You will not turn my loyalty towards any other than the Irgovaen and his queen," he growled.

He glanced at his companions and nodded at them, and suddenly I felt a violent surge as though something was sucking the air into him. I was just a second too late to realize what it meant, for he did something else. "Long live the Irgovaen and his queen! May death befall Lucifer and the abominations that are his descendants!"

The three of us were enraged by his big mouth, but before we could do anything, he exploded right in front of us, showering me with his blood.

I let out a foul curse. "What an idiot jerkoff! How dare he say low things like that! And instead of spilling any shit about the guy, he spilled his fucking blood! Now, it's all over me! Just who the hell is this son of a bitch and that stupid queen of his?!" I snarled grudgingly as I pulled a bit of my energy to dispose of the blood on me.

"Well, isn't this turning out to be fun and games?" Vrae rolled her eyes and sighed.

The other three seemed to get some courage from their late comrade and suddenly made a movement. Luckily, I saw that coming and locked them firmly in their place. "Just what the hell do you think you're doing? You three bastards ain't going anywhere until you give us something important," I said coldly, and then locked their voices temporarily until they decided to spill anything useful.

Well, rather that than hear them say anything as low as their dead comrade had said.

"Now what?" Vrae asked as she inclined her head, while Zade, who appeared to have found something peculiar, just stared at the three who were struggling to scream and glaring at us.

I ignored Vrae's question and approached him instead. "Is there anything?" I asked as I saw his expression.

He gave me a weird look. "Nothing. I was just wondering . . ."

"About what?" I prompted as I folded my arms.

"These guys, do you think they're like us or what? I mean, are they devils?"

I was startled and traded a puzzled gaze with Vrae. From the look on her face, I think she might be thinking the same thing as me. The two of us turned to him again. "You can't possibly believe that these guys are similar to the 'races' that you told us about earlier, now do you?"

He shrugged. "I'm not exactly sure either. I mean, they do look similar to the elf look-alike I told you about earlier. No wings. These guys don't have those small horns, but they do have peculiar pointy ears, and their eyes . . . you may laugh, but they filled me with awe, just like when I saw them in my visions. You didn't see what I saw, but that's it," he explained with uncertainty in his deep voice.

I observed the three attackers who were still glaring at us closely and a wave of awe went through me.

He was right. If it was just that they had no wings and horns–hell, all of us could hide our horns and wings and assume human form. That was how we mingled. But their eyes, now those were something you wouldn't see every day. They were so–hell, I didn't believe I was gonna say this–beautiful.

"Well, you got that one right," I murmured as Vrae abruptly sucked in her breath, and I realized that she too noticed the same thing. I turned to her. "But seriously, did our dear old Ry tell you any of this, Vrae?" I asked.

She shook her head. "No, as far as I remember, he didn't tell me squat about this, neither did he tell me about this Irgovaen and that queenie of his. If he had told me, I'd already have told you guys back at Amon's, Yve."

"Very cute as always, Ry," I sighed, and I glanced at the three prisoners. By then, I saw that they were no longer glaring.

Instead, their gazes were widening at us as if they had just heard something they'd never thought they would hear.

"*Vrae*," I called her.

She glanced askance at me. "*What?*"

I subtly jerked my head at the three captives. "*Look at them. They reacted when I mentioned Ry.*"

Vrae slowly turned her gaze to them. "*Are you positive? Maybe they just finally gave up and decided they want to spill some beans? Let's just hope that they won't spill filth like their comrade did. So, how's it gonna be?*"

I shrugged. "*Well, let's hear them out then. Just blow them apart if they spit dirt.*"

Vrae nodded. "*Roger that. Have it your way. We'll see what they've got.*" I turned my attention back to the three captives and lifted the lock on their voices, including the ones on their heads.

I cleared my throat. "You three look like you're in the mood to talk, so spill it out. Our patience is growing thin by the minute, so start talking."

The three of them exchanged a weird look, and then turned their eyes back to us. Their grudging expressions had changed drastically. "Okay, but first, may I ask you to release our locks? You have our word that we won't pull any stunt on you."

I arched a brow at their peculiar mood swing. One minute they wanted to kill us, and the next they acted formal and polite. Not knowing what they would say, I ignored Vrae who whispered hoarsely, "No, don't do it," and released their locks. I was, however, ready in position to lock them again any second should they did pull any stunt on us.

"Thank you," the closest one said, and astonishingly the three of them suddenly dropped to their knees and put their right hands on their chests. "Forgive us, Cherxanains. May the grace of our king the Irgovaen and his queen befall you three."

"What the . . . ?" I threw a baffled look at my sister and the Varkonian, who were standing with the same baffled expression on their faces.

I glanced at the three on the ground and cleared my throat. "Not that I'm irritated with your mood change, but do you know who we are? And this guy here is not a Cherxanain. He's a Varkonian," I explained as I pointed to Zade.

Unfortunately, he decided to joke in the wrong place and in the wrong time. He waved his hand to them. "Yo, my man."

I rolled my eyes and popped him on the head. "Not a good time for bad jokes, Varkonian." I snapped.

He yelped. "Ouch! You didn't have to do that. I was just trying to lighten the situation a bit." He pouted as he rubbed his head.

"Someday you'll learn to think with your head and not with your ass." I pointed at my head.

Vrae snorted while Zade curled his lips. "That's mean, but whatever. Do as you please."

I scoffed. "Whatever," I said, and turned to the three, and once again they surprised us. "Is that so? Well, may the grace befall you as well, Varkonian. Forgive our lack of tact and our attacks on you."

I stared at them for a second. What was this? A joke?

"They're definitely not like us. They're one of those 'races', right? But how do they know what to call us?" I asked Vrae as I held my gaze on them.

"I have no idea. Just hear them out first. At least they're not as hostile now as they were minutes ago, and they're in the mood to talk as well," she replied.

I nodded at her response. *"Okay, what about you, Zade?"*

He glanced at me. *"I'm with Vrae on that one. Let's hear them out and check whether they did react to Ry's name like you said."*

In the end, I decided to take the risk and concurred. *"Fine then, here goes."*

I cleared my throat and averted my gaze from my two companions to the three before me. "Okay, you three can stand up."

They rose to their feet.

"Do you know who we are?" I asked slowly.

The one in the middle stepped forward. "At first, no, we did not know who you are. But when you mentioned the Hieldhar Ezryan,"—we silently gasped— "and you both called each other by names, we realized who you are. The Irgovaen told all of us to treat you two and any companion you bring with the same way we did the Hieldhar, because that was one of the messages Hieldhar Ezryan left our king."

"Where is he? Is he still alive?" I asked in a low voice, not daring to raise my hopes high. Right then, I felt Vrae's gaze fall on my back, no doubt to warn me, but I ignored her.

He shook his head. "It was unfortunate, but we only know as much as you do, that seven hundred years ago he was burned down by the Heavenly Light of God Himself." The guy smiled sadly.

Disappointment sank in at his words, but I didn't show it.

"He was a very close friend of our king, the Irgovaen, and the queen. He was even considered to be the king's brother. Hence, all of us respected him," the guy on his right added.

I raised a brow at his statement. "Why is that? I don't even remember him ever telling any of us about this . . . Irgovaen, well, your king. And by the way, forgive us for insulting your masters."

They nodded. "Apologies accepted. We were tangled in misunderstandings. Besides, we were the ones who attacked you first," the middle guy replied. "Before we tell you anything more, I believe introductions are in order. My name's Rivorgad, this is Daviros," he pointed to the guy on his right, "and he's Arann." The last one nodded in greeting.

I put one hand upon my chest. "I'm Yverna, this is my sister Vrathien, and this fellow here is Zaderion." I indicated my companions who gave them a subtle nod in greeting.

They returned their nod, and Rivorgad continued. "Our king the Irgovaen and his queen were close with Hieldhar Ezryan, because nine hundred years ago, the Hieldhar saved him from the Dark Light of Rygavon."

"He what?" the three of us shouted in unison.

"What the hell is this? Ry pulled someone from Lucifer's attack?" I asked in disbelief.

Vrae stared at the three of them. "Lucifer attempted to kill your king?" she inquired, while Zade just gaped.

The three nodded at her while I was thinking about what they said. After a few moments, I looked straight at them. "You'd better take all of us to see him."

The three of them hesitated, but they accepted my request in the end. "Very well, we understand, because it's very unusual for any of you to stand in the way of your master. Perhaps our king will elaborate the details we're all vague on. But before that, can you get rid of . . ." Rivorgad tilted his head upward, indicating Amon's golem.

I turned my gaze to my companions. "Time to set the dops on them," Vrae said.

Before we did so, I stopped Vrae and Zade and faced our new pals. "Wait a sec. What difference does it make since they've already seen us with you all?"

Arann smiled as he shook his head. "Do not worry. The second you came in contact with us here, those beings have not been able to see you because you have all now gotten yourselves inside our shield. You only need to distract those creatures so they think the three of you found nothing inside the shield and decided to go elsewhere."

I arched a brow at his remark and immediately surveyed the surrounding area with my senses discreetly reaching the ether. For a while I didn't pick up anything, hell, not even a cockroach. Later on, I finally stumbled upon something like a very thin layer in the air, engulfing us all like a miniature dome.

"Gee, no wonder we didn't even realize we'd gotten inside," I mused.

Vrae patted my back, evidently realizing what I just did. "They're good?" she whispered.

I gave her an indiscernible nod. "Well, that's cool to say the least. I wish all of us were allowed to disguise ourselves. Sometimes a moment of silence is totally *worth* killing for." I flashed an evil grin at them.

"Fine, let's do it," Vrae inserted.

We called forth our doppelgangers and instructed them to wander around in the woods, pretending to look for more clues as to who had slain our underlings. After they had a good grasp of their orders, we immediately dispatched them.

As soon as they took off, the golems's eyes followed suit. The three soldiers then held out their hands. Before we took them, I hesitated. "Can we trust all of you?" I asked.

They pulled back their hands, and then to my surprise, they made a firm gesture and put their hands upon their chests. "We swear on the name of the Irgovaen and his queen that we will protect all of you, comrades of Hieldhar Ezryan, saviour of our king, with our lives, and we all are bound by it," they remarked in unison.

We were startled at their vow, but at least we knew that we could trust them a bit, so I decided to place a bit of trust in these guys. "Well, that's fair enough."

Before Vrae could say anything, I replied to their vow. "In return, we swear on the name of Rygavon and Hieldhar Ezryan"–Vrae cursed under her breath and I ignored her again–"that we won't pose any threat for any of you and your masters, friends of our leader and closest comrade, unless we sense that any of you want to attack us. And we are all bound by it," I said as I glanced at my comrades who secretly let out a relieved breath.

I looked back at the three soldiers in front of us. "Sorry, our vow seems to be unfair, but we have yet to know each other well enough to trust you guys completely. Even Ry would find it funny if we just jumped into a hole with complete strangers."

Rivorgad chuckled. "He sure would. So shall we go now?" he asked as they extended their hands again.

"Yeah, finally we can run from those golems for a while." My comrades laughed at my comment and took the hands of our new companion. Once we did so, they brought us, flashing us to somewhere beyond our knowledge.

Chapter 7

After seconds that felt like forever, we arrived at the so called other dimension, well, according to Zade.

And the first thing welcoming us was the pitch black darkness of a forest. It was a good thing that our eyes were able to adapt in any condition, though how in the hell a forest could be all black was beyond me. Hell, even the grass was black.

"What the hell is this?" I asked as I looked at the surroundings in awe.

"Welcome to our home. Everything's pitch-black here. Don't worry, you all will get used to it," Rivorgad said.

"Hey, it's not that I'm complaining or anything. Actually this is quite cool," I remarked as I looked around. When I glanced at my companions, I caught Zade gaping with the strangest look on his face, and Vrae stood there looking impressed.

"Well, thanks." Daviros grinned.

"Shall we go now? We're heading to our castle." Arann pointed at the road ahead.

"Okay, let's go," I said, and we all followed them.

As we walked along the black path that seemed to lead out of the forest, I almost couldn't stop my jaw from dropping as I gazed upon the cold beauty of this place and felt the absolute tranquillity of it seeping into my skin. Well, not everything could be put under the "beautiful" category, but this place held a certain lethal aura that was threatening and yet comforting, and yeah, beautiful.

As we wandered through the forest, I recalled what Zade had said regarding his vision. Sure enough, I glanced sideways at him again and saw his eyes almost bulging out of their sockets. *"You recognize this place?"* I asked.

"Yeah, Yve, now we can be sure that this place really is black and it wasn't some kind of mistake on my part," he replied as we continued to follow the natives.

Moments later, we were finally out of the forest and arrived at a vast field, a barren one. I lifted my gaze to the sky and found another thing that emphasized the difference between this place and the earth. Four moons hung in the dark sky like two pairs of pearls and shone brightly over the entire field.

"Now that's definitely not something you see every day," I thought in awe.

"What are we doing here?" Vrae asked, when another guy came out of the other side of the forest and stopped dead upon seeing us. No sooner had he appeared than he shot a bolt at Vrae. I rushed to her side and immediately deflected the bolt with one hand.

"Wait, Ziram! Hold your fire! They're guests of the king and queen," Rivorgad shouted at the newcomer as he ran to us.

"What are you all doing, bringing abominations to the king? Have you lost your mind? Kill them all, or I alert the others that you've committed high treason!" Ziram roared furiously as he readied to launch another bolt.

Vrae rolled her eyes. "I had no idea that bringing guests of your king could be considered as treason," she said sardonically.

Our new pals arched their brows, and from the look on their faces, they were trying not to blanch outright at her temerity.

Ziram spat in disgust. "Shut your hole, abominations!" he roared, and then he shot more bolts.

We took our stand and prepared to return fire, but before those bolts reached us, another guy appeared out of thin air and blasted them. We turned to the newcomer. "Cease your action, Ziram," he said.

The guy was six-foot-six with an obviously ripped body and broad shoulders covered in thick silver robes, and his light grey hair fell to his waist. Under the ray of the four moons that lingered in the sky, his pale skin made him look like a ghost.

Rivorgad strolled towards the new guy. "Daryth Helkann," he greeted.

The guy he called Daryth Helkann saluted his comrades. "Good to see you in one piece, Rivorgad, Daviros, and you too, Arann." His clear blue eyes then wandered from them for a second. Judging by the glint of sadness in his eyes, there was no doubt that he was looking for his late comrades.

I grimaced inwardly. *"I think an oopsie is in order."*

He let out a long breath. "I see that Vangurd and Xeithar didn't make it."

Ziram was enraged at his statement and readied himself to lunge at us, but once again that Helkann guy stopped him. "Daryth, you said Vangurd and Xeithar were dead, so why did you ask me to cease fire?" Ziram asked, half demanding an answer from the guy who appeared to be his commander. Perhaps here, "Daryth" meant the same as "Hieldhar".

Helkann glanced askance at his hot-blooded comrade. "It must be a very unfortunate misunderstanding that caused you to engage in battle. Perhaps before you learned about each other?" he asked his companions and us.

Vrae decided to explain, but as if she were reading my thoughts about checking these guys out, she explained all about the fight but didn't mention our names. Luckily, Rivorgad along with his comrades seemed to understand that despite their vows, we needed to see their comrades' reaction and corroborate her story.

"Daryth, I don't understand. They're not exactly explaining anything except when they murdered Xeithar and Vangurd," Ziram said slowly as he directed a cold glare at me.

Not wanting to stupidly ignite a fight, I just cast a blank look at him.

Helkann smiled at me and my companions. "Well, I see you have yet to say anything about your names. I don't expect you to grant their wishes simply by seeing their reaction when you mention the Hieldhar, Rivorgad. So, I take it these two ladies are Cherxanains Yverna and Vrathien?" he asked the soldier.

Rivorgad nodded apologetically. "Yes indeed, they are, Daryth. The one next to Cherxanain Yverna is Varkonian Zaderion." Helkann turned his gaze to Ziram. "His Highness sent me here to welcome his guests."

Ziram's eyes widened when he mentioned our names, and he dropped to one knee, whereas Helkann half bowed. "Forgive us for the late introductions. May the grace of the Irgovaen and his queen befall you. I'm Helkann, their commander, and he's Ziram. Please excuse his atrocity. He didn't know because he was out on patrol. The king knew about you the moment you set foot here, and he gave me the order to escort you inside immediately. It turned out Ziram ran into you first."

We returned their salute, and they straightened themselves. "No matter, we thank you for your hospitality. I'm Yverna, and she's Vrathien, my sister. This is Zaderion," I said.

"Once again, forgive us about your comrades," Vrae added.

Helkann smiled sadly. "It is unfortunate, but they'd fallen in the line of duty. Despite everything, they'd be thrilled if they learned who you are."

"By the way, it seems Ry really did say something to you all about us, huh? And you guys accepted it? No offense, just asking," Vrae said.

Helkann smiled. "None taken. I'm certain that Rivorgad told you the reason why our king and Ry"–I relaxed a degree when he called Ry by his short name–"became close. He was the saviour of our king, and he had been a good friend who will always be remembered with reverence. He treated us as his equal comrades, and this place was his haven. For that we will follow whatever his wishes were."

"Because that is also the will of our king," Arann inserted.

I gave them a respectful nod. "For that, we're all grateful. But right now we need to seek audience with your masters immediately."

He hesitated for a split second. I didn't miss that, and obviously neither did Vrae. "Is there anything?" she asked.

He shook his head and smiled. "There's nothing, I just remembered that I have to contact the others inside so they'll stand down and inform the king and the queen."

The three of us were alarmed at his words. "You *are* telling them to stand down, right? Not tricking us and then having them ambush us once we're inside wherever that is?" I asked flatly.

Helkann, to his credit, didn't even look offended. "Rest assured, we are telling them to stand down. If we just go inside, they all *might* attack you at once. I didn't get the chance to tell them about your presence, you see," he said calmly.

"Remember, the three of us vowed to protect all of you," Daviros inserted.

"And that includes us." Helkann and Ziram both approached us and firmed their gestures. Both of them took vows as their comrades had done.

Well, I sure as hell didn't count on that one. Standing there and hearing them vow like their comrades made me think just how much these people respected Ry, so much that they would just make vows to us.

I raised a brow and answered them with ours. "Very well, you may contact your people."

He nodded and closed his eyes, no doubt telepathically contacting his pals. Seconds later, he opened his eyes and without saying a word, he turned his back and faced the vast field.

All of a sudden, Vrae called me. *"Yve, this field's barren. What are we doing here?"*

I shrugged. *"How do I know? Maybe this place of Irgovaen's is indeed here, but . . ."*

"But protected with a protective shield? Is that what you mean?" she interjected.

I gave her a subtle nod. *"Could be. What do you think, Zade?"*

He eyed the five who had turned their backs on us, staring at who knew what. *"Just be on guard and see what happens. That's what I think. If they try anything stupid, just fight our way outta here."*

"It's good when you talk sense and brute force once in a while. Darvahl or the other guys wouldn't be that much fun." I grinned, and he returned it with a small laugh.

Suddenly, I felt a peculiar sensation as the air began to stir. *"Heads up, guys. Something's coming,"* Vrae warned us.

I turned my attention to follow her line of sight and saw that something *was* coming, or should I say, a huge fortress was coming. It emerged slowly from thin air, and we gaped as the whole place stood before us.

"Comrades of Hieldhar Ezryan, welcome," Helkann said, indicating the place with his hand, "to the Black Fortress of Irgovaen."

The fortress was an improvement on those black woods in every respect. Its walls were hundreds of feet tall and were made of black bricks. The gate was sturdy, made of pure iron, which would be pretty much bad news for us if it closed. I caught glimpses of the palace that resided behind the gate. It was huge and like every other thing here, it was black and made from some sort of stone like diamond, black diamond.

And I had been thinking that forest was something we wouldn't see every day.

"Shall we?" Helkann said as he pointed at the gate, which slowly motioned outward until it stopped. We looked at each other and then followed them inside.

The moment our feet touched the inner area of the fortress, there were people coming out. They stood there and stared at us as if we were some kind of freak show.

If it wasn't for the vow I'd just made, I would probably have wasted all of them by now–staring at us, at *me*, like that.

"Stop, Yve." Suddenly I heard Vrae's voice. *"Remember, we can't do anything unless they start it."*

I scowled. *"Thanks so much for the reminder. I guess we'll have to wait and see."*

"C'mon ladies, don't throw a party just yet. We're in the middle of nowhere here," Zade interjected.

"No shit," I retorted as we walked through lines of people who, judging by their appearances, were soldiers.

It was then six soldiers came at us with the strangest look of surprise and rage on their faces. I recognized them right away. They were the ones who had got away from D'arksin before I could hold them in place.

"Uh-oh."

One of them was about to lunge at us, but Helkann planted himself in the way. "Stop right there, Hyrion. They are guests of the king and the queen."

"They're the guests? But, Daryth! Xeithar, Rivorgad and the others . . ."

Rivorgad and his companions stepped into view. "I'm here with Daviros and Arann, but Xeithar and Vangurd have fallen. As you all have been informed by Daryth, the three here are the ones Hieldhar Ezryan spoke of."

It was as though somebody had just sucked out the air for a split second by a mere mention of Ry's name. Now, most of them went from a completely-ready-to-go-berserk state to a helluva lot friendlier. I still spotted a few whose eyes gleamed in uncertainty and utter distrust, though, but that was to be expected.

Rivorgad and the others saw our reaction when they mentioned Ry and had talked with us. They accepted us and vice versa, but these guys didn't, and they were bound to feel that way.

If all of them just accepted our presence here, I would have said that this was a trap or that they were really that gullible or, hell, maybe they really did revere Ry that much. But still, somebody else could've impersonated us and fooled them all–not that anybody had the guts to do it.

And besides, Ry would never run with people who were that stupid.

But then, despite the uncertainty some of them might have felt, they all stepped aside, making a clear path for the three of us.

"I shall tell you all what happened back there after we escort them to His Highness and the queen," Helkann said. "This way," he motioned us to follow him, Rivorgad, and the others into the palace. The main entrance was already wide open, and we all walked inside. The place was quite huge. We'd been walking for a few minutes after going through the main entrance, and we still hadn't reached the main hall.

I shook my head in disbelief as we walked. "Gee, Vrae, Ry is famous around here."

Vrae scoffed. "It doesn't mean he's alive, Yve. Don't think I don't know what you're hoping to accomplish by coming here. You heard what they said. According to them, Ry's dead as a rock around here too. Getting more truth about what happened between him and our master won't bring him back," Vrae said quietly as she kept a stoic look on her face.

"What I meant was that these people did know and respect him. I didn't mean or think he's still alive. Not even I would be that sentimental." I stared dryly at her, while Zade just stood there with blank look.

After a while, we finally arrived at a fairly massive hall. It looked opulent; the walls were decorated in carved black diamonds, and four pillars stood in their respective corners. Everything *was* black in this place, I might actually like it. In the centre were stairs that led to a pair of thrones.

We halted to a stop at the bottom of the stairs with more of the natives swarming around us. I strode towards Helkann and the others. "Why are we stopping? And by the way, nice place." I jerked my head, indicating the palace. *"If your pals don't stare too friggin' much."*

"Thank you," Rivorgad replied. "We shall wait for the others to inform the king and the queen that you've arrived and ask for their audience. Then we can escort you to their chamber."

I winced. "Okay."

Vrae suddenly patted my back and walked away. "Excuse us," I said to them, and then I followed her to a corner. "What?"

She whispered, "I'm getting more nervous by the minute here."

I rolled my eyes. "If you're really that nervous, why don't you take a channel? C'mon, we're all in on this. The only thing I'm worried about is that someone on the other side might notice we're gone, and that'd open a whole can of worms I have no interest in dealing with."

Vrae let out an undignified snort. "You don't say. You were the one who jumped to conclusions and followed these people here just because they knew Ry."

"You're blaming everything on me? Does Ry mean anything to you at all?" I muttered grudgingly.

She glared at me. "It's not that. Of course he means something, everything, to all of us, but that doesn't mean you can follow anyone who appears to know him everywhere! What if this turns out to be a trap? And according to Zade, we're in another dimension here. Have you any idea how we could save our asses if everything went south? 'Cause I have no fucking clue. I mean, come on, Yve, it's not like you to just jump into a hole without checking around first."

I scowled at her words. Damn, did she have to stab people anywhere she liked?

Exhaling in exasperation, I looked around to find Zade having a chat with a few of the natives. He was making friends. Good for him.

I faced Vrae and narrowed my gaze at her. "Just what the hell was that supposed to mean? I'm not going for chick-flick moments here and trying to share my feelings. Like I said to Zade, if being in this mess could get me one step closer to the truth of what happened to him, then so be it. If these people try anything clever, I'll blow them apart. That's part of our vow, so stop nagging like an old hag," I said coldly.

She opened her mouth, no doubt to throw some acerbic retort, but then, lucky for the both of us, Rivorgad returned. "Excuse me, Cherxanains. The king and the queen have agreed to meet all of you in private, since our people certainly make you somewhat nervous. But if we didn't contact them they may attack us."

Vrae cleared her throat. "Yeah, to tell you the truth, we are a bit nervous. Anyway, let's go see your masters. Yve, go and grab Zade." She jerked her head towards the Varkonian.

I nodded as I went to get the Varkonian. "Sure thing."

He saw me walking towards him and waved. "Come here, Yve. Meet Amran, Movarek, and Jezraeli." He pointed at the three guys with whom he had been chatting earlier.

They put their hands upon their chest. "May the grace of the king and the queen befall you, Cherxanain."

I nodded. "You too. By the way, nice to meet you and all, but we gotta go. Your masters want to see us." They nodded, and we left them.

While we were walking back to where Vrae was waiting with the others, I slightly elbowed the Varkonian. "You're getting along pretty well with these guys. Good thing you didn't notice how nervous we are, or in particular, Vrae," I whispered curtly.

He laughed. "It's a good thing you can be nervous once in a while. I'll find a new use for my jokes here."

When I raised my eyebrows, he exhaled heavily. "Look, Yve, we're all together in this. You wanna know about Ry, right? That makes three of us. Listen, I had visions about these guys, and I'd say that, after we got to know them a bit, they aren't so bad after all. And I know we can get outta here in case some trouble happens, though I doubt there will be any. Also, I could tell that you trust these guys enough in the first place. Otherwise, you wouldn't dare throw vows on a whim like you did, now would you?"

I snorted. "Thanks for trusting my judgment. Pal, you gotta tell *her* that," I whispered as we reached Vrae and saw Rivorgad waving his hand to a hallway.

"Cherxanains, Varkonian, forgive me, but we should go to the king and the queen. They are waiting."

"All right, that's why we're here after all."

"Come on, let's get this over with," Vrae interjected.

Helkann took a step back. "I'm not coming. I must explain this to the others. You can go with Rivorgad."

"Arann and I shall be here in your stead then, Rivorgad," Daviros added.

We nodded, and they gave us their salute. "Thank you, Daryth Helkann," I said.

"Just Helkann, please, Cherxanain," he replied with a smile.

"I will, if you'll call me Yverna, not Cherxanain."

He smiled and nodded. "As you wish, uh, Yverna."

"Later, Helkann," I said, and I left them with the crowd. We followed our guide further down the hall into the darkness of the palace.

"So, Rivorgad, can I ask you something?" I asked him while we were walking through the darkness.

"Sure, what is it, Cherxanain?"

I cleared my throat. "Look, first of all, you and your friends can call us by our names. You're not our underlings. You guys respect Ry, and you're not calling us abominations or anything any more because you take his words into consideration. That's good enough for us. So, are we cool? And try not to get all formal, if you don't mind."

He hesitated for a moment and then he smiled as he faced me. "Very well, Yverna."

"Great," I said, while Vrae and Zade just kept their silence.

"So, what is it?" he asked. "You said you wanna ask me something."

"Yeah, I've been meaning to ask, what were you and the others doing back there, I mean on our plane?"

He looked aghast at my remark. "So, you noticed that we're on different dimensions?"

I indicated Zade with a nod. "Well, thanks to Zade here who told us earlier, and it's not like there are four moons back on earth."

"Yeah, it's not like there's a pitch-black leaf on earth either, let alone a forest," Vrae inserted.

"Well, unless you're talking about that cake with cherries and everything, then we don't have a black forest," I muttered under my breath.

Vrae stared dryly at me, and I ignored her. Zade snorted at my comment, while Rivorgad frowned deeply. "Wait, how did

Zaderion know this? We've certainly never met before, and by the look of things, you've never encountered one of us either. He really knew?"

I nodded. "Yep, he's the one who told us, and that's a long story to begin with. Maybe you'll hear it when we're talking to your masters. So, back to my question, what were you guys doing on our plane?"

He inhaled in uncertainty. "We were ordered by the king to search for something."

"Search for something? What were you looking for?" Vrae asked.

Rivorgad's eyes gleamed in worry. "Actually, some weird events have been happening throughout our plane, and if I recall it correctly, this has something to do with the classified information Hieldhar Ezryan confided in the Irgovaen before his death."

"Classified information? Do you happen to know what that was?" Zade asked him.

"No, I don't. Only my king and queen knew about it, and perhaps Daryth Helkann. But, if I'm not mistaken, His Highness told me that this information could only be passed on to the two of you and whoever you bring with you. Perhaps then, he'll let some of us into the loop. But all and all, that is up to the king to decide."

"Okay, once again, who or what were you looking for back there?" I asked him as I looked ahead up the hallway.

"Well, we don't know for sure," he said hesitantly.

"You don't know?" Zade repeated as he arched a brow.

Rivorgad shook his head. "We were there because our intel came up with something. They said the chances are high that the one who's been causing these events I told you about was running to your plane."

"What exactly are these weird events you keep telling us about?" I asked.

He hesitated and then expelled a short breath. "Well, not only were they weird, they were worrying to say the least. I believe it started seven months ago or so in your time. Our soldiers have been slaughtered one after another. Their condition was bad, but all of them were always the same. They were put inside some form of protective shield, and the place where we'd find them was always pretty far from where the battle seemed to have taken place."

Hearing his explanation, the three of us exchanged an alarmed look, which he noticed. "Is there anything?" he inquired.

I nodded. "Well, we have to give credit to your intel department. They got it right. Whoever or whatever it was really did come to our plane."

He was aghast at my words. "How can you tell?"

Vrae answered him. "When we ran into you back there, we'd just finished checking the remains of *our* underlings, which were in the very same condition as your pals."

Rivorgad gasped in shock at her words. "What? Your subordinates were killed as well?"

Vrae snorted. "Hell, being killed was an understatement."

"Yeah, even the word butchered wouldn't quite cover it," Zade shrugged.

I frowned. "It quite covered it," I inserted without thinking.

Well, it did, right? From my point of view at least.

I glanced at Zade who raised his brows and Vrae who rolled her eyes. "Whatever, I won't start arguing with you on that one. Anyhow, we can be sure of one thing. You guys have nothing to do with the deaths of our subordinates," Vrae remarked.

He shook his head. "No, and speaking of that, that part confused me before, because you two"–he cast a meaningful gaze at me and Zade–"assumed my king and queen had attacked someone." He paused and smiled sadly. "It's a shame that Vangurd died and Xeithar killed himself. They would have been glad if they had learned who you three really were. They respected Hieldhar Ezryan and liked to talk to him from time to time."

"Well, I'm sorry I cornered him and made him think there was no other way." I offered him an apologetic smile. He shook his head in response.

"So," Vrae interrupted us. "Do your masters know who it might be?" she asked in a voice strained with curiosity.

He shrugged. "Even if the king knows, he's never let us in the loop."

Vrae nodded in understanding. "Maybe we'll know as soon as we talk to your king and queen, huh?"

"Indeed."

"By the way, do you have any speculation about what's been killing your guys here?" Zade asked.

Rivorgad was startled by his question. He was silent, as if choosing his next words carefully. Abruptly, he cleared his throat. "Well, we did suspect something. Maybe I'd better tell the story starting from eons ago before we even existed, when God hadn't even created heaven and hell. Our archive, well, the *restricted* part of our archive recorded that at that time God created one entity. It is said that this being was made of pure void. We're not even sure of its purpose or even if it existed at all."

"Well, if it's true, we can be certain of one thing. It *is* dangerous beyond anything we've ever known before." Vrae exhaled heavily.

All of us turned to her.

"And why the hell is that?" I folded my arms.

"Somebody in the Lasinth told me once that void was the source of all creation. Everything made of it could be poison or cure. Either way, it's the best of its kind," she explained.

"Just great, another joke created by the Master of Jokes Himself." I muttered grudgingly.

Vrae scowled. "What the hell ever, Mistress Obvious. Get over the acidic attitude for a second." She turned to Rivorgad who seemed amused with our banter. "So, what then? Do you guys have a name for this guy?"

"Yeah, actually we call this entity Avarnakh, meaning 'absolute void' in our language."

"That's a mouthful. After that, what? Did the Big Guy create some other yahoo to accompany this Avarnakh? He's usually big on balance and pairs," I interjected.

He snorted. "Not that we know of. Anyway, He created heaven and hell after that," he said as he nodded at us, "along with the universe within which was our plane. But before He created the archangels, including his current Right Hand, the Archangel Michael . . ."

"He created Lucifer first," we interrupted him.

By the look on his face, we could tell that he wasn't too fond of the name of the Fallen One, but what the hell. That would be his problem.

He nodded rather stiffly. "Yes indeed He did. He created the Fallen One, the Arcs, and the rest of the angels. Some say God created another race. Either it was before or after the Fallen One; we weren't quite clear on that. The thing was, something happened to them, and the race was wiped out by God Himself. After the Fallen One was, well, fallen, then your race started popping up, starting with Lilith."

"Yeah, we've heard. They say that race was our origins, but no one can tell." Rivorgad looked aghast at this, but he didn't ask anything.

I bit my lip as I let his explanation sank in. "So, where does your race fit in all this? And your masters, they've been around for that long?"

"No, our current king and queen are the twentieth rulers that have reigned over our kingdom. They've ruled us since Noah made his Ark in your plane."

"Wow, that's quite a long time, and I'm impressed that you know about that as well," I said with an inward grimace.

Damn, I was right. Leaving aside the horny part, all in all they *were* indeed an old couple. Since Noah–who would've guessed?

His story immediately occupied my thoughts, along with one told by a senior of mine. Czemoren was his name. He was once called to join a special unit named the Sahadim that was formed each time a new prophet or saint appeared. This unit consisted of a few soldiers hand-picked by the Echelons to seduce the humans closest to the prophet or saint into straying from the right path decreed by upstairs. Sometimes they'd even try to seduce the said prophet or saint himself. To be assigned to this unit, these soldiers needed to be the best in their respective fields. They had to maintain an extremely low profile in association with the angels and mortal sorcerers, and they had to have been in the high ranks for a very long time.

As the second condition stated, Cherxanains like Vrae, myself, and few others, not to mention Ry, could never be part of the Sahadim, since we ran into angels so often. They had learned our names. The sorcerers had heard rumours about us as well.

Anyway, Czemoren told me as he struggled not to laugh outright, that he had convinced Noah's wife and son not to follow him into the Ark, and then they died for it.

Sometimes I'd heard their annoying screams in the punishing block.

Rivorgad smiled. He definitely didn't know what I was thinking, but whatever. I had no intention of telling him anyway.

"Yes, it is a long time. The first king and his queen who ruled my kind was created not long after Lilith and some others. In other words, my kind was born sometime between the creation of the Fallen One and your race. As for why we were put in the different plane, well, that beats me. I have no idea myself."

"And this Avarnakh fellow, where does that guy fit in?" I asked.

Rivorgad noticed that I talked as if the thing were still around and kicking. "Uh, are you sure this Avarnakh exists? I mean, its existence was indeed recorded, and it bore a resemblance to the powers we felt from the remains of our fallen comrades, but still . . ."

"We can be pretty sure about that because of the protective shield that covered our underlings. It didn't give out any specific energy print, just blank, but if it were mixed with certain types of energy, like ours, for instance, it can be as deadly as a poison. And an energy with no print? For me that's no different from void or whatever that is," I said as I wondered where the king's chamber was.

"Damn, this place is way beyond huge," I was half bemused as I subtly observed the hall.

"There's something in that," Rivorgad agreed, and he also faced the hallway once again. "But, why did whoever that was do this?" he asked.

"Who knows?" I shrugged, and he exhaled heavily.

Vrae looked at Rivorgad. "By the way, you keep mentioning Lilith. Does that mean Lilith has anything to do with this guy? Or does she even know that guy existed at all?"

I arched a brow at her. Funny she brought that one up. Lilith was gone–well, not that she's dead or anything. She'd just gone into seclusion many centuries ago. As for why she did it, we never had a clue and never worried about it.

The humans who knew Lilith described her as Adam's first wife who left him because he didn't treat her as his equal. If only it really was that simple. Well, considering the fact that she was the very first being created by Lucifer and thus she became one of our race while Adam was a human, they were indeed not equal.

But from the point of view of me and my comrades, she was already a bitch.

Long ago, she went to Samael and became his woman, and as far as we know, the Big Guy never joined her with Adam in some stupid church, let alone in heaven. I didn't know where the humans heard all that crap about her being Mrs Adam and having Adam's family with him.

Maybe that was why there were few people, humans and devils, who worshipped her.

Well, if she *did* seduce the guy, we would never know.

But, we did know one thing about her. She liked to take names, credits, and stuff, and that really pissed off most of us, the ones whose ranks were higher than the soldiers who revered the old bitch.

We once thought she was the one who spread the bullshit about her being Mrs Adam. Again, names. We never really knew for sure on that part, though.

By the way, there was a history between me and her. She showed off to the warriors once, claiming that she made a king of a certain land into a ruthless tyrant. Well, it was unfortunate for her, but my fellow warriors weren't that dumb. They knew it was *my* doing, so one of them came and told me about it.

In the end, I came to her and bitch-slapped her before several warriors and underlings. Hell, even Vrae looked as if she was enjoying herself when she saw me did it. Right after I did that, we were immediately caught in a huge fight at the Kadarost forest. I recalled that we almost burned the entire forest down. Vrae called Ry when the fight nearly got out of hand. He came and separated us to prevent me accidentally killing her. Thank all hell he did, because as appealing as it sounded, I might end up facing the wrath of Samael or worse, our master himself, and I was so not in the mood to get my ass kicked for her, so I left with Ry.

The bottom line was I didn't care if Lilith was Samael's woman or Adam's stalker or anything. A bitch was a bitch, and that was how I dealt with bitches.

"I'm not sure either. Lilith was only mentioned because she was created by the Fallen One, although I heard that she has a certain importance–with what, I don't really know," he replied, pulling me from my contemplation at the same time.

I scoffed. "Well, probably that's because she doesn't really have any importance except to be a footnote bitch in your record."

Vrae and Zade snorted at my harsh comment. They definitely remembered the last thing I did to her.

Rivorgad smiled, but he appeared perplexed. "Is there anything I need to know?"

Vrae cleared her throat. "FYI, Yve here had one hell of a fight with Lilith, starting with her bitch-slapping the old slut several centuries ago."

"For being a bitch and a pain in the ass to boot," I interjected, and the three of us laughed quietly while Rivorgad winced in bafflement but didn't ask anything. Good for him.

"Okay, we can go through the tedious history lesson later. And speaking of that, would you tell us why we're also abominations to you?" I tilted my head at him.

He hesitated and then took a deep breath before answered, "Very well, I'll tell you. First off, amongst your kind, there is one who possesses the ability to cross over dimensions, well two, but the other one, he's dead . . ."

"What? Who?" The three of us were alarmed at his statement.

"Well, I presume you three are not aware of the fact that the Fallen One himself can do such a thing," he said in a theatrical voice, while our gaze widened in shock.

He went on, "At first, this plane wasn't our original plane. All of this started eons ago, when the Fallen One started to hunt and kill Irgovaens and their queens. He'd done it since the first Irgovaen and all the way until the nineteenth.

"Fortunately for us, the fourth Irgovaen left a curse in his last breath. He'd stripped the power of crossing over planes, not completely, but enough to make sure the offspring of the Fallen One can't do the same. All you can do is just teleport from one place to another, so the Fallen One remains the only one who can do that. Since then, the hatred has been passed down to us, because the Fallen One just won't stop doing what he's been doing. As for why he did it, we still don't have a clue. Perhaps the previous king did, but nobody knows for sure."

We gaped. Wow, this gave us a whole new kind of shock. The look on Vrae and Zade's faces told me they too still couldn't get over their utter surprise upon hearing this outrageous story.

"And there's one other thing," I said. "Tell us exactly how Ry first met your king."

Rivorgad hesitated when he looked at us, but decided to ignore us with a sorry-guys-but-suck-it-up kinda face. "That day, His Highness was in your plane, along with five of us as his guards. I believe it was around the time when Moses arose. His Highness was there because he was curious about his staff. He'd heard about him from the scout party he'd send from time to time to your plane to gather intel on your kind's movement, well, sort of."

"Why would he be curious about that thing?" I asked him.

Rivorgad slowly shook his head. "I'm not really sure, but from what I heard, it seemed that His Highness may have thought it, or perhaps something that is owned by prophets, would protect us from becoming objects for the Fallen One's hunting sport." I arched my brows at his choice of words but remained silent.

He cleared his throat and looked uneasy. "They didn't linger for long around the prophet's premises and left for a certain forest to depart back here. It was then that all his guardians were wiped out in no time by the hands of the Fallen One himself," he said. There was profound grief in his voice that indicated that he knew the dead soldiers, which I could relate to.

"What?" the three of us asked sharply.

As I let this sink in, a thought popped into my mind. If I remembered it correctly, I once ran into Ry not long after that time, and he acted a bit weird, pale and trembling a bit as if he'd witnessed or done something he wasn't supposed to, but how could it be? Amon would know about it if he did, wouldn't he?

I winced as the answer followed the question. *"He would know through the golem, unless Ry used his doppelganger,"* I mused, half mocking the liability of the thing yet grateful for it at the same time.

Besides, he said it was nothing, but it was not long after that when he started showing off that he had a special inside man doing some digging for him whenever we needed a bit intel.

I glanced at Vrae, whose wondering gaze was stuck on me and succeeded in pulling me from my thought. Well, maybe I'd save it for later. Luckily, Rivorgad didn't notice, and neither did Zade.

Our guide let out a long breath. "It was only a matter of seconds before His Highness met Azrael himself. Fortunately, Hieldhar

Ezryan, bless him, happened to be there, and with his powers he deflected a bit of the Dark Light of Rygavon from the distance. It was only a bit, but it was enough to distract the Fallen One. His Highness immediately went towards where his saviour was hiding, and then he teleported back here with him. And as far as I can tell, His Highness then prevented us from attacking the Hieldhar and told all of us that he was his saviour."

My brows knitted in disbelief. "And you guys accepted him just like that?"

He paused, as if considering what was best to say. "The two of them and the queen were locked up in His Highness's chamber for days after. Naturally, there were some of us who looked at him with suspicious eyes," he said quietly, his gaze on a distant past. "Well, it was mostly caused by him being an unholy. Furthermore, he was the Commander of the Fallen One's army. With that said, his closeness to our king put some of us on edge. But after that, he came here from time to time, and thus we came to know him pretty well and deemed him to be trustworthy." Rivorgad led us to a right turn.

My eyes widened when he said Ry came here. "Wait, so, you're telling us that the other one who's got this ability to cross dimension was . . ."

Rivorgad cast a sad gaze at the three of us. "Yes, it was Hieldhar Ezryan. At first, he didn't have it, but the king granted him that ability as a gift for saving his life. After that, they, including the queen, became close ever since. And he was close to all of us as well. At the end of the day, he was the one who saved the king's life. That's all that matters to us." There was a glint of respect in his eyes when he mentioned Ry's deed.

We fell into utter silence at his story and just kept walking. Moments later we halted, and he indicated a left turn up ahead. "We'll soon reach the king's chamber where His Highness and the queen are waiting for all of you."

As we proceeded, my thoughts turned to Ry. He never told us any of this. He'd once told me that I was the only one he completely trusted besides Vrae, and the same went for me. He was the only one in existence I trusted completely aside from her. But then again, from what I knew about him, maybe he didn't want to endanger all of us.

Yeah, if our master or any ass-kissers that love to kiss his ass, had been able to get their hands on this piece of information, hell, "fucked over royally" would be a major understatement for Ry and those close to him. *"Can't say if being burned by the Light of God could be a good thing for him or not,"* I thought bitterly.

We sauntered towards the junction and took the left turn. Hell, there had been many turns before this, and they both were in the end of the hallway. I wasn't sure why kings and queens were so fond of dead ends.

After we turned left, there was a pretty massive and sturdy door with a lot of engraving on it, some sort of language. Rivorgad stood in front of it and firmed his gestures. "Your Highness, My Queen, the companions of Hieldhar are here," he said clearly to whoever was behind the door.

A deep masculine voice that was full of power replied to him. "Bring them inside."

Chapter 8

Rivorgad placed his hand on the door, and it glowed before slowly swinging inward.

He went in and stepped aside to let us through. He then closed the door and motioned us to follow him. I glanced at the interior of the chamber as we strode further inside. The first things I noticed were ornaments and engravings all over the room, which again were black.

Well, I'd expect nothing less from a king's chamber.

We then came face to face with a couple. I almost couldn't stop my eyes from gaping wide open when I saw them. They definitely were not like any living beings I'd ever seen.

The male, I assumed he was the Irgovaen, was wearing a black shirt and tightly woven criss-crossed laces that held up his tight black leather pants. On top of them, he wore long, black silk, duster-like robe that was left to flow regally around his body. He was tall and extremely gorgeous with straight waist-length silver hair. His clothing highlighted his muscular body, and he, like some of his people, had pointy ears, white little horns and beautiful dual-coloured eyes. Those eyes were so beautiful that I could barely stop looking at him. I also noted that he had no wings.

I noticed his long white silver hair and couldn't help thinking he did resemble Ry in some way. That thought about him made me clench.

He stood near a long table with black armchairs, where there sat a female. No doubt she was the queen. She wore long black gown. Like the Irgovaen, she had had pointy ears but no horns. Her wavy silver hair was pulled in a single braid down her back. Her hair was so long, it almost touched the floor. She also had the same beautiful eyes as he, but with slight gold swirling on them. Both their skins were so white and pale that they practically glowed in the darkness of this place.

The queen stood up and they approached us.

Rivorgad knelt before them while we stood behind him. "They're here, My Liege. Now I shall take my leave." He rose up and started for the door.

The king raised his hand. "No, you may stay. After this I want you to summon the others who have made vows to be their protectors, but that's for later," he said, and he turned his gaze to us.

Rivorgad stood up and walked to the corner. I saw his baffled expression as he went by, but he didn't say anything. As he settled in a spot at the corner, the three of us stood in silence, staring the couple. As I observed them, there was this weird feeling as if I'd seen this guy somewhere before, but not this close.

But where? There was no chance of me ever having stumbled across this guy. How could this be possible?

The Irgovaen smiled. "We finally meet. I am the twentieth Irgovaen, and this is my wife. I'm Xaemorkahn and she's Varisha." He indicated the female, who also smiled at us.

Vrae cleared her throat. "It's an honour to meet you, Highness."

He raised his hand, stopping her. "You can call us by names. You are not our soldiers, but our close friends," he said with a warm, dazzling smile.

We exchanged a puzzled look and turned to him again. "Well, thanks, Xaemorkahn," Vrae said hesitantly.

He kept that friendly smile on his face. "It's my pleasure. Come, take a seat." He led us to the long table with several armchairs around it where his wife had sat earlier. We dragged three of the chairs out and took a seat.

"So, you must have lots of questions, right?" He inclined his head. He was pretty relaxed and not as uptight as I had expected, with him being the *king*.

I hoped he'd swallowed a lot of Ry's crap, enough to make him quite easy to deal with.

Deciding I'd try to prove my suspicions that he would act pretty much like Ry, I encouraged myself. "Yeah, actually, so many questions that we don't have a clue where to begin. By the way, I'm Yve, this is Vrae, and he's Zade."

Vrae gave me a look saying, *"You're talking to the big cheese. Could you at least watch your damned mouth?"* Zade evidently grimaced at my attitude.

I ignored them and kept my eyes on the king and his queen. Contrary to what Vrae had feared, he looked amused and abruptly let out a scoffing laugh, which made me frown at him. "What is it?" I asked.

He shook his head. "Nothing. I thought I might end up offending you if I didn't act all formal at first. It seemed Ry was right. You guys really aren't that uptight," he said as he laughed, and Varisha just concealed her soft laughter with her dainty hands.

Well, this is wholly unexpected. His underlings had acted as if they had a major stick up their asses, and their king acted, well, a bit like us.

This should be amusing. On that note, I cleared my throat. "Yep, Ry got that right. We are fun. Now, I don't mean to be rude, but how about we cut to the chase?"

When I glanced at the other three, they obviously thought I didn't realize that I was talking to the king of this place. Hell, despite what the king had said, Vrae still had that look on her face as if she were more than ready to strangle me. But screw them. We'd had enough trouble to deal with aside from formality.

What I didn't expect was the next thing that came out of his mouth. It was nowhere near protesting my lack of manner. "Okay," he said as he leaned forward. "So it seems my sworn brother Ry hasn't contacted you yet."

*　　*　　*

Somewhere among massive cliffs on the edge of the earth, an unspeakable malevolence stirred in the air, and a rift cracked open, revealing a big black cocoon-like form.

As the rift closed, the cocoon slowly spread open, forming a black pair of wings. From within, an unholy being emerged.

The wings transformed into a heavy midnight-blue robe that draped across his shoulders. His black armour hugged his lean well-built body. His impressive height made him all the more devastating, and his lethal aura radiated absolute terror.

He stared down silently from the cliff. A long time ago, those cliffs had been shores surrounding a massive lake which no longer existed. It was the one of few things that had saved his life before he was forced to leave in the end.

The cold wind of the night slowly teased his skin, caressing him like a gentle touch. As he closed his deep sapphire eyes to savour the wind, an image belonging to a beautiful unholy being like himself appeared in his mind. The longing and fear that lingered in him for her stirred, making tears of blood fall from his eyes onto his cold cheeks.

He'd been waiting for this moment for far too long. He was drowning excruciatingly slowly in anticipation and utter misery for the one thing that had held a firm grip on his mind for seven hundred years.

Was she, the one and only reason he'd fought his way back, still here? Or was it all just an empty hope on his part? Yes, he still had the rest of his companions, but without her he didn't really have any actual reason to come back or, more to the point, to live.

His mind wandered to the distant past, to the exquisite image of his beloved. The memory was so vivid, he could've sworn he looked right into the soothing darkness of her eyes and felt the depth of their warmth.

He could feel the smoothness of her long black hair that begged him to bury his face in it. His senses even recalled the scent of her sweet enticing fragrance that danced through his nostrils and drove his core mad in an irresistible addiction each and every time she was close. Above all else, he could almost picture her in his arms as he whispered in her ears the very thing he wanted to say a long time ago.

To let him protect her forever.

Then again, if he was to make this true, which was his own vow to himself, his first priority was to make sure she was still here. Only after that could he move immediately to warn his companions of the mortal danger that was headed their way, the ultimate threat that had already been set in motion against them all.

At the thought that reminded him of the moment when he had been forced to leave this plane and barely survive, there was ignited an agonizing pain that instantly burned his core. His lust for vengeance went wild in him as hundreds of images played over and over in the back of his mind–the truth of what had truly happened to him.

The truth that ultimately separated him from her, and that was the only thing which angered him the most.

The time to exact his revenge was finally in his grasp. His course was set. Opening his eyes, he smiled in anticipation.

Jumping off the cliff, he flew to the northern sky.

*   *   *

Rift of Bahyrdanam

Amon rose slowly from his seat as chills teased his spine at those words.

Rifts were rarely opened. If they did, usually it would be around domains of royals, not around some lake, let alone one that had been burned to oblivion.

His confusion was increased by another wave that broke on the surface of the Veil and revealed two more lines. His blood ran cold upon reading them. He hastily made sure none of the Echelons was in the mood to observe him, especially the one directly supervising him. After he was sure no one was watching, he looked closely upon the Veil.

Unknown unholy
Great Lake of Bahyrdanam

Amon frowned deeply at the sheer absurdity of it. *"Unknown unholy? What the hell? There's no unholy that can't be identified,"* he pondered in confusion.

He then read the next words, which didn't help him at all. Those words were once again swallowed into the darkness of the Veil. It was then that outrageous possibilities hit him one after another. "That was where . . ." he stopped in the middle of his words when another thought came into his mind.

"Could it possibly be?"

*   *   *

The three of us, along with the king's soldier, gaped at his words. "What did you say?" We asked simultaneously.

His eyes gleamed with wariness and vexation. "Dammit, brother, you really *didn't* contact them," he muttered under his breath. He sounded pretty calm when he was saying it, as if finding out that our best comrade and commander, who supposedly had died, now turned out to be alive, was an everyday thing for all of us.

I frowned at him referring to Ry as his brother. What was that supposed to mean?

He then lowered his gaze to the floor and his hair fell over his shoulder, covering one side of his face. After a few seconds, he lifted his gaze at us. "Well, apparently he didn't contact any of you, well, maybe not yet. By the way, we vowed to be brothers, so we called each other that. So don't be surprised in case you run into him and hear him addressing me as his brother," he explained.

I inclined my head. "Rivorgad here told us, not the vow part though. But let's get over that. What do you mean, he didn't contact us? Do you mean before or after he was burned down?" I narrowed my gaze at him.

He raised his brows. "Well, after, of course. Just so you know, he didn't die that time. And none of my men knows about this, because he asked me not tell them, not until we come in contact with you two and whoever it is you're with."

"No way! He's alive?" I asked with a happiness in my voice that I barely could hide.

Zade leaned forward. "So where is he? Is he all right?"

Xaemorkahn put his hand on the armrest and looked tense. "Yes, the last time we saw him he was all right. We'd had a bit of an argument on the day he left not long after he'd recovered."

"Why was that?" Vrae asked him.

He threw his long hair over his back and looked a bit frustrated but sad. "I was so against his judgment when he intended to go out there again by himself. But, bitter as it may sound, Ry sometimes has better views even than mine. I had no other choice but to let him go. In return, he asked both of us to tell our people that he indeed died by that Heavenly Flame of God. He told me that his–your–Echelons would spread that news the moment he disappeared. He said they'd use the evaporated lake as the only evidence of his demise."

"Yeah, those smart-asses have been trying to shove that BS down our throats all these centuries," I interjected.

He snorted. "Well, I'd expect nothing less from him. I heard about it too, and it seems he got it right again. Anyway, he healed and left soon after, but he was okay."

I leaned forward. "Tell us the whole situation when he got here after he was attacked."

Xaemorkahn sighed. "When he came here after that stupid Light burned his ass down. He contacted me the second he hit the woods, so I secretly fetched him myself. None of my men ever knew he was here, so don't even expect Rivorgad or the others to tell you squat."

I confirmed his words as I glanced at the Irgovaen's soldier. He just stared at the floor in silence. "No kidding, he told us the same thing those jackasses fed us."

Xaemorkahn frowned a bit. "Needless to say, he was injured badly by that attack. The damage he took, it was pretty massive. I'm still grateful to this day that he was able to get out from that attack alive, though barely. He'd escaped and came here practically on the verge of death, so my wife and I brought him in and took care of him ourselves."

"So that was what happened. Thank you." I gave them both a nod of thanks, and they smiled.

Vrae let out a slow breath. "And by the way, I meant to ask, did he come here often? I mean, after he saved you from the Fallen One?"

The king stiffened a bit at her mentioning our Lord. "Yes, he did."

"Why?" I asked.

He gave us a droll look. "He said that our archive has a lot more information than yours–no offense." He nodded subtly at us and lifted the edge of his lips.

I shook my head and returned his grin. Hell, the only one that would be offended was Amon, and that guy wasn't here.

"So every now and then he'd come here, digging stuff and exchanging news with me," he remarked as he tapped the armrest.

"And you became his inside man for all of this information as he was to you so you could get info on our master's movement," I inserted.

Both Vrae and Zade turned to me with ghastly looks on their faces.

Xaemorkahn arched a brow. "Yes, I did. And before he carried out his last order, he came here and spent hours, days, in our archive. I helped him search for something there. And he was terrified by what we found out and made me promise not to tell anyone about this except you two and whoever it is you'd bring alongside you."

"No wonder he went MIA few days before and only saw his doppelganger," I thought.

"He specifically mentioned the two of us?" Vrae asked as she pointed a thumb at me and herself.

"Yes, he did. It seemed that he suspected that you two would eventually cross paths with us. He knows things, that Ry," Varisha added softly.

"Yeah, that's him all right," I sighed.

Xaemorkahn raked his hair with his fingers. "That was why he told me to ask my people to treat you two and your companions the way they treated him. He said that when the time comes, he'll contact all of you. In the meantime, he warned me, all of us, to beware of the Avarnakh."

We exchanged an alarmed look at his words. He took a deep breath and released it as he inclined his head. "I told him at first that there was no way that particular being could be around, but given the recent events, I'm not so sure any more." A sad smile broke on his handsome face.

All of us fell silent for a moment, and he exchanged a weird look with his wife before he stared at the floor once again. In that silence, I realized that there was something peculiar about his story, the part where Ry was attacked.

Something . . .

No sooner had the thought came into my mind than the answer, which was no less outrageous, followed suit and stabbed my brains. Wanting to confirm this, I firmed my gestures. "Xaemorkahn?"

"Yeah?"

"Tell me something," I began as I leaned forward. "Which Light had burned him?" my eyes were fixated on him, while Vrae and Zade's questioning gazes were stuck on my face.

Xaemorkahn raised one brow, and he hesitated for a moment.

In his silence, Zade took advantage. "What are you saying, Yve? We all know whose Light got him," he remarked.

"Yeah, I know. But after all this, a bit of speculation does look like an appealing option to me, especially after the bullshit those jackass Echelons use to feed us up to this point," I replied without looking at the Varkonian.

When none of them tried to argue, I repeated the question. "Which one? You can call me crazy or say I'm imagining things, but that's what popped into my head, because I found it a little bit weird for you to mention the Big Boss's light as 'that stupid light'. Hell, not even we have that kind of audacity." I let my words ring in their heads for a moment.

Varisha suddenly touched her husband's arm. When he turned to faced her, she cast a tender look at him and nodded.

Xaemorkahn lowered his gaze, and I caught a glint of sadness in his eyes. Abruptly, he heaved a long breath and locked his gaze straight on us. "Just like Ry said, you really are perceptive in the matter of dangerous things."

I didn't say anything at his comment. I just put my hands on the armrest with my eyes on him.

He tapped his fingers on the table for a few seconds, as if deciding whether to explain it or not. After a second, he too firmed his gestures. "Before I tell you, please promise for Ry's sake that you won't do anything reckless. You have all become close to us because we care for the same person, and that person had become my brother, so everyone he cares for, we care for them also, whether you like it or not. So, what say you?"

I hesitated and stopped to think for a second. All of a sudden, I heard Vrae's voice in my head. *"Yve, I don't think he's joking about his vow to be brothers with Ry. To this point, all of them haven't done squat except welcome us. I'm not saying we should let our guard down, because that would be stupid. And besides, I think I know what you're trying to confirm. If it's the truth, then we have no choice but to stay low afterwards and not be reckless yahoos."*

Zade's voice followed hers. *"She's right, Yve, although I tried not to think about who really attacked him 'cause to tell you the truth, all this talk already scares the shit outta me, but I wanna know it all until the end. Just, get on with it. All of us have to."*

"Nice to hear that you're all on board, so here goes nothing," I replied with a blank expression on my face.

I put my hand on the table as Xaemorkahn had done. "Okay, when Ry comes into the game, we can hardly do otherwise. I promise . . ."

"*We* promise," Vrae interrupted as she looked at me and lifted the edge of her lips.

I exhaled a bit and added her comment to what I was about to say. "Fine, *we* promise that we won't do anything reckless after we hear your story." He looked relieved at my remark. Unfortunately for him, I wasn't finished. "Unless we are force into circumstances in which we have to fight, in other words, to do something reckless." I finished as I smiled wickedly.

He winced, and abruptly the couple and Rivorgad, who had stayed silent throughout our conversation, burst out laughing.

"I assume this laughing-your-ass-off thing you're doing means that smart-ass Ry told you something else about me." I grinned, while Vrae and Zade just exchanged an amused look.

The king cleared his throat and attempted to suppress his rich laughter. "Well, he did. He told us that we should be careful. Yverna's sarcasm could kill us either with laughter or with a headache. Actually, I find it amusing. Your play-safe style is rather interesting. It's actually good once in a while."

I rolled my eyes. "Thanks very much, Ry," I said under my breath, and then I levelled a you-better-watch-it stare at the king. "Unlike us, as the king, you'd better not start having a smart mouth; otherwise your people may think you got a very bad influence from us, with a real emphasis on the bad part." I shot back, and all of us laughed.

"You know, it's like talking to him again after all this time," Varisha pondered, and our laughter died instantly.

"So," I cleared my throat to break the silence. "Let's get back to it, shall we? Now that you have our word, why don't you start elaborating about the thing I asked you."

He inhaled a bit. "Okay. As you suspected, the Light of God wasn't the one that burned him. God indeed attempted to smack his ass down–there was no doubt about that–but Ry managed to get himself out of the way. It only burned his arm, and the next attack left an entire lake vaporized in its wake."

"Yeah, the said lake has become nothing but barren wasteland, uninhabitable since that day, whereas its surroundings are endless forest," Vrae added.

"After that, let me guess, either he ran into our master or our master was already waiting for him, ready with his Rygavon," I said in low calm voice I didn't feel.

Vrae and Zade sharply sucked in their breath.

He cast a sad look at me. "When we were working on his injuries, he was screaming terribly while he was barely conscious. But the strange thing was that to both of us it sounded more like something he was recalling rather than the pain of his wounds, which, I'm sorry to say, was brutal." My guts tightened in dread at his words. "Between his agonized roars, he . . ." the king stopped, and he glanced to his wife, who locked her sad gaze at me for a second before she turned to her husband again.

Maybe it was nothing, but still I had to ask. "What?"

Xaemorkahn hastily shook his head. "Nothing. He kept on cursing the Fallen One and his Dark Light. Of course, we never let anyone know about this. Even he hesitated to tell us the truth of what had happened to him until we told him about all the things he had said while he was unconscious and locked in all that pain and suffering. I didn't want to push the guy, but we needed to know. Fortunately, he understood, so he let us both in the loop.

"In the end, needless to say, he wanted us to tell everyone he was dead. That he was killed by the Light of God Himself. It wasn't exactly on our list of favourite hobbies, you know, to frame God for smiting him"–I winced at his choice of words–"but he asked it from us both, and considering the circumstances, it was the best choice to keep everyone in safety and for his sake as well. If he was thought to be dead, the Fallen One wouldn't look for him again. He made us promise not to breathe any of this and just stay off radar. If I didn't know any better, I could've sworn that he sounded like he was afraid the Fallen One would follow him here, though, to be honest, I have no idea how."

"I see," I said with the same calm voice, but before I realized it, blood rushed to my head upon hearing his story about what truly happened to Ry.

In a split second, the entire chamber was plunged into total darkness.

Xaemorkahn had just arisen from his chair when a sudden rush of pain hit me. It was as if something had just pulled my spinal cord with full force.

As I felt another wave of pain, the chamber was illuminated once more.

I yelped and let fly a curse as I rubbed the back of my head. Turning my gaze to my companions, I saw that Vrae looked totally pissed. Under her indignant glare, I realized that it was her. She had forcibly pulled the blood from my brain and at the same time forcefully calmed down my veins that were throbbing with anger.

I cringed and gave her a sorry-my-bad look. Averting my attention from her and the horror in Zade's eyes, I turned to find Xaemorkahn slowly sitting down again with an uneasy look on his perfect face, Varisha softly exhaled in relief, as did Rivorgad, who had gone ghostly white like a corpse.

I cleared my throat. "Sorry, didn't mean to do all that. I slipped." I smiled apologetically.

"Yeah, she's just that irritating at times," Vrae added, ignoring the is-that-necessary stare I threw at her.

Xaemorkahn shrugged. "That's okay. I understand. What I just told you wasn't exactly good news. Thank goodness our place is already dark; otherwise I might've mistaken that darkness earlier for somebody switching the light off."

I let out a scoffing laugh. "That's a good one."

He snickered, but there was something in his gaze that gave me the feeling that he hadn't told us all of it. I decided to ask him later and let him go on.

But instead of continuing his story, he said something else. "Well, leave that aside. I do have more to say about him, but maybe it's a story for some other time, because I presume you all got here without permission from your Echelons."

I frowned at his out-of-nowhere remark. "Yeah, we didn't exactly have a clearance to cross dimensions either, but what's that gotta do with anything?"

He smiled. "For now we need to make sure that your Echelons don't get all suspicious about you three. It will be best if we keep their noses, or better yet, the Fallen One's, pointing in other directions than yours."

And as annoying as it sounded, the king was right. We had no other choice.

"I'm with you on that one, 'cause running into him would most likely push me into *doing something reckless*," I said, emphasizing the last three words.

The couple and Rivorgad laughed, and the king stood up along with all of us.

"That's funny, but really we don't want trouble for any of you. Don't worry, we'll send four of my men, the ones who swore to be your protectors, to come and get you three, let's see, how about a week from now, your time? Maybe you all can arrange your rendezvous in the place when you all met for the first time, wherever that is."

We considered his offer and decided to accept it. "Fine, how about you, Rivorgad?"

He nodded. "I will see you there."

"Very well, Rivorgad, fetch Daviros and Arann to escort them back. After that, do what I've told you before. Comrades of my brother, have a safe journey, we'll see you again."

"But before we go . . ." I looked at the king. The others, who were walking towards the big door, stopped dead and turned to us. "I wanna ask you a few things first." I glanced at Vrae, who exchanged confused looks with Zade, but they didn't say anything.

"Yeah, what is it?" the king asked, inclining his head. His hair fell just over his broad shoulders, while his wife just looked at me with a puzzled gaze.

"Aside from us, there are four others who know about this matter–well, a bit of it. So are we safe to let them in the loop?"

He considered my question. "Do you trust them enough?"

I hesitated and glanced at Vrae, who nodded. I raised one brow but didn't ask her anything. It was quite weird though, for her to let Amon, who was one of direct subordinates of the Echelons, but he could be a bit trustworthy sometimes. After all, she did let him in the loop. I didn't know about those Valthors though.

Deciding to follow Vrae's lead, I gave him a nod. "Yeah, we trust them enough."

He smiled. "Then you can pass this information to them however you see fit, but I think you still have to do whatever is necessary to ensure your safety and everything we discussed here."

I lifted one edge of my lips in a wicked grin. "Leave that to us. You don't have to worry. Oh, and one more thing."

"Yes?"

"Did Ry ever mention Cain or Amon?"

Xaemorkahn cringed, and his wife's gaze widened, whereas Rivorgad was obviously confused by his king and queen's attitude.

I didn't miss the grimace. "What is it? You both know one of them, or better yet, both of them?"

Xaemorkahn looked at me uneasily. "Well, we do know about Cain. Our archive recorded bits of him, and Ry told me about him as well. To be honest, most of what we knew wasn't pleasant. As for Amon, Ry only told us that he's *your* Head Intel, but he can be trusted."

I secretly felt relief when I heard that Ry also thought the same.

"Maybe you can tell us later about what you had heard about Cain, but I meant to ask, from what you've heard from Ry and with you being his sworn brother and all, I'd think he told you more than he did with us. So, do you think we can trust Cain?"

He winced at my question, and his lips formed a faint smile. "I'm sure he trusts me no more than he does you," he said earnestly, but I caught a weird note in his voice.

"Thanks."

"Well, I can't really tell you whether you can trust him, but I know this. He is sometimes able to get hold of things he's never meant to. I wonder if it's one of the perks of becoming what he is. Regardless, I don't think it makes any difference whether he was trustworthy or not or whether you intend to tell him about this. For all we know, he's already got this piece of information, God knows from where." The three of us flinched. "Ry did tell me, though, that he would give a certain item to Cain regarding his last job."

I stared at him. So Ry told him about that too, huh?

"But whatever that item was," he continued as he rubbed his beautifully shaped brows, "he didn't tell me jack squat about it. He only said that I would know what it was when I met you and I'd passed on the information about his last gig. He seemed to think that both of you, for whatever reason, would pay Cain a visit, to take whatever it was he left with him." The king glanced at his wife, who once again levelled a quizzical stare at me.

We fell silent for a second and stared at him before he said anything more. Abruptly, he cleared his throat. "To tell you the truth, I don't really like the idea of Cain. Then again, Ry might have known something he didn't have a chance to tell me about. But can I ask you why you're asking me about him? Do you plan to go to him?"

I exhaled heavily. "Yes. We heard something really worrying from him, and as Ry told you, we indeed intend to take whatever it was he left with him."

Xaemorkahn was taken aback by my words. "You know? But how? Did Ry have a chance to tell you? Because from what I've surmised, nobody knew but us."

I shook my head. "No, he didn't exactly tell *me*," I said, and I glanced at Vrae.

She met my gaze and turned to the king. "Ry ran into me the night before he went up. He told me a few things, including the item he gave Cain," she explained.

He nodded. "I see. Anyway, we shall talk about this another day. Time is against us. If there's nothing else, you'd better go back." The king saluted us, and we replied to him in kind.

We then followed Rivorgad to the door. I was walking behind them when suddenly the king grabbed my hand. I stopped dead and threw a baffled look at him. "Xaemorkahn?"

"Yverna, listen," he began.

"Look, call me Yve," I said before I could stop myself. Well, he was Ry's brother. I guessed it wouldn't hurt.

"Okay, *Yve*," he said with a hint of smile. "There's something you should know."

"What is it?"

He lowered his voice to a whisper. "Ry was screaming your name when he was in pain. He kept saying—well, *screaming*—'don't you fucking touch her' over and over."

"What?" I asked, alarmed at his words.

Varisha took over. "That's the thing he hesitated to tell you all. Ry refused to tell us that part, but just between us, we could guess who he was cursing at. Anyway, we agreed that you need to keep this to yourself, because we fear that you may be in danger."

I stared at them for a moment. "Did he say why our master would go after me?"

The king shook his head. "No, he didn't. But whatever happened between him and your master, he was absolutely terrified for your life. So, just be careful."

I bit my lip as mixed feelings rose like a hurricane in me. Deciding it was no use to think about it now, I nodded. "Thanks, I'll be sure to watch my back." After that I ran to catch up with the others.

When we had reached the outside of the Fortress, our escort flashed us back through the darkness.

Chapter 9

We found ourselves standing in D'arksin woods once again.

After settling our rendezvous plan with them, we called back our doppelgangers that we sent out before. The moment they arrived, we debriefed them regarding the situation while the three of us were gone. Fortunately, nothing bad had happened.

Well, by "bad" I meant nothing that would warrant our heads.

When they were done with their report, we pulled them back. The moment the doppelgangers vanished, Daviros and his companions immediately returned to wherever they came from.

I curled my lips as I stared where those three disappeared. But guess what was tailing them here? The damned eyes of Amon's golems.

This just kept getting better and better.

I took a deep breath and released it. "Well, that was a whole new dimension of fucking riddles," I said as I stretched out my arms.

Vrae exhaled heavily. "Yeah, tell me about it," she replied.

We turned our attention to Zade, who seemed too shocked to even make a sound. He was just staring at the ground. I patted his back. "You okay?"

He was startled and then shook his head as he eyed us. "Nah, nothing. I just have to pull myself together after I was thrown into a hell named insanity. I think all that talk just broke my brains."

I snorted as I glanced at Vrae and back to him. "That's new. I thought you didn't have one to break."

Vrae laughed while he scowled. *"Hell, Ry's right. Forget Avordaen. Your sarcasm alone can kill us. Ry, help!"* He raised his voice to a falsetto as he screwed his face up.

"You know what?" I asked them. *"I've never dared to hope he's still alive. Turned out he is, even though he's a no show."* I passed the thought to them.

They half looked over their shoulders, making sure that Amon's golems didn't get to read anything weird on our faces.

"Yeah, I didn't see that one coming, but at least there's something good in all that all-hell's-breaking-loose talk," Zade grinned broadly.

I frowned. *"What are you talking about? Hell's breaking loose is always good. I won't put that talking under the 'hell's breaking loose' file, 'cause I didn't get to raise my own hell."*

"She's right," Vrae muttered under her breath.

He chuckled. *"You two are violent all right, but I wonder though if we've done everything we were supposed to. How in the hell can we find him now? Hell, that dumb war could come to pass, and we could be turned into stupid Votzadirs for all he knows."*

"It's funny you use that." I scowled at the term which I was so not in the mood to hear. *"But hey, forget the dumb war, I know what I would do when he shows up,"* I replied.

A thought then struck me and made me suppress an urge to laugh: hell, this must piss Amon off, not knowing a damn thing about what we were saying.

Vrae and Zade cast a puzzled look at me. *"Just what is it you'll do when he shows? You don't mean to have sentimental hours, now do you?"* Vrae narrowed her gaze.

I grinned wickedly. *"'Course not. I'm gonna chew him up, spit him up, and stick him under a desk,"* I retorted, and we laughed quietly.

Sobered up, I then ran my hand on my hair. "So, where to next? To the Aryad? Or do we pay Cain a visit?" I asked as I crossed my arms.

Vrae gave a one-shoulder shrug. "I'm not sure, I think we'd better . . ." She stopped dead. It was then I felt it too, and together we turned our heads to the left.

We sensed several sets of dark energy coming our way.

We traded annoyed looks and hid behind trees to see who were approaching us. Seconds later, seven lesser soldiers stopped in mid air and landed. They were members of the Levarchons, the special unit where those seven remains we checked belonged.

"What are they doing here? Patrolling?" Vrae asked.

"Don't know. You think they might be looking for us?" I looked in their direction from where I was standing.

One of the seven, who bore the emblem of the squad's leader on his armour, indicated his surroundings. "Cherxanains Wartiavega and Tyraviafonza and Varkonian Zaderion should be around here. Split up and search!" he exclaimed, waving his hand towards the woods.

This was bothersome. I rolled my eyes as they started walking in different directions.

"Damn, they are *looking for us,"* I grumbled.

"This sure is unexpected. Hold your fire, Yve. They don't know we're here," Vrae warned me.

I passed her a "duh" stare. *"You think? Good for them they didn't see us, 'cause I am so not in the mood to face nagging, especially from underlings,"* I replied as I braced myself for the worst, well, for them.

Just seconds before they flew, we felt unfriendlies appear from out of nowhere, followed by a few lights coming from their direction. Funny thing was, I didn't know if we could be considered as lucky, because those lights blasted our underlings into ashes.

Startled, we simultaneously looked at the light's direction, and I almost laughed out loud. Three halo-top bastards were here, just exactly what I needed to put an end to the "boring hours".

At the very sight of them, I felt Amon's pets were leaving, maybe to report this Arcs attack from a safe distance. Well, they sure picked the right time to haul ass from here. I didn't want them to hear anything about Ry just yet in case these yahoos mentioned him, let alone report it to Amon.

I arched a brow however, when I recognized who the Arcs were, because we'd hardly seen their asses on their Dad's green earth, much less around this place.

Raguel, Uriel, and Danyael, the elite executioners of the archangels.

I guessed we were lucky to meet them right when we needed something to rejoice about after the good news we just got.

Zade, Vrae, and I stepped away from the trees. "Well, well, well, the famous holy Arcs. It must have been so damn boring up there for all three of you to come down here and join us," I said snidely.

"Wanna play?" Vrae taunted, while Zade just braced himself for the fight.

Raguel and the other two took their stands.

"Hell spawn!" Uriel tilted his chin in disgust, mocking the three, of us while Raguel and Danyael readied themselves to attack.

"Heaven's poo!" I shot back lazily. Zade chuckled at my words.

Raguel narrowed his gaze at me, but Uriel raised his hand before Raguel could do anything. "You filthy beings, how dare you even be in our presence?! We will destroy you all so you can't do anything to Adam's descendants!"

I scoffed. "Vrae, better call Pride Boy"–I indicated his arrogance–"to come here and ask him whom he's been dating recently. Seems Uriel here accidentally kissed him."

The three Arcs weren't amused. Surprise, surprise!

"Where is your leader? Tell him it's no use to hide." He raked us with a scathing glare to which I didn't bother to reply.

I raised a brow at his question. "You mean Lucifer? Like he'd ever want to meet assholes like you three!" I taunted them, while Vrae and Zade just stared at them in silence.

Danyael narrowed his gaze at us. "Don't play the fool with us. You know full well we are not talking about the Son of Perdition. We are talking about your leader, the one who dared to overhear the Secret of Heaven. Furthermore he dared to steal a Forbidden Item that resided in the deepest part of Heaven!"

We were taken aback by his words, but we didn't show it. Well, it seemed the Big Guy was suddenly bothered by the fact Ry was still alive. I wondered why that was–not to mention his deed.

How and why in the hell could he get in that far?

Anyhow, I wasn't wasting a second and played along with them. "Ooh, you mean Ezryan? Well, either way, we will ask you the same thing. If you're having trouble in understanding it, I'll spell it out for ya: 'Like. He. Would. Ever. Want. To. Meet. Assholes. Like. You. Three.' Get me, jerk wads? By the way, dude, you say 'play the fool' once again, and I might think you mistake yourself for a human, because as far as we know, the only fools on this earth are they, and those herds are our playthings, unless you wanna volunteer to trade places."

Vrae let out a small laugh, but to our surprise the three suddenly smiled disdainfully at us. "You have no idea if your own leader is still alive, do you? How pathetic," Raguel said with a dose of venom I'd happily spit on his face.

Ooh boy, I so didn't have time for this crap. And here I thought they were about to say something a little bit creative.

I rolled my eyes. "Well, *you* have no idea if he's still alive, 'cause, FYI, he's not your leader. If you knew he was still alive, you'd be hunting his ass down way before now, would you not? But no, why would you? You guys had no idea until Michael or Gabriel told you, right? Yeah, I know, not being one of God's favourites sucks. We'll tell you from first-hand experience and give you our shoulders for you three chuckleheads to cry on. How's that? So, stop spitting shit or I'll wash your holes myself."

Uriel levelled his cold stare at me, and his lips curled in repugnance. "For a she-devil, you have quite a foul mouth."

My lips twitched in a disdainful smile. "Well, thank you. For a he-angel, you have quite a dull mouth yourself."

Zade and Vrae snorted at my words while the rest of the angels glared at us. "We do not have time for your nonsense. We'll just kill you all and give you what you deserve, you abominations!" Uriel roared, and he raised his hand.

I could feel his powers surging throughout the air. "Ditto, bud. Now, let the game commence," I mocked as I drew out my own powers.

Right after the words left my mouth, Raguel shot a bolt at us. We split up and each took an opponent. I chose Uriel, Zade was already engaging Danyael, while Vrae was already throwing multiple bolts at Raguel, who launched bolts of his own.

Uriel brought rains of stupid bolts upon me. I deflected those, and yeah, I laughed jeeringly at him when I did it. By the look on his face, he was pissed as hell, but, sadly for him, I loved doing it.

Vrae was having her fun up there in the air with Raguel, and like me she taunted the hell out of him as well. She evaded his bolts by doing several impossible aerial manoeuvres as she launched her bolts at him.

Zade kept on defending himself while Danyael shot multiple bolts at him. Abruptly, he deflected Danyael's attack and started his own.

It took no time for the fight to get bigger and bigger. The whole forest was soon brightened in the middle of the night.

Uriel's face contorted with anger as I rolled sideways to evade yet another pair of bolts he threw. Deciding I'd taunt him further, I thought to push him into manifesting his sword.

I quickly got up on my feet as he charged towards me with bolts flying. An evil smile curved my lips as I stood in place, deflecting each and every shot. Just when he was only five steps in front of me, I directed my right hand at him and conjured a big, pitch-black ball of solidified darkness.

It captured the Arc, and boy did he scream in there.

"Three, two, one," I counted under my breath as I took a couple of steps backwards and conjured a pair of thick black metallic gauntlets over my hands.

A second later, the black ball cracked, and lights peeked from it. Two heartbeats later, the ball shattered, and out Uriel came with a sword in his hand. And he swung it straight at me.

Raising my right hand again, the gauntlet collided with his sword. Well, by the war cry he kept roaring at me and the way he was hysterically trying to cut my face but ended up hitting my gauntlet, he'd definitely lost his calm.

"How dare you summon that filthy thing on me!" he shouted as he swung his sword downward, intending to chop me in half.

I caught myself before I rolled my eyes and got stabbed for it. Instead, I just made a face at him, which set him off just the same. "Well, duh, of course I dare. In case you've bumped your head and are having severe memory problem, I'm your enemy and live to seriously piss you off," I said, and then I backhanded his sword. It gave out a loud sound of metal colliding, followed by spouts of fireworks.

"Enough!" he bellowed as he swung his sword again. I blocked it with both gauntlets, and he pressed the blade against them.

I sneered at him. "And what if I say no?" I taunted him as I waited for him to add more pressure. When I felt the time was right, I removed myself from under his blade, using his strength to press my own advantage, and made him lose his footing.

However, his reflexes took over. Reacting on instinct, he rolled just before he fell and got back to his feet. He swung his sword at me just as he whirled around.

Unfortunately for him, I'd expected that.

I closed in on him just a split second before the blade reached my head. I intercepted the blade with my left hand and had my right one on his abdomen. "Boo," I whispered, and I shot one bolt into him.

Eyes wide, he fell with silver-white blood flowing from his mouth, but he wasn't dead.

Suddenly, I heard an agonized scream coming from Raguel. Turning around, I saw him falling. He crashed to the ground with Vrae landing snugly next to him.

I glanced to where they fought in the air and sneered. "Great, we have an angel falling from above. Nice work."

She snickered, and then we both shifted our attention to the last combatants, just in time to see Danyael rush towards Zade with his sword. The Varkonian jumped over the angel's head as he shot two bolts to his shoulders.

Danyael gasped and fell with the strangest look of surprise on his flawless face.

Zade landed smoothly on the grass and came to us. "Nice!" I said as I high-fived him.

He chuckled as he shook his head. "Well, I can't seem to beat you two when it comes to fighting fast." He grinned as he glanced at Danyael.

Vrae scoffed. "You might have a chance if you didn't fight him so seriously."

"You might want to stop glancing at me when you have an Arc coming right at you," he shot back.

Their exchange made me frown. Vrae splitting her focus in a fight? That was so not like her. But maybe she just had her moments –of what, I had no idea. Then again, this wasn't the time to give a damn over something so trivial either, for there was something I needed to tell these goons first.

A low groan escaped Uriel, pulling our attention back to them.

I scoffed in repugnance. As a rule, unless it was an open war, not a three-on-three like we just had, we were bound from killing archangels. I had no idea why Lucifer agreed to the damn rule in the first place, and yeah, it sucked. Although we were allowed to kill the lesser ones, the bigger cheese would have provided a bit more of a challenge, and we couldn't kill them.

All of us, his kind, had to abide by the dumb rule. So, instead of blasting their faces, we only incapacitated them to the point where they fell to the ground and stopped looking for trouble. Our Avordaen would chew them up slowly and could render them vegetables unless they got rid of it.

Luckily for them, we weren't cutting through their wings first or their halos. Yep, that'd introduce them to the word "mortality", and we could give them mortal wounds which would lead them to a mortal state where their friend Azrael would come, say hi, and then happily, or should I say sadly, escort their asses from here.

I raised one hand at Raguel and Danyael, both still passed out, and they floated. Bringing them towards Uriel, I then tossed them at him, and he got up in surprise. Before he could do anything, I manifested another solidified darkness in the form of a rope. It bound him tightly, keeping him from moving one more inch.

Now he could only glare grudgingly at me.

"Come on, Yve, what are you doing? Don't waste any time here," Vrae said as she stepped away and prepared to jump to the sky.

I stopped her. "Wait a sec."

Both of them came to a halt and turned around as I knelt near the Arcs. When Raguel and Danyael regained their consciousness, I quickly conjured similar ropes and bound them both. They looked like they were more than ready to tear us apart, but they were also trying to get as far away from me as possible.

I arched a brow. "Come on, why do you stop acting tough all of a sudden?" They gave me a wry glare as an answer.

I spat in disgust. "Okay, whatever. Anyway, I gotta warn you to stop looking for Ezryan, because he won't be generous like us. And tell Gabriel or Michael to get the hell outta Dodge and mind their own fucking business, or we'll make them and all of you wish you hadn't turned your backs on Lucifer."

They were still glaring. I stood up, faced my comrades, and jerked my head up. "Time to go," I said in an innocent tone that betrayed the fact I had just bound three Arcs with ropes made of solidified darkness, one of the very few elements that seriously pissed them off. Well, we always pissed them off, period.

"You're leaving them like that?" Zade asked.

I shrugged. "It'll disappear overtime. Let's go."

He nodded, and we immediately jumped to the sky, leaving the three Arcs helpless on the ground.

"Hey," Zade called.

"What?" I glanced at him as we flew, leaving the D'arksin woods–really leaving them this time, without interruptions like before.

He bit his lip. "Why do you think they're bothering about his whereabouts all of a sudden?"

I sighed wearily. "I have no idea. I wonder about that myself. I mean, hell, the timing was too damned good, right after we had just got all that new information."

"Not to mention Cain blabbering shit before this," Vrae said without looking.

I nodded in agreement. "Yeah, that too. Anyhow, we can hardly talk right now. Let's just get back there first." They nodded, and then we accelerated.

It was then I sensed something in the wind as I cut through the air. Somehow, it felt as though the wind was trying to whisper someone's unspeakable anguish. On that thought, a slight tingle ran down my spine, as if telling me that somebody was watching us somewhere in the darkness.

*   *   *

Moments passed after the three devils flew away before Uriel and his two companions could finally release themselves from the revolting rope that reeked with demonic power conjured by the she-devil they knew as the Tyraviafonza.

"She shall be vanquished for this! *They* shall be vanquished for this!" Uriel growled in fury. He then moved to check his brethren. "Are you two all right?"

Both Danyael and Raguel nodded weakly. "Yes we are," Raguel said.

"We should go and seek Michael's audience. They knew their Hieldhar has returned. We must corral them before they join ranks with him and find a way to use *it* against us," Danyael remarked with repugnance filling his voice.

Uriel concurred. "Yes, this is more dire than I'd anticipated. We have to get rid of their Avordaen first before we meet Michael."

Without more words, they directed their holy powers to drive out the dark ones and their visages and restore their strength.

After they'd done so, Uriel stood to his fullest height. "Let's go. Michael will decide what to do with them," he said, and then he turned to jump back to the sky.

Only that was the last thing he could hope for, because someone stood in their way.

"You!" Uriel snarled in wrath that was laced with utter disbelief, for he didn't expect the newcomer would dare to face them after what had happened to him.

The other two cautiously positioned themselves in battle formation on each side of Uriel.

The newcomer smiled evilly. "Me, Uriel. I don't think you can high tail it out of here, especially to bad-mouth Tyraviafonza and her companions. Because you see, it'll piss me off," he said with mounting disdain. "Then again, you people *always* piss me off."

"Enough! Die, abomination!" Uriel roared.

The three archangels charged towards the newcomer simultaneously. They expected him to hold back because of the deal that bound his entire race, but they were sorely mistaken.

The newcomer's stoic face turned, showing the true evil that he was. The last thing Uriel felt emanating from his opponent was a raw lethal power unlike all he'd ever seen. From the deadly glint in his eyes as he raised his hands, Uriel realized one thing.

This being was an unholy savage force. He'd flood the forest with *their* blood.

* * *

I frowned deeply as I tried to put my finger on the sensation I had felt minutes ago above the woods as we left.

"What is it?" Vrae asked. Well, for her to ask that, she obviously didn't sense it, or maybe it was just me getting weird vibes.

"Nothing. Come on, let's get down here," I said, pointing the ground.

We saw Zoran and Gevirash waving at us as we landed.

"Yo, what took you guys so long?" Zoran greeted us.

"Ran into anything?" Gevirash asked vigorously.

Zade, Vrae, and I glanced at each other. When neither of them said anything, I looked at the guards who stood there with their curious gaze locked on me.

"Well, we apprehended some extremely shocking information, which is not safe enough for us to tell you in the open. So I'll tell you other things first."

The guards looked a bit disappointed, but they got over it. "Okay, so what's this other thing you want to tell us?" Zoran asked, folding his arms.

I smiled wickedly. "We kicked Raguel's, Uriel's, and Danyael's asses big time."

"You what? You guys ran into them?" they asked in unison.

"Hell, yeah, we roasted them good and proper." We high-fived the guards and laughed.

Gevirash then cleared his throat. "But really, what business did those bastards have with you three?"

I swallowed a bit. "I'll tell you that later as well. Okay, I know it sucks," I said hastily, when they both scowled at me, "but we gotta tell this to Amon first, and as appealing as it sounds, actually I'd rather pass, but this one's quite big, so what do you guys say if we hook up with you boys later?"

They curled their lips simultaneously before Zoran sighed. "Fine, but don't forget to fill us in."

I winked. "Don't worry, we already promised to let you guys in twice. Okay? See ya boys later."

With that we left the guards, who looked at each other with a confused expression.

We quickly walked inside towards Amon's place. When we once again went inside his room, he was standing with his back facing us. "Amon?"

He turned to us. "Well, well, you three are finally here." Our gaze fell straight on him in silence. "First off, I nearly belly-rolled when I saw the Veil spouted the lines about you guys kicking those Arcs' asses," he began with a wide grin on his face, which we returned with our own. "But, Arcs aside, I want you to tell me something, and please tell me the truth. What did you find inside that protective shield, the one you entered after getting all those blue lights? And why the hell did you have to go there twice?" He gave us a quizzical stare.

I secretly felt relief, and I bet the others did too. It seemed Rivorgad and his pals didn't joke around with us; we did get ourselves inside their protective shield.

"Okay, but first, before we tell you anything, we gotta ask you to swear in the name of Rygavon that you won't talk about any of this to anyone but us, and I mean anyone," I said, emphasizing that last word.

He was aghast at my request and looked at Vrae and Zade, who gave him a stern look as if they were asking the same.

After a second, he bit his lip. "May I ask why the hell I should do that? I mean, come on, you all know you can trust me, even if it is a dangerous matter! Vrae, come on," he pleaded, but Vrae didn't budge.

"Sorry, champ. This piece of info is too big, and we don't even have all of it just yet," she smiled apologetically at him.

When he was about to argue, I raised my hand to stop him. "Just do it. We don't like it as well, asking you this, but you'll understand it later after we tell you all of it," I said.

He fell silent and then exhaled heavily. "Fine, I swear in the name of the Dark Light Rygavon of Lucifer that I won't talk about any of this to anyone but you Yverna, Vrathien, and Zaderion."

I inclined my head and added, "In any way."

He raised a brow, but didn't argue. "In any way," he followed after me.

I lifted the edge of my lips. "That's more like it. Now, if you two don't mind, please fill him in, I gotta take a breather for a second."

Zade cast a worried look at me. "You okay?"

I shook my head at him. "I'm okay. Just help Vrae with it."

He still looked worried, but didn't say anything. Instead he approached Vrae and Amon, and soon they were caught up in a heated discussion, with Amon looking shocked every five seconds.

As for me, I just stared at them in silence, and my mind was wandering off . . . to Ry.

I'd never tell anyone any of this, not even Vrae, and of course not Ry himself. As my mind conjured his image, I wondered where he could possibly be. I didn't know when this started, but he'd grown to be more than just a leader or my closest comrade.

Wasn't this hilarious? I, whom people revered as the Queen of Tyranny, fell for him, I mean, *him*? Yeah, the most savage devil amongst the seven legions of warriors and the Queen of Tyranny. Hell, our offspring should make everyone look alive and happy.

As if that would happen!

Suddenly, I heard Amon shout, "No way!" Zade and Vrae put their hands on Amon's mouth, shutting him up. Amon raised his hands and they released him. After just a second, they continued their discussion.

I inhaled deeply and kept my eyes fixed on the floor. Moments later they'd finished and approached me. I lifted my gaze from the floor. "Done? Now you know why we have to ask you to swear on it."

He nodded. "Yeah, I know. I'd never thought it would ever go this big," he remarked. I caught something weird in his voice, which made me frown. "Amon?"

Wincing, he eyed each of us in turn. "I guess this is the time for me to be straight with you guys. I figured the time's finally come anyway." He let out a long breath, as if he'd been waiting to get whatever it was off his chest.

But still, I so didn't like his tone.

Exchanging a puzzled look with Vrae and Zade, I turned my attention back to the Iverand. "Buddy, just what the hell is that supposed to mean?" I asked slowly.

He didn't answer. Instead, he glanced around the chamber cautiously, as if looking for something. After a moment, he fixed his eyes on us and motioned us to follow him into his private chamber.

That was weird. None of us were allowed to set foot inside there. Those too paranoid Echelons were scared that if the Iverand got too close with any of the soldiers and let us inside his chamber, we might try to squeeze classified information out of him, or hell, steal secrets of golem sorcery.

"As if any of us want to create those hideous things, even if we were dying to escape from their scrutinizing eyes!" I thought in utter disgust.

On that note, neither of us followed him immediately. "Are you sure we can go in there and not get busted?" Vrae asked.

"Just follow me," he mouthed.

I hesitated, but compelled by mounting curiosity, I decided to follow him despite Vrae's strained warning, "Don't!" When I paid her no heed, she and Zade came after me.

Amon opened the door and shut it immediately once we were all inside. I raised a brow at the sight of his chamber. It was pretty big with one bed in the middle of the room, and its headrest stood against the wall. A painting covered the wall across from the bed from top to bottom. It was a gruesome image of thousands of bleeding humans entangled in agony and burning in raging flames.

Definitely my favourite kind of theme.

"Dude, I didn't know you got yourself a chamber this nice," Zade said in awe, his eyes observing the chamber.

My lips curved into a teasing smile. "Careful, buddy, if your tone gets any weirder, Envy might be tempted to pay you a visit."

He blanched instantly. "No, thanks, I really don't want to see any part of him near me."

I laughed and glanced around. My gaze found four bookshelves that stood in two rows with countless dusty scrolls and thick ancient-looking books. Two shelves were on the other side of his bed, whereas the others were planted just few steps from me. I caught glimpses of golem images on several of them.

Vrae strolled towards me and stopped by my side. "Pal, you're in serious need of a life," Vrae remarked as her gaze fell on the scrolls.

Zade suddenly let out short coughs; no doubt it was his weak-ass attempt to hide his laughter. "Well, at least we know you know what you're doing in regard to those golems."

The Iverand screwed up his face. "Funny, I'm laughing," he replied sardonically, and then his features hardened again. "There's something I wanna show you. Well, at first, I wanted to ask you to vow that you wouldn't tell jack squat to anyone, but I gather there's no need for that any more."

"You gather right. Now cut to the chase," I pressed.

Amon nodded and strode across the room straight to the macabre painting hung on the wall. What the hell?

I let out a snort. "What, you wanna show us your next idea for barbecue?" I asked sarcastically.

He shook his head at my remark and tilted his head to the painting. "Definitely not. Come here and see for yourselves."

I sauntered towards the painting with Vrae and Zade. Once we stood next to him, Amon moved the painting with his powers. It moved outward with one side attached by its hinges, revealing a hole. What I saw behind it was something so revolting that I nearly destroyed it along with the painting.

It was a golem, one with six eyes intact. It sat calmly in the hole behind the painting. But there was something else, something that ignited my rage. It burned me viciously and almost made my self-control slip away and kill him right where he stood.

The damned clay thing gleamed in a brilliant light of sapphire. A very familiar feeling caressed my senses. It spoke of a presence that belonged to someone who wasn't even here.

Vrae gasped. "That's . . ."

"Ry's golem. How dare you?" I growled as I felt fury explode in an instant and ride me hard. "After all this time, you knew, and you hid it from us. How dare you?" I repeated as I slowly turned to the fucking Iverand.

"Yve, please listen to me," he began, with both hands raised as he took a step backwards. "I know you're mad. You have every right to be, but, like Vrae, I couldn't tell you before I was sure. But unlike her, Ry didn't exactly tell me any of this shit would happen. He just told me not to let anyone know what I might see."

"See what?" Vrae asked in a voice laden with venomous anger.

"This," he said as he stepped aside. The golem's chest glowed and split open. Sapphire light shot out and gathered just several inches in front of the source. It formed a transparent sphere. I could see something moving in it.

"Is this . . . ?" I couldn't bring myself to finish the question.

He nodded. "Yes, the last moments when he was supposedly dead. And this golem's force just got back now. Last time I saw it, only the hands were glowing."

I shot a glare at him, and he fell silent.

"But we know what's in it. He fell from above while he burnt. He went straight into that lake Bahyrdanam, and Big Boss upstairs obliterated him along with it," Zade said carefully with his wary eyes fixed on me.

"Unless," Vrae started slowly, "your golem saw something more, something that can substantiate Xaemorkahn's tale about Ry."

"Just see it, guys," Amon repeated.

As Zade said, the sphere projected scenes that I would have preferred not to see, but I forced myself to watch. I had to know, in case it was like Vrae said. I had to know so badly, I wanted to tear the golem's chest and grab the orb just so I could see it closer.

Hell, I wanted to go back to that day seven hundred years ago when he fell in flames with an empty hope that I might be able to save him.

"There, he's falling," Vrae whispered in a strained voice, whereas I held my breath and the tears that started to pool in my eyes upon seeing Ry's small image covered in flames.

I cringed when he hit the lake hard, and the next scene made me gasp in pain as I saw burning white light descend from the sky straight into the lake.

But the sphere didn't stop there as it was supposed to. I caught something small moving away from the burning lake. "Vrae, are you seeing this?" I asked in a low voice.

"Uh-huh."

The sphere caught up with the small image which I now had no doubt was Ry. He was running through the woods. The sphere showed nothing but seas of trees, and his small image appeared every now and then. A moment later it stopped in a certain part of the forest.

"There's nothing but trees. Was he trying to heal himself in there?" Zade mumbled. The answer was provided to us two seconds later.

More than half the woods exploded in black flames, and then the sphere vanished.

"Th–That's –that's the Dark Light," Zade stuttered in disbelief.

My hands balled into tight fists. "Now we can be sure Xaemorkahn ain't lying through his ass," I muttered grudgingly. As wrath rushed violently throughout my veins, I could feel pitch black spread on my eyes.

"You took the right decision to conceal this. I don't appreciate it at all, but that was the right move," Vrae said, while I struggled to suppress the vicious hatred burning me.

Amon gulped audibly. "Thanks. I know this is hard. Hell, it was hard for me too. I should've seen this coming. What good an Iverand am I if I couldn't even protect the only real commander we ever had in the last thirty thousand years?" He directed the question more to himself than to any of us.

"By doing this, you have protected him," Vrae said quietly.

Zade patted his shoulder. "Yeah, dude, don't beat yourself too hard on this. The Echelons could have busted you if you tried to do anything," he inserted.

Amon heaved a heavy sigh. "Thanks. Now let's get outta here." He closed the hole and sauntered back to his den with us behind him.

Once we were back outside. I couldn't restrain myself any longer. Without even realizing what I was doing, I grabbed his robe and planted my hands around his neck.

"Y–Yve?" he called with strangled voice. "Guys, a little help please? I really don't want to hit her lest we fight for real here."

"Yve, stop!" Zade said on full alert, for he had no idea what I would do.

I hardly heard them both as blood rushed to my head and the chamber was thrown into absolute darkness . . . until somebody popped my head pretty hard.

"Ouch!" I yelped. That one hit successfully made me rein myself in. In an instant, the chamber brightened.

"Where was your head?" Vrae snapped.

I winced. "Sorry about that. Thanks though," I said. I didn't notice where my hands were until a choked voice drew my attention.

"A little help here?" Amon gasped.

I hastily pulled my hands back with a grimace. "Sorry, got carried away for a bit."

He coughed and panted, "I'll live."

"That's the second time I popped you. Don't make me do it for the third time," Vrae warned me with her forefinger pointed at my face.

I gave her a cheeky grin. "Why not? You could win a prize or something for doing that three times in a row. You could use a silver tea set," I remarked gleefully.

She rolled her eyes. "What-the-hell-ever. So, now that we've kicked the nonsense out of the way,"–Vrae gave me a seething glare which I answered with an innocent look just for the fun of setting her off–"I wanna ask you something."

"What is it?" Amon prompted.

"Did the merry band know about *that* one or did you just shove the one you've made and shown to us all in their faces?" she asked, carefully not saying anything about what we saw in Amon's room.

The Iverand's face wrinkled in anger. "I have no doubt that they knew all along. Perhaps my showing them that one made them think that my golem didn't see what really happened. Contrary to their inane thoughts, *he* seemed to think that my golem would be able to catch at least a glimpse if something were to happen to him. Hence he asked me not to let anyone know about it," he said quietly.

"By the way, has it been like that the whole time? I mean, since he, well, left?" Vrae inquired hesitantly.

Amon shook his head. "No, to tell you the truth, this is the most bizarre thing that ever happened in all this time I've been doing what I do."

"So, what, it's just–what's the term–awoken?" Zade asked.

The Iverand shifted his position and unexpectedly used a blocked channel. *"The night he was supposedly gone, his golem ceased to emit his life force, but the golem wasn't automatically destroyed as it was supposed to be. I had suspicions that it was more like he was still alive but no longer here. It sounds all out crazy, I know. I couldn't find a better term to explain it myself,"* he said hastily, when he saw our reaction to his remark. *"That's why I didn't tell shit to anybody. But just now, you three confirmed that my deduction wasn't as outrageous as I first thought."*

Zade nodded in understanding. *"Yes, he'd jumped over that night."*

"But that still doesn't explain why this thing emits his life force now," I drawled, still fighting to suppress my fury.

The Iverand cringed at my tone, but he decided not to back down. Good for him. *"His golem here started to emit his life force just few hours ago, not long after you left to check those Levarchons' remains. And before that, the Veil spurted out something that went further in confirming that chances are high that he's still alive."*

My eyes widened at that. *"What did it say?"*

"Unknown unholy, Great Lake of Bahyrdanam," he replied.

Vrae, Zade, and I exchanged an alarmed look at that. "But that's where . . ." Zade started, and a wide grin broke on his handsome face.

"You tell me," Amon said meaningfully with a wink. *"Before that, the Veil mentioned the Rift of Bahyrdanam. So I guess it means that he just got back from wherever it was."*

I almost couldn't stop myself from heading straight to the place. Foreign hope stirred wildly within me. He really did come back!

"Well, all in all, the Echelons must not know about this just yet," Amon said.

Gritting my teeth, I levelled a malicious stare at him. "So, what happens now? Can I end them or what?"

Amon shook his head, and a sly grin broke on his face. "You wish, but no, not on your best day. I don't think we can do anything before *he* shows up," he said meaningfully. "Leaving that aside, I wanna ask you this. Another seven Levarchons were sent out to look for you three. Why the hell were they dead by the hands of the Arcs when you were standing so damn near?"

I rubbed my brows. "Now, that I'll be happy to tell you."

He curled his lips. "Yeah, tell me why you didn't come to them."

I rolled my eyes. "Look, we thought that we'd officially become fugitives, all right? We thought we were gone long enough for the Echelons to grow suspicious at us. And we didn't know that those bastards happened to be there to play baseball."

He raised his hands, as if surrendering to me. "Okay, so what now? You three plan on visiting him?" The look on his face was enough an announcement of whom he meant.

Cain.

"That's a definite affirmative, but maybe not now. Let's see, perhaps two or three days from now?" I inclined my head.

Vrae shot a questioning gaze at me, but then she shifted her gaze to the floor.

"Why wait that long?" Amon asked.

I took a deep breath and released it. "Look, we've been through so much tonight, and now it's daybreak. We need to lay low. *I* need to lay low. Not to mention him as an Imirae wielder"–I jerked my head at Zade–"and you as the Iverand. I think we can safely assume that you two have already drawn too much attention from the Echelons, let alone the two of us." I pointed at Vrae and myself.

They considered my suggestion, and then the men nodded. "Okay, you win. So, what will you do for now?" Zade asked.

"Me? I'm gonna get a good sleep and recover myself. And Amon, do you mind pulling your, ehm, friends off? I need some time alone, and I mean alone. Don't worry. You can put them back in when night falls."

"Nightfall! Are you saying you won't be going anywhere? Please, Yve, you know I can't do that. Even if I'm doing it, you sure you won't be going anywhere?"

I sighed grudgingly. "No, I won't. What? You want me to swear on it?" I curled my lips.

He was startled. "Look, as much as I want to do it for you, there's no way I could do that, not without raising suspicions. And my friends' distance is far enough, I'd say."

Vrae cut me off before I could argue. "Fine, Amon, how's this? Just extend their range around her really far, just for tonight, and for me as well." I raised a brow at her. "And since they'll keep circling around us, there's no way we could sneak up on them. Come on, we wouldn't endanger you. You know that." Vrae folded her arms.

Amon hesitated but then nodded. "All right, but only until nightfall," he said sternly.

Vrae and I exchanged a sly grin at his remark. Motioning to him, I patted his shoulder. "Thanks, it will be a whole lot more helpful if you do that every time I go to sleep. Your pals make me itchy to break something, and every time I wanna get a good sleep, well, let's just say that will definitely be counterproductive." I flashed a wicked grin at him.

Amon let out an exasperated breath. "Fine, whatever, just when you're gonna go to the dreamland."

"Thanks, I know I can count on you," I winked. "Oh, and before I forget, we left those Levarchons because we couldn't do anything to their remains. We'll leave you to decide what to do with them," I said.

Amon sighed heavily. "Yeah, I know about that. Vrae and Zade already told me about them. That was helpful of you to cover them, Vrae," he said as he faced her.

"No problem," she shrugged.

I clapped my hands. "All right then, what if we call it a day?"

"Yeah, keep in touch, guys," Amon said.

We nodded and left him.

*   *   *

Amon was just heaving a long breath and was about to sit when his skin bristled as a familiar breeze softly blew from somewhere behind him. He turned around and strode towards the source.

The Veil of Sights.

What he saw in there made him let out a fetid curse.

Three perished Archangels Forest of D'arksin

"Don't fucking tell me those three they fought are dead by leftover Avordaen. What are those three? Numbskulls?" Amon cursed as he considered what he could do to cover them for this mess.

But that thought instantly vanished, for he saw another thing on the Veil that made him expel an even fouler curse.

Unknown unholy Forest of D'arksin

He staggered back and slowly walked to his chair. He sank in his seat and covered his face with both hands. "Just what the hell is he doing?" Amon helplessly whispered the question. *"I hope those insane Echelons don't gut* them *over this,"* he mused with utter fear coursing through him.

*   *   *

We immediately went outside where Gevirash and Zoran were standing. As soon as they came into view, we began to explain everything to them, through blocked channel this time. And as we did with Amon, we also made them swear not to let loose anything.

Not that they ever would, but better safe than sorry.

We'd just finished with the story when my golem, Vrae's, and Zade's descended close enough to the barriers.

I looked up with a frown. "Guys, it looks like Amon's got something new to talk about," I remarked as my gaze went back to the others.

Zade nodded at the guards. "Later, guys."

He strode away, and Vrae and I followed suit. We were about to jump out of the barriers when two Machordaens came out of the Gate. "May the Dark Light Rygavon of Lucifer be with you, Cherxanains, Varkonian, and Valthors," they greeted us in unison.

No sooner had they shown up than the golems flew back to where they were a second ago, and that certainly was weird. Why would Amon pull those eyes back if he was so damned anxious to tell whatever it was? Surely two Machordaen passers who had no business with us wouldn't make him back off that fast. He could just send these guys away.

Unless these guys were indeed here for us, and he wasn't the one who had sent them.

We stopped before we could jump and returned their greetings. When I expected them to go away, they firmed their gestures instead.

"Do you have business with us?" I asked.

The one with long brown hair stepped forward. "Cherxanain Yverna, you have direct orders from the Echelons."

"So, they are *here for us,"* I realized, holding my breath and wondering what those bastards were up to this time.

"You are to report in regarding Nero. Your presence is expected at the Echelons' chamber, where you shall receive further instructions from Ravath DeVarren," the brown-haired one ended his not exactly helpful explanation.

I exchanged a puzzled look with the others and shifted my gaze to them again. "Ravath DeVarren? Are you sure you did not make a mistake? As for Nero, my mission to convert him is already completed."

The other with the deep scar on his left eye grimaced. "That is the instruction for you, Cherxanain Yverna. As for you Cherxanain Vrathien"–Vrae's eyes narrowed at him, definitely unhappy–"you have been given a new assignment. You are to ignite war within a certain kingdom in the east. You'll receive your instructions at your base."

"What is this? I was told that I would not receive another order until three months from now. Does this war hold any importance?" Vrae stared at them. As expected, they looked like they were more than ready to run back and hide behind the Echelons.

"That is the order we must relay to you, Cherxanain. It is imperative that you head for your base." The brown-haired one answered as he attempted to hide his fearful trembling.

I suppressed the urge to roll my eyes at them. "Very well, you can go and tell them we shall meet them where they expect us."

They nodded. "Very well. And there's also a call for you, Varkonian." Zade raised his brows. "Varkonian Darvahl summoned you. He demands you to go immediately to the Devorcae." Zade merely winced without saying anything.

After that, the pair gave us their salute. "May the Dark Light be with you."

"And with you," we replied, and they vanished. We exchanged a questioning look once again and said our goodbyes to the Valthors.

We sauntered past them, entering the Gate, and jumped off the cliff. Landing smoothly on the path, we proceeded to our respective destinations in silence, for we expected those Echelons to put extra ears on us, aside from Amon's damned golems.

Moments afterwards, Zade was the first to leave, and a while later Vrae and I arrived at a fork where we took separate paths. I proceeded to the one in the middle of the fiery maze, whereas she took the left.

For a while I strolled until I arrived at the punishing block for the lesser beings, mostly humans. Really evil ones were put in the deepest part of the basement, and I meant really deep. It was near the very core of the earth.

As I walked, I saw them being tortured with a kind of torment that wouldn't cross even the wildest dreams of the worst kind of humans. They were all screaming and pleading for me to help them.

As if I would waste my freakin' time on their problems.

I strode in intense silence as tons of suspicions swam in my head. What the hell was happening here? Suddenly the three of us had been summoned, and the reasons were evidently their stupid attempt to cover up whatever it was they really wanted. It was clear from them telling me that DeVarren would give me instructions about my work on Nero. First off, even though DeVarren was one of the Echelon members, each of them couldn't interfere with the other's work. Second, because of that first rule, that guy had nothing to do with my job manipulating Nero's marbles, because Bynethar was the one who'd given me that job.

Talk about being busted for hiding behind a totally inane reason! Just what in the world were they trying to pull?

Ignoring the screams that rang throughout the block, I kept on walking. Fifteen minutes later, I reached a huge gate made of earthly rock with the words "Echelons' Chamber" carved on it.

I firmed my gesture. "It is I, Cherxanain Yverna Tyraviafonza, come to fulfil Ravath DeVarren's request," I remarked clearly.

The gate moved inward with an eerie, scratching sound, and I walked in. As usual, the room where the Echelon members always gathered and planned their schemes was dark—not my favourite type of darkness, but more like the kind that pissed me off with the Echelons' elegant smell that sickened me to my bones all over the place. It was lit only with blue flames, similar to Amon's place.

The difference was that this place was bigger than his den and much colder too.

Damn, I'd never liked this place. Their arrogance knew no bounds, and that said a *lot* coming from me. I'd often wondered why they weren't doing Pride's job instead of showing off their superior attitude in this place.

I glanced around, and I swallowed as my gaze found five Echelon members in their respective seats above. All were present except Bynethar and the other six. *"Well, well, DeVarren, Weizar, Lazoreth, and . . . whoa, Kathiera and Faemirad? I wonder what the hell they're doing."*

Suppressing the urge to roll my eyes, I placed my left fist upon my chest and bowed a bit. "May the Dark Light Rygavon of our Lord Lucifer be with you, Honourable Ravaths and Ravathes," I exclaimed.

"And with you as well, Cherxanain," they replied in unison, and I straightened up with my fist still on my chest.

DeVarren abruptly arose from his seat. "Cherxanain Yverna, are you aware why I asked for your presence here?"

"I wanna know that myself, you dolt." I bit back the sarcasm. "Two members of the Machordaen informed me that I was to give a further report regarding Nero."

"And?" he prompted. The malicious look in his eyes was tangible enough for me to see from where I stood. That figured. They *were* planning something here, and I bet I wouldn't like whatever it was in the slightest.

I looked at them, expressionless. "I am not aware if there was anything else, Ravath. Although, I wonder . . ." I let it hang there and waited for their reaction.

"About what?" Weizar asked, with suspicions in his voice that would weigh a ton.

Once again, I had to keep myself from rolling my eyes. *"I wonder why you five are allowed to bitch at me about Bynethar's business at once."*

Refraining myself from blurting out the question that would totally get me arrested, I kept my voice as polite as possible. "Forgive me, but, I was only wondering where Ravath Bynethar is, because it is my understanding that he was the one who issued that order in the first place, and yet I noticed he isn't here. And as I've said earlier, I have completed my mission. Forgive my impudence, but is there anything lacking in my work over him, Ravath DeVarren?"

"Even if there is, which is impossible, that's no fucking business of yours. And I so damn hate being freakin' formal!" I snarled mentally, and I tightened my fist.

DeVarren folded his arms. "As expected from you, Cherxanain, you're never lacking in vigilance. And as for your questions, I'll answer them. Ravath Bynethar isn't here because he's taking care of his personal affairs."

"If he's not already dead or poisoned by you all," I thought with distaste.

He went on. "And as you've said, you have done splendidly with Nero. Now he's making enormous mayhem within his own kingdom as we speak. Have no worry about it."

Okay, so they'd explained things that no longer needed to be explained. In fact, they'd done everything but yell "boo".

Careful not to grind my teeth, I bit my lip instead, and damn, that hurt. "In that matter, may I inquire as to why I'm being summoned here?"

"We've been told that you were involved in the recent unusual events regarding the Alvadors and several Levarchons," DeVarren said.

Weizar tapped his finger on his table. "And also another matter regarding the deaths of the three Arcs you fought," he interjected.

That last bit slammed into me like a hammer.

"I beg your pardon?" I asked slowly. Unconsciously holding my breath, I winced in disbelief. I couldn't believe what I just heard! Did Amon know about this?

"You heard him correctly, Cherxanain." Ravathe Faemirad, a she-devil with gleaming blue eyes leaned forward. "We received a report which presents a very high possibility that the three Arcs whom you, your sister Cherxanain Vrathien, and Varkonian Zaderion fought earlier may have been slaughtered."

"Damn, this can't be good," I snapped as I mentally hurled all kinds of curses at them and this whole stupid situation.

Inhaling a really deep breath to maintain my poise, I thought about everything for a bit. This had to be what Amon was trying to tell us. Too bad he was late, and thanks to that, I had to be extremely careful here.

"Cherxanain, do you have any ideas as to who massacred the three of them?" Weizar asked sternly.

I kept my face as stoic as I could. "As for your earlier statement, yes, I was indeed involved. But, as for the deaths of the Arcs, I just heard about this myself."

"You really have no idea about this?" Weizar asked sharply.

I shook my head. "I have no idea whatsoever, Ravath."

Kathiera cast a cold stare at me. "Very well, we'll look into that later, since other events have also come to light before us."

"Has anything else happened?" I asked.

Faemirad suddenly made a movement. She threw her long hair back. "We received another report from the Iverand that you with your sister had voluntarily looked for the missing Levarchons and the Alvadors. And you two found them. Well done."

"I thank you Ravathe."

"To aid your investigation into the massacre, Varkonian Zaderion was summoned by the Iverand to examine the remains, and that was when an incident happened to the both of you. We're glad to know you two are fine."

"Whatever . . ." I bit back the snappy retort. "I thank you for your concern, Ravathe," I remarked as humbly as I could, for exasperation stirred and was beginning to change into a healthy dose of anger, and it was only a matter of time before that anger fought for control.

"If you'd stop nagging, I'll be happy to send you thank you cards every year. Or every morning if you'd let me get the hell outta here this instant."

"But there are several things that bother us. We received a report that you, your sister, and Varkonian Zaderion were attacked twice, first by unknown attackers and the second time by those three Arcs, but we have never gotten the details in regard to these battles."

"The fact that the three of us are alive is not enough for you lame heads to guess who got toasted asses and who were the winners? You are brainless. It's a wonder how you all became the Echelons in the first place.' I had to eat the sarcasm again, before it reached the point where I couldn't control myself and said it.

"We demand your explanation," Weizar interjected.

"I'm not a moron. What else do you want if not a bloody fucking explanation?" I snarled inwardly. I cleared my throat and carefully chose what to say and how to say it, because I really had to do some major cover-up here. "Very well, the first attack was indeed carried out by unknown attackers, but Cherxanain Vrathien managed to kill those beings. I cannot confirm this because apparently, after they died, every piece of them disintegrated immediately."

I hoped to hell they couldn't see through that bit of a lie and did not realize that the shield was still on even after our supposed attackers were dead.

"But the three of you came back there after you went elsewhere. Why is that?" Faemirad frowned at me.

"We came back there because we thought we might be missing something in our search regarding the deaths of the Levarchons and the Alvadors."

They nodded, although I could tell that they weren't satisfied. But what the hell! They could screw Amon's golems for all I cared.

"As for the battle with the Arcs, it all began when the Levarchons, who we learned later on were looking for us, came into the area.

At that time, however, we assumed they were patrolling, so we decided to rest for a minute, after we'd searched the forest and got ourselves attacked, and not bother them. That was when we saw the Arcs coming. They were so fast that we couldn't even react in time when they killed those Levarchons. But the three of us only defeated them. We did not kill them. We immediately headed back to the Aryad after that fight to meet Iverand Amon and report all we'd seen back in the forest."

When they kept their silence, I decided to try asking them whether they had a clue, although I bet they wouldn't share squat, even if they did. "Forgive my insolence, but I meant to ask, does our intel have any lead on who did it? Because I assure you, the three of us did not have anything to do with it."

Faemirad stared at me. "We're aware that the three of you are not the ones who did it, because the three of you are still alive and well."

At least she proved yet again to be one of the few amongst the Echelons with a brain. I hoped to hell they didn't conclude anything that even came close to mentioning Ry, though.

"But we indeed received information that the one who did this was, without a doubt, one of the devils," she went on.

I held my breath at that. What the hell was she saying?

"Surely not? With Iverand Amon watching us and the sacred deal, how could it possibly be?" I asked them.

DeVarren cleared his throat. "That is what we wanted to make sure. Do you know anything regarding this matter?"

I gave them a blank stare as an answer, which definitely would get their ire.

"You'd better be telling us the truth. We received a report that you, your sister, Iverand Amon, and Varkonian Zaderion were locked in the Iverand's den for hours before the three of you checked the missing Levarchons. Furthermore, there were indications that additional barriers were raised in there. Are you saying that had nothing to do with this matter?" Weizar interjected.

"No, dumbass," I mocked him in my thoughts again. "Certainly not, Ravath. We were there because we were discussing some unusual things we'd found in the remains. That was why we were there, to ask the Iverand whether he'd came across similar events before. If

he did, we could predict who the culprit was and send out a warning, maybe without involving Varkonian Zaderion in the process. It turned out that the Iverand said that there was no record of it, and Varkonian Zaderion had to check the remains. That was when the incident happened. Fortunately, none of us suffered serious injury."

Faemirad folded her arms. "If that's the case, you have done well, Cherxanain."

Ravathes Faemirad and Kathiera were two of the few whom I respected a bit. Even though they, especially Kathiera, always tried to devise some sinister scheme to get what they wanted, at the very least they were doing what Vrae and I called "brain-talking" and not "clout-talking."

If only their brains were put to use for the legions' sakes as a whole, not just theirs. That was why both their presences here didn't exactly spell good. They could be planning something that would lead to me and my companions getting disembowelled.

I bowed a bit. "Thank you, Ravathe."

"And could you elaborate about the additional barriers?" Kathiera asked suspiciously.

I winced but put on an innocent look that said "Isn't it obvious?" at her. "Well, the Iverand thought that we must keep secret everything we knew up to that point before someone gets a wrong idea and causes panic, for not even we have a firm grasp on what the recent events might entail just yet."

And that someone who always has the wrong idea usually sits among all of you.

Faemirad eyed me for a moment before she nodded with a look that could be considered as satisfaction. "Very well, that is a reason enough for the Iverand to do so."

"There is one more thing, Honourable Ravathe. I was wondering if you would enlighten me as to what I should do with Nero."

DeVarren sat. "He's no longer a concern, as I've told you before. We only needed to ensure that you know nothing about this troubling matter."

"So much for wasting my damn time." I clenched my teeth.

"And one more thing." Ravath Lazoreth suddenly rose from his seat. "Have you heard anything regarding Cain?" when he mentioned Cain, I glanced at the rest of the Echelons.

Weird! They all shot a warning gaze at him.

I, on the other hand, showed nothing on my face. "Regarding what, exactly?" I asked in an I've-never-even-heard-of-him tone.

He quickly shook his head. And after that long session of making-me-mad meeting, they dismissed me.

Man, I wished they'd ended it a whole lot sooner. Now I could barely feel my arm.

I got out and decided to pay Amon a visit. I had to know just how much he told those Echelons before we made him swear not to reveal anything.

I hurriedly strode to Amon's place, passing through the punishing block again, and this time I ran into Zabaniah, one of extremely few angels that were assigned in this fire hole. I watched the guy torturing some prisoners. As the most ruthless guardian angel in hell, his nature was pretty much like ours—well, like me, Vrae, and Ry. So, aside from Azrael, we pretty much could tolerate him.

He didn't look amused to see me and I wasn't amused either. "Having fun again today?"

"What do you want?" He folded his arms.

"Hey, just passing through. There's no need to be hostile. You know what? You should be a bit friendly to us because you are, after all, in our hole, mate, so suck it up." I jerked my head.

He let out a cynical snort. "And why should I befriend beings like you?"

I scoffed. "Come now, don't be bloody racist here. And don't be bragging that your origin was as a citizen of upstairs but you got foreign affair duties and you were assigned here, 'cause FYI, that would seriously piss me off, and the news is so out of date to boot."

He raised his brow and to my surprise, he laughed. "You sure are interesting, devil, annoying sometimes, but amusing."

I smiled wickedly. "Well, thanks. I live to give people headaches with my mouth. So what's new?"

"What do you mean 'what's new'? You think I'm some kind of gossip lady?" he snapped.

I let out a scoffing laugh. I then glanced around to check if there was anybody close enough to eavesdrop. When I saw no one, I approached him. "Do you know anything about Cain?" I murmured.

He hesitated. "You heard?"

I nodded at his question. "I don't know. He suddenly babbled things like that. I didn't notice when I was watching him being beaten black and blue after blabbering whatever that was, but after that, I did notice he acted a bit weird." The angel gave me a quizzical stare.

"Yeah? Weird how?" I asked.

"He muttered the name of your former leader, the one killed by God–and he deserved it, I'd say," he added nonchalantly.

I narrowed my gaze at him and he quickly cleared his throat. "But that wasn't all. He muttered that name once, and then he made a movement as if he were protecting or hiding something. I didn't give a rat's ass about it. I mean, what could he be hiding in that hole?"

I agreed with him. "Yeah, what?" I asked in wonder. Damn, we really should pay him a visit ASAP.

I was right to ask the ruthless hell angel. Zabaniah could be really annoying sometimes. Well, maybe we were racist to one another, but he'd proven to be useful sometimes. That was why I even looked him eye to eye in the first place.

I folded my arms. "Anyway, time to scram, buddy. Thanks for telling me this. See ya some other time."

He snorted. "Don't mention it, although I'd better not run into you again."

"Whatever," I said as I left him.

As I continued walking down the lane surrounded by flames, my mind was invaded with loads of questions.

At any rate, I could do nothing before I let everyone in the loop and after we got whatever it was Cain carried, we could hear the rest of the story from Xaemorkahn and most importantly from Ry.

Suddenly, I had a really bad feeling, and I couldn't shake it.

"Ry, where are you? Do you know what's going on right now?" I pondered in dread. Dammit, Vrae, and Zade better have their butts at Amon's when I got there.

The Echelons were watching over us, perhaps closer than I thought, especially after a devil unknowingly murdered the Arcs. They might suspect that one of us went rogue, but how, they didn't know. One thing for sure, this could get ugly. When that happened, what would Ry intend to do?

I hoped to hell he hadn't been exposed.

*   *   *

"What did you do to Tyraviafonza?"

Kathiera turned around to see a fellow Echelon member, Bynethar, standing behind her with his face as blank as usual. She gave him a dry stare. "Where were you and Xamian?"

Bynethar inclined his head. "I had something personal to take care of. Him? I don't know. I'm not his father. Again, what's this thing I heard about you and the others questioning Tyraviafonza? And Xamian wouldn't be happy too, since I heard you all went your way at Wartiavega as well."

"That is none of your concern, Bynethar," she said coldly.

The Ravath shot a warning glare at her. "It is, Kathiera, if you try to overstep your bounds. Wartiavega might not be my concern, because she's Xamian's subordinate, but Tyraviafonza is mine. If you have problems with her, you will and must discuss it with me."

Kathiera didn't waver under his dark look. "And could we trust you to keep her on a tight leash? You know as we all do that she knows too much, even when Ezryan was still alive."

Bynethar scoffed. "She always does, and she always uses whatever she knows solely to protect her interests, which never tangle with ours unless we, or more to the point, you, make it so. You know this for a fact, and yet you just can't stand to have a soldier outwit you. Thus, you always devise a plan to ensnare her and Ezryan too, in which you had succeeded."

Kathiera's eyes narrowed at his words. The Ravath had struck the right cord, and she felt shame and anger burning her. "Do not make false conclusions about me."

"Whatever you say, Kathiera. You can fool yourself all you want." Bynethar's lips curved in a sadistic smile. "Just beware. This is my last warning. She is *my* subordinate. That means if she makes a grave mistake, only I have the right to personally punish her. If she doesn't do anything and you tangle with her, believe me when I say I won't stand idly by, even if it means I have to go against you. No matter what rule restricts me, I will not back down."

"Is that a threat, Bynethar?" she said silkily.

Bynethar *tsked*. "Believe me; you won't like it when I start threatening people. No, it's only a fair warning, because you already know what you can and cannot do, but still you test me," he said in a dead-pan tone. "Even you know who is the more powerful between us even though you always pretend otherwise."

Kathiera sorted through his words and decided that it was best to feign surrender, because he was right, his powers far surpassed hers. It wouldn't do her any good to go against him in the open.

Raising her hands, she offered him a cold smile. "If that is what you wish, then I shall entrust her affairs into your hands."

He stared at her, knowing that those were false words. Each of them was trying to outsmart the other and hide their true intentions. Bynethar knew he must do something to find out what they wanted with his subordinate and how to cover her. She was one of the important pawns he needed if he was to reach his goal.

To exact his revenge on the devil before him.

She and the rest of the Echelons didn't even realize that he and one other Ravath had secretly been devising a plan to bring all of them down for the last four thousand years.

Inwardly, he smiled. *"You think you have everything under your control. You have no idea what we're planning. That prophecy is the key to everything, and I'm not about to let it be denied by people like you."*

He nodded at Kathiera. "Those are the wisest words that have come out of your mouth today. I'll be in my chamber if you need me," he said. "Oh, and by the way, if you're offended with me trying to put a fine line between our territories in regard to who her superior is, I suggest you bring it to the Lord," he said meaningfully.

"Careful, Bynethar," she said with warning thick in her voice.

"That's my line," he said as he started to leave.

She scoffed. "Fine, I just want you to know one more thing."

"And that is?" he asked with his back facing her.

"She seems to know about Cain's prophecy."

He glanced over his shoulder and saw her throw a sarcastic smile at him. "Still think you have her under control?" she asked, and then left him, thinking that he was completely ignorant of the fact she had just told him.

She didn't see him smiling in the darkness of the Echelons' chamber. *"You haven't guessed the worst, Kathiera,"* he thought. *"If I'm correct, then it's only a matter of time before she knows what happened to Ezryan seven hundred years ago. If that happens, I don't think even I can stop her from killing all of you."*

*　　*　　*

Kathiera appeared in a secluded part of the forest surrounding the Aryad. Walking in haste, she immediately reached a giant cave that was hidden behind a two-thousand-year-old oak tree that had been infused with magick. She mentally sent for the one who dwelled in it, another of member of the Echelons–Faemirad.

The roots covering the entrance slowly cracked open, admitting Kathiera inside. She strolled in and found her fellow Echelon standing in front of wooden bookshelves with scrolls in her hands. Kathiera glanced around. Her gaze found the desk in the corner and another door at the far end of the room, which was illuminated with several yellowish light orbs.

"What is it, Kathiera?" Faemirad asked, snapping Kathiera back from her wandering.

The Ravathe averted her gaze and crossed her arms over her chest. "I want to tell you something," she began. She proceeded to tell Faemirad about her encounter with Bynethar.

Faemirad's brows joined into a single hard line when she was finished. "It is suspicious indeed." Her finger went under her chin as she was deep in contemplation. "I think either he knows something or they both do."

"My point exactly," Kathiera said with a sly smile curving her lips. Inwardly, she felt a bit of relief. She knew she could always count on Faemirad to be on the same page, and usually she'd do whatever she asked. She just hoped that would apply to what she was about to ask her next.

"So," Faemirad finally broke her silence, "the most predictable thing here is that you'd ask me to keep an eye on either of them since we can't tell for sure. The question is which one?"

Kathiera snickered. The she-devil had volunteered before she'd actually asked. "If that's the case, I want you on Xamian's tail."

"What about Bynethar?"

"We'll worry about him later. He's too careful. If we do anything now, it'll just set him off, and then he'd cover his tracks. We won't even get a sniff of dust if he does that."

Faemirad concurred. "What about the three we questioned?"

"I wanna go to the others first. Let's see if they agree with what I have in mind," Kathiera said slowly, her voice turning icy cold.

A chill went down Faemirad's spine at her tone. At times like this, she knew she'd never like what Kathiera would say next. "And what exactly is that?"

Flame burned in the Ravathe's eyes. "Something that will excite their interest, of course. We're going to ensnare one of those three."

"I definitely know where this is going," Faemirad thought in amusement laden with fear.

"The bitch had it coming for a long time, anyway," she said with a cold smile as she levelled an evil look at Faemirad. "Tyraviafonza will finally get what she deserves."

*　*　*

Ezryan walked through the forest quietly.

He had just finished getting rid of the Arcs, and their stench was on him. Now he set to visit an old friend.

A very ancient one.

Not long afterwards, he reached the edge. He manifested a protective shield around himself and then flew towards the mountains. He watched closely over the forest below as he made his way through the air. After a few moments, he suddenly accelerated and shortened the distance to the mountains even quicker.

But that wasn't his destination. Seconds afterwards, he landed near a vast lake at the foot of the mountains.

As his wings turned into a deep sapphire-coloured robe that covered his body, he stared at the lake for a while. His perfect brows knitted, and he sighed.

Abruptly, he firmed his gesture. "Belphegor," he whispered clearly to the wind.

From out of nowhere, a crimson mist slowly appeared, making a silhouette of a person. After the form completed, the mist dissolved, and a shockingly handsome devil appeared before him.

His tall well-built body was covered entirely with a long heavy crimson-coloured robe. His long black hair flowed ever so smoothly, and seven horns jutted out of his head like a crown.

This fitted him, for he was Lucifer's son.

This particular devil before Ezryan was one of the few besides Lucifer himself that made most devil warriors flinch. Although he was the son of Lucifer, he'd held a grudge against his father and had been trying to dethrone him for thousands of years. Hence no devil ever tries to cross paths with him.

Even now after he went into exile, he was still revered by most. As for Ezryan, elders in the exile were proven to be a potential source of information for him. That was why he would visit those elders every now and again. With the exception of himself, only his two companions dared to come in contact with them, although not as often as he did.

Belphegor raised one brow at Ezryan's presence. "Well, well, talk about zombies coming back from the land of the dead. And to think you have the nerve to come here after daddy bastard whacked your ass. Ry, you must have harboured a death wish."

Ezryan lifted the edge of his lips in amusement. "Not really, Belphegor. So you know I'm still around?"

Belphegor shrugged. "Boy, what can I tell you? I keep tabs on certain things, and unfortunately you, my reckless young friend, are one of them," he said, and then he hugged him like a brother. A second later they separated. "Let's get inside. Those bothersome soldiers are annoying like flies these days," he said.

Ezryan didn't even move an inch, for he had one question that needed an immediate answer before he could continue to other matters.

The prince realized his guest wasn't following him and turned around. "What?"

Ezryan gulped with the fear that weighed heavy in his mind. "Highness," he started, but Belphegor raised a hand to stop him.

"He didn't."

It was several heartbeats later when that single statement registered, and even then Ezryan just stared in disbelief. This made the prince nearly laugh–if he didn't know this devil before him enough. "The bastard didn't do it. You can relax."

"But how . . ."

"I told you, I keep tabs on a few things, and they include you. I heard him that day, but he wouldn't do it, and I've checked it myself. Besides, even he has to know that she's way too valuable despite her tendency to make people nervous by knowing things she isn't supposed to. Luckily for them all, she keeps her mouth shut so long as no one threatens or corners her into any sort of ugly situation. So before you go screaming in despair at me, the answer is yes, she's alive."

Ezryan drew a short breath in relief. "Thank you," he said earnestly.

Belphegor shrugged. "No need to thank me. She's doing more than just fine on her own. Now let's get in."

Ezryan nodded, and Belphegor turned to face the lake and began chanting something under his breath. A second later, a palace made of crimson-coloured crystal emerged from thin air. It floated above the lake. There were stairs that led to a huge door. Those stairs reached all the way from the door to the ground around the lake.

Both of them walked towards the door, opened it, and then went inside. The castle disappeared the second the door closed.

Ezryan looked around the hall. This place was still the same as the last time he'd set foot inside it. Huge crimson-coloured pillars stood coldly in the corners of the hall. Belphegor led him to a circular staircase on the left that led to his chamber. As they ascended the stairs, he saw carvings everywhere, most of them full mockery directed at Lucifer and God.

When they arrived at the top of the stairs, a huge image carved into the wall greeted him. It was an image of Lucifer's death.

Ezryan sometimes thought he should either agree with his old friend's doings or be offended. He'd once thought about introducing Belphegor to Xaemorkahn, but he knew better. It would have been disastrous if they should cross each other's path.

They sauntered down a long hallway flickering with thousands of small pale white orbs. Belphegor led him towards a lone massive door at the end of the hallway that was his chamber. The prince opened the door, and they went inside. Belphegor strode casually towards a luxurious sofa in the middle of the chamber. He sank into it and indicated the one across from him with a nod at Ezryan.

Glancing at his surroundings, Ezryan sat as Belphegor settled in and relaxed. "So, what business do you have with me?"

Ezryan leaned forward. "I've come to pose some questions, and there are a few things I've been waiting to confer about with you."

Belphegor scoffed. "Of that I have no doubt. Since the night you almost died, right? Just cut to the chase, Ry."

The warrior cleared his throat. "I need to know whether you've heard anything about God's oldest creation."

Belphegor frowned in suspicion. "Where did you hear about that?"

"You knew that there's such thing?" Ezryan cast an alarmed look at him.

The devil prince smirked. "Well, tough luck, boy. You should know better than depend almost entirely on your so-called brother's resources." He laughed.

Sobered, the prince raked his crimson hair. "Although I'd give their intelligence department some credit. They know a whole lot more than dear old Amon without using any damned revolting golems. I take it that's why you took your butt out there every once in a while, right? And you even went there when that old bastard attacked you. The cowardice fit him real nice, by the way," he added.

Ezryan smirked at that last comment but didn't say anything.

"Talk about cross over! That was a smart move to jump over the plane like that. Now you can move freely because most of us think you're dead."

Ezryan scowled. "You knew that too? I'm surprised you've never contacted me, seeing that whatever it is you planted on me only works one way."

Belphegor rubbed his brow. "Because I figured there was no need for me tell you I know about it and then for us to gossip about it like a pair of teenage girls."

Ezryan snorted. "That's a really amusing thought. And I think your telling me now has nothing to do with you having a sudden desire to gossip and flirt around."

The prince burst out laughing. "That's why I like you. Your smart mouth is still as amusing as ever."

Ezryan shook his head in disagreement. "Nah, there's someone better."

Belphegor caught the knowing look in Ezryan's eyes. "Well, she does have a nice sense of humour, more than my bastard of a dad."

At the prince's remark, Ezryan chuckled. "Your dad is just weird to begin with, let alone his sense of humour. She'd be pissed if she heard you compared her with your suck-ass dad."

The North Prince grinned. "Well, I wouldn't argue with you on that part." He snickered, but he was brought to a pause when he saw the faraway look that dwelled in Ezryan's deep sapphire eyes.

At the warrior's sudden silence, Belphegor lowered his gaze and drew a short breath. "Have you decided then?" he asked as he lifted his gaze to Ezryan.

Ezryan winced as if he were just being pulled from a daydream, and then he turned his puzzled gaze to the prince. "Have I decided on what?"

The prince smiled evilly. "On her. I mean, you've always been sweet on her ever since before my daddy bastard toasted you."

Startled, Ezryan looked away before casting another sad look at the prince. "Yes, I've decided. I'll tell her when I meet her." A bittersweet smile curved his lips as the she-devil appeared once again before his mind's eye.

Belphegor laughed out loud. "That's my boy! Pity she doesn't seem to notice though. Or maybe she does, and we both had no idea since the only one who can see through her most of the time is Vrae, and I doubt even she could say whether her sister is into you or not," he teased with a short laugh.

His laughter immediately died when he saw a guilty look on Ezryan's face. "What?"

Ezryan slowly shook his head with the hint of a sad smile. "Nothing. I just . . . I wish I'd told her a long time ago. You have no idea how I regret it to this day that I didn't even have the will to shove away my fucking ego and tell her."

Belphegor shook his head. "You didn't tell her because you were afraid my daddy bastard would go after her if she did accept you. Hell, she being that close to you was enough to make those guys suspicious of her. I know you've never told her that they always ask you whether you tell her anything back when they beat the crap out of you, but somehow she always found out about things she was never supposed to–things that both helped and screwed you in the face."

"Just make sure you don't tell her any of that. She doesn't know, and I'll make sure she never does," Ezryan retorted.

Belphegor sighed. "You know, you worried too much. I heard you that day when my old bastard almost killed you. You called her name when you writhed there, just one step from death, just a breath away before Azrael come to get you." He jerked his head at the former Hieldhar. "I'm sorry that I couldn't get to you in time," he said quietly.

Ezryan laughed bitterly. "No matter. I didn't want you to anyway. He still doesn't know about our meetings. And speaking of that, don't you have anything better to do than watch my movements like a daytime drama?"

He shrugged nonchalantly. "Hey, beats looking for intel myself. Don't worry; I won't get a sneak peek at your sentimental hours when you're having them with her."

The warrior narrowed his gaze but didn't say anything.

The prince leaned forward in his seat. "Okay, enough with the jokes. Back to the game of Who Is Our Mystery Man, and by the way, I'm surprised that you'd bother to drag your ass all the way here instead of meeting her first."

Ezryan cast a wary gaze at the prince. "I'll see her after I get answers. So, have you heard anything about whoever that was?"

Belphegor folded his arms, and his crimson eyes swirled. "I've never actually seen it myself, but I overheard Lilith talked to the old bastard, maybe about a year before she went into exile. By the way, say hi to your girl for me when you meet her. Tell her I like what she did to Lilith. The old slut's still furious over it."

Ezryan cast a droll stare at the prince in front of him.

Belphegor grinned. "Yeah, I know. Anyhow, Lilith told Pop. Actually, she *screamed* at him about how anxious she was."

The warrior arched a brow. "Why is that?"

"She kept babbling about omens and saying something like, 'Stupid, that thing could be here any minute, we should run!' or

'Gotta find a way to kill it or at least seal the damned thing forever.' Yeah, something like that."

Ezryan bit his lip. "Are you sure they were talking about the same entity?" he asked with a frown.

Belphegor let out a slow breath. "I didn't even have a clue at first, but when she said 'that sack of void could pull me to oblivion before you could say fuck!' or something like that, right then I knew what they were talking about."

Ignoring the obviously exaggerated part, Ezryan's frown deepened. "Then you should have known about it before."

Belphegor nodded in agreement. "Yeah, actually I came across the old bastard's private records about a decade before I announced myself as a separate part of his flock. It was then that I found out something that made me sick of him."

Ezryan hesitated. His old friend could be deadlier than anything when it came to unleashing his rage. He built up his courage to ask, "May I ask what it was?"

Belphegor exhaled heavily. "This entity is called Arzia. It means 'The End of All Being.' Quite a classy name, I'd say. Classier than Avarnakh, the name your pal came up with." He sneered.

Ezryan scoffed. "You don't say. And that is classy all right. Classic scary, I might add."

Belphegor let out an undignified snort. "Tell me about it. The only thing I know about this destroyer is that since it was created from the void, it has the ability to neutralize almost all kinds of elemental attack."

"And wipe them to the oblivion whence they came," Ezryan inserted.

"Yeah, well, needless to say, it could just wave its hands and turn us all back to the *void* from whence we came, just like ashes to ashes, dust to dust," Belphegor said sardonically.

Ezryan chose to ignore that last remark. Instead he rolled his eyes at the prince and got punched for it. "You said almost all kinds of elemental attack?"

"Yeah, I did."

"Then there's an element or two that could countermand it?"

Belphegor lifted the edge of his lips in amusement. "I see you caught that one. Well, there is one element, but it's not exactly a countermand. Let me put it to you this way. Whoever wields the element has more of a chance to fight the destroyer in hand-to-hand combat, because in a way it is more like the destroyer's element and won't be erased like the others."

"So, which element is it? Water? Air?" Ezryan guessed, hoping that if he was right, then he could take most matters into his own hands, since he had both at his full disposal.

Belphegor shook his head. "Not water–too concrete. And there's definitely no air in the void," he said with a chuckle.

At Ezryan's half blank, half disappointed look, Belphegor inclined his head. "Actually, it's more up your sweetheart's alley. The only element I and a few other royals know that could almost match it is . . . the element of darkness," he said dramatically. "So, if we wind up fighting the damn thing, we definitely should call her."

Ezryan gulped at that. He could never imagine her fighting God's ultimate destroyer. He'd rather be gutted first before he would let the damned thing go anywhere near her.

"If that should happen, is there no other choice?" the former Hieldhar asked.

Belphegor could almost see where Ezryan's thoughts were heading. "Sorry, but you know that there's no other darkness wielder that exists in the entire First Legion, let alone the other six. Even among the royals, the number is extremely limited, and most of them I don't trust."

Ezryan lowered his gaze. "I understand."

Belphegor cleared his throat and pulled Ezryan back from his musings to the matter at hand. "But leave that aside. I also figured out that by wielding Rygavon, daddy bastard had condemned us all."

Ezryan frowned. "What do you mean? Him screwing us is nothing new, but that Rygavon was his from the beginning."

"Yeah, after he tampered with every other crap and thus bound most of us." Belphegor curled his lips in disgust.

Ezryan's eyes widened at his explanation.

"Just so you know, that thing wasn't originally his. As you probably know by now, when this Arzia was created, it was intended as the Big Guy's ultimate key to destroy everything, and I do mean everything–verses, planets, dimensions, everything. Raphael blowing his horn is just a signal before this being does what it was intended to do."

"And what's that gotta do with Rygavon?"

"Rygavon is one of the keys that sealed that thing and its ultimate weapon to destroy everything. In short, when it awakes fully recharged and then uses the thing, even I wouldn't have a chance to slap Lilith before I go."

Ezryan had to keep himself from laughing. "There's one thing I don't get, though. If its purpose is only to destroy everything like you said, why did God create it way before He made anything else and then hide the nature of it? It's barely recorded anywhere. Besides, it's only a destroyer," Ezryan said in bafflement.

Belphegor sighed heavily. "God is the owner here, remember? As much as I hate to acknowledge it, the Big Guy is omniscient, as in everything-omniscient."

Ezryan just stared blankly at that obvious information.

The prince then raked his hair. "But I guess, one of the reasons was that He'd predicted daddy bastard would act out of cowardice and try to pull a weird stunt over Adam's descendants, or even better yet, the Arcs. Or hell, maybe if he was crazy enough, he'd try to use that entity and the Rygavon as a means to take over all of Big Guy's creations and challenge Him or something. And that would certainly make the whole world become a gigantic amusement park. I think that's why we barely ever heard about its existence, to prevent it from being a puppet played by a twisted puppeteer."

Ezryan concurred. "That makes sense."

Belphegor took a deep breath and then released it. "It seemed daddy bastard knew all this when he was still the MVP of the upstairs team. But when *his* daddy dumped him because he was temporarily poisoned by testosterone, apparently he snatched it, and those Arcs weren't strong enough to face him. God could just create another one just like him, but why should the Big Guy waste any effort just to end him? There are lots of beings down here and up there itching to tear him to pieces."

"Including you," Ezryan added with a wicked grin.

He laughed evilly. "Especially me. Anyway, I also found out that there are three keys needed to seal its tomb. First off, like I said, it's the Rygavon. I'm not sure about the other two, but I'm pretty certain that one of them is here on earth, but as to the whereabouts of the last key, I have no idea. All I know is that once the three are joined, they will form the Arkhadim, the seals to the Arzia's tomb and its strongest weapon."

Ezryan suddenly winced as a thought came to his mind.

"What is it?" asked Belphegor.

"Do you think Solomon and his ring have anything to do with that seal?" he asked in a wondering tone.

Belphegor shrugged. "I am more concerned over that list of names he made, and now it's in the possession of the human who's been entrusted to keep the ring after his death, as if we didn't have enough trouble already."

Ezryan nodded slowly. "Yeah, I know what you mean. That is bothersome to say the least. Well, perhaps a few Machordaens or somebody will get the order to steal it."

"Right. And by the way, Ry, tell me first, what was it you stole from up there and then gave to Cain, and second, what did you hear?" Belphegor narrowed his gaze at the former warrior of his father.

Ezryan shot a brow. "That's a lot."

Belphegor gave him a "duh" stare. "You're one to talk. What you've done was too much to be called the work of two hundred years."

Ezryan scoffed. "I thought you said you're omniscient about me?"

At the young devil's playful demeanour, Belphegor curled his lips. "Well, unfortunately, it's not enough to cover anything concerning up there or other planes, and I know whatever you gave Cain, it must be the thing you took from that dull place. C'mon boy, cut the crap and tell me."

Ezryan hesitated. He lowered his gaze for a moment. Abruptly he looked the North Prince straight in his eyes. "Okay, I'll tell you. First, you wanna know what I gave to Cain. Like you said, it does have something to do with up there. The thing I gave him, is called Herathim, it . . ."

"It's a Forbidden Item. Some say the damn thing was a weapon, but for what no one can tell, especially because of the place God put it in," Belphegor interrupted in one breath.

Ezryan was aghast at the prince's words. "You knew what that was? You've never mentioned it before."

Belphegor narrowed his gaze. "The question is, Ry, how in the hell did you get that? It was located in the deepest part of Heaven! I wonder why those Arcs haven't chased you before. Why are they starting now?"

Ezryan arched a brow. "You know about that too, huh?" he asked.

The edge of Belphegor's lips twitched in a wicked grin. "I like what you did with them."

"Well, it was nothing. They perhaps counted on your dad to gank me for real. My returning here alive must be like a bitch-slap across Michael's face."

The North Prince chuckled. "Nice picture. Makes me wanna slap him myself," he inserted, and Ezryan snickered at that.

"I thought that it's too strange for them to be chasing you again and acting as if they already knew you survived daddy dearest's attack from the start," he said in repugnance. "Although I figure those ass-kisser Echelons would think someone went rogue or at least managed to slip through their fences. The old bastard won't like it when he finds out someone can weasel out of his deal, whose purpose was more to watch all the devils than to maintain the balance. He ever cared about the stupid balance," he remarked bitterly.

The prince then raked his hair. "It was the right move to whack them. Yve, Vrae, and the guy they were with will have to face those Echelons because of this though," he said without thinking, and then saw the uneasy look on Ezryan's face. This made him clear his throat. "I bet she invents a whole new kind of insult when she deals with them."

Ezryan snorted at his comment and then cocked his head when he caught something in the prince's words. "By the way, you said they were with a guy?"

Belphegor nodded. "Yeah, he bears the crest of Varkonian. Blonde guy, with a not-too-good sense of humour. Too stiff for the girls' tastes, I'd say. Why, you know him?"

Ezryan frowned as he tried to guess who it was, and then it occurred to him. "Yeah, if I'm right, then the guy they were with was Zaderion. His Imirae's a bit unique compared to the rest of his group, but he's okay. He runs with the girls from time to time, and he ran with me too back then. Most importantly, he shares the same view as us in the matter of 'Echelons are mostly jerks, so is your dad', so don't worry, he won't rat. Besides, he has a personal reason not to do so."

Belphegor frowned at him. "And that is?"

Ezryan shook his head. "Sorry, it's not my place to say. You probably will see it for yourself if we meet the sisters again."

The prince stared at him for a moment before he finally shrugged. "Whatever, so long as he's not a rat. Still, like I said, it was the right move to gank the light-heads," the prince remarked, and he rubbed his brow.

Ezryan once again lowered his gaze. Wariness and pain were evident on his handsome face as his thoughts wandered to the she-devil he loved.

Belphegor eyed his young acquaintance and realized what he was thinking. Abruptly, he expelled a short breath to distract the former commander. "Okay, back to the subject."

Ezryan was startled and turned his gaze to the prince. "So, why didn't Amon know about this thing you pulled again?" he asked.

Ezryan grinned. "His pals freaked out when I got too close up there."

Belphegor scoffed. "I figured as much."

His gaze darkened, and Ezryan's lips curved in a cold smile. "However, I'm sure he knows more than he let on to all of them, which means he kept his end of the deal I made with him before my supposedly last day in the living realm," he said. "The Veil, at least, should've known that I'm back in town."

The prince gave him a hard stare. "You reckon he'd save the golem he created for you? The Veil, without a doubt, has already stated that somebody showed up from who knows where. And what deal are we talking about here?"

"I asked him not to tell anyone about whatever he might see in my golem's sixth eye."

Belphegor nodded in understanding. "Because at the very least, it would surely record the bastard using his toy to burn the forest down," he said, "if not to the point where he cornered you nice and proper."

"Yeah, and since I'm not dead, my golem should be intact. If he even remotely realized what that means, he'd at least fabricate the eye's record, or better yet, create a new golem, destroy it to made look like I was dead, and save the real one."

A wicked smile broke on the prince's face. "I just wouldn't want to be in his shoes when the sisters, especially your lady, find out he knew all along."

Ezryan grinned at his remark, and the prince cleared his throat. "So, you get another question to answer: why did you do it? And by the way, question number two is still waiting."

Ezryan folded his arms. "To answer your 'why I did it' question, I'll need the answer from 'what I've heard'."

Belphegor rolled his eyes. "Whatever! Just fill me in."

Ezryan swallowed a bit. "You know Cain has spewed another prophecy?"

Belphegor rubbed his brow. "Yeah, I've heard. He sure knows how to amuse us. But I take it you knew he would spill that rotten shit beforehand. You just needed a confirmation from him."

Ezryan nodded. "Yeah. What I heard has everything to do with what he said."

"And that is?" Belphegor interjected.

With his deep sapphire eyes fixed on the prince, Ezryan shifted his position in his seat. "Well, here goes."

*   *   *

I entered Amon's place, just in time to see him examining something bizarre on his desk.

When he saw me coming, he abruptly stood up and whatever it was that was sitting on his desk vanished. "Yve, I heard you were summoned by Ravath DeVarren."

I *tsked* in disgust. "Not just him. Four others of them, except Ravath Bynethar and the others."

He was taken aback by my remark. "Five members? I thought only Ravath DeVarren wanted to meet you?"

I arched my brows. "And wouldn't you find it odd that he wanted me regarding Nero? Like he had anything to do with that human in the first place!"

Amon winced and looked as though he'd just realized something. "Now that you mention it, yeah. He didn't have anything to do with him. Ravath Bynethar did. So what did they want with you?"

I gave him a "duh" stare. "They wanted to know what we were doing–when Vrae and I found those soldiers' remains, us crossing over with Zade, the deaths of those stupid Arcs, everything! Luckily they haven't heard about you know who." I shot a meaningful gaze at him. "Which begs the question, *Iverand*, why the hell didn't you tell us sooner that somebody whacked the bastards?" I gave him a peeved glare.

He cringed. "The Veil just showed it to me right after you guys got out. I wanted to tell you through your golem, but those Machordaens beat me there."

I rolled my eyes. "I figured as much. Now, did the Veil give any clue to you as to who the lucky bastard was that ganked them? Just don't tell me they were killed by our Avordaen with their fluffs intact. If that's the case, I swear I'm gonna go back to where we left them and kill them myself."

He snickered at my acerbic comment. "No, I don't think you can. The Veil indeed gave me something that raised my suspicions, but still, there's no way that could be done. The deal . . ."

"Yeah, tell me about it. I wonder why they didn't just drop the bomb on us and say that *we* did it." I laughed bitterly at my own words. "Now tell me what you know."

"I wanna wait for the others first."

"Well, according to the guys who relayed those stupid orders, Darvahl could have sent Zade who knows where by now, and the same goes with Vrae–and that is if their orders weren't some sort of horse shit. Anyway, can't you tell me where the Echelons sent them?"

He shifted his position and looked uneasy. "That's what bothers me. Whichever it turns out to be, those two aren't supposed to have anything until two or three months from now unless there's something urgent, and there isn't."

I arched a brow. "Aren't they supposed to go through you whenever we get a gig?"

Amon scowled at my question. "Well, yeah."

I clenched my teeth. "Nice! That means those annoying bastards are trying to split us up. Can you try to contact them?"

"I can't use their golems if they are in their bases. I *can* if I either use doppelgangers or summon Machordaen or Levarchon to call them back in. That, I guarantee you, will make those Echelons grow suspicious even more than ever."

I scoffed. "Yeah, tell me about it. And that's the last thing we need right now. Damn it!" I swore under my breath. When he didn't say anything, I slowly expelled a long tired breath as another thought occurred to me. "Dude, before I forget, I wanted to ask you, just how much intel did you let loose?"

He was startled.

I repeated my question. "Amon, how much?"

He bit his lip and then lowered his gaze. After a moment, he looked at me again. "Well, I–I didn't tell them much. I told them all except the thing Vrae told us and the story about you three crossing over. That's it."

"That's it?"

"That's it. Hell, even I know that this matter's too big, I'll risk more than just my job here if I tell them any of this. Not to mention the you-know-what I just showed you," he remarked meaningfully.

I *tsked.* "You got that right, and by the way, someone sent a bird to the Echelons when you raised additional barriers in here," I remarked in disgust.

He blanched at my words. "You're kidding."

I curled my lips. "No, I'm not, smart-ass. They told me that. 'You'd better be telling us the truth. We received word that Iverand Amon raised additional barriers when the three of you were in his den.' Yeah, something like that. You're telling me you don't have any clue about this?"

Amon raked his hair in frustration. "No, and I didn't feel any of their usual rats around when I raised those additional barriers either. I made sure to add more alarms in case one of those showed up. There was nothing." He expelled a short breath. "Sorry, I should've known they could be that slick," he said apologetically.

I shook my head. "No, it's not your fault that they're sneaky bastards." I spat and let out a crude expletive. *"Ry, if you're really out there, we've got a situation down here."*

Grinding my teeth, I turned to Amon. "I'll go to the Valthors in case Vrae and Zade are already out and don't have the chance to tell us."

"I'll contact you if they come here."

I nodded and left the den. I quickly headed towards the Gate, but to my disappointment, neither of them was there, which meant they were still at wherever they were at the moment.

"So they haven't come out, huh? Dammit! Where the hell are they?" I cursed after Zoran told me that the two I was looking for never came.

Moments later, instead of them, I felt another presence that belonged to the one who made my coming here one sore mistake. It was the devil whom I'd been avoiding for four hundred years.

"Well, well, it's the Tyraviafonza herself. Isn't this a surprise?"

The three of us turned around and found a male soldier sauntering towards us from the woods. I tensed before I could stop myself at his arrival. His name was Baradyn, a fellow Cherxanain just like Vrae and me. At six foot six, he had the physical perfection of high-ranking devils. With amber eyes and shoulder-length blond hair, he radiated an aura that spoke his murderous threat. *"Don't even look at me the wrong way if you don't wanna be a stain under my shoes."* To top that aura, he commanded the earth and the wind. Because of the elements at his disposal, the Echelons often sent him to wreak havoc on the humans by causing what the humans thought of as natural disasters.

Furthermore, since he had contradictive powers, one of sky and one of earth, his enemies had nowhere to run. He could tear them apart with the wind or bury them alive. With that unusual combination, he was considered to be the only one whose powers almost matched Ry's, and he could be the next Hieldhar.

The two were rivals, but they would partner up in their jobs once in a while. However, from what I knew, Ry would always be on guard whenever he was around, despite the fact that the guy had never really posed a threat or anything.

Then again, just a short time after Ry's supposed death, this guy began to harbour some misguided and annoying thoughts, namely that he wasn't so different from Ry in certain areas.

Keeping my face devoid of emotions, I nodded at him while the Valthors straightened themselves. "Baradyn," I greeted him.

A glint of pain flashed in his eyes when I addressed him formally rather than using Rad, his short name—one thing I managed to ignore every time I did it. "Yve," he replied, as if he wanted to dismiss my formal attitude towards him. "Valthors," he saluted the guards, who gave a stiff nod.

I tensed even more at him calling me by my short name. Not that I had a stick up my ass, but he didn't know me well enough to call me that. Besides, for some reason I couldn't guess, Ry had told me to keep my distance from him, and I did.

These matters aside, I knew why he had started using that name in the first place, and that was why I'd rather not hang out with him. At first he was quite a fine guy to be around, until he started acting weirdly to me every time we crossed paths.

"So, what puts you in such a foul mood?" he asked.

I controlled the urge to screw up my face at him. *"Seeing you instead of the two I was looking for. That'd suffice."*

I shrugged. There was no need to tell this guy of the problem we were in, especially about the deaths of those Arcs. "Nothing important. What about you? What brings you down here?" I asked, trying to appear unperturbed in front of the Valthors.

But it turned out to be one very wrong move.

His eyes lit up. "Why, you suddenly show interest in me! Have I finally changed your mind?" he asked, not wasting a second. He said it not in a playful tone, but not in a serious one either. Hell, he asked the question as if he were asking my weekend plans.

But the worst thing was that he'd asked it in front of other devils, and I could feel them both staring at me, saying *"Is this guy asking what we think he is?"*

I cleared my throat. "What are you talking about?"

His full lips formed a smile. "C'mon Yve, you know what I mean. I've been asking it of you forever," he said quietly.

"Baradyn," I said in warning, reminding him that Valthors were present.

He caught my meaning, but unfortunately for me, he ignored it. "I don't care, I've been trying to make you see reason for four hundred years, and I don't care any more. I'd say it out loud before the Echelons if I had to," he declared fiercely.

My gaze darkened at him. "If you think you know me well enough to ask that of me, you'd realize that threats are not the way to talk to me."

He froze. "I'm not threatening you. It's merely a statement of what I would do to make you accept the reality."

Not even the Valthors made a single sound at his words.

I gritted my teeth. "What reality would that be? If that's the same unimportant bullshit you've been trying to shove down my throat, then no thanks. Besides, that wasn't the matter even before *that* happened. It never was. Only you would think that," I said with a heavy dose of venom, all the while trying to make it as subtle as I could so the Valthors couldn't guess what it was. Though I was sure as hell it was futile.

And it was added by another wrong move from him.

"Then why can't you accept me?"

That one question was as if a thunderbolt had literally struck my ears as I heard both Valthors gasp.

I inhaled as I tried to rein in my anger. Damn, he was lucky that only the Valthors whom I was familiar with were here. If it had been other than them or Vrae who saw this, he would have been dead meat. It wasn't his feelings that kicked me over the edge though. It was rather his reasoning. "Sorry to say this, *Baradyn,* but I'm not interested."

He kept his face unreadable, but the look in his eyes said it all. It was lacerated with pain, but aside from that, there was one thing I loathed that gleamed in there–overloaded pride in himself. Pride that could fill a mansion, pride that he was sure he could claim me.

That was the thing that made me overlook his disappointment and longing.

"You know that's not the real reason. Why can't you admit it? I know I'm more than capable of erasing *his* shadow, so why?" he asked slowly as he walked closer.

I nearly tore him apart at these words, but I restrained myself. It wasn't wise to fight before the Gate, because Valthors or no Valthors, Gevirash and Zoran wouldn't just stand there and do nothing if I were to start a fight. And I really didn't want to fight a bloody battle with them over this big-headed bastard. "Buddy, you're so full of yourself, no doubt the result of consulting with Pride. There's no other reason other than the one I just stated loud and clear," I said acerbically.

He shook his head in denial. "Yve, you can deny it all you want, but we know why you can't. You still can't get over him. He's dead. Get over it."

Blackness seared my eyes. I directed a murderous glare at him as I drew bits of my powers to prove my point. "Watch it, Baradyn, you're walking on *very* thin ice here, so you'd better be extremely careful to pick your next words. I've never had anything with him, and if he was still around, he'd gladly verify that for your inane and exceptionally slow mind," I said, betraying the vicious pain my own words carved in me, but I would die before admitting that to anyone.

To know that he had returned somewhere and that he might still view me only as his companion brought forth a foreign pain, but it was one thing I chose to endure alone. Admitting it would be the last thing I'd ever do.

"I don't believe it!" he exclaimed, and he started towards me, only to be stopped by two spears coming from behind me. The tips of those spears rested dangerously close to his throat.

"Believe it, Cherxanain Baradyn. Cherxanain Yverna has made her point loud and clear," Gevirash said. Both he and Zoran had their battle aura engulfing their bodies with the intensity that showed the strength expected from Valthors–guardians who watched over the Hell Gate and would kill all who might threaten their post, even if they had to face Azrael himself.

"Kill all, and throw the souls for the Hell angels to sort."

Baradyn took a step back. "What are you doing, Valthors? This does not concern you."

"Well, it does if you're about to start a riot before the Gate. There's a reason why we're both stationed here, and I assure you, it's for guarding and not sleeping," Zoran added.

Baradyn threw a disgusted look at them both, but he backed down. "Whatever you say, Valthors," he said.

Surprise and gratitude to them both surged through me. Other Valthors would simply have minded their own business and talked about this hilarious event behind my back. "You heard them. If you know what's good for you, you'd better go, like *now*," I added.

"So, is that your final say?" he asked. His longing was far more tangible right now.

I nodded. "Just so you know, you yourself provided the reasons for me not to accept you, and I'll say it again, if you knew me well enough, you'd never give me those reasons. I'm sorry, but there can never be an 'us', Baradyn. But, I would go as far as to say that I respect your strong will. Others gave up after I ignored them for one or two decades."

"Could I ask what those reasons were?"

"It's too late, and you wouldn't change my mind even if you promised you'd change those reasons," I commented mildly.

Defeated, he raised his hands. "Very well, I shall withdraw for now. But know this. I will not give up. I'll show you that I won't lose to a dead devil no matter how I respected him," he stated. A look of determination laden with that stupid, pardon the pun, Pride was written all over his face.

Inwardly I sneered at his ignorance, and I cursed him at the same time for his audacity. *"If only you know that he's so not dead . . ."*

I went ramrod stiff. "I warn you, this will be the last time I tolerate your stupidity for discussing our affairs in public. If you do that again, it means war."

His features went blank. "Duly noted. I shall go now." He strolled past the Valthors and went through the boulders at the entrance of the Gate.

I gulped, waiting for the Valthors to ask me to elaborate. Fortunately, they didn't.

Not wanting to pursue that sore subject, I decided to talk with them about some trivial things until my golem descended near the shield above us. "Yve, they're here," it said.

Both Valthors burst out laughing. "Gee, I think we can never get over how stupid their voices sound." Zoran jeered.

"Welcome to my happy life," I said indignantly. "All right, I'll go." I waved to the eye, which immediately ascended back into the sky.

Nodding at the guards, I walked past them and entered the Gate, hoping I wouldn't come across the demented bastard who went ahead of me.

* * *

Disbelief and cold rage appeared on every inch of Belphegor's rugged features after Ezryan told him everything he knew.

"Are you sure about this!?" the North Prince asked Ezryan sharply.

Ezryan cast a wary look at him. "That is what I've got. So you haven't heard any of this?"

Belphegor curled his lips. "I'm not saying I haven't heard it, but to think it really is happening right under our noses . . ." His voice faded. Abruptly, he tapped his fingers on his plush sofa. "Maybe someone knows about this a bit better than I do."

Ezryan frowned. "If you had heard about this, why are you suggesting someone else? Not that I'm against your judgment or anything, but we don't know whose side they're on."

Belphegor bit his lip. "Yeah, I'm aware of that, but come to think of it, maybe there's someone worth the risk to talk to."

A confused look appeared on Ezryan's face. "Like who? King Bael of the East?"

Belphegor snorted. "And why would that toad know anything? If I had to guess, Lilith definitely knows something besides the old bastard, but . . ."

Ezryan smirked. "But you won't pick either one of them."

"You got that right, I won't," Belphegor retorted.

"Then who are you suggesting?"

Belphegor sighed with a deep frown. "There are five people you might have a chance to talk to and a few others you wouldn't even dare to get within a several mile radius of their lairs, so I won't waste my breath mentioning them to you. All of them have their own sources."

Ezryan nodded slowly. "Okay, that's plenty of people. So who are they?"

"You know those guys–Vassago, Orobas, Seere, Dantalion, and Balam."

Ezryan scoffed. He should've known the prince's old gang were still keeping their eyes and ears on everything out there. "Them? Of course, why wouldn't they know anything about this?"

Belphegor rubbed his brow with his middle finger. "Boy, you don't possibly believe that you are the only one sticking his nose into someone else's business, now do you? I'm sure you know that those five, including myself, have been watching closely for any omens. Why did I say you might have a chance? Because I know you sometimes consult with them, if I could even call it that, I might add. Besides, you are also aware of the fact that they have been backing me up without my daddy bastard knowing about it."

He then raked his hair. "But I'm not saying all of them know about this–hell, definitely something, but not this. And we'd better pick the man carefully; otherwise we could end up causing a riot or not getting anything at all."

"Like Orobas who tends to freak out or Seere who'd rather slack off with his bling?"

Belphegor sneered. "Exactly my point!"

"So, who's it gonna be?" Ezryan asked with a grin.

The prince looked straight into his eyes. "Well, Dantalion might be busy playing governor, and Balam is usually doing research for only he knows what, which leaves us with one option. My buddy Vassago."

Chapter 10

It turned out I didn't meet that bastard Baradyn along the way.

My thoughts left him and wandered to more useful topics such as what those Echelons were hoping to accomplish by doing this to the three of us.

I absently walked until I arrived at the door. I immediately lifted the enchantments on the den's door and entered. Walking inside, I found both Vrae and Zade were standing before Amon's desk with the owner leaning on its side.

"Yve." Vrae called me as I closed the door.

"So you two are back. How's the east, Vrae?" I asked.

She gave me a dry stare. "East, my foot! There's nothing there. I got all suspicious about it in the first place, because as far as I know, there are indeed some small kingdoms but they're not that important. Never mind that. You know whom I met back there?"

I shook my head and shrugged. "No, who?"

"Ravath Havok and two others. Not Xamian, who was supposed to be there since he is my damn superior, and you know what? They asked me about everything, but none of it had 'e', 'a', 's', or even a fucking 't' in it," she snarled.

Amon snorted, and Zade stifled a laugh at Vrae's outburst. I raised my brows, and Vrae continued, "They asked me to elaborate on what we were doing."

I swore grudgingly under my breath. "That figures! They wanted the same thing with me." I turned to Zade. "What about you? What did Darvahl want?"

Zade rubbed his temple. "And why would he want squat with me when there's no job? No, he wasn't there. Ravaths Mezarhim and Gildam were at the Devorcae."

"What is this? Are they playing Let's Swap Echelons and Piss Them Off or what?" I snapped at his remark.

The Varkonian scoffed. "Hell, I have no idea. At any rate, we'd better watch our backs a whole lot closer, and I do mean closer," he said bitterly.

"You got that right," I inserted under my breath. As I tried to clear my head, a thought occurred to me about what the Varkonian had just told us. "Zade, you said two members?"

He nodded. "Yeah, why?"

"Wait a sec, buddy." I turned to Vrae. "You said that Xamian wasn't there, but was Bynethar present?"

Obviously perplexed, her brows joined in one hard line. "No, just Havok, Herron, and Falthan," she trailed off and her eyes widened. "I take it they didn't show at your place?"

I twitched the edge of my lips as I saw her catching up. Good. "No, they weren't there, just Ravaths Lazoreth, Weizar, DeVarren, and both Ravathes Faemirad and Kathiera," I ended meaningfully.

Vrae curled her lips. "That is not good."

"Fucking tell me about it. That's a fucking major understatement," I interjected.

Both males exchanged baffled looks, and Zade cleared his throat. "Girls, would you mind telling us whatever it is?"

"They're doing this without telling Ravaths Bynethar and Xamian," I said indignantly.

Vrae nodded in agreement. "Which could only mean they're plotting something against us. Who knows? The point is that both Bynethar and Xamian would never approve what those guys did–interfering with each other's line of work, let alone interrogating us with more than two members, without telling them in advance too, for that matter."

"Should we consult with them about this?" Zade asked.

Amon shook his head. "No dice. No matter how reasonable they are or how powerful compared to the rest of them, they're still Echelon members. Who's to say they won't rat us out or better yet, bust us themselves? We don't even know if the rest of the Echelons are indeed acting without telling them. Lucifer forbid, it may have been them who asked the others to do this. They're the most powerful among them, after all."

I concurred. "You're right. We keep this to ourselves."

"Right, now I wanna talk about something else," Vrae said with an uneasy look in her eyes. "They told me that those Arcs are dead. Did they tell you about this?"

I levelled a darkened gaze at her. "Yeah, they did," I grunted.

"They told me too. Any idea of who might've done it?" Zade asked nervously.

I scoffed. "I don't even have any idea who had reported it to them, much less who did it." I turned to Amon. "But Amon here told me he had a good idea."

Both the Varkonian and my sister simultaneously turned their attention to the Iverand. "What is it?"

Amon gulped. "The Veil showed something just after it gave out the news about those useless Arcs."

"And that would be what?" I prompted.

"The same one the Veil said was wandering around at Bahyrdanam–'Unknown unholy'." His nervous voice echoed clearly in my head, and no doubt in Zade and Vrae's too.

I choked. "Come again?"

"I don't know if this means he did it. The Veil didn't exactly make it clear either. It just said that this unholy was at D'arksin around the same time those Arcs died. Now, they certainly didn't go and die by themselves, so we could safely conclude that this unknown unholy offed them. But if that's so, would he still be alive? The deal . . ." He couldn't bring himself to finish the sentence, for he knew what it meant.

I swallowed and shook my head in denial. *"No, that doesn't mean anything. If it was indeed him, I'm sure he knew what he was doing,"* I said fiercely.

Vrae and Zade concurred. *"You're right. He wouldn't be so reckless as to let himself be whacked by the deal just because those three announced that he was still alive,"* Vrae said nervously as she gave me a wary stare.

I expelled a tired breath. "Fine, leave that stressful issue aside. I think we'd better go to Cain right now."

All of them turned to me.

Vrae raised her brow. "Why is that?"

I cleared my throat. "I heard something from Zabaniah."

*   *   *

Ezryan winced at a name he was more than familiar with. "Vassago, huh?"

Belphegor levelled a don't-even-ask stare at him. "If there's anyone who would know and who would be available at this obnoxious hour, as he would call it, well, it would be him."

Ezryan didn't dare to ask what those reasons were. If the North Prince before him said anything in a sharp tone, it was better to leave him be and not provoke him.

"But are you sure he's still around? I mean, from what I've heard, his name was written in that name list. What if the Valdam has already contained him?" Ezryan asked, casting a wary gaze at the prince.

Belphegor chuckled at his question. "Yeah, I've heard about that. He was said to have conjured every devil whose name was in that list and then contained them in a jar, right?" he asked rather dramatically.

Ezryan just looked at him with a blank expression.

Belphegor raked his hair with his fingers. "I'd really like to see his face if that human king really ever tried something like that, or more to the point, that Valdam of his. Boy, it's gotta be funny to look at him when he was piled up with the others in one jar staring out at us." He laughed at his own comment.

Ezryan just grinned and grimaced at the same time. "Really, get serious. The name list contains royals' names, commanders who keep most of us behind the line. Take them out of the game and we get mayhem among our own."

The prince just sat there looking calm. "And who's to say *our* mayhem won't affect the humans?"

Ezryan answered without hesitation as he smiled a bit, "Raphael would have to blow his horn ahead of schedule, especially if the Xarchons and the hellhounds go haywire."

Belphegor jerked his head as he grinned. "Exactly! So no worries, boy, Solomon knew that. He was making that list as a means to threaten us and at the same time guard his ring. I still don't have a clue about the entire name it contains, but what the hell, as long as we keep our distance, we won't get caught in the crossfire."

The young warrior sighed in relief. "Okay, so when is the best time for me to go see him?" Ezryan inclined his head.

Belphegor scowled. "'Me'? What do you mean by 'me'?"

Ezryan arched one brow in apparent confusion. "It means me. What, is there somebody else going along?"

Belphegor lifted his lips. "Yeah, me."

Ezryan snorted. "That's new! You wanna tag along and meet Vassago? I thought you never leave this place."

"I'm a loner, but who's to say I'm not allowed to have fun elsewhere with someone other than myself?" he snapped.

Ezryan raised his hands. "Okay, fair enough, but when?"

Belphegor stood up abruptly. "How about now?"

"Whoa, whoa, hold on a second here." Ezryan raised his hands.

Belphegor arched a brow. "What is it now? I thought you needed answers ASAP?"

Ezryan scoffed. "I do, but I need to go somewhere else to take care of a few things first, if you catch what I mean." He gave the prince a knowing look.

Belphegor burst out laughing. "Okay, just get back here right after you're done and please don't take too long, otherwise I might change my mind about taking you to that guy."

Ezryan nodded respectfully. "All right, thank you, Highness, I appreciate it. I'll be right back."

Belphegor sighed. "Okay, let's get out." The prince then escorted Ezryan to the main door of his castle.

Belphegor watched the former commander depart, and he closed the door.

The castle dissolved into nothingness as Ezryan flew across the sky towards where he last saw his beloved heading.

* * *

"Wait, Yve." Vrae stopped me before I could elaborate on anything regarding our plan to visit Cain.

I cast a puzzled look at her. "What is it?"

She grinned sheepishly. "Nothing, actually, my strength's starting to wane here. It's only two hours before dawn."

"So?"

"So, how about we really call it a night and get to Cain tomorrow? Besides, it will be too conspicuous if we were to be seen headed there right after the Echelons summoned us."

I considered her request and glanced at the other two. It was then I realized that I too was just as tired as she was. "All right, let's get outta here then." I turned to Amon, and we all said our goodbyes.

Once we had headed back outside, Vrae and I separated. She was going to her own sleeping spot—well, we weren't exactly sleeping together.

I felt it again, the feeling of someone watching, but something else pushed it away from my mind as I made my way up to the sky. I grew restless as Ry once again invaded my thoughts. An idea popped into my head, and I decided to go to where the Veil supposedly "saw" him for the first time.

The last place he'd been before he left us.

As I reached the dense clouds that were gathered above, I made up my mind. I stopped dead in the middle of the clouds and floated. After making sure that the clouds had me completely covered, I wrapped myself in a protective shield and summoned my doppelganger.

They were beings created by each of us using our creative powers. Usually, they were used to scout or to provide personal backup since we'd store our powers within them. Well, technically, those were the things we were allowed to use them for, not that anybody had the guts to use them for something else, like providing cover while the owner was off doing something else. All in all, creating them was one of many things we'd learned after stepping up to the Cherxanain rank. Any soldier who became powerful enough to reach that rank would be placed under the care of a devil who possessed the unique ability to adapt to the soldier's core ability and train her or him to harness and master new abilities.

These devils were called Kivarda. The reason why the would-be Cherxanain had to be trained was because each one of us had different core powers, which were basically everything that existed and burst to life the moment we stepped into the Cherxanain realm.

Some of us had absolute control over fire, while others could fully utilize water with ease. It was the same with everything else, wind, electricity, metal, sand, even mind-control like Farsanzi.

Still, there were a few who were considered an exception. Whereas lots of Cherxanains and Varkonians had the abilities I mentioned earlier, only a few had a firm grasp of particular elements.

In my case for instance, I commanded the darkness. Aside from the literal darkness which I'd accidentally unleashed when I almost lost my temper at Amon's den earlier and at Xaemorkahn's before then, I could bend the one within human souls and make them do my bidding, which was mostly violence.

Vrae, on the other hand, was one of the few who could manipulate living blood. She could make her enemies bleed just for the sheer fun of seeing them die from blood loss, or she could make sharp things out of the blood and use them to kill the owner. Sometimes she'd make the blood rush either to her enemies' beating hearts or brains and make them burst, or she would control the flow to alter her victims into whatever persona she wanted them to be–provocateurs, traitors, and such–whatever suited her as the Master of War.

But even rarer were those who had all the elements of the sky at their disposal. Most devils could only manipulate one element that dwelt in the sky, like water which transformed into clouds, rains, and hail, or electricity that could be turn into raging thunder. Some could command the air into a violent tornado or even manipulate the heat of the air to ignite fire, hell, everything. In the last thirty thousand years, there was only one who could bend all of these elements at will.

It was Ry.

Scoffing at my own thoughts about him, I exhaled as my doppelganger appeared and bowed slightly. "Shakra?" the doppelganger greeted.

I cringed a bit at her greeting. It was always weird looking at my doppelgangers, whose face and voice were my own, whenever they did that. It felt like I was calling myself master. Talk about a twist! I just hoped it wouldn't rub off on me, or my buddy Pride would pay me a visit which would involve him bitching at me.

Damn, I was glad these beings only got bits of my powers and appearance, not my personality, though if need be, they could impersonate me.

Shivering at the thought, I cleared my throat and put those ideas out of my mind. "Yeah, I need you to cover for me. I need to do something personal. Go up there and sleep."

Perplexed, she winced. "Sleep, Shakra?" she asked hesitantly.

I nodded. "That's what I was supposed to do here. Anyway, keep those eyes off of me," I said, without revealing anything more.

She gave me a salute. "I will, Shakra."

I nodded and scanned the dark sky once more as rain clouds started to gather. Luckily, Amon had put those eyes further away than ever. Plus, with the thick clouds forming, those eyes would be having difficulties detecting my doppelganger.

Directing my gaze to my place in the darkest part of the sky, I couldn't help but smile. I liked it up there. Despite the sun, that part of the sky would always be dark, which was in harmony with my own powers.

Besides, there was something about the solitude of darkness that kept my soul serene.

Inhaling deeply, I nodded at the doppelganger and flew back below the freezing clouds as lightning bolts began to blitz one after another while she went up there. Engulfed in a shield, I could feel those eyes stuck on my doppelganger as I put more distance from them.

Exhaling in relief, I headed straight for what still remained of the Great Lake of Bahyrdanam.

*   *   *

Ezryan stopped dead in his tracks, lifted his gaze to the darkened sky, and saw the one devil he held dear. She came through the clouds and headed to the north to the place where he'd set foot in this realm again.

His gaze showed how he was longing to meet her once more, to be with her. All this time, his memories of her were the most important thing that had kept him alive. He'd missed her lethal beauty, her sweet laughter, her dry wit, everything. But, most of all, it was her loyalty that he remembered the most.

As he stared sadly and yet felt more alive than ever, he braced himself and set out to meet her. Covering his presence with a protective shield, he took a lower altitude and flew to the very place she was.

＊　＊　＊

I dove straight to the small opening between the trees below as the rain started to fall.

Walking in silence towards the edge of the forest as my wings wrapped across my shoulder and my horns disappeared, I emerged moments later on the edge of a cliff.

The rain was pouring down hard on me as I scanned the massive valley and sucked my breath in awe. I still couldn't believe that these endless wastelands were once full of living beings occupying the massive lake that was had been bluer than the clearest sky.

Gulping, I felt unfathomable grief and guilt assail my soul. I inhaled deeply, and I let the tears that I kept for hundreds of years in mourning for the one I thought I'd lost roll down my cheek and be washed away by the cold rain.

"Ry," I whispered in a trembling voice into the night that was nearly ending. It drowned away in the sound of vicious gusts of wind and thunder. Would it carry my voice to him? Or was he truly here to begin with? If he was, where had he been and what was he doing all these centuries?

Just when those musings began to drown me, I suddenly felt a surge of power through the air. Lifting my gaze upward, I saw the rain abruptly cease and the clouds disperse really fast, revealing a clear dark night sky with the stars scattered all over it shining brightly.

Wincing at the abrupt sight, I frowned as I observed the valley, but I saw nothing. Perhaps it was all just my stupid imagination, wishing that it could be Ry. Perhaps it was just the time for the damned rain to stop.

Gritting my teeth as I fought back more tears, I inhaled deeply. "Ry, are you really here? How long do we have to wait for you to come back? Just how long do *I* have to wait?"

Just a heartbeat after those questions left my lips, I heard the one voice I thought I'd never hear again answer them.

"I don't want you to wait."

Gasping in total shock, I slowly turned around. There I saw an insanely gorgeous devil, whose face I'd been longing to see.

Ry.

He stood a few steps from me with a gentle smile I'd never before seen on him curving his perfect lips. "You don't usually stand in the middle of a storm like that." He inclined his head as he took a step forward. "How are you doing, Yve?" he asked in a surprisingly strained voice as though he was hesitating or something.

But–completely foolish of me–I could do nothing but stare. I was unable to say anything.

His brows knitted and his eyes gleamed in mischief. "What, didn't you miss me?"

I still didn't say a thing. I just stared at him, not believing he really was here before me.

He sighed and bit his lip. "What the hell!" He suddenly took several long steps towards me. I walked towards him as well without realizing what I was doing. My feet just brought me straight to him, and then we embraced in silence.

"I thought I'd never see you again," I said as I clenched my teeth and fists to hold the tears that already stung my eyes.

He gently ran his hand on my hair. "That makes the two of us. You've no idea how much I waited for this moment." His deep rich voice was filled with dead earnestness. It warmed me all the way to my soul.

After a moment that I wished to be eternity, we let each other go. "You're really here, aren't you? You're not going to disappear ever again?" I asked slowly with my eyes fixed at his deep sapphire ones.

He touched my cheek. "Yes, I'm here now. I won't be going anywhere."

I nodded in relief. That was when an unfathomable wave of annoyance assailed me. "How could you not tell us, not tell me that you're still alive? We had to know it from your brother!" I poked his armoured chest.

He smiled as he gently caught my hand. "So, you've met Xaemorkahn and Risha. And who's 'we'? Were you with Vrae when you met them?"

"Not just her. Zade went with us. Now Amon, Zoran, and Gevirash are in the loop as well. They know as much as we do, including our plan to go to Cain tomorrow night." I curled my lips.

He nodded. "Amon and those Valthors are okay in regards of what you guys know, but you can't tell anyone, not even Vrae, that you've met me. Not yet."

I cut a sideways glare at him. "I don't like it. You made her keep secrets and almost turned us against each other."

When he was about to open his mouth, I waved my hand in dismissal. "Yeah, as sucky as it sounds, I know you were doing that for our sakes. We can't tell who's eavesdropping on whom these days."

He closed his mouth, and a glint in his eyes told me he had more experience of this subject. That he did, maybe more than any of us could take. My chest clenched at that thought, but he pulled me away from it. He stared at me for a second before he shrugged. "Shoot."

"Well, I heard from one of your brother's people that Xaemorkahn gave you the ability to cross over."

He nodded. "Yeah, he did that. So?"

"So I wanna ask you this. Did you end up here when you just got back from wherever that was?" I indicated the place with a tilt of my head.

He paused at my remark. "The Veil really caught wind of me, huh?"

I screwed up my face at him. "Is that all you wanna say? The Veil really caught wind of me?" I turned my voice mockingly deep and quoted him. "Of course it caught wind of you. You know what that thing does."

He chuckled. "What do you want me to say? And by the way, did it only catch my presence, or is there something else?"

"You could say something else that's a whole lot more helpful, and yeah, there was another one, now that you've confirmed it. It caught your latest deed wasting those three rucksacks," I replied.

His brows knitted, and he cast me a baffled look. "What do you mean I've confirmed it?"

I smiled wickedly at him and moved my forefinger from side to side. "Nu-uh, I'm the one asking the questions for now, hot shot. You have yet to give me any friggin' detail. You ganking them and still being able to walk begs for a really good explanation, buddy."

He snickered. "How do you want me to elaborate it to you? Hi, sweetheart, I'm home. Guess what, I ganked three Arcs today, isn't that cool? Is that what you wanna hear?" He flashed me a crooked grin.

Trying to ignore the heat that was creeping up my cheek at his playful endearment, I raised my brows. "Well, that sure is great, honey. Will you get an extra bonus on your payday?" I retorted sarcastically.

Laughing with his eyes bright in amusement, he winked at me. "Yeah, plus I got extra days off too."

I shook my head. "Gee, buddy, and here I thought you might have lost your touch in the sarcasm department."

"And risk getting a lame-ass label from you? Not a chance," he said with a wicked grin that made my blood rush.

Suppressing a laugh, I waved to end the banter. "Okay, all right, there are a couple more things, though."

"And they are?"

I narrowed my gaze at him. "How come you're still here?"

He raised a brow. "I hope you don't mean it as it sounds," he said teasingly.

I gave him an apologetic smile. "Look, Ry, I'm sorry. I'm thrilled beyond belief that you're alive and now standing in front of me, but even you can't deny that. Not with that deal, cowboy."

He nodded with a hint of smile. "And the other?"

"The thing you asked me earlier–why I said you confirmed it."

"You wanna tell me what you meant by that?"

"You wanna tell me why the Veil identified you as 'unknown unholy'?"

Grinning at me answering his question with my own, he inclined his head. "So I'm 'unknown unholy' now, eh?" he asked, making a quote sign in the air. "At least it didn't call me 'unidentified object that flies'."

I curled my lips at him. "You know, that would be funny if the devil in question was Pride or some poor bastard from another planet. You'd better start explaining it to me before I strangle you," I threatened playfully, surprising myself at how easy it was for me to return to the carefree state I was always in every time he was around, considering we hadn't met for seven hundred years.

For a second, I wanted to curse at my bluntness, but then I realized that it was because of him. I didn't want to admit it, but he always made me feel safe to be myself.

He winced, and the strangest look of surprise blended with longing appeared on his darkly handsome face. "All right, all right, I'll explain it to you. After all, both are related," he said, and he stared at me. Weirdly enough, he chuckled.

"What is it?" I asked.

He shook his head. "Nothing, it's just that it's been a while since the last time I received one of your threats, and damn, I missed it. It's good to be back."

His words succeeded in bringing a wide smile from me, though I wasn't sure what he really meant by missing my threats. Perhaps because he had been all by himself out there, and that terrifying thought made my stomach clench.

I knew the feeling of utter loneliness that came crushing like walls all too well.

"It is indeed good to have you back, Ry, but you have to explain," I said in low voice, half apologizing for my insensitive-like-a-brick-wall demeanour.

He cleared his throat. "Well, the deal says we can't gank any Arcs unless it's an open war. Thing is, you guys are bound to it, and the Echelons watch your every move through Amon's golems. With that said, from where I'm standing, *you're* not allowed. As for me, they thought I was dead, so dead people can't exactly be bound to any crappy deal, now can they? Not to mention that when he attacked me, he'd somehow set me free from his stupid deal. I bet he never saw that one coming. I think that's why the Veil identified me as unknown unholy," he remarked calmly, but I caught a hint of anguish in his voice.

It was the same anguish that I too felt, the only thing that immediately rode herd on me whenever I thought about him.

Not wanting to bring that particular subject up, I forced myself to grin at him. "Yeah, you have a point. All in all, you're still alive. And after what I've heard from your brother and Amon, not to mention everything we know all this time about him, I really don't know if I want to be considered as his warrior any more." I lowered my gaze.

He touched my chin and lifted my head. His sapphire-coloured eyes cast a sad yet gentle look at me. We stared at each other for a moment. "So, Amon knew I was around even before the Veil?" he asked quietly.

I averted my gaze nervously. "Uh, yeah. He'd secretly kept your golem all this time and suspected that you were still alive, because it wasn't destroyed like it was supposed to. He showed it to us after we told him about our encounter with Xaemorkahn, Varisha, and their people."

"Well, I'd expect no less from his golem and himself," he said.

"Right, but what I don't understand is why Lucifer waited that long just to attack you? Not that I wanted him to do so a whole lot earlier than he did, but from what I heard from your brother, I'd bet he realized who saved his would-be victim. So what's the deal? He didn't want to attack you in the open, so he made those Echelons give you that order so he could kill you?" I asked with venom in the last five words.

He shook his head slightly, and his hair fell over his gorgeous face. "You never cease to amaze me, you know. Your guess is right as usual. He said he'd been waiting for that chance. He couldn't risk letting the soldiers know. He told me he had to keep them in line," he said matter-of-factly.

Sighing heavily, he forced himself to smile at me. "What if we save that kind of talk for later? You look tired," he whispered.

Something I'd never felt before began to inflame my blood. He'd never had that tender look on him before or talked with such a gentle voice. He'd always had this playful air around me, and full of sarcasm too. In the battlefield, "forever craving for a good blood bath" would be the perfect words to describe him.

Thinking it might just be me being delusional because my powers were waning, I arched a brow at him. "Whatever, I am a bit tired. Your showing up here threw my fatigue out of the window, though."

He scoffed and smiled patiently, but he didn't say anything. For a moment we were both locked in the steel of silence.

I intended to break the ice, but he beat me there. "What were you doing up there?"

"Up where?"

He gave me a droll stare. "Up there. Too damn near upstairs for my tastes. What, were you looking to do some stunt? From what I know, that is where you usually go if you wanna sleep, My Loner Queen." He spread both hands, indicating the place.

I rolled my eyes, but his playful endearment once again made my blood rush with heat for who knew what reasons. "Gee, you think I wanna do that ever . . . ever since . . ." I swallowed the rising pain, but still, I couldn't finish the damn sentence. I cleared my throat and forced a grin. "Never mind. The point is that I'm not looking for stunts. Well, maybe I'm just in the mood for taunting upstairs' citizens. It would be fun if they bite the bait."

"Yve . . ."

I glared at him. Well, I might be in love with him, but that didn't mean I would shed any damn tears in front of him, especially if he only viewed me as a comrade. Even if I longed for him, there was no way I'd do that. People didn't call me Queen of Tyranny because I tended to cry like a friggin' fool. "What?" I asked. My voice was thick with warning.

Instead of saying a damn thing, he just fixed his gazed at me with his lips still curved in that patient smile.

To my surprise, I felt his aura soften but radiate with supreme happiness.

Thinking that was another one of my inane imaginings, I let out a tired breath. "Ry, cut me some slack here. As if you don't know the things I'd do to piss those people off. And would you quit staring? Say something," I said, almost begging him before I couldn't stop myself from breaking into wrenching sobs like a damned weakling.

He started to open his mouth, but to my confusion, he shut it again. Abruptly, he braced himself. "What the hell," was all he said again, and to my utter disbelief, he did something I'd never expect in a lifetime.

He came closer and pulled me into another tight embrace that felt a whole lot different than before. It felt like . . . well, it might be an outrageous thing to say about him, but it felt like he longed to have me in his arms.

"Ry?" I asked nervously as I tried with all my might to ignore the heat of desire that threatened to overcome me.

"I'm so sorry for everything," he whispered in an agonized voice. His pain was a whole lot more tangible than before.

Flustered by his misplaced apology, I carefully placed my hands on his back. "Why are you apologizing? You did nothing wrong to me."

He shook his head as though he was adamant that he really had done something wrong. "Leaving you was the hardest thing I've ever had to do in all my life, but had I stayed or returned earlier with that bastard still out for my head, it would have put your life at risk, and I couldn't do that either. I never could, not if it meant I'd endanger you." He kept his strained voice low, but I could feel his mounting anguish in every syllable.

Gulping with my blood racing in my veins, I unconsciously held my breath. *"What is he trying to say?"* I wondered uncertainly. I felt his hand leave my back, and to my surprise, he gently placed it on the back of my head. "Ry, why are you telling me this?"

He pulled back and directed an intense stare at me that penetrated deep into my soul. "I should've had the guts to beat down my ego, to beat down the thought that I might risk disrupting what we had as comrades. I should've kicked all that aside and said what I wanted to say to you a long time ago. I should've been honest with you, for you are the only one who holds my full faith, and you've placed yours in me this whole time. I owe you that much, and I'm truly sorry for that. I'm so sorry that I needed a real kick in the ass just to make me realize it."

My core hammered so hard I was afraid I'd burst.

He tucked my hands into his and brought them up. "Forgive me that it took seven hundred years for me to say that I love you more than my own damned life, Yverna Tyraviafonza, the Queen of Tyranny, the one who holds my very soul within her grasp."

*   *   *

Belphegor stopped dead at the middle of the grand stairwell of his castle when he felt a familiar presence right outside. He had met its owner just before Ezryan had come to him.

"Your Highness Prince Belphegor," his guest's hollow voice echoed in the main hall.

The North Prince willed himself outside his castle and found the newcomer kneeling before him. Gesturing to his guest to stand up, he inclined his head. "Bynethar, what news do you have for me?"

The Echelon member stood up and sauntered closer towards the North Prince. "Your suspicions and Prince Vassago's seem to be true. The other Echelons are closing in on them. Even Kathiera and Faemirad are in on this." His deep voice was devoid of emotions.

Belphegor nodded. "Is Xamian taking care of the matters we discussed?"

"He is, Highness."

"I see. Well, after this, I want both of you to do whatever it takes to make sure the others don't get wind of whatever it is the Veil or those golems might reveal. And do it undetected. Amon will, without a doubt, take precautions about that particular matter, but not even he could hide the Veil from Kathiera's scrutinizing eyes."

"We will, but to tell you the truth, I still can't believe that Kathiera and Faemirad would do this just to get back at those sisters." A hint of resentment was evident in Bynethar's voice.

Belphegor let out a sinister laugh. "They've never liked Tyraviafonza and Wartiavega, not to mention Ezryan. What my cursed father did to him was to their benefit."

Bynethar's lips curved into a smile at the mention of his and Xamian's most reliable soldiers. "Yes, Tyraviafonza always has the knack of jerking Kathiera's chain, just as her sister can jerk Faemirad's, but I still couldn't believe that would make the two of them agree to something like this."

"Well, jerking the chain of jealous women in politics would definitely be reason enough, especially when they have too much of Pride and Envy in them. Though why they have too much of their shit is beyond me. Well, at least they don't start acting like Lust, otherwise I really would have to bang their heads on the wall," the prince said nonchalantly.

Bynethar had to bite his lip to keep himself from laughing. "That is certainly reason enough, no matter how trivial it sounds. And there is one more thing, Highness."

"What is it?"

Bynethar gulped with evident trepidation. He wasn't even sure if he could ask the question and get out in one piece. Bracing himself, he firmed his gesture. "Uh, it's about Ezryan."

As he expected, the swirling crimson of the prince's eyes spread as the monstrous aura emanated from him. Bynethar carefully inched away as he waited for Belphegor's response. Several heartbeats later, Belphegor calmed down, and his eyes went back to normal. "What about him?"

"Now that he's back, does he know about what Xamian and I are doing?"

The prince shook his head. "He doesn't even know that you two are in on this, and neither do the sisters. Maybe they will when the time comes. Right now, the only thing you have to worry about is the one I asked of you," he said.

Bynethar gulped again. "Will the sisters be all right with Lord . . ." The prince shot him a murderous look, making him quickly rephrase his question before he got gutted just for good measure. "I mean, the others could go to him . . ."

"Look, Bynethar, I appreciate that you give a damn about them, but if you really wanna do something about it, then let me ask you to do this. Protect them while they're at the Aryad, but try to be inconspicuous. If they're out here, they will be my responsibility."

Bynethar nodded with a whole new respect for the prince. "I understand. Now I shall take my leave." He started to withdraw, but Belphegor stopped him.

"Wait."

"What is it, Highness?"

Belphegor eyed him for a moment. "Are you sure you and Xamian wanna go through with this?" he asked quietly.

Bynethar's jaw ticked, and a vein stood out on his forehead as his stoic face contorted with evident rage. "Forgive me, Highness, but as I said to you, my allegiance left them and the Lord the moment they betrayed Laviett. They've all overestimated me, thinking I wouldn't take things too personally and that's where they were totally wrong."

Belphegor inclined his head in respect. "No, they *underestimated* you and Xamian if they think you two would forget about her."

Bynethar nodded subtly. "Thank you. What matters is that Xamian and I took an oath to avenge her and protect the others, which is why we turned our allegiance to you, Highness, something we should've done a long time ago."

Belphegor shrugged. "I don't blame you. I'm not exactly the Royalty of the Year type, more like the last-person-you-should-ever-talk-to type."

Bynethar let out a small laugh. "With all due respect, Highness, you are that type, for a good reason that is," he said.

Despite Bynethar's retort, Belphegor could hear the anguish in his voice. "Look, I know I said this to you four thousand years ago, but again, I'm really sorry for what happened to Laviett. She didn't deserve that."

Sighing, Bynethar averted his gaze to the ground to suppress the pain that was rising in his chest. Inhaling, he lifted his head. "Thank you, Highness. What's important now is to set things straight," he said, and then bowed a bit. "I will do as you ask."

"Good, now go." Belphegor dismissed him, and the Echelon member walked into the depth of the forest and disappeared.

Moments after he left, Belphegor still stood there with his eyes fixed on where the devil had gone. Bynethar sure had his eyes set on his course that was headed a really serious payback. He would too if his comrades had used his mate or his sister as bait to be gutted by the Arcs.

Above all, they did it by the order of their Supreme Leader, Lucifer.

Belphegor raked his hair. "Thank Hell I've never had either mate or sister," he said bitterly. "I absolutely want to choke that stupid bastard to death and then some." Belphegor cursed under his breath, and then he disappeared into his castle.

*   *   *

Those heartfelt words came out of his mouth with a conviction I'd never heard from him. It successfully shattered what was left of my defences, but still I forced myself not to cry. "You know, you could make any she-devil kill herself with an overload of happiness," I remarked with a nervous chuckle, barely keeping my tears from falling. But that had proven to be futile under his gentle, unwavering gaze.

My mouth opened, and I couldn't stop trembling as tears finally rolled down my cheek. "I . . . have . . . waited . . . for those words . . . for . . . far too long. I'm so sorry I've burdened you with so much grief." I stuttered the words and buried my face in my hands.

He slowly lifted my hands and tenderly wiped my tears away. His loving smile got even wider. "With that, you just made me the happiest son of a bitch that ever existed," he grinned.

A chuckle escaped my mouth. "You are so *not* a son of a bitch." I feigned annoyance and let out a scoffing laugh.

Once again we were locked in a tight embrace. He sighed contentedly as he ran his hand down my hair, and then he pulled back, eyeing my entire face. "I love you. That's all I know right now. That's all I've known ever since the first time I saw you, saw your smile, and heard your voice. Hell, I'll say it again and again until I drive you crazy," he remarked with a laugh.

"How, Mr Hieldhar, would I be crazy if you wanted to repeatedly tell me the very thing I longed to hear from you?" I retorted.

His rich laughter filled my ears. "That's what I wanted to hear," he said as he leaned his forehead against mine. As if savouring the skin contact, he closed his eyes and inhaled my scent, while I bathed myself in his masculine one. Very slowly, he opened his eyes and sealed my lips with his.

He rained down deep sweet scorching kisses on me as he tenderly scooped me in his arms and brought me to lie under the tree. Before I knew it, he was all over me. I didn't even realize at what point we removed our armour and left our bodies bare with nothing but our wings-turned-robes over them.

I should've burst into flame from shame for being this melancholy, or at least I should've shoved him away, for I'd never let myself be this close with anyone. All my life, I trusted almost nobody to stand at my back. I had certainly never lowered my defences this way, and for the most part I had taken, well, pride in that.

But with him, somehow, I didn't mind it in the least.

Now he'd stripped himself, and I wasn't talking about his present state, which was glorious. No, it was rather the deepest part of his heart, the side of him he'd never shown anyone else. Under his gentle eyes, I realized I could learn to be vulnerable around him. It was the least I could do, and I had to say, it was an absolutely nice change of pace.

Pulling back, he touched my cheek as he levelled an intense gaze at me. Very slowly, he nuzzled into me. "I've missed you," he whispered.

I looked up and smiled at him. "And I you," I replied.

He returned my smile with his own, but he looked so strangely weary, as if he were carrying the weight of the world all by himself. Lifting one hand, I reached for his cheek. His skin was so warm under mine. I motioned to whisper in his ear. "Why don't you rest for a bit?" I asked and moved back to gaze upon his flawless face.

Startled, he just winced and let me bring him down to my lap. Ignoring the heat that was creeping up my face at the thought of those thin black silk robes that were the only thing covering my body from his, I placed my hand on his forehead.

"You really haven't changed a bit. Always looking after me," he said dreamily with his eyes closed, as if savouring my touch.

"You do look like you could use some sleep after traveling through the dimensions and all that," I said in low voice.

He opened his sapphire eyes and looked up to me. Reaching up, he placed his fingers on my cheek. When I thought he'd stop there, he went downward and hesitantly tucked back my robes a bit. He then started to trail his fingers on my throat and onto my shoulder blade, giving me shivers at the contact. He stopped, as if waiting to see whether I'd give some kind of rejection. When I didn't even stiffen under his gentle touch, he trailed off from there to the valley between my breasts and all the way to my navel.

I gulped and tried not to move or avert my eyes. He had this look in his eyes as if he were curious and yet at the same time as if he were afraid he'd hurt me. Before I knew what his next intention was, he replaced his fingers on my navel with his lips.

He kissed his way up and sealed my parted mouth in mounting passion. I lifted my hands and grabbed his hair as we were locked in a senseless embrace.

"I thought I told you to rest?" I purred.

He grinned. "I am resting," he said, and he invaded my lips again.

It was then his robes fell aside, revealing one big blackened scar on his right chest. Gasping at the sight, I touched it. "Ry, is this . . . ?"

His hand captured mine, and his face went blank. "It's nothing," he said reluctantly as he covered the nasty-looking scar with his robes and moved away.

I grabbed his robes and re-exposed it. As they fell open, I saw that the same scar was on his back. Whatever our master stabbed him with went all the way through, and that thought made my gut twist as if the pain were my own.

He tucked his robes back on, but I caught it. "Don't you dare tell me it's nothing. It was him, wasn't it? *He* did this?" I pressed with an obvious hint in my voice as to who 'he' was.

Our master, Lucifer.

He finally conceded with a subtle nod. "Yes. The scar won't heal because he stabbed me right where the Flame burnt me the worst, and then he added his damned Rygavon on top of it. Nothing really. It's okay," he said soothingly.

Icy rage engulfed me at the sight. "I am gonna *gut* him so dead." I gritted my teeth.

He gave me a sad smile. "Why don't we forget about him for a second? I don't wanna let him ruin this moment," he whispered.

Raising one hand, he tenderly trailed his fingers on the side of my face. It still amazed me that he would treat me as if I were the most precious thing to him. It was as if he were afraid that I would break, which was a bit silly considering the fact that I had pretty much the same level of savageness as he did.

His hand left my face and gently took mine. Our fingers entwined, he brought my hand to his lips and kissed my knuckles. "I have so much to tell you, I don't know where to start," he said with a faint laugh.

I smiled. "You know you could always talk to me about everything, right? I told you that a long time ago."

He chuckled. "I know. Honestly, I'd rather do something else," he said with a wicked look that burned my blood. But it wasn't in me to just welcome anyone into my body on a whim, even I it was the only one whom I'd ever loved.

Despite everything I felt, including the overwhelming need to soothe him, this was our first time together again. As crazy as it sounded, I needed time to adapt to him as my mate, and knowing him, so should he need time.

We needed to adjust before we moved to the next level.

"Ry," I started, but his long fingers covered my lips. "I know. I was just teasing you. You think I don't know you well enough to know what you feel right now?" he asked gently.

A tidal wave of guilt assailed me. Yeah, he did know me enough, and I could feel that he was restraining himself like hell, but I still couldn't bring myself to do it. Damning myself, I forced a smile. "No, you know me that well. I'm sorry," I said apologetically.

"What for? You're here with me, and that's more important than everything. Well, I'll just go back to catching up on the things I mentioned earlier. I *can* talk to you, right?" He grinned at me, as he trailed his fingers on the side of my face.

I chuckled. "Yeah, nothing'll change. You talked to me from time to time back then, and to Vrae as well. Sometimes, you even made me think you guys had something going on," I said teasingly.

He kissed my forehead. "Nu-uh, she and I are just comrades, nothing more."

I nodded. "Okay, but now you talk to me if anything bothers you," I said as I levelled my gaze at his deep sapphire eyes.

"I will, but regarding Vrae, before you develop some wrong idea about what was going on back then between me and her, I think you should know something about our conversations," he said, half reluctantly, and half . . . suppressing his laughter.

I frowned at him. "What is it?"

He cleared his throat. "The only one whom I've ever told *willingly* about every single thing that bothers me on a personal level was you, and that's never gonna change," he said earnestly. "But, I did talk to her about one personal matter, just one." His lips formed a sheepish grin.

"And that is?"

"How to get you interested with me," he said with glee.

That succeeded in making me speechless for a split second. "No way. You're kidding," I replied with disbelief.

He shook his head with his lips curved in a wide teasing smile. "When it comes to you, I have no sense of humour whatsoever, sweetheart. Well, when I talk to you, then yes, but matters about you, those are dead serious for me."

"But she'd never told me anything. Wait a minute." I narrowed my eyes at him, and he pretended to look at something else that caught his attention, all the while trying futilely to suppress his wide grin. "No wonder we'd often run into you in weird remote places when we weren't on jobs, and then she'd hightail it out of there, saying she forgot something or whatever."

"And as you recall, in those times I'd tell you things I'd never tell anyone else. Hell, I'd even take you to the royals," he added.

He lost me for a moment, and then I covered my mouth as his words sank in. "Oh, no. I'm so sorry for being that clueless. That was so stupidly insensitive of me. I thought you just needed someone to talk to, because we know the circle of people we can trust is tighter the higher our place is on the chain of command. I had no idea. I'm sorry."

Laughing as he brought our entwined hands to his chest, he shook his head. "No need, I know you, and clueless or insensitive are a far cry from who you are. On the contrary, you know me so well, you would do anything to help and protect me, especially when it comes to the head games those higher-ups always try to pull. Being overly experienced in that area, you just couldn't keep yourself from helping me. Not just me, you do that to all of us. And I love that about you—the Queen of Tyranny who preys on the darkest side of humans and turns their loyalty against each other, and yet only few could challenge the depth of her loyalty towards her own," he said with obvious admiration in his voice.

My face went totally red at his words. "You're exaggerating, buddy. I'm not like that."

"And like everything else I love about you, you always refuse to take that particular credit," he inserted.

I scoffed. "That's because mortal members of the loyalty club are my playthings, and I throw them into the head-case department on a daily basis. And with Pride's weird tendency to bitch at me for reasons only he knows, do you really think I would ever take credit outside the things that are my job? Don't count on it. I'd never stoop that low, and I don't worship Lilith either. Not that I think I do all those things you said earlier, but thanks. Means a lot to me, especially coming from you, who, as we all know, do all of those things. You took care of us all those millennia ago. Now it's time for us to take care of you. It's time for *me* to take care of you, *capisce*?"

He nodded and smiled at me. "I get it. Thanks a lot, sweetheart."

I shrugged. "No problem."

"You know," he said as he cleared his throat. "If Pride's bitching always has this kind of effect, I might shake his hand," he said with a laugh.

I poked his chest. "Not funny, buddy. On that note, I might give his playmate a call," I shot back meaningfully.

"What do you mean?"

Giving him a wicked smile, I snuggled into him. "You forgot about your bad run-in with Slut every now and then?"

He actually laughed at me turning the name of one of Pride's siblings, Lust, into "Slut". "And I see you still call her that."

"A whole lot easier and fitting than 'Lust' in my opinion." I shrugged nonchalantly.

He chuckled. "Yeah, I remember. She always tried to throw herself at me. Well, she's an extremely minor part of why I stick with you. But just like you, Pride's attitude perhaps was one of the reasons why I couldn't admit it sooner."

"Yeah, that goes for both of us. I'm sorry for that too," I said apologetically.

Abruptly, he landed a quick kiss on my lips. "Okay, apology hour's over."

Sighing contentedly, I lifted my head and brought my face closer to his. "Yeah, let's just catch up and talk about other things."

"I couldn't agree more. We have a lot to talk about," he said, and he began kissing me again. We were locked in long deep passionate kisses, and then before I knew it, we started to talk and banter again.

We lost track of time until finally he tucked me within his arms, and we lay there in silence with his hand absently running over the top of my head.

"I'm glad that I could finally be with you," he whispered.

I just replied him with a subtle nod. I didn't know when exactly, but because of the daybreak, my powers waned enough to bring me down under. I fell asleep, huddled with him, without having human nightmares for the first time in centuries.

*   *   *

Amon was eyeing the scroll given to him by the alchemists outside. He had them spread out in front of him, while several others were scattered on his desk. Suddenly he felt the enchantments on his door lifted at once.

He snapped his fingers and those scrolls vanished as he stood up, right as Kathiera walked inside. "Uh, welcome, Ravathe. Is there anything I can help you with?"

Kathiera made a swiping movement, and the door was shut closed. "Save it, Iverand," she said curtly. "I want to know what exactly those three told you."

Amon feigned an innocent look as best as he could. "I beg your pardon, but which three are we talking about here, because there were several other people from *three* different divisions who just left here in the last hour alone?"

Her palm landed hard on his desk, making him jump. "You don't want to test me when I'm in this mood, Iverand. So again, what did they tell you? More to the point, did either Tyraviafonza or Wartiavega say anything of an importance? Anything that might have had a connection with Cain's prophecy?"

Amon inwardly cursed. Well, Vrathien *did* tell him something significant that definitely had a connection with that prophecy, but he was the one who told them Cain had blurted it out to begin with. *"No way am I telling you that, you bitch."*

"No, I just asked them to look for those missing soldiers. I realized that I had crossed the line when I did that while I'd received direct orders not to," he said slowly.

"You got that right," she interjected.

"But," he politely ignored her, "I've considered every possibility, and I figured the sisters were my best options. The Varkonian whom they requested was a good decision on their part as well. They found the soldiers immediately after they left the Aryad, while the

221

Alvadors who wound up being the victims couldn't find them after a week. Their golems didn't catch anything, and the Veil wasn't clear either, so I did what I had to before another unit went missing," he explained.

She stared at him for few moments, making him grow nervous, since there was another thing the Veil showed him, and it was perhaps the deadliest information the damned thing had given him in the last seven hundred years, one that, if he handled it in the wrong way, could cause several heads to roll.

Including his own.

"Speaking of the Veil, did it show you when the Arcs died?"

He nodded. "Yes, it did."

Her eyes narrowed dangerously at him. "It told you who did it?"

"No, it didn't. It just stated the same thing as when our soldiers died—unknown peril, D'arksin—and I know you're aware of the fact that the three couldn't have done it since they're still alive. There was no way they could've breached the vow of our Lord."

Her lips twitched. "You don't know that. They may know someone who could, and that's what I'm going to find out."

Those words were like knives buried straight to his gut. "Pardon my impudence, but there's no way a soldier could escape from that vow, Ravathe."

"That is for me to decide. You wait for my command. If things get worse, I may have them shadowed or even brought in for, shall I say, *further* questioning," she said, and an evil smile broke wider.

Amon gulped. "That is your privilege indeed."

"Just hope that you don't have anything to do with it, Iverand," she said, turning on her heels. She jerked her hand, and the door pushed roughly inward. Without even giving the Iverand another look, she walked out and slammed the door behind her, leaving Amon blanched with terror.

∗   ∗   ∗

It was a couple hours after nightfall when Ry woke me up with a gentle touch on my cheek. Damn, I'd never seen this side of him back then. Hell, maybe I was just too damned blind to see it.

He already wore his armour. "Yve, I have to go now."

I grabbed his hand. "What? I haven't even told you anything important yet." Because *he* was busy asking me a lot of things unimportant . . .

He smiled. "I'll see you again. The night you return from meeting Cain, I'll meet you here," he promised.

I fell silent and then nodded subtly. He cast a gentle look at me before giving me the sweetest kiss beyond my imagination. I'd be well over the edge had I not fought it. Reluctantly, he pulled back and carefully touched my cheek again. He slowly lifted his hand and stepped backwards.

A thought occurred to me and I caught his hand. "Before you go," I said with his hand in my grasp. "Do you know about Cain's prophecy?"

He nodded subtly. "It was about time for him to do so. And I figured that's how you know Vrae's been keeping secrets, because she felt the time has come to tell you."

My silence confirmed his words.

"Right, and so now you're going to Cain to take what I left him with?"

I curled my lips. "Yeah, and I thought you would say something more than that."

He flashed his dazzling smile at me. "I'll tell you later, after I know more."

"Okay, but where are you going anyway? Don't tell me you're going back to your brother now?" I asked with a frown.

Giving me one-sided grin with a totally wicked look that made my blood almost burst in my veins, he shook his head. "'Course not. I'm planning to meet him with you guys. I have an appointment with Belphegor. He's gonna take me to Vassago. We're looking into those slaughters."

I gaped. "You met Belphegor?"

He nodded. "Yeah, the dude already knew I was alive, and I think Vassago knew about that too. I know that Belphegor planted whatever that is to keep tabs on me, but I'm not sure about Vassago. Hell, perhaps all their drinking buddies knew about me being back in town–I've no clue how."

I shook my head in disbelief. "I can't say anything about the others, but those two are always full of surprises." Sighing, I then forced myself to look at him. "Say hi to them for me," I said quietly.

He nodded. "Will do, baby," he said with a bright gentle smile that ignited my own.

Under his bright eyes and warm smile, I had never thought I would see this day come to pass, the day where he'd embrace me in his arms and accept me for who I was.

Hell, I'd never thought I'd hear him saying that he longed for me.

Me, a callous and too damned full of–pardon the pun–pride bitch who used people's loyalty to their own kind as a plaything. I ripped them apart and bathed in their entrails. Hell, I'd dance with their screams for mercy as music. Even though that was what I was trained to do and was ordered to do, it was still an act I did with relish every damned day.

For it was also my damnedest nature. As I told him, those things were my job, and I didn't know when it started, but during the twenty-five thousand years I had been a Cherxanain, there wasn't a day went by that I didn't revel in the sound of my victims' roars of despair as they realized what they'd done.

But, after seven centuries of missing him, knowing full well his capability for both violence and loyalty to us, it made me think that he deserved another devil but me.

Hell, I'd spent too long playing with those humans. I'd even started to question my own loyalty from time to time.

To hear him saying those things earlier clawed me deeply, for I felt exactly the way he did. Him saying those words meant the whole world and beyond to me.

Looking back at what I did earlier, trying to pull myself together purely because I couldn't get past my stupid ego, I couldn't help thinking I might as well kill myself. He'd been torturing himself for far too long and I still patronized him for it.

In all honesty, I'd wondered why he didn't at least slap me.

Hell, maybe it was just like he said. We both needed a long time of grief and loss just to see how much we meant to each other, to finally get past the stupid thought of "what if the other's not that into me, and I'd totally be ashamed if that happened."

Suddenly, I felt a pair of warm hands on my cheeks, pulling me back to earth. "Baby, you all right?" he asked, his deep voice filled with concern.

Warmth spread through me at his endearment, which wasn't part of his usual playful banter. "Yeah, I'm all right," I said.

"What is it?"

Gulping, I firmed my mouth and changed my mind. I had already told him how sorry I was for not being honest with him and myself, but I still couldn't help feeling that I had to make it up to him somehow. He was out there by himself while I was here, regretting and bitching that he'd gone.

Still, I shouldn't talk about this now. He had more pressing matters to take care of, and even if I wanted to be with him as long as I could, I couldn't keep him much longer.

"No, it's nothing. I guess we'll talk later," I said, mustering a faint smile. I'd bet I ended up looking like I had stomach-ache.

He reluctantly gave me a nod and started to turn his heels.

"Ry?"

He came to a stop and quickly turned to me. "Yeah, what is it?"

"Be careful, and promise me you'll come back, okay?" I looked straight into his eyes.

He sauntered towards me and gently tucked a lock of my hair behind my ear. "You too. And don't worry. I will. There's so much I need to tell you. No matter what, nothing'll stop me from seeing you again."

He kissed me for one last time. Pulling back, he made a little swiping move in front of my face, and I felt something engulf me. "What was that?"

"Can't have you move around with my scent just yet, can we?" he winked.

I winced. "Well, thanks. That one almost escaped me," I said with relief. Yeah, if I really had that scent and somebody realized, the Echelons would be the least of my worries.

His wide grin faded to a faint longing smile. Abruptly, he stepped away, manifested his shield, and then flew through the thick canopy of the forest.

I gazed sadly at his direction. Shaking my head, I attempted to shove each and every sentimental thought from my mind.

It was a good thing I'd set my doppelganger up there for Amon's golem to stick with, and they couldn't see through protective shields either. Otherwise we would have been compromised.

As the night had fallen, I manifested my own devil armour and then I headed to the border of Croatoan. I looked for a safe spot and called my doppelganger.

Moments later, she landed before me. *"Shakra?"* she greeted.

I tilted my head at her. *"Hey, anything happen while I was gone?"*

"Nothing. The eyes kept floating around me. I did as you asked. I made them fix their attention only on me, Shakra."

"Great, thanks. I'm gonna pull you back."

She nodded. *"You're very welcome. Until next time, Shakra."*

I raised my hand and chanted the spell required to pull her back and slowly dissolved my shield at the same time. After I finished, I moved to block her as she faded into spirit form and went into me.

Releasing a deep breath, I glanced towards the sky and noticed that those eyes were up there. Ignoring them, I continued straight to the Gate where Gevirash and Zoran were standing. As I strolled through the forest, I couldn't help but smile happily as I kept saying the litany *"Ry's alive and he's come back to me!"* over and over in my head.

When I got near the Gate, I could see Vrae and Zade were already there.

"That sure is a weird place for you to show up," Vrae said, while the others nodded to me in greeting.

"Hi, Vrae, I'm good. Nice to see you too at this fine Gate. How are you?" I asked sardonically as I tilted my head to Zade and the guards in greeting. They all turned their laughs into a weird sound like a snort at my retort.

Vrae rolled her eyes. "You get a good sleep?"

I grinned. "Oh hell, yeah. You have no idea."

Vrae and Zade exchanged puzzled looks with their brows raised, which I ignored.

Her voice suddenly echoed in my head. *"You're in a good mood, no nightmares?"*

"Nope. And hell, it's so damn good not having stupid humans in my head for once."

Abruptly, Zade patted my shoulder. "You really didn't have those nightmares? At all?"

I looked at him and grinned as I shook my head. "Maybe I was too damned overloaded to even let those dreams get inside my head. What about you?"

He shook his head. "Nah, didn't get a chance to visit the friggin' dreamland. I got called not long after we split–Imirae wielders gathering."

I nodded. "I see. So we'd done everything in time."

He scoffed. "Yeah, tell me about it," he said, while the guards seemed to be in the middle of a heated discussion with Vrae.

They looked tense. I wondered why that was. "What's up?"

They turned their wary gaze towards me. "Haven't you heard? Those three Arcs were killed," Zoran said under his breath as if he'd just said a taboo word or something.

"Yeah, not just heard. The three of us were told about them." I jerked my head at Vrae and Zade. "What about it?"

Zoran swallowed. "Well, we heard two passers talking not long before you guys got here. They said there was a chance that you three would be taken in for that particular slaughter."

I glanced at Vrae, who confirmed his words. "Has Amon told you anything regarding that problem, like what exactly was on the report that was handed over to the Echelons?" I folded my arms.

"Yeah, he did. There's something not right with the damned report though. Apparently, in spite what the Veil had revealed, they weren't sure whether those guys really are dead, because there are no bodies. But from what he told me, they found something else that made me think we could be sure enough about those angels' whereabouts, and it ain't in the living realm. Not that I feel sad over their deaths or anything. Hell, I wanna laugh like crazy over their demise, and I know you do too," Vrae smirked.

I let out a snort. "You got that right."

Abruptly, she narrowed her gaze at me. "But this ain't funny. We could be the ones who get the credit here, 'cause they knew about our encounter with them."

I gave her a "duh" stare. "What? Did a rock hit your head and make you forget? Vrae, they told us about it, and hell, they confirmed it with us."

She didn't look amused, so I raised my hands. "Okay, just chill. Anyway, you don't have to worry. We're still bound to the One Million Deal Lucifer made. If we killed them in a three-on-three like we did . . ." I didn't finish my sentence and gave her a knowing look.

She caught my meaning, and she nodded. "We'd be toast by now. Yeah, you have a point, but still." She bit her lip nervously.

Zade and the guards looked worried as well.

I sighed. "By the way, you told me that Amon and the Echelons weren't sure of their deaths, so why in the hell should we worry over something that we're not even sure of? Hell, you told me there's no body."

Zade exhaled heavily. "Well, Amon told us what had happened out there up to the point those Arcs died, well, according to the Veil. Anyhow, seven other Levarchons were sent out to confirm our story that the Arcs did kill their pals. But instead, they ran into something else," he said in a theatrical tone.

I shot a questioning gaze at him. "And that is what? Those Arcs were actually dead of Avordaen poisoning? Damn, aren't they bunches of schmuck? So much for being Arc bastards, if they couldn't even get rid of our Avordaen."

Vrae scowled. "Would you be friggin' serious for a second? They weren't there, like we told you, no bodies . . ."

I cut her off. "Then tell me, why in the hell are you worried like the Echelons gonna kick your ass?"

She gave me a chiding stare in return. "Whatever, hear this. When those Levarchons arrived, they found their pals' remains."

"As expected, and?" I prompted. I had to know what exactly happen to those three.

Zade rubbed his eyebrow. "And they also found blood–*angels'* blood. I'm not talking about a small amount of blood splashed on two or three bushes. I'm talking about a lot of blood, so much that it flooded the area where we fought them. Trees were burnt to the ground, but those Arcs were nowhere to be found."

"So what? The Veil announced that they're dead. Maybe the guy who did them was the same as the guy who ganked those Machordaens and Alvadors. We have no clue as to what the guy looks like–yet."

Vrae curled her lips. "Unfortunately for you, this time the bastard wasn't involved, Mistress I-Like-Making-False-Conclusions. Aside from the fact it didn't fit the bastard's MO where we'd find its victims, those Levarchons checked. They found dark traces of Avordaen in the blood, and yeah, the blood burned them a bit in the process," she explained in a dead-pan tone and with a meaningful look in her eyes, as if saying, *"It's sounded more and more like Ry."*

She cleared her throat to prevent the others from getting suspicious. "Not just that, they also found several angel wings, which confirmed the Veil's sightings. Those bastards received mortal wounds with their fluffy out of the way . . ." she didn't finish her sentence.

I suppressed my nervousness and focused on finding a stupid retort instead, as I casually inclined my head. "They'd be playing chess with Azrael by now. That's cool. I wanna shake hands with whoever did it," I said with a grin.

Suddenly Vrae grabbed my shoulder.

"What the fuck?" I grabbed her hand.

"Tell me the truth. I could tell that somehow you know more, or at least you got an idea of who was behind this, and that couldn't have come from Amon," she growled.

Zade and the guards hurriedly tried to step between us. "Vrae, stop! Don't do this!"

She still didn't budge.

Gritting my teeth, I raked her with a seething glare. "I warn you, Vrae, let go off me," I said coldly as I strengthened my grasp on her wrist.

When she didn't say zap, a tic worked in my jaw. "Just what the fuck do you want me to tell you, huh? What? I invited those guys to play poker and have a drink, and then I poisoned their fucking Vodka?" I snarled.

Zoran snorted. Vrae shot a shut-your-mouth-before-you-get-my-hands-around-your-throat glare at him. He fell silent instantly.

"Tell me honestly. You can't throw horse shit at me and hope I won't notice. I've known you for far too long to be fooled like that. Tell me, I've blocked Zaderion and the others, so you fuckin' tell me now. I know you somehow got the intel about whoever did this. So,

tell me. Did. Ry. Really. Kill. Them?" She asked in my head and kept on glaring.

I paused at her question. Could I tell her?

"Dammit, answer me before I make you swear to tell me the damned truth! The Veil's implicating him and we're standing in the middle of it." She tightened her grip on me.

I took a deep breath and released it. *"You sure you've blocked them?"*

"Damn sure."

I closed my eyes tightly as I bit my lip. *"Ry, I'm so sorry."* I clenched my fists as I regretted what I was about to do.

Vexed, I curled my lips. *"Fine, yeah, it was him."*

Her eyes widened in disbelief. *"How do you know that for sure? Did he contact you?"*

I rolled my eyes. *"He himself told me that in front of my face! Are you happy now? Just don't tell anyone here. I'm not supposed to even tell you. He asked me to do so. Gee, you better give me more friggin' credit here. At least I told you right now and didn't wait for freakin' centuries to do it!"*

She looked as if she felt guilty at my comment, and then she grinned apologetically as she released her grasp on my shoulder and I released her wrist. *"I'm thrilled like hell, worried like hell too, but I'm good,"* she said. *"Now I know why you look so damned happy when you got here."*

"Don't tell them anything," I repeated as I glanced at the guards and Zade, who looked at each other, obviously confused.

Zade waved his hand in front of us. "Hello, girls, would you mind telling us what the hell did you two talk about?"

We exchanged looks with each other, and then Vrae turned to them. "Sorry boys, we'll tell you soon, but not now."

"Yeah, I can't tell you now and lose all the fun, now can I? Look, if we're lucky, the one who whacked 'em would come and say hi to us."

Zade and the guards looked disappointed, but they gave up. "Another friggin' secret! You gotta tell us soon, okay?" Zade feigned a pout.

I winked. "Deal." After that, we were caught up in a swift discussion about other minor things about the passers and where this Avarnakh guy had gone.

Vrae cast a meaningful gaze at me every now and then, which made me warn her. Dammit, she'd raise their curiosity if she went on with it.

At that time I wasn't aware that a shadow was watching us, watching *me* with a sad gaze.

*   *   *

Ezryan stood silently behind the trees as he watched over his old comrades.

He overheard them and was aware that he had almost compromised himself by killing the Arcs, but he couldn't risk them running into someone else and babbling out the fact he was still alive and had just met the North Prince. Still, he was grateful that those Arcs had run into his closest comrades.

He was also aware that Vrathien knew what he'd done, and he had no doubt that Yverna told her. Not that he blamed Yverna, because by the look on her face, her sister must've asked her to swear to tell her the truth or something. Otherwise, he knew that she'd rather be gutted than break her promise, and he wouldn't want anything close to that happen.

The former Hieldhar sighed, and before he took his leave, he cast a sad yet happy look at Yverna once more.

He was grateful to the marrow of his bone that he had the chance to be with her, really with her. He felt that he could never be more relieved than when he heard her saying she also loved him.

At that moment, he swore to do the very thing he had desired all those thousands of years ago.

To always protect her no matter what happen.

And when the time came, he would tell her and them what he knew and what danger was fixing its eyes on them in the shadow, waiting for the moment to strike and destroy them all.

He expelled a long breath, turned his head, and disappeared quietly into the depths of the woods.

*   *   *

I sensed it again. Something or someone was watching over me, like back there in the forest. But this time that feeling was accompanied by something that was far from anguish.

More like a crazed level of happiness.

I looked over my shoulder and stared at the trees. *"Ry, is that you?"*

"Yve, is he here?" Suddenly Vrae's voice popped into my head.

I cast a warning look at her. *"How should I know? I just felt something or somebody was watching. That's all, and don't ask that over and over again, all right?"*

Vrae raised her brow. *"Okay, whatever. Just asking."*

I rolled my eyes at her and turned to the males. "All right then, we gotta go now. See you boys later."

They nodded, and both Vrae and I left them outside.

As we walked, I glanced at my sister. "So Vrae, can we just go there, or do we need something to distract his guards? I mean, we can't guarantee there's no fool that won't try to eavesdrop."

Vrae folded one arm and held her chin with the other as she lowered her gaze and thought. Abruptly she looked at me. "I think it's the latter. Let's go."

I raised one brow. "What do you mean 'let's go'? We haven't planned anything."

Vrae just sauntered ahead. "We'll improvise."

I stopped her. "Vrae, stop!" She halted abruptly. "Come on! Stop dragging your ass!" she snapped.

"What's your problem? You suddenly go in a rush like this. What is it?" I shot back.

She suddenly turned and faced me, and weirdly enough, she grinned. *"You made out with the dead devil, didn't you?"*

Totally caught off guard, I blushed all over. *"What the hell? Is this the right time for that? And, duh, he's not dead."*

"It figures! So you did! I'd been wondering since way before he disappeared when exactly you two will be honest with each other."

I frowned. *"What do you mean? I felt nothing about him. We're just comrades. You know that. I thought you were the one who had a thing for him."*

"Nah, he is gorgeous, I give him that, but his nature isn't like me. He's more like you. And you know, I'd often wondered who'd break

the stalemate and tell the other, because back then when we were hanging out, I'd often caught you staring at him when he wasn't looking, and his eyes were stuck on you when you were busy with something else.

"I didn't do that!" I snapped. *"And I take it that's why you tried to hook me up with him?"* I asked, directing a chiding stare at her.

She grinned. *"He told you, didn't he?"*

I rolled my eyes. *"No, I wormed it out of him,"* I sent a mental jolt at her, which she gleefully blocked.

Heaving an exasperated sigh, I glared at her. *"By the way, how can you tell that I met him? I thought I got, well,* he *got everything covered,"* I said, ignoring her question.

She chuckled. *"You don't know? Gee, Yve, were you born yesterday?"* I frowned at her question. *"At first, it was a guess. You think I'd believe you guys wouldn't do anything once you got together?"*

I narrowed my eyes at her, and she just gave me a taunting grin.

"And then what?" I asked grudgingly. Well, I'd need to cover all the bases if I were to walk around inside with the Echelons' rats all over the place.

"Don't worry. Ry did a good job masking his scent on you. But, lucky for me, there are things that could never be masked from blood. I can tell from yours. It felt different. You could cover everything, but I still sense something different from the usual you."

"If that's true, that you could tell from my blood, then why did you force me to tell you that it was really him who killed them?"

She inclined her head with her lips curled. *"Duh! The fact that he was with you doesn't mean he really did it. For all I know, he was accidentally there when those Arcs were slaughtered. But all in all, he did a hell of a job covering his scent on you. When combined with the scent of the other guys earlier, I didn't even get a whiff of it at first. I just felt something was different with your blood. It was as if something so small and nearly untraceable ran through your veins, and yet it was all over you."*

"Something like what? Care to explain it?"

"Well, it's fortunate for me that living blood is my specialty. I could tell that it wasn't poison, only something foreign. Once we were in here, I could pick up his scent and traced it to whatever it

was in your blood, which turned out to be his 'feelings' branded on it, like it was protecting you."

I winced at her long explanation, and her last words made me warm with love for him. It'd always surprised me, though, that she could pick out emotional reactions merely from blood.

With her enemies, she'd used it to destroy them from every way possible. With me, it certainly didn't bode well, considering she loved to nag at the most impossible of times.

Like right now.

Rolling my eyes, I walked past her. *"Thanks for telling me that, but that ain't helping. Anyhow, come on Vrae, we don't have time for this."* She was still grinning at me, but then she started to walk. *"Okay, say hi to the guy when you meet him for me."*

After we'd done with that so unimportant talk, we walked down the fiery lane again. This time, towards Cain's place, and that was thousands of kilometres below, near the very core of the earth.

There were several tunnels that led to the underground. Each tunnel led to a certain level and ended on the level intended. After reaching the level, there was one hole leading out from the tunnel, and from there a path would lead to the ground on that level.

The tunnel we took was a tunnel that could be used only by people from our division. Special units like Machordaen or Levarchon used another tunnel. There was also a tunnel used by hell angels like Zabaniah. Echelons and other similar people used a secret tunnel only they knew about.

Vrae took a swan dive down the tunnel first, and then I followed her. It felt like hours as we just kept falling all the way underground. When we finally reached the bottom, Vrae stopped dead and landed right onto her feet.

I spread my wings and floated for a second, waiting for her to go outside. After she was out, I landed. My wings wrapped around my shoulders as I went outside as well.

This part of hell was a whole lot hotter, because the flame here was blue and not just some stupid magma. And yet, it was colder. It was silent here, because this place was where the great sinners of the human race were confined. Some of them like Cain even became useful to us.

We walked on for a minute and looked around. The torture here was more of a silent treatment, but from where I was standing, that was a whole lot worse, because you'd come to an existence where you wouldn't even know that you had ever been alive.

There were few of the things that made you come to realize who you were–probably physical tortures once in a while by the bored guards or something from your own past.

As for Cain, his guilt over slaying Abel and his hatred towards King Belial were the only things that reminded who he was. Even though the reason why he decided to help us devils was never clear, point was, he'd proven himself to be useful ever since we brought him in here.

We stopped a few meters from his place after minutes of walking. His guards were standing in front of his cell.

I glanced at my sister. "Vrae, if you have any idea or have improvised something, it's time to do it."

She folded her arms. "Well, we can always monkey with their brains."

I scoffed at that. "I thought we'd use something like jelly donuts."

She rolled her eyes. "That would work on humans about two or three millennia from now, Yve, not on them."

I rubbed my brow. "I know. I was just trying to joke with myself. So, how's it gonna be? What about the inmates?"

She scanned the surroundings, checking the guards. "Then we need to do it in a wider scope. It's time to go massive. Concentrate on everyone except Cain."

I chuckled. "It's been a while since I heard you use that term. Okay, on three," I said as both of us silently used our energy to freeze their memories. After we got our hands on whatever it was Ezryan had left with Cain, we'd erase their memories of ever seeing us here.

"Three . . ." Vrae whispered.

We released our energy on the entire block and every being in there, except Cain. A second later, all of them were moving like usual, but their eyes and brains would only see what they saw seconds earlier. Vrae and I stood in silence.

In reality, both of us were approaching Cain's hole. Those guards wouldn't get near us. If they did, they'd approach the fake ones and talk to thin air.

When we saw him, he curled himself up in the corner. I called him as I opened the bars. "Cain."

He woke up abruptly and smiled wickedly. "Well, well, Yverna and Vrathien, finally you two have come."

*   *   *

Ezryan stood by the lake again. He was just about to call Belphegor when an eerie hollow voice echoed. "Don't bother."

A crimson mist appeared from out of nowhere, and a few moments later it dissolved and Belphegor emerged from it.

Ezryan inclined his head. "That was quick."

"You mean my coming out or you getting here?"

The warrior chuckled. "Either."

Belphegor scoffed, looked at the sky, and then turned his crimson gaze back to Ezryan. "Shall we?" Belphegor asked.

Ezryan nodded. "Yeah. By the way, Yve sends her regards," he said with a knowing look.

"She did, huh? Nice of her." The prince grinned. "C'mon," he said, and then they both covered themselves with a protective shield.

They transformed their robes into wings and spread them. Together, they immediately jumped to the sky and flew northeast so fast that they were like a pair of swords that cut through the darkness of night sky with the speed of light. Minutes later they arrived at a huge barren field at the Gillian forest. Belphegor then indicated to Ezryan to stay back, and he stepped forward.

He lifted the edge of his lips. "Come out, Vassago. I've come here with an old friend," he called clearly into the wind.

Out of the blue, there was a shadow on the ground, forming a hole. No one was around.

Suddenly a devil emerged from inside the shadow. The second he was completely on the ground, the shadow disappeared.

With turquoise-coloured eyes and wavy waist-length blond hair, the devil was devastatingly handsome. His tall lean body was covered by a long deep-blue robe. On his head there was a pair of horns and a small crown with a turquoise stone in the middle. Clearly, he was another Prince of Hell.

He tilted his chin when he saw the North Prince. "To what do I owe the disturbance, Belphegor?" he asked, feigning annoyance.

"Shouldn't you say honour?" Belphegor snickered. "It's been a while, Vassago. How are you doing?"

Vassago shrugged. "I'm doing all right. So, where's the old friend . . ." he stopped dead when he saw the devil warrior who stood behind Belphegor.

He stepped forward and firmed his gesture. "Good to see you, Prince Vassago."

Vassago *tsked* when he saw Ezryan. "You really *are* alive. And to think you dared to come to Belphegor and now to me?"

Belphegor cut him off. "Yeah, I know. I told him he must've harboured a death wish."

Vassago sneered as he glanced at Belphegor.

Ezryan chuckled. "Well, it seems that the fact I'm alive isn't much of a surprise, is it? But thanks anyway. Neither of you let loose any of this." He nodded respectfully at the princes before him.

They exchanged amused looks. "Why would we do that? It's kinda fun to tell you the truth, you taking over his dad's position among the soldiers"–Vassago jerked his head at Belphegor–"even though we felt a bit sorry for your pals. But it's worth it."

"Anyway, let's get inside." The prince turned around, facing the barren field. He chanted, and then, from out of nowhere, a big castle made of turquoise stone appeared. There was a huge door with engraving all over it.

Vassago led them to the castle. The door was opened at Vassago's approach. The three of them went through it. The second the door was closed, a shadow engulfed the castle, and it dissolved into nothing.

They stopped in the hall of the castle, which looked exactly the same as the last time Ezryan had set foot here. The grand hall was luxurious, with pillars and statues made of turquoise stone everywhere. There were peculiar engravings all over the wall; they looked like a language of some sort.

Vassago turned around to face them once more. "So, I'll ask it once again. To what do I owe this disturbance?"

When Ezryan was about to open his mouth, Belphegor stopped him. "Let me," he said. Ezryan fell silent as Vassago's gaze darkened. "What is it, Belphegor?"

Belphegor gave Vassago a quizzical stare. "How about we go to your archive first?"

Vassago was startled, but then he agreed. "Okay, come." He led them towards some stairs. Like every other thing in here, the stairs were made of turquoise stone. They walked up the stairs for a minute. When they'd reached the top, Vassago led them to the left to an empty hallway and a freely carved wall.

The prince faced the empty wall on their left and chanted. After he'd done so, a small door appeared. He opened it and let his guests inside. He closed it, and the door vanished.

Ezryan looked around. He had never been to this part of the place before. Maybe Belphegor wasn't kidding. He did meet with Vassago every once in a while, maybe even more often than that. He knew about the existence of this place after all.

The archive was, as its name suggested, filled with old dusty books and records. There was a long table at the centre of the room and armchairs around it. Vassago took the one at the far side of the table near the window and asked Belphegor and Ezryan to take the other two at his sides.

He then folded his arms as his two guesses sat. "So, what is this all about? Don't tell me you came here because you wanna play fun and games."

Belphegor asked nonchalantly. "What if we do?"

Vassago arched a brow.

The North Prince then cleared his throat. "Just kidding. Actually, I decided to come here after Ry came and brought some sad news. It is practically listed under my obit files."

Ezryan snorted. The prince sometimes had a tendency to exaggerate things. Vassago rubbed his temple as he scowled. "Cut the crap, Belphegor."

The North Prince leaned forward and put one arm on the table. "You're too tense, you know. It's a wonder your hair doesn't have any greyish color by now."

Vassago narrowed his gaze while Ezryan just watched. He was definitely amused to hear their banter. Belphegor raised his hands. "Okay, okay, old man. So, listen to this, you're not gonna like it."

* * *

"It seems you knew we would come here." I folded my hands over my chest as I looked down at him.

Cain inclined his head. "I was told you would." He stood up slowly, but he stopped dead when a guard walked past his cell and acted as if he didn't even see me and Vrae. Turning his attention back to us, his lips curved in a sly smile. "Looks like you two did something to them."

We nodded, and abruptly he rubbed his palms. "So, your pal's around, right? The one who left me with that shit? Where the fuck is he?" he clenched his teeth.

I inhaled sharply. "Okay, he's out there."

He scoffed. "Well, where is he? I must have at least one shot at kicking his head, leaving me with this shit. That thing he left with me triggered an annoying connection with Abel's place, and that is the last thing in existence I need."

Vrae scowled. "You're saying that thing came from all the way up there?" she jerked her head up.

He suddenly lowered his gaze, and for a second I saw a glimpse of sadness in his eyes. "Yeah, where do you think Abel is right now?" he murmured.

Cain abruptly lifted his gaze and looked at us again. "So, you two are here to take it, right? I mean, I'd spilled the shit he wanted, and in return I was beaten into mush, thank you very much," he said sarcastically.

I felt sorry for the guy. Despite the humiliation, the thing he mentioned offered a chance to help us overcome upstairs' vermin, and yet he was beaten because of it. He could have just said no when Ry asked him to keep whatever it was.

Vrae folded her arms. "Thanks for spilling that shit. It was helpful." To my surprise, she smiled at him, and he started.

Then he rolled his eyes. "Whatever. So here it is." He approached the corner and started digging. I exchanged looks with Vrae and then looked at him again.

When he'd finished digging, he pulled out a small dusty pouch. It was a bit singed and it was tied up with a leather rope. Cain handed it to Vrae, but the second she touched it, she screamed and dropped the pouch immediately, letting out a series of creative curses under her breath, and held her arm.

Attempting not to pay attention or even let loose a grin at some of her weird curses, I patted her shoulder. "What is it?"

She inhaled deeply. "That thing is from up there all right. It burned my fucking hand even though it's still in that dirt bag." She held out her right hand she used to grab the pouch.

It was blistered. There was a fair amount of burn marks eating at her skin, and it was still smoking.

"Great, this kinda wound won't heal by itself, dammit." She cursed under her breath and quickly healed it as she cast an annoyed gaze at me.

I frowned. "How in the hell could he touch that and bring it down here?" I asked him.

Cain made a face at me. "How the heck should I know? Do I look like I play ball with those flickering halo-tops up there every other day?"

"Is that a trick question?" I retorted innocently, which set him off.

"Funny! I should introduce you to the bastard guards out front. Look, that thing popped in here, just as your pal told me it would, on that day I heard he'd died or something. Bottom line is, he left me with the damned thing, hoping I would become a fortune teller so I could tell you all some nonsense omens about the War of the Century," he snarled.

I averted my gaze to the pouch on the floor. When neither of them picked up the pouch, I knelt and slowly placed my hand upon it. Bracing for the pain, I poked the pouch.

To my utter surprise, I felt nothing.

I grabbed it and stood up. Vrae's blood-red eyes widened in shock when she saw me grab the thing as if it were just an ordinary pouch, not one that contained an item from heaven.

"What the hell!" She snapped as she eyed the pouch in my grasp. Both she and Cain gaped at me in disbelief.

I raised both hands. "Hey, don't look at me. I don't know squat here."

Vrae scowled. "Yeah, right, whatever. By the way, Cain," she said to him, "can you tell us everything you discussed with him?"

Cain curled his lips. "Why don't you ask him? You said he's out there, right? So ask him, and then tell him to come down here so I can kick his head."

Vrae rolled her eyes. "Whatever. If that's what you want, then we're done here."

"It's about time," he chuckled.

When Vrae started for the door, I stopped her. "Wait."

She turned abruptly, and I faced Cain once more. "He didn't tell you anything else? Maybe about something called Avarnakh?"

Vrae shot a warning look at me, but I ignored her.

Cain arched a brow at my question. "Ava-what? What the hell is that? You guys invented some new boring game or what?"

I snorted. "No, it's nothing. Anyway, thanks again, Cain. I'll kick his butt for you when I see him."

He snickered. "Good for him, and thanks, I appreciate it. Now, if you two don't mind, I'd like to have some well-deserved sleep here."

Vrae and I grinned at him, and then we stepped out of his hole. We sauntered quickly back to where we had stood and had frozen the memories of the guards and the inmates earlier. We stopped and glanced around at our surroundings, in case someone or something realized what we just did.

After we were sure nobody was poking their noses at us, we exchanged knowing looks at each other and then subtly held up our palms, removing the ban on their memories. This way they'd think that we had left without doing anything.

After we were done, I entered the tunnel and flew straight up with Vrae following behind me. Moments later we jumped out of the tunnel. I sighed. "Well, that was fun."

"C'mon, we gotta go and see what's in there," she said, pointing at the pouch in my grasp.

I nodded, and we went out quickly. A lot of questions flooded my thoughts as I wondered how Ry had managed to get whatever it was inside the pouch.

Chapter 11

Minutes later Belphegor finally finished with the explanation, leaving Vassago in utter disbelief. His jaw dropped.

Ezryan was just staring in silence while most of his thoughts were wandering once again to Yverna and her safety. Had she managed to get the Herathim he left with Cain yet?

Vassago managed to regain his composure. Closing his mouth, he glared at the North Prince. "Are you . . ."

"Positive?" Belphegor cut him off. "Deadly," he said and glanced at Ezryan. Vassago fell silent for a moment.

Abruptly, the prince tapped his fingers on the table. "But that can't be. We know that wasn't supposed to happen until, like . . ."

"Several millennia from now?" Ezryan asked. His thoughts were back on the discussion in front of him. Both princes stared at him, and he looked back at them. His face was stoic.

Vassago curled his lips. "Well, yeah, several millennia from now! And by the way, how in the hell did you manage to get your ears on those? Let alone taking Herathim!"

Ezryan hesitated before he answered, careful not to bring the wrath of the Princes of Hell upon himself. "That, Your Highness, is my secret. I can't get you involved in that." When the princes were about to say something, he raised his hands, stopping them. "I've endangered many devils already by letting loose this information. Forgive me, but this is my decision," Ezryan said, firming his gesture.

Both princes were surprised by his audacity for a second, but then they let it go and decided to respect their young friend.

Vassago sighed. "Fair enough, but really, why do you need Herathim if you alone could get this information?"

Ezryan hesitated, and then he put his hand on the table. "When I heard that earlier intel I told you about, I couldn't be sure just yet. Since I didn't know any other way to confirm it, I remembered the other use of that Herathim. That thing also can trigger a connection to up there, and not just everyone can have this particular connection."

Belphegor sneered his understanding. "You'd need someone like Cain, the Son of Adam who was condemned by God Himself and was marked by Him when he was still alive. The most important thing is that he also has a very strong connection with up there in the form of guilty feeling because he killed his brother, Abel. After millennia of being tortured, and despite of his sin that makes him get beaten each time a human does what he did, he still can't forget that feeling, which makes him a perfect medium for that connection."

Vassago showed understanding in his expression as well. "And that connection's still so strong even though he's not too fond of other humans."

Ezryan nodded. These two people before him often made him feel awe, like now. They did know about certain things.

Belphegor folded his arms. "Hence the BS prophecy he spilled then. He could get that because you had triggered a connection between him and up there by giving him the Herathim. Man, I bet he wants to kick your ass for that."

Ezryan chuckled. "He didn't know about the stable connection it'd trigger, but I said if there was any complaint, he could have his way if he wanted to kick me or whatever after he made the prophecy and confirmed everything I'd heard."

Belphegor scoffed. "You're slick."

Ezryan shrugged, while Vassago once again tapped his fingers. "But still, we only have an approximate time here, not the exact one."

"Yeah, not to mention daddy bastard once again amused us. I wouldn't have guessed that by wielding that thing, he's not only stealing Big Boss's ultimate weapon and condemning us all twice, with him having testosterone poisoning first, like there's nothing better to do than getting all jealous of humans," Belphegor spat in disgust. Vassago snorted at his words, but the North Prince ignored him. "And now he'd also literally accelerate the time for our ultimate destruction, and that Arzia thing's getting active by the minute." he ended grudgingly.

"And now it's after its weapon, in anger I might add." Vassago stared warily at them both.

Ezryan inclined his head. "Yes, although from what I've gathered, it intends to take back Rygavon in order to continue its deep slumber and not wake up until Raphael gives the signal to do what it must."

Vassago agreed. "Indeed. Well, Belphegor, at least something brainy is chasing your dad." He laughed at the prince, who rolled his eyes without saying anything.

Belphegor cleared his throat. "By the way, if those Arcs plan to wage war against us, what could they do? They'll never have a chance to take us down, not to mention that your scary pals aren't the only ones in existence, and their lesser ones are mostly no match against ours."

"Unless Boss Man Himself interferes and unleashes the light-heads who had entered the House of Prosper, for instance," Vassago added.

Ezryan shook his head. "No, they'll need something more than that, because, I assure you, if He unleashes them in an open war, they'll only make my two comrades and me have more fun," he said with wicked smile.

The two princes only nodded and exchanged amused looks. They both know full well the capabilities of the warrior before them and his comrades. The three of them then fell silent. Minutes later, Vassago abruptly stood up as if he'd just realized something.

He walked towards the bookshelf while his guests watched curiously. "You said that Rygavon was one of three keys to seal that Arzia thing?"

They both exchanged questioning looks, and then Belphegor answered him. "Yeah, I found it written in the old bastard's private records. Why, you remember something?"

Vassago didn't answer. Instead he suddenly searched his pile of books and records, muttering under his breath. Moments later he'd found the book he wanted after he'd ransacked several sections, and he put it on the table. It was an old thick black dusty book with peculiar carvings on its cover, and it was tied with a leather rope.

Belphegor suddenly stood up when he saw it. From the look on his face, he was about to explode in anger. "But that's the Book of Lost Knowledge! You had it with you this whole time?" he asked sharply, but Vassago just lifted the edge of his lips, while Ezryan just stared at the book before him. He'd heard myths surrounding this book, and only a few amongst the devils knew about them.

Legends had it that the book contained Forbidden History written in the first language spoken in the universe. Long ago, there was an advance race of devils. It was said that they were the origins of the devils that existed at present. Their resources were unimaginable. So far and deep was their reach that they even managed to gain much information regarding God, His angels, and other things that no unholy or mortal should have knowledge of.

Some say they even wrote about Adam and his descendants, who hadn't even been created that time. Some of this information was so vital and dark that it wasn't supposed to be recorded in the first place.

When their audacity no longer knew any bounds, they recorded too much and they intended to let loose the book's contents to the race that was similar to current humans. At this point, God wiped out the race entirely, and their language became the Lost Language. Not long after, Lucifer was banished and spawned his devils.

There was some speculation that this book also contained information about him, but no one really knew. In fact, nobody could really guess everything written in it.

Vassago grinned at them both as he untied the book. "What could possibly be more help to us if we are about to fight something that's said to be older than anything than the info written by those who might actually have seen it?" he asked as he opened the book.

Belphegor still didn't look amused. "You have a point, but that still doesn't explain how and why in the hell you took it. I've been wondering where it was, dammit!" he snarled.

Before Vassago could say anything, he caught a puzzled look on Ezryan's face. "I'd seen it among Lucifer's old files several times. On the night I decided to separate, I intended to take it with me because I knew some things in it were dangerous to him. I didn't want him to hide it in case I couldn't find out what they were. He didn't have a clue I knew about it and wanted to take it with me. But, that night, it was, poof, gone!" He exclaimed, evidently upset.

"Even though I decided to separate anyway, I figured I may have enough on him. I've still been looking for it until now, and to think you've been hiding it all this time!" Belphegor shifted his gaze from Ezryan and gave a wry glare at his old friend.

Vassago exhaled heavily. "You could at least be a bit grateful to me, you know." He levelled an offended stare at the North Prince.

"Why is that?" Belphegor asked in a surly tone.

Vassago stared dryly at him. "That night, from what you've told me, I figured you might want to steal it before you wage war against him, so I waited for you there. But before you came, I overheard him. He intended to either destroy it or move it to a safer location. When he was out of his archive, I sneaked through the shadows and stole it. You can laugh now, knowing that he went hysterical like a girl when he found out it was gone."

Ezryan swallowed his laughter at the prince's acerbic comment.

"If I'm not mistaken," Vassago went on, ignoring Ezryan, "he then went to your place and mine and secretly looked for it when you were at *his* place. I went elsewhere to hide the book, well, temporarily. And then from what you've told me, I knew that you went there after I took it. I kept it all this time because I thought he'd be coming to your place or here perhaps, whenever he could, to look for it."

He then folded his arms. "I thought there was no need for me to let him get his hands on this. And from what we've gathered along with our pal here," he said as he tilted his chin at Ezryan. "I think we may have a use for this book one day, and it's not safe to pull it out from safekeeping. Believe me when I tell you, now is the first time I ever laid hands on this book since then." He ended his explanation.

"You could've at least told me that you had it, asshole."

Vassago ignored Belphegor's insult. "And let you nag at me like an old bitch every now and then? Begging me to give it to you so you could read it before going to sleep like a boring middle-aged human? As if, *asshole*," he retorted calmly.

Ezryan winced at his caustic retort while Belphegor scowled. A second later though, Belphegor relaxed again. "Fine, let's get over with it."

Vassago sneered. "That's more like it. Now," he said as he handed the ancient book to Belphegor, who lifted the edge of his lips when he took it. "Let's take a look at it. We might find something regarding the three seals of Arzia, Herathim, and we might even find something on what stunt upstairs' army would pull against us."

* * *

Vrae and I quickly went back to Amon's place. Damn, I hoped this thing wouldn't emit any energy that tied it to up there.

Sometimes, I was grateful that most of people here wouldn't bother others that had nothing to do with their own work. Imagine if one of them had 'poking nose to someone else's business' on their to-do list. Vrae hastily opened the door, while I was trying to hide the small pouch from sight.

Amon and Zade were both in there. We hurriedly entered the room and closed the door. They exchanged questioning looks and then shifted their gaze to us.

Zade held Vrae's shoulder. "What's happened? You didn't waste your time in there."

Vrae was panting when she answered him. "The thing he left with Cain. It was . . . from up there. I couldn't touch it."

Both of them looked aghast.

Amon frowned at me. "So, it's still with him then? You both couldn't take it? Now what are we gonna do?"

I chuckled. "She didn't say anything close to 'we couldn't take the damned thing' now, did she?"

Zade shot a questioning gaze at me. I grinned and then pulled out the pouch. I shoved it in front of their shocked faces. Amon was taken aback. "But how can that be? You can grab it and she can't? Why?"

I bounced the pouch and then grabbed it as if it were a rubber ball. "I did some thinking about that. There's only one way to find out. You two, touch this."

Amon arched his brows, while Zade just gave me a have-you-lost-your-mind stare.

"Come on, if it burns you, then you can't grab it. It won't kill you. C'mon." I shoved the pouch to them.

Zade swallowed a bit and then slowly extended his hand. When his finger touched it, he raised a brow, and then he grabbed the small pouch.

Amon stared in disbelief. "What the . . . ?" He threw a puzzled look at Zade, who looked as bewildered as he was. He answered Amon's unfinished question only with a shrug. Amon approached him and slowly tried to poke the pouch.

When his fingers came in contact with that dirty little bag, he yelled and tossed it away, holding his hand as Vrae had done when she touched it before. The pouch fell to the ground and I grabbed it. "Well, this is all I need."

All of them looked at me.

Vrae shot an upset gaze towards me. "Why in the hell did you need to barbecue our hands?"

I scoffed. "It's not that, Vrae. Don't you see it? You and Amon can't touch it, and Zade and I can? What do we have in common? I'm not an Imirae wielder, and neither are you or Amon. So what was it?"

Vrae's swirling red eyes widened in understanding. "You both have those nightmares."

Zade's jaw dropped. "You mean, because both of us have those nightmares, we're able to touch this thing?"

Amon just gaped.

Suddenly an unlikely thought came to my mind. "And guys? I don't wanna sound too friggin' happy because I can touch shit from upstairs or because I have stupid humans in my head, but I think I know why *he* managed to get this and gave it to Cain."

The three of them gasped. "You're saying, *he* . . . ?" Zade's voice faded as he asked the question I had provoked.

I shrugged. "Well, unless *he* figured some other cool and sweet way to do it, yeah, I think so. I don't have a clue why having stupid humans in his head could help him slip through those Arcs and take this, but I'm pretty sure this was the cause."

All of them gaped in disbelief.

Vrae scowled. "Yve, considering the situation, I think we need something better than 'pretty sure' before we go ask him, 'Yo, buddy, did you manage to get this because you have vermin in your head?'"

I raised a brow at her words. "Fine then, *totally* pretty sure," I shot back, and both males snorted.

Vrae rolled her eyes. "Whatever, this just keeps getting better and better."

Amon suddenly cleared his throat. "So, how about we open that thing and see what's inside?"

I looked at all of them, and they nodded at me. I took a deep breath and released it.

"Okay, so here goes," I said as I untied the pouch slowly. When it was opened, all of us looked inside it. There was something shiny. I pulled it out and showed it to all of them.

Vrae frowned as she stared at the small, shiny object on my palm. "What's this?"

*   *   *

The two princes were scouring the book while Ezryan just looked at it in silence. They both were caught in a heated discussion as they flipped one page after another.

Suddenly, as they just turned the pages without looking at them, Ezryan saw something that made him wince. "What the hell?" he blurted before he could stop himself.

Both princes stopped and looked at him. Belphegor shot him a questioning look. "What?"

Ezryan hesitated and then asked for their permission to take the book. "May I?"

The princes exchanged a look, and then Belphegor nodded his permission.

Ezryan slowly motioned the book closer to him. It showed a picture of something he'd last seen seven centuries ago. He pointed at the image. "*This* is Herathim," he said firmly.

Belphegor and Vassago exchanged a surprised look and then faced him again. Vassago pointed at the picture. "Are you sure about this?"

Ezryan rubbed his chin, feigning contemplation. "You're right. Considering I was the one who took it, yeah, I shouldn't be so sure about this," Ezryan remarked in a rather innocent tone.

Belphegor snorted, and Vassago narrowed his swirling turquoise eyes. "Boy, you better be grateful we've known each other for too damn long, otherwise you'd have your ass toasted for your attitude right now."

Ezryan raised his hands in surrender, and a grin curved his lips. Belphegor elbowed Vassago's arm a bit as he laughed. "Come on, I dig his style, and I know you do too. Don't be so tense like a human having PMS."

Ezryan had to refrain himself from bursting out in laughter, and Vassago glared at his old friend as he curled his lips.

Belphegor sighed. "How's this? Consider this a bit of a payback for taking and hiding this book from me, and let's call it even."

Vassago raised a brow, and then he grinned. "Fair enough."

Ezryan exchanged amused looks with the North Prince. "I owe you one," he mouthed, and Belphegor just shrugged.

"Okay, back to business. So, this is Herathim, huh?" Belphegor asked as he looked at the picture.

Ezryan nodded. "Yes. This is what I found in the place called 'The Deepest Part of Heaven'," he said dramatically.

Belphegor rolled his eyes and then looked straight at him. "I take it you wouldn't tell us how in the hell you found this and brought it along with you?"

Ezryan shook his head as he smiled apologetically. "No, I'm afraid I can't do that."

Belphegor looked disappointed but said nothing. Instead he stared at the picture once again. After couple of seconds, he frowned at it.

Vassago noticed and patted his back. "What is it? You found something?"

Belphegor jerked his head at the picture. "Does that look like a weapon to you? I mean, from what we've gathered, it's *supposed* to be a weapon, right?"

Vassago looked at the picture, and then a deep frown lined his brows as well.

Ezryan just stood there and looked at the picture. He had never got a chance to look at it closely, since he had to move his ass pronto after he stole it. After that, he'd put it in a small pouch and given it to Cain.

As the both of them studied the picture, Vassago tapped his fingers on the page. "Well, if you ask me, that thing doesn't look like something that can be listed as a weapon. Man, by the look of it, it's even smaller than a fruit knife. Good luck trying to attack some flies with that."

Ezryan nodded. "It was small enough to be put inside a small pouch."

The North Prince scoffed. "Well, if the army from upstairs wanted to whack us with this, we should run and duck for cover."

Both princes burst out laughing, while Ezryan just smiled as he continued to look at the picture closely. Suddenly he winced as if he'd just realized something and began turning the page.

At first he turned it backwards. When he didn't find anything, he turned the next page forward and the next and the next until he stopped dead when he found two pictures facing each other on two pages.

His jaw went slack and he turned his gaze to the two royals in front of him. They sobered up and looked at him.

Vassago pouted when he saw Ezryan's expression. "Would you stop playing The Truth Is Out There?! I hate it when you do that, especially when we were laughing."

Belphegor snorted. "I thought you didn't like to laugh."

Vassago narrowed his gaze at Belphegor, but the North Prince ignored him. Instead, he looked straight at Ezryan. "What is it? You've found some . . ." His voice faded as Ezryan pointed at the page with pictures on it.

One of the pictures was a ring with a silver stone in a shape of six-pointed star attached to it. He recognized it immediately as the Ring of Solomon. But that wasn't the one that the former commander meant to show him. Following Ezryan's finger, he fell silent as his eyes fell upon a picture of something he hadn't seen for ages.

It was a picture of a piece of metal in triangular shape. In the middle was a fiery eye known among devils as The Eye of Hell. Sorcerers of the Old World referred to it as the *Ocularis Infernum,* while a few others, including some humans who had seen another form of it, an ordinary eye inside a triangle, called it The All-Seeing Eye.

Upon seeing the picture, the North Prince lifted his gaze and stared at Ezryan, who looked back directly into the prince's eyes. "That's one of the seals. That's Rygavon."

*   *   *

I spun the small shiny object as we examined it closely. The object was some sort of small gold knife that was broken all the way to its hilt. There were crescent moon shapes on both sides of the hilt, and it had a short handle.

"This thing looks like a pendant," Amon said.

Vrae shook her head. "No, I think it's more like a key or something."

I rolled it and noticed something. "I don't think it's just a key. It's a *part* of one."

Vrae stared at it, while Zade looked at me with a quizzical stare. "How can you tell?" he asked, indicating the thing with a nod.

I showed them the tiny piece of metal jutting out in the middle of its base; it looked like it could fit onto something. Similar metal was also on the centre of the outer part of the hilt. "See these? It looks like something could fit on the hilt and the tip."

"You're right, it does," Amon said.

"Done?" I asked all of them, and they nodded. I put it back into the small pouch and tied it back up.

"You think *he* knows what this is and what the things that fitted on its handle and its tip are?" Zade asked.

I shrugged. "I bet he knows what that is, otherwise he wouldn't have bothered to go all the way up there just to take it."

"And that connection thing Cain mentioned, I think he knows about that as well," Vrae added.

Amon sighed heavily. "I still don't have any idea where the hell could he get his hands on that kind of information."

Zade and Vrae were staring blankly at the floor, probably thinking the same thing. As for me, I had an idea of where he got it. He told me that was where he'd go, and I was surprised Vrae hadn't thought about it.

Long before he saved his sworn brother Xaemorkahn, the three of us–well, usually the two of us–would go to the elders in their exile, including Belphegor and the others. Of course Lilith wasn't one of them. Almost none of the devils wanted to cross paths with them because of their savageness that made them far deadlier than anything if lesser devils dared to bother them. Not even the Echelons wanted to seek their advice if they had other options.

As for the three of us, we never really bothered whether they were scary or anything. I had a thought that our natures perhaps weren't so different: we were all savage. And they also weren't that uptight.

Amongst all of the royals, we'd often go to Belphegor. Though it sounds like we were looking for trouble meeting someone who opposed Lucifer, we never cared much about it. In fact, I'd be surprised if his name wasn't on top of Ry's list of sources aside from Xaemorkahn. After his disappearance, Vrae and I never went to the elders any more. We thought there was no need since he was no longer there.

As for me, it would bring too many memories of him, and I really didn't want that.

All this time, no one apart from the three of us knew about his secret little meetings with them, and it had to stay that way. I decided to tell Vrae later and directed my thoughts elsewhere.

What were the other parts of this thing? What would it do?

*   *   *

Kathiera had just arrived back at the Aryad after her visit to five of the other Echelons, and now she was heading to the private chamber of another member. She strolled down the left path past the Echelons' chamber and passed through many forks before she finally stopped in front of a door with ten layers of spells covering it.

Immediately she dispelled all of them and knocked twice. The devil inside opened the door. "Kathiera?" he said in surprise.

The Ravathe nodded in greeting. "Can I come in, Lazoreth?"

"Sure," Lazoreth said, and he stepped aside to let her in. "What is it?" he asked after he had closed the door and re-erected the protective spell on it.

"Bynethar is up to something, if he hasn't stumbled upon our plan already."

Lazoreth frowned. He didn't get what was making her frustrated. The Ravath in question always seemed like he was up to something nasty, like killing people. "Isn't he always?"

Kathiera shot him a glare. "That's not funny. I think he knows something concerning the recent activity of Tyraviafonza, Wartiavega, and Zaderion."

Lazoreth considered her a bit. "Tyraviafonza didn't reveal anything with that mocking attitude of hers, and yes, I agree that she's up to something she's not supposed to be doing, but what makes you think that Bynethar is too?"

"He came to me earlier, and his attitude in covering her was far too peculiar," she said.

Lazoreth arched a brow. "That's it? I'm sorry, but if he was referring to the fact that we banded together to question Tyraviafonza, he had a point. Besides, he's always like that. No one could ever guess what's on his mind. Just as long as he doesn't find out what our plan is, I don't think it's necessary to do anything that could raise suspicion."

Kathiera shook her head stubbornly. "No, I can feel it in my gut. He has ulterior motives this time."

Inhaling in patience, Lazoreth decided to humour her. "All right, then what will you have me do?"

The Ravathe levelled a dead stare at him. "Summon one of your Ladurgas."

Lazoreth frowned at the mention of his personal guards. "To do what?"

"Have him shadow Tyraviafonza."

Lazoreth let out an undignified snort at her request. "That is beyond ridiculous, Kathiera. Why would we need to do that? Her golem's more than enough. If you wanna keep an eye on her, check her golem at the Hall."

"That won't be enough. She could easily trick her golem, and Amon will do something to cover her if he's in on whatever it is that she's up to."

Lazoreth fell silent as he considered her words. In the end, he had to admit that she was right. Tyraviafonza was more than capable of evading her golem.

"Relax. I've gone to the others, and they agreed with me," she inserted.

Lazoreth sighed. "Who?"

A victorious smile curved her lips. "Mezarhim, Falthan, Havok, Herron, Gildam, and of course, Faemirad. With that many, I'm sure you know that the rest will follow."

"What about Xamian?"

"At this point, he's as suspicious as he gets, just like Bynethar."

He had to concur. Xamian was full of mystery from the get-go. Lazoreth inhaled as another thought came to him. "Fine, but why her? Why not her sister? She seems to be the one who has her ears sticking to whatever rumours are out there these days."

Kathiera nodded her agreement. "Indeed, but most of the time, she doesn't have a clue as to what Tyraviafonza know when it comes to the plans we devised."

Lazoreth stared at her for a moment before she drew a long breath. "You wanna know the truth? Honestly, I'd like you to shadow Bynethar while you're going after her, but I know that is not possible. He would know."

He snorted. "You got that right. That's even more ridiculous."

"Whatever. So again, I want you to shadow Tyraviafonza. She knows something."

At her words, Lazoreth almost had to admit that the female soldier had roused his interest as much as the two Echelons did. That particular Cherxanain somehow always had her hands on things she shouldn't, just like her dead Hieldhar. In the end, he nodded his agreement. "Fine, I'll have one on Tyraviafonza's tail."

Kathiera smiled in cruel satisfaction. "Good. She'll never know what hit her."

* * *

The princes were staring at the 'Eye of Hell' in silence, while Ezryan just stood there feeling uneasy.

All of a sudden, Vassago sighed. "Well, we've found out exactly what the Herathim is. It's one of the three seals of Arzia."

Belphegor pointed at the Ring of Solomon. "And you're right, Ry. The Ring of Solomon indeed has something to do with it. It's also one of the seals."

Vassago folded his arms. "And from what we're looking at right now, those three can be put together, forming a key which looks like a miniature sword."

"It's also a weapon, maybe with some kind of mechanism. Fortunately, even though daddy bastard managed to wield that Rygavon and also that Eye of Hell that he'd use to bind most of us, he still doesn't know how to use it. If he did, then we could only kiss this world goodbye." Belphegor interjected.

Ezryan nodded. "Well, it's indeed a weapon, but Arzia's, not the Arcs'. Although, I wouldn't have guessed that thing was one of the seals, but still, we've found something useful now."

Belphegor tapped his fingers on the Rygavon's core picture. "Now that we know something about that sack of emptiness, how's that gonna help us? Return the thing to it so it could go back to its vacation in dreamland?"

"Or we just hide them? Who's to say it wouldn't change course and destroy us all ahead of schedule?" Vassago added the question.

Ezryan fell silent as he was thinking the same thing.

"Either way," Ezryan said as he pulled an armchair and sit, "we already got two out of three, so to speak. The problem is the ring. How could a devil take that? As much as I wanted to steal it myself rather than letting the lesser devils do it and then having the ring go AWOL, there's no way devils can take it."

Belphegor shook his head. "No, not with the lists of names in the hands of the Valdam. *You* can try after we are sure it doesn't have your name and you haven't been compromised. You should stay dead to those Echelons. Otherwise daddy bastard would put you into a jar himself."

Vassago exhaled a bit. "Well, as annoying as it sounds, maybe I can try sneaking up through the shadow and take it."

Belphegor scoffed. "Don't you know? That stupid Goetia had your name in it."

Vassago scowled. "What? What the hell is this?! How did he know about me? Come on! This is not fair! How did Solomon get to know that much about us?"

"Not to mention that King Belial, Duke Dantalion, King Balam, and the rest of the princes are in it as well," Ezryan interjected.

Both royals were taken aback by his words.

Belphegor frowned. "You haven't told me this before. I only heard that he'd created a name list that contains royals' names, but I have very little intel on who the people are, and they aren't so clear either. I know that Vassago's in it. I also know that the other three are in it too, and that toad Bael, but Belial, Balam and Dantalion?"

Ezryan cast a wary gaze at them. "Last time I checked, there were seventy-two names in Ars Goetia alone. Who knows what he'd written in the other lists," he said bitterly.

Belphegor gave him an upset look. "I thought the name list was only Goetia! From what I've gathered, the other lists don't have our names in them."

Ezryan shrugged. "Like I said, who knows? I don't know for sure. But one thing I do know, those names are the names of royals, so it's safe to say that mine won't be in it."

Vassago then pulled an armchair and sat on it as well. He looked frustrated. "Great, so now what?"

Belphegor averted his gaze from the other two and stared at the image of Rygavon. Suddenly he tapped his fingers on it. After a moment of silence, he abruptly looked straight at both of them. "We do what we can–get hold of two out of three, and then we can worry about that stupid ring."

Ezryan nodded, but Vassago frowned at his old friend, looking unhappy. "And who do you think would steal that Eye thing, huh? You? Belphegor, get real. Your pop would deck you a whole lot faster than Solomon could turn you into strawberry jam."

The former Hieldhar snorted at the prince's comment, but he hastily averted his gaze when Belphegor cast a dry stare at him. Displeased with his old friend's sarcasm, Belphegor let out a tired breath. "Did I say anything close to 'I have a dying wish, and that wish was to become strawberry jam'?"

This time, Ezryan really had to struggle just to keep from bursting out laughing. He then cleared his throat to put an end on the princes' awkward banter. Both of them turned to him and asked the warrior in unison. "What?"

Ezryan raised his hands. "Gentlemen, may I ask you to change the subject to the seals instead of blabbering about some random strawberry jam? We don't have much time here."

The princes exchanged looks and regained their composure. Belphegor looked a bit bemused. "Okay, so what are you suggesting?" he asked.

Vassago just stared blankly at them both.

The warrior heaved a sigh. "I think, before we can do anything to either of those, we have to do some stake out first."

Belphegor crossed his arms over his chest. "No doubt about that, but let me ask you this. As the only warrior who managed to stay alive after being burned by that stupid light, do you have any idea how we can get close enough to him and take the Eye?"

Ezryan considered his question for a second, and then he answered, "I've been thinking about that, and as a would-be victim of that thing, I daresay I can't face him alone, but together, I think we might have a chance. Not just to face him, but to seal the destroyer, after we do him in," he remarked.

Vassago bit his lower lip. "Okay, but who's the 'we' here?" He made a quote mark in the air.

Ezryan caught a weird note in his voice, no doubt to remind him about their earlier discussion as to who had the power that nearly matched the destroyer's. Vassago too realized this, and his thoughts wandered to the she-devil he hadn't seen in seven centuries, the one who possessed the element they needed.

Ezryan gave them a half-hearted smile. "We'll have to get the sisters in on this. Maybe they'd have someone in mind as well, and my sworn brother. As for the last one, I'd like you two to decide."

"That's quite a lot, but why do you need us to decide on the last guy?" Vassago asked.

The warrior gazed warily. "Because I have a hunch we need one or even two more royals at our backs."

Belphegor nodded slowly. "Okay, but I wanna ask you one thing, boy. You sure you're okay with dragging your lady and her sister into this?"

Ezryan's face showed that he'd rather be disembowelled than drag the other half of his soul, with whom he'd just been reunited, to an imminent death. He then heaved a weary breath. "I really don't want to, but from what you've told me about that God's Destroyer, I think you'd agree we don't have that much of a choice. Besides, I know she'd kill me herself if I told her to stay out of this. Besides, both of them already know exactly what happened to me, and I know they'd be willing to turn their backs on him after what he'd done."

"And above all else, we don't have any other fire power that's stronger and more trustworthy than them. Oh, yeah, congrats, boy, you're finally together." Vassago grinned wickedly.

Ezryan chuckled at the prince's totally unrelated comment. "Thanks, Vassago, and like you said, that's why we need them both."

"And you're sure we need your brother?" Belphegor asked in a tone that suggested he was suppressing an urge to vomit.

Ezryan shook his head at the prince's unreasonable animosity towards his sworn brother. "Can we move past that already? You know we need him. His power's the only thing that can effectively negate your pop's. So, unless you have something that's labelled 'made in heaven' that we could use without getting stupid burns, I really don't think we have much choice," he explained calmly.

"Okay, all right," Belphegor mumbled.

The three of them then fell silent. Abruptly, Vassago looked at his guests as he raked his hair with his fingers. "I have an idea as to who the last guy could be. I bet he'd want to give us a hand." Vassago's guests exchanged a puzzled look with each other and then turned to him with faces that demanded an answer.

He smiled evilly at them both. "I'll ask Seere to come here and join us."

The North Prince let out a scoffing laugh at his old friend's idea. "You're joking, right? The man's barely able to make up his mind just to kill a fly, let alone my daddy dearest."

Vassago rolled his eyes. "Dude, just because he's indifferent about evil doesn't mean he ain't capable of doing it. If we could just give him a good enough reason, he'll do it. Besides, we want that ring, right? He'll come in handy on that part."

Belphegor rubbed his temple. "Fine, suit yourself. Ask him," he muttered. "Now, what are we gonna do?" he asked Ezryan.

Vassago suddenly raised his hand to stop Ezryan from answering. "Before that, I wanna ask you, are we gonna try to kill him to get that stupid Eye, or will we just incapacitate him temporarily?"

Belphegor scowled at his question. "What difference would it make? The deader he becomes, the better for us."

Vassago ignored him. "So, what's the plan here? Because I find it hard to imagine we'd try to make him rest in pieces with just that bit of firepower."

Ezryan hesitated before he answered. "The latter, I guess. Like you said, we'll need a whole lot more than that if we want to end him. Besides, *it* didn't mention anything about us ganking him," he said meaningfully.

Vassago nodded. "Okay, I'll try to contact Seere ASAP. You wanna come along?" he asked Belphegor, whose face looked as though he'd rather be gutted than meet that particular Hell Prince.

Belphegor gave him a droll stare in return. "Yeah, I'm coming with you. In the meantime, what are you gonna do, boy?"

Ezryan stood up slowly and then inclined his head. "I'll check the sisters and see if they already took the Herathim. After that, maybe we'll cross over first to inform my brother. Can I ask you a favour? Let me know when Prince Seere joins us. If we all meet before the sisters and I go, it would be better."

Belphegor tilted his head at Ezryan. "Will do. Just tell us whatever happens over there. My surveillance detail's not exactly clear whenever you cross over. It's kinda blurry on few things."

Ezryan rubbed his temple and scoffed. "Your surveillance detail, huh? Whatever, just don't see through anything private."

"Well, you can sue me if I do," Belphegor shot back nonchalantly.

"Okay, remember to find a good lawyer when I do."

Vassago chuckled at his comment.

The former Hieldhar raked his hair. "Yeah, at any rate I'd better take my leave now, Highnesses," he said as he saluted them, and they replied.

Vassago and Belphegor walked behind him towards the door. Vassago went past him and chanted to open the sealed wall.

Ezryan went out once it opened and departed, back to the one soul he couldn't take his mind away from.

Chapter 12

We separated after minutes of discussion, and since no one except Zade and I could touch the thing Ry had left with Cain, I took the liberty of keeping it with me.

Zade and Vrae went together elsewhere. They told me they had something to do, so I went out and told the guards everything except the fact that Ry had showed up and put an end to those Arcs. I asked them if there were any passers, and oddly enough, they informed me that there were several Chonars, soldiers that were directly commanded by those Echelons whose main job was to spy on suspected rogue devils and then take them in. It wasn't usual for them to pass through, especially through this Gate. And there was something even more bothersome. They also said that some devils were suspected to be traitors, but they didn't say who. The guards told me to warn Vrae and Zade about this and once again reminded me to be careful. So I gave them a nod of thanks and left.

There were a couple hours left until daybreak, and since I promised Ry to meet him after I took whatever that was he left with Cain, I went back to that forest. I immediately flew into the clouds and left my doppelganger to take my place amongst the darkness of the sky.

After I finished with my cover, I headed straight to the forest. As soon as I arrived, I looked around the trees closing in around me, but he was nowhere to be found. So, I settled under the same tree where we met the day before. I leaned on the tree and covered myself with my wings as my mind filled with one question: did he really get those nightmares as well?

When I was distracted by all these thoughts, suddenly I felt someone was approaching. I uncovered myself and then waited to see who it was. I felt who it was immediately as the newcomer emerged from behind a huge tree across from me.

It was Ry.

He walked towards me as I stood up and hugged me tightly. He pulled away to give me a rain of hot kisses, and then we separated. I untied the pouch from my armour's belt, showing it to him. By the look on his face, he seemed pleased. "You got it? Great, sooner than I thought."

I curled my lips. "You have to tell me something, Ry," I said seriously.

He cast a gentle look that melted me. "What is it? Is something wrong?" He reached and squeezed my shoulder gently.

I was about to ask the question when a frantic call rang in my head, averting my attention from him. The call was from my doppelganger.

"What is it?" he asked.

I raised a hand. "Wait, wait," I said as I shushed him. *"Shakra! Something's coming at me!"* she exclaimed.

Judging by her louder voice, it sounded as though she was coming closer to where we were, and possibly bringing whoever chasing her. Fuck, shit, and damnation! Couldn't the bastard pick a better time or hell, not pick a time at all?

"Do they attack you?" I sent the thought to her with a frown while Ry stared at me.

"No, but whoever it is, it's getting too close to be a mere additional surveillance. From the feel of it, it's no Chonar," she answered. *"I don't know who or what it is! Regardless, I'm coming to you."*

"All right, I'll be here," I replied, but then immediately fell into deep thought. "What the hell?" I mused in confusion. But that pondering was interrupted by a sharp "shush" from Ry, followed by a chill down my spine. Something or someone was here.

"Shield!" he whispered hoarsely.

We simultaneously manifested our shields just as my erratic doppelganger arrived. *"Come, I better pull you back before whatever that is realizes who you are."*

Then again, chances were high that whoever it was had already realized that she was my doppelganger.

She nodded to Ry and myself, and then I pulled her back before I dissolved my shield, showing to whatever bastard was on her tail that she was me, just wanting to evade him.

Looking at Ry, I nearly opened my mouth when I saw the horror on his face. That was not a damned good sign! He abruptly glanced at me and gave me a hand signal to wait before he took off. Well, I hoped he found out who it was.

A second later, dark clouds were forming above me and the surrounding area. In no time, a storm was coming down hard, forcing me to expand my energy around me in order to block it.

It seemed Ry had decided to use his elemental powers. Weird, since it would definitely be overkill if he summoned the sky elements just to off one bastard.

I waited anxiously for him for at least one and a half minutes when suddenly the clouds were dispersed, just like when we had met the previous day. Moments later he came through the bushes and I ran towards him. "Are you okay?"

He captured my lips with a quick kiss. "I'm fine."

"Who was it?" I asked, noting the glint of trepidation in his eyes. "Ry?"

"Uh, look, I wanna ask you something, and please, be honest with me. Don't hide things just because you don't want me to worry about you," he said quietly.

I gulped. That was so not good. "Okay," I nodded, "but who was it back there?"

He hesitated, and then glanced in the direction from where he came. Then he looked at me again. "What does that guy want with you?"

"Who?"

Inhaling deeply, he released his breath with worry etched on every inch of his dark face. "Lazoreth. That was his Ladurga."

*　*　*

Lazoreth strolled quickly past the other end of the Echelons' chamber. Various curses accompanied his every step. A few moments later, he reached Kathiera's private room. He lifted the four layers of spells that covered her door and knocked frantically. "Kathiera! Kathiera!"

She opened the door. "Lazoreth, What is it?"

Lazoreth burst into the room and closed the door. He was about to talk when he noticed Faemirad. "Why are you here?"

"She's here at my request. Why are *you*?!" Kathiera snarled.

Lazoreth drew a short breath. "My Ladurga. He's dead!"

Both females were alarmed at that. "She knew?" Faemirad asked.

"No, even though I have no doubt that she realized something was following her since she flew away from it, but it wasn't she who killed him," Lazoreth said in a dead-pan tone.

"Who was it then?" Kathiera snapped impatiently.

The Ravath's gaze darkened, and he shook his head. "I don't know. Whoever it was, they masked their powers before they killed my minion, and they did it well."

Kathiera cast a puzzled look at him. "Can't you at least tell who it was? Angel or . . ."

"No angel would interfere with our matter," he interrupted her. "Besides, they'd know if she was in the immediate vicinity, and she would too. They wouldn't miss each other."

"Fine, but can you determine of what rank they were or what element they used?"

Lazoreth had just opened his mouth to answer when her words registered completely. "Wait a sec here. They were strong enough to be a Cherxanain. Chonars are out of the question. Xarchons are nowhere outside," he muttered, half talking, half thinking, until he arrived at an outrageous thought, one that made him bristle in disbelief and horror. "Come to think of it, they killed my Ladurga with ice made of rain."

"Then it was a Cherxanain with the power of water. Not Wartiavega," Faemirad said.

He shook his head. "I'm with you on that one, but that's not the case. The rain stopped right before my Ladurga really died."

"So? It's just a coincidence," Kathiera interjected.

"Not that, no, because you see, the rain started before they killed him, and then it didn't stop on its own. They *stopped* it," he explained.

The two stared at him as his remark began to sink in their minds. "They stopped it as in . . ." Faemirad trailed off.

"As in they dispersed those damn clouds," he finished her words.

Kathiera shook her head in denial. "There's no way they could do that!" she snarled. "That means whoever that was had the power to control the sky, not just water!"

"She's right," Faemirad interjected. "There's been none since . . ." Her voice faded as her eyes widened in horror.

Lazoreth eyes were seared with dark red. "Yes, there's been none since Ezryan. That bastard might still be alive."

* * *

I stared at him. "It was a Ladurga who followed my doppelganger?"

He nodded. "Yes, I was lucky to notice him before he saw me."

"But why?" I asked with a frown. Dammit, did I really screw up back in their chamber?

He placed his firm hands on my shoulders. "Has something happened? Something that warranted surveillance straight from him?"

I shrugged. "Nothing big. They just questioned me, Vrae, and Zade, but I don't know for sure if either of us screwed up somehow."

His brows formed a single line. "They questioned each of you?" he asked sharply.

"Yeah, three on Vrae, two at Zade's, and five ambushed me. Don't ask. I know that's obnoxious," I inserted when he almost open his mouth. "But they didn't do anything outrageous aside from the more than obvious glare of suspicion they threw at me."

"Okay," he said slowly, before he cocked his head as if a thought had just occurred to him. "Was Xamian or Bynethar there?"

I let out a small laugh. Our thoughts still worked on the same page, it seemed. "What is it?" he asked with the hint of a smile.

"Nothing. You just asked the same thing I asked myself after they questioned us, and no, they both weren't there."

His frown deepened. "What were they hoping to accomplish by doing that?"

"Beats me," I said with a shrug. "I don't think I did anything that warranted a Chonar on my tail, let alone a Ladurga."

He gulped, and wariness was written all over his flawless face. "All right, I hope we find out before anything happens."

I nodded. "Yeah, but what's Lazoreth doing? He's never done this before."

"That's what worries me. He's up to something. Be careful," he said with concern in his deep voice.

I barely heard his words as I absently put my hand under my chin. "It doesn't sound like him, though," I muttered.

"What's that?"

His question snapped me back to reality, and I shook my head. "No, nothing," I said with a disturbing thought. There were three among the Echelons who could do this, but I could only think of one. Could it be?

Gulping at the thought, I decided to change the subject. "Now, I wanna ask you something else," I said as I played with the pouch as if it were a rubber ball. I opened my mouth to speak, but fortunately I recalled his words about Belphegor keeping tabs on him. Catching myself, I switched to a mental channel. *"You could touch this, yeah?"*

He realized that I didn't want to be overheard, but he did seem to be confused by my question. *"Well, of course. How could I give it to Cain if I couldn't?"*

I folded my arms over my chest. *"Right, so listen to this. Vrae and Amon can't touch it, but Zade and I can."*

As I'd expected, he didn't seem to be surprised. Even if he was surprised, obviously it was with something else. *"What do you think is causing that?"* His strained voice was clear in my head.

I gave him a "duh" stare and explained everything that happened when they tried to touch it, and in the end I told him about me and Zade getting human nightmares and my suspicions of him having those in *his* head.

His gaze widened after I told him about it, and for a moment he didn't say anything. He just averted his gaze to the ground in silence. Abruptly he let out a long breath as he closed his eyes. Then he looked at me, and his gaze shown glimpses of a look that combined sadness with, weirdly enough, happiness. *"So you figured it out, huh?"* he asked in my head.

I nodded. *"What I don't get though, is why Cain would ever agree to help you? Not that I'm not grateful that he did, but I still don't get it."*

"You didn't ask him?"

I rolled my eyes at his question. *"The only thing he told me was to ask you, and that he was so gonna kick your butt. Duh, since when did you know him to be helpful with anything?"*

He cast an amused look at me. *"Well, at first he didn't want anything to do with the shit I deal with."*

"But?"

"But I swayed him in the end by telling him that he could get back at the Echelons if he helped me. Believe me when I say that he couldn't wait to do that anyway possible. Since he's locked up and no one's ever come to offer something like that to him, well, let's just say that his options were quite limited."

I winced at his words. *"So Cain really holds a grudge against that bunch, huh? But still, the only ones getting help from his grudge are us, not him. To get back at the Echelons, he didn't have a choice but to wait for who knows how many millennia."*

Ry shrugged. *"He looked like he was more than ready to wait that long. Hell, I'd be pissed too if I was locked up, being used by people who took advantage of me and beat the hell out of me whenever they saw fit."*

Pain rose in my chest at his words. They certainly didn't lock *him* up, but they did abuse him in more ways than one, and I so didn't want to recall any of the things they did to him before he was forced to leave seven hundred years ago. Since I was the only one who knew about it, I didn't want to remind him of those brutal moments. *"I get it. So, he was willing to wait until we turned Votzadirs and rebelled against them, huh? That's one pissed off guy."*

He nodded, with a heartfelt look at my mention of Cain. *"Well, Cain aside, I certainly can't say I'm happy that you have those dreams as well, because that would certainly lead you into danger beyond anything we've ever encountered before. Both Arcs and our own Echelons are against us, not to mention Belphegor's old man."*

Staring at my lips, he gently touched them, sending shivers down my spine. Very slowly, he leaned down, and rested his lips on mine. He was bit hesitant at first, but then heated with passion, he kissed me until I was left breathless.

When I was nearly lost in mounting desire, he reluctantly pulled back, and his sapphire eyes fell on me. "Yve, I wanna ask you something. It's perhaps too damn weird for me to ask this while we're just started, well, you know," he said meaningfully.

I frowned at him. "Well, shoot. After meeting with Cain, I'd say hardly anything could beat him in the 'weird' department."

He scoffed and shook his head. A faint smile formed on his lips. "No, seriously."

"Yeah, seriously," I retorted.

At my nonchalant reply, he firmed his gesture. "Okay, here goes. Um, I know that this is a bit too soon, and not even those who'd been together for long would do it in a whim, but . . ." he fell silent, making me frown at him.

"Uh, but what?" I asked carefully. By then, I didn't really pay attention to the hints he was dropping.

Until he said it to my face.

Inhaling deeply, he gulped. "Okay, what the hell, let's just get this over with," his deep voice was full with determination. "Will you, Yverna Tyraviafonza, be my soul mate for eternity and bind yourself to me in blood and soul?"

*　　*　　*

A woman walked into the forest outside a small human city which, unknown by its citizens, was governed by a duke of Hell. With her six guards fanned out around her, she transformed into her true self, a she-devil wearing an ocean-blue robe that covered her armour, on which a single star crossed with twin spears was embossed.

The crest of Kivarda rank.

"Rea, have the Machordaens been informed?" she asked.

The guard she called Rea nodded. "They have, Kivarda Aleeria. They all should be waiting for us just in the heart of these woods."

"Good. I can report to the Echelons and get back. Finally. It must be great to come home to the Aryad after six weeks in there. I have nothing against the duke, and I respect him, but it seems we lingered among the humans for far too long. They made me really nauseous," Aleeria commented as she feigned a shiver.

"Indeed. Even mere Fierytarians like us can barely stand them. How in the world the duke does it, let alone rule those primates, is beyond me," a guard named Jadam inserted vigorously.

Rea snorted. "What does that explain? You can barely stand anything."

All of them stifled a laugh at Rea's remark, and the seven of them continued their journey farther. They went deeper into the forest until moments later they reached a small barren field. There waited seven Machordaens.

They approached and saluted her and the Fierytarians. "May the Dark Light of Rygavon be with you, Kivarda, Fierytarians."

Aleeria and her guards answered his salute and eyed the Machordaen. "Long time no see, Teghari. It's good to see you all again."

Teghari smiled and nodded. "Likewise, Kivarda. So, shall we?" he indicated the path leading to the edge of the forest.

Aleeria inclined her head. "C'mon," she said, and she followed him, while the rest of the Machordaens took up positions ahead of them.

"So, Teghari, what's the deal with the extra details? Are the Arcs gonna ambush us?" asked Phyara, the Fierytarian who walked in caution at the far back of their formation.

Teghari almost answered her with the truth. He would have done so if it wasn't for the vow he made to the Cherxanain sisters. He was silent for several rapid heartbeats before he answered. "We don't exactly know what's what. The Iverand just sent us here, but he didn't mention anything about Arcs," he said, ignoring the meaningful gaze that was coming from his team.

Personally, he inwardly sighed in relief. Well, at least he hadn't breached his vow. It would suck like hell if he suddenly dropped dead after telling them why he and his team were sent as an additional security details for Aleeria.

"Okay, the Iverand's not helping. No offense, Teghari, but that guy really needs to broadcast something useful one of these days," Aleeria said under her breath.

Teghari grimaced, for he knew it all too well. "None taken, Kivarda."

They had not stridden far from where they had met when a cold eerie wind suddenly blew. *"Halt! Something's here!"* Aleeria's sharp warning echoed in the minds of her guards and Machordaens.

Rea, Jadam, and Teghari, along with a Machordaen named Hakal, quickly formed a defensive formation ahead while the rest spread in their positions around Aleeria. *"Kivarda, are you sure there's something here? I don't feel anything,"* Teghari said as he observed the surroundings.

"Same with me. That wind sure was eerie and a bit off, but I didn't sense a thing," Rea interjected.

Aleeria took her battle stance as she scanned the woods ahead. *"No guys, something's here. We can't see it, but trust me it's here. I caught its faint presence along with that wind earlier,"* she remarked with apparent dread.

They were all locked in dead silence, waiting for whoever or whatever Aleeria felt to appear. *"Hey, Teghari, shouldn't we tell them?"* Hakal asked, after he blocked the others.

Teghari didn't answer immediately, for he was also dying to tell them what he knew. But if it turned out not to be the one those Cherxanains told him about, the something that was out there killing soldiers, he would've died for nothing. On the other hand, if it was indeed the same being, he would die when he should be around to protect the Kivarda.

Point was, he just couldn't say a damn thing, period.

"Keep your silence, Hakal," he said in an even tone as he continued eyeing the woods. *"Elam,"* he called to another of his team who stood guard at the rear with the other Fierytarians. *"If this thing the Kivarda sensed is indeed the one I told you guys about, I want you to stay on guard. Be prepared to leave at my command and bring the Kivarda out of here at once."*

Elam almost turned to give a you-can-shove-that-command-right-up-your-ass look at his leader, but he caught himself as he glanced at the Fierytarians around them. *"May I ask why the hell you would give me that shitty command? She can leave with the Fierytarians."*

"She is our responsibility, and that damned thing will be too much for them to handle alone! Even with our aid, I honestly doubt it will do any good, but at least there are Machordaens at her side. You'll come with him too, Hakal." Teghari glanced at the soldier near him with his senses fully alert.

"Fine, whatever. Just don't die or I'll kill you myself," Hakal replied calmly.

Teghari grimaced inwardly. *"Thanks for the support. You guys have greatly brightened my day,"* he said sardonically.

"Likewise, buddy," the two said in unison.

"Look, if anything happens, the Iverand would know. Let's just hope he can send us backup if needed," Teghari said. That was when Aleeria saw something that caused her to draw on her full power. "Heads up!" she shouted without warning.

All of them abruptly lifted their gaze to the tree ahead and sucked in their breath, for they saw something above it that was beyond anything they'd ever seen. None of them could move. They were too transfixed by the being that floated ahead and slowly landed.

It was such a marvellous sight, one that promised ultimate chaos.

The Fierytarians and the Machordaens were snapped back from their trance by five bolts that flew past them. "Spread out!" she barked. They were moving to battle formation when they saw the impossible.

The five bolts Aleeria shot at their enemy just vanished. Whatever it was just made a swipe, and all of the bolts disappeared.

Teghari cursed. *"This confirms it. This must be whatever killed those Levarchons. No angel looks like that or has that ability."* He took his battle stance. "Fire at will!" he roared as he too threw multiple bolts, all the while knowing how his attempts would be no use.

Not after it depleted the Kivarda's attacks like yesterday's garbage.

Gritting his teeth, he realized he had no other choice. As the rest of his squad and the Fierytarians let loose their battle cries and lunged at once upon their assailant, Teghari came to Aleeria. "Kivarda, please, you have to leave."

"Not a damn chance!" she snarled as she launched another bolt.

Teghari *tsked*. "Forgive me, Kivarda," he said, and then he turned his attention to his soldiers and the Fierytarians. "Elam, Hakal, you have your orders! Rea, get the Kivarda out of here!" he said sternly.

"You have no right . . ." Aleeria started.

"Nyra, Yadok, Ridan! You heard him, go!" Rea shouted her orders, interrupting her.

"Thanks, Rea," Teghari sent the thought.

"Don't mention it."

Teghari and the rest of the soldiers spread out and blocked Aleeria from the creature's sight, while the Kivarda's angry shouts trailed off into the woods. But as he and the rest simultaneously shot multiple bolts, the being simply stood and dissolved their attacks. Suddenly it spread its wings.

For a split second, Teghari's attention was swept back into the surreal nature of the scene. Before he could react, the winged being moved swiftly and landed in front of him. He barely heard his comrades' desperate screams as he saw a terrifyingly beautiful smile and caught glimpses of six wings that glistened like water under the moonlight.

Its magnificence was the last thing Teghari noticed before everything went dark.

*   *   *

"Uh, Yve? Are you all right?"

Ry's voice pulled me back from a trance. I winced and stared at him like he was some sort of a ghost. Was it just a dream?

He just said the one sentence I didn't even dare to think I'd ever hear from him! Eyes wide, I swallowed in disbelief. "You really asked me that?"

He blushed, igniting my own smile. He appeared so innocent with that sheepish look. "Well, I understand if you want to think about it first. Hell, I won't even be mad at you if you say that I'm being hasty or even paranoid because of what has happened," he said quickly. "But I just, well, I just need to ask you that," he remarked with dead earnestness.

Biting my lip, I almost couldn't hold my tears from falling. I'd never dreamed that there would come a day when he would say this to me. Inhaling before I broke into a cry of joy, I levelled an intense look into his eyes. "You know, you're right to say that most people wouldn't do it in such a short time of being together," I started, and I caught a glint of pain in his eyes, but he was still bracing himself for whatever I'd say. "But, you definitely forgot that not everyone went through what we did."

His eyes bright, he gulped. "Does this mean . . . ?"

I kissed him blindly. "Do you need any further explanation, Mr Commander?"

Smiling with his eyes bright, he played with a lock of my hair. "I just don't want you to be disappointed afterward," he said quietly. "Honestly, I don't want to bind your soul's freedom against your will, but I detest the thought of you being reborn and being with someone other than me a whole lot more."

I smiled at his heartfelt words that warmed my soul. "I'd say I've had seven hundred years to sort things through, and yes, I wouldn't like that either," I replied with a wink.

He still hesitated with his next move, made me wonder if I really was that scary or something. "Ry, really, what is it?"

Shaking his head, he gave me a gentle smile that melted me. "I just can't bear the thought of being apart from you ever again, but like I said, I understand if you think I'm just being paranoid and you don't want to rush this. Don't push yourself on my account."

Heaving a sigh, I cupped his face. "Babe, which part of 'I've had seven hundred years to sort things through' escapes your understanding? And when I said I wouldn't like that either, that means there's no other soul I'd rather spend the rest of my life with than you."

He winced, but before he said anything, I wrapped my hands around his neck, pulling him down to me. "Ry, I'm glad that you love me enough to consider my feelings so much that you'd even go as far as to give me chance to think about this. I know that you barely could hold yourself yesterday when we met again, but because you know what it means to bind one soul to another, you asked that of me. That's just who you are–considerate, honest. Hell, you weren't even mad at me when I dragged my feet before I admitted that I too love you more than my damned existence."

"Yve," he started to pull away, but I held him in place.

"No, let me finish this. Believe me when I say that I too love you more than my damned existence. When I realized that you were alive and had been wandering for seven centuries out there, alone, after barely escaping with your life, you have no idea how much that fact almost destroyed me with guilt–profound guilt that I wasn't even there with you to protect you. Guilt because I didn't realize that Lucifer would come after you sooner or later, even if you didn't help your brother escape his clutches," I said as I slowly pulled back to stare at his deep sapphire eyes.

He raised one hand and placed it on my cheek, silently urging me to say more. "But that also made me feel a foreign hope I'd never known. To know that I could see you made me feel alive again, because I slowly died inside every millennium I went through without you. Vrae and the others, they were there, but without you I still felt this gaping hole nobody could ever fill. When you said that you loved me, I knew that I'd do anything to protect you and never let you go," I said in a dead-pan tone with my eyes stuck on his. "Never again."

Raising his other hand, he placed it on my other cheek as he lowered his head, and with his eyes closed, he leaned his forehead onto mine. "You're not damned, not to me."

"Hon, I know thousands of royal families that would say otherwise."

He smiled, but weirdly enough, it was more like he was suppressing an urge to laugh. "Protecting is my department, sweetheart, and that would include protecting you," he said, and he started to laugh with obvious happiness on his face.

He abruptly hugged me and lifted me as he whirled on his heels. After he finally put me back on my feet, I grinned at him. "You look like you just won a jackpot or something."

Returning my grin, he shook his head. "Nu-uh, I got more than just a jackpot, baby," he said with a laugh, and then he cleared his throat. "So, you're ready?"

I smiled at him. "Sure thing."

"Okay," he said, and then he scratched his right palm, forming the symbol of devils' binding link, an encircled upside-down trident, while I also prepared my symbol.

We looked into each other's eyes as we held our palms together, letting our blood blend as we repeated our vows in our native tongue. The second my blood came in contact with his, the symbols on our palms burned in black and sapphire flames. With this, my blood and powers were assimilated in his veins as his blood and powers were in mine. As we felt our blood streams burn, he kissed me with a kiss so tender and so full with passion that my head spun.

In that moment, glimpses of his memories invaded my mind, but strangely enough, I felt that he covered most of them, especially the painful ones I knew he'd experienced. I could only feel a modicum of his pain and loneliness course through me, but I saw almost nothing.

I inwardly smiled bitterly, for I also did the same thing with my memories. We were still like we were before, it seemed. We believed in each other more than we did our companions, but we still kept back the most painful things we should've shared but wouldn't just to protect one another.

He seemed to feel that I had deliberately masked some things from him, especially my encounters with Baradyn. But just like me, he understood the reason without asking and simply revelled in our union.

We separated minutes later and I looked at my palm. The flame had disappeared, but the burning symbol remained. Now our bond had become eternal. I saw it go under my skin and glow for a moment before completely disappearing.

Satisfied, he took my hand and kissed my knuckles. "Oh, one more thing."

"Yeah?"

He cleared his throat. "Since we're more than likely reborn into another form than this one, I wanna do something else. If we are indeed to become humans," he stopped and embraced me, "I swear I'll look for you, even if it takes me to the end of the world. No matter what happens, my soul will never rest until I find yours," he whispered softly.

I winced at his vow and felt love for him swell in my heart. Returning his hug, I answered his vow with mine. "I too swear that my soul will never rest until I find yours."

He smiled widely. "I'm a little bit perplexed though," he said with a frown.

I cocked my head. "Why is that?"

He gave me a mischievous grin. "You're willing to unite our blood and soul even though we're not exactly mates yet."

I curled my lips indignantly. "Male, and here I thought you would think seven centuries apart had brought me past that 'mate' part."

His grin grew broader. "That's why I love you."

Rolling my eyes, I cast a serious look at him. I intended to ask him why he'd never said anything about his head problem. "Never mind that. So you indeed have those dreams too, huh? I wonder why you've never told me any of this before when you should have."

He directed a tender look at me. "You know I always place my full faith in you, but that doesn't mean I'd let anything happen to you."

I sighed at his overprotective attitude. "I know you wouldn't, even when you don't say it. Somehow I know you always keep the most dangerous of troubles to yourself. Unless one of us happens to be with you when something occurs, you wouldn't tell us jack squat about anything." I held his hand and looked straight into his deep sapphire eyes. "But don't you ever do that from now on, not to me. We've bound our souls together. That means my soul is part of yours as yours is part of mine. That means that your problem is my problem."

He kissed me deeply right after those words left my mouth. Pulling back, he tucked a lock of my hair behind my ears and smiled at me. "I know. That's why I'll tell you what's been happening since we separated yesterday."

I raised a brow. "Good, I wanted to ask that myself. So?"

He recounted everything I wanted to know about what he had done at the prince's. Aside from that, he also told me everything about Herathim, the ring, and—the part where I gaped in disbelief—the Core of Rygavon and its origin. I also heard something more about that void thing, the one they called Arzia or something, I only remember its meaning, which was really classic.

And Lilith seemed to know something about this after all, not that I cared, but Vrae's suspicions and Rivorgad's words were proven to be true after all. She did have something of importance–for once.

When he told me about the princes' banter, I laughed out loud. "Those two never cease to amaze me. In spite of their reputations, they sometimes can be more ridiculous than anybody. Who would've thought?"

Ry chuckled. "Yeah, I really had to restrain myself from laughing. I'd never imagine you or Vrae babbling about some random strawberry jam."

"No, I wouldn't dare to imagine something like that myself, because that'd be awkward as in 'weird' awkward," I added, laughing again.

Damn, it felt like forever since the last time we had laughed together like this. To talk and banter as if nothing could ever bother us in the world and all that crap with the Echelons and Lucifer was no more than a meaningless nightmare–it was like a dream . . . I hoped this peaceful moment would last, yet like most hopes, it was bound to end.

Bittersweet feelings swirled inside me as he explained the rest. After he'd finished, he fell silent. Clearly he was deep in whatever downing thoughts were going through his mind.

I went back to what he said about not wanting to tell me about his nightmares. *"You know, for a second I thought you didn't want me to tease you about all those humans you have going in your head."* I grinned.

His attention shifted back to me and he smiled. "Maybe that too, but first things first. No harm comes your way unless the bringer wants to die a slow, painful and disastrous death."

I gave him a sullen look. "Yeah, I know. It's a total wonder why they still call me the Tyraviafonza, considering the way you treat me."

He raked my hair gently with a wicked smile. "Luscious, not even I dare to cross you, and they say I'm all-powerful with the whole sky practically at my disposal."

I snickered and then ran my hand from his hairline to his chin. "Well, it's too bad, because I might have an idea as to what to give you whenever you think to *cross* me," I purred teasingly.

He looked straight at me with a gaze so intense it melted me from inside out. "I can't wait to see it, and you better mean it, sweetheart." His words came out in a husky voice. It rolled off his tongue like the sweetest honey as a wicked smile curved his lips that were made for long deep kisses.

I shivered a bit, not out of fear, but because of the feeling his gaze aroused in me. The intensity of his gaze towards me was so tremendous that I felt he wrapped me up entirely with just the protective look on his devastatingly gorgeous face.

He then poured another rain of scorching kisses on me again. As I revelled in the feeling of being in the shelter of his strong arms, he drove me to the edge with his hot kisses and blinded me with passion that grew wilder with each kiss and touch he gave me.

Slowly he nipped my earlobe. "You're up for a challenge?" he whispered.

My blood rushed at the warmth of his breath as I leaned on his cheek. "What do you have in mind?" I whispered silkily.

He pulled back and spread his wings. "C'mon, let's go up and see if we could piss off our buddies up there enough so they'd come and play with us," he said wickedly.

I arched a brow. "They're no buddies of mine, hon, and I thought you didn't like me being up there? And by the way, do you really want to invite them to *our* party?"

"What I don't like is the thought of you being up there on your own without me, and no, I'd prefer they didn't show up. I just want to be up there in the sky with you," he said calmly, but I caught a note of protectiveness and longing in his voice that touched me deeply. That alone told me how worried he had been when he had learned about my suicidal habit of taunting upstairs' citizens.

Smiling, I nodded. "All right, I'm sorry about that. C'mon, I'm ready."

An evil grin broke out on his handsome face, and then he stood behind me, hugging me tightly. Without warning, he jumped through the tight canopy of the forest and flapped his wings, taking us straight to the sky.

We stopped once we reached the highest place, with the clouds surrounding us in darkness. By the tightness of his hug, I felt that he was afraid he would lose me. And that same feeling swelled in me. I would never want to let him go, ever again.

He slowly buried his face in my hair and inhaled deeply. "How I missed your scent. I wish I could just stay here with you forever and let go of everything." He whispered in my ears. His rich deep voice sent shivers through my body.

"I like the sound of that," I replied quietly.

He was playing with a lock of my hair when my eyes caught a slight ray of moonlight. I turned my head to see it, but it was covered by clouds. He seemed to realize what had caught my attention, and he waved. The clouds dispersed, revealing the big full moon that shone like a gigantic pearl that shone brightly, illuminating the night sky. Its pale white surface looked unbelievably beautiful as its light shone out amongst the darkness.

"Would you look at that," he said in amazement as he pointed at the moon and gently rubbed his cheek on mine. For the first time in my entire existence, I realized how breath-takingly beautiful the scene was. It was absurd for me to feel this way, for I saw that moon every time I went to sleep. But being here with him within his arms made me notice even the most insignificant things around me. Like that moon.

How peculiar, and yet somehow it felt like a refreshing change.

Ry placed his warm palm on my forehead. He tenderly ran his hand from my head to my hair and back again as he sighed in complete contentment with his arms tight around me.

"I never realized it could be this beautiful," I said quietly as he laid my head on his shoulder.

I felt him nod gently. "I don't know how many times I'm gonna say this, but I missed you so damn much," he murmured.

I felt him wrap his strong arms around me protectively. "I missed you too. More than I could bear," I muttered as I looked at him.

It was then that I remembered the last thing Xaemorkahn and Varisha told me. I didn't want to ruin this moment, but I just needed to know. I had to.

Was I the real reason Lucifer had gone after him?

"Ry, there's something I want to ask you," I started. Tears had begun to sting behind my eyes. Clenching my fists, I braced myself as I heard his reply.

"What is it?"

"Xaemorkahn and Varisha told me about this one moment when they were tending you after you got shot by the Rygavon."

"And?"

"They told me that you were screaming at someone not to touch me. Who was it?" I asked, with an utterly disturbing idea of who it might be.

He fell silent, and for a moment there was no sound but the faintest whisper of the night wind around us. "Ry, please be honest with me. Did Lucifer go after you because of me? Did I do something that ticked him off?" I whispered. I could never forgive myself if I truly was the cause.

Instead of giving me an immediate answer, he slowly tightened his arms around me, and I could feel his trepidation. "No, you had nothing to do with it. It was me he was after from the get-go," he said.

"But?"

I felt his arms clench. "But he threatened to kill you. Right before the Black Light came to kill me, he said something about you jerking the chain of the wrong people, though I really had no idea what he was babbling about, and I still don't. Maybe he said that while I was fighting off his damned Black Light to jerk *my* chain. That sounds like something he'd definitely do," he said bitterly.

I let out a nervous scoff. "How in the hell did he know about the two of us? Not even I knew the way you felt about me back then."

He shook his head. "I have no clue and I don't care. I just damned glad he didn't make true of his words, or so help me, not even Azrael could stop me from butchering him."

I levelled an intense gaze at him. "Don't say that. I'll never let him touch you. I don't want to lose you. Ever," I said fiercely.

He gave me a smile so tender, it melted whatever uneasiness threatened to consume me. "You won't," he whispered.

Our lips met in a passionate kiss as he moved his wings to wrap us both. Not only that, I felt something else gathered around us. When a cool breeze slightly teased my skin, I realized that he'd moved the clouds around us. He continued to rain down on me with deep sweet kisses that seemed endless. Pulling back, he looked into my eyes with a look as if he wanted to devour me. I met his gaze with the same intensity to show him just how much I missed him, just how much we'd lost.

Even now I still couldn't believe how he'd wormed his way into my heavily guarded heart. I believed even less that somehow I'd unknowingly stolen my way into his.

Most humans believed that we, the so-called bringers of evil, had no hearts, much less the ability to love. In some aspects, maybe that was true, but even we were bound to meet with our destined mate, the one with whom we could share our buried secrets, our deepest darkness, and count on them not to betray us.

But very few would go so far as to bond our souls forever like we just did.

Perhaps this was meant to be. I always thought that he needed someone at his back. All this time, it never crossed my mind that he wanted that someone to be me and that I too wanted to be that someone for him, even though I knew he deserved so much more than just me. Yeah, me, a devil who toyed with trust and beliefs, who should never be counted on to be at anyone's back, let alone his.

After thousands of years being his comrade, I knew that despite everything he did per the Echelons' orders, he was struggling to keep himself together. He would never want to admit that, and I respected his wish, even though I was dying to get whatever it was off his chest and soothe him.

This second time I'd met him again, I began to notice that he had that same weary look on his face. Every now and again I caught a glint of worry in his eyes, like dread he was trying to conceal.

If back then his eyes would sometimes bring me sadness that he didn't trust me enough to tell me what he was thinking, now that look really made me want to scream and beg him to share whatever burden he was carrying on his back.

As if he read my thoughts, he kissed my forehead. "I love you, and that's the only thing I've ever feared I'd lose," he said out of the blue.

"What do you mean?" I asked as I stared at him.

He returned my gaze, but I could see that he was looking at something beyond me as if he were recalling something in the faraway past. "All these thousands of years, everything that I did, I saw, I've been through without you, this lump of–I don't know–fear or something would always appear with the one threat that would always try to drive me over the edge, one that wanted to devour everything I feel about you until it completely perished," he said quietly with turmoil and anguish in his deep voice.

"I can't bear the thought of losing you ever. You're the only reason I've fought my way back. You're the only one that kept me going." His deep voice was strained, and his words reached deep into my soul.

"Ry," I whispered his name, as I fought the tears that threatened to fall.

Very carefully, he trailed his finger on the side of my face. "In my entire life, you're the only one who makes me feel things that I've never known existed. You made me realize who I could become and what extent I could reach. There's nothing I wouldn't do for you, especially to protect you, because I love you too damn much. That's all I need, all I know, and all I have left," he said in a rather fierce voice. "Even if I had to face Rygavon head on, I'd do it if it meant you'd be safe. I just can't lose you."

Yeah, and he did that all right. No way in hell I'd let him do that again.

I turned around and cupped his face in my hand with my eyes fixed on his sapphire eyes. "You won't. I'm here now. I love you, and I will never leave you. You said you'd face Rygavon to protect me. Guess what? You did. You've been there, and that scared the hell out of me. So don't even think that you'd be facing it alone if it came to a situation where you had to do it again."

He opened his mouth to reply, but I raised my marked hand to stop him. Black light illuminated the lines from beneath my palm. "That is what this mark means. No buts, period," I stated firmly as I stared at him. "And you know what's not fair?" I asked him.

Wincing, he shook his head. "What?"

"You just said all the things I wanted to say." I narrowed my eyes at him.

Smiling wickedly, he landed a quick kiss. "Good thing I did. I've been dying to tell you all that and get it off my chest."

"Nice to know I've helped you," I replied silkily.

Bringing his devastatingly gorgeous face closer to me, he masterfully claimed my lips again. As he eagerly explored my mouth, we dissolved our devil armours despite the fact that we both were floating dangerously close under upstairs' scrutinizing eyes.

Amongst the scattered stars, I finally accepted him. Under his massive black wings, warm blue flame was ignited and engulfed us as we were joined for the very first time.

We ignored even the slight rays of the blazing sun that escaped through the clouds for hours until I slipped away into true peaceful darkness.

∗   ∗   ∗

"We're here, Iverand."

Amon glanced at his guests, but most of his attention remained on the Veil. The damned thing had just blurted out more grim news that was far worse than he thought.

Whatever that thing was, it had just killed Aleeria, her Fierytarians, and a Machordaen team, the ones Yverna sent out to recover the remains of its very first victims. When they were under attack, the golems had given out an alert, but before he could send reinforcements, it was over, again with no sightings of who or what did it.

He turned to face his guests, the two female devils who walked in and shut the door. They were the only pair he trusted among the Intelligence Division who wouldn't rat anything to the Echelons–something he had rarely found in the last fifteen thousand years.

The two were Lenora and Ravendy, the soldiers who were, by all of Hell, referred to as the Eyes of Truth.

Originally Varkonians, each possessed an unparalleled ability to uncover deceit. Whereas Lenora could unravel the distant past, Ravendy was able to foresee far into the future. While seers could only have their premonitions if something big was about to happen, these two could use their abilities on massive crowds or an individual, either at will or triggered by whoever they had their mental eyes on doing something that crossed the line.

Not even the Echelons dared to lower their guard, let alone speak without thinking, for they feared the two would see into either the past or the future in regard to whatever matter they spoke about.

The two looked like twins with matching gold robes and armour, Ravendy had amber eyes, and her long brown hair was pulled neatly into a single braid on the right side which she brought to her front. She stood with her calm demeanour that mirrored the depth of her wisdom, result from gazing into whatever it was she found in the future. No one knew whether it was paradise or hell on earth.

Lenora, on the other hand, had long-braided amber hair that fell over her left shoulder to her front, and her dark brown eyes shot a feral gaze, but it was obvious that it was her thick shield to defend herself. Some said that it was caused by her constantly seeing countless of betrayals that led to brutal slaughters that she grew suspicious of almost anyone. She could no longer work together with other soldiers, because not only would she expect them to betray her in the field, but she would also taunt them, believing she was revealing their nature to betray her.

Sadly, some of her comrades couldn't control themselves and gave in to the temptation to be rid of her–all because she was driven by her paranoia.

The only one among the Varkonians whom she trusted and who could calm her whenever her hysteria kicked in was Ravendy, who, in a sense, matched her in terms of powers. Thus they each were given their own unique station. Two thousand years before the supposed death of Ezryan, the Echelons moved them to the most secluded section of the Lasinth, where they barely meet with anyone but Amon.

He invited the two to take the chairs in front of his desk. "Come sit, Ravendy, Lenora," he said as he too sat.

Both of them took their seats. "May we ask why you requested our presence, Iverand?" Ravendy started.

"And using a shield too for that matter," Lenora added. Her voice was so low, Amon could barely hear her.

"I'm sorry. We need to tread carefully in this. Before I tell you anything, first I wanted to know whether you two have seen anything in the last six months."

The pair exchanged a knowing look and then turned their eyes back to him. "The Veil revealed something, did it not?" Lenora asked.

"The Hieldhar has returned, hasn't he?" Ravendy inserted.

Amon's eyes widened in awe. It seemed there was no hiding anything from this pair. But this also stirred fear for them in him. "All right, what exactly do you know regarding the Hieldhar?"

"He did not die," they said in eerie unison.

"The Lord was the one who attempted to kill him, not the Almighty," Lenora whispered in horror.

Ravendy nodded her agreement. "Yes, I'd foreseen it, and Lenora saw it as it came to pass, but we couldn't tell anyone until now. I saw that you would summon us, and only then could we speak of it." She narrowed her gaze at him. "You already knew. Yve, Vrathien, and Zade know about it as well."

Amon raised his hands. "Fine, I'm busted. Why didn't you tell me this the last time I summoned you?" he asked.

Ravendy lowered her voice, almost like Lenora did. "Last time wasn't the moment. Now is, because you asked what we knew in the last six months."

Amon was about to open his mouth, but he saw that their rambling truth was yet to end. He was right to keep his mouth shut, for they blurted out something that not even he would ever have suspected. "You also need to know one other thing–the very reason why the cursed Echelons removed us both from everyone's eyes."

He gulped. This was one of many things he had wondered about for a long time, but neither of them would speak of it before. "You saw the Echelons did something, didn't you? Did they kill someone to hide whatever it was?" he asked.

They simultaneously nodded and cast a miserable look at him. "Not just any soldiers. The Echelons had been attempting to kill the Hieldhar for four thousand years. It just so happened that someone lent a helping hand, and you know who it was," Lenora said.

Amon gulped. He definitely knew where she was going.

Ravendy inclined her head with a sad look all over her face. "Yes, it was the Lord."

*   *   *

Ezryan landed smoothly under the tree where he had met Yverna hours earlier.

Carefully, he laid her gently on the grass and tucked her robes safely over her body. He ran his hand down Yverna's long black hair that was as smooth as silk under his fingers. He still couldn't believe his fortune that this remarkable she-devil who'd stolen his heart would feel the same towards him. To think that one day he could be her soul-mate was beyond anything he could ever dream.

She just never realized how precious she was. Unlike most devils of her nature, she would do anything in her power for those she cared about, those who earned her loyalty and gave her theirs in return.

It was true that she could be most vengeful in the event she got wronged, but all the things she'd do to protect her companions often made even him speechless in awe. And she did all that, spontaneously, calmly, without a second thought.

That was one of many things he learned from her. It was also the very thing that had drawn him to her in the first place.

She'd never admit it, and each time he'd tease her about it, she'd just evade the topic by saying that it would be disastrous or something similar if she didn't do whatever was needed to protect her companions. What she said had merit, but he knew that was just who she was–a protective, caring, and lethally beautiful she-devil.

She could be deadly and gentle, which made him wonder at times just how she could be both with all the shit they went through, hell, with the shit that was their nature. Not to mention all the things that had happened to her in the past, all the horrors and betrayals that demanded her blood be shed and the blood of others she protected . . .

For those reasons alone, she shouldn't even be able to let anybody be in her circle or, more to the point, to give her trust to others. It turned out that her loyalty was one of the many things about her that would often strike him deep, as well as her understanding nature that never passed judgement on anyone except those who'd crossed the line.

And she was the only one who could make lower his guard and reveal his true self.

When she found out what was happening between him and the Echelons, she kept it to herself and never breathed a word of it, not even to her sister, just as he would have expected from her. She was the only soul among the legion who knew that the Echelons would beat him whenever he'd done his job as they requested to a T, but the result wasn't quite in their favour. Hell, they'd torture him if there was a soldier went rogue. It didn't matter if the renegade wasn't in his legion, they'd still blame him. At least, he thought that those were the reasons when they did it to him, no matter how insane that sounded.

Whenever he was by himself, away from his companions after he'd received a long brutal beating, she was the one who sought him, instead of him looking for her or Vrathien hooking her up with him. Hell knew he didn't want anybody to ever see him in such a humiliating situation and appearing so damned vulnerable. In moments like that, she'd asked him to show her his wounds. If it had been someone other than her, he'd have told them to mind their own business, but even then he found that he couldn't say no to her, and he'd let her heal him. Those wounds would indeed heal by themselves, but the Echelons would always do so much damage, more than his body could heal in a short period of time. She knew that and just couldn't leave it be.

She just couldn't pretend that she didn't know anything. Contrary to what most of their people and the humans thought, it wasn't in her to know something like that and just look the other way. That was one of many incredible things he loved about her.

As he stared upon her exquisite sleeping form, his thoughts drifted to the moment when he'd just landed on the edge of Sarokh River at the edge of Kadarost forest. Immediately he buckled from the pain he'd received from another vicious beating, another of the punishments the Echelons brought down on him because one of the devil witches named Zarkhyn had gone rogue and slaughtered a whole herd of Alvadors and Machordaens.

He had just removed his armour when he heard a crack somewhere near him. Flashing his armour back, he felt a painful hot lash sear his flesh. He ignored the pain as he readied himself for whoever was coming. If they wanted a fight and thought he was a sitting duck because of his wounds, it would be the last mistake of their lives. At least that was what he was prepared to do until he heard a familiar voice from behind the trees.

"Stand down, Hieldhar. It's me."

Relief washed through him at the only voice that could bring him solace. Hers.

But that feeling quickly faded when he realized something was off. He just didn't know what. "Yve, what are you doing here?" He forced a smile at her despite the weariness gripping him.

She sauntered towards him with a gait that showed how lethal she was, but that was the sexiest thing he'd ever seen. For a split second, he'd forgotten the vicious pain in his back and front. Unfortunately, that single moment of distraction ended when he snapped back to reality as she knelt next to him. "Just looking to do some fishing," she said casually.

He arched a brow at her random retort. "Fishing?"

She rolled her pitch-black eyes. "What do you think I'm doing here?"

"Well, I . . . Wait," he said as he finally realized what was wrong. "Aren't you supposed to be at the Zerthurian kingdom?" he asked in alarm.

She shrugged. "I am. Well, technically. I had my doppelganger stay there."

"Yve . . ."

"It's night, Hieldhar. The humans are sleeping. So, chill."

"I know. It's not the humans I'm worried about. The Echelons were still on to you up until few weeks ago. They strictly forbade you to leave before your job's done."

"Then you'd better not waste any more of my time. Now stop talking and remove your armour," she said sternly.

He had to suppress an urge to laugh at her stern words. In the entire First Legion under him, only she could boss him around and not get punished or even scolded. Then again, she was the only one who dared, whereas not even her sister would.

Well, she was the Tyraviafonza after all. Still, he couldn't even begin to think of how he didn't mind it in the least. He felt like he could endure anything from her. Yes, her, the she-devil notoriously known as the Queen of Tyranny, who made even the Xarchons tremble at her presence, and yet he'd never felt any cruelty from her whenever they were away from the battlefield. Nothing but the depth of her tender kindness.

How peculiar was that?

"I'm fine," he replied.

She curled her plump lips, soft beautiful lips he'd do anything to kiss. Only that seemed to be far beyond his reach. What he wouldn't give to claim this precious she-devil's heart.

Despite the fact that he could always count on her to stand by his side whatever the circumstances, in some sense she wasn't even there. As for her, she too depended on him to be by her side whenever she needed him.

Unfortunately, it wasn't in the way he'd wanted.

"Don't make me tie you down with my darkness, Hieldhar. That would be more painful for you and definitely less productive for me if I were to heal you," she rebuked.

He cringed and then yielded to her playful threat. He removed his armour once more but left his long leather pants in place. Against his instincts not to let anyone see him when he was vulnerable, he let her see the savage mutilation that had been done to his bare body.

She didn't even grimace at the gruesome sight. Moving to his back, she touched one of the worst wounds there. "I toasted the bitch before I went. You can relax," she said quietly.

He'd heard about it and nodded. "I know. You made a good well-done toast out of her."

"Nah, I prefer it crispy," she said with a small laugh. A laugh that calmed the wrath that was searing his soul after the humiliation he'd endured, one of many things about her that gave his soul a strange sense of peace despite her morbid humour.

"You're not gonna ask me what their excuse was this time?" he asked with a hint of bitterness and shame in his voice.

She ignored him for a moment as she continued to heal him. Sighing, she stopped for a second. "Do I really need to ask? Besides, I thought I just gave you the answer before *you* asked," she said nonchalantly.

Indeed she had: Zarkhyn, the devil witch, who had fifteen entourages of deadly witches and warlocks under her command.

"There's nothing I'd like more than to kick the Echelons' asses for their stupidity, but then again they wouldn't be the Echelons if they used their heads," she went on.

He laughed at that, ignoring another jolt of pain that shot through him. "I'd love to see you kick their asses. Pity we'd have a riot if I let you or better yet, if I did it myself."

Apparently, she felt his muscle clench when he laughed. "Stop laughing, Hieldhar. You'll just hurt yourself," she said sternly.

"Yes, ma'am," he replied gleefully.

They both fell silent for several heartbeats, until she suddenly spoke about something he thought he'd concealed from her. "Look, I know the real reason why they're doing this to you," she said bitterly with a hint of reluctance in her soft alluring voice.

He felt as though his breath was knocked out of him. He'd never told the actual cause to her, and not even the Iverand knew about it, so how did she?

"What are you talking about?" he asked slowly.

She let out an aggravated breath. "Really, do you need to ask? Who do you take me for? It was all clear after you killed Darov, when in reality they'd expected you to capture him so they could torture him until their rabid dog instincts were satisfied. Not only did they start to beat the crap out of you for inane reasons, they began sending you on suicide missions. Don't think I don't know all about it," she snapped, when he began to open his mouth. "They thought you heard something from him and that you killed him because he asked you to."

He was completely lost for words and merely stared at the ground before he shifted his gaze back to her. "But he didn't tell me jack, and I killed him because he nearly chopped my head off! How did you know they wanted whatever that was from me, anyway?"

She shook her head. "I won't tell you any time soon. What I can tell you generally is that I know why the Echelons went after him like a bunch of rabid dogs."

"And that is? All I know is that they wanted him because he killed those guys."

She scoffed. "Well, the reason why he killed those fifteen Xarchons was nothing. He was merely fighting his way out to get away from the Echelons, who sent *them* to kill him, which I think they forgot to tell you."

The look on his face was all the confirmation she needed.

She wrinkled her nose with a repulsed look. He would've smiled at how beautiful she was despite her funny expression if his mind wasn't forcing him to focus on the problem at hand. "Unfortunately for them, he was too powerful to be faced by mere Xarchons."

He winced at her words, because Xarchons were a helluva lot more powerful bunch than average soldiers and a hundred times more savage. It was wrong to call them "mere Xarchons". But in regards to Darov's powers, her words may have had some merit, because the deceased devil had nearly succeeded in killing him, which was a surprising feat in itself.

Then again, he'd never thought that a Cherxanain could master elemental sorcery and could have had three elements at his disposal that almost matched his own powers.

Sighing, he rubbed his temple. "Well, what exactly did he do?"

She fell silent, as if considering what she should say next. "Darov told me what his intention was before all that commotion started. What I didn't expect was that they'd turn on you after his death, and for that I'm so sorry. But it seemed like he'd foreseen it, because he told me to tell you that if things turned from bad to worse, he asked for your forgiveness for not making things easier on you. He had to do it. Well, he did respect you as his commander, Ry, in spite of the fact that he, to quote you, 'nearly chopped your head off.' He was a First Legion after all."

He gulped at that. "You should've told me. What did he say?" he pressed.

She stubbornly shook her head. "No, I can't tell you. They could kill you for real over it. It's safer if I'm the only who knows about this, and as long as they still don't know for sure whether you know something or not, they won't really harm you more than this, Zian," she said gently, calling him by the term for brother in their native tongue. It was a term she reserved only for him and one he'd always cherish. That single word would warm him whenever she used it, but lately it pained him more.

Because he wanted her to see him as much more than a mere brother-in-arms.

He closed his eyes as bittersweet love for her surged through him. "There's nothing I can say that would change your mind, is there?"

"Nothing indeed," she said simply as her hand moved from one wound to another.

He swallowed. "I was supposed to take responsibility for all of you, especially you, since you tend to walk on treacherous ground." He forced a small laugh.

She dropped one hand on his shoulder. Her skin warmed his cold soul, a feeling he revelled in whenever he was with her. "You've been guarding all our backs for thousands of years, and you bear more responsibility than you should. It's only fair that at least one of us guards *you*, especially in the head games those bastards favour so much."

"Thanks, Yve, really," he said earnestly.

"Don't mention it," she murmured.

Both of them fell silent again as he felt her healing power surge through him like cool water in the harsh heat of hell. It was all the help he could hope for. The damage done to his body was too much, and his powers were all that made him strong enough to go out here in the first place.

As he felt her powers seeping through his body, one question that had been bothering him for a long time slowly came to his mind, the one that she'd always refused to answer every time this happened. But, he still couldn't let it go. "Yve?"

"Hmm?"

"I know I've been asking you this a thousand times, but still, I gotta ask. How do you do it? How can you always know whenever I'm down?"

She didn't say anything but just kept on healing him.

"Yve, look, I'm glad that you're helping me . . ."

"Then stop asking."

He turned around, looking straight at her. "Yve, please," he said as he took her hands. "I can't let this go if it means you're endangering yourself. Tell me who's been keeping close eyes on me? Please tell me, because there's just no way for you to know what happened to me while you were in that kingdom."

Pulling her hands away, she grasped his. "Ry, don't you trust me?"

"I do. With my life," he replied earnestly.

A surge of pride went through her at his words, and another feeling started to warm her soul. It was so gentle, and she wasn't sure what it was. "Then believe me when I say the thing you don't know could endanger a lot of people. I know you. If I tell you who it is, you'll just pay them a visit and ask them not to tell me anything any more. All because you worry so much, and that would draw the Echelons' rats towards you. And then, you and my sources will all go straight into the meat grinder."

He fell silent and just stared at her. He couldn't even find even one argument because every word she said was true. She did know him, in fact, far too well.

"Ry, my sources communicate with me using methods not even I can understand, but it's absolutely safe. So, just leave it be, okay?" she asked with a voice so alluring, he found himself concede to her request. "Okay?" She repeated.

He nodded. "All right, fine."

Smiling, she let go of his hands and went back to healing his injuries. He was hoping she'd hold his hands a little while longer, but he didn't want to ruin the moment by surrendering himself to any kind of urge.

Moments later, he could feel his powers slowly climbing back to their fullest. He then looked at her over his shoulder. "Yve, I'm okay now. You can stop."

She ignored him.

Shaking his head, he grabbed her hand that was on the deep bleeding gash on his side. "You know you don't have to do this, and more to the point, you're not supposed to. I don't want those Echelons to mess with you too. Nobody's supposed to know."

And I definitely don't want you to see me this way.

"You should've told me that earlier, but then again, it wouldn't make any difference. So I suggest you save it, Hieldhar," she snapped as she continued healing the wound.

He inhaled to find the strength he needed to at least be firm with her without truly hurting her. If only he could find it . . .

Exhaling, he looked straight at her. "You do realize I'm your commander, don't you?"

She *tsked* at his words. "Oh? That's how you wanna play it? You wanna pull rank with me now? As you wish," she said.

Before he knew what her intention was, he felt her hand leave his back, and she knelt before him with her left hand upon her chest and her right hand on her knee. "Then what would you have me do, Hieldhar?" she said with a slightly bowed head and in a tone that surprisingly showed her sincerity in acting as his subordinate.

That little act successfully made him flinch, and his gut tightened with a foreign pain. He couldn't bear to see her put a distance between them in any way. Before he could stop himself, he gently lifted her head so he could look into the darkness of her eyes. "I don't ever want to see you act like this to me again."

She pressed her lips. "Then don't ever make me, *Hieldhar*," she said with that same weird sincere tone, no doubt to made her point.

Once again, he raised his hands in surrender. "All right, all right, I'm sorry."

Her eyes went blank, and then she smirked victoriously as she continued to heal his mutilated back. "Really, after the hundreds of times we've been through this situation! One would think you'd have stopped arguing after the third time I'd done it," she muttered under her breath, making his lips curve with a smile.

Soon she had healed all the wounds on his back and moved to his front. But his body had recovered more than enough to mend itself. There was nothing more he wanted than to spend more time with her, but he shouldn't do it.

Bracing himself, he met her gaze as she directed her powers to the wounds on his chest. "Yve, thanks, but I can take it from here."

"I didn't hear you," she said in singsong voice.

"Yve . . ."

"You'd better shut it before I really tie you down, Hieldhar," she threatened again.

In the end, she'd won the argument. Even though every sane part in him screamed in his ears to shove her away before she caught the Echelons' attention too, or worse, before they moved her to a place that would forever separate him from her, he couldn't bring himself to do it. He could never shove her away. Not her.

Because he didn't know when it began, but before he realized it, her existence was the only balm for his battered soul. Removing her from his life would just be the same as killing him, and that was why he'd never let anyone know, not even her. Not if there was a possibility she would look at him differently and distance herself. He could never live with that as well. It was true that he'd never want either the Echelons or even the Morningstar to bring any kind of danger to her door, but she was the only one who could rip his soul apart.

"There, it's all done," she said finally, pulling her hand from his chest.

"Thanks, I appreciate it," was all he could say to her, when in truth there was nothing more he would've wanted than to embrace her and never let her go. Hell, he would crush her into him if he could.

Her earlier playful hostility vanished from her beautiful face, and a warm gentle smile replaced it. It was the one smile that had been branded forever in his mind, one of the very few things that could make him rein himself in from going on a rampage against those Echelons.

"Any time, Zian. But really, next time something like this happens again, well I hope it won't, but that doesn't seem likely, so when it does, you'd better remove your armour the moment you see me coming and not argue if you don't want a taste of why people called me the Tyraviafonza. And besides, we've been through this over and over, for Hell's sake." She narrowed her gaze, feigning annoyance.

His body burned at her playful threat, and it had nothing to do with all the pain she'd just healed. Unfortunately, he knew her too well to know that she didn't mean that threat the way he did in his thoughts.

Deciding it wasn't the best time to let his mind wander to a place that definitely would make her slap him, he grinned sheepishly at her as he raised both hands in surrender. "Okay, I will, My *Lady* Tyraviafonza."

"Good," she smirked.

"Do I have to remove my pants too when that moment comes?" he teased.

She rolled her eyes. "Your pants can stay where they are, Hieldhar. They're so not my business," she snapped.

Before he could say anything more, she tilted her head as if she'd heard something he couldn't.

"What is it?"

She gave him an apologetic smile. "I'm sorry, I'd love to stick around and chat, but my dop's calling. Something's happening in the palace. I'd better get back," she said. "Take your time to heal properly, Ry."

He nodded reluctantly. "I'll see you another time."

She smiled and started to leave him. To his surprise, she turned on her heels and knelt again. Raising her hands, she cupped his face. "Just be careful, okay? My thought goes with you, Zian." She kissed the top of his head and looked at him once more.

Before he could stop himself, he embraced her.

She fitted perfectly in his arms, and her fragrance was just intoxicating. How he'd dreamt about this moment for so long! To finally have her even for a moment was just like finding true peace for his soul.

They stayed that way for several heartbeats until she gently patted his back, and he was snapped back to planet earth.

"Ry?"

He nearly jumped out of his skin at her voice. Very slowly he pulled away from her. No. No, no, no! What had he done? Cold went through him. The split-second peace he had felt turned into raw fear. He couldn't guess what her reaction would be. Every fibre in his being instantly hoped that she'd just let it go. "Uh, yeah, I'm sorry for that. I didn't mean to . . ."

She put her dainty fingers over his lips. "It's okay, Zian," she said quietly with the hint of a smile. "I'd better get out of here." She stood, turned around, and left him for real this time. He knelt there, staring at her as she disappeared back into the woods from where she came.

His mind then drifted back to the present, right to the wondrous scene before him. He was dying to know what she knew then, but now it didn't matter any more. Those damned Echelons thought he was dead, and he intended to let them think that for as long as he could, because being with her and being able to protect her were the only things that mattered to him now.

"I'll never let anything happen to you, not after I've just got you. Even if I have to go through thousands of lifetimes, I will find you and protect you forever," he thought in unspeakable anguish,

knowing that he would lose her in *this* lifetime and there was nothing he could do about it.

Despite what his own kind thought about him–that he was one of the most powerful devils aside from the royals and Lucifer himself–not even that could help him outrun the ultimate fate drawn by God Himself. That too made him constantly question one thing to himself.

Was he strong enough to protect her?

He'd shoved the question out of his head whenever he was working on something, mostly when he thought that she'd scold him for questioning himself. That thought would instantly calm him and made him smile even if he was staring straight into the cold bottomless darkness in the eyes of Azrael himself.

Now, he just wished the time could stop. He wanted it to stop desperately, so he could hold her in his arms until he drew his last breath. So he wouldn't have to let her go ever again. Nevertheless, he knew that no matter how desperate he was for her, his wishes would never come to reality.

Carefully pulling her closer to him, he gently kissed the top of her head. "I love you," he whispered, before his powers waned as well and brought him under with his arms safely around her.

*   *   *

Amon felt like he had been struck by a giant boulder at what he just heard from the two females sitting before him. "That was what happened?"

Lenora and Ravendy nodded with that miserable look still hanging on their faces. "It went down just like we've said, Iverand." Ravendy's hollowed whisper reached Amon's ears, giving him goose bumps.

"So when the Lord attempted to kill him, it was because of them?" Amon asked, half disgusted, half terrified by the revelation.

Lenora shook her head. Her pale face looked even worse by the minute. "No, as you know the reason why the Lord went through so much trouble just to vanquish the Hieldhar was another matter entirely. It just *appeared* as though the Echelons and the Lord were banded together to kill him because of the same problem. Well, maybe they intended for the Lord to kill him for them, but it just so happened that the Lord had a problem of his own."

Amon winced at her saying "as you know". So they both knew that Yverna and the others had told him about Ezryan's different-realm acquaintance who should have been the victim of their master had the Hieldhar not saved him.

"Anyway, that old matter has nothing to do with the disaster we're facing now," Ravendy commented, and Lenora nodded vigorously.

"Besides, the Hieldhar knew nothing of the matter, even though those cursed Echelons thought he did. Yve was the one who knew about the problem, but she told nobody, not even him," Lenora inserted.

"And what is that matter?" Amon asked.

Both of them shook their heads. "We cannot see it any more. We only know that it involved the late Cherxanain Darov and Yve. Since he had died and Yve had concealed it to the extent that not even our powers could see, all has been lost," Lenora remarked with regret filling her even voice.

"Like I said, that had nothing to do with what we're facing now," Ravendy repeated.

Amon tapped his finger on his desk. "Fine, so what are we dealing with here? Aleeria, her Fierytarians, and one squad of Machordaen have fallen victim to whatever that is out there, and I still don't have a damn clue."

The two exchanged a peculiar look and turned back at him. "You've heard about it, haven't you? The story of God's ultimate destroyer?" Ravendy began.

Amon gulped. "The Avarnakh? It's just a myth, isn't it? They don't know for sure either if it really existed, never mind doing all that slaughter. Well, the only thing that supports that destroyer theory is the non-existent energy print."

Lenora suddenly let loose a hysterical laugh. "Just so you know, that damned thing is far from the typical bullshit called myth. And its true name is Arzia, not that choking sound you called it."

Amon tried to ignore her doomsday demeanour. "Right, so it exists. How the hell do we face it? Should I alert the legions?"

Both female frantically shook their heads. "It's not safe!" they stated simultaneously.

Amon rubbed his temple in frustration. "So what the hell am I supposed to do? Sit on my ass here watching the damned Veil telling me about one slaughter after another?" he snapped.

A faint smile broke on Ravendy's face. "No, you will not be alone in this, Iverand. The four of them are attempting to seal the destroyer, but we cannot intervene."

"For they will be committing several acts of treason in the process. That's why we said it is not safe," Lenora added.

Amon literally choked at that. "Treason?" he whispered.

"We shall tell you what they have to do and the people they must work with, but we must conceal this as best as we can. Let their destiny and ours unfold as they are supposed to. Aside from that, I want to ask you something, Iverand. Would you mind if we help you?" Ravendy asked.

Amon shook his head in confusion. "I wouldn't," he said with narrowed eyes.

She waited for several heartbeats and dropped the bomb she intended to throw at him. "Would *you* mind helping *them*?"

He froze. He didn't like her tone. Not even a bit. It was as if she were insinuating that he would betray the four who were somewhere out there and then run back to the Echelons.

Lenora would taunt people to betray, but Ravendy?

Then again, in a sense he understood the necessity of the question, and that was a two-sided blade. Dare he openly rebel against the Echelons? Or would he turn his back on those who had been betrayed one time too many and yet still try to save them all with their lives hanging by a thread? Could he even *think* of forsaking them?

Amon gulped. "I honestly don't know. I don't know where I stand any more, and treason is another matter entirely. Hell, I don't even know what treason means these days. Is it treason when I disobey the Echelons or when I walk away from the legions and the commanders whom I've sworn to protect from this hole?"

Ravendy inclined her head respectfully. "It is understandable that you have these doubts, Iverand," she said soothingly.

Amon raked his hair. "Will it bring the wrath of the Lord upon the soldiers?"

Ravendy shook her head, looking glum. "No, it has nothing to do with the soldiers. And I'm so sorry, Iverand, but it seems you have no choice but to help."

Amon arched his brow at her grim words. "What makes you say that?" he asked, and he scoffed bitterly. "Wait, why am I even bothering to ask? You've seen it, right?"

Lenora nodded with a cold look at him. "She has, so if you really want to know, you'd better stop patronizing her this instant."

"Len, it's fine. He doesn't mean it that way," Ravendy calmed her down, and then she glanced at him. "Yes, indeed I have, but I'm sure that alone is not reason enough for you."

"So, is there anything more?"

Ravendy swallowed. Her trepidation was apparent. "Yes, I shall tell you everything that I know, for the two who matter the most to you are also helping them . . . to the point they will sacrifice their lives," she said in a low whisper.

He looked as if he had just been gutted. "You mean . . . ?" he stopped midsentence. He couldn't ask it. Not them! It was impossible!

Lenora's gaze darkened. "As you've suspected, but it's meant to be. That's the thing about fate. You can't do anything to stop it. If you try, it will alter the paths to the future, the ones Rave's foreseen. These paths must unfold and join without fail. Disturb them even for a bit, and we all die for real. No coming back from hell."

*   *   *

Belphegor landed in the forest outside the human city of Zodura with Vassago and Seere alongside him.

The three of them walked extremely cautiously straight into the heart of the woods. They kept walking until they found what they were looking for–the remains of the fallen Kivarda and her guards. The bloody limbs and countless bodies were scattered, and most of them weren't recognizable any more.

When they arrived, someone was already there, standing before one particular corpse that seemed to be in better condition than the rest. "You're here?" Vassago said to the stranger.

He ignored the prince for a moment and just stood there, clearly lamenting the fallen one whose corpse he was towering over. The body still wore armour with a distinctive crest visible on it–a star pierced with two spears, which could only mean one thing.

It was Aleeria's body.

Sighing, the stranger subtly nodded. "Yes. The news reached me too late, I'm afraid," he said quietly. "She had just left my palace and headed back. How could she have died here?" he asked it more to the wind than to the three behind him.

"Dantalion," Belphegor said, approaching closer to the grieving duke.

"What is it, Highness?" Dantalion asked. His gaze still lingered on Aleeria's corpse.

"When you first got here, did you happen to see or sense anything peculiar–anything that might lead to who or whatever killed her?"

The duke frowned deeply. "I felt nothing more than a gust of eerie wind that brought along the scent of her freshly spilt blood and the rest of them."

Belphegor exchanged looks with the other two princes before he turned his attention to Dantalion once again. "Is there nothing else?" he pressed.

At the North Prince's persistence, Dantalion recalled the moment he was flying here. Did he miss something because his full attention was focused solely on the blood scent he'd smelled? His black eyes were fixed on Aleeria's lifeless face as he began to lose himself in deep contemplation. Several heartbeats later, he finally remembered it. "There is something," he said as he turned to the princes.

"And that is?" Seere prompted.

"There was this peculiar smell, really faint. I barely picked it up among the scent of blood that dominated the air at that time."

Vassago frowned at his remark. "What did it smell like?"

"At first, it could've been mistaken for the air, but there was something else. It smelled like darkness."

Vassago cast an alarmed look at Belphegor and turned back to the duke. "*You* willed that element. Is there anything more specific?"

Dantalion nodded. "Yes, it smelled like the darkness of the night–empty. No evil, nothing, which was peculiar since even though darkness conceals everything, it would still leave traces behind.

Then again, since it was darkness, naturally there was no holy power I sensed from it," he said, levelling a grim stare at the three. "Tell me something, was the one who killed them the Arzia?"

*　*　*

When I woke up, night had just fallen. I felt a slight movement near me. I turned around to see what had caused it.

It was Ry. His unwavering gaze was fixed on me. Very carefully, he touched my cheek as if he were afraid he might hurt me.

I smiled at him as I held his hand. "What is it?"

He kissed my forehead and smiled broadly. "I wanna take you to see Belphegor and Vassago. They just contacted me while you were asleep. Seere's already there too."

"That was quick," I retorted.

He looked like he was trying to swallow his laughter. "Tell me about it. I even caught Belphegor cursing under his breath when Vassago told me about it. I'd wager Belphegor wouldn't look so happy," he said, and he cleared his throat. "So, you wanna come?" he asked as he held out his hand like a human asking for a dance.

I chuckled as I took his hand. "Okay, but shouldn't we ask Vrae to join us? Maybe Zade as well, if he doesn't have anything else to do. Besides, they've been in on this already."

Ry considered my suggestion. Suddenly he lifted the edge of his lips and gave me a quizzical stare. "Vrae can tag along as usual . . ." His voice faded.

I could've sworn I heard a weird note underneath it.

Narrowing my gaze at him, I tried to guess what was on his mind, but to no avail. "Is there anything? What? You think Zade wouldn't be okay if he came in contact with Vassago and Seere, and above all, Belphegor? Or could it be that you think he would squeak out our whereabouts to the merry band?" I asked suspiciously.

He hastily shook his head. "No, it's not that."

I frowned at his strange demeanour. "So, what is it? Come on, tell me. If we're lucky, Vrae may already be with Zade and save us the time to look for him."

He hesitated. "They were together before you guys parted?"

I nodded. "Yeah, they said they had something to take care of. What, are they doing something weird?"

He snorted and then cast a quizzical stare at me. "No, it's not that, baby, trust me."

When I stared dryly at him, he frowned. "You don't know?" he asked hesitantly.

I gave him a blank stare as an answer, and then he sighed heavily. "Vrae, I don't believe this. I thought you'd told her already," he muttered.

I raised my brows at his comment and then let go of his hand. "What are you talking about? Are we even talking about the same thing here?"

Abruptly, he raked his hair as he grinned at me. "Baby, I bet they're still together right now. And according to what you said, they didn't have any gig to do except taking care of *something*," he said meaningfully.

I frowned for a second, and then the realization hit me. "You're saying they're together as in 'together' together? You're kidding me, right?"

He nodded as he laughed. But although it was funny, I found something a little bit off here. "Ry, you can't be serious. Unless those Varkonians were mutating into something else when I wasn't looking, an Imirae wielder isn't supposed to be together with anyone except another wielder, because it'd slowly destroy the Imirae in their blood."

Yeah, and if Zade ever lost his ability, he would have his ass handed to him on a plate, and he was also endangering Vrae by taking the risk. I realized that the decision was theirs, but not even that would stop me from scolding them if they were endangering each other.

He cleared his throat and cast a gentle look at me. "They know the downside of this relationship, and I happened to know about this as well. I respected them enough to let them decide whether they'd keep it a secret or tell you or end it. It turned out they have yet to take one of those options. I did suggest to them that they tell you though, because, like it or not, if they were busted, the Echelons would think that you also helped them to hide it. It might be as well that you knew. Then you could better protect them and, more to the point, yourself."

I smiled at him. "Back then as our leader, you could've report them to the Echelons, but you didn't."

He shrugged. "Nah, I didn't see the point of doing it, and I definitely don't see it now," he said nonchalantly. "But I do see the point of making either one of them nervous as hell every time I get the chance." He winked mischievously.

I slapped him playfully. "You evil, you."

He took my hand and placed a kiss on my knuckles. "Never admit to be otherwise," he said with a wicked grin.

Choosing to ignore that dazzling grin before I had us both stripped again, I turned my attention to something else. "But there's one thing I don't get, though."

"What is it?"

"Why couldn't I pick anything up from her before?"

A wicked grin broke on his ruggedly flawless face. "The one thing they both asked me the minute they found out I knew about them was how to completely mask their energy."

I smiled helplessly. "Right, because you're the master of that department, more than those Echelons could ever know."

"Well, thanks." He gave me a crooked grin. "And besides, you've barely run with her in the last four millennia. Anything going on with her would surely be gone when you guys meet."

I curled my lips. "Right, and by the way," I said as a thought occurred to me. "You just answered one question I was wondering about."

"What is it?"

"It was when we fought those Arcs. Zade said Vrae kept looking at him every now and again, when I know that it's so not like her to split her focus in a fight. Even though she'd taunt her opponent, she wouldn't pay attention to anything else unless there were enough of us to allow her a small window to do so. Now that you've told me about this, it's all clear."

"Well, that would be your answer."

"Right, so stupid me, I thought it was because she wanted to make sure nothing happened to him because we're responsible for guarding his ass in the field."

He grinned. "Nah, you're definitely far from stupid. Who would've thought a Varkonian would mate with a Cherxanain, anyway? Not even Kathiera or Bynethar would think that."

I gave him a droll stare. "Great, so what now? Are we gonna check their whereabouts first before we catch them doing whatever it is they might be doing?"

He scoffed. "Either way, we should get going. Get your shield on."

I nodded as I noticed he already had his shield around him, maybe because he was supposed to be dead. With Amon's pals around and with the Alvadors, who might've positioned themselves who knows where, it wasn't safe for him if he didn't keep the shield around himself all the time. Either of us could run into them anywhere and any time.

Perhaps he'd dispel the shield when it was safe to do so, in places like Belphegor's.

His gaze went to my belt. "You still got the pouch?"

I untied the thing and showed him.

"Make sure it's safe, okay?" he said.

At his request, I tied the pouch back to my belt. After I'd finished tying it up, he gave me his hand again. I took his hand, and we flew southeast. Moments later, we landed.

Ry told me to stay back for a second. When he started to step forward, an idea popped into my head, and I stopped him. "You know what? I wanna surprise them. You can show up later, because Zade doesn't know you're back just yet."

He grinned. "Okay."

I returned his grin with my own. "Just tell me where they are and follow me, but keep your distance."

Ry pointed north to the forest and told me that they were supposed to be hanging around in that direction.

I walked for a while with tripled caution. They'd notice that someone was approaching. I had no doubt that Vrae would do what the humans call "shoot first, ask questions later", and I was so not in the mood to do a "Cain vs. Abel" scene with her.

I finally felt a presence after I had walked several meters. Ry was few steps behind me. I stopped dead behind a big tree.

Suddenly a single blast of Avordaen came at me. It hit the tree, making me cringe in surprise. It was then I heard Vrae's voice. "Who's there?" she shouted.

I sighed heavily. "It's me!" I shouted back, and I stepped out to see her standing there with Zade, whose expression was a strange look of fear.

Maybe he thought I would report them or kill him where he stood.

Mentally rolling my eyes, I noticed both of them were using protective shields, which made me think they just did what I did with Ry before we came here. I stared blankly at them. "Well, have you two finished taking care of whatever that was?" I asked, feigning ignorance.

Vrae looked like she was about to be gutted as she exchanged a wary look with the Imirae wielder standing beside her.

Zade looked at me as he approached. "Yve, please, I can explain."

His words made me unable to resist teasing them a bit. "You can explain to the Echelons later," I said as I narrowed my gaze angrily–I mean, *pretending* to do it angrily.

It was funny, though I felt a bit disappointed. Vrae's face looked as if she thought I'd do what I just said. There was fear on every inch of her face.

"Did everything we've been through up to this point show that I would do something as so-not-classy as that?" I thought in disappointment.

Deciding to end the joke, I grinned. "Just kidding, don't worry."

Both of them blinked, and then Zade burst out laughing in relief, but not Vrae. "You think that was funny? You're lucky I don't shoot you again!" she snarled as she shot a maybe-I'd-really-kill-you-for-being-so-annoying glare at me.

"Hey, whose fault was it that you didn't realize that was bull fucking shit? Have I ever done anything that's even within a thousand miles of betraying you that made you think I would do something as low as that?" I shot back nonchalantly.

She was still glaring even though Zade tried to calm her down. I shook my head. "Sorry, I couldn't resist doing it when I saw your faces," I said, keeping myself from laughing.

When neither of them said anything, I cleared my throat. "Well, here's what you should have been asking me from the start: who told me about you two and this place?"

They traded a baffled glance for a split second before their eyes widened. But before I could tell them anything, I suddenly felt at least four unfriendlies headed our way.

"Hide!" I said sharply, and I quickly positioned myself behind the closest tree. We simultaneously masked our powers and stared cautiously in the direction ahead of us, where we saw four Arcs. Camael, Remiel, Zerachiel, and Raphael, were landing.

"Well, well, it keeps getting better and better, don't you think, Vrae?" I asked her sarcastically.

"You got that right. Even Raphael bothers to jump in. You think they came to ask about Ry?" she asked, not knowing the guy was standing not far from us. Fortunately, he still had his shield on him when these losers arrived.

"I would think so," I replied as I stole a glance at Ry's direction. Hell, I hoped he'd stay put while we took out the light-heads. I couldn't contact him without alerting them.

The three of us stepped out of the shadows. I crossed my arms over my chest as I silently drew my powers.

Zerachiel jerked his head as he curled his lips at our appearance. "What are you doing here? You abominations . . ."

"' . . . should never be in our presence, and we will kill you all so you can never do anything to imbeciles . . . ' yada yada yada." I cut him off from saying his BS and rolled my eyes. "You all should hang around brainiacs more often, so maybe, just maybe, you'll find some new sentences that come even within a mile of being called insults," I taunted, and I averted my gaze to Zerachiel. "Why don't you just go into a hole somewhere and pretend you do have dominion over something? Or maybe take care of some bastard tykes out there? I mean, you're *supposed* to be a human-sitter," I said as I put one hand on my hip and cast a bored look.

Raphael glared at me in repugnance, to which I didn't even bother to respond. "Where is he? We know you know he's come back."

Oh, man, this was why we couldn't help taunting them. They talked like a human toddler that's barely able to walk.

I laughed darkly. "Well, we know *you* know he's come back. So congratulations, at least you got your news right for once."

"He dared to kill angels–Arcs no less–even though it wasn't an open war! He's broken the deal between us and the Son of Perdition!" Raphael roared.

'Wow, they know about that. It was a good thing then that we're the ones who ran into them,' I mused in my thoughts, feeling a little relief.

I expelled an irritated breath. "That's the point. That deal was between you morons and Lucifer, so in that regard, why in the hell should he bother with that crap? That's your business and Lucifer's, not his. Well, it would be his if you asked *him* to make that deal."

Yeah, right, like something as ridiculous as that would ever happen.

Remiel looked as if he were about to explode from rage. "Cut your jest off! We don't have time for you foolishness! Where is your leader?"

Vrae snorted at his question. "See, you people always try to ask questions when you don't even know how to ask. If you wanna ask someone some questions, you should've never bothered to insult whomever it is you're asking. Didn't the Big Boss ever teach you that? 'Cause being the ones who spend most of eternity with the Guy, or hell, near His den, you all sure displayed the Most Civilized Demeanour of the Century."

All of a sudden, Camael drew his energy. There was light in a small ball shape that appeared from his palm, and it floated as if to threaten us. "You will tell us where your leader is or you will suffer severe consequences," Camael said coldly as he kept that ball of light above his palm.

I glanced at Zade, who smirked. Well, he could try to laugh for once.

"The lady's right. You should invite more brainers to your party so you can learn the word that has the letters i-n-s-u-l-t or even t-h-r-e-a-t. Really, as the ones who've been hanging around the Big Boss's library, you guys seriously need to learn how to talk and how to pull that stick from your asses," he said snidely.

Vrae and I exchanged amused looks, and then I turned to him. "Nice."

Seconds later, we heard growls of rage come from them, and we turned our heads to their direction just in time to dodge the bolts they threw at us.

I glanced at Vrae who was shot at by Remiel while her mate was busy rolling sideways to avoid Camael's rains of light. I was somewhat cornered by Raphael and Zerachiel. Well, at least Amon's pals weren't here. Otherwise they would suck the fun until it went bone dry.

I deflected Zerachiel's attack, rolled to the right, and threw multiple bolts at Raphael. Vrae was running towards Remiel as she shot him with her bolts with her right hand and maintained a shield in front of her with her left. Remiel kept hurling bolts at it.

Camael and Zade went to the air and were doing aerial manoeuvres as they tried to land severe attacks on each other.

All of a sudden, I felt a tree drawing near behind me. Great! I was so not in the mood to be cornered by lowlifes like them. I sensed another ball of light shot by Raphael come right at me. I turned and punched it. After I sent his energy away, I immediately jumped to the sky and shoved away another attack shot from Zerachiel.

"Hey, Raph, why don't you take these punk asses with you and take your loserness back home so you can play with your little flute? We don't mind hearing flute songs!" I yelled, half aggravated and half taunting him.

Raphael clenched his teeth as he and Zerachiel followed me to the air and blasted lights at me. "I will make you eat your own arrogance!" he yelled in fury, and both of them started to attack randomly because of their uncontrollable anger.

I laughed sarcastically. "Well, that won't help much since we all know we can't possibly taste, let alone eat, arrogance. Maybe you should talk to Pride about that. Ask him if you could eat it," I said as I kept charging and rolling in the air.

"If it turned out you could, I'll take you to Gluttony and you could eat it together. Let me know how that turns out!" I yelled as I did another manoeuvre and kept my distance so I wouldn't bump into Zade, who was still taking care of his own company.

Vrae suddenly relayed her plan to us on how to wrap this up and stopped running. Zade distracted Camael before he landed right next to her. I blasted Raphael and Zerachiel's bolts and flew towards them.

I took a dive and landed with my back against Zade and Vrae's. The Arcs were hastily charging towards us from every direction when Vrae whispered, "On three."

When they were close enough . . ."Three!" she yelled, and we simultaneously jumped over their heads, making them run into each other, and then we caught them off-guard –or at least that was what we were hoping.

They threw their hands in the air and deflected our bolts back to us.

Landing with our wings spread wide, Zade punched his bolt away, while Vrae flipped hers with her wings. I raised a hand and intercepted mine, absorbing it back. "Well, you guys have improved since our last dance."

Raphael's eyes couldn't get any colder. "You will perish, abomination," he said. I could feel him and his crew pull their powers to the max, but that wasn't the only thing that moved in the air.

Something far even more malevolent teased my skin.

"Now, die!" Raphael said, and the four of them raised their hands. Suddenly, as if they had just been surprised by something I couldn't see, they all abruptly froze.

"Raphael?" Camael asked. His voice was laden with uncertainty and –was that fear?

I started to look in Ry's direction when I saw what made the angels stopped moving. No wonder they suddenly couldn't move a muscle. The air around them began emitting small lights that flickered around them.

Electricity. Where the hell was it coming from?

"Fear not, Camael. No abomination could do anything," Raphael retorted, and then he turned his attention to the woods. "Show yourself!" he snarled.

Ry walked towards us from beyond the shadows with a cold expression on his face. Damn, if a look could kill, Raphael and his pals would've been shredded by now. "Get your story straight, you sons of bitches. I don't have any intention to hide. And you definitely need to learn to show respect too while you're at it."

The small charges in the air slowly formed an outline that tightened around the angels. I gulped in awe. One wrong move and they'd get electrocuted, if not toasted. I'd never known he could do this. Usually, he'd only use it after summoning the clouds first, gathering the ions in the air, because elements of nature were connected to each other.

For him to manipulate it freely out of thin air was just . . . wow!

Ry stood there looking calm while his body was emitting an aura so lethal, I could almost breathe from it and let it drive me into insanity.

"You!" Raphael growled as he saw him approaching.

Ry scoffed. "You know, I'm kinda having a weird flashback here, because that's just the same stupid look and reaction your brother Uriel had," he said mockingly, but in contrast to his morbid humour about the dead Arc, the darkened gaze he fixed on Raphael said it all. He'd set his mind on doing some serious massacre.

I inhaled in anticipation. It had been too long since the last time I saw him like this, and it sent chills all over my body.

"Now, before you bastards bug me and my companions here even further with your I'm-a-saint-and-you're-dirt attitude, I'll tell you this, and make sure you brand my words onto what little brains you have." He stared down at the Arc who was still withering. "Get the fuck out of our way, or Adam's descendants will be destroyed ahead of schedule and you won't get to play your horn first, Raphael," he said with heavy dose of venom in every word.

He jerked his head and gave a wry glare. "This is a warning. Let Michael and Gabriel know what I have done."

After that he shot multiple bolts. They went through the wings of Camael, Remiel, and Zerachiel. Paying no attentions to their screams, he withdrew the electricity he used to bind them and sent a few more bolts directly into their bodies before they could get away.

They roared as they bled even more. Their insides were being melted slowly and, I have to say, painfully. Raphael moved and tried to help his comrades, but I held him still, so the only thing he could do was watch as his companions died. Their agony was ended by an explosion of hot blinding white light, followed by a rain of flesh and blood showering us. We quickly covered our bodies with a defensive shield so that none of it could land on our skin. Instead, all the blood and flesh hung in the air, blocked by our shield.

We got rid of the angels' remains and saw Raphael glaring at Ry as he kept muttering something between his panting. Ry then dropped to one knee to level his gaze with Raphael. "You all pushed me into this, but I know you have your function, so I'll let you go."

"Just kill me like you did them! I won't accept pity from abominations!" he yelled.

Ry went on as the three of us were mesmerized by him. "Shut up! I don't have time for your masochistic self-destructive obsession," he said as he extended one hand and tried to put it on Raphael's head. He struggled to move away, and I once again had to hold him still, this time by putting my foot on his back and pinning him to the ground. When he wasn't moving that much any more, Ry raised his hand and chanted.

I don't know what spell he used. All I saw was that Raphael's eyes suddenly turned back in their sockets, and he screamed in excruciating pain as smoke came out of his head. Moments later, Ry stopped and stood up, leaving Raphael shaking on the ground as he kept muttering something, and his eyes were still turned into the wrong direction.

I only could say one word: Wow!

Ry then faced us and gave his hand to me as he looked at Vrae and her man. "We're done here. We better shag ass before someone comes." I took his hand while Vrae took mine. Zade grasped his mate's hand and Ry's. We concentrated on Ry, and suddenly everything went black.

We reappeared in another forest. I scanned the surroundings and frowned. I knew this place. We were at Gillian, somewhere near Vassago's. He took us here?

I turned to Vrae to see her standing there with apparent shock on her face, while Zade smiled as he approached his former commander, well, technically. "I'll be damned. It's the Hieldhar himself," Zade said as they high-fived and hugged each other. "It's good to see you again, dude! How have you been doing all this time?"

They separated, and Ry shrugged. "Well, same old, same old," he said with a grin.

After that Ry turned to Vrae, who still stood in silence as if she were seeing a ghost. The three of us walked towards her. "Vrae, you okay?" I asked.

Suddenly she dropped to her knees. "You really are alive."

I gulped a bit at her evident happiness that was tangled with guilt, but I kept that thought to myself before she made me join her in tears. We helped her to get on her feet.

"Yes, I'm back now. I'm so sorry I've burdened you with that little secret and made you vow over it, and I can't thank you enough. But you're okay now," Ry said in a slightly sad voice.

Zade suddenly grabbed Ry's shoulder. "Oh yeah, about that, dude, I just remembered something," he said as Ry turned to face him.

Suddenly Zade punched him right in the face. Ry staggered back a bit as he wiped a bit of blood from the edge of his lips.

I started at him, but Vrae got there first. "What are you doing?" she asked sharply, but Ry stopped her.

"Thanks for that. Are we even now?" he asked calmly.

Zade sighed and then extended his hand. "Yeah, we're even." Ry shook Zade's hand, and they grinned at each other. Vrae and I exchanged a puzzled look and shifted our gaze back at our men.

Zade cleared his throat. "But, dude, don't you ever do that to her again. I'll beat the crap out of you, even if I have to die in the process. I'll never let you do anything to make her say the word 'vow' without me by her side," he said as he put his hands on Vrae's shoulders and held her protectively.

"So that's what this is all about," I thought with a surge of relief.

A newfound respect towards the Varkonian surged through me. He was willing to stand up to Ry to make sure nothing happened to my sister. She cast him a tender gaze that was full of affection, to which he replied with the same intensity. It made clear to me how deep their relationship was.

Ry nodded respectfully towards him, and then he walked to my side. He took my hand and squeezed gently. I glanced at Zade, who saw Ry's demeanour. He looked surprised at what Ry was doing, but he didn't say anything. If I didn't know any better, I could've sworn he was pleased to see that.

All of a sudden, Ry clapped his hand. "Well, it's good to see you two again and all, but unfortunately we gotta bring an end to the sentimental hour," he said. They grinned and nodded, and then he went on, "Because now, there are more pressing matters."

Vrae frowned. "And they are?"

Our former leader, though he still was in every other aspect, smiled evilly. "Before I tell you what's what, how about we meet our *very* old friends?" he asked meaningfully.

I saw my sister's gaze widen in understanding. "You mean *them*? You were with them after you met with Yve?"

"You haven't told me you knew Ry showed up, Vrae," Zade said.

I curled my lips in vexation. "Yeah, and she wasn't supposed to know that just yet," I snapped at her.

Vrae stared dryly at me, and I ignored her. When I looked at Zade, he seemed like he had just realized something. "You mean, when she asked you who the Arcs' killer was, and then you two didn't want to tell us anything . . ." his voice faded.

Ry cleared his throat. "Yeah, the one who wasted those Arcs was me. Well, I couldn't possibly let them wander around announcing that I was still alive through loudspeaker now, could I?" he asked nonchalantly.

We burst out laughing at his rhetorical question.

Ry then cleared his throat. "Anyway, I just obtained a lot of dangerous intel, and I can't explain all of it by myself, so I wanna take you all to see them."

Zade gave him a quizzical stare. "And who are they exactly?"

Ry lifted the edge of his lips in a sinister smile I hadn't seen in a long time. "Three Princes–Belphegor, Vassago, and Seere."

Vrae smirked at his words while her man gaped. "You . . . you met *them*?" Zade asked. Clearly he was having a hard time believing that a common warrior, even one as high-ranking as Ry was, would be able to set foot in their stronghold without being blown to oblivion.

My sister patted his shoulder as she grinned. "Don't worry, hon. If you get to know them a bit, they're actually not that bad."

Zade gulped audibly as he gazed helplessly at her. She just smiled, trying to comfort him before he fainted, I guess.

I exchanged an amused look with my own mate. "Come on, don't waste a second here. We might run into one of our subordinates," I cautioned.

"Are you guys sure it's okay for me to tag along?" Zade asked in a trembling voice.

Ry shrugged and gave him a weird look. "Well, I'm not so sure. The three of us already know them."

Zade bristled, but Ry didn't seem to notice. "At any rate, if you're not doing anything to make one of them mad, you have nada to be afraid of, but remember this: sometimes they can be a bit cranky, so just watch yourself," he remarked seriously.

Vrae rolled her eyes and playfully punched his shoulder. "Don't scare him like that! Those royals aren't exactly that bad," she said as she curled her lips at him.

Ry sneered at her. "Hey, better safe than sorry."

The Imirae wielder winced and looked as if he were sorting through everything. When he realized Ry was just playing with him, he shoved Ry and gave a half-hearted laugh. "You scared the shit outta me! But I'll remember that. I'll try not to piss my pants first when I see them."

"Yeah, 'cause that will certainly make Belphegor chop you into confetti before you can say 'hi' to him," I added.

Zade stopped laughing immediately, and Ry chuckled. "Come on," he said as he indicated the direction where the prince who dwelled in this forest lived.

I caught up to Ry. "Babe, we're meeting at Vassago's?"

"Yeah," he answered as he looked at me.

I frowned. "Why is that? I thought Belphegor never left his place, especially not to meet the other princes."

He smiled at that. "I thought so myself, but it turned out like he said to me, 'I'm a loner, but who's to say I'm not allowed to have fun elsewhere with someone else beside myself.' Yeah, something like that."

I snorted. "Have fun with someone beside himself, huh? He's still a bit narcissistic as usual, it seems."

He laughed. "Yeah, but I won't say a thing, because, for your information, Yve, he and Vassago know about us. They could be watching over us right now for all we know."

My brows knitted, forming one hard line. "What! How?"

Ry grinned helplessly. "Beats me, baby. You know those two can be more mysterious than anyone if they want to. Maybe the only one who can match their know-all-but-spill-nothing habit is the Big Boss Himself. Well, Lucy dearest doesn't count of course."

I burst out laughing. "That's what you call him now? That's nice, Ry. Tell me if you want to put some girly bling on him," I said, glancing at the couple. They just looked and grinned at each other as they heard our conversation, but they didn't say anything.

Minutes later, we arrived on the barren field by Gillian forest. Ry stepped forward and said clearly to the air as he firmed his gesture, "We're here, Belphegor, Vassago."

Chapter 13

From out of nowhere, crimson mist slowly appeared, forming into the shape of a person. When the form was complete, the crimson mist faded, revealing Belphegor, who still looked as handsome as ever, but that wasn't the X-factor of why I liked meeting this guy.

All I could say was, damn, I wish I could have an aura as lethal as that. I felt it all over my skin, and it made me ache to kill something. Maybe it was a good thing Ry was my mate. He could suppress my sometimes overwhelming desire to kill better than anyone. All these centuries, I had restrained myself from doing unnecessary kills by remembering him, and as sentimental as it sounded, it worked. I never told this to anyone though.

Seconds later a shadow came forth covering the ground in the form of a hole. Suddenly the other prince, Vassago, emerged from inside it and stood next to Belphegor. When Vassago was completely on top of the soil, the shadow faded.

They jerked their heads at us. "Girls, long time no see. How are you two doin' out there?" Vassago asked as both of them approached us.

Vrae and I grinned at the princes. "We're doing all right, Belphegor, Vassago. Have you two been having fun without us all these millennia?" I asked as I crossed my arms over my chest.

Belphegor scowled. "You're no fun. You two never came by my place after this little jerk hid his ass," he said, jerking his head towards Ry, who snorted at the prince calling him a jerk, while Vassago just stood there with an amused look on his face.

Vrae grinned. "Sorry about that, Highness. We were kinda busy," she said, smiling apologetically.

Both princes shifted their gaze ton Zade, who went rigid as a statue. Vassago raised a brow. "What is he, a stone? He hasn't say zap for minutes."

Vrae laughed, and Belphegor looked curiously at the Imirae wielder. "No, the man you called stone is my mate, so please try to be nice, Your Highnesses," she said.

"I know that this guy's been running with you guys, but I'll say he's okay if he turns out cool to deal with." Vassago shrugged.

Belphegor scowled. "I don't know. Judging by the 'I'm a stone, I'm invisible, and I'm not talking' demeanour he's doing right now, he looks like he's trying to impersonate my pop's statue down at the Echelons' chamber. Oh, wait, that's a stone." The North Prince waved his hand in dismissal.

Ry and I had to look elsewhere as we struggled to keep ourselves from laughing. The prince was exaggerating things again.

Zade–good for him–encouraged himself and laid his fist upon his chest. "Forgive my impudence, Your Highnesses Prince Belphegor and Prince Vassago. My name's Zaderion, Vrathien Wartiavega's mate."

Both princes looked surprised and amused at his salute, but that look turned one-eighty degrees into boiling rage as Zade started to say something inanely wrong. "May . . ."

A fissure rattled the air and grabbed our attention. Moving faster than I could blink, Ry went towards Zade just in time to place a palm over his mouth, stopping him before he completed the rest of his sentence.

"You do know my history with my daddy dearest, don't you, boy?" Belphegor slid a cold glare at him.

"With that alone, buddy, you should know not to say things like that around here, 'cause none of us do," Vassago added calmly, but I caught a note of promised disaster underneath it.

Half-panicked, Zade quickly nodded his understanding, and Ry released him. "Thanks, dude," he panted with relief.

"No problem. Sorry I forgot to remind you about that," Ry said with a grin.

Zade waved. "Apology accepted."

Ry nodded with that gorgeous grin still hanging on his face as he sauntered to my side.

Both princes exchanged a wicked smile and faced him again. "Well, it is a surprise that you found yourself a mate after you stopped visiting us. It's even more surprising that he's a wielder," Vassago said, indicating the Varkonian crest on Zade's armour.

"Yeah, I'd say nice work, Vrae. I bet those Echelons would be pleased if they heard about this," Belphegor added.

Zade hesitated when he heard this comment, while Vrae just smirked, knowing that they weren't serious.

Obviously, Zade didn't see it, because he firmed his gesture. "Please, Your Highness, don't let anyone know about this," he said.

Vassago put his hand on Zade's shoulder with a friendly gesture. Well, luckily for Zade and Vrae, Vassago wasn't as weird as his pal. "Relax, we're many things, but we ain't disloyal."

"Unless it comes down to my sorry-ass dad," Belphegor inserted.

Ry, Vrae, and I snorted at his words, and Vassago cast a dry stare at us.

We changed our laughs to small coughs, and Vassago rolled his eyes. "Dude, that's your trauma," he interjected.

Belphegor shrugged as he too looked at Zade. "Don't worry, I was just joking. Just take good care of her. We've both known her for a long time, and she's been one of a very few good friends of ours. Not to mention that you, being a wielder, are bound to face a whole can of worms you don't want to deal with."

Vrae tried to step between her mate and the prince, but Zade stopped her. "We know the risk, but I give you my word, I'll protect her with my life, and there's nothing can stop me from doing so other than Boss Man up there."

Both princes looked satisfied with his answer, but the smug smiles on their faces were replaced with a hint of surprise in a split second. They exchanged frowns, and then weirdly enough, Belphegor glanced at me.

What the hell?

Ry gave me a puzzled look which I answered with a shrug. As if nothing had gone down between them, Vassago turned to both Vrae and Zade and started talking to them, while Belphegor draped one hand around my shoulder. He dragged me away with Ry behind him.

When we stopped, Belphegor grinned at me. "So, you two are together now, huh? That's great, Yve. I wish you could've been his mate before daddy bastard whacked his ass. He's been whining all these centuries."

I raised a brow as I glanced at Ry, half curious at the prince's words and half hoping Ry would tell this guy to stay away from me. "Huh? What are you talking about?"

Ry quickly stepped between us, and the North Prince lifted his hands as he laughed. In turn, Ry held me instead. "I never. Don't say anything as absurd as that, Belphegor. It's not funny."

Belphegor laughed. "Sorry, just wanted to harass you a bit." I looked back and forth at Ry and Belphegor, but they didn't say anything more, so I stopped asking. But I fully intended to ask what happened earlier between him and Vassago.

"Say, Highness," I started.

"Yeah?"

"What's with you and Vassago back there?" Ry and I asked in unison. He flashed me a crooked grin, which made him look too damned dazzling for his own good, and I answered him with a faint smile. Well, his mind had always been in the same page with mine, though more often than not, his was usually much more complicated.

Belphegor cleared his throat, and we turned to him. "So, you wanna know what that was all about, huh? Hmm, let's see. First off, have you had some bad run-ins lately?"

I frowned at him. "Well, just some Arcs, but they hardly count as bad run-ins. Besides, he did them in," I said, poking Ry's armoured chest.

Belphegor rolled his crimson eyes. "Not them, sweetheart. Someone or something else. My grandma can take them down in her sleep."

I choked at that. "You don't have a grandma."

He waved his hand in dismissal. "Details, and that's beside the point."

"But, what's with Zade? Did he do something?" Ry interjected. By the look on his face, he was definitely trying not to laugh at the prince's earlier comment.

Belphegor shook his head. "No, that was because Yve here had her bad run-in when she was with him. We picked up faint traces of her healing power in him, but strangely enough, we felt bits of it in her too, which means she was compelled to use it because her injury couldn't heal on its own. Well, maybe Vrae was there when whatever it was happened."

Ry turned his full attention to me. "Something happened to you both before we met?" A deep frown lined his perfect brows, and his deep, sapphire eyes gleamed with concern.

At that point, I realized what Belphegor was talking about. I related to them both what had happened. When I was done, I saw that neither of them looked even the slightest bit surprised, and hell, that bugged me a lot. Just what could surprise these two?

"So, what's the deal?" I asked.

"Well, you just confirmed what I discussed with Ry," Belphegor said.

I turned to Ry, who looked more than ready to kill himself, and that seriously freaked me out. "Zeian?" I asked carefully.

His eyes lit up for a split second, and then he glanced at Belphegor, but before they could explain anything, our three pals approached us.

The prince leaned over to reach my ear. "All I can say for now is, congratulations, you just ran into Big Boss's ultimate destroyer's handiwork," he whispered.

It felt like a hammer struck me in the gut. My eyes widened in surprise as the others came to us. "Yo, guys, we've been out here for too damn long. Let's get inside," Vassago said as he turned to face the barren field and chanted.

From out of nowhere, a massive castle made of turquoise stone appeared before us. Come to think of it, it had been too long since the last time I set foot in this place. We followed Vassago into his castle. The four of us dispelled our shields once we got inside. Ry caught up with Belphegor. "So, where's your other pal?" he asked.

Vassago heard his question, and then he glanced at Belphegor who didn't look happy, not even one bit. I saw Vassago smirk before he turned his gaze back to Ry. "He's in the archive. He's not that interested in being a welcoming party," he said with a shrug.

Vassago's archive. I'd never been there before.

We continued until we got inside, and the castle was swallowed by shadows. Vassago led us towards the stairs, and we ascended to the next floor. When we reached the top floor, we went to a hallway, where we faced a wall that was free of the carving that decorated almost all sections of the castle.

Vassago chanted. A second later, the wall opened up and Vassago let us inside. In the room I saw many books and old dusty records, fitting the chamber's name.

In the centre of the chamber, there was a long table with armchairs placed around it. One of the armchairs was occupied by a devil I recognized as another Devil Prince. He wore a ruby-coloured robe and a crown with a ruby stone in its middle.

It was he who commanded twenty-six legions of demons–Seere.

We stopped dead as we looked at his ruby eyes that swirled when he gazed upon us. He stood and then approached. "Well, well, well, I won't get a chance to see this every day. The famous savage sisters set foot here again, but most surprising of all is you, Ry," he said. Obviously, he was ignoring Zade.

Ry smiled reluctantly at the prince. "So, does that mean you knew I was still alive all this time, or did you just hear about it from Belphegor and Vassago, Seere?"

Seere jerked his head. "You don't possibly believe Belphegor here would waste his breath to tell me, now do you? Vassago ain't exactly that nice either," he said nonchalantly.

Prince Vassago stared dryly at him but said nothing. "For Vassago's guest, you certainly can't shut your hole," Belphegor said as he gave Seere a wry stare.

Seere didn't say anything but simply ignored him.

Ry raised a brow. "Okay, great to know that I'm being watched by royals. It's good to be famous once in a while," he said as he cast a meaningful look at me, which I answered with a smirk.

Vassago then asked all of us to take a seat. He took the armchair at the far end of the table, while the other Princes sat on his sides.

Ry put his hand around my waist and led me to the seats next to Belphegor, who took the one on Vassago's right side. Zade and Vrae sat on two armchairs next to Seere.

"So," Vassago said as he eyed each and every one of us, "now that we're all here, how about we get down to business?"

Ry raised his hand to stop the prince. "Before that, I wanna show you something first."

The royals glanced at each other, looked puzzled. "What is it?" Vassago asked.

Instead of answering him, Ry turned to me. "Yve, give me 'that', would you?"

I nodded and untied the small pouch. I handed it to him, and he reached inside it, pulling out the Herathim it contained and putting it on the centre of the table for all of us to see.

The royals stood in disbelief as they looked at it. Belphegor, who definitely couldn't hold his curiosity, went ahead and tried to touch it. Not sure of what would happen, I intended to stop him, but Ry placed his hand on mine and shook his head. We watched Belphegor again. His fingertips were now only inches from the key-like object. When he touched it, the effect was shocking.

There was a jolt of electricity in the air, Belphegor yelled "What the fuck!" and there was a loud "BOOM!" followed by smoke.

When the smoke dispersed, I saw the table was broken right in the middle, and the others stepped away from it. Belphegor staggered back as he stared down at the hand with which he had touched the object.

My jaw dropped. His hand was bloodied and no longer covered with flesh. It had shattered in bloody little pieces all over the table and the floor, and he was absolutely furious over it.

Ry approached the North Prince. "Are you okay?" he asked, while the other two princes smirked at him.

Belphegor glared at Ry. "I never thought it would be as annoying as that." He pointed at the sliced table with his finger, well, more like the bloody bones of a finger.

My mate cast him a rather innocent look, which without a doubt made the prince even more upset. "What can I say? You know that thing's from up there, and yet you couldn't restrain yourself from touching it."

Vrae motioned to the table and examined the bloody pieces of flesh and skin. "The effect sure was much greater than when I touched it," she said as she looked at me.

I confirmed her with a nod. "Maybe that's because it was still inside the pouch, and you were the one who touched it," I answered her.

All of them looked at me.

Ry nodded in agreement. "Yeah, Vrae isn't exactly you Belphegor. Perhaps the more powerful you are, the greater the effect would be when you touch it," he said to the prince.

Belphegor arched a brow. "Thanks for complimenting me for being more powerful, but yeah, she's not exactly me. Does she look like me? She's not even a male."

All of us snorted at his oops-I-couldn't-hold-myself joke. Vassago rolled his eyes and waved his hand at the table. The broken table repaired itself that instant.

We then turned our attention to Belphegor. He just stared blankly at his wound, and flesh appeared from out of nowhere, starting on his fingertips and continuing all the way to his fleshless arm. After he was done, the blood that was splattered all over his arm vanished without a trace, along with the flesh, skin, and blood on the table and the floor.

"Where's that thing?" Belphegor asked, looking at the table. The Herathim was no longer on it.

"It probably fell off the table when that explosion happened," I said. I looked around and found it two seconds later. Without thinking, I immediately picked it up and put it on the table.

Not until I saw Ry's and my companions' eyes widen in fear and shock spread all over the royals' faces did I realize that I just did what I shouldn't have done. Apart from my companions, no one should know I could touch it.

Belphegor stared at me. Damn, if a stare could kill, I'd be mutilated by now. I stood there and exchanged wary looks with Ry. The North Prince cleared his throat as he glanced at the other princes, who kept their silence. "I assume you will explain to us why in the hell *you* could touch it?" he asked as he came near me.

I gulped as I tried to screw up my courage. There was no way I could tell them what really happened. Who knew what they would do if they learned about our human problem?

Ry suddenly stepped between me and him. "She shares my blood," he said, looking straight into the prince's eerie crimson eyes.

The three princes cast a look of disbelief. Even Vrae and Zade did so too.

Vassago gazed blankly at him. "You're saying that whatever it is that makes you able to touch this thing"–he pointed the harmless-looking Herathim on the table–"lies in your blood?"

Ry glanced at me and then shifted his attention to the prince once more. "Probably, or maybe it's something in my powers. Who knows? All I'm saying is this has nothing to do with her. I share my blood and powers with her, and then she can touch it."

Belphegor jerked his head. "So that's what you two were talking about when you were playing mute film?"

"Damn, they were *watching us, "* I swore in my thoughts.

Ry hesitantly nodded. "Yes, that was it."

Belphegor cleared his throat, and strangely enough, I saw his eyes gleam with glee. "Show the sign to us."

Ry raised his brows. "And why do you want to see it?" he asked suspiciously. No doubt he had the same suspicion I did, that the prince was up to something that was so not important.

"Because I can," Belphegor replied smugly.

Annoyed, Ry then gave me a subtle nod, which I answered with a just-get-it-over-with look. I stepped forward and joined my palm alongside his. The tip of his finger touched mine, and the sign glowed beneath our skin.

Both Belphegor and Vassago winced at the sight, while the others just stared at us. After a moment, we pulled our hands apart.

"Happy?" Ry asked.

The royals exchanged a quizzical stare, and abruptly they laughed out loud. "Boy, who would've thought you'd do this with her so soon, I mean, I know you've been whining, but whatever," Belphegor said between his laughter.

He kept saying Ry had been whining. I wondered if it was a stupid joke or not. As absurd as it sounded, I decided not to ask him.

Ry cast an annoyed looked at him, and Seere cleared his throat. "Enough! Let's get to it, shall we?"

All of us pulled up the armchairs and took our seats once again. This time neither of us dared to lay a finger on the Herathim.

"Wait, before we go anywhere," Ry started. "I wanna tell you something. After that I need you two"–he nodded at Vrae and Zade–"to answer me."

Both of them exchanged a frown before they looked back at him. "Sure, what is it?"

Ry then told them about the Ladurga following my doppelganger. At his words, the princes stared at each other, but I could slightly feel their powers reaching the ether. Good, they were checking it right away.

"Vassago?" I asked.

He didn't respond for a moment before finally shaking his head. "None around here."

"There was only one that Ry killed," Belphegor added.

Ry glanced at Vrae. "You two find anything peculiar while you were out there?"

Zade cast an uneasy look at him. "I can't say for sure. As far as I know, no one's tailing us, but I might not know if a Ladurga was around."

"Vrae?"

She frowned in deep thought and then shook her head. "No, I'm sure none of that lot was following us."

Seere tapped the desk. "Let's keep it that way. Someone from that bunch stirred Lazoreth into sending his Ladurga. We'll take care of that later. We have other matters."

Ry leaned forward. "All right. So, Highnesses, what do we have right now? Have you discovered anything new about Arzia and its seals?"

Zade looked puzzled. "What's Arzia?"

Vassago and Belphegor exchanged a look, while Seere crossed his arms over his chest. Vassago then turned to Ry. "You tell them about it, up to the point where you left us."

"And Yve can add their side of the story because we know you let her know, although we weren't that amused when you told her about our little banter involving Solomon and the death wish," Belphegor inserted as he curled his lips.

Ry grimaced. "Yeah, sorry about that. We'll explain it to them."

I scoffed at Belphegor. "Your Highness, you don't get to threaten my man. That privilege is for me and me alone. And yeah, we talked about it and laughed about it, so thanks for making us have a very nice chat."

Vassago raised a brow, while Seere suddenly whistled. The other couple looked at me, obviously shocked to hear my audacity, whereas Ry just looked elsewhere as if he hadn't heard anything, but I saw him shiver in his attempt to hold his laughter.

Belphegor scowled. "The lady has spoken. We should know better than to take away her *privilege,* otherwise she would bring down her wrath, boys," he said, half mocking and half meaning what he was saying.

Seere looked amused. "Well, I don't know what you were talking about, but I wasn't the one who provoked her, so keep that figure of speech to yourself."

Suddenly the crimson color on Belphegor's irises spread all over his eyes as he glared angrily at the prince across from him. "If you don't know what we were talking about, then why don't you keep that hole of yours shut?" he asked in a low deadly tone with a frightening dose of venom that Seere obviously ignored.

I frowned at them both. I'd never seen Belphegor act like this. Then again, I'd never known what had happened between them. Even though I'd heard that they both never liked each other to begin with, judging by the looks on their faces, they looked like they were more than ready to kill each other right here, right now.

Vassago and Ry might have known something, because they didn't even try to put a stop to their little word fight. Both of them just looked at each other warily. Well, Ry never told me what the issue was, and it did intrigue me from time to time, but watching them like this, I really didn't want to know what their dispute was about.

Zade subtly cast a questioning look at my sister, which she answered with a shake of her head, indicating her own cluelessness.

Vassago expelled a weary breath and ignored the other princes. He looked directly at Ry and me. "Ry, Yve, start with the news flash. We don't have all day to waste on this fight between middle-aged women."

Belphegor glared at him but managed to calm himself. The crimson color on his whole face returned to the centre of his eyes.

Ry nodded and started on Zade. "I believe you know about Avarnakh?"

Zade nodded. "Yeah, the three of us heard about it at your brother's place."

Belphegor sneered. "You know about his brother, then?" he asked me.

"Yeah, we ran into his soldiers, had a little fight and a chat, and then we crossed over. It was then we learned that my man here was still alive. We also heard a something about that void or whatever that dirt bag is that had apparently been running amok and slaughtering several of their people like it does here."

Vassago was taken aback. "That thing's been killing in that other dimension? It should be really angry."

Vrae put one hand on the table. "But what's that thing gotta do with this Arzia?"

"I just found out about that myself. Ry told me about Avarnakh aka Arzia a while ago."

They gaped in disbelief. "You're saying Arzia is that void thing?" Vrae asked.

"That's its true name. I just heard about it from Belphegor," Ry added.

Later on we told them both, and we repeated what we found out from Ry's brother, including what had happened when we checked those soldiers. Every now and again the princes would add some details. We stopped at the part about the seals.

Seere looked uneasy. "So, basically you two are dragging me into this because you want to steal Solomon's ring, knowing full well that the Valdam of that thing has that annoying list?"

Vassago cast a dry look at him. "That's the general idea for your part, because we know how much you favour shiny things. We want you to follow your indulgence. Is it heavy?"

Seere sneered. "You sure you just want me to do my favourite pastime? If I didn't know any better, I could've sworn you just wanted me to be put in a friggin' jar."

Vassago gave him an annoyed stare, while Belphegor smiled evilly, as if he were really looking forward to seeing Seere inside a jar. "I hope the Valdam does that to you *after* we get our hands on the ring."

Seere glared at Belphegor. His eyes were loaded with the same hatred I saw gleaming in Belphegor's. I rolled my eyes but didn't say anything. Gee, couldn't these royals act a bit more as befits their rank and not fight like a pair of girls trying to get a boy's attention?

I expelled an aggravated breath. "I'll do the stake out and the stealing if it safe enough. Just tell me how to do it without screwing it up, because stealthy moves aren't exactly my forte. I'd prefer to break in, making a big entrance in the process, kill everybody present, and then take it."

Ry looked straight at me. "If you so choose it, you won't be doing it alone. I'll go with you," he said.

I frowned. "Are you sure? You shouldn't be seen by anyone, especially his dad." I jerked my head towards Belphegor, who rubbed his temple.

Ry gave me a soothing smile. "There's no way I'd let you go in there alone. And it's all right, there's no one aside from us who knows that I'm around. Well, maybe the Arcs do, but what the hell, they can dance with Azrael for all I care."

We broke into laughter at his sardonic comment, but I still wasn't sure if this was safe enough. But he was right. I didn't like the idea of jumping into the guardian's lair alone.

Vassago looked puzzled. "You sure you want to do this? We don't know whose names are written in it."

Ry nodded. "I'm sure. We at least know that the list had you two in it," he said, tilting his head at Vassago and Seere. "So as much as I like you to help us out, Seere, you can't get in that close. You can't go with us, and the two of you aren't going in either," he said to Vrae and Zade.

Vrae scowled. "Mind if I ask why the hell not?"

I caught Ry's meaning. "Look, we're not going into a bonfire festival here. There's no need to add the number. Besides, we're not royals, so the chances are slim that Solomon even bothered writing down our names, and even if he *did* bother, the impact won't be as severe as the repercussions if the royals were caught."

Zade did not look too happy with what I said. "That's not good enough. I mean, we're not royals either, so at least take me to back you up," he insisted.

Ry shook his head. "No, Zade, you're an Imirae wielder. You're being watched a lot more closely than them."

Vrae hastily cut Ry off. "Then take me."

I sighed. "No, can't do. Unlike me, those jackasses tend to give you orders in groups. And with the recent events, I bet they'd ransack Amon's place and your base to check your whereabouts if you ever went MIA, Vrae. Even if you were using a doppelganger, they'd know it wasn't you the moment they sent our subordinates," I said as I leaned back and tapped the chair's arm.

Ry tilted his head at them. "Just watch your backs and wait until we've got it, okay?"

Defeated, they both nodded without a word.

Seere let out a slow breath. "So, it's decided then. I'll show you the art of stealing treasure." He gave us a smug smile.

Belphegor didn't look amused. Instead, he looked like he was disgusted with Seere. He turned to us. "Okay then, it settled. If anything goes wrong, come to me immediately."

I felt a wave of newfound respect for the North Prince. I'd never known him to explicitly say anything that even remotely indicated that he gave a damn about us, not even in a very Belphegor kinda way, which would be funny.

"And where will you be? Back at your place?" Ry tilted his head at Belphegor.

Vassago answered him. "The three of us will be here."

I traded a surprised look with Ry. Well, it wasn't every day we heard that the three of them hung out, especially not Belphegor and Seere. Nevertheless, we didn't say anything.

Vrae frowned at us, evidently displeased with the plan that didn't involve her. "In the meantime, what are Zade and I supposed to do? Pick a fight with an Echelon?"

Belphegor lifted the edge of his lips. "That's a good idea. It might be good to kill your boredom. But no, look, why don't the two of you gather intel as much as you can? While you're at it, try to inconspicuously keep the nose of those Echelons, and more importantly my pop's, from this place–or more to the point, from all of us–if you could manage it. Ask Zabaniah and his pals if you have to. They might hear something."

"Besides, before Yve and I go in, we'll meet my brother first, and since I know you two have met him before, you both can tag along," Ry added.

Both of them cast a gleeful look at us, but that delighted look disappeared from Vrae's face and was replaced with suspicion as if she'd just realized something. "And after that?" she prompted.

Ry startled. "What is it?"

Vrae narrowed her gaze. "There must be something more for us, right? You didn't bring us here just because you wanted to give us the Biography of Arzia. You could have told us elsewhere and not bothered to take us here."

Ry exchanged a half amused, half wary gaze with the royals. Then he faced her again. "Actually, I'm hoping all of us can go in and try snatching Rygavon," he said as he turned his gaze to me.

My jaw dropped in amazement. "Wow, that must be the most shocking and interesting thing I've ever heard from you," I said.

The royals winced at my response.

Vrae looked unsure. Hell, she looked like she was about to slow dance with Azrael. "Are you positive we can do this and walk out in one piece?"

Ry cast a helpless look at her. "We'll definitely be toasted a bit–no denying that part–but alive, yes. Besides, I intend to ask Xaemorkahn along."

I put my hand on his shoulder, and then he looked at me. "Why are you taking him? He's been Lucille's target since before the Stone Age."

Belphegor snorted at my nickname for his demented dad, but he didn't say anything.

Ry snickered. "I know, but he's not a wimp. He's the Irgovaen, and he possesses fire powers that are pretty much like theirs," he said as he jerked his head towards the princes. "And knowing him, I know that he would be willing to put a stop to Lulu's habit of annoying his kind."

Belphegor chuckled. "You two should've told me you've been inventing new names for the old bastard." We grinned at him. "By the way, I don't like the idea of getting your so-called brother into this," he went on.

"And why is that?" Ry asked, but by the tone of his voice, I was absolutely sure he knew the reason, which was why Belphegor gave him a "duh" stare.

"You think? He's not one of us. I hate his guts by nature and I damned know he does too."

Ry just rolled his eyes. "Are we through playing racist around here? I thought you hated your pop enough to cooperate even with someone you hate by *nature*," he said, a bit aggravated by the reasoning the North Prince offered.

Startled, Belphegor fell silent as he gave Ry a dry stare. I shook my head and glanced at Zade, who had a wary look on his face. "You're sure about this?" he asked.

Ry nodded subtly. "Yeah, it's not like we're gonna try to kill him, because that would be the most foolish thing in the long history of foolishness. It's your call, though, whether you him want in or not. After that, we'll move to find and seal the Arzia," Ry said.

"Count me in, Ry. I'm not gonna sit and watch that sack of void keep on slaughtering our underlings one by one. And to top it off, that thing hurt him"–she tilted her head towards her mate–"and Yve. If stealing his weapon can put an end to that thing's history, then so be it," Vrae said without hesitation as she glanced at me.

Zade cast a protective look at my sister, and Ry smiled at her determination.

"She's not going in without me," Zade added, and then he exchanged a look with my sister.

We all then turned our attention back to the North Prince, who sighed heavily and shrugged. "Fine, all right."

"So," Vassago said, clapping his hands. "Now that we're all agreed to this insanity, let me tell you another news flash."

We all looked at him. "And that is?" I asked.

Belphegor raked his hair, looking rather frustrated. "There was another massacre in the east," he said.

I swore under my breath. "Again? Does it have to be this annoying or what?" I asked grudgingly.

Ry frowned. "Did you see it? Where was it?"

Vassago gave me a gloomy look. "We didn't manage to see the one who did it. However, we saw the aftermath. It was at the outskirts of a small human city called Zodura."

Vrae cocked a brow. "Weird. The city of Zodura is Duke Dantalion's domain, is it not? Who were the victims, anyway?"

Belphegor lowered his crimson eyes. "That thing butchered Machordaens, one team."

"If I'm not mistaken, it was the fourth squad of your legion," Vassago inserted.

I exchanged an alarmed look with Vrae. "That's Teghari's team," I said.

"You know them?" Seere asked.

Vrae and I explained to them that not too long ago we had ordered him to recover the first victims of that thing, and now he himself got butchered as well.

Belphegor cringed. "Those guys are unlucky bastards."

A tic worked in my jaw. "Is there anyone else?"

Vassago nodded with a glum look. "Yes, there was also a Fierytarian squad and . . . Aleeria."

I stood up slowly as profound rage burned my bloodstream. Vrae looked like she was ready to break out in a rampage as well. Shaking her head in denial, Vrae eyed each of the princes. "That thing killed Aleeria? No way! There must be a mistake here. She was supposed to be somewhere in the west with her Fierytarians," she said slowly.

I looked straight into Vassago's turquoise eyes to search for a glint of hope that Aleeria wasn't the one who had fallen, but I found nothing.

Ry slowly stood by my side, draped one hand around my shoulder, and gave a gentle squeeze. Very quietly, he asked me to sit. I sat as anger began to boil within me.

Vassago inhaled deeply. "We're sorry, Yve, Vrae, but they were the ones we found." He gave me a half-hearted smile.

I exchanged grieved looks with Vrae as my mind drifted to the deceased female soldier. Aleeria was once our close comrade, and Ry knew her as well. She was the Kivarda who became our mentor once we became Cherxanains, and she was like an older sister to both me and Vrae. We had seldom heard about her again since she was reassigned to the far west to do a secret job. The Fierytarians were devils assigned as personal guards of Kivardas.

Damn it, this thing kept making me angrier and angrier!

"I will *rip* that damned thing limb from limb," I said as icy wrath rode me hard.

Ry held me as he whispered, "You will, and I will be there with you."

I nodded and then tried to calm myself down. "What else, Highness?" I asked Vassago in a rather sharp voice.

The prince shrugged. "We have yet to hear that anyone else has being massacred, aside from those I've just told you about."

"As for that thing, the three of us intend to keep scouring the book and other things in here while all of you cross over," Belphegor said as he entwined his fingers under his chin.

"Okay, we'll try to dig up as much info as we can on the other side. Be safe here, Highness, in case our pal decides to pay a visit." Ry suddenly stood up, followed by Vrae, Zade, and myself.

"Will do. You guys be careful yourselves. Don't die before you even discover the fun of stealing things," Seere added.

We chuckled, and then Ry turned to the royals. "Do you mind if I take this?" he pointed at the key-like object on the table.

Belphegor shrugged. "Suit yourself. We can't do anything with that anyway."

"Fine, we'll take it with us," Ry said. He took the thing, put it back into the pouch, and then handed it to me. I cast him a questioning look, and without another word, he just gave me a subtle nod. Hesitantly, I took the small thing and tied it to my belt once again. After that we gave a nod to say our thanks and goodbyes.

The three princes rose up slowly, Vassago walked past us and chanted to open the wall. As soon as it opened, we stepped out and left them. We saw the castle evaporate into shadows.

"Ry," I called him, and he turned to me. "We're supposed to meet Rivorgad and the others in about two or three days."

He smiled. "Xaemorkahn's soldiers that you guys ran into were Rivorgad and his pals, huh? How are they doing?"

"The last I checked, they were fine. You know them?" I asked him out of curiosity.

"Yeah, I pretty much know almost every one of them," he shrugged.

"Oh . . . oops," I blurted out before I could stop myself.

Ry looked puzzled. "What is it, Yve? Something wrong?"

I grimaced at his question. "Uhm, well, one of them who was called Xeithar or something wasted himself when I tried to squeeze some info out of him."

"And I killed the one named Vangurd," Vrae added.

Ry bit his lower lip. "Then the fight was a bit bigger than I thought. Well, it couldn't be helped then," he sighed.

I cringed. "I'm sorry," I muttered.

He just shook his head. "Don't. It's okay. They understand. My brother and Risha do, so just take it easy. We know the situation when it happened, and we got over it. They died doing their job as soldiers. They won't regret it," he said. "So, what was it you were gonna tell me?" he asked as we changed course towards the northeast.

I cleared my throat. "I just wanna ask if you're really gonna take us there, when we were supposed to wait for them."

He gave me a quizzical stare. "Didn't they tell you guys about me?" he asked.

Vrae answered his question with another, "You mean the part where your brother gave you that cross-over ability?"

He nodded. "Yeah, that part. I'm taking you guys there myself. I don't want to waste a second. Besides, Belphegor and the other two might have found something new by the time we get there," he said, and he offered his hands.

We took them. "Focus to me," Ry said. We did what he asked, and instantly everything was swallowed in darkness.

Chapter 14

Amon arose from his seat and stretched his sore body. Sighing heavily, he leaned on the wall. He had just finished debriefing the Machordaen team who found Aleeria, her Fierytarian unit, and the team he'd sent to back them up.

When he saw the Veil spouted the news and realized that their golems were melted, he almost couldn't stop himself from confronting those Echelons and blowing their heads off. Their soldiers were dying, and now even a Kivarda had fallen victim to whatever the being was that had gone on a rampage out there, but those stupid we-are-the-high-and-mighty-and-all-else-are-brainless Echelon members, especially Kathiera, kept pushing him to spy on the three elite soldiers who had done nothing but try to stop the current disaster.

Well, yeah, as he was told, they had at least committed three acts of high treason in the process and were about to commit several more, but they were doing it to prevent another soldier from becoming that void thing's victim, while those Echelons were asking this of him to prevent *them* from becoming the *soldiers'* victims.

Personally, he'd rather bid their asses goodbye and join the three devils out there, but he had his own part to play, and if he wanted to protect those three, he should do it.

Raking his hair, he sighed in frustration. He really could use at least one sane Echelon on his side. He *tsked* at the slim possibility of it. Yeah, right, people at the punishing block wanted ice water and not even *he* could get some.

"What the hell are Ravaths Bynethar and Xamian doing? Just where the hell are they?" he muttered. It was then something pulled his full attention from his musings.

There was a gulp, and a small wave broke the surface of the Veil.

Amon pushed himself to walk towards it and read the words on its surface. They made his sombre mood go instantly from bad to worse.

Three Perished Archangels
One Disabled Archangel
Two Cherxanains
One Varkonian
Unknown Unholy
Forest of Karan

He let fly a curse. "No fucking way. Not now. Not another dead Archangel," he said as he staggered back. "And they're together. Great! This is fucked up, dammit!"

Taking a deep breath, he quickly dug in his memories to find the one spell he hadn't used in a long time. How to mask the Veil before its broadcast energy reached the Echelons.

Once he remembered it, he immediately positioned himself in front of the Veil and raised both hands as he started the spell, all the while hoping the Echelons wouldn't realize what he was about to do. Unlike the last time he'd done it, they'd now put him directly under Kathiera who was more than capable of breaking through his sorcery.

The only ones more capable than her in that area were Bynethar and Xamian, but not even he could guess their agenda or their whereabouts at the moment.

After he'd finished the spell, he exhaled and gazed upon the slight glint of a very thin shield he'd just cast over the Veil. "I hope she doesn't pick up anything," he muttered. He took a step back and saw the glint disappear, leaving no trace of shield over the Veil. He was about to turn back towards his desk when an unfamiliar tingle went down his spine. Frowning, he turned his attention to the door to his den, but the shield on the door was still there.

What the hell was this?

He was still staring at the door when he heard a distinct click coming from another door in the room. It came from the Hall of Golem.

His blood ran cold at the sound. He headed straight to that door and burst into the Hall, but he didn't find anyone inside. There was no hint of who had been here without his knowledge.

Swallowing hard, he looked around the Hall but still found no one there aside from the herd of golems sitting silently in their holes.

He sauntered back to his den and closed the door, all the while bewildered at what had just happened. *"What the hell was that? Did somebody see what I've just done?"*

*   *   *

We arrived once again at that pitch-black forest. All of us let go of each other's hands. I came to Ry's right side, and he put his hand around my shoulder. We started walking, and the others followed.

"So, Ry," I said as I looked up at him.

"Hmm?"

"Did you intend to kill them from the start, or was that just because they pissed you off?" I asked him as we walked through the forest. It was a good thing our eyes worked perfectly in the dark.

"Let's just say it was a bit of both." His voice sounded smug as he grinned widely.

"Man, I still don't get it how you could do that without getting toasted," Zade said.

Ry glanced at him over his shoulder and then looked forward again. "You guys know that old bastard attacked me, right?"

"Yeah," Vrae and Zade said in unison.

"After that thing hit me nice and proper, something happened. I didn't know how but I'm a bit grateful for it. That attack has broken something and made me no longer bound to his deal that tied up the devils. So in short, I'm not a bound devil any more. I'm a free one, and I have to say, it comes with some cool perks," he said as he gave me a crooked smile.

If I didn't know any better, I could've sworn I heard a bit of sadness in his voice despite his nonchalant words. Out of instinct, I reached down to his hand and entwined our fingers together as I looked up to him. He was startled and met my gaze as we walked.

I smiled at him without saying anything. I just felt that I needed to comfort him. He would never lose me again.

He cast a gentle yet slightly sad look at me as he strengthened his grip on my left hand. I raised my right one to show him my palm, to remind him of the vow we made. His expression went blank, and then he flashed me a dazzling smile. His hand left mine, draped over my shoulder, and gave a gentle squeeze.

Moments later, we found that barren field where the Black Fortress should be standing.

Ry told us to step back, when suddenly one of Xaemorkahn's soldiers appeared from out of nowhere as Ziram had done before. He was about to attack when recognition hit him. He dropped to one knee and put one hand upon his chest. "Hieldhar?" the soldier asked in disbelief.

"Yes Arlain, now stand up," he said.

The soldier arose, still looking shocked. "The Irgovaen and the Queen will be thrilled. Thank God you're alive."

We cringed a bit, and the soldier, who had seen us when we were here before, grimaced. "Forgive me, I didn't mean to offend you," he said apologetically.

"No, it's nothing. We're grateful as well that he's still alive," I said.

He nodded and then looked back to Ry. "Shall I lead you inside?"

"That would be nice, but I don't think it would be a good idea. Why don't you just go and tell Xaemorkahn we're here, but don't tell the others. I don't want an unnecessary riot just because I'm still alive. Xaemorkahn can tell them later," Ry said.

Arlain looked a bit disappointed, but he nodded anyway. "Very well, you can wait here, Hieldhar," he said as he started to turn around.

Ry called him, "Arlain?"

"Yes?"

Ry gave him a scolding look. "How many times I told you, just call me Ry."

The soldier looked uncertain, but he honoured his request. "Uhm, all right, Ry."

Ry grinned. "That's more like it, and by the way, it's nice to see you again."

Arlain looked as if he couldn't believe his own ears, but he didn't say anything further. Genuine happiness appeared all over his face, and he bowed a bit.

He was just turning around when Xaemorkahn suddenly appeared from out of nowhere with his wife beside him.

Arlain gasped in surprise and dropped to his knees with his left hand on his chest. "My Liege! My Queen!" he said in greeting.

"You may stand up, Arlain," Xaemorkahn said without paying attention to the soldier. Arlain stood up and stepped aside, allowing the couple to walk towards us.

By the looks on their faces, it was clear to me that they had been longing to see Ry once more. "Brother!" the king said as he approached Ry in delight, and Ry too walked towards him.

"It's been too long," Ry said as he hugged his sworn brother.

They let go of each other and then Ry shifted his eyes to Varisha who embraced him like a sister. It was when I saw them that it dawned on me that both of them cared for him more than they appeared to, and that made a newfound respect towards the pair grow in me.

"Ry, how have you been?" she asked him with a smile as they separated.

"Well, nothing has changed since the day we parted, Risha," he said, returning her smile.

Xaemorkahn snorted. "Since the day you left us without any useful information, you mean," he interjected.

Ry smirked as he raised his hands up. "Whatever you say, brother, whatever you say."

Xaemorkahn let out a relieved breath at the sight of his sworn brother, and then he faced us. "Welcome back, you three. Didn't expect you'd come back early though, especially not without the escorts we've agreed on," he glanced at Ry, who grinned at him. "But it's good to see you again."

I folded my arms across my chest. "Yeah, we were kidnapped by your brother here. And yes, it's nice to see you both again. How are our, uhm, escorts doing?"

Varisha laughed. Her voice was like a melodic song to my ears. "They're doing all right. Of course, they haven't been told that you're all here ahead of schedule and with him as well. They should be going to your plane later. We'll just explain to them then," she said, tilting her chin towards Ry.

"Oh, that's great." Vrae inclined her head, while Zade just watched in silence.

"Let's get inside," Xaemorkahn said, but when we saw Ry was about to argue, he cut him off. "Through a safe route, brother, don't worry. Your secretive habits still doesn't show any improvement, it seems." He shook his head at Ry, who just shrugged and lifted the edge of his perfect lips.

The Irgovaen then turned to Arlain, who looked a bit bewildered at his king's demeanour around us. "Arlain, go back inside and give a word to Rivorgad, Arann, and Daviros. Tell them to go to my chamber and then continue your shift guarding the gate. Don't let anyone knows that Ezryan and his companions are here just yet. I'll tell them myself. Is that clear?"

Arlain assumed his firm gesture as he put his hand upon his heart and nodded. "It's crystal clear, My Liege, My Queen. I shall take my leave, Cherxanains . . ."

"Nu-uh, no title with us," Vrae and I said in unison.

"With any of us," Ry added. He glanced at his brother, who shrugged.

Arlain hesitated and glanced at his king and queen, who replied with a subtle nod. And then he did what we asked. "Very well, I shall take my leave, Ry, Yverna, Vrathien, and Zaderion."

We nodded, though I was sure each one of us felt a bit uneasy at the soldier's formal attitude towards us. It was like the rest of them did, well, except Rivorgad and Helkann.

"Come," the king said as he held his wife's hand. He then raised his right hand.

Out of the blue, our surroundings changed. We were no longer outside his fortress. I recognized the room to be the king's chamber.

He had flashed us inside without warning. And the most surprising thing of all, he brought us without making any physical contact with us. Hell, even Ry wouldn't be able to flash me anywhere without touching me first.

Zade let out a low whistle that was answered with a smile by the king. "After this realm became my domain, I put a heavy shield on it so you can't get here unless you know where to find this place. Even if by stupid luck an unfriendly managed to come here, whoever that would be would have to face me, and since I can do anything here, well, Ry can tell you the details," he said smugly.

"No, there's no need for you to show off. We got the point already." Ry waved at his brother, who grinned at him. Shaking his head, Ry then turned to us. "That is why Lucy never tried his luck chasing him all the way here. Belphegor would be willing to dress in pink before he ever tried that," he added. We burst out laughing at his comment, which really made me imagine Belphegor wearing pink.

Xaemorkahn shook his head. "Really, brother, of all things you could pick as an analogy, you picked *that*? Him in pink! I bet he'd be furious over something as stupid as that."

"Hey, at least they laughed," Ry shot back.

The King rolled his eyes. "Whatever. And I can't believe you actually refer to your former boss as Lucille."

"Well, he tends to exaggerate things on occasion," Zade said with a grin.

Vrae giggled. "Sometimes he's even worse than Yve and me. Trust me, coming from us, that says a lot."

Varisha let out her melodic laugh again. "Yeah, we noticed." Her husband then made a gesture towards us to follow him to the table and armchairs where we had sat days before.

We had barely touched the seats when we heard a familiar voice outside the door. "My Liege, Daviros, Arann, and I, Rivorgad, are here."

"Come, sit," Xaemorkahn said, so we along with his wife sat while he walked towards the door. "Come in," he said in a firm voice.

A moment later the door opened, and our previous escorts walked in. Arann closed the door behind them, and then they sauntered towards us. At the sight of Ry sitting there with the three of us, their jaws dropped.

"How is this possible?" Daviros asked in disbelief, while Rivorgad and Arann just eyed Ry in shock.

"Hi, you three, it's nice to see you again." Ry smiled as he gave a nod in greeting.

"You really are alive," Arann looked totally grateful, as if Ry had saved their entire race, I thought. Maybe Xaemorkahn did hold something that was extremely vital to his people.

Suddenly the three of them stood shoulder to shoulder, and as they put their hands upon their chests. "It's good to have you back, Ry."

Ry stood up, mimicked their gesture, and replied. "It's good to be back here," he said as he gave them a nod.

Their gaze then shifted to us. They made the same gesture, and we answered them.

The king then motioned for his soldiers to join him near the door. There we heard them talking in low voices. The three soldiers then came to us again, gave their salute, and then walked out of the chamber. From the bits I'd heard, Xaemorkahn also told those three not to tell the rest of them that we were already here with Ry.

After Xaemorkahn dismissed the soldiers, he joined us. He then cleared his throat. "Now, that we've done the reunion and all, let's get to the matter."

"Wait, Xaemorkahn, before we go anywhere, can I ask you one thing?" I asked as I put one hand on the table.

"What is it?" he asked.

"You know Belphegor?" I asked calmly.

Weirdly enough, he grimaced a bit. "Uh, not really, I just heard stories about him, and I don't think crossing paths with him would be a good idea. Even though we detest the same enemy, it doesn't mean we can work together."

I chuckled. "Okay, thanks for the explanation. I just thought you two knew each other and had met."

The king rubbed his brow. "Trust me, even if that psycho Lucy was suddenly willing to bow to Adam's descendants, Belphegor and I would never want to meet with each other."

I let a nervous laughed. "That's nice–Lucy bows to vermin. It will never happen."

He nodded. "Uh-huh."

At his curt response, I bit my lip. *"Whoopsie, Ry, I think that just put a solid end to your brilliant plan to introduce them and ask both their help to screw Lucille over."*

343

I glanced at Ry, who didn't say anything. I looked back at Xaemorkahn, who seemed to be waiting for another question from me. When I shook my head, he tilted his chin a bit and then shifted his gaze to Ry again, but before he could say anything, this time Vrae interrupted him. "Wait, you promised us you'd explain everything the second time we get back here."

Xaemorkahn chuckled. "There's nothing for me to say. You can ask him. All I'm going to say will be just repeating every word he said to me before he left us both."

"Okay," Vrae nodded in understanding. When neither one of us asked him more questions, Xaemorkahn turned his dual-coloured eyes to his brother.

"Tell me, what news you have now?" he asked seriously.

Ry leaned forward. "We discovered something about Avarnakh."

The pair gasped at his words. The four of us then related most of what we knew to all of them. To my surprise, Ry withheld the part about the seals. At first, I wanted ask him about that, but since he was the one who did most of the talking, and this was his brother and the brother's wife he was talking to, it was up to him.

"How in the name of Xiveira did you know all this?" Xaemorkahn ask sharply, while all of his men and his wife just stared at Ry.

I raised a brow at the unfamiliar term and directed a puzzled look at Ry. "Xiveira was the fourth Irgovaen," he explained.

"Oh, I see," I muttered.

Ry exhaled heavily before he gave his brother a quizzical stare. "I found out only a few things on my own. Well, your pal was the one who told me most of it."

Xaemorkahn gave him an arched stare in return. "And who might that be? I don't recall having such a *pal* before," he said, eyeing him suspiciously.

Ry rubbed his chin and put on an act as if he were doing some thinking. Then he answered, "Your pal, you know, the one you said you'll never want to meet even if Lucy was suddenly willing to bow to Adam's descendants?"

Xaemorkahn curled his lips at that. "Oh, him! And you believe him over this?"

Ry raked his hair. "Well, considering he detests his dad enough to even let me stay alive and set foot inside his castle, yeah, I believe him. Besides, I've told you before about some of his sources."

The king expelled a tired breath. "Yeah, I know, I know. So, now what are we supposed to do, Ry? I doubt a mere kick in the ass could do anything to God's Ultimate Destroyer."

"Well, we could always call Azrael," Ry said innocently.

His brother raised his brows. "That's morbid. And I doubt even he could do anything."

Ry raised his hands in surrender. "Okay, okay, so listen to this. From what I heard, that sack of void supposedly has three seals."

"And?" Xaemorkahn prompted.

"We already know what they are."

"And?" Varisha joined our conversation.

Ry crossed his arms over his chest. "One of them is the Ring of Solomon,"–the King's gaze widened in shock, but Ry ignored him–"the other one is Rygavon,"–Varisha gasped this time, but Ry still chose to ignore her–"and we've already got the last one. I stole it."

The king gulped as he tried to regain his composure. "From where? What is it?"

Ry glanced at me. I reached for the pouch on my belt and untied it. "From the deepest part of heaven," Ry said as he took the pouch from me.

Xaemorkahn froze at his words. "You really stole it?" he asked in a rather low voice as Ry took the object from inside the pouch.

Ry shrugged. "Well, as you know, they asked me to do some eavesdropping. I just showed a little initiative."

The king rolled his eyes. "Very funny! So, I take it this is the reason you're still alive after your ass got burned by Heaven's Flame?"

"Yeah, it was a bitch trying to get the hell out of there after I took it. Luckily, it was worth the effort," he said nonchalantly.

Xaemorkahn reached for the Herathim, and I raised my hand to stop him. "Careful with that. Belphegor had his hand explode when he touched it," I warned him.

The King hesitated at my warning, but he braced himself and slowly closed the distance between his fingertips and the Herathim, ignoring his wife, who also attempted to stop him.

When he finally touched it, to our amazement nothing happened. "Whoa," I said as the others stared at him. The king just shrugged, indicating his cluelessness in this.

"Can't you touch this, Yve?" he asked as he examined the object.

Ry was the one who answered him. "She and Zade can, but for some reason that even Belphegor can't figure out, Vrae and the rest of them can't touch it."

The King inhaled and released his breath. "You think that this thing came from up there and that you guys from down there had absolutely nothing to do with it?" he asked sarcastically.

Ry rolled his eyes. "Yeah, we bet on it."

The King handed the object back to me. I put it back inside the pouch and tied it to my belt. Well, maybe he'd tell them later the reason later.

"So, what's the meaning of this, brother? Some of you can touch it while the others follow the laws of nature?" Xaemorkahn asked.

Ry glanced at us, and then he looked at his brother again. "You both know about my human problem, right?" The pair nodded.

"Well, it turns out he let them both in the loop and not me. Great," I brooded, a bit indignant, but then again I realized that maybe he figured it was safe enough to tell them without the risk of jeopardizing us, his comrades. No Lucifer would be coming this way after all.

Ry seemed to notice what I was thinking, because he gave me a sorry-about-that look for a second before he continued. "Yve and Zade have been experiencing those nightmares as well," he remarked.

The king winced at the news and looked at Zade and myself for confirmation.

We nodded. "Yeah, we both have," Zade said.

"Have you figured out the cause?" Xaemorkahn asked.

Ry shook his head. "No, there's nothing reliable this far."

"I see, and you think that's why you three can touch this? Because you know that I don't have anything close to human in my head." The edge of Xaemorkahn's lips twitched.

Ry shrugged. "Probably. That's the only plausible reason I could think of right now."

The King bit his lip. "And what do you plan to do next?"

The four of us exchanged a knowing look, and then we averted our gaze back to the King. "Considering the slaughter that has been going down up to this point, we've planned to put a stop to it," Ry said.

Xaemorkahn gave him an arching stare. "Put a stop to it as in sealing that thing?" He asked calmly, but I caught a weird note in his voice.

I nodded at him while Ry just returned his brother's stare with silence. "Ry and I planned to try stealing the Ring of Solomon," I explained.

"What about the Fallen One's weapon?" Varisha interjected, her voice trembling a bit.

Ry let out a tired breath. "As for that, I need your help, brother."

"No!" Varisha said sharply, shaking her head and staring angrily at her husband, as if warning him not to accept Ry's request.

I put my hand on hers and tried to comfort her. It might be weird that I, whom people called the Tyraviafonza, would do something as unthinkable as comforting someone's sorrow, but I understood her. After my reunion with Ry and everything we'd done and he'd said to me these past days, I myself would never let him go into something like this if I had a choice.

She looked at me in fear, and then to my surprise, she held me and wept in silence. "Why?" she whispered to my ear, and her frail body shivered. I glanced at her husband, who looked as if he were in excruciating pain that tore all the way to his core when he looked at his wife. He fell silent for a moment, and then he closed his eyes, perhaps to brace himself. He motioned to his wife and put his hand soothingly on her shoulder. She didn't move but still hugged me.

I looked at Ry and shot a warning gaze at him. Perhaps it was right not to bother the couple with this problem. He just returned my gaze with an I-got-no-other-choice look, one I'd never seen on his face before.

I turned to Xaemorkahn. His features were tormented, but he didn't say anything for a moment. He shifted his sad gaze towards Ry, and he didn't look pleased one bit. "Why are you asking this of me? You know I despise him, but this?" he asked slowly. His deep voice was filled with an unfathomable pain.

Ry looked tormented as much as the King. "I'm sorry. I didn't mean to bring you bad news just to suffer over it."

"You're asking me to leave my wife and my people and walk into an imminent death for what? To stop a God-knows-what entity that no one knows how to end?" he asked in an irritated voice.

Ry expelled an exasperated breath. "Forgive me, brother, but all deaths are imminent." We all stared at his answer in disbelief, and the King glared at him while his wife tightened her grip on me.

"That's not exactly a good thing to say right now, Hieldhar." I glared at him.

Ry closed his eyes as if to find strength to ignore me. Ugh! He went on, "Before you blame me for everything I'm gonna say, hear this first. It's not like it's only the two of us who are in on this. They,"–he indicated Zade, Vrae, and myself–"along with Belphegor, Vassago, and Seere,"–Xaemorkahn grimaced a bit at him mentioning the Three Hell Princes–"are also in on this, and I assure you, none of them would ever betray us. I swear it on my own life," he said earnestly.

The king's jaw went slack, and he relaxed a bit, despite the idea of him working together with Belphegor. Even Varisha finally let go of me and turned to look at her husband.

"You don't have to swear it, brother, not over those *princes*," Xaemorkahn said, with obvious repugnance laced into his last word. He then stared directly to his brother's eyes. "I know I can't say that this thing has nothing to do with us, because it's been wreaking havoc here and killing my people God knows how."

Again we cringed at the mention of the Big Guy, but the King chose to ignore us. "I mean, that thing is the only one I can't detect. I could sense it when all of you arrived, and that's been extremely disturbing to say the least." Letting out a long breath, Xaemorkahn then raked his hair. "And now you're telling me this, one of the very few possible solutions to put an end to that thing's hunting season."

Ry kept his silence and simply returned his brother's stare with the very same intensity. When I saw them, I couldn't think of anything to say except, "Damn, if a stare could stab, I bet one of them would already be blind by now."

Suddenly, Xaemorkahn let out a frustrated breath, as he looked a bit disgusted about whatever was on his mind. "Does Belphegor know your plan to bring me along in this?" Xaemorkahn asked. He sounded doubtful, and yeah, disgusted.

"So that's why he looks like he just lost a fight with one of Amon's golems all of a sudden." I bit back the sarcasm before I answered him, "He knows."

Xaemorkahn considered my answer and Ry's request, and then he turned to his wife. Suddenly he stood up and looked at all of us as he gave his hand to his wife. "Excuse us. We need to talk in private."

We nodded. "Sure," Ry said hesitantly as Varisha arose and walked with her husband. They went to another door in the corner of the chamber, and there were carvings all over it that made it similar to the wall.

After they disappeared from our sight, we all relaxed a bit. "That didn't go too well," Zade said.

"Indeed," Vrae said as she sucked in her breath and released it.

Ry suddenly took my hand in his. I gave him a sullen look. "'He's not a wimp either; he's the Irgovaen who possesses fire powers pretty much like theirs. And knowing him, I know that he would be willing to put a stop to Lu's habit of annoying his kind.'" I quoted him in a low irritated voice.

He said nothing. Instead he pulled me gently and tucked me on his lap. "He indeed hates Lucille's guts, and you know, I understand completely why we have to ask him, but do you really have to be so irritating that you even said a completely unnecessary phrase like 'all deaths are imminent'?" I went on.

He rocked me gently in silence for a second before he answered, "I'm sorry if I irritated you, but as you said, that was necessary," he said, and then he kissed my shoulder.

I curled my lips. "No, I didn't say that was necessary. I said I understand why we have to ask him. And *the* completely unnecessary phrase you said was the one with seven words." He looked puzzled, and I rolled my eyes at him. "Do the words 'I swear it on my own life' ring a bell?" I asked sarcastically.

He laughed. "Oh that," he said.

I cupped his flawless face and stared at him. Vrae and Zade started to talk to each other. Perhaps they didn't want to intervene.

Good for them. "That's all you wanna say?" I narrowed my gaze angrily at him.

He cringed. "Sorry, baby, but I had to reassure him. We need him, trust me."

I leaned on his broad shoulder. "I know, but do you have to swear it on your life? Even your brother said you don't have to."

He raked my hair as he chuckled. "Now you don't believe in them too?"

I lifted my head from his shoulder and patted his chest. "It's not that! I mean, why your life? You know we can't just go around throwing out vows unless it's necessary. You don't need to go that far just to assure your brother. He doesn't like it, and I don't either, not one bit." I glared at him.

He sighed heavily, and then in a voice so calm and soothing he answered, "Look, Yve, I'm sure you know why, and believe me, I'd rather swear my life on protecting you forever than swear it to make old hags forget their unreasonable fight for a second and focus on the bigger problem at hand. I mean, gee, they haven't even see each other's hides yet," he said sardonically, and then he let out a tired breath.

I was startled at his words saying he'd be better off protecting me. Gee, he'd been saying those things since we were, well, officially together. As I felt another wave of longing run through me, I leaned against his shoulder, a bit closer to his neck this time. I sighed as his masculine scent teased my nostrils as I wondered how he'd been doing out there all alone.

Deep sadness overwhelmed me as I realized something. It had been awful enough for me longing for him, and yet at that time I thought he was dead, so I just held onto his memory without having any hope to be with him for real. I couldn't even imagine how he'd been dealing with his situation back then. He knew the others, in particular me, were out there, but he couldn't meet us. And judging by the way he kept on repeating his words that he'd protect me over and over again, I guess there was no telling how much he'd been missing me.

Poor Ry! I wish I'd been there for you.

I circled my hands around his neck and nuzzled closer into him. I could feel that he was startled by my mood change, but I chose not to say anything. He too chose not to question it and just embraced me tightly, and I revelled in the feeling of being in his arms.

Moments later, I tried to lighten the situation. I recalled the last thing he said. I cleared my throat as I ran my hand through his hair. "By the way, I don't think it's wise to call them old hags. I particularly don't think that they need to see each other's hides, because, forget us, Varisha would beat the hell out of you if she gets to see or even *hears* something as impossible as that."

He chuckled. "Baby, I think that instead of beating me, Risha would sue Belphegor first for getting a sneak peek over something *that* private. Better yet, she'd beat the crap out of my brother for having an affair, and not normal to boot."

Even Vrae and Zade, who weren't involved in our banter, suddenly burst out laughing.

"I assure you, Ry, I will beat you first." From out of nowhere we heard the Queen's melodic voice snap at him. I quickly got up from his lap and sat on the armchair I sat on earlier. We turned towards the door where she stood.

He grinned at her as she closed the distance. "Oops, you heard that, huh? Sorry."

"We both did, because we didn't exactly go to another dimension to talk in private, you know," her husband said sarcastically as he followed her.

Ry grimaced. "Yeah, I know."

Xaemorkahn rolled his beautiful dual-coloured eyes, and then he stood next to his wife. They grasped each other's hands very tightly. Maybe they had decided to make that difficult choice. If what Ry said about his brother was true, then most likely that was what he would do.

"I just hope we don't blow this–I don't blow this. I owe them more than anything for saving Ry." I branded those words deep in my own thoughts.

The king expelled a frustrated breath. "We've decided."

I inhaled a bit before I heard the rest. Zade and Vrae just stared blankly at the couple, whose faces looked totally miserable.

"And?" Ry prompted.

Xaemorkahn bit his lower lip, his brows knitted. "Okay, I'm in."

Ry stood up and approached his brother. He was obviously grateful that his brother had been wise enough to make that choice. Ry hugged him, but Xaemorkahn just went ramrod stiff. After that he let the King go and extended his hand. "I won't let you down, Edros."

Relaxed, Xaemorkahn slowly shook it. "I know you won't."

That term Edros caught my attention, but I stopped myself from interrupting them I glanced at Varisha, who was still rigid next to her husband. She was definitely reluctant to let him go. Just when I was about to make a gesture to tell Ry, he already motioned towards her.

He tucked her hands in his. "Risha, you're a sister to me. I swear to you, I won't let anything happen to him."

Smiling sadly, she looked up to level her gaze at him. "I know, little brother." And then she hugged him. "Just make sure my husband gets back to me in one piece, okay?"

He patted her back gently. "I will."

Nodding, she let him go. Xaemorkahn then led her to the armchairs on which they sat a while ago. Once they were seated, Ry returned to his seat next to me. Eyeing each one of us, he inhaled deeply and released his breath. "Now, I'm gonna tell you what I haven't told Belphegor and the other princes. I doubt any of them knows about this, at least not yet."

We exchanged puzzled looks and then looked back at him.

"What is it?" I said. I could sense the anxiety in my voice, but I forced myself not to feel it. He in return grinned helplessly. "This is gonna be difficult, so I need you guys to bear with me," he began in a tone that seriously freaked me out.

I narrowed my gaze at him. He swallowed a bit before he answered, "Yve, Zade, it's about our nightmares."

Chapter 15

Duke Dantalion arrived outside Vassago's castle. The Prince immediately came out with Belphegor, and Seere pulled up the rear. "I didn't think you'd actually come," Vassago said without as much as a preamble.

Dantalion's gaze went dark. His grief for the fallen Kivarda and her guards was still evident in his eyes. "I don't think I have a choice, now do I, Highness?"

"You have options. We're not pushing you to do anything. Unless you want to hinder us, our alliance still stands," Seere interjected.

Belphegor rolled his eyes. "Don't tempt him, stupid. It's not like he's that type of bastard," he snapped.

Dantalion nodded respectfully at the North Prince. "Thank you for having that much faith in me, Highness," he said, and then he turned his eyes back to Vassago. "So, about the question you've posed earlier," he started.

Vassago straightened his features. "What say you?"

Dantalion lowered his gaze, contemplating on how best to give his answer. Abruptly, he lifted his head. "I will do anything in my power to help you in all other matters, except leaving my palace to join your quest in sealing the Arzia, and naturally that includes facing the Lord. Forgive me."

"Would you mind elaborating?" Vassago asked.

Dantalion's lips curved in a bitter smile. "I cannot afford to leave now. It's rather ridiculous and awfully bad timing, but lately something foul has been stirring in my castle. Whoever is mastermind behind it, he's turning my people against each other, and his motive's yet to be unravelled."

Seere glanced at Belphegor. "Yve's not the one behind that, is she?"

Dantalion almost smiled at the name. "I assure you, Highness, she's not anywhere near my castle, nor even is Vrae. Besides, she

353

knows not to mess with my domain. Even if she was ordered by the Echelons, she wouldn't do it. Not that she doesn't have the ability, but we darkness wielders tend to stand behind the line, since it's hardly productive to blend darkness with its own. What I know is that if this is indeed a soldier's work, it has to be someone outside the First Legion, because we all know Yve always boldly and effectively involves herself whenever she's on the job."

"Not to mention that she always goes straight for the big cheese," Vassago inserted.

Belphegor concurred as he shot a "duh" stare at Seere. "Yeah, and in case you haven't noticed, someone's keeping her busy these days," he snapped meaningfully, and then he turned his eyes back to the duke. "With that said, somebody else is screwing with you, it seems. Be on guard then, Dantalion. If it is a soldier, they might be targeting you. Perhaps this time those marvellously idiotic Echelons are upping their playing field. Who knows what my asshole of a father has ordered them to do."

Dantalion chuckled. "I will alert my legions. They've been restless as well these days," he sighed.

Vassago nodded. "Fine then, we will not involve you. But be ready. We'll be sending the two of them along with *him*. Just guard them well."

The duke bowed slightly. "I will. I hope you succeed."

*　*　*

We were taken aback by his words.

"I thought we were gonna do some digging. Turns out you already have?" I asked him in confusion.

He shrugged. "This piece of info won't do us any good if the princes know something about it before we do. Besides, knowing them, they'll find out through other ways."

"Care to elaborate on that?" Vrae asked.

Before Ry could answer her, Xaemorkahn cut him off. "Wait, wait. You said you don't know anything about your nightmares."

Ry gave him a droll stare. "No, I said 'there's nothing reliable so far'."

His brother scowled. "Don't play the word game again. So you're saying you do have something but whatever it is, it's not reliable?"

Ry scoffed. "Yeah, something like that. Okay, I'll tell you. After I left,"–he gave a meaningful look at Xaemorkahn and Varisha–"I crossed over several times to our plane"–he glanced at me–"and few other places," he said as his gaze fell on all of us.

Xaemorkahn jerked his head. "Where? You came back here?" he asked. There was a hint of doubt in his voice.

Ry shook his head. "No, I didn't, 'cause like you said, you would've noticed."

Xaemorkahn nodded slightly. "Right, because if you had done so without me feeling anything, I would vote that my entire people to take refuge elsewhere and sadly bid this fine realm goodbye," he said, half mocking, half seriously thinking about what he'd said.

Ry scoffed. "That's funny, but I'm sorry to disappoint you. No, I didn't, so scratch that 'taking refuge elsewhere' idea and shove it where the sun doesn't shine."

"That would be your place, Ry, and I don't like *that* either," Xaemorkahn shot back.

Ry flashed a shit-eating grin at the King.

"Okay, screw that. So where had you been?" Xaemorkahn jerked his head at Ry.

"I went to the Zihargan realm." He gave his brother a quizzical stare.

"You went where?" Xaemorkahn asked. He blinked and looked as if he didn't get what Ry just said. Well, I for one heard what he just said. The problem was that I didn't know what or where the hell it was.

"Um, guys, one quick question," I said, and all of them turned to me.

"What?" Ry and Xaemorkahn asked in unison.

"What's the Zihargan realm?" Vrae asked, cutting me off.

I raised a brow. "Well, thank you for your help, Vrae," I muttered.

"You're welcome." She kept her eyes fixed on Ry and Xaemorkahn, who exchanged knowing looks.

"Zihargan was our original realm," Varisha answered as she put her fragile-looking hand on the chair's armrest.

I raised a brow. "Oh, I see."

Zade leaned forward as he raised a hand. "Whoa, whoa, hold on a second here, guys."

"What is it?" Ry asked.

Zade scoffed. "What do you think? You're telling us that you can also go to any realm that exists as well as this one?"

"No, just the realms my brother here takes me to, and if I have the map on me, so to speak, I can go wherever it is," he said, crossing his arms over his chest.

We all stared at them in disbelief. "All the same, basically, you're saying you can go to other realms? Wow," Zade said in awe.

Ry chuckled. "Now if you've finished with the 'wow, other realms' moment, let me explain the rest."

Zade raised his hands, telling Ry to go on with that amazed look still on his face.

Ry then cleared his throat. I noticed a glint of wariness in his eyes. "When I was there, I came across something."

"And what was it? By the way, I still don't understand why you even bother to go there. I mean that place, well, you know . . ." Xaemorkahn said hesitantly. He looked as nervous as Ry was.

I wondered why. Something happened over there perhaps. When I glanced at them both, they just stared meaningfully at each other, but they didn't say yahoo, so I didn't ask.

Varisha cast a baffled look at her husband. "Did we have something that relates to humans in there?"

Xaemorkahn shook his head at her as he gave his wife a tender gaze. "As far as I know, we don't, which is why I'm also gonna say that this does raise a disturbing question," he said as he turned his attention back to his brother. "Just what made you go there?"

Ry shifted his position. "Well, I had a hunch that something might still be in there, so there I went."

"And?" Varisha interjected.

"I was right. At your old place, I found some records. Apparently my memories can be dependable sometimes."

"And what were those records?" I asked him.

"I found out that the event where one entity is reborn into another, aka Votzadir, isn't just happening on us."

All of us exchanged confused looks and then stared back at him. "Wait, wait, what do you mean? This kinda thing happened before? I don't recall ever having that kind of . . ." Xaemorkahn's voice faded, before he continued with just one word, "Record."

His peculiar eyes fixed on Ry, and they gleamed in utter amazement. Ry just gave him a subtle nod in return. I had to keep from rolling my eyes at this sign language we had no clue about. I really hoped he'd explain it to us, or else I'd beat the crap out of someone. Fortunately, he did continue his explanation.

"A long time ago, before we were even created, supposedly there were these advanced races. You guys know one of them. We believed they were our originals."

"And what of the other pack?" I asked.

His answer made my jaw go slack. "It was another advanced race as well. To make it easier on you, let's just think they were like us and humans."

I winced. "Wow."

Zade and Vrae just stared at him in disbelief.

"We had guessed that those races were some sort of experiment, if you wanna put it crudely." Xaemorkahn rubbed his brow.

Exchanging a disgusted look with me, Vrae scowled and cursed under her breath.

I *tsked*. "Yeah, tell me about it, another *joke*."

Ry bit his lip, and then funnily enough, he grinned. "But let me tell you something else. Apparently Mr Almighty up there kinda blew up on that particular experiment."

I snorted. "Gee, never heard of *that* one. Was He for real?"

Ry let out a small laugh. "Don't bet on it, baby. Perhaps He was counting on it to be a grand failure before He went all the way to create the next generations."

Staring dryly at him, I folded my arms. "Wanna tell us why the hell He had to be such a sweetie pie?" I asked with a heavy dose of venom.

Flashing a wide grin at me, he shook his head. "I assure you, He's everything but *that*."

I narrowed my gaze at him, and he raised his hand in surrender. "Okay, so those devils and humans, simply put, were too advanced. The success of their creation was matched only by the great failure and disaster they caused."

I gave him another puzzled look.

Smiling patiently, he rubbed his chin. "You know those ancestors of ours, so to speak, gathered and planned to spread forbidden knowledge, right?"

I frowned. "What? You mean the Book of Lost Knowledge?"

Nodding, he then cleared his throat as he eyed Vrae, Zade, and me. "I still don't know what exactly that book contains, but Xaemorkahn, I mean the Irgovaens before him recorded something." He glanced at his brother. "They did have some overall record about it. You see, when they were gathering intel on Big Boss that time, there were rumours, or so the records said, that there was some vague prophecy spread amongst those guys."

Vrae, Zade, and I were eyeing him in shock. "You're saying that Cain's BS . . ." I stopped midsentence because of the absurdity of it.

He nodded again. "I think their prophecy, whatever that was, was the precursor of this Votzadir matter, or in this case, *they* went Votzadir before Cain came up with the full version of it." He then exhaled heavily. "I didn't find out what caused it, but the record had several footnotes, something I failed to notice before. Apparently, after that vague prophecy, a few of the originals had a thought."

"And that was what?" I asked slowly.

"Some of them, the ones who got the chance to go Votzadir, got paranoid. They were afraid they couldn't remember who they were, let alone get a firm grip on their powers."

"So what did they do about it?" Vrae asked.

He shifted his position and looked deeply uneasy. "Well, they made some sort of, uh, copy of their memories and the core of their powers and handed those to each other," he said.

I winced at his words. "Come again?"

"They made a copy of their memories and powers," Vrae murmured as her gaze turned to me and Zade.

"And handed it to each other?" Zade finished her question.

He gave us a helpless grin. "Yeah, I know how it sounds, but that was what I got. It seemed that they believed they would get both copies when they become Votzadir. Think of it like their ticket to return."

"That is one hell of a ticket, I'd say." I cringed at the thought, but another occurred to me. "Oh, hey, wait a sec." I raised a hand.

"What is it?" Ry asked.

"They could only get those copies on condition that they did meet with each other, right? So, let's say they did come back, how did they meet with each other? Did they just cross their fingers, hoping they'd meet?" I raised a brow at him.

"No, it looks like those orbs they created and handed to each other drew them to meet eons later after all of them were reincarnated."

"Oh, okay, because I'm so not in the mood to hang ourselves on hope only." I feigned a shiver at my own words.

He chuckled, and then he went on, "That's what I got from those records. Soon after that, well, we were already told about it. Big Boss up there got totally mad at them and wiped them off the map. But apparently, eons later some unexpected things came up. It had to do with what I just explained earlier about those orbs being their anchor towards each other. It turned out that there were several of those advanced humans who transformed into those originals, I mean, literally transformed, in the flesh, fully recharged, and with their IDs," he said dramatically.

My jaw went slack at that.

"Are you serious?" Zade asked, half amazed, half not believing what he just heard.

Ry expelled a tired breath. "I'll say it again, that was what I got, and yeah, I'm not sure about that, which was why I said 'nothing that's reliable' minutes ago. But I really hope this thing turns out to be the real deal."

When neither of us said anything in response, he continued, "That was why these advanced humans were also blown to kingdom come, or in their case, drowned to kingdom come, because some of these Votzadirs turned out to be the humans' protectors–well, for some of the humans–and the others stayed what they were, devils, real ones or otherwise. So they were fighting each other over humans, and in the end their conflict wiped out not just them, but also most of the humans. The rest were the Boss Man's handiwork. I guess that was one of many fucked up reasons I couldn't even begin to fathom why the Big Boss created us and the humans today. All of the predecessors were gone," he ended bitterly.

"Nice," Vrae rebuked.

"Wait, wait. When you said they were drowned, do you mean it was Atlantis?" Zade asked him. Vrae and I abruptly turned to him at his question. Even I found the idea absolutely incredible.

The King and Ry just gave us a confirming nod without saying anything else, which baffled me even more. "And when I said Boss Man did the rest, He didn't just toss all of them along with their island. As you know, He also destroyed the survivors, wiped out their memories, and rearranged their cultures, language, and, well, virtually their entire legacy, along with that notorious tower they built. Hell, perhaps He was just looking for the right moment to destroy the damned thing. I'd bet the day those so-called Atlanteans built it was one of Pride's best moments," Ry added sarcastically.

I winced at his tone, but I recalled it well. The Tower of Babel was, as he said, one of Pride's glorious moments. There was no doubt that he'd harvested a lot of souls just from the ones who built the tower alone, not to mention those who worshipped it.

Well, Pride and his siblings had indeed been around that long, but as far as we could tell, no one knew how each of them became what they were now—one of us.

Few of us had guessed that someone or something or, hell, people from upstairs had sealed them all at some point. Perhaps Lucifer and the royals knew, but then again, nobody bothered to ask, because they tended to crawl under people's skin, like Pride, who enjoyed bitching at me. Now that I'd heard this, they might have been sealed around the same time that tower got destroyed and were freed when our race came to be.

"So, Babel, huh?" Vrae asked.

He nodded. "Yep, as you may recall, there are still fragments of the island out there, but there's almost no trace of its existence nor any concrete detail on what happened with the citizens. Instead, all that's left are obscure stories about them."

"But we believe that even if there were any survivors with their memories of who they truly were still intact, there's no way they'd tell the next race of humans about the existence of their advanced technology, lest history repeat itself," Xaemorkahn explained.

"Which is what the Boss Man was counting on. But still, memories or no memories, the survivors kept singing songs and telling stories of their perished homeland throughout the generations. Even though humans nowadays, who came from both Adam's and Noah's lines, view it merely as a fairy tale for children, it seems to be enough for them," Ry added.

I bit my lip and stood up slowly. "So, Atlantis and Babel aside, you're saying that maybe this is our chance to reunite when it happens to us? This is our ticket to get a grip on our powers and memories?"

Ry's sad gaze met my eyes, but he didn't say a thing, and I knew what it meant. We had no other choice.

Vrae scowled. "Wait, hold on you guys. Why can't you just keep them with you without making backups? I mean, I don't know, but you're not sure if you all won't remember a damn thing now, are you?"

I made a choking noise. "I don't know, but think about it. If we carried these powers and all of our memories and we stuck them into Adam's descendant's infants, don't you think their brains would just pop before we even get the chance to say hi?" I asked sarcastically.

She rolled her eyes at me while Ry just snorted. He looked rather pleased. Whether that was because I caught on quick or because he liked my sarcasm, I really had no idea.

"Like she said," Ry tilted his head towards me, "that's not an option. The lesser soldiers might have a chance without splitting their orbs, but then again, none of them possesses the elements we do. If we wanna guarantee we can get through this, we have to try making that copy. To us, maybe it's like our QuiMarrae," he mentioned our powers' orb. "Besides," he continued, "according to the records I've found, before one entity can become another, its true body has to die first. In that regard, there's no telling that our powers will die unless we make that backup," he said.

"I'm in," I said without hesitation.

Vrae cast a glare at me, which was replaced with miserable look when Zade responded pretty soon after, "Count me in."

Vrae looked at us both, and from the look on her face, she definitely wanted to argue. But when she glanced at Zade, who gave her a meaningful gaze, she restrained herself.

"All right," I said slowly. "How's it gonna be, Ry?"

He hesitated and then answered, "We'll have to do some exchange here."

I arched a brow. "You mean exchange like those old devils did?"

He cast a gentle look at me and nodded. "Yeah," he said. Before he continued, I stopped him. "Wait a second."

"What is it?"

I cleared my throat, feeling a bit nervous. "What difference would it make? I mean, why don't we just make those copy things and carry them ourselves?"

"Yve, if we made the copy of our powers and carried it ourselves, when the true body dies, the QuiMarrae will vanish along with it, because they're linked to each other. If we carry each other's QuiMarrae . . ."

I caught on to his meaning. "The QuiMarrae will stay intact as an orb, because it's not linked to our bodies. Rather, it would join the spirit core of the new host and stay separate from our bodies."

He smiled at me finishing his explanation. "And as you know, our spirit core wouldn't be gone even if the visage was no more."

"Fine, so what do we do now?" Zade asked as he rubbed his palms.

"Whoa, hold on, buddy," Ry said as he raised both hands.

Zade and I turned to him. "What?" Zade asked.

"I'll try it first. After we create our QuiMarrae, we must split it in half, so two people"–he held out two of his lean fingers–"are carrying a part of one QuiMarrae." He pulled in one finger and only held out his forefinger.

"Okay, and . . ." I interjected.

He lowered his hand. "And here's the order: Yve, you give your orbs to Vrae and me. Zade, you do the same. That way you can get at least one of them when you meet with either of us. "Ry pointed at Vrae and himself.

My sister let out a scoffing laugh. "Dude, in case you've forgotten, I'm not going Votzadir, so forget the idea of giving their juice to me." She gave him a harsh look as she shook her head frantically.

Ry just grinned at her in return. "Well, then you might be a little happier after you hear this. You won't be thrown into another dimension who knows where if you have something to lock you here, i.e., their orbs."

Vrae started and then looked at us gleefully. *"Well, at least something good came out of this,"* I said in my thoughts as I felt a bit relieved.

"Although there's a bit of drawback," he added.

We cast a quizzical stare at him. "And that would be what?" Vrae asked nervously.

Ry bit his lip. "As long you have one of the QuiMarrae, you can't have your true form, as in the flesh and blood. But, you might be tied up to whoever comes across you first."

She hesitated and then nodded slowly as she glanced at her mate, who gave her an encouraging look.

"Okay, what about you? To whom will you give yours?" I asked as I stared blankly at him.

He cleared his throat. "I'll give more than half of my powers and a bit of my memory to my brother." He glanced at Xaemorkahn, who looked surprised by Ry's decision.

"More than half of your powers?" There was a hint of doubt in Xaemorkahn's voice.

Ry gave him a subtle nod. "Yeah, I can't give it to Yve, Vrae, or Zaderion. Somebody on the other side may sense it when we get back, and it'll only bring them more trouble than help. As for my memories, I'm only giving you bits of them, enough to prevent me from blowing anybody apart because I'm freaking out," he grinned half-heartedly.

"And what becomes of the rest of your memories?" I asked him.

He answered me with the soothing smile that I had come to love so much. "I'll give it to you. I wanna make sure I remember everything the second I come in contact with you." My eyes widened at his words, and then I replied to him with a gentle smile.

He had trusted so much in me in the last few days already.

"Of course," he went on. "I'd rather have anything about you in my head, but then finding you would be much harder, and I can't possibly know what you may look like after you change. This way, we'll be drawn to each other," he said. After that, he let out a slow breath. "Now, after we're done with the story . . ."

Before he finished, I cut him off. "Wait, I just noticed something," I said. All of them turned to me. "Did you happen to find out why Cain's prophecy turned out not to be his one of a kind BS? If this thing happened before, you'd think somebody up there might already have arranged it, as a sick joke perhaps."

Ry frowned at my out-of-the-blue question. "I don't know. Even if it turn out that someone up there did pull the strings, I don't think it was meant to happen. I'd rather think that our originals came across something they weren't supposed to, and their prophecy only contained the omen of their doom, the omen that Big Boss was gonna kick their asses to another dimension, not the omen of them going Votzadir. Maybe, just maybe, they *intended* to be Votzadir," he said emphasizing the word intended.

Which made us gape again.

"What makes you think that, brother?" Xaemorkahn asked.

"I can't tell you why, because I'm not so sure either. The record was vague. I just had a wild hunch," he said hastily.

"That must be one hell of a hunch–to think that our kind, never mind our *originals*, ever wanted to become one of *them*," Vrae muttered.

"For survival maybe? Or to get some payback after Big Guy intended to wipe them off? If it turned out eons later that some of them had survived, it would be like shouting, 'Wiping us off the map is way above your pay grade' to the people up there," I sneered.

Ry and Zade chuckled at that. "I bet we may know the rest after we get a hold on what is in that book those princes are scouring right now," Ry said in a wondering tone.

"Right, so basically, we've now come across something we're not supposed to about that sack of void, which can be considered as upstairs' dirty little secret–which could be classified above top secret if I may say so." I gave them a meaningful stare, raked my hair, and then went on with my speculation. "So naturally Cain gets hold of the omen of our destruction, but this time, because something like this has happened before . . ."

"Cain provided us with the omen of our destruction along with our ticket to survive it. Vague though it is, it was enough for you to do some digging of your own," Vrae concluded as she glanced at Ry.

"It seems I can't hide anything from you both, because that sums up almost exactly everything that came to my mind." Ry grinned broadly.

Vrae and I beamed at his words.

Zade raised a hand. "Okay, now can we get down to business or explain some more things that certainly will make my head explode?

And guys, I hate to break it to you, but our time's limited. There's no way we can be sure our doppies won't cross someone's path."

Ry nodded at him. "I hear ya, so now I'll try it first. After I'm done, you two follow." He jerked his head at me and Zade.

He then raised his palms and placed them facing each other in front of his chest as he chanted a spell we recognized as one to temporarily pull our source of powers into an orb form and then double it. After he finished with the incantation, there were two orbs floating in front of his chest. He shoved the original core back into his own body, and then he concentrated on the remaining orb. This time, he muttered another spell I didn't recognize.

I gave him a questioning look as he split the orb very slowly. The moment it was separated, I saw his perfect face covered in sweat. That must be one hell of a spell.

Ry then tilted his head towards his brother, indicating to him to come forth. Xaemorkahn hastily came closer and then carefully extended his hands. Ry handed him one of his orbs with extreme caution.

The moment Xaemorkahn received Ry's orb, he chanted his own spell, which caused some sort of force field to appear and blanket the orb.

Vrae, Zade, and I just watched the king in silence. A QuiMarrae orb was a frail thing, which was why after we created it, we needed to protect it immediately as Xaemorkahn was doing right now.

I shifted my gaze to Ry, who was blanketing the other orb he held. After he was done, he expelled a breath of relief as he wiped the sweat from his forehead. Looked satisfied, he turned to me as he approached. He stopped and handed the orb to me.

I took his memory orb very carefully and then held it in front of my chest. It divided into two smaller orbs and shoved itself slowly inside my palms. A warm sensation ran through me as I felt the orb bury itself and then vanish completely.

"Done," he said, and then he touched my cheek tenderly as he smiled at me. I returned his smile with another.

He let out a weary sigh, and he turned his gaze to Zade and then back to me. "You two can try it now."

"Err, one quick question," I interrupted.

"What?" he asked.

"Do we have to use the same spell you used just then? Because FYI, we don't know jack about that." I folded my arms.

He shook his head. "No, Yve, you just have to use the regular spell. I used that particular spell because I had to separate my orb in a slightly different way. Well, you know." He gave me a crooked smile that made his gorgeous face even more devastating.

"Okay, no more questions. Let's do this." I placed my palms in front of my chest as Ry had done.

I glanced at Zade, who stood up and copied my gesture. Then both of us muttered our usual incantations. Everything just went down exactly the way it did for Ry. This time, when Zaderion and I separated the orb, Vrae and Ry hurriedly helped us. They covered our orbs with protective shields, and the orbs vanished inside their palms.

Ry let out a long breath and rubbed his palms. "We're done here for now, brother," he said as he looked at his brother, who nodded at him and took his wife's hand.

That instant we were back outside his fortress.

"Wow, I still can't get past the fact that you're able to take us out here without making any contact." I gave him an impressed look. He gave me a smug smile in return.

Ry then asked us to take each other's hands like before. After that he faced the couple. "I'll come to you before we start the plan against the Fallen One. Be safe, brother," he gave him a salute.

The King nodded, and his wife smiled. "Have a safe journey, all of you."

"Yeah, thanks guys," I said as we gave them a salute.

Everything then went black as Ry took us back home.

Chapter 16

Cain bolted awake with vicious pain hammering his head. Cursing, he leaned on the wall of his cell. He was still rubbing his head when suddenly his mind conjured the one image he tried his damnedest to forget.

Abel. His face pale showed the blood flowing from his mouth, while he stared at him in horror and utter disbelief before he drew his last breath, calling him, *"Brother . . . why?"*

Letting out another fetid curse, he closed his eyes and placed his palm over them. But no sooner had he relaxed than he felt something was wrong.

Usually the guards came down his cell to beat the hell out of him because some human had murdered another or because they heard him cursing or just to poke his joints with the blunt side of their spears for fun—*their* fun.

He decided not to think about it seriously, for the few seconds he could go through without their crap was all the peace he could hope for down here. Unfortunately for him, it turned out that there was something that made the guards oblivious to his foul curses. Well, not exactly something.

It was more like the two devils who were now standing right outside his cell.

"Cain," one of them called.

Removing his hand, Cain opened his eyes, only to see two of the very people he wanted to butcher. He gritted his teeth. "What did I do now? If you're here just to kick me for no good reason, believe me when I say I will kick back this time. Guards be damned!" he snarled viciously.

The two just stared at him. "Calm yourself down, and don't go all hysterical like a girl. Do you think we came here just to waste our time beating you? We have guards for that. There's no need for us to go at you."

Suspicious, Cain narrowed his gaze at both his visitors. "Then why don't you do just that, Honourable *Ravath* Bynethar? C'mon, call those guards on me," he taunted.

The addressed Ravath rolled his eyes, knowing that Cain was doing it to jerk his chain. "You do realize we have made the guards and the rest of the inmates oblivious to us?"

Cain winced and recalled his meeting with the two devil sisters. Bynethar just did the same trick to everyone but him. But that didn't tell him anything as to what Bynethar sought by coming to his prison. Furthermore, he came only with one other Ravath, whereas all their colleagues had come together and turned the guards loose at him when he blurted out that damned prophecy.

Slowly getting up, he neared the bars. "So, what are you two doing here, Bynethar, Xamian?" he asked, inclining his head to the other Ravath present.

Both Ravaths exchanged a look and shifted their attention back to Cain. "We know how you ended up with that prophecy," Bynethar began.

Cain startled. "Duh! Like it's a damn secret," he retorted acerbically.

"Don't worry, Cain, we're with him," Xamian said.

"Him who, exactly?"

"Ezryan."

That one name was enough to make the blood leave his face, but he decided to play pretend before he said something that would lead to more beatings. He really didn't need any of those right now. "Dude, are you both high? Last time I looked, he'd been dead for seven hundred years."

At the end of his tether, Bynethar abruptly raised his hand and grabbed Cain's throat. "We're not here to listen to you bitching, Cain. We know what he did, we know that he's back, and we're with him. Why do you think we weren't present when the others beat the crap out of you?"

"You were drunk at somebody's party? Lilith's perhaps?"

Bynethar almost choked him, but he reined himself in before he could ruin what he was supposed to do here. He then let him go. "You're hopeless."

Cain rolled his eyes. "Hey, I'm not the one coming down here blabbering bullshit."

Xamian cast an indignant look at him, but despite the guy's obstinacy, both he and Bynethar could appreciate him trying to protect *their* subordinates. God knew he didn't have any obligation to do so. "Cain, look, just hear us first, because we really don't have much time here."

Cain shot a feral look at the two. "Then leave me the fuck alone."

Bynethar aimed a punch at the bars. "Listen to us, dammit! The sisters have already met with Ezryan, and they've shown that item he gave you to the North Prince. They, along with us both, have secretly turned our allegiance to him and few other princes."

At the unexpected news, Cain relaxed a degree, even though he was still suspicious. "Don't even try to trick me into saying something that will result in you two throwing punches, or so help me . . ."

"What? You'll whine at us?" Xamian mocked.

Cain glared at them. Bynethar then raised a hand to stop their mouthing at each other. "We don't give a fuck about what you think. We came here on the Prince's behalf. He sent us to ask you one thing."

"And that is?" Cain prompted.

Bynethar's lips curved in an evil smile. "What would you do to get the hell out of here for good?"

$$*\quad*\quad*$$

I felt hard flat ground under my foot as everything became clear. We were at the Kadarost forest, miles away from Gillian.

Well, I had no clue why he'd brought us all the way here, but then again, maybe he was doing it for safety, considering the fact that he'd whacked those angels there, and I bet by now our underlings or worse, *their* underlings, were already swarming that forest.

"Is everyone still with me?" Ry turned to the three of us.

"Yeah," Zade responded to him. "Gee, man, this is the fourth time I've been back and forth across dimensions, and I still can't get used to it." He sucked in a deep breath and then released it.

"That makes the two of us." Vrae rubbed her temple. Well, she looked a bit dizzy.

"Make that three," I added as I looked at Ry. He raised his brows and then gave me a breath-taking smile as he gently ran his hand on my head. I grinned at him, and he withdrew.

"All right, guys, we should split up for a while. Call back your doppelgangers and then go back to the Aryad. After everything's clear, meet us back at Vassago's." Ry pointed far southeast where Vassago's palace was located.

"What do you mean by 'us'?" Vrae asked.

"I'm taking her with me," he said in a casual tone, and then he looked at me as if everything had been made obvious and understandable by saying that. Not even I could read his thoughts.

"Why is that again?" Vrae raised a brow.

I cast a sour look at her in return. No doubt she was thinking something that was utterly ridiculous judging by the look on her face. I shifted my gaze and looked at Ry, who, weirdly enough, seemed amused.

"Vrae, I'm not taking her to 'take care of something', I assure you of that," he said. He made a gesture as if he were putting his words in quotes and keeping himself from laughing.

Vrae blushed at his words.

Zade cleared his throat to draw our attention. "So, why is it then? Don't you think it would be dangerous if she went MIA?" He tilted his chin at me.

Before Ry could answer, I cut him off. "It's not a problem. Like I said when you two tried to volunteer yourself in the ring heist we're trying to pull, our higher ups won't notice if I'm ever a no show, unlike you two," I said as I folded my arms over my chest.

I looked at Ry and saw a satisfied look all over his face. Well, at least I managed to keep up with him this time.

"You heard her," Ry said calmly. The other couple were trying to argue, but they couldn't find anything reasonable to say, so they just sighed in defeat.

"We take a channel after you three are done," Ry said, pointing his head. We nodded and split up.

Learning from our earlier experience when Uriel and his pals suddenly appeared and threw blazing bolts at the Levarchons, we immediately searched for trees that stood several feet from each other, ones that were enough to hide ourselves and our doppelgangers when they got here, but not too close to each other in case unfriendlies came and shot at us.

It wouldn't be fun if they launched bombs of light at us and we were huddled on the same spot, it would be like saying "come kill us all in one blow" to those halo-tops.

We called the doppelgangers back, and asked if they had stumbled upon anything. Lucky for us, each of them said they ran into nobody. After we were done, we pulled them back and got rid of our shields.

"Remember, just go back there, give no reason for them to say you've gone MIA, and then they can't ransack everything." I heard Ry's voice clearly in my head.

"And perhaps you could ask Amon if anything happened while you two are at it," I added hastily.

"Yeah, whatever, just don't get busted, guys. See ya later," Vrae said. Her tone was a bit irritated, but Ry didn't say anything in return.

After a while, we felt their energy tracks were completely vanished. *"What now, Ry?"* I asked him. He was hidden behind another tree several feet from me.

He didn't say anything for several heartbeats as he came into view. Abruptly, he looked straight at me. "Yve, I wanna ask you something."

"Yeah?"

"Since I left, have you ever been to the sea? I mean one that's never been tainted by human blood? I know you hadn't been back when I was still here."

I winced at his question. "Okay, now you're being random on me. Where did that come from anyway?"

He shrugged. "Just asking."

Not sure where he was going, I narrowed my eyes at him to look for a hint. When I didn't find any, I shook my head. "No. That part on my job hasn't changed since you . . . left. I only got a peek four times when Vrae and I played the humans into long-term war across the ocean. Most times, they wouldn't even let me be seen by the other side. It's true that I could escape and go whenever I wanted, but even in those very short moments, I saw only blood and piles of bodies wherever I looked, so I kinda skipped the chance to do anything much more productive," I explained, half revelling at the memory and half feeling utterly disgusted by the humans.

Sighing, I glanced askance at the sky, as the memory of the last time I'd been to the beach flashed in my mind. I remembered only three things–a revoltingly sweet stench of blood, scattered limbs, and guts, along with the reddened sea.

I gulped as repugnance and longing pressed my chest. Shoving aside those thoughts, I shifted my gaze to him again. "Besides, seas are full of damn salt. No way am I getting soaked in that. Not to mention the sea spirits whining and pulling jokes to drown people, and Hell forbid, Focalor could be there too," I said in disgust as an image of a Hell duke emerged in my mind.

Notorious for his tendency to throw his victims to the sea, Focalor was a duke of Hell and a total scumbag.

He flinched a bit at Focalor's name and nodded. "I see."

Not getting whatever he was driving at, I put both hands on his shoulders. "Ry, tell me what's going on in that head of yours, or I'll beat the crap out of you." I poked his chest playfully.

He feigned a scared look. "No, please don't do that, My Lady Yverna. I'd rather you go with me to take care of something." He grinned. Suddenly, his mischievous grin was gone and was replaced with the hint of gentle smile. "Actually, I was kinda hoping you'd say that."

I arched a brow at him. "And why on earth you would hope for something like that?"

He leaned down to my ear. "Because I wanted to take you to one."

"Take me where?"

Before I could finish the question, his lips found mine and we were locked in a scorching kiss, until a fissure drew my attention. Pulling away from him, I turned around to find . . . a beach.

I inhaled sharply, and the scent of salt and cool breeze teased my nostrils. The sight was magnificent. It was unlike any beach I'd ever laid my eyes on. No blood, never mind dead bodies or limbs. And the sea! I'd never seen such a beautiful thing. The water was as blue as sapphire. Lake Bahyrdanam a long time ago was beautiful, but it had nowhere near the purity of this place that had never been tainted by anything. It was like gazing upon an endless field of deep blue silk that waved in symphony with the wind. The rays of moonlight that fell on it made it look like pearls that scattered from here to somewhere beyond.

The best thing was that not a single spirit was here. I couldn't even feel any of them.

"I've never known that there was a place like this," I whispered in awe.

Standing behind my back, he wrapped his hands around me and held me protectively. "That's why I wanted to show this to you. I think those warm eyes of yours deserve to feast on something other than revolting things like human corpses," he said in my ear.

I shivered as I bathed in his heavy scent of pure masculinity. "The water is so blue, just like *your* eyes," I purred as I held his hands before his remark sank in. I couldn't believe that he thought my eyes resembled anything close to warmness, while others just saw them as they were—cold, unyielding, bottomless darkness.

Somehow he saw someone different within me. One who deserved his trust, or more to the point, his heart. It had been a long time since he had left. Not once had I dared to think that he'd view me as a being other than what I was, and yet he did. It was more than I'd ever dreamed.

I was a heartless devil with cruelty as my crown and countless human souls as my jewels, yet he said that I'd claimed his heart. Above all, he also claimed the heart that I thought had perished eons ago—mine. Any other day, I would think of this as utterly hilarious, but with him, it felt like I'd finally found what I'd been missing my entire life, the other half of my soul.

"Yve, is something wrong?" he asked as he lifted his arms and turned me around to look at him.

I shook my head as a wave of surreal happiness washed through me. "Nothing. It's just . . . it all feels . . . so unreal."

"What is?"

I stood on tiptoes to reach his height. "Being here with you," I said, and I captured his lips with mine.

After moments of pure bliss, we parted, and once again he flashed his dazzling grin at me. "Well, I was lying when I said I wasn't taking you to take care of something."

"Who cares? They've been taking care of *their* something a lot longer." I shrugged.

Letting out a deep laugh, he sealed my lips in quick kiss. "Well, I won't argue with you there." Taking my hands, he walked backwards, and a wicked smile broke on his handsome face as he brought me closer to the breath-taking ocean behind him.

"Ry?" I asked slowly with a smile curved my lips. His deep sapphire eyes met my pitch-black ones. I could hear my core thundering against my ribs under his intense gaze, and the sweetest desire threatened to overcome me like utter madness.

"Come, walk with me," he said. Tucking my right hand in his, we started walking along the line of the water.

Several minutes had passed since the first step we took, and I still couldn't take my eyes of the sea. "How did you find this place? More to the point, how did you know this place exists at all?"

He chuckled. "Well, those stupid Echelons should've given you a chance to at least wander around to some parts unknown, not just the forests or, hell, the lake that's now AWOL because of me."

I scoffed at that with my eyes still fixed upon the ocean. "Well, having Amon's golem on my tail all the time is definitely one good reason not to go anywhere too far, not to mention the Echelons' personal dogs showing up every now and then."

He lowered his gaze. "Yeah, I'd be pissed too if I were in your shoes."

My left hand balled into tight fists. "They stopped right after you left. I did suspect something was off, but I didn't think that that had to do with Lu personally going after you and that they stopped because they thought you were gone for good. If only I'd looked into it further . . ."

"I'm glad you didn't," he interrupted. "You could've been caught, and if they did catch you, they would punish you for whatever reason," he said seriously, and then surprisingly he took my hand that was beginning to bleed without me even noticing. "Yve, you should watch it. You're just hurting yourself." He turned my hand to face up and healed the four small bleeding holes in it. The wound disappeared immediately. He then let go of my hand.

"Sorry, didn't realize it," I shrugged, and then I flashed a sheepish grin at him. He definitely watched over me more than I did myself, and that warmed me with a comforting sensation that was foreign to me. It felt like I was truly safe.

When I was within the shelter of his arms, it was the first time I'd ever felt protected, but now, with his full attention to me, it was as though being with him alone was enough to make me feel safe. True, it was trivial to heal small wounds like that, but for him to even notice when I myself didn't told me how much he cared and that he was always looking after me.

"Baby?"

I winced and was pulled back from my thoughts. "It's nothing," I said quickly and returned to our talk. "Well, there's indeed a possibility of getting caught. And it wasn't exactly you who boiled the lake to oblivion, Ry. People up there did it." I pointed heavenward. "Anyway, I didn't know you had the time to wander off. Shouldn't those bastards have kept a close eye on you because they were scared you'd do something against them or at least go AWOL?"

He tucked a hair behind my ear and scoffed. "Okay, I confess," he said with raised hands. "I did play some hide and seek with the Echelons' lapdogs to find this place."

I stared at him in horror. "What?"

He grinned. "Yeah, actually Weizar nearly caught me a couple hours before I finally found it."

I cupped his face. "That's not funny. You were lucky he didn't bust you," I said. "Then again you did deserve some time off from those bastards."

Well, I could relate if he wanted to find some place where the Echelons couldn't scrutinize him. At least, at first I thought that was the reason, until he winced and shook his head. "Yve, this isn't for me. I didn't exactly need to find a place like this for a meditation spot."

Directing a confused look at him, I placed a hand on his shoulder. "What do you mean?"

He cleared his throat. "I told you, your warm eyes deserve something that's far better than corpses."

It took five seconds for his remark began to register. "You did it for me?"

"Well, I was kinda hoping I'd catch you after I went up there, but Lu beat me to it. The bastard messed up my entire plan to bring you here and, well, you know, tell you that I love you," he said with that sheepish look I adored so much. "A totally bust-up lake wasn't the place I had in mind to do that."

Before I could stop myself, I jumped at him and wrapped my hands around his neck. We both fell to the sand with me on top of him. "Thank you. It's so beautiful," I said with my face buried in his hard chest.

He ran his hand gently on my hair. "It's nothing. It's the least I could do for you."

I got up and landed a quick kiss. "Why don't we stay here for a while?"

"You read my mind again," he said with a smile.

"Say, what's Edros?" I asked, recalling his words to his sworn brother.

He was silent for two seconds before he looked up at the sky. "It's his language. We've never say it in front of his men though."

"Why not?"

"He wouldn't mind, of course, but I thought it would burn few ears no matter how much they respect me. Not even the fact that we're sworn brothers are known to them."

A fact I could understand, but still didn't explain anything. "Okay, so, what does that term mean?"

"It means brothers through hell and beyond."

That made me sat up and stared at him. "That sounds dead serious, not that I don't trust him, but does he really use such highly respectful term with, well, a devil?"

He smiled. "Your doubt's understandable, that's why I asked him not to use that to each other unless there are only the three of us."

"If you don't mind me asking, why would he use it in the first place?"

I felt his chest tighten for a heartbeat. "Ry, it's okay if you don't wanna talk about it," I said quickly.

He relaxed again. "No, I'm fine. I'll tell you, Seian."

Smiling at his endearing remark, I carefully laid my head on his chest. "Okay."

"It happened after Xaemorkahn and his people left their previous realm," he began. "It was about five decades after I saved him. Lucifer somehow managed to cross over to his realm when I wasn't there."

I rose up and threw a shocked look at him. "I thought that ability was stripped from him."

He nodded. "It was. That's the thing. Xaemorkahn suspected that he picked up his trail when he escaped together with me, because originally he did have that ability. All he had to do was gather his powers to find the exact location of the portal to his realm and the powers needed to jump over. Luckily, he didn't have the core power to jump any more, so he had to gather his powers over time, and he had only one shot. He succeeded."

I stared in horror. "He destroyed his place?" I asked quietly.

He nodded bitterly. "He wreaked total havoc over there. Fortunately, Xaemorkahn had home-field advantage. He'd sensed him coming and teleported most of his people out."

"Most?"

He grasped my hand that rested on his flat stomach. "Some of his elite soldiers died fighting Lucifer off, including Helkann's predecessor, Raghal. They did it to buy time for their king so he could open the portal. And I must say that teleporting that massive a crowd wasn't an easy task to do."

"I'm sorry," I said with an earnestness that surprised me. Xaemorkahn's soldiers had grown on me too. Helkann and the others were fairly cool to be around, and losing a commander was something I understood far too well.

He gulped as if he had been reminded of something painful. "Yeah, me too," he said. I caught a note of sadness in his voice. Had something even more horrific happened?

"Ry? You okay?"

Agony and guilt flashed in his eyes. "Aside from Raghal, Lu also killed someone else."

I bit my lip. Oh no. He sounded like he knew well whoever it was that died. "Ry?" I called carefully.

He glanced at me. "He killed my brother's son, Xarhad, the only heir to the throne."

It was like a knife buried deep in my gut, and my body started to shiver. "He killed . . . ?"

"Yes. While my brother was holding the portal open, Risha was protecting their people, calming the women and children. But Lu went on his way through the soldiers, and when he almost killed her, only Xarhad stood in his way. Of course, Lu easily overpowered him."

"After that what happened?" I asked slowly.

Ry pulled me closer. Surprisingly, he draped his hand over my shoulder and held me protectively. My body stopped trembling, and he kissed my hand. "My brother took his people to his current realm. Apparently, that was one of the many realms his ancestors took him to, and it was heavily guarded compared to his previous one."

"How did he find it?"

"From what I know, his ancestors prepared it as a safe place in case one day they all needed to seek refuge. Anyway, after he had his people situated, he came to me and brought me there. Ever since then up to seven centuries ago, I'd been visiting him. I was pretty surprised at first that none of his people blamed me or even showed any sign of hostility after what had happened. I'd expected them to think that I told Lucifer just where to find them, or worse, that I'd brought him there myself."

I gave him a comforting smile. "Well, I'm sure they know you don't have anything to do with that."

"Well, my brother wouldn't want to have anything to do with me. Hell, he'd kill me himself," he added with a grin.

I poked his chest. "That's not funny," I said sternly, and I laid my head back on his chest.

He laughed. "That was why he put his fortress and city under a heavy set of shields. Even if Lu could get there, he wouldn't know where to look," he said quietly. "Not long after that, I went back to Zihargan by myself, hoping there might still be survivors left."

"And?" I asked carefully.

His gaze saddened. "I found none. Lucky for me, Lu had already left, which made me able to search the place thoroughly. Lu, however, butchered most of them. There was almost no one died in one piece. Few of them were still in decent enough state, and two of them were Raghal and Xarhad. I gathered them, and brought them to my brother to be sent properly with their people's custom."

My chest clenched at what he described. The horror, and pain to see those close to him lying dead at his feet. That was one of very few things I knew about him, one that could shatter him. Though appeared calm and often seemed nonchalant, he protected us all the best he could, ever since he'd first seen others that fought by his side died in battle.

But once again, he couldn't keep the people who'd provided him with secret haven from getting slaughtered by the very being who wanted his throat.

"After they had sent Raghal, Xarhad and the rest of the bodies to oblivion so their souls could go to the after realm of their ancestors, my brother began calling me with Edros, which is the highest respect their people can give one another. Sometimes, I still feel like a total bastard that doesn't deserve to be treated so highly."

Smiling at him, warmth spread through me with care for the couple. "Why did you do it? Brought back their son and Raghal and the others? Did Xaemorkahn ask you to?"

He shifted, red crept on his face, making me feel tremendous urge to hug him. "No, he'd never asked that of me, but I figured that was the only thing I could do for him since I wasn't there to help."

"Then you totally deserve to receive such treatment, Zeian. They all see you as who you are, like we do, you are our companion until death. Besides, running from Lu technically qualifies 'as through hell and beyond'," I said teasingly.

Kissing the top of my head, he pulled me to lie on his chest. "Well, thanks."

I cleared my throat. "Okay, I want to tell you something too."

"What is it?"

"You asked me before why I went up there."

He stared at me. "I was wondering about that, yeah. I didn't think that you not wanting to see the remains of that lake was a sufficient reason for you to go sleeping up there."

His words made me fall silent for a moment before he ran his hand on my hair. "Yve?"

I sighed. "Okay, I admit it. Maybe somewhere deep down I kept hoping I'd see you falling again and that I could save you," I muttered. "I know how stupid that was. I won't be mad if you wanna laugh." I forced a grin.

He stared at me for a while, making me nervous as hell. "Would you say something?" I asked as I looked away.

Raising his hands, he cupped my face and turned me to him. "I won't laugh, because you did save me."

I was perplexed to say the least. "I didn't do anything," I said as shame assailed me.

He just smiled at me. "I told you, didn't I? You were the only reason I've fought my way back. If it weren't for you, I'm not sure I had the strength to do it."

I shook my head and laid it on his chest. "No, you had it in you. You always have. You'd be back to save us, your brother, Varisha, all of us, because you know what?"

"What?"

I lifted my head and returned his smile. "That's just who you are, and I love that about you," I said gently. "Well, maybe I motivated you a bit more, and I'm glad for that," I inserted with a small laugh, and I rested my head on his shoulder.

He chuckled. "I'd say you motivated me a whole lot more."

We lay there in a moment of true peace and just stared at the sky and the sea. "It's quiet here," I said absently.

His grip tightened. "Yes, it makes me wonder whether that day Lucifer tried to kill me was a mere nightmare," he said with faraway look.

Sadness began to choke me. "Ry, it was real, all of it." His hand trembled at that one word. "It may be a cruel truth for us both, but in a sense, I'm thankful for it," I said.

He turned his head to me in disbelief with curiosity all over his face. "Why is that?"

"Forgive me saying this, but had we not been separated that long, I might not have realized the one thing that matters most."

"And that is?"

I levelled a dead serious look at him. "How much I love you."

His eyes widened and went still as I gently embraced him. "It was only after you were gone that I realized I love you to an extent that is beyond words, because maybe I was that stupidly blind to my own feelings. But now I feel like I've been given a second chance because you came back to me. I will do anything to protect you, and I will remain by your side no matter what happens," I whispered in his ear.

He returned my embrace and tightened his arms around me. "You're not blind, but you do need a bit of a push in the right direction every now and then," he said with a grin. "And I will keep you safe," he said as he levelled his sapphire eyes on me.

Unconsciously, I held my breath as I returned his deep stare that penetrated all the way to my soul. I saw his eyes gleam with happiness and a longing that was so tangible, I nearly broke into wrenching sobs. It was as if that feeling were reaching out to me from deep inside him even though we'd been together for real now. Then again, being together just for a few days wouldn't be enough to erase the longing and loneliness he felt for all the time he was out there without us–without me.

And what was worse, knowing that I was here but he couldn't come to me.

Suddenly I felt his shield extend and wrap me as well. "Ry, since when you can do this?" I asked in awe.

Still staring at me, he answered, "Since a long time ago. I did this when we first met again. Apparently you were too overwhelmed with my reappearance to notice I did it." He lifted the edge of his lips.

"Whoa!" was all I could manage under his dazzling stare.

"And I could do this as well." He blinked.

Without warning, my armour was gone, and so was his, leaving our bodies with nothing but robes to cover them. "Hey, don't do that," I said, completely shocked.

"You're not impressed?" He muttered his question as his face was now getting really close to mine.

"Nu-uh, I'm not impressed with trespassers," I whispered.

He gave me a wicked smile as he looked at my slightly parted lips. "So, I'm not welcome?" his forehead was touching mine as he spoke, and he closed his eyes as if to savour the contact.

I trembled a bit. "That depends . . ." I trailed off. I felt like a moment longer like this, I'd be breathless.

"On what?" his hands now cupped my face.

"On what you're trying to trespass on." I only could manage to mutter my answer, when suddenly I saw a huge smile spread across his stunningly handsome face. "Then it means I'm welcomed."

In the next second, we were both stripped from our robes. Right there our bodies entwined within blue flames that ignited at his passion. But this time he was fiercer, though with the same gentleness and care. It was as if he lived to devour me.

And I loved every second of it.

Hours later, I was still safe within the shelter of his arms. That feeling was there again, the one that says he'd never let go of me ever again.

At that thought, I felt a sting behind my eyes. Before I could stop it, tears fell towards his hard chest where I laid down my head.

He suddenly straightened up a bit and looked at me with his hand on my shoulder. "What's wrong? Did I hurt you?" he asked in concern.

I shook my head. "No, *I* hurt you." The tears were now rolling down my cheek freely, even though I managed to keep my voice steady.

He looked confused. "What do you mean? You've never hurt me."

I stared at him in despair. "I know I said that in a sense I was thankful that I could realize my feelings because we were separated, but still I couldn't shake the guilt that I wasn't by your side for you. You were out there alone, knowing I was here, but not able to see me, not able to be by my side, while all I was doing was cursing and bitching at everything and believing that you were gone for good. If only I hadn't given up on you and tried to look for you a lot harder, we would've . . ."

Suddenly he put his finger upon my lips, stopping my endless ramble. "Don't beat yourself up, Yve. You couldn't possibly know that. I'm sure you heard the reason from my brother, and I've said it too. I didn't want to put you in danger. I never would. What do you think I'd feel if I couldn't control myself and I went to see you, and then, because of my own selfishness, you got killed? I'd rather die in the most excruciating pain that exists than be the cause of that," he said as he ran his hand carefully down my hair.

I looked at him in horror hearing his words. He smiled comfortingly as he wiped my tears. "And now," he went on, "I was able to come to you after I made sure it was safe enough and everyone including Lucifer himself–well, most of us–assumed that I was killed. So, please, *please* don't ever blame yourself over this."

Sniffing, I tried to calm myself and gave him a smile with the hint of promise that I would do what he asked me to.

"That's my girl." He smiled a devastating smile and kissed me again. After minutes had passed, he embraced me, and I laid down my head on his chest like I did before.

I exhaled heavily. "I can never argue with that look of yours," I said dreamily as I trailed my finger down his chest to his navel.

"It's a good thing then. Otherwise I'd panic out of my wits whenever I see you cry, Seian," he said with a small laugh.

We then lay there on the soft grass in silence, looking at the endless sea of stars as he gently ran his fingers through my hair and muttered a song I didn't recognize.

Perhaps it was something human?

I decided to put the question aside and simply revelled in this moment. But as with every other good thing, this peaceful moment didn't last as long as I wanted, for I felt tremendous unfriendly energy coming from somewhere far behind. As expected, he picked it up too because he manifested our armours at once as we arose.

"Who's that?" I asked him.

His face looked extremely cautious, and I felt his grip tighten on my shoulder.

"I don't know, but it's definitely someone from upstairs. Let's get a better look." He hitched his thumb and pointed to a nearby tree.

I nodded, and I opened my mouth to ask whether I need to put up a shield when I realized his shield was still around me.

We floated without a sound, and the second we reached the top of the tree, we saw something that made my jaw drop in shock.

To the far northeast of the forest, where Karan forest was located, our eyes caught a pair of very blinding lights that descended from above and stopped dead in the middle of the air. Those lights destroyed everything that stood helplessly around them within several miles' radius. Now the trees around them had become nothing but ashes.

"Well, well, looks like the bastard pair didn't waste a second to come down here," he said in disgust. It was then I realized what, or more to the point, who those lights were.

Gabriel and Michael.

It had been a long time since the last time I met them. I barely remember what they looked like when they came down or on what occasion.

I stared at them, curious what they would do after they found Raphael, and like Ry, I couldn't help but feel disgusted.

The next second, Ry suddenly pulled my arm and took me straight down. We landed, and then he led me to a big tree. We circled it cautiously, and then we stood with our backs against it.

"Ry, what is . . ." I couldn't finish my question because something else answered me.

A hot blinding light followed by a hurricane wind swept through the forest. It brought along a weird harmful sound that invaded my hearing. I crouched as I put my hands over my ears. Ry held my shoulders, and when I saw him, he looked extremely wary seeing the situation I was in at the moment.

"It penetrates my brain!" I gasped. Ry immediately wrapped us in his massive wings once again.

The voice was almost gone the moment he did that. I could barely hear it now. I sighed in relief and cautiously took my hands off my ears.

"Better?" he asked.

I nodded and then cast an annoyed look towards the direction of that pair of lights. Ry looked at them as well with a distasteful expression spread all over his face. "It seems they wanna announce their arrival and are hoping we would prepare full royal welcome," he said sarcastically.

"No doubt," I said, panting a bit. "I have to say though that they've never done anything like this before. What do you think caused that weird annoying sound? You don't think it was something belonging to Raphael, do you?" I frowned.

"No, I don't think so. It something else," he answered wonderingly.

"What do we do now?" I could feel the wariness in my own voice.

He fell silent for a moment, and then as he took me slowly to the highest branch of the tree, he answered, "We'll wait. I have a hunch that the arrival of those two and that stupid sound they were playing with will attract another bastard." He gave me a meaningful gaze which I understood immediately. The one he said would come was his attacker, who was our ultimate ruler.

Lucifer, the Son of Perdition himself.

* * *

The Iverand's den shook tremendously as a destructive scream suddenly thundered all over the place. Vrathien covered her ears, and so did Amon. "Amon, is that what I think it is?" she asked. Her voice was trembling.

Looking at the she-devil in front of him, who was a whole lot more powerful than himself, Amon nodded. His body was shaking even more tremendously than hers. "Lucifer comes forth. What do you think drew him?" He stopped dead as he noticed something that had never happened in the last ten thousand years on the Veil.

The Holiest of Archangels
First of the Fallen
Forest of Karan

"Amon? What is it?" Vrathien asked. She looked back and forth from the Veil to Amon, who was now gazing at her in complete horror.

The torturous scream was still thundering.

He slowly pointed at the pitch-black surface of the substance. Vrathien followed his finger, but since she didn't understand the Veil's language, she just threw him a questioning look. "What? I don't know squat about how to read the damn thing!" she snapped.

He raised his hands to cover his ears again. "They've finally here. At Karan forest, where you said the four of you left those dead Arcs." His voice was trembling in fear.

"Yeah?" she prompted.

"Now those two have come," he said in broken voice. As the scream lessened bit by bit, both of them lifted their hands from their ears.

"Who? Amon, who's coming?" she repeated her question.

"They . . ." but before Amon could say a thing, Zaderion stormed inside. His face showed that he was also in complete horror.

"Have you heard?" He panted and gasped as he gazed at them both. "They–Gabriel and Michael–they've landed at Karan, and now Lucifer comes forth to meet them. Most of Karan has been destroyed by their arrival!" Zaderion said. His gaze was widened in shock.

Vrathien looked frightened but disgusted at the same time. "They're really here. I thought they'd take more time before they shagged their asses and fetched their buddy Raphael."

Suddenly she looked as if she were having a heart attack, and then she looked at them both. "Do you think those two would tell Lucifer about 'him'? I mean, we don't know whether Lucifer knows, but if he doesn't and now he's meeting them . . ."

Amon and Zaderion gasped. "I hope to hell your sister and he already got the hell outta there, Vrae," Zaderion said.

"Yeah, if Lucifer wasn't involved, I know the two of them could take those Arc bastards, but if Lucifer is in the game, he'd better be going with her by now." She expelled a wary breath.

The three of them slowly turned their gaze towards the door.

∗   ∗   ∗

From out of nowhere, a thunderous scream that I hadn't heard in ten thousand years echoed throughout the woods.

Ry opened the cover of his wings a bit, allowing us to see what was coming. "Here comes the old bastard. He's not in the mood, it seems," he said with repugnance as his gaze wandered far away to the west.

I followed his line of sight and saw a black light fly towards the pair in the distance. The light went so fast, I was barely able to see who was inside it.

Everything in that light's way was reduced into ashes, spreading the reek of death. The black light stopped dead in front of the other two lights, adding more destruction to the already destroyed forest below them.

"It's a showdown," I said as I held my breath a bit.

"Come on, let's get outta here. I'm sure those two didn't come here to have some stupid twisted reunion with him, especially now that they've found one of their pals has become a comatose . . ."

"They'll be coming after you," I finished his sentence.

He nodded, and then he gave me a wicked smile. "It's not me I'm worried about. It's . . ."

Before he could finish, I put my finger over his lips. "Don't. If you worry about us, then you worry about *us*, not just *me*, okay?" I stared at him.

He was startled and took my hand to place a gentle kiss on my knuckles. "Okay, so shall we? We're going low this time. We can't risk flashing ourselves and attracting those three. We can't do that anyway. The place is shielded," he said.

I concurred. "Right, let's go."

He cast a wary and yet disgusted look once again in those lights' direction. We went down and flew together through the trees towards Gillian forest where Vassago's castle stood silently in the shadows.

*   *   *

The three lights slowly descended to the ground, where a few feet from them Raphael lay injured. He was still shaking, just as he was left by his assailants.

The second they reached the soil, the lights disappeared.

"Lucifer," Michael said in a tone of disgust, which was answered only with a smirk by the Son of Perdition in front of him. Gabriel stood in silence beside his comrade.

"Nothing changes, it seems. Disdain and crap, more disdain and more crap, no brains," Lucifer said lazily. "Is there none of you bothers to take 'How to Talk like Civilized People' lessons?" He stared in repugnance and crossed his arms over his chest with his black eyes flared in hatred. "So you just used that annoying LeQuirrem just to call the devil, old me?"

Gabriel cast a hostile glare at his former brother, the one he'd admired a long time ago. "Don't flatter yourself. We weren't using that thing to alert you, and just so you know, we don't have to be civilized with the likes of you."

Lucifer rolled his eyes. "Whatever. I don't need appraisal from people that are lower than myself anyway. What do you want? If you wanna bring down the apocalypse ahead of schedule, I'm game." He smiled evilly at the two Arcs who had once been his comrades.

Michael's gaze darkened with impatience. "That is enough, Lucifer. We did not come here to hear your jest."

"Never said I was jesting with you," Lucifer taunted with a heavy amount of venom in his voice.

Gabriel clenched his teeth. "Uriel and the others were killed! Raphael has been severely injured! You said in our pact that no devil is allowed to kill archangels unless it's an open war, and there's been none in the last ten thousand years! Are you trying to tell us that you have no more dignity, that you can't even keep your own word?" His voice trembled in potent anger.

For once, the arrogance on Lucifer's face was gone. Glancing at the helplessly shaking Raphael, Lucifer shot a lethal glare at the other two. "That has nothing to do with me or anyone under my command," Lucifer said in an awkwardly calm voice with a hint of warning in it. But despite his steady voice, his hands were balled into tight fists, as if he were threatening to launch an attack.

Michael suddenly gave Lucifer a completely and utterly distasteful look. "Are you saying you have no idea that one of your own commanders is going around slaughtering Arcs, just like that *other* one?"

"Or are you saying you no longer have any control or connection over that particular devil? That is, assuming, you do know that he's still alive and thrives," Gabriel inserted with a low laugh.

A weird glint flashed in Lucifer's menacing stare. "This is my business. I'll take care of it. There's no need for your annoying criticisms, so get off my back. And take along that useless flute sucker outta here before I kick his face myself," he said with the same calm voice, only now it carried an obvious hint of a threat.

Gabriel and Michael both stepped back. Even though it was only an inch, it didn't escape Lucifer's glare. A smug smile returned to his face, making the unchallenged beauty of his face looked more than ever twisted.

"What's wrong? You were hoping I didn't know squat so you could throw crap at me, weren't you? Well, sorry to disappoint you." He let out an evil laugh that echoed throughout the remains of the forest.

Michael hesitated before he replied, "If that's the case, we'll leave him to you."

Lucifer lifted the edge of his lips. "Who do you think you are, 'leave him to me'?" he mocked.

Gabriel smiled disdainfully. "We are the ones who stay in grace, unlike some people." He gave Lucifer a meaningful glare.

Lucifer's gaze darkened dangerously. "Very funny! I see you've worked your way up to creating something that's worth a bit of my anger, Gabriel. What have you been doing? Hanging out with some prune or with some random slut?" he asked nonchalantly.

Gabriel almost exploded in rage. "You . . . !" was the only thing he could say, because Michael stopped him.

Lucifer shrugged. "Hey, don't look at me. You asked for it."

Michael was still holding Gabriel down when he asked, "Very well, leaving that matter aside, I want to ask you about Arzia."

Lucifer's face was completely unreadable. Not even the holiest of the Arcs could tell what he was thinking.

He stared at them for a moment and then answered, "Yeah, that thing has become quite bothersome these days. Tell Dad, it was a bang-up job He did with that pet of His." He gave the Arcs a stare.

"You were the one who broke its seals to begin with! Don't you dare place the blame on Him!" Gabriel roared.

"Yeah, yeah, it's not like He'll get a scratch or anything if I insult Him a bit. And as if *you* could do something to stop me from mocking Him!" Lucifer laughed darkly. "If that thing comes and picks a fight, then so be it. It's not like it could do anything now that your pal became a vegetable," he went on.

"You are aware of the destruction it could cause, are you not?" Michael said as his patience grew shorter by the moment.

"I knew things well enough before I was dumped down here, unlike you chuckleheads," Lucifer said, his anger beginning to kick in as well.

Michael was about to argue when the clattering voice caused by his friend Raphael grew louder, and he could no longer ignore him. "If you say so, then we will take our leave. Just remember to take care of your flock or we will," Michael put a closure to their meeting.

"And I will be happy to stomp on your filthy Commander's face," Gabriel added in a disdainful tone.

"Just get your pal out of my face this instant before I make you call Azrael for help," Lucifer said in a bored voice.

Michael and Gabriel left Lucifer. They walked towards their brother, knelt beside him, and put their hands on his chest. Suddenly the blinding light that covered them when they arrived appeared once more. It wrapped them, and then they ascended to the sky. Seconds later, they vanished.

Lucifer could no longer control his wrath. He screamed furiously as the black light engulfed him. His scream thundered, and the earth itself shivered in fear. The sky launched lightning bolt after lightning bolt, followed with a deafening sound in response to the evil he spread. He too ascended to the air, but instead of continuing to go up, he gazed around, as if searching for something. When he faced north, he stopped. His face showed that he may have found what he was looking for. Immediately he flew across the night sky, bringing horror alongside him.

Chapter 17

We were only a few miles from Gillian when suddenly we heard that familiar scream echo. It was followed with lightning bolts that kept on coming one after another.

"Looks like the meeting is over," Ry said. I felt his grip on my hand tighten a bit as he sped up.

"He knows," I stated as I looked at him. He just nodded in silence. His expression was still as unreadable as ever. "Where do you think he'll look first?" I asked as we were now entering the forest.

"I reckon he'll come to Belphegor's," he answered quietly.

I raised a brow as I considered it. "I can understand if he suspected Belphegor gave you shelter just to piss him off, but are you sure he'd want to even step foot around there?" I asked wonderingly, because as far as I knew, those two would never see each other's faces.

"He'll do anything to show that he's still the most powerful amongst us. The most powerful yes, but for those who know his stink, he ceased being the most respected ruler a long time ago," he said bitterly.

I fell silent as we reached the barren field where Vassago's castle was located, but before our feet even touched the ground, shadows jutted out from below and then evaporated, revealing the castle within. We looked at each other as we landed. By the time our gaze fell on the castle, Vassago had appeared. He looked really pale.

"Come in! Hurry!" he said harshly. Without another word, we quickly followed him. After the three of us were inside, I could feel the castle once again dissolve and hide us in the shadows.

"You knew?" was all Ry asked Vassago as he led us towards his archive room. His face was still full of wariness when he nodded.

"Yeah, that was why Belphegor left moments ago. We suspected that when those three were having a date, then the fact that you're still alive and well would no longer be a secret. So Belphegor thought his dad may be coming to his place first, looking for you. Thus he decided to wait there, and he asked me to tell you both to lie low in here for the time being, and no buts about it."

Neither of us said anything at the Prince's statement, though I still wondered how the hell these princes watched over Ry. Then again, I shouldn't complaint at times like these.

"Belphegor went to cover my ass, huh? Remind me to thank him," Ry said gratefully as he looked at me. I took his hand which still held my left one in my right.

"Don't worry, I'll add a thank you card when you do that," I inserted.

We arrived in front of the archive's wall. Vassago chanted to open it. Seconds later, it opened, and we walked in.

Seere was already inside. The wall was closed once we were in the archive. Vassago headed towards the seat at the far end of the long table, while Ry led me to the pair of seats beside Vassago.

Seere was still seated at the other side of the table, right where we had left him. "Welcome back," he said, tilting his head in our direction.

We nodded back at him as we took our seats.

"You saw them?" Seere asked.

"Just a bit," I answered. "They're getting more annoying by the century. Last time I looked, they didn't have that toy that nearly made my eardrums bleed."

"It's called LeQuirrem. It was supposed to be used for calling among them. Maybe they don't know how to call Lucille fast enough without using that thing," Vassago shrugged.

"Vassago, do you think it's really safe enough for us to be here?" Ry asked quietly.

The Hell Prince frowned at him. "You heard what I said and what Belphegor told me, so don't even think of giving me your crap." Vassago tapped his forefinger on the table.

While Ry just cast a respectful gaze at the Prince, I leaned forward to get the Prince's attention. "Thank you, really," I said.

"No problem. We saw this coming when we learned your man here was still alive. Besides, if we stick to our side of the fence where our purpose is to piss Lucifer off, sooner or later we'll have to take chances like this one," Vassago chuckled.

Ry's gaze fell to a big old book in front of him. "Have you found anything new?" he asked as he pointed the book.

Vassago exchanged a peculiar look with Seere, and then they shifted their gaze upon us. "Yeah, but we have a hunch that you already knew," Seere answered as he leaned back.

"And apparently our hunches were proven to be true," Vassago added.

"Knew about what, exactly?" Ry asked. His face remained stoic as he locked his gaze on Vassago.

"About those races and the connection between Cain's prophecy and the real reason why you two were able to touch Herathim," Vassago answered.

I cringed inwardly. *Oh crap, they figured it out.*

Ry reached out his hand slowly and took my hand under the table. I could feel him tightening his grip, but he didn't say anything. I saw his brows knit as wariness spread all over his gorgeous face. He stared at the book.

After moments of silence, he turned his gaze to the princes. "How can you tell?" he asked. His expression looked as if he were waiting for them to murder him or something.

"The moment you came in contact with us, we sensed something that, fortunately, not even those Echelons could sense," Seere smirked.

"And that is?" I asked carefully.

Vassago lifted the edge of his lips with a smug look. "You did what our dear ol' ancestors did. You two exchanged QuiMarrae. Perhaps Vrae and her mate and even your brother were also involved in this."

Ry cast an impressed look at the princes, but his eyes still gleamed with dread. "Well, I guess it sums it all up. That was fast. I thought once we were back, you'd be asking why the hell we did that."

"You think we just sit here and drink? The book pretty much covered it. What we don't quite get is how you knew about it and why you just went and did what you did," Seere interjected.

I swallowed a bit. Damn, we really couldn't hide anything from these princes. Luckily, they were on our side.

"All right, you caught us with our hands red. And as I've said before, I can't tell you how I've got it." Ry raised both hands in surrender.

I inhaled sharply at that. He didn't tell them that he found it in Xaemorkahn's true realm. I guessed it might have pissed Belphegor off if he learned Ry chose to go there. The guy just despised Xaemorkahn's guts.

"So, what are you gonna do with us?" I asked calmly.

"Well, since we cannot afford to have people like that on our side . . ." Seere trailed off.

"We'll have to kill you." Vassago suddenly rose up from his seat.

What in the hell . . . ! I took a step back. I couldn't believe what I just heard!

Faster than I could react, Ry rose up from his seat and immediately put himself between the princes and me.

The next second, I felt his battle aura emerge around him, sending a tingle down my spine, though his face remained devoid of emotions.

I saw Seere's face . . . and frowned. He looked like he was gonna laugh.

And I was right. Not just him. Even Vassago burst out laughing. "Sorry, kiddo, just wanted to see how far you'd go, that's all," he said between his laughter.

"What was that supposed to mean?" Ry still remained vigilant as he stared cautiously at the princes.

Vassago sat back and cocked his head. "Look, you two. It's not like it'll change anything that we know both of you, and who knows how many others will hit the jackpot of becoming Votzadirs?" he said quietly.

"We just wanted to make sure that you will serve your purpose in becoming one," Seere smiled evilly.

"And that is?" I asked.

"Bring them down," Vassago sneered.

I exchanged a puzzled look with Ry, and then we turned our eyes to them.

"Bring *who* down, exactly?" Ry asked suspiciously. His lethal aura dissolved slowly as he also returned to his seat. The tingling in my spine lessened bit by bit.

"I believe you two are aware of the fact that those Echelons weren't meant to be the supreme rulers right under Belphegor's dad.

But a thing or two happened, and they were made the Echelons." Vassago folded his arms across his chest.

"Yeah, that's why I have to keep myself from kicking their faces myself every time they summon me in," I inserted in disgust.

"Well said," Seere chuckled.

Ry frowned deeply, knowing both princes still had yet to elaborate a damn thing. "That still doesn't explain anything. If you wanted to bring them down, those Echelons wouldn't stand a chance against you or any other royals."

"That's true, but we're not controlling any of you directly like they do, if you two know what I'm saying." Vassago cast a meaningful gaze at us.

"Yeah, royals such as you have legions of their own, and that doesn't involve warriors like the two of us." I pointed at Ry and myself.

Ry gave them both a quizzical stare. "What are you getting at here?" He tapped his fingers on the table.

Seere levelled a wicked look at Ry. "A long-term revolution."

*   *   *

"All right, Amon, we'd better be off now," Vrathien said as she put one hand on Amon's table. The Iverand was sitting behind it.

Amon bit his lip as he looked at her and the Imirae wielder who stood next to her. "Okay, you're gonna be meeting them, right? Just tell me everything you get. The latest news you brought nearly made my head explode, but it's worth it," he said with a grin.

"No sweat, just watch your back." Zaderion nodded at him, and then he and his mate began to withdraw.

"Watch yours too," Amon replied. "Oh, by the way, Vrae."

Vrathien paused and turned around. "What is it?" she asked.

"Just be careful, okay? I don't think that boss-man would want anybody aside from him to know he tried to kill our pal, but who's to say that he won't pull a weird stunt on you and your sister? Heed my advice and lay low, though I'm sure you already know. Just reminding you, that's all." He shrugged and smiled half-heartedly.

"I know, thanks." Vrathien smiled and nodded. And then she and her mate turned to the door once again.

"Say hi to them for me," Amon added.

"Will do." She waved her hand without facing him. Both of them went out through the door and quickly walked down the path between the fires.

When they reached the usual Gate, they quickly exchanged news with the guards. After they were done, they headed to Gillian forest.

"Luckily, Amon agreed to extend the range of his pets, not to mention that he also agreed to do that to some random soldiers just to distract the Echelons," Zaderion said quietly.

"Yeah, I need a whole new perspective if I want to look at him now." Vrathien grinned at her mate.

"I know what you mean. By the way, are we safe enough if we go there by the usual route? You told me back there at Amon's that Lucifer would be looking for Ry with his eyes bloody, right?" Zaderion asked. His face looked wary.

Vrae considered him for a moment. "You're right, and it would really not be good for us if we bumped into him. Let's go low, as fast and quiet as possible." Vrathien jerked her head towards the forest down below.

Zaderion concurred. They immediately reduced their altitude and proceeded just above the woods.

As they had feared, the Son of Perdition was now outside the castle of his rebellious son, Belphegor, and face to face with him for the first time in fifty thousand years.

* * *

The Vagarim Lake beneath Belphegor's castle was changing color from a beautiful dark blue into pitch black that was full of the stench of death as his father now stood before him.

Annoyed, Belphegor waved his hand towards the lake without releasing his angry stare from his father. The color of the lake instantly back to its original one.

"No need to show off. You'll impress nobody but maggots around here," Belphegor said in disgust.

Lucifer's gaze darkened. "Is that all you wanna say to your dear old father after fifty thousand years?" he asked lightly.

Belphegor snorted. "That's new. I thought I'd ceased to be your son after I've been mocking you for that long."

Lucifer smiled in menace. "Indeed you had. But it's nothing new if you're still one of the royals amongst us," he said calmly. Belphegor could sense something deadly in the eerily cold voice of his father.

"What's your point? Just spill the rubbish, because I don't have all day. I have to get back to my studies," Belphegor said mockingly.

Lucifer still didn't budge despite his son's disrespectful demeanour towards him. "And with whom do you work your studies these days? Is it Ezryan?" Well, he indeed didn't want to waste any more than a second to tell his point in coming here.

Belphegor remained stoic. "Ezryan? What's a dead guy got to do with those light-asses? Then again, I understand your fear that he could've survived, because the one who wasted him was in fact you, right? Not Big Guy up there? Just imagine what most of us, most of the soldiers would do if they ever heard that their commander was obliterated by the hand of their own master. They would probably go rogue at the very least." Belphegor let out a low laugh. "But the coolest part would be the sisters who are his closest comrades," he added and smirked.

"Enough," Lucifer cut him off. "I just wanna ask you if you ever crossed paths with him lately." He gave the North Prince a threatening glare.

In return Belphegor just ignored him. Luckily, as far as he knew, Lucifer knew nothing of his regular meetings with the warrior and his comrades. And he hoped Lucifer didn't know their whereabouts right now.

"Why would I cross paths with him? And what do you mean by 'lately'?" Belphegor crossed his arms across his chest.

Lucifer's face suddenly broke into a twisted smile. "Because I know he comes to your place every now and again. And what's more, someone has been going around slaughtering Arcs without getting toasted."

Belphegor's face still remained expressionless as he rolled his eyes, though in his mind he was cursing his father. "And whose word might that be? Really, after all this time you could at least show me that you've grown some brains. And yet, here you stand, wasting your breath, producing groundless information about some warrior who dared to set foot in few miles radius of my castle. And yeah, I've heard about those Arcs, but that's hardly my fuckin' business." He grinned tauntingly. When Lucifer didn't say anything, he tsked and went on with his audacity. "No wonder you chose those lame-head devils to be your direct Echelons. They're even more brainless than you are," he chuckled.

"You're saying that if I ransack your place right now, I won't find him or his stench inside?" Lucifer asked in a low lethal tone.

Belphegor gave him a "duh" stare. Well, Ezryan was indeed not inside his castle at the moment. "Do I speak in language you're not getting here? Or have you spent so much time in that hole of yours that you don't even get what I'm saying? Do you need me to spell it out?" he asked sarcastically.

A deadly glint flashed in Lucifer's eyes. "Not really, but rest assured, if your word is proven to be wrong, your castle would be the least of your concerns," he laughed darkly.

"Bring it on, bitch," Belphegor replied in the same low dead-pan tone.

The next second, everything happened so fast that even Belphegor was barely able to see it. Once he realized what was happening, Lucifer was already strangling him with his claws pressed his throat. "Mind your tongue with me, boy," Lucifer whispered slowly in a cold voice that threatened gruesome death in his ear.

Belphegor went rigid at the menace. "Have it your way, bastard. We've been standing behind the line for too damn long." Belphegor gave Lucifer an intense look of hatred as his father pulled away from his ear.

Lucifer was startled, and then he released his grip. "Remember this moment when I could have killed you." His gaze narrowed.

Suddenly a chilling breeze came from out of nowhere, blowing the same stench of death. This time, it went through the woods around them and reduced more trees into ashes.

"I said you'd impress nobody but maggots around here, didn't I?" Belphegor didn't even wave his hand this time. He just kept staring at his father and instantly undid the damage his father had done. The trees around them transformed back to their original state at once.

"And yeah, I'll remember this moment, when you could've killed me but instead you were killing the greeneries and ruining my place. As if you'd be bothered to fix the damage yourself." Belphegor let out an aggravated breath.

Lucifer smiled evilly. "Whatever you say, boy. Just remember, I'll let you go for now, but I always can rip your throat any time, anywhere."

"I said, bring it on," Belphegor replied through clenched teeth. For a second he couldn't help but gaze on the small triangular pendant dangling on Lucifer's chest.

The All-Seeing Eye, the very object he must take, Rygavon.

Belphegor hurriedly shifted his gaze back to his father's face. Fortunately for him, Lucifer hadn't noticed.

Lucifer then lifted his grip from Belphegor's throat. "Very well, I'll look for that treacherous insect elsewhere," Lucifer said as the black light wrapped around him once more.

"Just go, will ya?" Belphegor said lazily.

Lucifer let out an evil laugh that once again echoed throughout the woods, and then he departed.

The second his father was no longer in his area, Belphegor inhaled a deep breath and released it. *"Damn it, Ry, I hope you're at his place by now,"* the North Prince thought with a curse under his breath.

After he made sure his father wouldn't be back at any second, Belphegor hastily flew towards Gillian forest. He was so fast that he left cut marks on the trees he passed through. He was careful not to destroy them, because it would certainly draw attention if someone were to see the straight path it formed between his palace and Vassago's castle.

And the last thing he needed was for that someone to report it to his wretched father.

* * *

"What do you mean 'long-term revolution'?" Ry asked.

"Well, it's . . ."

Vassago suddenly raised his hand, stopping him.

"What is it?" I asked.

"Someone's coming," Vassago said simply as he arose from his seat.

I instinctively looked at the door. "Is it Vrae and Zade?"

Vassago nodded. "Belphegor as well," he added as he walked towards the door and then chanted in front of it.

After the door—well, the wall—opened, he turned to the three of us. "Wait here while I fetch them."

"Okay," I nodded. I felt Ry's fingers once again gently lace with mine.

I turned my attention to him from Seere, who averted his gaze from the door where Vassago had stood seconds before back to the old book in front of him.

Ry just tightened his grip without a word, which made me itch to hit something or, better yet, destroy it. It was really frustrating when you didn't even have a wild guess what the supposed half of your own soul was thinking. His face remained stoic, but I could see a glint of unfathomable wariness in his eyes.

I wished I could tell him right here and now that he could tell me anything, or at least give me a clue as to what he'd been worrying about. Call me nosy, but he really should learn to trust me more before he died from too much stress, well, so to speak. Perhaps old habits die really hard. He was still keeping all his troubles to himself.

All of a sudden, he whispered hesitantly, "I know you're wondering what I'm thinking right now, and I will tell you later, okay? Let's just wait for the others."

Surprised by his words, I nodded.

Moments later, the door opened, and Vassago came in, followed by Belphegor, who looked really pissed off, and Vrae, along with Zade. Both of their faces were pale as if they had barely escaped from something.

Ry let go of my hand, and then he stood up. "Hi, you guys," he greeted them, while I only nodded. The three of them just gave a nod in return without saying anything and took their seats.

"Oh and before I forget, thanks Belphegor, I owe you big time," Ry said with sincere respect in his gaze.

"Yeah, thanks," I said as I followed him.

Belphegor just sighed and waved his hand in dismissal as he gave us a smug smile. "No problem. I managed to piss that old bastard off right to his face, and I must say getting that opportunity once in a while is really highly entertaining."

"That's tough talk, considering your pop could've put an end to you before you could even blink," Seere commented to Belphegor without even looking at him. "And I see he marked you pretty good."

I had caught a glimpse of the deep red marks on Belphegor's throat but refrained from asking, for Seere's bland but bad comment alone had already triggered Belphegor's temper. A tic worked in Belphegor's jaw as he reached for the book. "At least I don't pick up shiny things like some stupid bird," he shot back as he stared scornfully at Seere.

Seere gave a sideways glare at Belphegor in return.

"Enough! Wrap it, ladies." Vassago cut them off before they could continue their inane battle of words.

Belphegor shrugged. "Have you told them?" he asked.

Vassago nodded. "Our prediction was correct after all. Not just these two; it looks like Vrae and Zade are also in on this as well."

My sister and Zade frowned at each other, obviously having no idea what these princes were talking about.

"Err, can I ask what's going on? 'Cause we're completely clueless here," Vrae said.

"Let me answer her," Ry said, before either of the princes could open their mouths.

"Be my guest," Vassago shrugged.

"You gotta tell us the details of your own meeting with Lucy, though." Ry's gaze fell on Belphegor, who gave him a smug smile in return.

After that, he told the pair everything Vassago had said to us up to the point where they were entering the archive.

When Ry was finished, Vrae's gaze fell slowly to the table, while Zade just leaned back to his chair looking helpless. Even Belphegor just stared in silence.

"That was all there is. They all knew what we were doing at my brother's place," Ry said quietly. "Fortunately, for us," he went on, "they're on our side of the fence, so you needn't worry they would attack your mate, Vrae," he assured her.

She just nodded but still didn't say anything in response.

"But what did all of you mean by 'long-term revolution'?" I repeated Ry's question from moments earlier.

"Just a second, baby. Belphegor needs to do some explaining first," Ry interjected.

I winced. "Oh yeah, I forgot."

Belphegor threw Ry an annoyed stare and then expelled an exasperated breath. "Fine! Frankly, I'd rather you lct them answer her first. Then you can hear my part of the story, but anyway, let's get started," he said.

Belphegor then filled us in about everything that had gone down between him and his father. "Like I said, I managed to piss that old bastard off right to his face." Belphegor's face broke into an evil smile.

"Yeah, nice one! Apart from nearly getting your throat shredded, that was nice," Ry said, half relieved, half wary at the North Prince.

"Cool," I added in disbelief. Well, Belphegor's conflict with his father had already begun millennia ago, but this was the first time I'd ever heard of him literally face to face with that old bastard. And facing someone like Lucifer wasn't something anyone could call a walk in a park.

"Thanks." The North Prince gave me a smile that, in a way, was much more dazzling than Ry's. He then cleared his throat. "So, it's time for your answer isn't it? Vassago, shoot." He jerked his head at Vassago, who arched a brow at him but agreed to his request.

Vassago sighed. "All right, you were asking about the 'long-term revolution'. Hmm . . ." he mumbled to himself. Either he was pretending to do some thinking or he had forgotten he was supposed to give us the answer we needed.

"Cut the jest, will ya?" Seere rubbed his brow.

"All right, all right. What we meant was, well, actually this is gonna be a bit aggravating," Vassago said carefully.

Ry, Vrae, Zade, and I exchanged a clueless gaze at the prince's demeanour.

"Aggravating how?" Ry asked him hesitantly.

"Well, we believe the four of you are aware of the existence of those races, am I correct?" he looked at each one of us.

"Yeah," I confirmed slowly.

Vassago grimaced. "Right, so we weren't sure if you know about this part as well."

"Which part?" I frowned at him.

"He's reluctant to tell you that some of those Votzadirs in the past turned to the human side of the line," Seere cut him off before Vassago could even move his lips. Both the other princes glared at him, but Seere just simply ignored them and continued staring at us.

I looked at Ry, but he didn't even turn his head. "We know about that. What's your point?" he asked calmly, but something in his voice made me feel that he was worried.

Of what, I had no clue.

Vassago and Belphegor looked surprised for a second, but their surprised expression vanished as soon as it came. "So, we don't have to waste another second then," the North Prince said as he rubbed his palms.

He then cleared his throat. "Basically, we don't have to talk about this now, since we have another pressing matter at hand, that Arzia thing. But, we don't know squat of when Cain's BS might come to past, so we figured the sooner we told you guys, the better."

"And now we know all of you already exchanged QuiMarraes, you don't need to make a new one. Everything new will be added instantly into those orbs held by each of you," Vassago added.

"We get it. Now would you explain to us what your point is?" Ry repeated.

Vassago expelled an exasperated breath. "Fine! What we wanted to tell you was that there's a big possibility that all of you here who got to share in going Votzadir might do the same as the Votzadirs did in the past. Become fans of the humans, I mean."

Vrae and I scoffed at that. "Now that is utterly ridiculous," Vrae said. Obviously she detested the idea that any of us would be on the humans' side of the fence.

I chuckled at her comment. "Yeah, I admit there is a possibility. I mean, Ry told us some of them did, but I don't think we would be one of them."

The three princes exchanged amused looks, but when I glanced at Ry, he didn't even look gleeful. I saw a weird glint in his eyes as his gaze grew darker. "You're saying, you'd rather we became human defenders? Is that it?" he asked slowly.

Vrae and I immediately threw him a wry glare. "Come again?" Vrae asked. Her brows were knitted, and her face showed that she was unbelievably outraged by that idea.

Unfortunately for us, the princes confirmed his worries. "As usual, you always catch on quickly. You should be careful with a habit like that, you know." Belphegor sneered.

"You have got to be kidding," Vrae mumbled reluctantly as she gave all three of them a sullen look.

"Sorry, Vrae, but that's what most likely will happen," Vassago smiled sadly at us.

An outrageous thought just came into my mind, and I gazed at Ry, hoping I would find some answers if not a confirmation. And I got it all right. His sapphire eyes were overwhelmed with unfathomable sadness.

Biting my lip, I averted my gaze to the royals. "Wait, so you expect us to go 'Yeah, humans!' which will eventually lead us to confront the Echelons, because we all know they won't give a rat's ass about what Cain had said, let alone follow it." I frowned at the princes, who were obviously surprised by my words.

Seere lifted the edge of his lips, and his ruby eyes swirled. "Well, well, you two are a pair indeed," he said.

Vrae looked at me, to Seere, and then back to me again. She definitely had a hard time absorbing this idea into her head. Looking furious, she scowled at me, well, at the rest of us except her own mate, who apparently was in too much shock, because he didn't say anything at all.

"Very funny, Yve, and why in the hell do you have to be with humans just to confront the Echelons?" she asked in an irritated voice.

Zade made a movement for the first time and held her shoulder. "Vrae, I'm sure you know that becoming one with humans provides a risk of getting tainted with one of their natures, and that is to protect each other, especially one's own bloodline. Well, it's not that tainted. I mean, that's also what we do to a certain degree," he said carefully as he gazed at the table.

Vrae curled her lips. By the looks on her face, it was obvious for me that she knew this for a fact.

"Besides," I went on, "if I recall it correctly, Votzadirs who confronted the humans' new pals sounded like they were on their boss's side, well, you know . . ." I said, and I gave them a half-hearted laugh.

"So, in the end, we either choose the humans or the Echelons, is that it, one way or the other?" Zade asked.

"Naturally," Ry answered him. He then gave the princes a quizzical stare. "This is ironic, the Hell Princes gathered here and hoping devil warriors turn to the human side," he said bitterly.

"Tell me about it," Belphegor chuckled. "But hey, like you said before, you're gonna help us wage war with those lameys millennia from now. And just so you don't feel so much like dirt, maybe at some point in your human life you'll enjoy it more than you ever imagined," he winked.

I raised a brow. "And where did you hear unsubstantiated information like that?" I asked him.

Vassago scoffed. "Trust me, we know."

"Yeah well, for once I gotta agree with him," Seere added. His gaze fell on Belphegor, whose crimson eyes stared directly at him without any stabbing comment for once.

Ry arched a brow. "You have some inside info on them, huh?" Vassago just shrugged without saying anything.

"Wow, this is a whole new level of insanity," I muttered in disbelief. And then I considered the princes' words for a minute. "Basically, you just want us to topple them, right? So, whether we become human pros or not, it doesn't really matter, correct?"

The princes exchanged a puzzled look and then nodded.

"So, we can forget about the distressing human part for now and just keep the 'kick Echelons' asses until next winter' part in mind," I said in a lighter tone.

Belphegor was startled and then burst out laughing. "You really are unbelievable."

"So, how's it gonna be? All of you in on this?" Vassago asked.

The four of us looked at each other for a second and then exchanged a subtle nod.

"Right, now let's get back to the matter at hand," Seere said as he put his elbow on the table, leaned forward, and rested his chin on his fist.

"We're going after the ring." Belphegor smiled darkly at us. His handsome face looked so evil, and he slightly let out his murderous aura, making me almost unable to restrain myself from accidentally destroying something.

"Fine, let's hear it." Ry crossed his arms over his chest as he leaned back in his seat.

I gulped a bit to get rid of the sensation derived from the evil I felt from Belphegor. "Just make sure you have enough roles for all of us."

Chapter 18

Vassago stood up from his seat and took the book. He flipped the pages until he reached a page on which I saw a picture of an object I recognized as the Herathim. He flipped the pages twice again, and then there were another two pictures. One was the ring we were about to steal, and the other one was the Core of Rygavon.

Dang, I still couldn't believe we were about to take that thing off Lucifer's neck.

"The three of us have been scouring this book to see if we could find any spell or anything else that the Valdam could use against us," Vassago said.

"Or worse, conjure us and make us into peanut butter," Belphegor added lazily.

I snorted. "Peanut, is it? What happened with the strawberry?"

He scoffed. "Not now, honey," he said as he glared at Ry. My mate snickered and ignored the North Prince's angry stare.

I glanced at Vrae and Zade who were exchanging a puzzled look. I restrained myself from telling them what I meant in case I ignited a sarcasm war with Belphegor.

Ry cleared his throat. "So what did you find?"

Vassago then asked for a tiny object from Seere, who handed it to him. He used the object to mark the page. Then he continued to flip the pages. He stopped at a page that contained an unfamiliar symbol that was painted so big that almost the whole page was covered by it.

"What's this? It looks like a seal or sort," I said, pointing at it.

Belphegor tapped his forefinger on the picture. "This is the infamous Key of Solomon–well, infamous to us, that is." He gave us a droll stare.

"The writers certainly knew almost everything. They even recorded something that existed millennia after their extinction," Ry said in amazement.

"Or Solomon just got himself another kind of forbidden record like this one, probably handed to him by one of those Arcs. He was, after all, the only human who ever lived that was trusted to possess both forbidden knowledge and ability. Perhaps he was told how to contain our kind, and then since no one knew otherwise, he announced it as Key of *Solomon*." There was obvious venom in his cold voice.

"Yeah, it would be no surprise if that was what happened," Vrae said bitterly.

From out of nowhere, we smelled the stench of an animal followed by the faint sound of a horse. I saw Vassago exchange an annoyed gaze with Seere and Belphegor.

"Do you have to be this annoying, Orobas? If you wanna talk, then just talk. Now my archive's full of your stench," Vassago said, obviously upset.

"Orobas? He's here? Today sure is crowded with princes," I mused.

Suddenly, an evil laugh echoed in the room, and a hollow voice that I've never heard before replied to him. "Consider this a bit of payback, Vassago, and I see Belphegor and . . . well, well, well, I never saw this coming, Seere? You're here too, with Belphegor? This is very rare indeed. I wonder what conspiracy you're working on right now."

Belphegor shook his head, while Seere's face was full of utter disgust. "C'mon, cut the crap Orobas, what's your problem? Why don't you come here and have a chat?" Belphegor sounded strangely amused as he looked up at the ceiling.

"Thanks for the offer. You know that in this state, I can't appear before you because Vassago's spell prevents it, even though I can reach this place because of Vassago's permission. And I can't possibly go there right now."

Vassago frowned. "Yeah, now that you mention it, what did you mean by payback?"

The hollow voice let out a scoffing laugh. "I know that Ry is still alive."

"I'm here. Long time no see, Prince Orobas," Ry said as he glanced at me.

"Yeah, nice to see you too, but what I don't find to be so nice is that you all gather here and didn't even bother to give me a warning!" the voice growled.

"And why should we?" Seere asked.

"Don't even start, Seere!" the voice snapped at him. "I was just having an unexpected visitor, and not a pleasant one I might add," he hissed.

Belphegor swore under his breath. "Don't tell me that old bastard . . ." his voice was fading.

The voice let out a low laugh. "Yeah, regards from your daddy asshole. He snapped furiously and almost destroyed my place. You're a lucky bastard, Ry, because both Sitri and Stolas don't seem to know you're alive. They've became much of an annoyance these past centuries, especially Sitri. If he knew you were alive, he would've told Lucifer," the voice said.

Absently, my hand went to Ry's and grasped it tightly. He glanced at me and simply gave a soothing smile which calmed me a degree.

"And now? Do you know where he's heading?" Vassago asked warily.

The voice went mute.

"Orobas!" Belphegor called.

"He's already made Sitri shit his pants, and in a moment Stolas will get the honour," the voice answered.

"Has he come over to my place?" Seere asked.

The voice snickered. "No, maybe because not even in a million years would he ever think that you could be in the same room for five minutes with Belphegor here, so he figures you don't have anything to do with this."

"And now, head's up, boys! He's coming. Tell me how the meeting turns out, Vassago. And don't worry, my scent will be gone as usual. Catch you on the flip side, boys, and nice to see you, ladies," the voice turned polite all of a sudden.

Vrae was stunned. She didn't say anything. I lifted the edge of my lips. Well, he did sound like the princes here. "Yeah, nice to see you too, Prince Orobas," I said.

Yeah, right, like I knew what he looked like. I gotta ask Ry. It seemed he'd been visiting royals without me or Vrae. No wonder he could get his hands on dangerous intel.

Seconds later, that low evil laughed echoed in the room once again, and the stench completely disappeared.

"Now what?" Belphegor asked. "You can't tell he's here until he *is* here."

Vassago scowled. "Just ignore him. I know he's telling the truth, but like you said, I can't tell he's here until he is. Lucky he doesn't find the idea of scouring the shadows to be productive," he said bitterly.

"Just stay here and don't do anything stupid when he does show. This room will prevent any signs of your presence from getting out, so rest assured, he won't notice you all here as long as you all stay put." He gave us a crooked smile and sounded really proud of the protection he provided in this place.

"Will do. Now can we please get on with the plan?" Belphegor asked without wasting a second.

"Wait a second, Belphegor." Ry raised his hand. All of us turned to him.

He gazed at Zade and Vrae. "Sorry, you two. You just came here, but I need to get you both outta here."

"No fucking way, Ry. You can't kick us out of the way and put yourself and my sister in danger all the time. You can't do this!" she snarled in fury as she hit the table.

Zade frowned deeply as he tried to calm Vrae. "What's your excuse this time?" he demanded.

Ry's face showed that he was really sorry he had to ask this of them, but I caught a glint of determination in his eyes. There was no way for them to change his mind if his mind was already set to do something.

"You heard what Orobas said, didn't you? He's coming here, and we can't risk you both. Besides, we need someone inside to hear if there's something happening and give us warning. I don't like it either. If Orobas hadn't said anything, I wouldn't ask you this," he said with sincere apology in his voice.

"He's right, Vrae. I bet after that old bastard gets here, and if by some luck he doesn't realize that we're right in front of his nose and that makes him crazy, who knows what madness he'll get up to? He could go looking for you and Yve for all we know. It'll be too suspicious if both of you disappeared right when he was looking everywhere for Ry." Belphegor jerked his head.

"And I'll say it again to you, Vrae. It'll be no surprise if I never show, but not you or Zade, okay? Like you said, you're my sister, and I won't risk you," I inserted with a smile at her.

Well, it wasn't like I heard her calling me her sister in front of other devils every day.

She looked enraged, and for a second I swore I saw a glimpse of helplessness in her eyes, but with Belphegor backing us up, she had no other choice.

"Fine, just watch your backs," she said grudgingly as she and Zade rose up from their seats and gave their salute to Belphegor and Seere, while Vassago followed them to the door. Zaderion gave us a subtle nod of goodbye.

"Take care of her, will ya?" I said to Zade.

"Don't worry, you know I will. Catch you later, guys," he said reluctantly.

Vassago then opened the door and walked them outside. Moments later he came back and the door was closed. He sighed in relief. "There were no signs of your dad anywhere, Belphegor, so I think it safe enough to assume those two will get out far before he gets here," he said as he took a seat.

Belphegor rubbed his temple without saying anything.

"Okay, so, Ry and Yve, you two decided to go in, right? We figured that one thing you two gotta be extremely aware of is this seal." Vassago tapped his finger on the seal's picture.

"Check the floor *and* the ceiling before you enter any room, because they can make this on either one. Putting this on both won't be necessary," Seere added.

"How can you tell?" I asked.

"Because some of the owners of the things I intended to steal got a bit creative and put this in their treasure rooms. It was fortunate I have demonikyn of my own. I unleashed a few of them into the room, and when they got caught, I could tell that there was a seal inside," Seere chuckled, obviously proud of himself.

"That would come in handy. I wish I had some of those. Will doppelgangers do the trick?" I asked.

"No need to use them. They could help in the worst case scenario where either of you should get in a fight at the Valdam's place. Remember, you two will be breaking into the Guardian of

Solomon's ring here, not into some lame-head human's treasure room," Seere warned us.

"So, what do you suggest we use?" Ry asked, tilting his head at Seere.

"I'll let you two take some of my demonikyn, since I can't go in there myself." The prince lifted the edge of his lips.

Ry nodded in understanding. "That's a good idea, thanks."

"Are there other things we need to be aware of?" I jerked my head at the book.

The princes gave each other a knowing look, and then Vassago shook his head at us. "That's all we have at the moment, we can formulate the plan after you two do some scouting."

"Naturally," I said in bored voice.

"By the way, do we need to destroy the whole part where the seal is painted on?" I asked him.

Seere shook his head. "No, a little damage on the circle part that cuts it off is enough. There's no need to make a riot over a stupid seal like this. Otherwise it would defeat the whole purpose of a stealth move, wouldn't it?"

I scoffed at his rhetorical question. Indeed he had a point, but something in this little heist we were planning started to bug the hell out of me. What was it?

"So, when will we do this?" Ry asked, pulling me back from my musings.

"After we've directed his dad's nose somewhere else," Vassago said, and Belphegor nodded in agreement.

"You won't be doing anything when he could be here any second. You get out now, and he's already out there for all we know. You stay here, and he's a no-show. Either way, it will be wise for the two of you to stay here for a while," Belphegor said reassuringly.

I saw Ry considered for a moment, and then he concurred. "Okay, but if in two days he's not shown up, we're going in."

Belphegor shrugged. "Suit yourself."

"In the meantime, what will you two be doing?" I asked Belphegor and Seere. Well, they wouldn't be staying here, would they? They'd argue with each other all the time like some middle-aged human women–in front of us if possible, and I so didn't want to see that.

"I'll be around," Belphegor said. As expected he was a bit reluctant. He glanced at Seere, who sneered at him. The North Prince just snorted and then averted his gaze back to us.

"Belphegor and I made an agreement that we'll stay out of trouble for the duration of your stay, and after we commence our plan against his dad," Seere said as he raked his long hair that fell to his back.

Ry gave me a mischievous look that made me let loose a grin. "That's good to hear, because no offense, but I really don't want to show any groundless fight between you two to her." He jerked his head towards me.

Vassago scoffed. Belphegor just narrowed his gaze at Ry but didn't say anything. Seere on the other hand just shrugged.

"Fine, we'll stay put," Ry said finally.

Vassago then rose up, followed by the rest of us. He walked to the door and opened it. He let us went through it and closed it behind us.

Moments later, he guided us through his castle. He led us away from the free-carving turquoise wall that led to his archive. We walked for several minutes, and I saw parts of this castle that I've never seen before. This place was mostly made of turquoise stone like the owner's eyes and the color of his robe. I saw weird engravings in almost every corner of this place. The floor felt a bit cold on my feet, and it was so clean and shiny that it reflected us as we walked on it.

"We're here. This is your room, Ry," Vassago said, when we arrived at a huge marble door.

"Thanks Vassago," Ry said gratefully. Vassago gave him a subtle nod and was about to lead us further inside the castle when Ry stopped us. "Wait, what about her?" Ry asked, indicating me.

Vassago chuckled. "I was waiting for you to ask," he said as he grinned at me. "You can share the room with him, Yve." He gave me a teasing smile. I glanced at the other princes and saw them do the same.

Embarrassed, I nodded slightly as I muttered my thanks to Vassago. And then he left us with the other princes, leading them to their rooms, I guessed.

Suddenly, I felt Ry's grip in my hand, his fingers crisscrossed with mine. "Come on, let's get inside," he whispered in my ear. I shivered a bit and then looked at his eyes and smiled at him.

"Okay, a bit of good sleep will be nice before we commence the suicide plan."

He placed a soft kiss on my head, and after that he led us inside. Once we went through the door, my jaw dropped in amazement. The room was extremely immaculate, and it had a certain tranquil and majestic beauty I'd never seen in any chamber belonging to any king of humans.

I heard the door close behind me, but I didn't turn around. I was too absorbed by the grandeur of the chamber, when suddenly Ry held me from behind. We stood still for a moment as I closed my eyes and savoured his hold on me, and somehow I thought he did the same.

I felt his cheek touch my temple, and he inhaled the scent of my hair. "Finally we're alone and free from all that talking," he murmured.

I made no movement but stood still in his arms. "I thought that talk was essential."

He laughed quietly. "It is, but for me this time, this second, the most essential talk is when I talk about us," he murmured.

I felt him loosen his hold and slowly turn me around to face him. I opened my eyes and met his soft gaze and smile. He then gave me a really tender kiss that lasted for a full minute. Suddenly I felt him gently lift me off the floor while his perfect lips still locked with mine.

When he put me down, we separated, and I realized that we were standing at the side of an enormous bed. I gave him a puzzled look. "You want me to sleep on it?" I asked him. My voice hinted doubt.

He shrugged. "You said you wanted a good sleep," he teased as he stroked my cheek.

"Yeah, I did, but I never sleep in one of these unless I'm in human form." I flinched.

Ry considered me for a second and then he sneered as if an outrageous thought had occurred to him.

"What?" I demanded.

He gave me a crooked smile. "Then why don't you try to do so here. Consider it practice before the actual deal."

I looked at him in horror. "No. Way. I'm *so* not doing that," I said, curling my lips.

He just smiled patiently at me and without saying anything, he transformed into his human form I'd never seen before. I held my breath as I saw him. He was astonishing as ever. Whether in the devil form or in human one, he looked just as gorgeous. His tall lean and muscular body was now covered in elegant, sapphire duster robe, much like the one his brother wore. His chest was left bare as the robe waved at his side. He had tight black leather pants on his lower body. His straight hair fell more freely on his shoulder now because there were no horns jutting out of his head.

"Come on, just when we're alone," he encouraged me. I couldn't find the strength to resist him, to say no to his stupid request.

Feigning annoyance, I pouted. "I doubt you'll look this stunning when you become an actual human."

"Come on," he repeated.

I grimaced. "I don't look that good in human form," I said, trying to weasel my way out of this.

"No, don't you dare try to escape," he grasped my hands. Giving up, I closed my eyes and transformed. When I'd finished, I opened my eyes, covered my body in a black bed robe, and then gave him a sullen look. "There, happy now? Although I doubt it. I told you I don't look that good in human form." I curled my lips.

But as I looked at him, I realized he definitely thought differently. He stared at me as if he'd never seen me before. Well, technically he never had seen me in this form, but whatever . . .

"Ry? You okay? Gee, I really look that hideous, don't I?" I grimaced.

He slowly shook his head with a stunned look. "What are you talking about? You should've told me you'd look this beautiful, you know," he said in astonishment.

I frowned. "What are *you* talking about? You definitely gotta get yourself an eye exam," I suggested in disbelief.

Did he really think I looked that good, or was he seeing things here? I do look quite good in human eyes, but in his?

He laughed and then dragged me to a huge mirror which I hadn't noticed before. Then he held my waist as he pointed the mirror. "I don't have a clue as to why you would think of yourself as 'hideous'," he chuckled.

Slowly inhaling the scent of my hair, he leaned down to my ear. "You look absolutely stunning. No wonder those kings fall one by one at your feet, making me jealous sometimes. They get to be with you more often than I do. The only thing I'm grateful about is that they couldn't get their hands on you," he said quietly. I could feel the sincere relief in his voice.

I smiled at our reflection on the mirror. "Of course they couldn't. Who do you think I am? My job is to excite their cruelty, not to be their low concubine," I laughed.

"Yeah, sorry, my mistake," he giggled. "So, beautiful, are you ready to sleep?" he teased with a totally devastating wicked smile on his lips.

"Definitely," I nodded. And then without warning, he lifted me again, and I let out a low gasp of surprise.

"What are you doing?" I asked him, half trying to get him put me down.

He just walked holding me as he gave me a wicked smile without saying anything. Eventually we were back at the side of the bed. He put me down gently on the middle of the bed, and he joined me. He then carefully cupped my face in his hand and gave me a soft gaze.

His forehead met mine, and we both closed our eyes to savour this moment. I could hear him inhale slowly as I felt his hand stroke my hair.

"I just . . . I wish I could believe in this moment of being with you. It still feels so surreal to me," he whispered.

I held his hands that were still around my face. "You *are* with me. Nothing can separate us ever again, if I can manage it," I muttered fiercely.

"I'll do everything in my power to protect you," he said as he began to withdraw, putting some distance between his face and mine.

We both opened our eyes, and he kissed me with another tender kiss. One gentle kiss after another invaded my lips. Slowly, I felt his hands move to untie my bed robe and sweep it off my body. The warmth of his skin made its way into my soul as his touch went all over mine, while my own hands shoved away the duster robe he wore loosely around his masculine body. Our human bodies entwined as he made love to me on that comfortable enormous bed. He made love to me over and over, and I savoured each and every time. Several hours later we both were drifted into sleep as he held my shoulder and I laid my head on his bare muscular chest.

Chapter 19

I woke up several hours later. When my senses came back, which took a few seconds because of the human form I was in at the moment, I felt a gentle rake on my hair. I slowly lifted my head and turned to see Ry smiling at me. "Did you have a good sleep, beautiful?" he asked, his hand that was raking my hair now on my cheek.

I yawned a bit and then gave him a satisfied look. "I did, thanks." I smiled back.

"Come here," he pulled me so I could rest my head on his chest. After that, he continued raking my hair as he started to mumble that usual lullaby. I felt something different in his touch, but since he didn't say a thing, I wasn't sure what was on his mind, so I decided to ask.

"Ry, what's wrong?"

I could feel him slightly shaking his head. "Nothing, baby, don't worry," he said calmly.

Like hell I would believe that. "If there's anything on your mind, please tell me," I pleaded as I lifted my head from his chest so I could look at him in the eye.

"Nothing, really." He shook his head. I curled my lips at him and he simply answered me with a gentle smile.

I hated it when he did that; I almost couldn't find the strength to argue with him.

Trying to ignore his breath-taking smile, I kept on pouting. That was when something popped into my mind. "You're not sure if we can get out from the heist alive, are you?" I asked him lightly. I didn't want to trouble to his thoughts any more than they already were.

He started. "I'm sorry, I didn't mean to trouble you, but it seems now I can't hide anything from you, can I?" he said softly.

So I was right. He *was* worried about that. I touched his cheek and then gave him a soothing smile—well, at least that was what I hoped it would look like, not a gloomy one. "Don't worry. Nothing is gonna happen to us. You've got my back and I've got yours, okay?" I assured him in a lighter tone.

He nodded, although that bleak expression remained on his face. Suddenly he cleared his throat. "I wonder where that old bastard is right now. Seems there's no sign of him anywhere. I hope that means that he's not coming here any time soon," he said, changing the subject.

I decided not to question him and played along instead. "Don't know. I just hope that his going AWOL doesn't mean he's going after Vrae." I levelled a wary look at him as I got up.

"I'm sure they'll be just fine." He held my hand as he too stood up from the bed . . . and transformed into his devil form.

"Finally!" I rejoiced in my thoughts. I followed him and did the same. Devil must remained devil after all. When I looked at him, for a second I could swear I saw a glint of disappointment in his eyes, but he just smiled as he extended his hand.

"Shall we go? I wanna look for Vassago to ask if Belphegor's dad came by."

I scowled as I took his hand. "I hope to hell that he's just given up and gone back to that hole of his, or at least that he's trying to look for us without involving any other people," I snapped bitterly.

He let out a long tired breath. "Me too. If he indeed didn't show up, I was wondering if I could scour the book as well. I've been curious since I saw it few days ago," he replied.

I frowned. "Okay, but can you explain one thing to me first?"

"What is it?"

"I didn't get to ask Belphegor further about why both he and Vassago seemed to be bothered by the bad run-in that Vrae, Zade, and I had."

His face went blank, and then he reluctantly looked away from me. "Ry, what is it?" I asked him carefully.

"To tell you the truth, there is something," he began.

I swallowed. Something was never good if he started it with either "to tell you the truth" or "there is something", and this time he used both. "Yeah?"

"Before I came to you, I discussed most of those things with Belphegor, and then after that I talked about them with him and

Vassago. Both of them didn't tell you this because, well, maybe they'd expected me to tell you or for you to ask."

"And sorry, Hon, but you still have yet to explain anything," I interjected.

Sighing, he levelled his gaze at me, and what I saw in his deep sapphire eyes was a glint of helplessness I'd never seen in him. "Belphegor told me that there's only one element that perhaps could match the destroyer's, because in essence it bears a resemblance more like the void itself."

"And that element is?"

He inhaled deeply and released it. "Yours. The element of darkness."

That news hammered me hard, but maybe deep down, I kinda expected it. "That was how I could drive out whatever it was that got into me when I checked those Alvadors, wasn't it? I even managed to pull it out of Zade when he used his Imirae on it. This was the cause."

He nodded subtly. "Please promise me you won't tell Vrae? She'd freak and think that we'd asked you to face the destroyer head on, while you know those princes and, above all, I would never let that happen."

Warmth engulfed my body at his heartfelt words. I inclined my head and placed a palm gently on his cheek. "I know you wouldn't. Don't worry, I promise."

He put his hand over mine and brought it to his lips. "I wish that it wasn't you, but now it has come to this, I can only promise that I'll never let that touch you," he said earnestly.

I landed a quick kiss. "I know that. Now come on, it's time to get out of your guilt fest. You said you wanted to get your hands on that book."

His face lit up, he led me to the door, and we went out of the room. "Vassago?" he called the owner of this place. His deep voice echoed clearly throughout the corridor.

"Yeah?" Vassago suddenly appeared from out of nowhere.

"Any sign of him?" he asked cautiously.

Vassago shook his head. "Not even a scrap of his robe was found around here," he answered in an aggravated voice.

I sighed in relief. I glanced at Ry and saw that he looked a bit relieved as well. He gave Vassago a quizzical stare though.

"So, what now?" Vassago asked. Ry was startled, and then hesitantly, as he bit his lip, he asked, "Where's Belphegor?"

"I'm here." Out of the blue, the North Prince appeared beside Vassago.

"Gee, these princes really need to stop doing that," I thought as I restrained myself from rolling my eyes.

"What is it?" Belphegor crossed his arms over his muscular chest that was covered with a crimson heavy robe.

Carefully, Ry told him what his intention was. Belphegor exchanged a weird gaze with Vassago, but they didn't say anything. Instead, he nodded to give his permission.

"Thanks." Ry gave the princes a subtle nod. Vassago then led us towards the archive.

Once we arrived in front of the wall, as usual Vassago chanted to open it, and we went inside. Just before Vassago closed the door, Seere appeared, blocking the door with his hand, and then he joined us.

"So, what was it you wanted to look for?" Vassago asked as he closed the archive door.

Ry led me to an armchair, and I sat while the other two princes stood next to him as he began to open the book. Vassago immediately followed the others and stood at his side. I quietly looked at him. He seemed too absorbed with the old book he was now staring at to answer Vassago's question.

He carefully opened the book, still in silence. I glanced at the princes, who obviously weren't sure what was on my mate's mind. Their eyes swirled as they gave each other a puzzled look.

"What is it?" Belphegor repeated Vassago's question.

"Nothing. Like I said, I'm curious. That's all," he said lightly.

Belphegor scowled. "Okay, whatever. Now, while you're doing whatever it is you're doing, let's get to the plan. Seere," he said as he nodded at that other prince.

Seere glanced at him and then manifested a firmly sealed scroll from out of nowhere, while Ry just kept continuing his search for whatever it was. Seere opened its seal with some sort of chant and laid it on the table. I saw a glimpse of something that looked like a blueprint.

The prince then held his hand upon the parchment. Soon the old piece of paper glowed ruby-coloured and a transparent image of the blueprint started to emerge from it.

"What's this?" I asked as I stood up from my seat.

Seere gave me a smug smile. "This, Yve, is the blueprint of the place where the Valdam keeps that bloody ring," he said as he pointed at the image.

Ry looked up from the book and frowned at him. "You didn't say anything about having a blueprint before. From what you said earlier, I thought you didn't have anything connected to the place."

Seere winced. "Well, I didn't remember I had this, because it was practically shelved for quite a long time."

I gaped in awe. "Just how in the hell did you get your hands on it?" I glanced back and forth between Seere and the image.

Seere raked his hair and his ruby eyes swirled. "Well, simply put, I once intended to steal something from there, and of course it wasn't the ring, because that would be utter madness," he chuckled.

From the corner of my eyes, I saw the other princes exchange aggravated looks at each other. Seere then cleared his throat. This time, Ry shifted his attention from Seere to the image in front of the prince.

"Back then I went here," Seere said as he pointed the rectangle that denoted a room on the upper left corner of the blueprint. The part he pointed at illuminated in soft ruby before separated itself from the rest. It then transformed into a larger image resembling a chamber full with boxes with various size and designs. Piles of scrolls were also seen scattered all over the place.

"At the time this wasn't the ring's place, and because of the lack of security, I was able to get out before the Valdam noticed."

He lowered his finger and the image of the chamber was back in its place and in its earlier form, the rectangular shape of a room.

Belphegor scoffed at Seere's explanation. "And when exactly did this happen? If this blueprint was made over a thousand years ago, then we can all just forget it."

Seere didn't even bother to turn his gaze towards Belphegor. "And tell me, just what the fuck do you know about the art of stealing?" he asked calmly, but I had no doubt he was trying to keep himself from yelling.

Belphegor gave Seere an upset look in return. "Nothing. I have plenty of other important things to keep me occupied besides learning how to sneak into human houses and chambers acting like a low thief. As if my life hinges on that!" he shot back in the same calm voice, although I could hear a bit of rage in it.

"Enough both of you," Vassago said sharply, and the two princes fell silent. I looked at Ry, who gave me an apologetical smile as if he'd rather I didn't see it.

I shifted my gaze from Ry. "So, what was it you were gonna tell us? Something you wanna say about stealing and this blueprint, yes?" I asked.

Seere cleared his throat. "Yeah, Belphegor here just reminded me that I have to explain a few spells connected with stealing treasures, like the one I used to make this," he said, pointing at the transparent blueprint which glowed a ruby color.

"You see, every time I scout and enter a place of treasures, I mark every corner of it along with every single thing the place contains, forming a blueprint like this one here. In addition to that, I also make a timely connection between the blueprint I have and the actual place, so whenever it changes, either the place itself or things inside it, my blueprint will change as well." He smirked at Ry and me.

"Hence you know the ring has been moved here. You know something changed inside it. That is useful," Ry said, and Seere gave us a smug smile in response.

I observed the blueprint, intending to put his words to a test. I pointed at one of other rooms, the one in the south.

Once I did that, the room I was pointing at separated itself and appeared as a transparent miniature of the real place. As I looked carefully at the image and everything it showed, I realized how detailed this blueprint was. I was so occupied with checking the image that I hardly heard anything else Seere said, although I thought they were discussing something other than the heist.

Seconds later, I'd gone through almost every room in that blueprint. When I pointed at the chamber located at the southeast and the chamber's detail image appeared, suddenly I felt a hand placed on my shoulder. When I looked to my right, I saw Seere's ghastly expression as he stared at the image.

"What is it, Seere?" Vassago asked.

I stepped aside but kept pointing at the image to give Seere some space to check it. "I've got it, Yve," he said, so I lowered my hand.

"This room isn't supposed to look like this," he went on as he pointed at the room I was looking at earlier.

Ry frowned at him and then joined him to check the image. "Something has been changed in here. Is that what you're saying?" he asked while staring at the chamber's miniature.

Seere hesitated before he explained. "Physically everything's still the same as the last time I looked into it."

"You mean, something invisible has been added in here? If that was so, then how can you tell?" I asked.

"That's one way to put it, yeah. All of the things inside it haven't been removed, added to, or lessened. But instead of something concrete, the Valdam's been adding something else," he answered.

"Duh, you still haven't explained anything helpful," I rebuked him in my thought.

Seere held his palm upon the image once again. This time, his other hand stuck to the projection of the chamber. In a second, other things did appear on that projection. Several tiny things I recognized as the Key of Solomon showed up, some were on the floor, while others were made on the ceiling.

Vassago swore under his breath. "Nice! Now how in the hell can you two get in there?" he asked in irritated voice as he pointed the blueprint which glowed innocently in ruby.

I glanced at Ry, who looked equally upset. I shifted my weight to one leg as I observed the blueprint once more. It was then an idea popped into my head. "Hey, guys?"

All of them looked at me. "I don't know if this will work but, is there any way we could take this blueprint along when we're about to going inside?"

Seere considered my question. "Well, I'm not sure, since nobody has ever asked, and usually I wouldn't allow anyone to do so either, but yeah, that's a good idea. Maybe I can try making a copy and lift some of my protective spell while I'm at it, so you two can use it." He inclined his head.

I faced Ry, who obviously had caught the general idea as expected. "Thanks a bunch, Seere," Ry said, giving a subtle nod of thanks.

Belphegor didn't look amused though. "So the only plan for you two here is to simply break in and, because you two know the locations of the seals, you're just gonna undo them, is that it?" he asked. He was definitely not pleased.

I shrugged. "Well, do you have another idea? Besides, we're not sure just yet that this room is the one the Valdam uses to keep that bloody ring, and if this is indeed the one he used, he might change the seal every once in a while. With this, we can tell for sure if he's done so," I said as I tilted my chin towards the image.

Seere shook his head. "Actually, it wasn't just the ring that made me realize it was there. Since its powers are so enormous, it practically blanketed the place, so I can't tell where exactly it is. And not just that. The Valdam also put several Keys of Solomon around the place. No human would have any need to put seals in that massive an amount, one or two maybe, but fifty seals? He's gotta be a Solomon fan if he didn't have any particular need for it but is still using it."

When neither of us said anything, he went on. "And now judging by the whole loads of spells and seals this particular room contains, I think we can be pretty sure that ring is in here. I don't know why the Valdam decided to raise the power level now, but anyway, it's there," he ended in a worried voice.

I bit my lip. "Okay, but that's not gonna change anything. Who knows, the Valdam might be using these seals just to distract us, and the real thing is stored somewhere else with a little less security? Anyhow, unless we find something better, this will be our only plan," I stated firmly.

When none of them said or did anything other than cast a worried gaze at me, I expelled a tired breath. "Look, I know this is risky, but for now it's the only thing we have, and since time is a luxury we don't have–not with that thing screwing around and your dad not having shown his hide–tomorrow we're going in." I gave them an assertive look.

All the males in the room exchanged a look of surrender, and then Ry nodded at me. "All right, we're going in, because I don't see the need for you to see his father's hide." He jerked his head at Belphegor.

Hearing his comment, we all burst out in laughter. After a moment, Seere cleared his throat. "Okay, I'll do some mojo with this tonight. Tomorrow, the ring's all yours." He lifted his finger off the image, and the chamber went back to its original lined shape. Seere then raised his hand again, and the image slowly descended onto the piece of parchment. It glowed a little brighter before the light completely vanished. He resealed the scroll and dissolved it into thin air.

Ry–who knew what was on his mind?–went back to his search in the book, so in my attempt to get his attention, I tapped my fingers on the table. Luckily, he did avert his gaze from the old book. "What is it?" he asked.

"Nothing. I was just wondering what time would be best for us to go. Would it be tonight or later before dawn?" I crossed my arms across my chest.

Belphegor gave me a droll stare. "You sure you still need some scouting now that you'll be bringing Seere's map along when you get in?"

When I was about to answer, Seere held out his hand to cut me off. "No, she's right. I didn't exactly cover everything in this blueprint. Other things surrounding the area aren't here, but you guys can do it just before you get in though."

I inhaled a little and then released my breath. "Okay, oh and by the way, now that we'll be carrying this with us, we don't need your demonikyn any more, do we?" I asked him as I made a gesture towards his blueprint.

Ry immediately shook his head. His white-platinum long hair fell just slightly over his perfectly sculptured face. "No, we still need them. If it's all right with you, Seere, I think we still need them to check the outer area of the place and in case we're separated, unless you could make two of these, because I really don't want us get lost and then by dumb luck, one of us, or better yet, the two of us get trapped in one of those seals." His swirling sapphire eyes fell on Seere.

The prince nodded at Ry's suggestion. "Yeah, I've considered that as well. I'll make two copies. With my demonikyn, you won't need to go scouting the place in advance."

"If there are two of these, then we won't need them inside, thanks." A grateful smile broke on the edge of Ry's lips.

"Now everything's settled, when will you two go there? You at least need some time to look around," Belphegor said.

Weirdly enough, Ry once again shook his head. "There's not enough time before dawn. I say both of us wait until tomorrow night and use what time we have now to fully regain our strength," he said as he closed the book and glanced at me.

Arching a brow, I gave him a droll stare. "May I ask what is on your mind? Not even I dare think of breaking into a place full of the Key of Solomon without taking a *really* close look at it first."

Ry simply cast an understanding look at me. "I know. I wouldn't want to do this either, but the clock is ticking, and we have to do this as fast as we can, *I* have to do this," he said. There was a hint of impatience and extreme caution in his deep, masculine voice.

Vassago frowned deeply at him. "I get what you mean when you say we don't have much time, not with Belphegor's dad looking for you in outrage and those stupid Arcs out there as well. Not to mention that mongrel Arzia's been wreak havoc around here, but what do you mean 'I have to do this'?"

Ry looked as if he realized he'd just said something he wasn't supposed to, and then he cleared his throat. "Nothing, never mind," he said hastily.

"Boy, who do you think we are? Some human idiots?" Belphegor narrowed his crimson gaze at him.

Seere snickered. "Just accept it, Ry. We know you're hiding something. It's not like we've only known you since yesterday."

"Thank you, gentlemen." I gave them a nod of thanks for backing me up in asking what was running through his mind.

"You're welcome," Belphegor said. His crimson eyes were still swirling at Ry, who definitely looked uneasy.

Ry grimaced. "It's nothing. I've just misspoken. That's all," he insisted.

I rolled my eyes. "Right honey, is it 'misspoken' or 'slipped'?" I asked him in an accusing tone, and I gave him a chiding stare as I tried to ignore his jibe.

"I assure you, it was misspoken. I didn't mean it that way." he gave me a crooked smile that almost melted me. If I didn't know any better, I would've thought that was what he intended . . .

"Whatever, if you don't wanna talk now, you gotta tell us after we get the ring." I stared directly into his eyes, hoping I was the one who melted him and not the other way round.

He sighed heavily. "You just won't take 'it's nothing' for an answer, will you?" he asked slowly.

I made a face at him, pretending I was thinking. "Hmm . . . let me see, no, I won't take 'it's nothing' or 'never mind' or anything else that doesn't give us anything useful as an answer," I said sarcastically.

The princes let out a snort at my words. "Give it up, Ry. There's no way you could weasel your way out from her," Belphegor chuckled.

Ry then ran his hand through his hair. "All right, after the ring." He raised his hand in surrender.

Seere put one hand on his hip. "Now, if there's nothing else, I'd like to go back to my chamber and start the mojo. Would you mind, Vassago?"

The owner of this place still stared at Ry for few seconds before he headed towards the door. All of us followed him, and we all separated after we got outside the archive.

"Yve, Ry," Vassago called us when we were just walking several steps from them.

"Yeah?" Ry and I whirled around to face them. Seere was already out of sight.

"Belphegor and I agreed that you two have to stay in your chamber as long as you're here, and Belphegor will do the same. My chamber's protection spells may not be as strong as the archive's, but they still have some strength, perhaps enough to cover your powers while you're here," he explained.

"Just to make sure that when daddy bastard decides to pay a visit, he won't notice us, or so I hope," Belphegor added bitterly.

I glanced at Ry, who seemed to be considering their request. A second later he nodded. "All right, I understand. We won't be going anywhere until tomorrow night when we'll be off to get the Ring."

"Yeah, don't worry, we'll be in there like a dead human in a coffin, getting in but not getting out," I inserted sardonically as I gave them a are-you-satiesfied look.

"That's an overstatement, but yeah, it pretty much covers the idea of 'stay in your chamber'. Well, you know." Belphegor grinned at us.

"Fine, you two can go back now. We'll head back to ours," Vassago said as he jerked his head towards the hallway in the direction to Ry's and my chamber.

"We'll see you downstairs tomorrow night." Belphegor tilted his chin.

We both answered him with a subtle nod, and the next second, both of them disappeared without a trace. "Come on." Ry took my hand and led us back inside our chamber with me still wondering what was inside his head.

Chapter 20

We stayed in our chamber for the rest of the day, hardly doing anything in particular. Ry still didn't elaborate on why in the hell we didn't go out there scouting before we had to sneak into the place.

And there was something else which I didn't know if it could be called the worst or the best thing that happened during our stay. He had us transform into our human forms again.

I didn't even have a clue why he seemed to enjoy himself every second he looked at me in this form, which, to be honest, I detested to the core of my being. Luckily, it wasn't as if he'd come to realize that he preferred me in this stupid form.

He barely talked about the plan too, and that irritated me, but when I looked at his handsome face and the hint of doubt that we would succeed in carrying out this whole brilliant suicide plan, I decided not to add his worries. So, I had a chat with him as we lay on that enormous bed.

We talked about many things—what he'd been doing after Lucifer attacked him, why he decided to save his sworn brother, how he even knew that Xaemorkahn was there, what it was like up there when he went to steal Herathim, and so on. As expected, he didn't give me a detailed answer to each of those questions, but at least he was willing to share the general idea with me.

He even told me that he'd met this guy named Varhorren or something when he was out there in one of those dimensions, I forgot which. This guy was also searching for that Arzia thing, because it had slaughtered his companions and, more to the point, his family. The amazing part was that this guy supposedly lived from around the same time as that Xiveira person. Talk about an old man.

Aside from that, Ry was most reluctant to tell me about his state after Lucifer's attack. When I thought about it, perhaps he just wouldn't want me to feel guilty all over again for not being there with him. Most likely I would cry my tears out if that happened, and

I figured he just didn't want to make me feel that way again, so I braced myself and insisted that he should tell me.

As he'd predicted, that familiar wave of despair stirred in me as he told me about the mortal danger and the searing pain he was in after the Dark Light burned the crap out of him. I held my breath as I fought the tears to prevent them flowing out like before, otherwise he probably wouldn't talk about his troubles or burdens ever again.

Our small talk made us lose track of time. When the night had fallen outside, we realized that Vassago hadn't even once come to our door. I hoped that was because Belphegor's pop never turned his nose this way, or worse, towards Vrae and Zade.

"Come on, Yve," he finally said as he transformed back into his true form and walked towards the door and opened it.

I did the same with my form. "Okay," I said, and then followed him. I walked through the door that was held open by him. After that we went down the hallway. When we had passed the wall where the archive room was located, we finally reached the stairs that led to the hall below. As we reached the bottom of the stairs, we saw the three princes were already waiting for us.

"It's about time you two showed up." Belphegor jerked his head at us. There was a mischievous glint in his crimson eyes which I chose to ignore.

"Sorry, we weren't exactly staring at the clock all day when we were locked up inside as you had suggested," I retorted as I gave him a sarcastic grin.

Ry sniffed and simply nodded at the other princes.

"So are you ready?" Vassago asked.

I exchanged looks with Ry. His sapphire-coloured eyes swirled as he gave me a soft gaze. He lifted his eyes from me to the princes. "We're ready. He's not coming any time soon, is he, Belphegor?" he asked meaningfully.

Belphegor shook his head. "Vassago still hasn't sensed him up to this point, so I guess you're good to go."

I nodded, feeling a bit grateful. "Right, that's convenient."

Seere suddenly made a movement. He manifested two parchments out of thin air and handed them to Ry and myself. "These are the copies you wanted. Try opening them. Unlike mine, there are no complex locks, so you can open them simply by willing them open," he explained.

Hesitantly, I willed it open, and just like he said, the blueprint glowed, but weirdly enough, mine glowed pitch black, while Ry's emitted a sapphire-coloured light.

I glanced at Ry, who looked satisfied. "So, this is what you meant by no complex locks. You added a simple yet effective one."

Seere arched his brows. "Again, you catch on quickly. It's irritating sometimes, you know."

Hearing their conversation, I realized what Ry meant about the lock. Seere had made a lock that could only be opened by the first person to open it. Hence each parchment emitted our signature powers.

We spread the blueprints in our hands, but when I expected transparent images would appear like the original one belonging to Seere, I was wrong. Instead of images jutting out of it, the blueprint stayed in the parchment, but there were several dots that sparkled all over it.

"I take it these are the seals?" I asked as I pointed at the dots.

Seere nodded. "I made it a little simpler than the one I have, but with pretty much the same principal. If you pointed at one room, the detailed image would appear. If you want to close it, just close the parchment, like the usual human map. There's something quite neat though. If someone other than you opened the parchments when it's locked, they would only find an empty parchment."

"It's quite neat. Is there anything else we need to know?" I asked him as Ry and I closed the parchment. Sure enough, nothing weird happened to the parchment except that it stopped glowing.

Seere shook his head. "Nope, there's nothing else."

Ry nodded and gave his salute to the three princes. "Very well, everything's settled. Thanks, Your Highnesses. We'll be back with the ring ASAP. Let's go, Yve." Ry pulled me along.

"Not so fast, you two," Seere held his hand up to stop us.

Ry paused and turned to the prince. "What is it, Seere? Is there anything else you wish to tell us before we go in?"

"My point exactly. I'm escorting you two as close as I can," he said as he exchanged firm looks with the others.

I crossed my arms across my chest and frowned. "Why? You'll be risking yourself if you go anywhere near that place."

"I know that, but there's been a change of plans. The three of us agreed that I have to take you two through the rift. We don't have the slightest clue as to when the old bastard might show his hide here, and according to Vassago, you'll only have ten seconds warning before he actually lands here. Needless to say, that's not enough time to do anything."

Vassago confirmed this. "He's right. Anyway, he'll leave his doppelganger to escort you back here through the same way. It won't be dangerous for him if it's only a doppelganger."

"All right, let's get on with it then. You both be careful if he does show." Ry jerked his head towards the door.

"No sweat, just stay alive and don't get caught." Belphegor lifted the edge of his lips.

Seere abruptly chanted something, and the air was ripped open in our faces. He turned to us. "I've opened the rift. Come on." He jerked his head at the gaping hole behind him and then stepped inside it.

We glanced at Vassago and Belphegor. "We'll be seeing you two later," Ry said, and he entered the opened rift. I waved towards the princes and followed Ry.

And as if to prove the princes' suspicions, the thunderous tormenting scream that we had heard few days before when upstairs' scum landed suddenly echoed as the rift slowly closed behind us.

Ry swore under his breath. "He's coming. Can he sense us in here?"

"Don't worry, we're safe," Seere said calmly.

When the hole was completely closed, pitch-black darkness engulfed us. "We'll be walking through the darkness of the rift for a while. Just follow me and stay close. One wrong move, and you might fall into another realm, and the worst case scenario is that you won't be able to come back for the rest of your existence," Seere warned us both, and he started walking ahead of us.

I bit my lip and felt Ry squeeze my hand. "Okay, stay close, no problems at all," I said as Ry pulled me, and we followed him.

As we made our way in the darkness, I couldn't help my thoughts as they wandered off to Vassago and Belphegor. "Do you think they'll be all right?" I muttered to Ry, who walked by my side. He looked down at me and just gave me a warm smile. But even that couldn't hide the fact that he felt as worried as I was.

Seere kept on walking as he answered my question. "They will be okay. As long as Vassago got Belphegor in his archive and Belphegor's not looking for trouble, I think it's safe to presume that they're both just fine," he said in a flat voice.

"Oh, okay," was all I could say after hearing his explanation. I sighed a bit in relief. I couldn't bear to think how I would face them if something bad happened to them because they were helping us. Not just that, they had given us shelter after we'd unofficially become fugitives.

We followed Seere for a while, not knowing what was happening back at Vassago's castle after our departure.

*   *   *

"Get in!" Vassago whispered harshly to Belphegor as he held open the archive's door.

Belphegor hastily went inside and stopped dead near the door to face his friend. "Okay, but be careful with that old snob. And try not to get killed. You're no good to me dead." He let out a scoffing laugh.

"You'll be the cause of my death if you don't let me shut this fucking door now! Just stay here, and don't use any damn energy or he'll sense you. I'll take care of that old bastard." Vassago gave him a chilling stare as he started to close the door.

"Yeah, yeah, stop the scolding already." Belphegor jerked his head at the door. Vassago started for the door, glanced at the North Prince, and then he shut the door.

The second Vassago closed the door, the castle shook tremendously, and deafening screams echoed in every corner of his place. Clenching his teeth, he hurriedly willed himself outside through the shadows.

When he hit the ground outside his castle, an extremely lethal presence welcomed him, as if its owner were waiting to devour him. Reeks of death immediately engulfed Vassago as he glanced around warily. The grass on the barren field was reduced to nothing but ashes, the soil was blackened, and every living being within few miles' radius around had been obliterated.

"Vassago." A chilling low voice came from the all-powerful devil before him—Belphegor's father and mortal enemy, Lucifer.

Bracing himself, he closed the distance between him and Devil King. "My Lord Lucifer," he greeted the Son of Perdition as he knelt before him and put his arm upon his chest.

"It has been a long time since we last met." Lucifer hissed his greeting with the same cold voice as he gave him a scathing glare.

"Indeed, My Lord. It truly is an honour to have you here in my exile," Vassago said humbly to his Lord.

In his thoughts, he swore and cursed the Devil before him. Yeah, like he didn't know jack shit about him. It had been too long since he had ceased to have any actual respect towards his master. At the moment, however, he couldn't afford to jeopardize his companions, most of all, Belphegor. He was involved too damn deep in this shit, but that was the least of his concerns. His loyalty and honour would never let him do anything close to betrayal.

"Is it, Vassago?" Lucifer let out a low evil laugh.

Vassago winced at his question. "Is it what, My Lord?"

"I'm asking you, is it true? Is it really an honour for you to have me here before your fancy shadow castle?" His voice turned even colder than before.

Vassago was never someone to take lightly, but even with all his power, he couldn't overcome the threatening aura that enveloped this one Devil. The danger he felt was like walls closing in around his body as if they wanted to crush him.

"Well of course, My Lord." Vassago tried to sound aghast at his question. Well, frankly, it did surprise him.

"Is it indeed?" Lucifer scoffed. "So I take it you know what has been going on around here, the slaughter of archangels and my meeting with the pair of scum, Michael and Gabriel?" He suddenly changed the subject, or so it seemed.

Wanted to play it careful, Vassago kept his face as stoic as possible. "I did hear some vague news about it. From what I heard, the culprit is still on the loose, and forgive me, My Lord, but I also heard a disturbing rumour. Fortunately, it's an unsubstantiated one, so I take it I should not be bothered," he said as calmly as he could.

"Disturbing rumour? Was it really just that, or did someone that was involved in it give you insights?" he asked sharply.

"Forgive me, My Lord, but I'm not sure I follow you," Vassago said, while attempting to keep his voice steady, all the while cursing in his thoughts. *"Crap, does he really suspect me or does he throw this bullshit at everyone he meets?"*

"You do know all about my despicable son's activity, do you not? In that regard, I believe he would take drastic measures just to anger me." More lethal aura spread from Lucifer's body, an aura that was so deadly, it practically showed the wrath of hell.

Vassago waited for the very thing he knew Lucifer wanted to say to him. "Drastic measures, My Lord?" Vassago prompted carefully as he grimaced.

"Protecting Ezryan, for instance?" he asked. At the moment he mentioned Ezryan's name, his body emitted an even deadlier aura that felt like it was fracturing the prince's spine from within.

That second, Vassago literally trembled despite his efforts not to. He wondered how his old friend could stand all this tremendous energy. Either Lucifer had held back during his encounter with his son, or Belphegor did have what it takes to behold such a murderous aura.

"More of this shit and he might as well choke me to death." Vassago cursed in his thoughts, all the while making an almost desperate attempt to hold his ground. Clearing his throat, he then answered Lucifer's question with another, "Ezryan, My Lord? He died, did he not? Surely he didn't manage to get himself out of the way of God's Light? Well, even if by the most ridiculous luck, he did manage to escape, we'd most likely have heard news of his whereabouts way before now, wouldn't we, My Lord?" Vassago asked as politely as he could.

Yeah, like he wasn't the one who tried to waste the young devil commander . . .

Hearing Vassago's question, Lucifer shot him another deadly glare, and without warning, Vassago's body suddenly floated a few inches above the ground as his feet straightened and he was no longer in his kneeling position.

"My Lord?" his voice trembled. He had no idea what the intention of his master was. Out of the blue, Vassago felt tremendous pressure on his neck that blocked his windpipe. "My . . . Lord . . . please . . . what have . . . I . . . done?" Vassago choked the question out of his throat.

"It's not a question of what you *have* done. It's rather what you haven't," Lucifer said lazily.

"Could he be any more fucking vague than that? I'd appreciate him a bit if he wasn't playing with my throat and looking pretty while doing it!" Vassago bit back his words as he tried to get some air into his lungs.

"What you haven't done, Vassago, is convince me that you indeed know nothing about Ezryan's location and furthermore, about the dispute that went on between me and him." Lucifer held his hand with his palm facing outward. Using his powers, he pulled the choking prince closer to him.

"What . . . do . . . you mean . . . My Lord? Please . . ." Vassago pleaded. He was trying his best not to retaliate and save his own life, well, for few seconds at least . . .

Upon Vassago's plea, Lucifer's gaze darkened, and instead of loosening his hold on the prince's throat, he put on even more pressure, and this time he willed his power to slowly crush Vassago's innards.

It took no time for Vassago to cough and choke in his own blood. He felt a sharp pain invade his eyes and his eardrums, and hot fluid began to flow out of them.

"Are you ready to speak, Vassago?" A beautiful yet twisted smile broke on his face.

Vassago almost gave up to the dire situation he was in. He could barely see anything aside from his master and hear the wind blow next to his ears. He almost couldn't stop himself from attempting an attack and thus escape from a grand opportunity to meet Azrael. The prince cursed his own master in his thoughts. *"I've gotta hold on, dammit!"*

The pressure was nowhere near lifted off of him, and he vomited blood while at the same time he tried his hardest not to faint. But not even he could stand any more of Lucifer's atrocities towards his insides without using any of his powers. "My . . . Lord . . ." he muttered in desperation.

Lucifer narrowed his gaze angrily as he realized he'd failed once again to gain the information he needed. "Fuck! Where the hell did that little scum go?" His thunderous roar nearly made Vassago's eardrums bleed.

Not that he needed any more bloodshed on his part.

All of a sudden, the pressure was no more. Vassago dropped to the ground and landed on his knees. He was still coughing when he saw Lucifer shoot him with a lethal glare that mirrored his desire for carnage. "Very well, you've proven that you have nothing to do with that despicable traitor. I will leave for now, but mark my words carefully. If later on I find out otherwise, I'll have your entrails for decoration inside the Echelons' chamber," he said coldly.

After giving this crystal-clear threat, he rose up to the sky and flew away, bringing along every horror and death on the forest below him.

"Go blow yourself!" Vassago swore under his breath as he immediately willed himself into his castle.

When he got in, he barely made it to opening the archive's door with the remainder of his powers. The second the door opened, Belphegor rushed outside just in time to see his old friend fall before him.

"Vassago!" he yelled, just in time to catch the prince as he collapsed onto the immaculate floor of his castle. The withered prince slightly averted his gaze at Belphegor as he kept on bleeding profusely. "Come on, I'll take you to your chamber!" Belphegor said, and they both vanished.

A second later, Belphegor had his friend lying on the bed in his luxurious chamber. The North Prince immediately checked Vassago's wounds. "Not good. Your innards are crushed like crispy potatoes, along with all stupid poison he left behind. That old prick, he'll fucking pay for this!" he cursed as he used his powers to heal Vassago, who still had blood flowing from his eyes, nose, ears, and mouth.

"Dammit, Ry, Yve, don't you dare fail us, or worse, die on us," Belphegor said in his own thoughts as he continued to use his healing powers on his withered friend.

Chapter 21

"Here," Seere said as he opened the rift in front of us. "This is the closest I can get you." He stepped out of the hole, followed by Ry and myself.

We had arrived at the edge of a cliff, from where we could look into another forest below and a fortress surrounded by it.

As I looked at it, recognition slammed me hard like a huge rock. "That fortress is the place? But that's . . ."

"Yes, the Great Fortress of Asael. I see you still haven't forgotten this place, Yve," Ry said quietly as he gave me that soft, soothing gaze of his.

I cursed inwardly. How could I forget? This place was where I received my first duty as a Cherxanain to bring forth humans' cruel nature. I could never erase the beauty of carnage that once happened in that place. Just through one simple whisper, I made the human king, what was his name? Oh yeah, Norgan. He went insane, well, so to speak. He acted out of pure anger and hatred, and he ended up slaughtering everyone. Not only his enemies when he was out in the battlefield, he also garrotted and impaled anyone around him, and I meant anyone.

Friends.

Allies.

Family.

And the last life he took was his own, when he finally came to realize what he had done. And so, he gutted himself, and I watched him bleed to death as his entrails splattered all over.

I, without meaning to use the name of the old bastard friend of mine, took the *pride* for being the cause of that. But maybe because that was my very first job and seeing that horrendous scene, it made me feel somewhat uneasy. Ry knew about this, and this was one of few things I'd never tell anybody about, even my sister.

"You know this place? You didn't say nada when you looked at the blueprint before," Seere said as he left the rift open and started calling forth his doppelganger.

"That's because I didn't exactly make one of those blueprint. I barely remember what the layout looked like, let alone in line shape. Besides, the details I saw hardly had any resemblance to the place back then." I pointed at the fortress.

I glanced at the prince and, weirdly enough, for a second I could've sworn he gave Ry a knowing look.

Knowing about what, I had no idea.

The moment his doppelganger appeared, Seere gave it brief instructions and then faced us once again. "Well, be careful, you guys. I'm leaving my doppelganger here. He'll wait for you, but if you need him, just shoot red sparks, and he'll come to your aid. See ya later," he said as he turned towards the rift and started to walk back in.

"Wait, he has those demonikyn as well, right?" Ry asked him. He stopped and turned to look at us. "Yeah, not as much as mine, though. Why?"

"I intend to ask him to let them loose before we enter the place. You said it yourself–you didn't include the outer surroundings in this." Ry showed the map he carried.

Seere nodded. "Sure, like I said, I summoned him to aid you both anyway."

"Thanks, give our regards to those two. We'll be back soon." Ry gave a salute to the prince.

"Will do." We watched him move himself into the hole and vanish the second the rift was closed, leaving nothing but thin air behind.

Ry then turned his gaze towards the doppelganger and spoke with him for a minute. After he was finished, he came to me and held my waist. "Come on Yve, we have no time to lose," he said, and then he began to make his way towards the fortress.

"Okay," I said. He held my hand firmly as we walked side by side, followed by Seere's doppelganger down the single narrow path away from the cliff.

"Can't we just flash ourselves straight there, or at least fly? There's nobody around that can sense us, let alone see us, and the

Valdam's also a human." I looked at him as we drew close to the massive fortress.

He scoffed. "Yeah, and run into some unknown spells out front? Baby, we haven't even started yet." He laughed and then jerked his head at the doppelganger that walked silently behind us. "That's why I asked him to check it out first. Once we get in, he'll be back here waiting for our return."

I sighed wearily. "I know. I heard you with Seere before, but I'm just saying, couldn't we at least fly so we can land few meters from the gate, not walk several kilometres from here. I mean we're wasting our time here, and meanwhile Belphegor, Vassago, and Seere could be dead for all we know."

"No, they won't," Ry said calmly, but I could see his eyes gleamed with wariness.

"I hope you're right," I muttered.

Neither one of us said anything as we approached the fortress. We encountered nothing peculiar on our way there, just pebbles, grass, and some other things on the side of the road.

Minutes later we finally hit the bottom of the hill and reached the area around the fortress. The trees were as close as ever. The three of us split up and hid behind trees just a few meters from the main gate. I positioned myself to Ry's right, and Seere's doppelganger stood just a few steps from him.

"Zha'kra Ezryan," the doppelganger called him with Seere's heavy voice.

"What is it?"

"Shall I spread the demonikyn now?" The doppelganger gazed at the huge and firmly shut gate.

"Well," Ry said as he looked around us. "I don't feel anything weird right now. Yve, you sense anything?" he turned from the doppelganger to me.

I opened my whole senses to reach the ether to check if there was any uninvited presence around. After a moment, I could sense nothing aside from Ry and Seere's doppelganger, so I shook my head. "Everything's as still as a doornail."

"All right, we better move. You may unleash some of them. We'll move to the far left wall. It would be ridiculous if we went through the front door."

I chuckled. "Yeah, I imagine the Valdam would welcome us, boil us some tea, and give us some nice cookies."

"And then make a jam out of us," he inserted as he laughed quietly. I glanced at the doppelganger that stared at us in horror. Obviously, he'd never seen devils take the phrase 'you'll be locked in a jar for the rest of your existence' as a simple joke.

"Very well, far left wall it is," he said, and he made his way slowly. We followed him and then stopped dead just at the edge of the forest.

We gave our surroundings a final once-over. When we were certain nothing as annoying as a human ambush was around, or worse, Arcs wanting to play, Ry gave a "go" to the doppelganger. "You can start using them from here. Make sure the way is indeed secure from here up to the wall. Once we're inside, you can wait for us back at the cliff."

He nodded, and without another word he extended his arm forth just at his waist height with his palm face down. By the look on his face, he seemed to be concentrating on something. Sure enough, his palms glowed ruby like a conjurer's aura. In the next second, several tiny things popped out from them and transformed into some small beings that looked like devils.

The doppelganger spread those demonikyns between where we stood and few feet ahead of us. At first, we saw none of them trapped or stumble on anything out of ordinary. Several heartbeats later, Ry told the doppelganger to lead the way as he unleashed more demonikyns. Then he moved forward and signalled me to follow after him.

We cautiously followed him as the doppelganger kept on spreading the demonikyns all the way until we reached the wall. Fortunately for us, nothing happened. Ry faced the doppelganger and asked him to take away all the demonikyns he'd unleashed after we stepped onto the upper part of the wall.

After that, Ry and I flew together and landed on the wall. We turned for a moment to see the doppelganger pull back all the demonikyns and move away from us. As we watched him disappear behind the trees, I began to feel uneasy about all this.

We turned around, and Ry pulled out the blueprint Seere had given us. He stared at it for a second before it glowed in sapphire and opened.

"This is the gate." He pointed at a gate symbol that glowed at the bottom center part of the parchment. "We're here, on the far left wall." He went on and pointed at the line at left side of the gate.

"Okay, and here's the room where Valdam holds a fire sale with those seals," I said as I gestured at the room image on the upper right.

"Yeah, and the way there isn't exactly a cakewalk either. See these?" His forefinger traced the blueprint image without touching the parchment, starting from the wall where we were standing right now up to the ring's room–well, assuming it *was* there. Like he said, it was no cakewalk. There were seals and some other containment spells almost every step of the way. Not to mention small icons of swords, spears, and other things that looked like traps for humans. Fortunately for us, traps for humans didn't mean much against devils.

I rolled my eyes at the image on the parchment. "Might as well blow this whole place to the ground."

Ry chuckled. "That's a pretty good idea actually, if we don't consider the possibility that that ring might be taken away by that Valdam just before the fortress collapsed, or it might get buried, or worse yet, destroyed with the rest of them. Yeah, that's a pretty good idea."

I scowled at his comment. "I know, just thinking out loud. There's no need to be Prince Charming of the Year."

He laughed at my retort. His deep rich voice soothed the uneasiness I felt about commencing this plan a bit.

"Should we split up?" I asked him.

He inclined his head, and his long silver hair fell over the side of his breath-taking beautiful face. "No, we split up only when we are forced to do so, okay?"

I looked at him, and even though his face remained stoic, I could see glimpses of wariness and his intention to protect me every step of the way in his swirling sapphire eyes. A wave of passion warmed my soul as he gazed deeply into my eyes. Smiling, I gave him a subtle nod. "All right, sounds good to me. So, shall we?" I jerked my head towards the ground.

He nodded. "Come on."

We jumped from the wall and landed silently on the grass below. Still holding open the blueprint, Ry eyed the hallway part.

"Ever been to this part of the fortress before?" he asked.

I shook my head and then looked around the place. When I saw a dark hallway at the right wing, I pointed at it. "I'd only been to the king's and the royal family's wing. The room where the ring is must be where they kept treasures. I remembered Norgan, the human king, told me about this place. It held many traps, and of course he assumed I was a human fool just like he was. Hence he forbade me to get any closer to this place. He didn't wanna risk losing his *advisor*," I ended sarcastically.

He let out a scoffing laugh. "All right, anyhow, according to this blueprint, we'll be fine for at least fifty feet, so stay close to me," he said.

"Okay, come on," I replied, and then both of us moved deeper into the hallway. The odour of thick dust hung tight in the air with barely any stench of human anywhere, let alone signs belonging to any living being.

It was hard to believe there were humans in here.

We glanced around in extreme vigilance as we made our way towards the room where the ring was hidden.

Moments later, when I was looking behind us, suddenly Ry held his hand out in front of me. "Stop!" he said sharply.

"What is it?" I asked as my eyes fell on him.

He pointed to the ceiling up ahead. "Look."

I turned my gaze in the direction he was pointing, and what I saw would pretty much explain why he stopped me in the first place. There was one seal on the ceiling.

I raised a brow. "Only one? And here I thought we'd be facing more of those things," I said as I put one hand on my hip.

"And you're right. Look over there." He pointed few steps farther.

There was another one, but it was covered under quite thick dust. It was hardly visible from where I was standing. We couldn't tell if there were seals on the walls because of the old paintings that hung on them, and the floor was covered with carpet thick with dust, as if the guardian or whoever took residence here never bothered to make this place decent enough to live in.

"Real cute," I said irritably as I narrowed my gaze at the sight.

I faced Ry, whose brows formed one hard line as his eyes went back and forth between those seals and the blueprint in his hand. He extended his long forefinger and put it on the parchment. I stepped next to him so I could see the blueprint. Now it showed the place where we were standing at the moment. It turned from its long rectangular shape into an exact image of the darkened hallway.

What I saw there really annoyed me. There were other seals on the floor beneath the carpet, on the walls behind those stupid paintings, and on the ceilings as well. It looked more like a giant containment for devils than the hallway of an abandoned human fortress.

Ry let out a weary breath. "We'd better play this part carefully, Yve," he said quietly.

I curled my lips. "Undo these seals carefully and, more to the point, silently, you mean."

He nodded.

"Let's get it started then." I took few steps away from him, transformed my black robe into wings, and ascended slowly to the ceiling. I unleashed a bit of my energy to break the seal as quietly as possible, followed with a cracking sound. A small charred hole formed on it.

"That should do it," I said, but I was not entirely sure. I wanted to test it, so I flew into the centre of the seal and hesitantly went back to where Ry was standing. Luckily, as Seere had told us, the little hole I made was enough. I could fly through it.

"This one's done. Show me the next one." I landed on the carpet, and my wings transformed back into black robes. The pile of dust on the carpet was blown away as my feet touched it.

He shook his head. "No, I'll handle the rest. Open your map," he said as he folded his map and slipped it underneath his robe.

I shrugged and pulled out mine. "Well, go ahead and knock yourself out."

He replied with a grin. I pointed out to him every seal that was painted in the hallway. It took quite some time to undo them all, not to mention there were pairs of seals here and there. Ry almost walked into one of those the moment we had reached halfway that led towards the ring's room. He'd just undone a seal on the ceiling and was about to move on when I noticed something on the blueprint. I didn't see it in the hallway because of the rug spread on top of it, but the map showed that there was another seal waiting silently to catch him. I stopped him in time before he stepped on it.

At times like this, the guardian really irritated me. Whoever he was, he was really wasting our precious time, not to mention stupid booby traps for humans. We encountered several stupid traps where sword and spears were shot at us from inside the wall and the floor in exchange for the seals.

After quite a long time, we finally managed to get through all the stupid booby traps. There was nothing in the hallway for a few feet afterward. We stopped in front of a sturdy door made of gold. It still had its ancient grandness despite all the dust that covered it.

I folded the map and eyed the door. "It looks like a normal door." I examined the gold door closely with Ry standing next to me.

"Let me check the blueprint." He extended his hand to me.

"Sure," I said, and I handed him the parchment.

He unfolded the blueprint and eyed it. Seconds later, he averted his gaze and looked at me. "There's nothing on the door, but . . ."

"But what?" I prompted.

Ry's swirling sapphire eyes moved to the blueprint again. Then he exhaled heavily, and judging by his dismal face, I dared say it wouldn't be pleasant. "Taking that ring will be a tad bit difficult," he said.

Without saying anything, I stepped beside him to get a better look at it. "What is it?"

When I could see what was on it, I finally understood what had disturbed him, and I almost couldn't stop myself from destroying the entire room. The seals seemed to have doubled and now covered nearly every inch of the room.

Chapter 22

From what I remembered when I checked the blueprint at the gate, there were only five Keys of Solomon, but now there were several magic circles that'd bound any inhuman visitors. That certainly was a nuisance.

"Now how in the hell do we get pass this crap?" I asked Ry, rather upset at the sight.

He sighed abruptly. "Okay, there are seals on every side of the room, in gloriously large numbers I might add, so in theory, there's no way we could destroy one and not get caught in another . . ." His voice faded.

"Ry?" I asked carefully. By the look on his face, he might've come up with something.

He shifted his gaze to me. "Step aside, Yve, against the wall." He jerked his head at the wall on the right side of the door and shoved the parchment underneath his sapphire robe.

I gave him a puzzled gaze. "Why do I have to stand against the wall?"

He gave me a persistent look in return, so I did what he said without arguing any further. He walked to the opposite side of the room and stared at the door. Suddenly, he summoned forth his doppelganger.

Strangely enough, his doppelganger was powerless.

"Zha'kra?" His doppelganger asked. He obviously didn't have any clue why his master would call him and strip him off of his powers.

"Sorry, gotta take all of your juice for the moment," Ry answered him.

"Is something the matter?" he answered with the same deep voice as Ry.

Ry nodded. "Behind this sturdy door, there's an item we need you to take."

The doppelganger glanced at me and gave me salute. "It's an honour to meet you, Shakra Yverna," he said.

I winced at his greeting. "Uhm, likewise," I replied as I glanced at Ry and arched a brow at him.

Ry cleared his throat, and his doppelganger looked back at him. "The reason why I temporarily stripped you of your powers is because behind this door there are several Keys of Solomon, including some on the side that faces the door."

I grimaced as I cursed inwardly for not paying more attention to the seals' positions inside. No wonder he'd asked me to step aside and stand against the wall. It wouldn't be funny one bit if he opened the door and I got trapped inside.

With that thought in my mind, I shivered as I continued to look at them both. "I see, Zha'kra. If I still had my demonic powers, I'd most likely be trapped. Thank you," he said as he gestured his gratefulness.

"Don't mention it. So now, like I told you before, there's an item, a ring. Supposedly it has a stone in the shape of a six-pointed star attached to it." He held his forefinger and his thumb close together to indicate a tiny thing.

"You want me to take it?" he asked.

"I want you to take it," Ry said as he folded his arms across his chest.

"Very well, is there anything else I need to know before I enter the room?"

"Well, there are traps for humans, if that's what you're asking."

He cringed. "Right, and with my powers gone, I'd better not trigger those, had I?"

"Don't worry, I'll tell you which way to walk." Ry once again pulled out his blueprint.

Looking uneasy, the doppelganger nodded. "Anything else I should know?"

Ry shook his head. "I guess there's nothing else for now. So are you ready?" The doppelganger nodded, and a determined expression similar to Ry's whenever he set his mind on something appeared on his face.

"Okay, here goes. Be careful," Ry said. He then averted his gaze and stared at the door. Slowly, the big golden door was pushed opened. As the sturdy door moved steadily, I saw the doppelganger's eyes widen as he began to see what was on the other side. "There are so many treasures in here," he said in amazement. Well, just as the dead human king told me once about this place, they did keep treasures here.

Actually, it surprised me that these treasures had been left untouched. I thought human robbers would already have helped themselves until nothing was left but dust. I guessed it was no wonder Seere was attracted to it. He'd enjoy playing with them.

"There it is. There's a glass box containing a small golden ring with that stone of a six-pointed star attached to it, just like you said." The doppelganger nodded at the centre of the room.

As Seere had told us, the ring emitted an unfathomable yet strong aura. I could sense it where I stood. If I didn't know any better, I'd say the aura was of the holy . . .

The doppelganger cautiously walked in. When he finally got inside, he exhaled in relief. "I can get through the seals!" he shouted.

Ry brought his doppelganger to a stop. "Wait. I wanna try taking it before you walk there and take it by yourself. Be my eyes," he said.

"Very well, Zha'kra." I heard the doppelganger answer from inside.

Ry then closed his eyes. I felt his powers reaching out to me as he attempted to snatch the ring. As a result, I heard something that sounded like a small explosion, but the sound continued for several seconds. When the sound stopped, I gazed cautiously at Ry. "What was that? Something exploded in there?" I asked.

He finally opened his eyes and gasped. "No, there was fire ignited out of nowhere, and it engulfed the air around the box as if it were held by an invisible wall. And the ring made no movement to leave its place." Cursing under his breath, he glanced at me. "It figures. I guess it won't be any cakewalk, huh?"

I scoffed. "Well, what did you expect? Did you think the ring would be fed up with the Valdam and decide to come to our hands while mumbling a happy song? Not to mention all those spells. The Valdam seems pretty possessive," I said sarcastically.

The edge of his perfect lips twisted into a breath-taking smile. "Look who's back, the Queen of Sarcastic," he chuckled.

I rolled my eyes at him. "Ry, we gotta think here, not fight the 'Battle of Sarcasm'. The result would be 'Withered Princes', and then our asses fried well-done."

At my comment, he let out a low laugh. "Okay, you can proceed," he said to his doppelganger as he pulled out his blueprint again.

"Very well, Zha'kra," his doppelganger replied.

For a while nothing else happened. Ry told his doppelganger to walk in a straight line. I just waited there and looked around cautiously, hoping there'd be no more surprises.

"I got it!" I heard the doppelganger say.

We both exhaled in relief. "Okay, walk slowly in the same straight line, and you'll be fine." Ry stared towards the door as he waited for him.

I heard the faint sound of the doppelganger's footsteps as he slowly approached. When I was starting to feel relief, I suddenly heard something like an iron fence on the move inside the room.

"What is it?" Ry asked sharply.

"There's a fence came down. I can't open it without my powers!" The doppelganger shouted.

I exchanged a confused look with Ry. "I thought the map showed that there was nothing in his tracks, so what is it?" I asked.

Ry shook his head. "I don't know. The map still hasn't changed. I guess something did escape Seere's magick."

"Here, take it!" the doppelganger yelled. Ry and I saw the ring roll across the floor and out of the room. Ry stared uneasily at the small thing. Worry gleamed in his eyes as he faced the door once again. "Okay, thanks, you're done here. Go back."

"Yes, Zha'kra." With that, I felt his presence fading, and then he was there no more.

I glanced at Ry and saw an indignant look on his face. He then closed the door using his powers. The door moved slowly outward and shut firmly seconds later.

I looked back and forth between him and the ring. "Is it safe?"

He took a step towards the ring and knelt next to it. "I don't know. I can feel something emanating from it. It doesn't feel like that Herathim, but I don't wanna take chances. This thing is used to trap unholy powers. I'll wrap it," he said, and he produced a small pouch similar to the one that held the Herathim, only smaller. Grabbing its base, he used it like a cloth and wrapped the ring. He tied it and gave it to me. "Here."

I took the pouch and lifted aside my robe. I tied the pouch to my belt next to the Herathim and tugged my robe over them. After I was done, I walked towards him. "And all these problems over one stupid ring! I wonder what we'll face next. A jam party?" I asked sarcastically.

Ry just expelled a tired breath as an answer. "Come on, let's get outta here."

I nodded and together we quickly headed towards the exit. Thank Hell we'd already tossed those seals out of the way.

But when we reached the end of the hallway and were just a few meters away from the left wall where we'd jumped in, someone who was no doubt human appeared in our path.

The Valdam. The Guardian of the Ring of Solomon.

Without warning, he chanted something and threw multiple bolts. We deflected them at once.

I hurled all kinds of curses under my breath. "He's certainly learned or *turned* into something not human. There's no way any human could do that."

The Valdam glared and started to reach under his dark green robe as he scanned us from top to bottom. His hand ceased to move when his eyes reached the crests on our armour. "Well, well, a Hieldhar and a Cherxanain. You have a lot of nerve coming here, especially since neither of you are *royals*," he spat with mocking disdain. "I don't need to pull the Goetia on the likes of you."

I screwed up my face at his overblown confidence. "The likes of *you* shouldn't have the guts to say you could face us without some stupid spell you picked from that stupid scroll. You're damn well gonna need it, jerk."

Suddenly the human stared at me from hair to toe and then looked back up. "Alianna?" he asked in disbelief.

I winced at the name he blurted. What the . . . ? That was the alias I had used when I lived here! How did he . . . ?

I narrowed my eyes at the human and was hit by a violent wave of recognition that went through me like a sledgehammer. Those bright green eyes . . . It couldn't be . . ."Norgan of Giseiah!"

I took a step back as my mind went blank for a split second. How in the hell did he end up here? He was dead!

His expression went from utter confusion to complete and pure wrath. "You! You made me do all that! My family and my friends! My allies and my soldiers! How dare you, bitch!" He bellowed in burning rage and chanted something else. His voice trembled and was filled with anger so potent that I couldn't believe came from, well, a human. Or more likely, an ex-human.

I could almost lick it out of the air.

Not ready for what was coming, I stood there, glaring at the . . . whatever he was now. One thing I was sure. He was my victim.

When I saw him send another blast at me, I dodged it, and it missed me by just a few inches.

"I'll get you, bitch!" he roared as he kept launching those blasts at me. I had just evaded his last bolt when I saw other bolts flying at him from his left and hitting him hard. He staggered back and glared in the direction those bolts came from.

Ry.

He didn't look too happy. His sapphire eyes were swirling in anger. "How dare you called her bitch, you wretched excuse for a human! Nobody calls her that and dies in one piece," he said in low deadly voice.

Norgan cursed foully as he sent another blast at Ry. "You're dead wrong if you think I'm just a mere human, you low demon! I am the Valdam!" he roared.

Ry and Norgan exchanged more bolts and more angry words. I was about to join the fight when I noticed something. A protective shield was forming rapidly above us. Soon it would engulf the entire fortress and lock us both!

"Fuck this!" I cursed through my clenched teeth. I turned my gaze towards the two who were still caught in the heat of battle. Suddenly, I saw Norgan do something no human or undead could have done. He vanished, reappeared a few feet to Ry's right, and shot three bolts straight at his right knee, thigh, and stomach before he could react.

"Ry!" I shouted, as I saw him buckle. He groaned in pain and placed his right hand on his stomach. He quickly rolled sideways to face Norgan and managed to deflect two more bolts in time.

I couldn't believe my own eyes. The bastard had just teleported! How in the hell did he do that?!

Still, it was no time to be surprised. Ry forced himself to his feet. Shifting my gaze up, I saw the protective shield, and then hurled a curse. The shield was already completed.

I threw multiple blasts towards the shield as my gaze went back and forth between the battle and the layer of dome up there. When my bolts reached it, they just disappeared.

"Shit!" I snarled, and I was about to shoot more when I saw Seere's doppelganger floating around. He too hurled bolt after bolt, but to no avail.

I turned my attention to Ry, who readied himself and deflected four more blasts Norgan threw at him. It was then I saw the human shoot six blasts simultaneously.

Ry deflected the first three shots, but it was all he could do with one hand. He finally pulled his right hand, which was now covered in blood, from his stomach to handle the rest, but he buckled again. More bolts headed towards him, and his attention was averted to his knee that was covered in blood.

Time suddenly felt slower as I saw the blasts coming steadily at him. I couldn't possibly shoot those bolts without causing a big explosion that might hurt Ry, so I did the first thing I could think of. I flew as fast as I could to put myself between Ry and those bolts. I focused bits of my powers on my palm, ready to bounce the blasts back as I was getting nearer. But when I got there, I was too late.

*   *   *

Ezryan gritted his teeth as the pain in his side bit harder into him. He felt several bolts heading towards him, and he hastily looked towards the human or whatever he was fighting when he saw his worst nightmare laid bare before his eyes.

Yverna took those bolts for him.

"No!" he bellowed in despair as she fell to the ground.

The guardian, whom he now knew as the human king who had once lived in the fortress, lowered his hand, and rage contorted his face. "The bitch got what she deserved, as will you, low demon. The Arcs will be here soon, and you will die," Norgan said disdainfully.

Something broke within Ezryan at those words. He paid no attention to either the shield that had completed its form and engulfed the entire fortress or the harsh pain that was clawing at his entire right side.

Slowly, the former Hieldhar returned to his feet. Massive dark clouds gathered right above the fortress. "You shall die an extremely agonizing death for what you did to her, and I will make sure you can never be reborn," he said in ice-cold rage as he raised his right hand towards the dark clouds.

From out of nowhere, lightning bolts flashed one after another, lighting the dark velvet night, followed with crashes of thunder raging in the sky.

The Valdam stepped backwards. His gaze went from the unholy before him to the thunder clapping furiously in the sky. "What are you doing?" he asked as he nervously averted his green eyes back to his enemy. He started throwing multiple bolts at the devil, but those bolts didn't even reach him. All of them were blown away several feet from the devil as if he were protected by some sort of invisible wall.

Paying no heed to the bolts the Valdam hurled at him, Ezryan levelled a murderous gaze at the Ring's guardian. "Just shut up and die," he said in the same cold voice.

Abruptly, lightning blazed above the Valdam. Ezryan directed his raised hand from the sky and pointed straight at the former king. Lightning followed his hand and shattered the shield, went straight to the former human king.

The Valdam roared in excruciating agony as the lightning burned him from inside out. But all of his screaming couldn't save him from the flame that was cooking his organs, violently melting them. Fifteen seconds later, he turned into ashes that were blown away by the night breeze. There was no trace of him. It was as if he had just ceased to exist. The clouds above disappeared immediately following the Valdam's death.

Ezryan quickly forced himself towards his beloved. "Yve! Yve, baby, wake up!" Ezryan shouted as he rocked her.

She just lay still and made no response to his desperate call.

"Zha'kra!" The doppelganger landed next to him. "Shakra Yverna, she . . ."

"Not now," Ry said as he placed his hand on Yverna's abdomen and started to reach into her. He might not recognize the spell the dead Valdam had used, but he hoped to hell he could recognize his energy. If he was able to do so, he could countermand whatever it was and heal both her and himself.

But his hope was nothing more than an empty one. Slowly, he pulled back his hand. "No, it can't be . . ." was all he could say. He didn't recognize the energy, and he realized he couldn't risk using his healing powers. He'd be damned if he used it on her and she ended up dead because of it.

He held her as he bit his lip. Despair and anger consumed him so much that he didn't even notice the blood flowing from his lip that he bit. He would never let her die. Not like this!

Without another word, he took her in his arms and turned to the doppelganger. "It's no use. We gotta move Hurry!" he said as he tightened his grip on the she-devil.

"But your leg . . ."

"We're not going through the rift. We'll go straight outside Vassago's domain."

"What about Shakra Yverna? Will she be able to hold through it?"

"I'll use my life force. She'll hold."

The doppelganger nodded and put his hand on Ezryan's shoulder. The three of them flashed themselves directly to Gillian forest near the barrier of Vassago's castle. They arrived a second later, and Ezryan transformed his robe into wings. He almost couldn't hold himself to fly as fast as he could and get the help from the princes to cure her. There was no way he could remove whatever effect those bolts had given her. It was laden with whatever it was the spell ignited. He cursed his own stupidity to the point where he wanted to kill himself right where he stood.

A moment later he landed, and he ground his teeth as another violent jolt of pain shot through him. He dropped to his knees, but he managed to tighten his grip on Yverna before she fell out of his arms. "Zha'kra!" Seere's doppelganger came to his aid.

"I'm fine," Ezryan said through clenched teeth, and he turned his gaze to the empty field. "Vassago! Belphegor! Seere!" he shouted.

Belphegor and Seere appeared immediately.

"What is . . . ?" Belphegor didn't finish his question, because the sight of Yverna lying helplessly in Ry's arms and the devil kneeling with his leg bleeding answered him.

"No fucking way!" the North Prince cursed as he ran towards them.

"The Valdam shot her. I don't know what to do. His energy felt weird, and I didn't recognize his spell or his energy," Ezryan exclaimed desperately as Seere pulled back his doppelganger.

Belphegor took Yverna from the former Hieldhar, who reluctantly let her go. "Come on, there's no time!" Seere placed his hand on Ry's shoulder, and they all vanished.

They reappeared inside Vassago's chamber where the owner was still lying on his bed.

"Vassago?" Ezryan asked in disbelief as the North Prince hurriedly walked towards the enormous bed carrying Yverna, and then he carefully laid her there.

"There's no time for a detailed explanation. I can't believe I'm gonna say this, but what the hell . . . Seere, I need your help with her." Belphegor stared at Seere.

The addressed prince nodded gloomily. "With all the spells carved along the pavement, she was shot by the fucking Valdam," Seere merely stated the fact in a bleak voice.

"Just shut up and get your ass over here," Belphegor snapped.

This time, Seere didn't even give him an acerbic retort. "Okay, let's get to it then. Belphegor, if you would do *that* spell, I'll do the other," he said firmly, gesturing towards the North Prince so he would take up position next to him.

Reaching Yverna's side, Ezryan clenched his fists. "What can I do?" his voice was broken with pain.

"Sit your ass down. We'll take a look at your wound later. Luckily, it's only your right side. The poison won't spread as fast as it should when it penetrates organs. Don't move too much, and don't try to heal it. You'll only accelerate it. You can't do anything about her either. Let Seere and me take care of her." Belphegor cast a firm gaze at Ezryan.

Looking as if he'd rather get gutted by them, Ezryan slowly stepped away to the wall and slid to the floor with his sapphire eyes fixed on his mate. Both princes stood at Yverna's side and began muttering something.

Just seconds after they began, Yverna started to shake tremendously, and she began to vomit blood. Ezryan immediately leapt to his feet, ignoring the surge of a painful hot lash on his knee, and motioned towards her.

"Don't touch her!" Belphegor snarled.

Ezryan glanced up and saw that the situation wasn't going well on the princes' part either. Belphegor cringed as he kept getting cuts out of thin air, as if something intangible kept slicing him over and over mercilessly. Seere had his own troubles. His life force was starting to slip away from him as if it were being sucked out of him by something unidentified.

"You're still there, Belphegor?" Seere asked in a broken voice, all the while trying to stay conscious and get rid of the deadly poison in Yverna's body.

Belphegor gave him a weird grin and cringed from pain at the same time. "I could ask you the same thing. Don't pass out now. You'll kill the three of us if you do. If that happens, I'll drag you off the punishing block and dropkick your ass myself." His voice was trembling as he tried to use light sarcasm even though all parts of his body were screaming in absolute agony.

Watching the three of them in excruciating pain, Ezryan couldn't do anything but hope with all he had that nothing worse would happen. This was entirely his fault. He couldn't believe one single human or whatever he was could get him off-guard like that. That was incredibly stupid! How could he have dropped his guard like that?!

As he leaned against the wall, looking at the two princes struggling to help his mate and the other one who was still unconscious, he cursed his own helplessness, all the while wondering if there was anything he could do to help.

A few hours later, the princes finally stopped, and both of them simultaneously dropped to the floor. Ezryan hastily shot to his feet and dragged himself towards them in spite of the pain that had spread out of his stomach.

"Belphegor! Seere! You all right?" he asked sharply as he knelt beside them. His question was answered by the withered princes with coughs of blood.

"We're feeling totally superb," Belphegor said sarcastically as he wiped the blood off his mouth.

Ezryan grimaced at Belphegor's answer and then turned his gaze to Seere. "What about you, Seere? You okay?" Ezryan asked quietly.

Seere scoffed and gave another blood cough. "Just about. I'll live though it." Seere then dragged himself away to the wall and leaned against it.

Belphegor exhaled and slowly brought himself to lean against the bed. Raking his hair, he glanced at Ezryan. "Sit down, Ry," he said.

"No, we'll deal with my wounds later. You guys are exhausted," Ezryan said firmly.

"Boy, don't make me come over and punch your stomach. I know the poison's already spread out from there. So come here, sit the fuck down, remove your armour, and stop arguing. I'm so not in the fucking mood," Belphegor said harshly.

"Just get here, Ry," Seere added.

Gulping, Ezryan slid to the floor, lifted his robe, and removed his armour, exposing the bleeding flesh on his right side. Both princes then chanted with their hands raised towards it. Very slowly, Ezryan felt two foreign powers seeping into his skin and spreading through his abdomen to his leg. A few rapid heartbeats later, the pain disappeared and Ezryan could move it again. "Thank you," he said quietly.

Both princes scoffed. "Don't mention it," Seere said.

"Damn, boy, I think I'd better go to my room upstairs. I'm too wasted." Belphegor looked at Ezryan with his eyes almost closed.

Seere slowly moved his right hand over his eyes. "Yeah, me too. A good long sleep will help a lot if we wanna recover from this."

Belphegor expelled a long-suffering breath. "At any rate, thanks, bud."

Unable to believe his ears, Seere removed his hand from his eyes. "Wow, all the way from asking for my help up to saying thanks? Forget Arzia, I think the world's gonna get spontaneous combustion."

Belphegor cursed foully.

Seere answered his expletive with small laugh. "Just kidding, don't sweat it. I wanna help her too. And thanks for cooperating and not using the chance to off me where I stood."

Belphegor snickered. "Huh, I get what you were saying. The world's *definitely* getting spontaneous combustion with you saying you wanted to help her," he said with firm tone.

Both of them chuckled, leaving Ezryan with an expression on his face that was a mixture of amusement and confusion. When they'd stopped laughing, Ezryan grinned. "Thanks, both of you. I owe you both my life," he said with respect in his voice.

Belphegor waved his hand at his words, as if swatting off flies from his face. "What are you talking about? Don't sweat it, boy. Anyhow, take care of these two. I'm off. See ya later if I'm still alive." He vanished.

"I'm off too. Hopefully, and I mean hopefully, I'll wake up." Seere let out a heavy breath before he too dissolved into nothingness.

Clenching his fists and all the while hoping that both Belphegor and Seere would be all right, Ezryan rose to his feet and got rid of the blood on his right leg. He cringed at the sight of Yverna's face and body, which were covered by blood. He immediately dissolved the blood with his powers.

His expression changed. He seemed as though he was in an extremely agonizing pain as he slowly took a position beside her. "I'm so sorry," he whispered. He placed his hand on her head and gently ran his fingers over her smooth hair. "Please wake up." His voice was broken as he took her hand in his grasp and felt her cold skin. As he kissed her fingers, he heard a groan.

Shifting his position, he looked at Vassago, who moved a bit. Abruptly, the prince jolted awake with a loud scream. He immediately stopped and panted as if he had just awoken from a horrible nightmare.

"Highness? How are you feeling?" Ry asked him with concern in his voice.

Shivering, the prince slowly turned his gaze to the young warrior. "Ry? When did you get here? Where's . . . ?" he didn't continue his question when his swirling turquoise eyes fell onto Yverna who had yet made no signs of waking up.

"Yve! What happened?" he asked slowly as he looked at Ry and his firm grip on Yverna's hand.

"It . . . was my fault." Ezryan looked down at Yverna's beautiful hand. The coldness of her skin left his soul in torment.

Vassago slowly got on his feet and went around his bed. He walked towards Ezryan. "How do you mean? Did you both trip a wire or something?"

Ezryan shook his head. "No, we didn't trip any wire."

Vassago stood next to Ezryan and put his hand on Yverna's forehead. Then he moved his hand to her abdomen and let out a sigh. "She was shot by the Valdam, wasn't she?" he asked quietly.

Ezryan grimaced and tightened his grasp on Yverna's limp hand. "Those bolts were meant for me. She took them." His voice was broken with despair as the image of Yverna dropping to the ground after she got shot played over and over in the back of his mind.

A grim expression spread on Vassago's handsome face as he looked down at the sleeping she-devil. "Don't beat yourself up over it. This is what she would want. You know that."

Heard what Vassago said didn't make things any easier. Ezryan felt despair and guilt consume him even more than before. "I should've protected her. What's the use of me being around her if it's not for that?"

Vassago shook his head as he let out a tired breath. "You both are way too much alike. You can't wait to look Azrael in the face so you can protect each other. I can't say putting this matter aside will be easy with an attitude like yours, but now isn't the time to enjoy your torment. So I suggest you shove aside that suicidal thought of inviting Azrael in here. Some other poor sap needs that daddy reaper."

Ezryan just remained quiet as Vassago's comment stabbed his mind. The prince was right. He couldn't dwell in guilt forever. More dangerous matters were on their way. If he wished to protect her, he must concentrate. Otherwise, Yverna might kill him herself, or at least launch her sarcastic attacks at him for being shameful. At any rate, he couldn't go on like this. He should get a grip on himself now that Belphegor and Seere had been able to save her.

Closing his eyes, he inhaled deeply. "Thanks Vassago," he said as he faced the prince.

Vassago rolled his turquoise eyes. "Nah, what are you thanking me for?"

Ezryan scoffed at his question, and then suddenly the warrior realized something. "By the way, Highness, why were you unconscious when we got here? Was it . . . him?" he asked carefully.

Vassago scowled and told Ezryan everything that had happened. After he finished, Ezryan grimaced. "I'm sorry you had to go through all that."

The prince *tsked*. "Really, can't you say anything other than 'thank you' or 'I'm sorry' or 'forgive me'? I'll say it again if you didn't understand it the first time. Shove. The. Damn. Suicidal. Thought. You hear me?"

Ezryan fell silent, but from the look on his face the prince could tell that the warrior still felt guilt for what had happened to him. The edge of his perfectly sculptured lips lifted in a sarcastic smile. "Don't feel that important. We're doing this because of our own choices. Besides, we–Belphegor, Seere, Orobas, and I–already chose to oppose the old bastard long before you got into that dispute with him. Unlike Belphegor who, with the gloriously moronic mind he has, decided to rebel openly against his dad, the other three of us have been doing it secretly, so don't mind what happened to me. Just focus on our remaining plan, for all us," he said firmly.

Wincing, Ezryan gave Vassago the subtlest nod. "Very well, for all of us," he replied.

"That's more like it. So, now I assume those two are in their rooms recovering from healing her, right? And you too?" Vassago indicated his leg with a tilt of his chin.

Ezryan lowered his gaze. "What did you pick up? Belphegor's and Seere's healing powers?" he asked quietly as shame went through him.

"The trace of the spell they used on her is on you as well."

Ezryan nodded. "Yeah, they both left soon after they finished. They were both in pretty bad shape."

Vassago cursed foully. "Of course they were! That ex-human bastard, why he didn't just stay dead in the first place?" he said indignantly.

Ezryan was taken aback by his comment. "You knew who the Valdam was?"

Vassago appeared confused by his question. "Well, of course. I think most of the royals have known about that low bastard for some time now. Why do you ask?"

Ezryan shook his head in bafflement. "Well, because we didn't know jack about him at first. Why didn't you tell us? And what's with the spell he cast on us? And why couldn't I handle the after-effects of any of them?" Ezryan asked relentlessly.

Vassago frowned. "That's a lot of questions. By the way, with 'was', you're saying the Valdam's dead?"

The warrior's gaze darkened. "I tossed a lightning bolt at him."

Vassago grinned. "N-I-C-E. Okay, first, I for one didn't know who exactly the Valdam was. I just heard he was some guy who once lived in that fortress, but we did know for certain that this guy was already dead before he became the Valdam."

"You got that right," Ezryan murmured.

Vassago raised a brow at him. "Why is that? Did he go zombie on you and act grossly undead or what?"

Ezryan shook his head. "No, he just appeared human, but he could throw bolts and teleport, an idiotic combination between disturbing and annoying for an undead or whatever he was."

The prince gaped at Ezryan's explanation. "He could do what? Teleport?"

Ezryan nodded. "Yeah, that's how he managed to shoot my damned stomach and leg. He'd caught me completely off guard."

Vassago cringed. "Uh, okay. Second, we didn't tell you both because, well, you didn't ask and we assumed you knew about him."

Ezryan *tsked.* "Yeah, right, classic, 'you didn't ask'. Our safety was jeopardized by 'you didn't ask'. That's terrific. You've successfully made asses out of you and me. Great! I didn't ask because you guys looked like you didn't know much about him. Hell, no offense, but you didn't even know your own name was on that damned Goetia."

The prince grimaced. "Sorry about that."

Sighing, Ezryan shook his head. "Nah, it's a stupid mistake on my part too. And I didn't know him, Yve did."

Vassago cocked his head. "She did?"

Ezryan nodded glumly. "Yeah, when we ran into him, he recognized her and vice versa. Apparently, he was the human king who ruled the fortress, her very first victim. He definitely was not happy about it, and I fried him for it," Ezryan said with a hint of anger.

The prince let out a low whistle. "Right, one well-done Valdam because he pissed you off! So now we don't have to worry about him using that Goetia. Great!"

"Highness, the spells," Ezryan pressed.

Vassago cleared his throat. "Right, about them, well, only a few among the royals know about them and the counter spell."

"That's new. How in the hell did you guys get a hold of such a spell in the first place?"

"It was a matter of balance, I think, that became one of the major factors which led us to that spell," Vassago said slowly as he averted his gaze to Yverna's sleeping form.

Ry shook his head in confusion. "What does that mean?"

"It began with David receiving that damned ring, along with a set of spells to contain us."

"Received? From whom? People from upstairs?"

Vassago nodded.

"This thing came from up there? The energy sure didn't feel like that Herathim I took." Ry crossed his arms across his chest.

"Of course not. One of the high and mighty bastards upstairs possessed a jewel-maker to make it and then infused the thing with some undetectable crap."

"For what?" Ezryan asked. He couldn't imagine what purpose upstairs' bastards wanted to achieve by going through all that trouble.

Vassago snickered. "The rumour said that the ring was intended for Solomon in the first place. It possesses powers enough to restraint lesser devils such as Machordaen or Fierytarians like the ones guarding Aleeria."

"And the spell?"

Vassago laughed bitterly. "Now that's what I meant by balance," he said.

"Just cut to the chase, Highness."

The prince raised his hands, feigning surrender. "That set of spells used by the Valdam was created by Mariel and given to David by Gabriel and Michael. Even though David wore the ring for some time, only Solomon had had the privilege to use the spells."

"Wait, who's Mariel? One of the Arcs? Never heard of her." Ezryan averted his gaze elsewhere as he tried to dig up his memories of every known archangel.

"Never will. She died with her mate. She's probably the only rogue Arc that betrayed her brethren by giving her help to our kind, and she mated with one of the soldiers as well."

"She did what? Mated with one of the soldiers? *Our* soldiers?" Ezryan asked sharply. Well, he'd never hear about this.

"Yes, you knew who he was," Vassago said.

Ezryan just gave a clueless expression in return.

Vassago only answered Ezryan's puzzled gaze with one name. "Darkan."

The expression on Ezryan's face changed from a questioning look to utter disbelief. "Darkan? *The* Darkan? The ninth Hieldhar of the First Legion who wasted five hundred thousand Arcs from the House of Prosper all by himself?"

"Yes, the one who led Gabriel and the other scum to the conclusion that they needed to force that stupid deal upon the soldiers." Vassago's gaze darkened as he remembered that annoying moment.

"That Darkan really was something. But still, nobody knew about them?"

"At first neither devils nor angels knew what Darkan and Mariel had been doing all those centuries. Hell, I'd wager Lucifer's ugly ass that not even Gabriel and Michael knew about it."

Ezryan let out a low whistle and lowered his gaze. "So what, they forced her to create that spell to contain her mate's people and then killed them both?" he asked.

Vassago shook his head. "No, they didn't force her. More like tricked her into it. She just got instructions to make the spell. She wasn't told its function or who would use it after she was done."

"Let me guess. In the middle of the process, she got all suspicious about the spell and eventually found out what the Arcs were intending to do, didn't she?" Ezryan asked quietly.

Sighing heavily, Vassago nodded slightly. "Yeah, needless to say, that pretty much covers what happened. She tried to find out why such a spell should be made and, furthermore, given it to a human. Regardless of what the human's duty would be or the fact that it was Big Boss's will, she was against the idea. It might destroy the balance or something. Hence I said the problem of balance was one of the factors which enabled us to know about the spell.

"Above all, she didn't want anything bad happen to Darkan. In the end, she couldn't do a thing to openly rebel against Gabriel, Michael, and the others. So, the only option for her was to secretly warn Darkan."

Ezryan grimaced. "And that was when they found out about what they'd been doing."

Vassago closed his eyes, as if remembering his old friend. "Yes. Both of them hastily warned us about that spell, and Mariel gave us two sets of spells to countermand it. After that, they decided to run away, but they didn't want to hide in one of our places. Despite our warning that they wouldn't be able to run or hide from those pals of hers unless they stayed hidden in our castles, they still ran off. Only three days later, we heard that they both . . . died."

"No wonder there's no record concerning Darkan other than the fact that he wasted that many Arcs. Hell, not even the cause of his death was recorded," Ezryan said in a bleak voice.

He then turned to gaze at Vassago's face. Something told him that there was something more to Darkan's story.

"Hey, Vassago, you mind telling me something?"

"What is it?" Vassago replied without looking at him.

Ezryan bit his lip. "Correct me if I'm wrong, but you seem to know more about Darkan than you've told me," he said carefully.

Vassago laughed bitterly at his words. "You really don't know when to stop, do you?"

Ezryan winced. "Well, I'm . . ."

Vassago raised his hand to stop him. "I said no more apologies from you, didn't I?"

Ezryan closed his mouth immediately.

The prince sighed. "You're not wrong. I did know more about him and Mariel. Not just me. Belphegor and Seere knew them both as well. They sought us from time to time."

Ezryan was taken aback by his words. "The three of you got close with an angel? That's new. And you were all fine with what Darkan was doing?"

Vassago bit his lip. "What they were doing, that was all up to them to decide. All we did was just protect them both. You see, the three of us knew Darkan way before he got involved with Mariel. And when we got to know her, we had to agree that she wasn't like any of her kind."

"Because she fell for Darkan?" Ezryan asked quietly.

Vassago averted his gaze to the ceiling. "She once said to us that she'd rather be one of the devils. We're condemned to the depths of hell, but we do have a bit of compassion towards each other. Unlike devils or hell or humans, angels are cold, so cold that they have almost no feelings towards their own kind. I remember one of the things she said. 'It really is counterproductive, isn't it? We were supposed to be the example of the heavenly love of our Father, and yet we're not allowed to even feel anything. I don't know if this is the Holy Father's test or not. Regardless, I'm still grateful that I met Darkan and had the chance to know the world he lives in. I will treasure every single second I spent with him until the moment I die.'"

Then both of them fell silent. Seconds passed with neither one saying anything. They just stood there watching Yverna, who was still in a deep sleep.

Abruptly, Vassago turned to face Ry and smiled. "You know, Darkan was a lot like you back when I knew him–young, powerful, loyal, and fearless. He knew things and had a dry sense of humour. Well, the only problem was that he'd mated with an angel. He wasted too many Arcs. I don't have a problem with that, but, unfortunately for him, even though Mariel was that loyal to him, to the three of us who protected him her being a different kind from us was one of the causes that ultimately brought them to their deaths."

"So, you're saying that you and Belphegor don't mind having me around because I remind you of him?" Ezryan asked carefully.

Vassago snorted. "Boy, we're not that sentimental, but perhaps deep down having you around was like having him back. We knew him a whole lot longer than we've known you. With him, it was like having a sworn little brother with whom we were having fun. With you and Yve, really it was like having both of them back. Although, I wouldn't say Yve's as sentimental as Mariel, but their loyalty towards those they care for is, without a doubt, the same."

Ezryan smiled at Vassago's words, at least until he heard the next part. "Boredom can lead to many things, you know. For us, perhaps having young acquaintance once in a while is a way to get away from it." Vassago's voice was drifting away.

Ezryan frowned. "That's what started it? Boredom?"

"Yeah, more or less. And along with everything we got through our boredom, we got to know Darkan, Mariel, you, Yve, and the others. Hell, we can even get the chance to piss off Belphegor's dad. Who knows what'll happen next?" Vassago laughed.

"Unbelievable! I don't know if I should be flattered or offended." Ry shook his head.

Suddenly, a soft groan escaped from Yverna's mouth. Ezryan quickly dropped to his feet as he closed the distance between Yverna's pale face and his. "Baby! Baby, wake up," he whispered in her ear, all the while terrified for her life.

Chapter 23

I heard a familiar deep masculine voice calling out to me in the distance. *"Baby! Baby, wake up!"*

Who . . . was that? Was it . . . Ry? I couldn't tell where he was.

"Please wake up!"

Wake up? What did that mean? Was I . . . sleeping?

I opened my eyes and some light invaded my eyesight. I immediately covered them.

"Yve? Baby, how are you feeling?" That familiar voice was calling me again.

I groaned suddenly as I felt a sting on my body. "Ry? Is that you?" I asked slowly.

From somewhere near me, I could hear someone drew a relieved breath. "She's awake. Thank you Belphegor, Seere."

I felt a warm hand grasp mine, and then I heard another familiar voice. "This is great. I'm glad she's okay. Now I want to check on those two. Will you be staying here or going back to your room?"

"I'll take her to our room. Oh, and say thanks to them both for me."

"Will do. See ya later." And with that, I felt that other person vanish from the room.

"Come on, I'll take you," the owner of that deep voice said to me. That was Ry's voice. There was no mistake about that now.

That warm hand slipped away from mine and gently lifted me off the bed. While I was still unable to see my surroundings, I could feel that we went to a different room. His tight hold on me was like a warm shelter as he walked a few steps and then stopped. He put me down, and I ended up on another comfortable bed.

"The light still hurts your eyes?" Ry asked.

I nodded.

"Okay, hold on a second." I suddenly felt that we were plunged into pitch-black darkness.

"Better?" he asked again. From his voice I could tell that he was worried as hell.

I opened my eyes inch by inch and was grateful that no lights burnt into my eyes. And thanks to my genetic makeup, even in this darkness I could see his beautiful face.

He was sitting in front of me.

"Hey . . ." I said slowly as I extended my hand to touch his cheek. When I did, his warm hand was placed on top of mine.

"Hey, how are you feeling?" He kept asking me that, I wondered why . . .

"A bit weird, but I'm fine. And you?"

He smiled warmly. "That's good to hear. And don't worry about me. I'm fine."

"That's great," I said slowly as I began to remember something. I didn't know what it was, but for a split second I thought he was in grave danger.

"Ry, you really are all right, aren't you?" I asked him cautiously.

I felt him tense slightly under my touch. "Really, I'm fine. What's the matter?"

Perhaps it was my imagination . . .

"Nothing. For a moment I thought you were in danger. Maybe I was having a bad dream." I let out a small nervous laugh.

But he didn't laugh, and he didn't say that it was me having a bad dream. His eyes widened, and abruptly he held me tightly. "Ry, what is it?" I asked.

Well, something was definitely bothering him . . .

He shook his head. "I'm just really grateful you're all right. That's all." His voice trembled in relief.

Had something happened . . . ?

I turned my head a bit. "Why wouldn't I be? I'm fine, really. Ry, you're scaring me. What's wrong?"

He pulled away, and a puzzled look appeared on his handsome face. "You . . . You didn't . . ." He didn't finish his sentence.

"Yeah? I didn't what?" I prompted, not liking that sad gaze he directed at me.

He hastily shook his head. "No, it's okay, it's nothing," he said as he slowly embraced me again, tighter this time.

That feeling again, like he was afraid he'd lose me . . .

After few moments, he finally let me go. "Okay, you should get some rest," he said as he gave me that warm, breath-taking smile of his.

I nodded and moved a bit to lie down, but when I was about to put my head on the pillow, I felt something inside my robe. I pulled it out and found a small pouch tied next to the pouch containing the Herathim. Where the hell did I get this?

Frowning, I untied it and reached inside. When I touched whatever it was, a blinding pain invaded my head. I dropped it, holding my head, and screamed my lungs out as everything went white before my eyes.

"Yve! Yve, what is it?" I heard Ry's voice near my ears and felt his hands on my shoulders.

In the next few seconds I thought I heard his voice still calling out to me, but it seemed to be slipping away as thousands of images ran over and over torturing my brains.

I saw . . .

The Great Fortress of Asael . . .

The Ring of Solomon . . .

Ry took it . . . And then . . .

Bright green eyes . . . Norgan . . . He was still alive . . .

And about to kill Ry . . .

"Yve, what is it? Please answer me." I heard Ry whispering with panic in his deep voice while everything around me became clear once again, and the pain suddenly stopped.

I gasped and tried to steady my breathing as I slowly turned to face him. He was all right. Then that last piece of image I saw in my head didn't happen. Thank Hell for that.

"Ry, are you all right?!" I asked sharply.

I saw him look both surprised and confused by my question. "I should be asking you that, Yve. What happened just now?"

"More importantly, I want you to answer me. That bastard Norgan didn't get to shoot you, did he?" I asked him.

He stopped dead at my question as if he hadn't seen it coming. Seconds later, he answered me. "No, he didn't. I killed him. Yve, have you remembered all the things that happened to us back in that fortress?" he asked me slowly.

I exhaled in relief when I heard him. That supposed-to-be-dead human really was dead right now.

But what was going on? There was something missing here. There were missing pieces. "Have you remembered all the things?" Okay, I had to admit, I'd just got them back, but not all of them. Yet I could feel it. There was something . . .

I didn't answer his question. Instead, I looked around at the bed and found that little thing that had fallen out of the small pouch I'd just untied.

The Ring of Solomon.

I took it, and another pain hit me, as agonizing as that first one that tormented my head. I let out a low groan as I tried to hold on against another wave of sharp pain that invaded my brain.

Once again, everything went white, and I saw . . . those bolts . . . hit him . . . He buckled . . . and Norgan shot more of them . . .

I ran . . .

Those bolts . . . went through me . . .

With that last image, an exploding pain that was far more terrible than before made me scream. Ry abruptly held me tight once more, and his strong muscular body was trembling around me. Suddenly, the pain was lessening bit by bit as I felt Ry's powers reaching out to me. It was then I realized what he was doing.

He took the pain from me and put it inside him.

Ry's body shook tremendously, and he was sweating profusely as he groaned in pain. Very slowly he let me go. "You . . . okay . . . ?" His voice was broken.

"Ry? Ry, why did you do that?! I'll take them back!" I hastily raised both hands to place them on his forehead.

But he stopped me before I could do so. "Don't," he said.

Ignoring him, I tried to force my way in to take the pain back. "No way. I am not letting you take the pain, not after all that happened to you when I wasn't even there!" I yelled.

He suddenly sucked in a deep breath, closed his eyes, and then released it. For a moment he just stayed still without making a sound.

"Ry?" I called him carefully.

He opened his eyes and looked at me, smiling. "There, the pain's already gone," he said weakly.

I sighed in relief. "You're all right!"

He ran his hand gently on my hair. When that warm hand of his touched my cheek, I placed my hand on it. "Don't you dare do that again," I said to him in a low angry voice as I narrowed my gaze at him.

When he didn't say anything, I went on, "How could you do that? You know how I would feel if anything happened to you! Why didn't you leave that pain with me? I'll say it once again, I am *not*–you hear me?–I am *not* letting you be in pain, in suffering, or any damn shit after all that happened! I will never . . ." I didn't get to finish my words, for Ry suddenly took me into his arms.

"Baby, you already saved my life from that human. I'd rather be dead for real than see you in pain."

"But . . . you were . . . I didn't . . ." I couldn't say the words. Tears flowed freely from my eyes as guilt burnt into the core of my soul.

He tightened his hold even more. "What's past is past. Don't blame yourself over something you didn't even have a clue about. You got shot, that was another matter. *I* saw it. It happened in front of *me*, and it was *me* you shielded. You got hurt. That's definitely absolutely counterproductive to the main purpose of my return."

"And what purpose might that be?" I asked him slowly as the tears began to fade.

He looked me in the eye. "To protect you," he said firmly.

I wasn't able to find any words to argue further as I looked into his protective stare and he held me once more.

"Hey, why don't you change into human?" He smiled teasingly at me.

I raised my brows at the sudden change of subject. "Again? Aren't you bored seeing me human, even though it's just a form?" I curled my lips and pretended to be upset.

He shook his head. "I'd definitely never get bored if the human is you. Come on," he insisted.

I sighed. "Why are you being so persistent?"

He shrugged. "I wanna hold you as we sleep, and to be honest, holding you with horns jutting out of your head will make things a bit difficult if we are to sleep in this bed." He winked mischievously.

I scoffed at his words. "That would make a good excuse, even though you know I could just make the horns disappear without turning into that," I said, feigning annoyance. I transformed and put that black bed-robe on again.

After I did, I watched him do the same, and he looked as stunning as ever. This time, there was no duster robe covering his fine body, just the same tight pants he wore before.

"Come here," he said as he gathered me into his arms. Together we lay on that enormous bed in serene silence.

Just a few seconds after I placed my head on his bare chest and felt his warm hand raking my hair gently, darkness took me, and I drifted into the realm of dreams.

*　*　*

"How's it going?" Vassago asked Belphegor, who was lying down in his bed covered in blood, for he had still been coughing and vomiting blood for the last half an hour since Vassago had come to see him after he and Seere had healed Yverna.

"Completely annoyed and having my ego severely injured because an ex-human moron managed to get me and Seere into this trouble using only that stupid chant," Belphegor said lazily.

Vassago snorted. "Stop acting tough for a second, will ya? What about the poison? Is there still much left in your body?" he asked quietly.

Belphegor let out a long-suffering sigh and then shook his head. "No, not much left, but it still needs time and a considerable amount of energy and focus if I want to completely get rid of it. That stupid spell!" Belphegor cursed.

Vassago was startled at his friend's comment and lowered his gaze. "Do you regret it? That we let Mariel live for a while and, furthermore, protected her?"

Belphegor raked his hair and looked a bit frustrated. "Indeed, it's true that if we'd killed her before they made her formulate that spell, that Valdam wouldn't have had any spell to use against us, much less been able to hurt us this badly."

"But?" Vassago prompted as he slowly raised his gaze off the floor to his friend.

Belphegor gave him a bitter look. "It was Mariel. Besides, there were too many things we got through with Darkan to shove him away or kill them both. I couldn't just dismiss their loyalty to me, and I know you and Seere couldn't either. And don't forget, Yve would tell you to get real," he ended with a sarcastic tone.

Vassago gave him a puzzled stare. "Huh? What are you talking about?"

Belphegor returned his stare with a shocked glare. "You forgot already? Well, I remember she used to say this thing about regret. 'Get real, devils never know regrets, never did and never will. It's our bliss.' Remember that part?" Belphegor grinned.

Vassago laughed. "Oh yeah, right, I do remember that one. Really, she's completely different from Mariel, and yet she reminds me of her a lot."

"Yeah, and their attitude towards each other is just like Darkan and Mariel, don't you think?" Belphegor asked, looking up to the ceiling, as if recalling something far away in the past.

"It feels as if both of them were reborn into a different form and are reliving it all over again," Vassago said wonderingly.

Belphegor nodded. He felt it too. But he wasn't about to let his mind drift to that grievously sickening area. Abruptly, he directed his gaze towards Vassago. "Hey, you think she'll be all right? The after-effect of us healing her would be . . ."

Vassago gave him a grim smile. "The effect seemed to be over by now. She's no longer screaming, that much I can tell. Don't worry. Ry will take care of her, just like Darkan did with Mariel."

Belphegor suddenly let out a disgusted breath. "Really, I don't think Mariel got to know what the effect would be. If she did, there's no doubt she would've gone rogue right under Michael's wretched nose."

Vassago crossed his hands over his chest. "Yeah, I still get the shivers, you know, whenever I remember about those Fierytarians, the brothers and sisters who protected Adalmar."

"Yeah, to think it could gradually wipe out the memories of the ones closest to them, and worse, make them kill each other is unthinkable even for us."

"Fortunately, you and Seere could get to Yve before the effect got that far. You heard them both, right?" Vassago asked slowly.

The North Prince scoffed. "Yeah, I heard them all right. Aside from Ry making her into human form over and over, she's fine."

Vassago snickered. "I mean besides that, Belphegor."

Belphegor rolled his swirling crimson eyes. "I know. Yve just temporarily lost a few hours of her memories. That's a relief, but her losing her memories is not that surprising."

"You should've told Ry though. He's tormenting himself. Hell, I'd bet if Yve didn't recover her memories, he'd have killed himself right there." Vassago gave him a chiding stare.

"Sorry about that. Seere and I forgot because we were busy pouring too much blood rain from our mouths," Belphegor said sarcastically.

Vassago laughed at his sarcasm. "Yeah, you have a point. By the way, we don't have much time left to commence our next plan against your dad and ultimately face that stupid void-whatever. Make sure to get your full strength back before that," he said seriously.

Belphegor snorted. "You're one to talk. Like you've recovered already? And speaking of that bastard, you seem eager to finish him off or at least yell in his ear that you've been opposing him alongside me from the very beginning and that he's too much of a damned idiot to notice," he sneered.

Vassago scowled. "He is a bit of an idiot, but he's no weakling. Those injuries I sustained from him were quite a problem. And I admit I have to agree with you. The deader he becomes, the better for us," he said in a disgusted voice.

Belphegor laughed out loud. "Finally, we're on the same page. But anyhow, all of us need to be at our max, otherwise the deader ones will be us, and quite frankly, I won't enjoy that." He ended with a made-up expression as if he were thinking about something extremely repulsive.

"Me neither. By the way, have you sent Bynethar and Xamian to *him*?" Vassago asked meaningfully.

Belphegor nodded. "Uh-huh. I'm still waiting for them to report on that part. Xamian should've taken care of the Veil as planned."

"All right then, I'll check on Seere. You get some rest."

"Yeah, yeah, stop nagging, will ya? You'll look older than you already are." Belphegor produced an expression on his face that made Vassago roll his eyes. When Vassago said nothing in return but simply stood up, he went on, "You yourself also need some rest, don't forget that. We must not let them both die, no matter what the fate says," he said in a much fiercer voice than he'd intended.

Vassago, who had been about to leave, stopped dead at the North Prince's comment. "You still can't get over their deaths, can you?" he asked quietly.

Belphegor just scoffed at his question. "Just check on Seere, okay? I wanna get some well-deserved sleep here if you don't mind."

Vassago smiled slightly at his friend's reluctance to answer him. "Yeah, I know. Me too. Fine then, I'll leave you to your rest, see ya later." And with that, Vassago vanished.

Suddenly, Belphegor coughed a mouthful of blood. When he saw his own blood on his hand, his mind drifted to Darkan and Mariel. "I'm so sorry, you two," he whispered to the silence surrounding him as his thoughts now turned to Ezryan and Yverna in the other room. "I'll never let them relive your deaths." Belphegor's voice turned cold as he laid his head on the pillow and placed his hand over his eyes.

Vassago's castle emitted light everywhere just like his place, so he created pitch-black darkness and made it blanket the entire room. He expelled a long tired breath before hc surrendered to his worn-out body.

*　*　*

"Seere?" Vassago carefully called his old friend who lay still in his bed and let out shallow breaths. There was no answer.

Vassago slowly approached one side of the bed to take a better look at his friend. Once he did so, he gasped in shock. "What the hell? Seere!" he called the prince sharply.

The sight was unbearable. Seere was as pale as a corpse, and there were cuts all over his body that hadn't even stop bleeding. But worst of all was his life force. Vassago was barely able to sense it, as if it were being sucked out or was flowing out of Seere's body against his will.

"Crap! I can't heal him like this. Ry!" he called the young warrior sharply.

Ezryan appeared. "Highness?" he asked, and when he saw the state Seere was in, he too gasped in shock.

"No way! Is he . . . ?" Ezryan asked sharply.

Vassago pulled him to the side of Seere's bed and cast a wary stare at Seere.

"There's no time to explain. I need your help in this, because in my current situation I won't be able to heal him without having the poison attack me as well."

Hesitating, Ezryan glanced at the withering prince, who was lying miserably in his bed. "Are you sure? I don't know anything here. Both of them didn't even let me heal Yve before."

Vassago shook his head. "Don't worry, I'll only use your energy to heal him, not let you do all the work by yourself. Besides, this process won't be as delicate as when they worked on your girl."

Still unsure, Ezryan nodded. "All right, tell me what to do."

Vassago grabbed Ry's right hand with his left and held it upon Seere's body. Then he chanted something. Ry couldn't recognize the spell, but he just stayed there as he felt his own energy flowing.

Seere suddenly groaned, and more blood flowed from his body, but this time the blood wasn't red. It was pitch-black, and its stench was as if his innards were beginning to rot. Their noses wrinkled as the immense stink passed through their nostrils.

"What the hell is this foul smell?" Ezryan asked in a low voice as he tried to focus his energy under the severe pain that assailed his head along with that stench.

Vassago looked like he was about to be ill himself. "The poison has begun to eat his entrails and everything else as we speak, and that has made him unable to heal in this state. Don't hold your breath just yet. We still need a few hours before we can get rid of most of the poison in his body."

Ezryan cursed at his words. "Nice. I just hope I won't screw this up at all."

And there they both stood in an effort to heal the prince who stood only steps from death . . .

*   *   *

I woke up in the dark, only to find that I was alone in our chamber. How long had I been sleeping? I looked around, but Ry was nowhere to be found. I saw the darkness orb hanging several inches above my head. Ry must have left it behind to make sure I was covered in the darkness.

I raised my hand and willed for the orb to come into my grasp. Once I got the orb and dissolved it, the light suddenly went wild in the entire chamber. I covered my eyes as I thought of Ry. Where could he possibly be?

I moved a bit and felt that ring inside my robe. Pulling it out and staring at it, I expelled an aggravated breath and then shoved it back inside. I changed into my devil form and slowly made my way to the door. Feeling a bit uneasy, I opened it and went out to find a dark empty hallway.

I extended my powers to reach the ether and locate Ry. But after seconds of trying, nothing came back. Just then I remembered what Vassago had told me about the protective spell he'd put all over the place. Great, this meant that nothing I could do to search either one of them would do me any good. Only the other princes could get over these protective spells.

Should I call him?

I started to wander alone inside the huge castle. Where could he possibly be? And where were the princes? After a few moments wandering around, I decided to call one of princes.

At first I thought of calling Ry, but before I did so it occurred to me that he might be a bit tied up with the princes. That's why he left me alone in the first place, because knowing him and his protectiveness, there's no way he'd have left me alone.

"Belphegor?" I called carefully to the darkness.

He didn't appear anywhere. Weird.

"Ry? Vassago? Seere?" I called again and a bit louder this time, and once again there was no answer.

What the hell? They weren't coming, and without knowing their location or being summoned by one of them, there was no way for me to go to wherever they were at the moment.

Suddenly, my call was answered. I felt a familiar fissure go through the air as I heard Belphegor's voice loud and clear. "Yve."

I caught his presence and willed myself to where he was. "Belphegor?" I called him as I approached his bed. He was still lying in it.

"I'm here." He waved his hand lazily and gestured at me to come closer. "What's up?"

He looked a bit tired. Wait a sec . . . If I recall it correctly, Ry did say something about Belphegor and Seere while he was talking with Vassago. What was it?

"Thank Hell, she's waking up. Thank you Belphegor, Seere."

Did both of them heal me? I supposed they did, because I doubted I'd be walking right now after those stupid bolts I got.

"How are you holding up?" I sat on the edge of his enormous bed.

He laid his head on his palms and glanced at me. "Nothing new. What about you? Feeling okay?" he asked me.

I nodded. "Yeah, thanks for that."

Belphegor winced. "You remember what happened?" He got up in his bed slowly as he kept his gaze at me.

I inclined my head to him. "Well, I vaguely remember Ry was thanking both you and Seere after he said something about me waking up. Now that everything that went down in that stupid human fortress has come back to me, I knew that I wasn't in generally good shape when I got here with Ry."

Belphegor snorted. "No, you were practically as still as a corpse, and your mate was almost choking himself with guilt."

My eyes widened at his words. Seeing my face, Belphegor burst out laughing. "Just kidding, but it was true that Ry almost tore himself apart when you weren't waking up."

Hearing what he just said, I could hear Ry's every word in the back of my mind when we were having our little discussion after he took me to our room.

Ry . . .

Belphegor let out a tired sigh. "Would you stop making a face as if this is the end of the world? I swear you two are so alike. Keep that expression, and I'll start calling you Ms Doomsday one of these days."

I scoffed. "Yeah, whatever. By the way, where is he? I don't see Vassago or Seere either."

He gave me a frown. "Ain't he supposed to be with you? Last time I looked, Vassago went to check on Seere."

"Well, he's obviously not with me, hence my asking. Vassago and Seere weren't answering my call either."

"What?" he asked sharply. He then lowered his gaze, as if thinking about something. Abruptly he lifted his gaze and grabbed my hand. "Come on!"

The next thing I knew, we were in another chamber and an extremely rotten smell engulfed us.

"What the hell is this rancid stench?" I cursed as I looked directly towards the people who were standing by the bedside.

Vassago and Ry. They were sweating profusely.

"Stay here!" Belphegor said to me.

I made no movement as I saw him slowly approach the two people who were obviously trying to heal the one lying on the bed.

Seere.

His bed sheet was covered with pitch-black blood. Now it was clear to me what the source of that odour was. It was his blood.

Belphegor stood and looked closely at Seere. He rolled his eyes as he ground his teeth. "This is great," he said sarcastically.

He turned his gaze to Vassago, who was staring at him. "How long have you two been in that pretty stance?" Belphegor smirked.

Vassago let out an expletive so crude that Ry actually cringed at it, and I winced. "If you so much as snap your fucking finger in front of my face, I swear I'll kick your ass so bad you'd have to pour shit through your mouth," he growled at the North Prince, who screwed his face up at his threat.

"As usual, gross." Belphegor sneered. Sighing, he cleared his throat. "Enough stupid jokes! Do you need me to back you up or not?"

Vassago scoffed. "Yeah, right, like you won't pass out if you try mixing your fucking energy with what poison is left in him." He jerked his head at Seere, who groaned slightly.

Ry laughed and cringed at the same time. "But a little help with the blood stench would be great. I doubt if I can stand here even a few minutes longer without unloading my own stomach."

I immediately stepped forward and dissolved the blood. But since there was so much of that hot black fluid flooding Seere's bed, I couldn't eradicate it all at once. I kept on getting rid of bits of it until eventually there was no blood or stench left in the chamber.

Ry gave me a nod of thanks. "Bless you, baby."

I winked at him. "Any time. Just remember to wake me up next time you have to go anywhere."

Startled, he smiled at me. "Will do."

Vassago rolled his turquoise eyes. "If I'm not interrupting anything between you lovebirds and whatever weirdness you two are taking part in, would you please get back to the matter at hand? We'll end up killing him here," he said.

"Sorry." Ry then went back to focusing his energy on healing Seere. Moments later both of them finished and I once again dissolved the blood flowing out of Seere's body.

Belphegor caught Vassago and Ry, who were dropping to their knees. I hastily ran towards them.

"Ry? Zeian, you okay?" I asked him under my breath as I touched his forehead with mine.

He was panting and gasping before he answered me. "It's okay, I'm fine."

I gently ran my hand on his hair that was damp with sweat. "Come on." I brought him to his feet.

As he stood up, I looked at Belphegor was still holding Vassago. "Are you all right, Vassago?" I asked carefully.

"Obviously, I feel like I'm bathing in candy," he said, and he slowly got up to his feet as well with Belphegor helping him.

Suddenly Belphegor hit Vassago's head. "Bathing in candy? Puh-lease, I thought you would have something better than 'bathing in candy'." He shivered in disgust.

Vassago glared at him and then looked at us both. "Thanks Ry, and you Yve, for not letting us puke, 'cause that would be so not cool."

I shook my head. "No problem. So, can I take my man back?" I asked as I held Ry, who was leaning on me with his eyes half hooded.

"Sure, if there's anything else we'll let you know." Belphegor gave us a subtle nod as he supported Vassago.

"See ya later then." After that, I teleported us both back to our room.

* * *

Seere groaned slightly as he opened his eyes and found his two old friends standing next to his bed.

"Yo, stupid, you're finally awake." Belphegor sneered.

Seere *tsked* in disgust. "What the fuck are you doing here, moron?" he snapped as he moved and tried to get up in his bed.

Vassago placed his hand on Seere's shoulder. "Dude, just what the hell do you think you're doing?"

"I'm getting up, thanks to you and Ry," Seere said as he slowly shrugged off Vassago's hand.

At his words, Vassago blinked as he pulled his hand away. "Uh, so you were awake the whole time?" he asked.

Seere shook his head. "Nope, not the entire time, but I did feel your energy and Ry's, and the whole excruciating agony that annoyed the hell out of me."

"I see. By the way, I want to ask you something," Vassago said quietly.

Seere didn't even bother to look at him. "Sure."

"How did you mess up so badly that you ended up with those poisons eating you up?" Belphegor asked him, before Vassago had a chance to open his mouth.

"Shut up." Seere gave him a chiding stare. "FYI, it's not like I intended to mess up. It's the effect of using *that* part of that stupid counter spell." He glared at Belphegor.

The North Prince just scoffed. "Are you looking for an alibi to cover the fact that you did fuck up your part?"

"You . . . !" Seere started to get up, but Belphegor held up his hand to stop him. "That was a joke. You were supposed to laugh. I know about the effect, you shithead. I'm not some new-born devil. But next time you can't even use your damned energy, call for help, dammit! I'm not letting myself get torn up by guilt, especially over your ugly ass! And above all, I certainly don't have time to clean up your fucking stench and look at your ugly bleeding pose!"

Surprised by this outburst, Seere winced and then weirdly enough he laughed. He was laughing so loud that he even did a belly roll in his bed.

Belphegor hit Seere's head. "Ow! That hurts!" Seere yelped, and then he abruptly turned to the North Prince. Vassago just stood there restraining his urge to laugh.

"It serves you right! What the fuck are you laughing at anyway?" Belphegor pinned him with a dry stare.

Seere sobered up immediately. "Nothing. It's just that I don't know if I should be flattered that you're concerned about me or be offended by it."

"What . . ." was all Belphegor could manage, and Vassago burst out laughing. "Yeah, I know what you mean," Vassago said as he held his stomach.

Vassago finally sobered up. "Enough jokes. You two are all right, aren't you?"

"Well, we're breathing normally and not bleeding, if that's what you're asking." Belphegor jerked his head, while Seere just nodded, confirming what Belphegor had said.

"Good. I wanna make sure all of us reach our max again before we do the 'Death Match of the Century' plan on your dad."

"Sounds like a plan to me. So, if that's what you want, then excuse me. I want to have a bit of well-deserved sleep." Seere waved his hand, gesturing the other princes to leave his chamber.

Vassago held his hands up. "Okay, whatever, dork. Catch you later." He disappeared.

"Make sure you wake up, or else I'll beat the shit out of you so much that not even Zabaniah would want to look at you." Belphegor laughed evilly, which was answered by a scathing glare by Seere. "Just get your ass out of here, otherwise you'll be the one on the receiving end of that beating." Belphegor let out another low laugh before he too willed himself out.

Irritated but amused, Seere rolled in his bed. Suddenly, as if his mood were changing, he let out a low curse. "Just a little more, then we'll make sure the prophecy happens. There's no way the prophecy will be denied!" he snarled, and then too tired to move, he let himself be pulled into a deep sleep.

Chapter 24

We spent three days recuperating from our wounds. Even the three princes who didn't come with us to get that stupid ring also needed time to gather their strength.

Well, Vassago for one couldn't be blamed. He'd put his life on the line to cover for us. After Ry told me everything that happened during Vassago's little meeting with our dickhead master, I was so not going to be one of his soldiers ever again.

Damn, he even went that far towards one of his own retainers just to deep-fry my mate!

On the other hand, I couldn't thank Belphegor and Seere enough for saving me. They wouldn't be injured that badly if they hadn't gone through all the trouble to heal me.

And Belphegor's remark was also proven to be true. For the last forty-eight hours, I'd been telling Ry to stop tormenting himself for the fact that I took those stupid bolts for him. My telling him finally worked, after I told him I'd tear myself apart if he didn't quit making the please-give-me-death-because-I-had-failed-you face every time he looked at me.

I made him tell me what he meant by saying he needed to be the one take the ring as well like he promised, and his answer was as vague as ever. He just gave me hints that he wanted to go in the princes' stead so he could protect me. I did have the feeling that his reason was far more complicated than it seemed, but since he told me nothing more than that, I decided not to push him further.

Now, after all of us gained our strength back, we immediately planned our little party with Belphegor's dad. But before that, we agreed to call my sister, her mate, and Ry's different-dimension sworn brother.

Belphegor and Seere were both staying at Vassago's, so I left the ring in their care while I looked for my sister and her mate and Ry went to fetch his brother.

I flew off to the Gate where Zoran and Gevirash were standing–or were supposed to be standing. Instead of them, two soldiers wearing dark grey robes and masks stood there looking tough. But the one thing that made me arch a brow was the symbol on their robes–the All-Seeing Eye guarded with trident.

Chonars.

What the hell were they doing here posing like that?

"Name your business before you go through this Gate, Cherxanain." One of them who had a bronze mask on his face spoke sternly. Did they have some sort of death wish or had these two never heard about me before? Even Chonars should know better than to take that tone with me.

However, I kept my temper in check before I accidentally shredded them to pieces in a fit of anger. That would certainly open a whole can of worms which I absolutely had no interest in dealing with. At least I had to find out what had happened to those two.

"Name your business first for standing here. Last time I checked, the Valthors for this Gate didn't wear crappy masks like yours. Hell, I don't even know if they'd include guarding a Gate in your job description nowadays. Is poking your noses into other people's business not enough entertainment for you posers?" I could feel the coldness in my own voice as I kept my face as stoic as I could.

The other one with silver mask answered. His cold voice rivalled mine when he spoke. "The Valthors in question have been taken into custody."

Now, that was one serious way to pick a fight with me.

Trying to keep as stoic as possible and my temper on check, I scoffed. "Why is that? You couldn't find shit somewhere else, so even stuck-up Valthors became targets for your poking-nose-on-shit practice?" Suddenly the one with the silver mask let out a murderous aura around him as he spoke. Not that his aura felt that murderous . . .

"Just because you are a Cherxanain and your reputation as the Tyraviafonza precedes you, it doesn't mean you can pull that tough act with us Chonars."

"Stop it, Ovren. Our job is to guard this Gate for the time being, not getting killed in the process." The bronze-masked guy held his hand out in front of his pal.

Well, they did know me, and only one of them had the sense for survival. How hilarious.

"Stop being such a wuss, Kyvorg. Even though their rank surpasses ours, they aren't as strong as us in reality, otherwise we wouldn't be the ones called to rally them and all other soldiers in if any of them does something stupid, would we?" Ovren sounded so cocky when he asked his pal.

"Is that supposed to be a rhetorical question? Because I assure you, your pal here isn't being a wuss. Let's just say he does know who he's talking to at the moment." I twitched one edge of my lips.

"And what would make you different from the rest of the Cherxanains?" I saw Ovren narrow his gaze at me behind his mask as he made a taunting gesture. Was this guy a newbie in the Chonars division or what?

I glanced at Kyvorg, who took a bit of a step back at his pal's stupid question. Ignoring him, I focused on that stupid Ovren. "Look, I don't have time to do some Grand Moron Contest with you. Just answer me, why were they taken? They're much more entertaining than those other statues at the other gates." I spoke calmly while in reality that Ovren moron was testing my patience.

"That's none of your business, Cherxanain." Ovren jerked his head as he crossed his arms over his chest.

"Oh boy, this moron is so getting my fucking punches."

I gazed dryly at him and directed a bit of my energy towards the soil beneath his feet. He was still standing there in his tough stance, when suddenly the earth opened and he fell into it. He was so off guard that he couldn't even react as the earth closed again just around his neck. And then I locked the earth so that he couldn't bust himself free. Now only his head was visible.

"What the fuck? Let me go!" he yelled.

Kyvorg gaped at the sight of his partner's head and looked at me. I held my hand up and wagged my forefinger at him. *"Don't* even think about it. Don't worry. I still know my limit in teaching you slow people a lesson. You showed me your respect, and therefore you earned a bit of my appreciation, but not this shithead. Somebody needs to put him in his place." I let out quite a bit of my aura as I lowered my gaze towards Ovren.

I knelt before the stupid Chonar's head. "You may be right about one thing. *Most* Cherxanains aren't as strong as you people. But you are extremely wrong about one vital part."

"What?" he shouted, but this time his voice was trembling. There was fear in his voice. His sense might be working after all.

"There are a few Cherxanains that are much more powerful than the others. One of them is myself. Your assumption that I'm no different than other Cherxanains is your first mistake, but your greatest one is your stupidity for not taking what you've heard about me seriously. There's a reason why they call me the Queen of Tyranny, and that is, I assure you, not by posing," I said coldly as I narrowed my eyes angrily.

I took off his mask and his grey eyes widened as I held up my hand.

"What . . ." was all he could manage before I broke off one of his horns and then gouged one eye out. His screams echoed throughout the woods.

"Cherxanain, stop!" Kyvorg suddenly pulled out his own energy as he made a stance to shoot me.

I raised my brow at him and got up to my feet as I got rid of the blood that coated my fingers. "Relax, he'll live, and for the record, I'm not going rogue or anything. I just made him realize why my reputation as the Tyraviafonza precedes me. Just FYI, it's not only by manipulating human fools. My enemies' dying screams are the one song I relish as I bathe in their blood and entrails. I already carried out lots of painful torments that you couldn't even dream of, so I give you one piece of advice here. Don't *ever* test me." I emphasized the word "ever" as I lowered my gaze again towards Ovren.

This time, the moron didn't even look back.

"Now we have an understanding. So, again, why were they taken? Come on, just out of curiosity here, and for your info, I'm here to see the Head Intel. Happy? Your turn, c'mon, tell me about the guards." I folded my arms over my chest as I ignored Ovren who was gasping and panting near my feet.

Kyvorg cringed at the sight, and obviously he tried to ignore him for a while. "V–very well, Cherxanain, the previous Valthors are suspects for attempting high treason."

I laughed at his words. "They can't even move their asses from here. What treason could they possibly do?"

Hesitantly, Kyvorg answered. "Well, we received an intel that they've been acting suspiciously over the past week."

I winced and stared blankly for a second at his answer. 'They were acting suspicious?' That was so unheard of. I cleared my throat to refrain myself from laughing at their faces again. "Come on, don't joke with me. How suspicious could guardians be who aren't even allowed to leave this spot? Did they piss on your best shoes? Or damage your hearing with their self-invented gossip?"

Kyvorg laughed nervously before he could stop himself. "Not exactly, Cherxanain. We aren't that clear on the details either. Both of us are just assigned to guard this Gate and check everyone who goes through closely. Every *single* one."

This was really weird. The info we had passed to them was a bit like attempting treason, but that was all. It wasn't like they breathed this matter to anyone. They couldn't do that. Unless . . .

Letting out a tired breath, I nodded. "Okay, thanks for the latest gossip. Valthors attempting treason makes all sense in whole the world." I shook my head. "Okay then, now I'd like to go inside." I jerked my head at the Gate.

Kyvorgad then moved away, gesturing for me to go through. Without another word, I walked past him and waved my hand a little. The earth that was locking his pal opened and Ovren was thrown out as the earth closed again. When I walked towards to the boulder, his eye and horn were back to normal. I heard his gratitude the moment I passed the Gate.

Not that I cared. He'd finally learnt where his place was.

I walked as fast as I could towards Amon's office. As before, I went through the blue-flamed door with other intel divisions along the way.

I was about to open the door when I heard Vrae's furious voice from behind it. "What the hell did you mean they were jeopardized? There's no way for that to happen, and I don't think they're dumb enough to talk about it if there are people coming through!"

And then Zade's voice followed. "She's right, come on, tell us! Damn, both of them won't be happy if they hear this."

Deciding this was the right moment to make an appearance, I opened the door and the three of them froze. I slowly closed the door and then faced them. "Yeah, Amon, that bastard pair out front told me about them, so I'd like to hear it too. Why the hell would they take Valthors of a fucking Gate and furthermore accuse them attempting high fucking treason?" I asked coldly.

Amon rose up from his seat and then sighed. "Hi, Yve, I'm fine. Thanks for asking. How have you been?" He curled his lips.

I rolled my eyes at his ill-placed sarcasm. "Bad timing for jokes, Iverand. Answer our question, and I'll tell you how *I* have been these past few days." I replied quietly but with warning thick in my voice.

"Yve . . ." Vrae abruptly spoke.

I raised one hand to stop her. "Sorry, not now Vrae. We can get into 'hi, how are you doing these days?' chit-chat later. Now, Amon, tell us," I said sternly.

He lowered his gaze. "Fine, like you said earlier, those two are suspected of high treason. I don't know who gave the intel or how they came to that outrageous conclusion. Personally, I'd bet DeVarren's ugly ass that those two were under surveillance since a few days ago, hell, perhaps even longer. And the only chance I could think of for them both to be jeopardized is if they'd sometimes assumed that there was no one around and foolishly talked about the matters you guys told them about this past week. If that's indeed the case, then they both are done for." By the look on his face, I could tell that he was also frustrated.

I *tsked* as another thought came to my mind. "Nice! I'd suspect that much if they are indeed that stupid, but I don't think so. It's surprising that you really think they'd be that stupid, Amon." I raised my brows at him.

Zade was taken aback by my words. "What made you say that? You know something we don't?"

I expelled a disgusted breath. "Although they do indeed both look like Morons of the Year, they're not. That's the problem. Even they can comprehend the importance of the matter at hand. So in that regard, I'd say they'd use a blocked channel whenever they wanna talk about this, not to mention that it was them who told me that there were Chonar bastards going through their Gate, when they hardly ever do that. It was as if those Chonars were checking something. Considering that fact, I think it safe to think that they'd be even more careful than we are."

The three of them fell quiet for a couple of seconds before Vrae decided to break the silence. She folded one arm across her chest and rested her chin on her other hand.

"So, you're saying, if they communed in private and yet they still got their asses fried, then the ones who were watching them . . ." Her voice was fading as she narrowed her gaze at me.

I nodded as I gave her a wary look. "Yes, it's those Archanian dickheads." I let my statement hang in the air.

They were the Chonars' last line of defence, the only ones with the ability to break through mental channels. No one could secretly commune once they were under their scrutinizing ears. Well, that was the case for soldiers with lesser powers. What most of them didn't know was that they *could* be blocked too. One just had to know how to.

Luckily, everyone in this den knew the way–a little trick we'd learnt from Ry.

Mentally smiling at the thought of him, I cleared my throat. "So, Amon, tell me one more thing." I turned my gaze to him as he stood still listening to everything I said.

Zade suddenly let out a nervous laugh. "Wait, if that was what happened, then we . . ."

"Just a second, Zade, I'm getting there," I interrupted him. "Have they found out who gave them the info? That is, *assuming* the matters those stupid Echelons accused them of are the same as what we gave them insights to," I gave him a meaningful gaze.

His eyes widened as he caught my meaning. "No, as far as I know, there's no one yet reporting any shit about us and what secrets we hold."

My gaze was still stuck on him for few seconds as I kept my face as stoic as possible.

What the hell? Were they waiting for the right time to catch us off guard? Or did both of them not say our names when they talked about whatever it was? Were we also under surveillance?

That was to be expected if they were keeping their eyes on those Valthors.

"Very well," I said quietly and proceeded mentally. *"I hate to say this, but let's assume that we are also under surveillance. So from now on, when we're together, let's talk over that channel, okay guys? That way, even if they indeed placed those dickheads on our tails, they won't get anything."*

The three caught my meaning and nodded. Vrae then sighed in frustration as she ran her fingers through her long hair. *"Now, leave those Guards aside, 'cause I've been meaning to ask you this. What have you been doing with your man and those three?"*

Amon grimaced. *"The princes,"* he blurted out.

I frowned at his spontaneous remark. *"You told him?"*

Zade and Vrae shook their heads. *"No."* They turned to him. *"How did you know about those guys?"*

The Iverand winced. *"Sorry, I forgot to tell you that your working with them was one of the things they told me about."*

Vrae nodded. She seemed to understand whatever the Iverand was talking about. *"And they would be . . . ?"* I asked.

She turned to me. *"Lenora and Ravendy."*

I grinned at those names. *"It's been a long time since I've last seen them. How are they doing these days?"*

"Still as vague and somewhat miserable like doomsday as usual. Kind of like you," Amon said with glee.

I snorted. *"Well, what's life without disaster?"*

Amon suddenly levelled a chiding stare at me. *"Speaking of disaster, they didn't tell me how in the hell you guys could get anywhere near a prince, let alone three of them. You know if you struck a wrong cord with those guys, it would mean disaster,"* he snapped.

I rolled my eyes at him. *"Get over the theatrics. We knew them even before Ry almost got deep-fried by Belphegor's dad; hence we can walk away from their places alive."*

"We? You mean you and Zade knew them as well?" Amon asked sharply.

I looked at Vrae and was welcomed by a warning gaze. Okay, no telling the Iverand about her boyfriend. *"What I meant by 'we' is Ry, Vrae, and myself. Zade only got to know them a few days ago because he was with us."*

He blinked several times before he stopped. *"Oh, okay. At least this would explain why Ry could get his hand on dangerous kinds of information. I still can't believe that even you guys are allowed to cross paths with them. That's way beyond cool."* Amon sneered.

I scoffed. *"Thanks. Now I'll answer your question."* I looked at Vrae, who seemed to be holding her breath in anticipation.

Zade swallowed and looked at me closely. *"Ry and I went to get that ring,"* I said as I crossed my arms over my chest.

"You did what? You managed to get the ring?!" All of them yelled simultaneously in my head, causing a real sharp pain and buzzing sound to ring in my ears.

I shook my head as I placed one hand on the side of my head in an attempt to clear my hearing and my head from the pain. *"People, give me some fucking warning before you go wild in my head and tear my eardrums apart,"* I snapped, feeling totally annoyed.

They grinned apologetically, and Vrae cleared her throat. *"Sorry about that. So, you get the ring, and then what now? You guys plan to take the last seal?"*

I nodded to confirm her. *"Yes. That's why I came here in the first place, to fetch you two. Ry has gone to get his brother. Belphegor and Seere are both at Vassago's."*

Vrae nodded and turned to face the Head Intel. *"I see. In that case, we shouldn't waste any more time. Please cover for us, okay, Amon?"*

When I saw him do nothing more than just give a subtle nod, I arched a brow. *"You already filled him in, Vrae?"*

She winced. *"Uh, yes, I did. Besides, he knew from those two. Don't waste your time asking me how they knew, because they just did, as usual."*

"Right, that's what they do. And you've got nothing against it, Amon?" I asked him quietly. Well, if he did, then we had no choice but to kick him out of the loop.

He slowly shook his head and smiled at me. *"No, they asked me that, and I've got nothing against it. Don't worry, I'm not lying. I may respect the big bosses, but Ry's my pal too. I'll cover for you. Besides, my ass is out of harm's way, because we know they still can't find some other unfortunate bastard to fill in my position, right? So don't worry about me. For all our sakes, put an end to that stupid void dirt bag."* He winked.

This time I looked at him with newfound respect, and I gave him a nod of thanks.

"So now, shall we go?" Vrae asked me. I hesitated for a second and then shook my head. *"Not yet. I wanna meet those two first."*

"Then I'll go with you," Vrae said as she firmed her gesture. I nodded slightly to approve her coming with me, but I raised my hand up when I saw her mate was about to offer his company. *"No, not you, Zade. At this rate, I'm sure you understand why, right?"*

He curled his lips in disapproval, but then he sighed, knowing he couldn't argue. *"Fine, I'll go to my own base. Shall we meet at the usual Gate?"*

I snorted. *"With the bastard pair standing there looking pretty? No, we'll meet near Gillian. And if it's no problem with you, can I ask you to go through another Gate? We won't be using any doppies this time, so I'd like to avoid any unnecessary problem with going anywhere in packs."*

He sighed. *"All right, I'll go through the southeast Gate. We'll reconvene in two hours at Gillian."*

"Fine, we'll see you there. By the way, Amon, where did those bastards take them?" I averted my gaze from Zade.

"Last I heard, both of them were taken to the Araine level."

I let out a curse. *"Already putting them both in death row? They sure don't waste any damn time, do they?"*

He sighed helplessly. *"Even though in theory they might be relieved of all charges, we all know that's not gonna happen, don't we? And in terms of devils on death row, I won't expect Malik to intervene."* He averted his gaze to the ceiling as he mentioned the archangel, he who judged the most unforgivable of sinners, the archangel who became the sole Valthor of Hell, Malik.

"I've never known him to be that helpful anyway," I replied sarcastically.

Suddenly another thought went through my mind. "Oh yeah, Amon, do you have anything to say to them?" I asked him carefully.

He looked a bit hesitant as he lowered his gaze. He abruptly looked me in the eye and shook his head ash a smile broke on his face. "No, thanks for the offer, but maybe a simple 'hi and good luck' would suffice," he said calmly, but the look in his eyes betrayed his voice. There was a glint of despair that lingered there that made my stomach churn in guilt.

I swallowed a bit at his answer but decided not to ask anything further. "All right then, catch you later, Amon." I inclined my head to him.

He nodded. "Be careful, you guys. You're no good to anybody dead, and I'd miss your insults if you were." He folded his arms over his chest.

"Don't worry, we won't miss the chance to insult you," I said as I opened the door and went outside with the other two. I then closed the door, leaving Amon inside.

"Catch you on the flip side." I tilted my head to Zade. He waved and left us both.

We walked in silence on our way to reach the Araine level, which was located just two levels above the lowest basement where Cain made his eternal residence, well, so to speak.

Because it wasn't like he agreed to be put in there.

In order to reach that particular level, we once again went to the tunnel we used when we paid Cain a visit. I dropped off first with Vrae behind me, and we came out two holes higher than the last time.

"We're here." I looked around as soon as I went through the hole leading to the place. The surroundings were pretty much the same as Cain's block. Brick roads and flames were all over the place. There were no cells here, and the people were locked up together with chains. They were devils awaiting the death sentence.

There were several levels for people on sentencing row for humans and devils. Both races had to be powerless, so the devil who became a convict was to be stripped of his or her powers. Some were reserved for eternal beatings. Others, like Cain, were condemned to maddening silence. But only a few were preserved for actual death. What I mean by actual death is that people who received this punishment would no longer exist, not on earth, in hell, or in heaven. Their existence would just be wiped out. In other words, they'd be pulled into oblivion.

And that was what awaited our Valthors. Damn, if only I'd known, I would never have messed with their stuck-up lives.

There were twenty devils standing in one line and they were all chained up together. I looked around and saw six guards watching the prisoners closely.

Vrae and I walked for couple minutes before we finally found them, standing few feet in front of us. Funnily enough, they were talking and looked as if they were waiting for their turn to buy some lunch.

I exchanged a wary gaze with Vrae and then approached them. Right before we got to them, I called Vrae. *"Vrae, could you please ask the guards if we could take those two to talk in private?"*

She was startled but changed her direction as she replied, *"Okay, leave it to me."*

I walked past the other convicts as she proceeded. When I got behind Zoran, I patted his back. He abruptly jumped from surprise. "Yve, hey, how have you been?" he asked casually.

I arched a brow at his question. "I'm feeling awesome," I answered him sarcastically.

"Hey, Yve," Gevirash greeted me.

Damn, could they look at least a little bit concerned for themselves?

"Guys, I'm sorry. I really am," I said quietly.

Zoran waved his hand. "Nah, what are you apologizing for? It's a nice change of surroundings. Really."

"And with lots of others too," Gevirash added.

I made a face at their jibe. "Guys, these 'lots of others' are waiting for punishment! Damn punishment that you two don't even deserve at all! Not one. Fucking. Bit!" I drawled fiercely.

They both grinned at each other and then faced me again. "Yeah, but you still can't deny that this is a change from our surroundings, can you?" Gevirash grinned widely.

"Well, these spoiled the day a bit, but all and all, not that bad," Zoran said, indicating his chest and Gevirash's with a nod.

I frowned. They were already chained, so what was on them? Could it be . . . ?

A wave of disgust and anger assailed me. I slowly raised my hands and pulled aside the dirty convict robes Gevirash was wearing. There I saw that my suspicions were true.

The centre of his chest was blackened with a pattern burnt into the flesh. It was a seal to suppress his powers, and both of them had been branded with it. Now their powers must be constantly burning through their bloodstream.

I took a step back. "Guys . . ."

Zoran raised a hand to stop me. "Look, Yve, we both are totally grateful that you as a Cherxanain would have any concern about us."

Gevirash supported Zoran's words with a wide grin. "Yeah, we really are, and we noticed that about you. Not all other super 'high and mighty' ranks"–he made a quote sign in the air–"out there would trouble themselves with mere guardians, unlike you, your sister, and a few others."

"Well, you both do make me laugh from time to time. That in my book, gentlemen, makes you more than mere 'guardians'." I forced a grin, as I also made a quote sign.

"Well, vice versa. You do make us laugh from time to time yourself." Zoran snickered.

"Okay, enough jokes, oh, and by the way, Amon said hi and good luck." I raked my hair with my fingers as I looked at them closely.

They fell silent for a second and then smiled slightly at me. "How nice of him to remember us," Zoran said. I noted something weird beneath his calm voice, but I couldn't tell what it was.

Sighing, I tilted my head to them. "How long have you two been down here?"

"Not too long. We were just standing there making fun of each other, when six Chonars dropped by and four of them seized us." Zoran's voice was so calm. He could be mistaken for someone reporting the weather forecast.

"One of the two remaining said this, 'Gevirash and Zoran, Valthors of this Gate, you two are under arrest for attempting high treason'." His voice was heavier in an attempt to duplicate whatever Chonar had said those words. And then his voice went back to normal. "You know, if it hadn't been Chonar bastards who said that, we might have thought of it as a practical joke," Gevirash chuckled.

"Hell, we almost laughed in their faces, well, I mean their masks. You know those guys, so secretive that they never allow people outside their group to see their faces." Zoran added.

"Like we would want to see their ugly faces," Gevirash interjected, and then both of them high-fived.

When they raised their hands to me, expecting me to high-five with them, I expelled a long-suffering sigh and slapped my palms with theirs. "You two just don't know when to quit, do you? And for your info, I broke off one horn and gouged out one eye of one of the Chonars standing at your post." I couldn't help grinning myself.

They both gaped. "Wow, you should've told us. We'd come to see it even if it meant pay-per-view." Gevirash looked really amazed at what I'd just told them.

Zoran looked impressed himself. "Yeah, and here you stand asking us to look all gloomy like we're attending someone's funeral, but you do that yourself."

I was laughing when suddenly a well-built guard approached us with Vrae walking next to him. "Cherxanain,"–he bowed a bit to greet me–"I understand that both you and Cherxanain Vrathien have something to discuss with the convicts. Please take your time and go over that corner, but please note that you don't have more than thirty minutes," he said as he pointed the far corner of the hot flaming basement.

"Thanks for your understanding. We assure you that we won't take too long." I gave the guard a nod of thanks, and then he responded with another salute before he undid the chain that tied Gevirash and Zoran.

"Come on," Vrae said as she quickly walked towards the corner indicated by the guard. The three of us followed her, and as soon as we reached the place, Vrae abruptly stopped and turned around. "Now that we're quite far away from those guys, let's be quick. You two, how's it going?" she asked.

Zoran shrugged. "Well, it's like the old days."

Vrae frowned. "Like the old days?" she gave them a chiding stare. "Would you care to elaborate on that?"

I snorted. "If you expect them to act as if they had any realization that they are about to face death penalty, I tell ya, you're wasting your time." I shook my head. Both of them grinned broadly at my words.

She scoffed. "Okay, so let me ask you this. Have they told you what they are accusing you with? Is it the same thing we gave you insight to, or is it something else?"

Gevirash made a face, while Zoran just grinned at Vrae and me. "We suspect so."

My brows knitted. "You suspect so? They didn't even tell you guys why you both got dumped down here?"

"They don't need to." Zoran suddenly stopped grinning and looked serious for once. "We told you about those Chonars going through our Gate, right?" he asked me.

"Yes. That's why I assumed you two would be extremely careful about your surroundings. You'd even commune mentally if you ever wanted to discuss the things we told you about."

"Well, thanks, at least you know us that well." Zoran lifted the edge of his lips.

"So, what do you guys think made them bust you? Did you two mention anything about us or them?" She gave them a meaningful gaze.

I looked at them both, then at Vrae, and back to them. "Uh, Vrae, have you told them about *him* and our very old friends?" I narrowed my gaze at her.

She didn't even look at me. "Yes, I have. You were busy at that time, so I took the liberty to tell them about the rest of the things that have been happening, including our plans. I didn't tell Amon at first, because I wanted you to be there when I do, since I don't know how he would react. Don't worry. They agreed to watch the passers closely for us. They already told you about the Chonars, right?"

I rolled my eyes at her question. "And you even wonder why they got busted," I said sarcastically.

"Hey, at least we got the Coolest News of the Century," Zoran said in a nonchalant voice.

"Yeah, and we've been meaning to say this. Congrats, Yve, you finally got to be with him." Gevirash winked teasingly at me.

I felt my face turn partially hot at his words, and then I shook my head. "I can't believe you guys are okay with this."

Gevirash suddenly gave me a stern look. "I told you, right? You, your sister, and a few others, and–let me add it this time–especially *him*, don't act all high and mighty with us. Even if he doesn't think of us that way, we consider him a good friend of ours." He folded his arms across his chest.

"If we can do anything to cover for you guys, even at the cost of our lives, then so be it," Zoran said in a sing-song voice.

"At least for once we can do something more useful than some stupid security job," Gevirash laughed.

"That's why we didn't even mention your names whenever we talked about it through a channel." Zoran inclined his head.

"Yeah, and because we suspected that whoever was watching us might be poking their ugly noses in your direction, we made it seem as if we were the ones who planned the whole thing, along with some other exaggerations as well," Gevirash added.

"In other words, by taking us down here," Zoran interjected.

"Those shitheads ate the whole shit we offered them, along with the garbage can!" they said simultaneously, and they high-fived again.

My eyes widened at their words. "You guys even went that far!"

To think they'd help us this much.

"Don't mind us, you two. You both coming here is good enough for us. At least we got the chance to explain things so you don't have nightmares from guilt," Gevirash laughed.

"Come on, get the hell outta here. It's been almost thirty minutes. Say hi to your man for us when you meet him." Zoran winked at me.

"Yeah, at the very least we got the chance to say our goodbyes to him," Gevirash added with a shrug.

Even Vrae was speechless at their words.

"Guys, if only I'd known, I wouldn't have involved . . ." I didn't get to finish what I was about to say because both of them raised their hands to stop me.

"Don't take this from us. We wanted to be some help to you guys once in a while, and when we saw this chance, we simply took it," Gevirash said rather sternly.

"Besides, don't take back your words just because of us," Zoran's face turned dead serious as well.

I arched my brows at his words. "Which words might that be?"

"'Devils never know regrets, never did, and never will'," they both said in unison.

Damn, they even remembered that one, when I myself didn't even think about it.

I swallowed a bit. "Okay, if this is what you want, thank you guys, really. We won't forget what you've done for us. I will tell him you said hi."

"Okay, see you two girls later, oh and tell Zade and Amon we said hey to them as well." Zoran pointed himself and Gevirash.

I hesitated when he mentioned Amon. "Uh, is there anything else you guys want us to say to Amon?" I asked.

They exchanged a quizzical stare and then shook their heads at me. "Nope, thanks for the offer though, but an easy hey will do."

Frowning deeply, I closed my eyes and sighed. After a couple seconds, I opened them. "Okay, I'll tell him."

Looking at their bright expressions and hearing their simple wishes, especially when they had every right to ask for more, I couldn't do anything but to give them a half-hearted smile.

We walked slowly in the direction of the tunnel and parted with them both along the way. As we saw them get locked back up with the others, deep guilt and respect towards their sacrifice swelled inside me.

"An easy hey will do."

No more words to the only one devil who had the same blood.

"See you two girls later."

Zoran said those words lightly, knowing full well that we'd never see each other again, knowing full well that they'd no longer exist.

It was then I swore that I'd make damn sure we succeeded.

Chapter 25

We quickly went back up and dropped by Amon's den to tell him everything those two had told us. Walking in haste, we reached his den in no time. Vrae lifted the enchantments, and we went in to find the den's owner sitting at his desk with his head down. Damn, I could almost say I felt sorry for him. He'd done nothing but cover us, and those bastards planned to slaughter his brothers for it.

"Amon?" I called him carefully as Vrae closed the door.

He jumped a bit and lifted his head. "Oh, guys, hey," he said, sounding tired.

I bit my lip as I sauntered towards him. "Amon, I'm sorry about . . ."

"Don't. As much as I hate to say it, I heard you guys down there. They wanted this, and besides, the Echelons were already zeroed in on me–well, at least the Ravathes were."

I exchanged an alarmed look with Vrae. "What do you mean?"

"Well, they did say they'd do something if they find out or even suspected that I was in on this. I just didn't think they'd do *this*, which is pretty stupid of me," he said sadly.

"Yeah, that is a new low, even for them," Vrae said in disgust.

I glanced at her. She had a point. It seemed as though that wretched bunch was in hurry to ensnare somebody.

But who?

Judging by the Ladurga Ry had killed, the simple answer should've been me, but that would only be the case if I was the only one with it on my tail. Vrae and Zade said they didn't see any of them on their tails, but what if they didn't realize it?

Those thoughts were swirling in my mind when I felt someone lift the enchantments on the door. I untied the pouch containing the Herathim as Amon quickly opened a drawer behind his desk. I threw it into the drawer, and he slammed it shut. We turned around and saw two masked soldiers burst into the room.

Chonars! They had their spears at the ready in their grasps.

"What is the meaning of this?!" Amon asked sharply.

One of them with a grey mask raised a hand at him. "Back down, Iverand. This does not concern you."

"Or you," the other, wearing a metallic black mask, tilted his chin at Vrae.

I frowned at that. What the . . . ?

"Like hell it doesn't! This is my chamber, and I demand that you explain why you're here with weapons drawn, to a Cherxanain no less!" Amon snarled.

Vrae placed herself at his side, while I stared at them. "Answer the Iverand. Why are you here?" I coldly repeated Amon's words.

They pointed their spears at me. "We're under orders to bring you, Cherxanain Yverna Tyraviafonza, into the Interrogation Chamber."

I clenched my teeth. That place wasn't for friendly questioning. It was for torturing.

"This is outrageous! On whose orders?" Vrae demanded.

Their answer didn't make things any clearer. "We act under the order of the twelve members of the Echelon."

I inhaled deeply at that. Twelve members. So it meant that Bynethar and Xamian were also in on this. Well, I'd like to see those assholes' faces up close and personal.

"On what grounds?" Amon interjected.

"We are not at liberty to explain," the one with the black mask said flatly.

I snorted. "Don't you mean you know nada about it?"

Vrae elbowed me. "You're not helping."

I scoffed as I stared at the masked soldiers. It wouldn't be the best choice for me to fight these goons and give the happy bunch a reason to throw me to the death sentence row. With that compelling thought in mind, I decided to play along. "All right, fine, I'm coming with you bastards," I said calmly as I strolled lazily towards them.

"Yve!" Vrae said sharply as she grabbed my hand.

"I'll be fine. Take care of *that*, would you?" I asked meaningfully. "Catch you later."

The Chonars lifted their hands and started to grab mine before I shot a cold glare at them which made them hesitate. "You do that, and don't blame me when you lose them."

They pulled back immediately.

I sneered. "C'mon, I dare you. No? Oh well, I always know you douches are good-for-nothing lapdogs. Even lapdogs have more balls than you do," I said as I walked to the door.

"Yve," Amon called with a note of helplessness in his voice. "This isn't the best time for jokes."

I glanced over my shoulder. "When will it be?" I asked as I forced a grin and left the den without even looking at them.

∗   ∗   ∗

Zaderion hastily walked out of his base and headed straight to the Iverand's office.

"This can't be happening. It can't be!" he said over and over in his head. He'd received the urgent message from Amon just minutes ago when Darvahl debriefed him on his latest job. Now he was condemning himself for not being there when it happened.

Arriving at the den, he heard his mate's frantic voice from the inside. "We have to do something, dammit!" Vrathien snarled for the sixth time.

"Vrae, I heard you, and you're not helping." Amon tapped his fingers on his desk. "I just don't get it. Why the hell are they doing this? And for what?"

Zaderion clenched his fists and started to lift the enchantments. Vrathien opened her mouth to continue her tirade, but Amon shushed her. "Somebody's here."

They waited until the last incantation was lifted and Zaderion burst inside. "Hey, guys," he said as he closed the door.

Both Amon and Vrathien exhaled in relief. "It's you."

Vrathien was nearly about to throw herself towards him when she realized Amon was in the room and caught herself. "Zade."

The Varkonian restrained himself from embracing her. Instead he just gave her a light squeeze on her shoulder. "Calm down, Vrae. Now tell me everything."

At his request, both Amon and Vrathien explained the situation in turn.

After they both were done, Zaderion raked his hair in frustration. "At least with this we know one thing. Bynethar and Xamian are indeed *in* on this. We can't trust those two," he said bitterly.

Amon ground his teeth as disturbing questions invaded his mind. Biting his lip, he looked at the two devils. "For now you have to get out of here before those bastards think of something to pull on the two of you."

"But . . ." Vrae started to argue.

"Vrae, I agreed to call Zade, but nothing's happened to her yet. So you two better get the hell out of here," Amon pressed.

Vrathien stubbornly shook her head. "I'm staying."

Amon frowned in sympathy for the she-devil. He'd be frustrated too. Hell, he was already past that moment when the Echelons put his brothers on death row. "Look, how about you get out of here and find *him*?" he asked, emphasizing the last word. "I'll watch over her golem. If there's anything, I'll contact you both."

Zaderion nodded in understanding. "We'll be nearby. C'mon, Vrae."

Vrathien didn't move, and her hands were balled into tight fists. She hated it when she didn't know what to do. Even in the most life-threatening situation, she was always able to face things calmly and find a smooth way out, but now she didn't even know what to think, and it was her sister whose life was on the line.

"Amon's right. Ry. I've got to find him. He needs to know this," she thought. Exhaling in defeat, she levelled a dark look at the Iverand. "All right, we're out of here. Keep that thing, would ya?" she asked quietly.

"I will," Amon said as Zaderion opened the door, but outside they found the last two devils they would have expected.

Bynethar and Xamian.

*　　*　　*

I walked down the path towards the Interrogation Chamber which passed the Echelons' with Ry filling my thoughts. I really hoped Vrae didn't try to find him and tell him about this. He'd storm this place all by himself, and as powerful as he was, I didn't think even he could go unscathed.

"Guys, won't you say anything?" I asked lazily, trying to put away that scary thought.

"Save your breath, Cherxanain. We're not here to be friendly with you," the grey-masked one said from my right.

I rolled my eyes as we continued walking towards the farthest corner of the Aryad. "Duh, who says I want you to do that? That's just plain disgusting. So, tell me, who was it, *really*, that gave you the order to seize me?"

They fell into dead silence again. Dammit.

"C'mon," I taunted as we took the left turn at a fork. "You're lapdogs who just put a high-profile Cherxanain like me under custody. Most people would just brag without even being asked. C'mon, say it."

The one with the black mask scoffed at my words. "Talk all you want, Cherxanain, while you still have that title."

"Ooh, one of you talks like you've grown a set. Keep it going, buddy, while you still have that tongue. Who the fuck was it?" I repeated.

Their mouths were closed again, and this time they kept silent all the way until we reached a steel door at the end of the path. There was nothing on it, no flame, no name, nothing to indicate what monstrosity rested behind it, only countless bloody scratches, belonging to those who struggled futilely before they were thrown in there, most of whom didn't come out alive.

"This is the end, *Cherxanain*," the black-masked one said as he strode towards the door and knocked on it while the other remained by my side.

"You wish," I grunted.

The door slowly moved inward, and a familiar voice came from the other side. "Bring her in."

*   *   *

Vrathien almost burst out in anger, but she fought to rein in her temper. The two walked past Zaderion who shut the door behind them.

"May I ask why you two are here?" Amon asked with a hint of venom in his voice.

The newcomers seemed to be oblivious to the tense atmosphere in the room. "Where did they take Tyraviafonza?" Xamian asked.

That single question nearly made Vrathien explode in rage. "Where . . . ? Pardon my impudence, but weren't you two of those who ordered her to be taken under custody and then be brought to the chamber?"

Xamian stared at her. "What the hell are you talking about? We didn't order anything. We've just heard."

"There were two damned Chonars barged in here," said Amon, "levelled their spears at her, and took her out."

Bynethar raised a hand. "Never mind that. What chamber? The Echelons'?"

"No," Zaderion said as he shook his head. "They took her straight to the Interrogation."

Both Ravaths exchanged an alarmed look before their eyes went to them again. "I want both of you to come with us."

*   *   *

Those useless Chonars had left the room and now I was standing in the middle of the chamber with two black metal poles and chains attached to them at my sides.

The floor was dark with dried blood from who knew how many soldiers. The stench of death engulfed me like sickening poison, yet it had a sweet fragrance that almost drove me to the edge. But the only thing I could think of was that the Echelons didn't torture just mere soldiers. They'd tormented *him* too, countless of times.

The thought that Ry had stood here being punished for something that wasn't his fault made my chest clench with fury. Above all, he'd gladly taken the beatings, for they'd threatened to seize us, his companions, if he didn't.

Looking up at the row of chairs, I saw that all of them were here. Wait, not *all* of them. Bynethar and Xamian weren't anywhere to be seen.

So they *weren't* in on this, after all. Good for them.

This left me with one conclusion. Kathiera. That bitch was still going at it, it seemed.

I forced myself to give these bastards a proper salute. "I, Cherxanain Yverna, have come to fulfil your request."

"You still have the nerve to salute us, I see. We are glad you're facing this as calmly as we expected," Kathiera said.

Well, she sure didn't waste time with the theatrics.

"May I inquire as to why I'm being summoned here?" I asked in the best manner I could afford to give them.

Lazoreth rose up from his seat. "We command you to explain your lies."

I frowned. Now what in the hell were they getting at? They couldn't possibly have guessed that we were with Xaemorkahn's people, could they?

"I honestly do not understand what you're implying here, Ravath."

At my words, Lazoreth shot a murderous glare at me. "I'm talking about your lie, when you said that you know nothing as to who killed the Arcs and breached the vow made by our Lord, and by extension, your words regarding your ignorance of Cain's prophecy may be a lie as well."

It felt like a punch straight to my gut when I heard him. No, it couldn't be . . .

"I still don't understand which part was the lie," I insisted. "And I don't know anything about Cain's prophecy or even that he'd produced one lately."

Faemirad too arose. "Let me put it to you this way, Cherxanain. When a Ladurga was assigned to follow you, it wasn't like we acted on our own. All the Echelons had agreed on this, because we feared that you may face another attack by the Arcs."

Yea, fucking right . . .

"Not only you, we've also assigned two more to protect both Cherxanain Wartiavega and Varkonian Zaderion," she went on.

I stared at her. They sent ones to Vrae and Zade!

Calming myself down, I forced a smile. "That is so considerate of you. I thank you for your concern."

"Cut the false act, Yverna," Mezarhim said coldly.

Okay, they were provoking me. Like that would work. "I still don't get which part you referred to as my lie," I said with a would-you-bastards-get-to-the-point look.

507

Lazoreth ground his teeth. "Whoever was with you killed my Ladurga."

I feigned a shocked look, but perhaps it showed up as a mocking one. "Truly? I wouldn't know, because at the time I wasn't even sure what was on my tail, Ravath."

"Did Mezarhim not say it clearly? Cut the false act, Yverna," Kathiera interjected. "It was someone with the power of the sky," she said coldly.

Gulping, I sorted through her words. So they did find out when Ry eradicated that Ladurga. Whatever they were getting at didn't mean I'd just give him up. I'd die first before I did that.

"Pardon my impudence, but I'm sure I do not need to remind you of the absurdity of that. Hieldhar Ezryan was the only one with that power. Unless someone else has reached that level, it is simply impossible to kill your Ladurga with the sky elements."

Falthan tapped his fingers on the desk. "I assure you, there's no such soldier up to this point, so that only leaves one option. Ezryan is still alive, and you know where he is."

"If he survived, then it is good news," I said innocently. "Unless there's something we soldiers didn't know about."

"Silence! Where is he?" Kathiera asked. Her icy voice echoed in the chamber.

"I simply don't understand why you're all so furious over this," I said, at the end of my tether. "Or like I said, unless you all have something to do with his supposed death?" I shot a meaningful look at them all.

It seemed the time had come for us to reveal a few of our secrets.

Their vicious auras simultaneously burst forth, filling the entire room with cold rage that burned like the flame of hell itself. "We demand you to tell us where he is," Havok pressed.

I raised my hands. "I don't know anything about that. But, Ravaths and Ravathes, are you sure this is the wisest course of action? If the soldiers hear that you have something to do with the death of the Hieldhar, I don't think they'll just stay put."

"So you do know something about it, or more to the point, his whereabouts?" Faemirad asked silkily.

"Did I say anything of the sort?" I retorted.

Kathiera suddenly raised her hands. "No more useless words." The chains caught my wrists and jerked my arms up. "This is your last chance. Where is he?"

"I don't know, because last time I looked, he was supposed to be dead."

Kathiera's sadistic laugh echoed. "Fine, brace yourself," she said. My robes were bound with invisible rope, and my armour dropped, leaving only a thin piece of silk covering my body. "We have a long day ahead."

I ground my teeth as she made a swiping movement. It was followed by a searing flash of pain tearing my chest. I screamed, but there was no sound, and there was nobody to hear it but them.

Ry . . .

* * *

A rift cracked open somewhere near Vassago's domain. Ezryan and Xaemorkahn walked out of it, and the rift cracked closed. Looking around, he frowned. His mate and the others were supposed to be there.

"Brother, what's wrong?" Xaemorkahn asked.

"I don't know yet," Ezryan answered. "They're late. I just hope it's nothing," he mused, and his thoughts went to the Ladurga he killed. It was then a tidal wave of dread assailed him, making him buckle.

"Brother!" Xaemorkahn exclaimed in alarm as he knelt beside him.

Ezryan didn't seem to hear the king. His mind was full of his mate and that dread attacking him. "Yve!" he called her name like a prayer as he pressed his chest.

A horrible feeling twisted his gut. There was no doubt something had happened. He just didn't know what.

He was about to walk towards the nearest tree when Vassago and Belphegor suddenly came from out of nowhere. At the presence of Xaemorkahn, the two princes tensed immediately, but they tried to ignore him. "Ry, why don't you come in . . . ?"

"Wait, Highnesses, it's Yve," he whispered.

Belphegor cocked a brow. "What's with her?"

"I don't know. I'm checking her now."

Vassago tsked. "At least get inside my barriers. You'll be like a sitting duck out here. C'mon, Ry."

The former Hieldhar immediately followed the princes and settled down on the grass. He chanted a spell, and five seconds later, his spirit walked out of his body and flew towards the Hellgate.

* * *

"Yve!" Amon called her in anguish as he saw her golem lacerated with countless scars. His tight fists trembled, he cursed his helplessness. "Come on, guys! They're killing her!" he whispered through clenched teeth. Another deep cut stretched over her golem's chest, and he flinched. "Hang on, Yve!"

He was so tense at the entire situation that he didn't realize someone was there. "Amon," the newcomer called.

Turning around, he saw the devil he'd least expected floating there. "You!"

* * *

Bynethar led the way towards the Interrogation Chamber with Xamian, Zaderion, and Vrathien behind him. "When we get there, do as we told you earlier. We'll take care of them," Xamian said to the other two.

Vrathien nodded without a word. She still couldn't believe that these two were in league with them. Their explanation back at Amon's den was hard to accept, but two names left her with no choice but to do it.

Princes Belphegor and Vassago.

"There," Bynethar said as they saw a steel door at the end of the road. He raised a hand and the door violently burst inward.

Walking past the doorway, he immediately planted himself in front of Yverna. Even from there he could sense each of the wounds the other Echelons had brutally carved on her.

"Bynethar, how dare you interrupt us!" Mezarhim roared from his chair.

The addressed Ravath flipped him off. "Silence! I'm the one who has every right to be here because she's my subordinate! How dare you do this to without my consent?" he snarled as Vrathien and Zaderion walked towards their companion.

"Yve! Yve, wake up!" Vrathien frantically called her sister.

With one swipe Bynethar cut Yverna loose, and she fell into her companions' arms. "Get her out of here," Xamian said from behind them.

Zaderion carried the unconscious Yverna in his arms with Vrathien in tow, leaving the two Echelon members behind them.

Once the soldiers were out, Xamian slammed the door shut. "You all have gone too damn far," he said with anger in each of his words.

The ten members of the Echelon jumped down from their high seats. They landed, surrounding the two in the middle.

"You two better explain yourselves." Mezarhim demanded as he spread his wings threateningly. The others followed his gestures.

"No matter how powerful you think you are, you're outnumbered," Kathiera said. Despite her attempt to appear calm, she could barely hide her victorious smile.

Bynethar and Xamian drew their powers at their hostile stance. "We totally don't care whatever stupidity you've all got going, but know this, you've overstepped your bounds by going to our subordinates without our consent, and it means full-scale war. We could care less who out-powered whom. Got that?" Bynethar snarled.

At their combined powers, the other members aside from Kathiera and Lazoreth took a step back. It was unwise to have all hell break loose in the chamber, inside the Aryad no less. It could shake the soldiers' already-fragile loyalty towards them if they caught wind of this internal dispute.

Kathiera raised both hands. "Fine, you win. We'll withdraw for now. We'll take this matter before the Lord. Just wait for the call."

"Whatever you say, Kathiera. While you're at it, you can go on and declare that as of now, Xamian and I are no longer members of the Echelon," Bynethar exclaimed.

At his sudden declaration, all the Echelons traded baffled looks. Kathiera inclined her head with smug smile curved her lips. "If that is what you wish. Then you won't hinder our next action towards your *former* subordinates, will you?"

Xamian levelled a disgusted glare at her. "You just don't know when to stop, do you?" he asked. When she didn't answer him, he shrugged. "They're already out, anyway. We're leaving. You can do whatever you want, but I know you have enough sense not to do anything stupid."

"Just leave. You no longer have any say before this council," Faemirad said.

Bynethar blew them a sarcastic salute before he and Xamian turned around. They walked tall through the doorway, leaving the rest of the Echelons in the chamber.

∗   ∗   ∗

"C'mon, Zade," Vrathien pressed as they flew further from the Aryad. The Chonars almost stopped them, but once they were well out of the Gate's range, the Chonars couldn't follow since they were guarding it.

Yverna was still unconscious, but blood didn't stop flowing from her mouth. Vrathien wanted to immediately teleport straight outside Vassago's domain, but her sister had already lost a lot of blood. She wouldn't be able to survive it.

They were only halfway to Vassago's castle when four people intercepted them. Belphegor, Vassago, and Xaemorkahn, with Ezryan leading them, were flying like madmen.

"Yve!" he called out as they reached her.

All of them landed carefully with Yverna in the middle. Vrathien looked at each of the newcomers. "How did you guys . . . ?"

"Ry found Amon. He told us everything," Belphegor explained. A wary glint flashed in his crimson eyes as his gaze went to each deep scar on Yverna's body.

Vrathien frowned at the prince's words, but she restrained herself from asking as she heard him mumble a foul curse upon the gruesome sight while Zaderion and Vassago circled around Ezryan, who began healing his mate.

"C'mon, Yve, wake up," Ezryan murmured in anguish as he kept sending his healing powers into her body.

All of them were waiting anxiously when one of Vrathien's golem's eyes flew down. "Vrae," it said in its revolting voice, and the Cherxanain lifted her head. "Kathiera and Faemirad are on their way here. I suggest you tell Ry to get the hell out of here before they see him. And in case things get even worse, I'll do what we've discussed."

Vrathien gritted her teeth before she nodded. "I understand. Thanks for the heads up."

"No problem," the eye said, and it flew back to its position above them.

The royals exchanged a worried look. "Time for shields and a little distance," Vassago said as he, Belphegor, and Xaemorkahn started to walk away.

But Ezryan didn't seem to notice, for he kept healing his mate. Vassago sauntered towards him and placed a hand on his shoulder. "Ry, c'mon, let's go."

As if in some kind of a trance, Ezryan was still on his knees, and his hands were firmly planted on Yverna's bloody chest.

"Ry!" Vassago repeated.

The former Hieldhar didn't even blink. "I have to heal her," was all he said.

"Get a grip, boy," Belphegor interjected.

Vrathien moved and placed her hands over his. She was trembling when she drew her powers. "Ry, c'mon, I–I'll heal her," she said. Her tears already stung her eyes.

"She's right, brother," Xaemorkahn inserted, and he slipped his hand under Ezryan's. The devil reluctantly ceased his powers and stood up, following his sworn brother and the other two princes.

* * *

The door to his den burst open violently, and Amon stood up straight.

"Iverand, there you are," Kathiera said silkily, while Faemirad closed the door behind them. "Now that all nonsense is out of the way, let's get down to business, shall we?"

"What do you mean, Ravathes? What do you want me to do?" Amon asked in a slightly trembling voice.

Faemirad stepped forward. "Show us Tyraviafonza's golem."

Amon frowned at her peculiar request. "Her golem, Ravathes?"

"Just show us, Iverand," Kathiera snapped impatiently.

"But shouldn't we notify Ravath Bynethar first?"

Kathiera sneered sadistically. "News flash! As of this moment, Bynethar and Xamian are no longer Echelon members."

"They declared it themselves. Like she said, all that nonsense is out of the way," Faemirad interjected.

Amon was taken aback by their words. Both Ravaths renounced their seats in the council? That definitely wouldn't bode well for their subordinates.

Inhaling to calm himself down, Amon left his chair. He had no choice but to grant their request, which he was sure would involve something not good. "Follow me," he said as he led them to the Hall of Golem.

Opening the door to the hall, he stepped aside to admit the two females and then closed the door. "Her golem's up there. What exactly do you want me to do?"

"Kill her through it," Faemirad said flatly.

Amon stared at them both. How in the hell could they know that he had the ability to do it? No one aside from the long line of Iverand, masters and apprentices of golem sorcery, should know about it!

"I don't know what you're speaking of, Ravathe," he said, trying to appear calm while his core viciously pounded his chest.

Kathiera *tsked*. "I admire your loyalty to your deceased master, but you answer to the Echelons, Iverand."

A lump of fury swelled in him at the mention of his master. The she-devil talked as if she had nothing to do with his master's death. *"If only I had your golem,"* he thought with clenched fists. "I do answer to the Echelons, but I cannot do something that is beyond my powers," he said firmly.

"How long are we gonna pretend you can't do it? Do we need you to swear it?" Faemirad pressed.

Amon gulped. He couldn't postpone it any longer. He had no other option but to hope these two had no idea of his other ability, the one Bynethar and Xamian somehow had the knowledge of.

"All right, I give up. I shall do as you demand," he said with raised hands.

"It remains to be seen, doesn't it?" Kathiera asked icily.

The three of them flew straight to the left corner of the columns and rows of small caves where thousands of golems rested. Each glowed with their core powers. They stopped in front of a female golem that had cuts all over it. The wounds weren't as deep as before, and it continued to heal. It seemed Ezryan was halfway through healing her, but he hoped Vrathien manage to talk sense into him and get him the hell out of the way after that message he sent her earlier.

"Her sister's healing her, it seems," Kathiera said. Her gaze was fixed on the sixth eye of the golem. It showed them Vrathien and Zaderion kneeling around Yverna, who was still unconscious.

"I was half expecting to see Ezryan," Faemirad inserted.

Amon gulped at her words but pretended not to hear them. "So what now?"

"Now let's see how you kill her. I've always wondered how you Iverands could do it but wouldn't. I bet you're anxious to test it. Here's your chance," Kathiera said lightly.

We wouldn't do it for a damn good reason, you bitches.

The Iverand nearly lost it, but he caught himself and then secretly contacted Vrathien through her golem as he placed a hand on Yverna's. "As you wish."

He chanted the destructive spell that would vanquish the devil through the life force stored in the golem. Each word came out like stammered gibberish, but he managed to keep calm and finish the spell. His trembling was worsened as he saw Yverna start coughing a mouthful of blood and having violent seizures as her sister frantically called her name and the Varkonian attempted to hold the unconscious Cherxanain down.

Inhaling deeply, he started to chant the last two lines of the spell. He glanced askance at the two Ravathes, who smiled victoriously upon the sight of the tormented Cherxanain, and began his own move. *"Let's see if you two dumbasses notice this."*

*   *   *

"No! No! Yve!" Ezryan started to struggle at the sight of Yverna violently coughing blood, while Belphegor and Vassago firmly hold him back with Xaemorkahn next to them.

Belphegor gritted his teeth despite the fact that he knew what was happening, but he still didn't like it. "Calm down, Ry. She's gonna be all right."

"The hell she is! She's already wounded. We don't know for sure!" Ezryan snarled.

"Just wait," Vassago said as his turquoise eyes turned to the three eyes hanging not far above the three soldiers.

A moment later the three eyes belonged to Yverna's golem exploded on their own, and the seizures abruptly stopped, although blood was still flowing from her mouth.

"Yve?" Ezryan asked with a trembling voice. "Vrae, talk to me!"

Vrathien gulped as she reached out to the ether and found her own golem. *"Just wait for a second."*

"How is she?" He yelled with dread. It was then his ears caught static, but he couldn't pick out the source. His attention nearly went to it when he saw Vrathien gasp sharply and her eyes widen with the strangest look of surprise.

"Vrae!" Ezryan called again. She didn't answer him. Instead she spurted blood, and her body began to tremble violently just like her sister's just did.

"Dammit, those bitches just won't stop!" Vassago said through clenched teeth.

"Vrae! Vrae!" Zaderion called as he attempted to hold her down.

Her blood-red eyes turned backwards in their sockets, and she went limp. After that, her golem too was destroyed.

At the sight, both Ezryan and Zaderion fell to their knees and bellowed in despair.

* * *

Amon lowered his hand. His gut churned with guilt as both Vrathien and Yverna's golems were melted in their holes.

"Excellent work, Iverand. Now, we shall leave you alone," Kathiera said with a satisfied smile on her cold face. She and Faemirad went down. Amon got rid of the remains of the golems before he too jumped down.

"Is there anything else I can do for you?" he asked flatly. The absence of emotion in his voice made Kathiera raise a brow. "Volunteering much today? I thought you cared about the soldiers?"

"I thought it was you who reminded me that I answer to the Echelons?" Amon retorted.

Faemirad grabbed Amon's collar. "Don't start being a smart mouth, Iverand. That is not very wise."

"I don't mean to, Ravathe," he said in the same flat tone of voice.

"Good," Kathiera interjected. "Now let's just leave him be, shall we?" she said to her companion. Both Ravathes sauntered away from him towards the door. Faemirad opened it, and they walked out.

Amon dropped to his knees and landed a hard punch on the floor which cracked it. Anger bled out from every fibre of his being as he directed his gaze to the door. "One day, they'll be the death of you two."

*   *   *

The princes could no longer hold Ezryan in place. With dread killing him inside and out, the former Hieldhar ran to Yverna's side and held her in his arms. "Yve! Seian, wake up. Baby, wake up, don't you dare die on me! Not by them! C'mon," he said repeatedly as he started to heal her again. "Zade, talk to me. What the hell's going on?"

Zaderion trembled as he too attempted to heal his mate. "I don't know. Amon told us he would only do this in case the worst should happen, but not to Vrae."

Belphegor and Vassago walked towards the male soldiers with Xaemorkahn behind them. "Move it, you two." The North Prince said. "You won't be able to wake them up that way. You might heal their wounds, but the spell has a little bit of something in it."

"In case those bitches try anything funny," Vassago interjected.

Ezryan traded a puzzled look with Zaderion. "I don't understand."

"Like I said, move it," Belphegor repeated. He and Vassago placed their hands over the females and muttered something. Five seconds

517

later, Vrathien gasped sharply and coughed. Zaderion immediately held her. "Vrae? Vrae? You okay?" he asked as he cupped her face.

Vrathien nodded slowly. "I'm fine." She turned to her sister. "What about Yve? Is she awake yet?"

"She will be in just a . . . ." Vassago said as Belphegor continued to chant whatever it was. "Second." The moment that one word left his mouth, Yverna too awoke. She coughed violently and gasped for air. Ezryan immediately pulled her into his arms.

*   *   *

I struggled to breathe for a few moments when I realized that somebody held me tight. A warm hand was placed on my cheek as that somebody helped me to sit. I could finally breathe a little better and looked up to the sight of the very face I'd do anything to see.

Ry's.

His face was so close to mine, and worry was written on every inch of his face. "Hey," he said as he ran his hand on my head, "how are you feeling?"

I rubbed my temple as a wave of pain assailed my head. "Weird. I was just . . ." the rest of my words were swallowed as I remembered the last moments before I blacked out.

Jumping out of Ry's arms, I frantically scanned the surroundings and realized that we were out in the woods.

"Yve?" Ry asked carefully.

"Those bastards. Where are they?" I asked in alarm.

"Relax, they're not here."

I shook my head, trying to comprehend things. "What happened? How did I get here?" I asked as I turned and found Belphegor and Vassago with Xaemorkahn standing a few steps behind them. "Oh, hi, I didn't see you guys over there." I grinned at the princes, who answered with grins of their own. I then greeted Xaemorkahn. "Nice to see you again. How are Varisha and the other guys doing?"

He nodded at me. "It's nice to see you too. They're doing fine, and Risha wishes you well," he said. "How are you feeling, Yve?"

I winced. "Like I said, weird." I turned around and found Vrae huddled with Zade. There were traces of blood around her mouth. "What happened to you?"

"You're welcome," Vrae said curtly.

I frowned at her. "Come again?" I asked, and I glanced at Zade. My gaze went back and forth between them. "You two got me out of there, didn't you?" I asked quietly.

"To sum it all up, yeah," Zade said with a smile.

Ry stood up and circled his hand around my waist. "C'mon, Yve, sit down. You just went through a lot back there," he said.

I conceded as nausea went wild, making bile rise to my throat, and I sat again. "Well, thanks a lot, guys. I owe you," I said with a relieved sigh.

"Like I said, you're welcome," Vrae repeated lightly. "You shouldn't have let those assholes take you though, but I can understand your judgment."

I shrugged. "Well, it sucked to say the least, but it was worth it. How did you guys bust me out anyway? With those guys and all?"

They exchanged a strange look before they told me everything. My jaw went slack after they finished. "So basically, Bynethar and Xamian faced off with their colleagues?"

"Yep. We don't know where they went after that, but they said they'd take care of everything," Vrae explained.

"But where are they now?"

Belphegor was the one who answered me. "I ordered them to do something."

"And that is?" Ry prompted.

"Bust Cain out of his hole. We've arranged for them to stay at Dantalion's."

Vrae winced. "Wow. They agreed to do all that? Even the duke?"

"Not that big a deal." Belphegor shrugged. "Leaving that aside, it looks like Amon's made it." He tilted his chin upward.

Zade nodded. "Yes, maybe too well," he said with his eyes on Vrae.

I followed Belphegor's gaze and got confirmation of what they told me. Both my golem and Vrae's were no longer there. His was still around though.

"Sure we're all right?" I said, indicating Zade's golem's eyes with a jerk of my head.

"We should be," Zade replied. Abruptly he cocked his head. "Oh, that's right, I almost forgot," he said. His hand went underneath his robes and pulled out a pouch.

The one contained the Herathim.

"Here." He gave it to me. I took it and tied it to my belt. "Thanks."

"For a second, I thought Kathiera or somebody would bust me with this. Luckily, they were too preoccupied with Bynethar and Xamian. Hell, they even went to Amon."

I raked my hair and heaved a sigh. "Yeah, I didn't know he could do all that, but it seems like it played out in our favour, huh?"

"All right, guys, you ready to come inside or shall we just have a picnic out here?" A sudden question from Vassago made me turn my head. "Oh hey, I almost forgot about you," I said with a grin.

Belphegor chuckled. "Really funny, but there's something we need to take care of first." The light humour in his voice was gone, and the air suddenly tensed as the Hell princes and the Irgovaen made eye contact with each other.

As if to break the freezing ice between the two, Ry abruptly cleared his throat. "Your Highnesses, meet my brother."

When neither one of them made any movement to at least acknowledge each other's presence, I rolled my eyes. "Please, you guys seemed fine when you were asking about my and Vrae's well-being. Now that we're okay, are you back to the racist game? Pardon my insolence here, but you guys are supposed to be royals. Could you at least act that way and keep your egos in check, at least for the time being? We have your pop"–I nodded at Belphegor, who grimaced–"and a destroyer to deal with."

Right after that question left my lips, I felt Vrae's thick warning gaze fall on my back, which I ignored. We absolutely had no time to do some round of Ego Death Match here. There was too much at stake.

Fortunately, my question seemed to have the effect I wanted. They slowly averted their tense gaze from each other for a moment, before one of them looked at the other and gave a subtle nod of greeting. I exhaled in relief. At least they agreed to be friendly enemies.

That was better than them having a sudden death match.

Xaemorkahn turned to me and surprisingly he grinned. "Are you always this stern, Yve?" he asked.

I returned his crooked grin with my own. "Only with cool royals."

He then glanced at Ry, who smiled wickedly at him. "Now I know why Ry can't take his mind off you."

"Huh?" I asked him, and he hastily shook his head.

Arching a brow, I clapped my hands and got their attention. "Now, that's settled, can we get inside before your friend's old man catches us having a standing party out here? I for one wouldn't enjoy that at all," I said firmly.

One edge of Vassago's lips was lifted. "I wouldn't enjoy that myself if you know what I mean. Okay, wait a sec." He turned to face the field and chanted to bring forth his castle.

It was strange to see that these royals had some things in common, and yet they hated each other just because they were from different races. I'd expect that from humans, not from our kind. Well, of course our hostility towards the fluffs upstairs might be an exception.

The second his turquoise-stone castle appeared, we immediately went inside. Vassago led us directly into the archive, where we found Seere standing beside the table with the Book of Lost Knowledge open and the ring laid beside it. Looking at Seere, it seemed he and Belphegor had been playing nice, which was quite good. A few days earlier I would have thought they'd be killing each other when no one was looking.

Ry's hand was still around my waist as we entered the room with Vrae and Zade. Xaemorkahn was the last one to enter. When he closed the archive door, that same tense aura came back. This time it was worse than before, because this time there were three Hell princes in the room, and they made the air tighter with their auras.

Vassago chuckled at this situation, making Seere turn to him. He inclined his head to them. "You'd better behave, because Yve here made a request for us royals to keep our egos in check, at least for the time being." He repeated my words outside, which made me blush for a bit. Ry made a very poorly timed decision to hold my shoulder as he pulled me closer and laughed slightly in my ear.

At Vassago's words, Seere suddenly laughed. I glanced at Xaemorkahn, who stood there looking uneasy. "All right, Yve, I'll behave. We have common enemies anyway."

After that, Xaemorkahn and Belphegor did the one thing we never thought either one of them would do. Belphegor approached the Irgovaen, and suddenly they extended their hands at the same time. Xaemorkahn hesitated for a second, and then both of them shook each other's hand for a brief moment and then let go.

Seere didn't do the same. Hell, he didn't even move. He just nodded like Vassago did. After all that awkwardness, Ry walked me to the armchairs, followed by Vrae and Zade, who looked so pale I thought he would collapse at any moment.

"You okay?" I mouthed the words at him, and he replied with a nod.

Belphegor moved back to where he had been standing earlier next to Seere, as Vassago indicated one seat for Xaemorkahn to sit and positioned himself next to Belphegor.

When all of us except the three of them sat, I pulled out the Herathim from the tiny pouched tied to my belt and put it next to the ring.

"So now we have two out of three." Belphegor began to talk as he pointed at the two seals on the table.

Vassago pointed at the core of the Rygavon's picture which was painted in the book. "We all know where the last one is, so we'll explain what we have in mind."

*   *   *

"Hey, do you think they'll give us our favourite food before they do us in?" Zoran asked his partner, as the line became shorter by the minute.

Now there were only five people in front of them before it would be their turn to enter the room at the end of the line where the "actual death" punishment would be inflicted on them. And there was no sign that they would be relieved of all charges and thus saved them from that miserable fate.

Gevirash shrugged as if he didn't care about that particular fact at all. "Dunno. You think we should ask?"

Zoran grinned. "Don't think they'll give it though."

When both of them said nothing further, that wide grin was wiped off of Zoran's face. "Hey, do you regret it, that we ended up here?" he asked quietly.

Gevirash exhaled and eyed the ceiling for a couple seconds before he faced Zoran again. Smiling, he then lifted his arm that was chained up. "Nope, not at all, I for one still want to keep things as they are, like we told those girls. You? Wait, no way, could it be that you changed your mind?" He suddenly narrowed his gaze.

Zoran stepped on Gevirash's foot as an answer and Gevirash yelped in pain. "What the hell was that for?"

"That was for asking stupid questions." Zoran curled his lips.

Gevirash scowled. "I was just checking. No need to step on my foot. I want the whole of my body in perfect condition before they do what they do!" he growled.

He shook his foot and put both his hands on his knee. "Besides, you were the one who started it! Asking me stupid things out of nowhere about regret!" he snapped.

"I just wanna make sure that you're there when they wipe us clean, that's all," Zoran said slowly as he lowered his gaze.

Gevirash hesitated at his partner's words, and then he took Zoran's hand in his. "Don't worry, you can call me sentimental or whatever, but I swear it to you, I'll be standing next to you when it happens," Gevirash said firmly.

Zoran grinned. "Thanks a lot. I appreciate it. I won't call you sentimental or whatever for saying that to me."

And then they exchanged a wide smile and started to joke again. While they were bantering with each other, the line shortened. Now, there were only two other devils standing in line in front of them.

"Hey, look! Two more, and then they'll call us in." Gevirash jerked his head towards the other two.

After he said that, one was seized by the two guards who stood in front of the door.

"Congrats, you're the champion!" Gevirash laughed as Zoran stepped forward.

Zoran snorted. "Yeah, right."

Looking at their so-not-appropriate manner for people who were about to face the worst sort of death penalty, the guard who had earlier given them permission to talk with the Cherxanains frowned deeply as he studied their attitude.

"What on earth could make these two act so carefree as that? It's as if they don't have any fear of being pulled into non-existent being," the guard wondered.

Zoran's turn finally arrived. When the guards seized him, Gevirash pulled one of the guards. "Take me along with him. We're both in for the same shit, so we'll both face our punishment together."

The guards hesitated, and then one of them went inside. Seconds later, he came back out of the room and seized Gevirash as well. "Your foolish wish has been granted."

Nodding, Gevirash grinned at Zoran, whose eyes widened in disbelief. "See? I'll be standing next to you," he said nonchalantly.

At that moment the guards shoved them through the open door. When they got inside, they saw that only ten members of the Echelons were there and about to sit on rows of chairs surrounding them above.

"Wow, look! It's not every day we get to meet people from high places," Gevirash said sarcastically.

Zoran chuckled at his sarcasm. "Nice. By the way, shouldn't Havok and Gildam be the only ones here? What are the others doing stepping in on death convicts' problems?"

"No clue. B and X aren't here though. Either that's good news or extremely bad," Gevirash retorted under his breath. "I wonder where those two are."

Mezarhim stood up, interrupting their exchange. "Valthors of the Gate, are you aware of the reason why both of you have been brought before us?"

"Are we supposed to play dumb with them?" Zoran whispered, making Gevirash have to restrain himself from laughing out loud.

Clearing his throat, Gevirash then faced all the Ravaths and Ravathes present. "We're somewhat wondering about that ourselves, Honourable Ravath."

Zoran laughed quietly but hastily coughed to cover it. Gevirash stepped on his feet this time, and he grounded his teeth to keep any sound from escaping through his mouth.

"So both of you are unaware of the discussion that happened just three days ago during which we heard that you were planning with a few other devils to work together with despicable angels to attack our Lord Lucifer?" another Ravath named DeVarren asked sternly.

"Well, that pretty much covered it. Now we know for sure that they did eat the shit," Gevirash said in his thoughts. "Oh, that? We actually didn't think much about it, Ravath. We were under the

impression that we were doing was what most people call joking. We had no idea it would cause such an uproar," Zoran said innocently.

"Don't you play dumb with us! How dare you make unforgivable insults like that towards our Master!" Mezarhim growled in fury, and the others threw horrible curses. "Who are the others? Do Cherxanain Yverna and Cherxanain Vrathien have any part in this?" another Ravath named Havok abruptly stood up from his seat and asked them sharply. He wore dark-blue robes that were left untucked to reveal his muscular chest, and his fine long legs were covered with black leather pants,

Gulping a bit, Gevirash decided to keep on playing the stupid bystander. "The savage sisters? Good Hell, no, Honourable Ravath, we'd most likely be their victims if we foolishly joked with them about this."

"Yes, well, we cannot say that we're innocent for joking about things like that, but you can perhaps understand our situation, Honourable Ravath. Perhaps it's been too long for us to have remained in the same post for the last ten millennia. Maybe we were so bored that we didn't even realize the things we made jokes of." Zoran's voice sounded more like an utter mockery than he'd intended.

"Know that you won't be fooling anyone around here. The fact is that those sisters started going through your Gate more frequently since that incident with the missing soldiers, and they talked about them with you two, mere guardians. Perhaps, they also told you something related to what you've been discussing within the past week," DeVarren said coldly as he narrowed his gaze, as if trying to find the truth behind their jest defence.

Gevirash sighed. This time he almost couldn't stop himself from cursing the Echelons right in front of their faces. "We didn't have any intention whatsoever of making fools out of anyone at all."

"Except for you guys," Zoran muttered, causing Gevirash to struggle to keep himself from laughing like crazy.

Gevirash then cleared his throat. "The sisters did indeed tend to come and go through our post, but that doesn't mean they wouldn't kill us right where we stood if we ever joked about something like that in front of them."

Zoran giggled a bit. "The only thing that'd make them kill us on sight is if we didn't make more outrageous sarcastic remarks about our dear old Master. And the fact they came and went more often through our Gate just proved that we're much cooler than the other Valthors."

"Would you stop? I can't enjoy my formal and humble role here if you keep trying to make me laugh like hell!" Gevirash snapped in a low voice to warn his partner.

Finally, Zoran decided to sober up and fell silent.

Falthan rapidly tapped his fingers on the handrail. "It is futile to defend them, Valthors. The sisters had been sentenced to death before you two were summoned here."

At his words, both guards exchanged an alarmed look. Zoran bit his own lip so hard that blood flooded in his mouth.

Kathiera shot a cold glare at them both. "Why don't you tell us what they talked to you about when they visited you. Tell us everything from the start?"

Zoran nearly exploded in rage. He would have done so had Gevirash not planted one arm on his shoulder. "Brother, stop. We can't do anything," Gevirash warned in a trembling voice.

"Yve and Vrae . . ." Zoran whispered with his eyes fixed on the floor.

Gevirash subtly nodded. "I know. Let's just hope Amon could prevent it. This is the end of the line for us. We just have to make sure that we don't destroy the reason why we got here in the first place."

Zoran gulped. "Fine, I won't."

"Well, Valthors? Do you have something to say?" DeVarren asked loudly.

With raw determination in their eyes, they lifted their heads and stared right at the Echelons. "We do not have anything further to say, Ravath, other than that the sisters would never do anything and thus we do not have to defend them from anyone," Gevirash said.

Kathiera rose up slowly from her seat. Her red silk robe fell loosely around her body making her regal appearance look more breath-taking than the lesser devils. "You still don't acknowledge your fault, and we shall see whether your claim about the sisters and in addition Varkonian Zaderion is indeed true. If it's not, we will send Zaderion to where you two are headed after this," she said quietly, but her melodic hollow voice echoed throughout the chamber.

Suddenly all of the Ravaths and Ravathes stood up and said two words in frightening unison. "Hecykra Araizenia!"

Actual death.

Smiling lazily, the two convicts exchanged amused looks with each other before another pair of devils wearing blood-red heavy robes approached.

Without a word, those devils raised both their hands and pulled their energy to the maximum. Gevirash and Zoran didn't even bother to look at their executioners. Instead they kept their eyes locked on each other as they felt those devils launch their deadly attack upon them.

A blinding hot and painful light engulfed both of them. Their flesh slowly melted from their lower bodies as the light burned them all the way to their core. Seconds later that felt like eternity, their entrails sputtered all over the place and despite all the agony, both of them kept on grinning at each other.

As if they felt their final moments were drawing closer, they murmured a few words as the absolute agony was eating them from inside out. "Thank you, guys, and farewell, brother."

They still held on to that peaceful expression when they muttered their last words towards each other right before they were completely obliterated. "See you on the other side, little brother," Gevirash whispered.

"I'll be right behind you, big brother," Zoran replied.

And then they were no more.

Now only ashes, dust, and the smell of blood remained, the signs that they ever stood here, that they ever existed.

Completely baffled by their attitude, Ravathe Kathiera slowly lowered her gaze towards where they both had been standing moments earlier, while the others started to make their way out of the chamber as they spoke amongst themselves of what idiots those guardians were.

Only Ravathe Faemirad approached her. "Is there something on your mind, Kathiera?" she asked.

"Nothing, it's just . . . their attitudes confused me, that's all," she replied quietly.

Faemirad nodded in agreement. "Yes, I won't deny that their audacity wasn't like people who were innocent in this matter nor people who were just playing some pranks."

Kathiera's expression changed. Her gaze darkened slightly. "I don't think they were either innocent or playing pranks," she said in a voice so low it sounded like whisper in the wind.

"So, are you saying that those two were covering someone else involved, who in this case are Yverna, Vrathien, and Zaderion?" Faemirad moved gracefully in front of her, making Kathiera turn her beautiful blue vivid eyes from the spot where those two guards had been standing to her colleague.

Kathiera hesitated, and then she looked down once again as her perfect brows knitted to form one hard line. She was thinking hard.

"Hey, you okay?" Faemirad asked carefully.

Kathiera turned her gaze to her abruptly. "I can't say anything about any of those three right now. The sisters are already dead anyway."

"But?" Faemirad prompted.

"But I do have this feeling I can't shake that our Head Intel and that ungrateful former human bastard know something. Whatever they've got going may still be in progress." Her melodic voice suddenly turned icy cold.

Faemirad was taken aback by her words. "You mean Amon and Cain? Why? I did hear that the guards once sighted both the sisters at Cain's level, but they didn't do anything. They just left."

"Knowing both of them, I wouldn't say that they just left there without doing anything. They were too efficient, not the sort of people who just wander around without a purpose. And they did visit Amon a little more frequently than usual, including that one time Amon strangely raised a stronger shield. Even though these last few days it's only been Vrathien and Zaderion going there, while Yverna has tended to wander off on her own, still, their movements have raised my suspicions. And Yverna's answer in regard to the barriers around Amon's place wasn't exactly flawless," Kathiera added.

Faemirad bit her lip. "Actually I've been thinking about this ever since our Lord Lucifer met with that despicable pair. The Lord indeed told us nothing regarding this matter, but I do think Amon and the three of them may have known something. Why Gabriel and Michael descended, for instance."

Kathiera nodded in agreement. "Yes, I thought so as well. There are too many incidents involving them in this matter, although from the intel I've received, both Varkonian Zaderion and Wartiavega were at Amon's den around that time, whereas Tyraviafonza was wandering off in the woods."

"Yes, and all three of them didn't give us anything at their previous questioning," Faemirad said as her mind wandered to the moment she participated in questioning Yverna.

"Indeed. Anyway, I want to have a little discussion with both Amon and Cain. Don't tell the others. It's imperative that I investigate this matter myself before I openly discuss my suspicions."

Faemirad nodded. "I understand. And if you don't mind, I shall help you. I don't like the idea that two of our very best soldiers, to whom most of the other underlings give their allegiance, were plotting against us. Not to mention that there's one Varkonian on their side."

"Thank you. Let us go to the Iverand again. At any rate, we can't let the others know, because once they do, it'll be difficult for us. Our judgment as the rightful Ravaths and Ravathes can be questioned if they are proven to be innocent in this matter, but then it would be much worse if they are guilty," Kathiera said fiercely as if the thought had deeply offended her.

"I know, but aside from the three of them moving around, do you think Bynethar and Xamian have anything to do with this? Now that they've renounced their seats, there's no way we can find out what they're up to," Faemirad said nervously.

Kathiera wrinkled her nose in repugnance. "I agree with you, but so long as they're both out of the picture, we have nothing to worry about. I've been feeling this unfathomable suspicion of them both, especially Bynethar ever since *her* fall." She said the last two words in a low voice as if they were taboo.

"But has he actually done anything?"

Kathiera shook her head. "No, and that's what's been bugging me. But leaving that aside, we mustn't waste any more time here." She started to walk quickly towards the door with Faemirad following behind her.

Hundreds of questioned swam in the back of their minds as they made their way towards the Iverand's den.

*   *   *

Amon was alone in his chamber, sitting in silence as he stared into nothingness with a bleak expression all over his face.

Suddenly he landed one punch on his desk. "Dammit, you two! Why did you have to go that far?" His voice was trembling as he struggled to keep the tears that already stung his eyes from falling. Only a handful of devils knew about his relationship with those two.

They were half-brothers.

Millennia ago when the three of them were still of the same rank, they often carried out their orders together, but ever since he got transferred into the Intel Division and soon after became the Head Intel, they had hardly seen each other. The only way for all three of them to simply say hi to each other or share words about their well-being was through other devils.

Yverna, Vrathien, and Zaderion. And now, Ezryan returned. But then, his brothers no longer existed. If only he hadn't told those girls anything or hadn't agreed to tell his brothers any of this, they would still be . . .

Finally, he couldn't hold it any more. He put his arms on his desk and buried his head in them as he started sobbing quietly. "I'm so sorry. Forgive me, you guys, I couldn't protect you. I couldn't do anything . . ." he muttered miserably as he clenched his teeth.

"Please all of you. Don't fail them." His mind wandered off to his comrades. His body shook tremendously as rage and despair swelled deep inside him.

Chapter 26

I hadn't had the chance to tell Ry and the rest of them about the guards and their punishment which would have been carried out by this time. As the princes elaborated their plan, my mind drifted to them both.

Had Amon visited them yet? But then, considering his position, I didn't think he could.

Well, at the very least, I'd mentioned him as their brother in case they wanted to tell him something. As brother to brother, not as devils of lower ranks to their superior, just for once.

And yet, their carefree attitude was still the same, so much so that I sometimes forgot that they were brothers of our Head Intel. But then that fact didn't do anyone any good.

"Yve, what's wrong?" Ry's deep voice whispered in my ear, pulling me back to reality. He took my hands that I had placed on my lap into his and grasped them.

I looked down at our entwined hands as I bit my lip. "Gevirash and Zoran . . . they're . . ."

"What? What's with them?"

I slowly turned my head to face him. "They both . . . died."

He was surprised by my words. I felt his grasp tighten and saw his expression change. His beautiful sapphire gaze darkened with sadness. "Why?" he asked quietly.

"They were busted. Or to be precise, they distracted the Echelons from investigating us any further."

"Distracted the Echelons? How?" his deep voice was hollow as he lowered his gaze down towards our entwined hands.

I told him that there had been Chonars going through their Gate when usually they wouldn't be, and I had met Chonars who were standing at their Gate. I also explained to him about my suspicions that they were under Archanians' surveillance and ultimately, what'd they done to make the higher-ups think they were the traitors . . . and what punishment they would receive.

A tic worked in his jaw. "Did Amon know about this?" There was unfathomable grief in his low voice.

I nodded slowly. "He knows, but he couldn't do anything about it without jeopardizing us, without compromising you. He couldn't even visit them for the last time as brothers."

His grip tightened even more as I saw him close his eyes, as if silently thinking about those two.

"You two! What have you been whispering over there?" Belphegor's stern voice made me jump in my seat, but Ry didn't seem to hear him. He kept on closing his eyes for few seconds before he opened them.

"Sorry. Yve just told me something. Please go on with the plan." He jerked his head at the North Prince.

Belphegor gave a frown. "What is it, Yve? What aren't you two telling us?" he asked suspiciously.

All of them focused their eyes on us, making me feel really uneasy. Ry abruptly sighed. "We, or should I say, the three of them"–he indicated Vrae, Zade and myself–"may have been put under quite heavy surveillance since their encounter with Uriel and the others, although we can't tell that for sure just yet."

Vassago snorted. "Whoever has eyes on you won't dare set foot around here. I know those Alvadors, or even Ladurga, for a lot of things but never courage. What makes you think that all of a sudden anyway?"

Vrae was the one answered him. "Amon's brothers died of actual death punishment, or at least, they should have by now. They both tried to make the Echelons eyes stick on them instead of us. It seemed as though both of them were unknowingly placed under Archanians' noses just days after we'd last seen them. Today we heard that they were busted and immediately given that sentence. The Echelons moved on Yve after that."

Not even Seere blinked at her explanation. All the three princes fell into a deafening silence, and Xaemorkahn's stoic face turned slightly sad.

Belphegor slightly ground his teeth. "Their stupidity just knows no bounds it seems. Amon's brothers were just fucking Valthors, and still they bust them?"

Vassago exhaled and then averted his gaze from us. "There was nothing we could do. They died protecting you all, so what do you guys say if we give Lucy a good long bitch-slap across his wrinkled face?" he asked firmly.

I nodded at Vassago's words. "Sounds like a damn good payback," I said.

Belphegor grinned at me, and we went on with the plan. After hours of discussion, we agreed to begin the plan the following night, and then we went back to the rooms Vassago had provided for us.

But there was one particular thing I absolutely couldn't agree with, and that was why I was now standing in my and Ry's room with one hand on my hip and my angry gaze locked on his handsome face.

He had agreed to be the sole bait to lure Lucifer out.

"After these few days we've been together, after *seven* hundred years we'd been apart, you know I could never let you do something like this. You know it would kill me if anything happened to you. So what, are you trying to make me kill myself?!" I asked in a low trembling voice that was thick with anger. I was desperate for him to change his mind.

He just returned a bleak expression and smiled patiently at me.

I tried my best not to fall for his attempt to make me accept the suicide part in the plan that was reserved for him.

"Yve . . ." he started.

I averted my gaze from him, all the while fighting back the tears that already stung my eyes. "No way! Don't you dare 'Yve' me! No matter what you try, I will never let you do this. If you still don't change your mind, then read my lips. I. Am. Going. With. You."

He sighed and shook his head. "We're a pair, aren't we? Looks like Vassago was right after all. We both can't wait to get Azrael waltzing in to protect the other," he chuckled.

I slowly turned to look at him. "Get Azrael waltzing in, is it? Whatever, he did get a score on that one, and I'm really surprised you haven't noticed that by now," I rebuked him with curled lips.

His strong arms suddenly wrapped around me. "I wasn't gonna argue with you. Though it's totally against my better judgment to say this, I'm gonna let you go with me. I swear I'll protect you this time," he whispered in my ear.

Unable to believe what he had just said, I moved a bit so I could look directly into his swirling sapphire eyes. "You won't argue with me or worse, make me pass out and go alone while I'm out?" I asked him.

He shook his head as an answer.

"Seriously?" I pressed. I felt my lips form a smile I couldn't help making.

He shook his head and held me tight once more. "I just want to spend as much time as I can with you." His deep masculine voice sent shivers all over my body as he let me go. His soul-penetrating gaze bore into my eyes.

And suddenly I felt our armour disappear.

I couldn't breathe as his lips slowly swept over mine and then went down my body. He opened his wings, took us floating in the air, and covered us both with it.

The next thing I knew, we made the fiercest and yet the most tender love I'd ever felt.

Blue flames engulfed us for hours before he opened his wings and we descended onto the floor. Right after we landed, he lifted me and walked towards our bed as he went on giving me one sweet kiss after another. When we reached the bedside, he slowly put me down. He was still kissing me when he whispered to me to change form into human. As I felt my head spinning from the heat of his passion, I obeyed without arguing at all. He continued making love to me for hours on end until I fell asleep from sheer exhaustion.

I woke up few hours after midday and found him smiling at me.

"Hey, beautiful, you had a good sleep?" he asked as he took a few strands of my hair and played with them.

I let out a moan before I nodded. "Yes I did, handsome, thanks. What about you?"

"I had one of the best nights in my life," he replied. His hand moved from my hair to my cheek.

I frowned at him. "'One of the best nights', Ry?"

He nodded with dreamily wicked face that made him even more devastating. "Yes, because I plan to make many more nights like it after this." He winked teasingly at me.

I smiled broadly at his words and landed one quick kiss on his perfect lips. "I know I love the way you think and look for a reason."

"Of course you do." He grinned at me and gently put his warm hands around me, pulling me down to his bare chest. I could hear his heart beating as he raked his fingers over my hair.

"Hey, do you think we'll succeed?" I asked him quietly.

I felt his chest tighten for a second and then relax again. "Take my word for it. I assure you everything will be just fine. I won't let anything happen to you."

"To *us*," I corrected him. "Don't forget that I'll be taking part and more importantly, your brother's in this as well."

He chuckled. "You're right."

We laid down in silence for few seconds before we decided to go downstairs. All of them might already be there.

"Baby?" he called right after we'd both transformed into our devil form and manifested our armours.

"Hmm, what is it?" I looked at him and saw his troubled expression.

"You're okay with this, aren't you?" he asked quietly.

I frowned at him as an answer. "Why are you asking me this all of a sudden?"

He shook his head. "Nothing. It's just that once you guys are in on this and that old man has seen us, there's no turning back. You guys will be hunted down and . . ."

I put my fingers over his lips. "Stop right there, Ry. We won't discuss this any more. We know what we're doing and the repercussions of doing it, so don't ask that sort of question again, okay?" I gave him a wicked look. "You'll only waste your breath, hon."

He gently kissed my fingers and flashed a dazzling smile at me. "Although it was me in the first place who suggested to the princes that we need both you and Vrae, I actually don't like the idea, not even a bit. So, I just need to ask you one last time, that's all."

I slowly wrapped my arms around his neck and held him. "We'll follow you no matter where you go. Even if the entire legion hunts you down, I will be there with you," I whispered in his ear.

He landed a tender kiss on my head, and I let him go. "Come on, let's go downstairs." I jerked my head at the door.

He nodded. "Okay," he said as he tucked my hand into his, and we went outside.

We wandered in the darkness of the castle and headed to grand stairwell. As we walked down to the grand floor, we heard familiar voices discussing something.

"So, they're already there," Ry said, when we'd reached the bottom of the stairs. We found all of them stood surrounding a round table with chairs.

"There you are." Belphegor waved at us. We gave the elders a subtle nod of greeting as we approached the table and stopped near Vrae and Zade.

Ry tilted his head at Xaemorkahn. "How are you holding up, brother?" he asked. Xaemorkahn smiled slightly in return. "I'm fine, thanks. I believe you're just fine?" There was something odd in his voice that I couldn't fathom.

Inclining his head, Ry grinned. "Yeah, just like old times."

Vassago cleared his throat. "We only have two hours before the Death Match begins, so we need to get on with it."

Ry mumbled his apologies, and then they went on with the plan. "Uh, I need to interrupt for a second, Your Highnesses," Ry said abruptly in the middle of the heated discussion.

"What is it?" Seere asked.

"There will be one small change in the 'I give my ass on a silver plate for him to fry' part."

Belphegor raised a brow. "What small change?" he asked sternly. For a split second I saw his eyes fall on Xaemorkahn. If I didn't know any better, I could've sworn he hoped for the king to be the bait as well.

"She said she's going with me," Ry said firmly, and the others gaped in response.

"Come again?" Vrae asked.

"I'm going with him," I repeated his words, ignoring Vrae, who was glaring at me.

The princes exchanged strange looks with each other, and then Vassago shrugged. "Do as you like. You'd go anyway even if we said no, right?"

"That's right. I'm glad we're on the same page, thanks, Your Highnesses." I grinned at them. Xaemorkahn's beautiful eyes were widened in disbelief as he looked at Ry and me.

"Yve, you . . ." Vrae started. I immediately cast a warning stare at her. "Don't, Vrae. I don't wanna argue with you, but you won't change my mind either. What would you do if Zade was to do that fun part of the plan?" I asked her.

My question had clearly caught her off guard, for she closed her mouth and lowered her gaze. Sighing, she looked at me. "I'd go with him no matter what," she muttered. Zade held her protectively at her words.

I nodded. "Then we have an understanding. Please go on," I nodded to the princes.

Belphegor crossed his arms under his robes. "Okay, Xaemorkahn told us about the nature of his powers, so the best chance we have would be . . ." and after that Vassago elaborated to us the next part of the plan.

First, we'd lure him to where Seere's stronghold was hidden: Logerrian waterfall. Seere said that he had planted a lot of traps around the place. We planned to combine several of the traps with some of Xaemorkahn's spell, whose powers, for some unfathomable reason, would negate Lucifer's.

We were done with the planning details around nightfall. "Let's go people," Vassago said. We all nodded and immediately headed towards the castle's front door. All of us went through it and then waited outside while Vassago chanted to hide his castle back in the shadows.

"Come," Seere said, and then he chanted.

"We're going through the rift. We can't pop into his domain without hitting any stupid wires or fly straight there in packs without any of those Alvadors noticing. Not to mention, if you guys are indeed under the Archanians' ugly noses, it'll be a bit of problem for you once we're outta here. At the very least, Amon's pals will still be waiting for all of you outside the barrier around the place," Belphegor explained, when he saw our puzzled expressions.

"Wait a sec." Xaemorkahn approached Seere, who had just finished opening the rift.

"What is it, brother?" Ry asked.

Hesitating, Xaemorkahn's gaze fell on Seere. "If you don't mind, you can project the location of your domain into my head so I can move all of you at once. That way we won't have to walk cautiously through the rift."

Seere's eyes widened. "You can do that?" he asked, a bit excited.

Xaemorkahn nodded firmly. "If it's about moving quickly through dimensions, realms, and the like, I can do that in a blink of an eye, well, as long as I know where I'm going, that is."

Lifting the edge of his lips, Seere then gave Xaemorkahn a subtle nod. "Okay, let's see what you got, tough guy." After that he closed the rift back up.

Belphegor looked like he'd rather feed his entrails to rabid dogs than trust Ry's brother. "Wait a sec, Seere. Are you sure about this?"

Vassago rolled his eyes at Belphegor's question. "Oh, shut up, Belphegor. This isn't the right time to announce that you're actually a woman," he snapped.

Belphegor opened his mouth for a second and then hastily closed it again as he made a face at Vassago. "That's harsh, but whatever. You'd better not pulling any stunt on us." Belphegor narrowed his crimson eyes at Xaemorkahn.

The king simply expelled a tired breath. "I could say the same thing to you since we're conspiring against your father."

"You . . ." The crimson color started to spread all over his eyes as he let out that murderous aura of his, but before he could say anything further, Xaemorkahn raised his hand to stop him.

"Relax. Ry, Yve, Vrae, and Zade are all here. I wouldn't do anything to harm them," he said calmly.

"Then it's settled, right, Belphegor?" Ry asked Belphegor.

Startled, the North Prince just let out a disgusted breath. "Fine, whatever, do as you please," he snapped.

Seere then turned his swirling ruby eyes to Xaemorkahn, whose eyes widened as he obviously was seeing Seere's domain in his head. Moments later, Xaemorkahn blinked a few times, maybe to clear his head from whatever effect he got after Seere sent that image projection into his mind.

Exhaling heavily, Xaemorkahn then looked at us with his beautiful eyes. "You ready?"

Most of us nodded, and then without warning our surroundings suddenly changed. There was a huge waterfall a few meters from us and a vast lake at its bottom. I felt big stones under my feet and looked around.

The trees of Iradin forest that was located next to Gillian were standing around us, as if warning us about what we were about to do.

"Cool," Seere said, while the other princes just stared without saying anything.

Vassago then cleared his throat to get our attention. "Listen up, people." We gathered around him as I glanced at the trees that were locked up around us. "We'll separate in three groups like we agreed before. Ry, you go with Yve. Xaemorkahn, you're going with Seere, Vrae, and Zade to spread the traps. Your group has got the most people, so you should be able to cover a lot more ground. As for me, I'll go with Belphegor to intercept Ry and Yve when they're being be chased by the old bat."

Belphegor sneered. "Nice, I'll tell him later he's evolved into a big ugly old bat."

Vassago rolled his eyes. "Whatever, so you guys ready?"

We all nodded in response. "Move out!" he said, and all of us quickly flew off to different places.

Ry and I headed towards Hirian Lake, which was near Lilith's domain. We decided to wander around and made sure Lilith saw Ry. Belphegor suggested that part because he believed the old hag knew that Lucifer was frantically searching for Ry. Rather than suicidally walking into his den, Belphegor suggested we use Lilith instead. She would tell Lucifer, and then our dear old master would come out and follow us right into the trap. And the rest depended on our combined powers.

At least, that was the plan.

We sped off across the sky for half an hour until the watery smell of the lake reached our nostrils.

"That's it. C'mon, we'll go low and land near the lake," Ry said as he jerked his head in the lake's direction.

"Okay." I followed him, and we landed just a few yards away from that massive hole filled with water. It sure was beautiful here.

Too bad the devil occupying the place was an extremely annoying out-dated hag.

Ry took my hand into his, and then we walked towards the lake. No sooner had we reached the beautiful lake than we sensed an unfriendly watching us in the shadows. This time, the unfriendly was also a devil, not angels like before.

I recognized the repulsive aura that was eyeing us. It had been a long time since I fought the owner.

Mistress of Samael, Lilith.

"She's here," I spoke cautiously through a blocked channel, as I pretended not to be aware of my surroundings. Ry gave me a subtle nod.

"You think she fell for it? Or would she go after us herself?" I asked him as he took me to walk around the lake.

His sapphire eyes cast a wary gaze to our surroundings. *"I sure as hell hope so. There's no point if the one chasing us was her instead of him."*

Suddenly we felt her threatening aura withdraw little by little, and then it headed outside the area.

"She's going for him. Now Yve, let's go back!" Ry yelled a bit in my head and took me to the sky.

From out of nowhere, she manifested in front of us. Her eerie pair of white eyes cast a murderous glare at us. Her long white hair fanned around her head, and the wind plastered her black gown against her body. "Where do you think you're going?" she asked in a low deadly voice. Her lethal aura reached out to us as it spread the acid-like stench throughout the woods. The trees melted into dust just seconds after I felt her aura reach the woods.

I let out a disgusted breath. "Obviously, far away from your stink. I like my nose, so I don't want it to be tainted by your foul smell," I said as I flipped my wings in the air and pulled my energy in case she decided to attack.

I felt Ry draw out his energy as well. *"Baby, we don't have much time. C'mon, just blast her out of the way, and then let's get the hell outta here."*

"Roger that. So, on three?"

"On three!"

Lilith laughed evilly as she raised one hand and formed a small yellow light ball. "Shut up! And you, Ezryan, how dare you wander around here with Lucifer himself looking for you, anxious to rip your head off. I didn't know you had that many balls."

I could feel a tic work in my jaw. "You talk to him like that again and you'll be the star of a 'ripping head party'." I started to move as I readied to attack.

Ry placed his arm in front of me to stop me from attacking, and then he chuckled. "Well, of course you don't know. There's only one devil I'd give the privilege of knowing about that private part, and that devil is her. As if I'd give that privilege to you, hag." His voice was full of mocking sarcasm. His words made me want to laugh and flattered me at the same time as I saw him gaze disdainfully at the old she-devil.

Lilith growled furiously as her white eyes were covered with a blood-red color. "You will not make mockery of me! You'll regret this, you worms!"

"FYI, we already did make mockery of you. And by the way, who are you calling worms? You spent your time talking with worms lately? Hell, no wonder you're so not right in the head," I said sarcastically as I drew my powers to the maximum.

"Ready, Yve?" Ry's voice echoed clearly in my head.

"Ready," I replied him.

"Die, maggots!" Lilith roared as she launched her energy ball at us.

"Three!" Ry and I yelled in unison, and we shot our own Avordaen at her.

Our powers collided and caused a tremendous explosion that destroyed the woods within several miles' radius. Even the lake was no longer there. All the water was evaporated by the extreme heat of the combustion. Every living being in the lake and in the woods lay lifeless below us.

I felt a strong grip on my hand, and the owner pulled me back towards Logerrian waterfall so fast that it almost felt we were flying at the speed of light.

For a few minutes I could feel Lilith's foul aura following us, but somewhere along the way it stopped and was replaced by something far more horrible. I turned my head around slightly to confirm what I felt, and then I saw it.

The Dark Light headed towards us and melted everything in its way into ashes and dust.

Lucifer.

I heard Ry curse as he accelerated and suddenly pulled me to fly low. I started to launch bolts at the trees to make our way through.

"He's destroying the woods behind us!" I yelled as I kept on shooting the trees.

"I know! Hang on and keep making way!" he replied.

From out of nowhere I saw a hole in the rift up ahead with Vassago and Belphegor in it. Ry took me straight into it, and then Vassago closed the hole immediately.

Once the hole was closed, Vassago let out a relieved breath. "That was an extremely close call. If you had been out there two seconds longer, you'd be Ry-kebob." He shook his head at the imagery.

Belphegor suddenly hit Ry's head. Ry yelped as he rubbed the spot. "Ow! What the hell was that for?"

"What took you both so damn long out there?" Belphegor curled his lips.

"Lilith decided to play with us for a bit," I answered him.

The North Prince arched his brow at my response. "What are you talking about? That old prune would rather enjoy the show than fight the battle herself if she had Lucifer headed straight to her," Belphegor said in a wondering tone.

I shrugged, wondering about that as well. "Beats me, I wondered about that myself. We got the chance to make fun out of her though," I chuckled.

Vassago suddenly clapped his hands together. "Okay, enough jokes. We gotta go to the rendezvous point with Seere and the others. I'll take you both to them while Belphegor's gonna lure him towards the trap. C'mon." He jerked his head the other way and indicated to us to follow him.

We walked for few minutes through the rift and then stopped. At that point Vassago made a hole on the rift, allowing Belphegor to step out. Then Vassago resealed the hole, and we continued to walk further. Moments later we stopped again, and this time Vassago opened another hole, and we all stepped out of it.

Xaemorkahn and the others were there, and we found ourselves standing in the big cave behind the waterfall. The water made a deafening sound as it fell, creating a thick curtain of water in front of us. The air was so humid and the smell of greenery hung low. All of us stood cautiously as we felt Belphegor's presence flying around the edge of the woods outside.

"Here." Xaemorkahn handed a tiny gold bracelet to Ry and me.

I spun the small bracelet thing in front of my eyes. "What's this for?"

He pulled another bracelet very similar to the one he gave us from beneath his black robe. "These will release a containment seal, pretty much like the Key of Solomon, but infused with my own set of spells. The good news is this will incapacitate him after he can no longer move once he gets into one of the traps. The moment we disable him, all of us must throw these at once after I finish the spell to activate them and give you guys a 'go'. That way, we'll temporarily hold him in place and hopefully buy us enough time to flee as far as we can and as fast as we can."

I nodded at his explanation. "Oh, okay. By the way, you said that was the good news. What's the bad?"

He shifted his weight, looking uneasy. "One of these will only hold him for twenty-four hours. So it's imperative that we don't lose any of them to one of his attacks."

Zade frowned at Xaemorkahn's explanation. "That's quite a long time. Why should we be worried?"

"Because we'll need every minute we can get to put the seals together and locate that empty-thing bastard after we're done with him. That may take a few days, and I assure you that we can't do it if your master is bothering us, and he will be since he'll have seen your faces."

I sighed helplessly and then shook my head. "Well, at least it'll hold him in place. That's good enough, but I wanna ask you something."

"What is it?"

"If by dumb luck a few of the underlings or worse, the other royals, came to him, could they bust him free?"

All of them turned their wary gazes simultaneously at me.

"That's a happy thought." Zade laughed nervously, while his mate just stared at me.

"Well, brother?" Ry asked him, after he fell silent at my question.

Xaemorkahn kept his stoic expression as he looked directly into my eyes. Abruptly, he expelled a long tired breath. "Good question, but no, they won't be able to release him. I'm the only one who knows the counter spell. Unless he has some tricks up his sleeve, the only choice for him is to wait for the spell to wear off with time." Everyone was so relieved that the feeling was tangible.

"That's more like it." Seere lifted the edge of his lips.

"You have it, Vassago?" I turned to the prince, who nodded and pulled the gold thing out of his robes. "Xaemorkahn gave it to me and Belphegor when you two went to Lilith's."

"Okay, now let's wait for him." I averted my gaze from him to the outside beyond the waterfall.

From out of nowhere, we suddenly felt the threatening aura belonging to Lucifer approach.

"Head's up guys. He's coming. Mask your presence so he won't sense us," Seere said in a low voice as he took his stance.

We all did what he said and anxiously waited.

Chapter 27

Belphegor turned around. "You're here," he said slowly as he levelled a disgusted glare at his father.

Lucifer glanced around the waterfall. I had no doubt of whom he was looking for. The one he had wanted to shred for nine hundred years.

Ry.

"Where is he?" our, well, Lord asked harshly.

From behind the thick curtain of water, I could see Belphegor roll his eyes. "Really, couldn't you at least elaborate before *politely* asking someone something? Who are you talking about anyway? Seere? I'm just about to meet him myself."

"Don't fuck with me!" Lucifer roared. "Ezryan! Where is he? He came this way and then vanished around here!"

Belphegor made a face as if he were extremely offended. "Why would I ever want to fuck with you? I'd rather take one of the female soldiers. I'm normal, and they don't stink. And what's with this constant calling 'Ezryan, Ezryan'? You have a hard-on for him or what?"

We all saw and heard what Belphegor said with our heightened sense of hearing and sight. When I turned to look at Ry his face blushed as he lowered his gaze, while Seere rolled his eyes and Vassago let out a curse.

"How dare you level that low mockery at me!" he barked, and without warning he threw one bolt after another at his son.

Belphegor flew sideways to avoid the attacks, all the while trying to direct the bolts at him, not at our hiding place. "Yeah, I dare! You have problems with that?" he snarled as he made a taunting gesture at his dad. The cave shook tremendously as a few of the bolts hit the rocks around the waterfall.

"Not good. A few more bolts and we'd be exposed sooner than we planned," Seere said as he ran a once-over at the cave.

"Guys, look, Belphegor's moving to the trap I set at the bottom of the waterfall," Xaemorkahn said, pointing at the prince, who had indeed begun to fly down.

"Hey, he really won't get caught, will he?" Vrae asked nervously as we saw Belphegor start to close the distance between the trap and him.

Instead of answering Zade's question, Xaemorkahn started to chant. I raised a brow at his action and cast a puzzled gaze at the princes and Ry. "Well, if it goes like he explained to us, the trap can only be activated by his spell, so unless he has bad timing and activates the trap while Belphegor is standing on it, that punk will get caught."

Vrae still bit her lip as we saw the huge battle outside. Belphegor kept avoiding his father's attacks and blasted one or two bolts of his own.

Lucifer still hadn't walked into the trap in the lake as he shot a bolt from nearly point-blank range just a few inches from his son. That alone made Belphegor fly away from the lake and continue being chased by his opponent.

"Fuck this!" the North Prince cursed under his breath. *"Ry, summon one of your dops and have Vassago transport him through the shadows. Make him appear just for a few seconds, enough for the old bastard to see him. Once he falls for it and chases the doppelganger towards the lake, you guys are welcome to fry the bastard."* We heard Belphegor's voice through a blocked channel. I glanced at Ry and Vassago who were nodding at each other, and then Ry called forth one of his doppelgangers.

"Zha'kra?" the doppelganger asked. Without wasting a second, Ry briefly explained what he want from the doppelganger. After he'd finished, Vassago opened the way into the shadow realm and they both vanished.

"Now we're ready. One more word, and he's done for." Xaemorkahn abruptly turned to face us after he was done with the chanting.

"It'll be any second now. Look down there closely," Seere said as he cast a wary gaze at the two combatants.

Just five seconds later, we saw the doppelganger appear from head to waist and stay there until Lucifer caught sight of his presence on the lake. Luckily, the water masked his doppelganger odour, and then, as the North Prince expected, his father immediately let out a thundering scream that nearly bled my eardrums and changed direction from chasing his son to Ry's doppelganger.

"Wait, wait . . ." Seere said as our master made his way towards the lake. Vassago suddenly appeared near us out of thin air.

When Ry's doppelganger went back into the water, Ry quickly summoned him back. Once the doppelganger had disappeared under the water, we slowly pulled our energy right up to the maximum. The second Lucifer hit the water, the princes shouted in unison, "Now!"

We all went through the waterfall and simultaneously launched bolts directly at our master.

I actually hated to corner one opponent like this. It was really way off the grid for me. I was usually the one being cornered, not cowardly trapping someone like this. But then again, his powers were way superior to ours combined.

And I was right. We really had to give him credit. He was all-powerful. Despite being off guard and surrounded, his reactions were so fast that he managed to blast all of our attacks and almost succeeded in landing one clean shot at me, but it was deflected by Ry.

The moment Lucifer saw him and his brother, his wrath was ignited. "You!"

"Yes, it's me. I'm back. You got issues with that?" Ry asked sarcastically, as he sent more bolts at Lucifer. All of us kept on blasting him to force him back into the lake, the closest of the traps we had near him.

Each one of us made a series of aerial manoeuvres as we dodged and shot Lucifer at the same time.

The battle went on for hours, and none of us succeeded in landing one solid hit, while the waterfall began to crumble and disintegrate as our bolts hit it.

Zade shot two bolts at Lucifer. Our Master dodged his attacks and launched a bolt at the same time. Zade moved to avoid it, but he was a split second too late. The bolt went through Zade's side and made a wide gaping hole in the left side of his stomach. His face paled in horror as he fell from the sky bleeding profusely.

"Zade!" Vrae screamed as she immediately flew to her mate, paying no attention to the battle we were in. I saw Lucifer seize that moment to shoot Vrae, while Ry grabbed Zade before he hit the ground hard and safely set him down. I rushed to pull Vrae out of the way and made it just in time before the bolt hit her as well.

"Gotcha!" I said under my breath as we saw the bolt that missed her.

I glanced at the other princes, who launched a massive amount of bolts at Lucifer, but our master blasted all of the bolts before they reached him.

"Thanks, Yve," she panted. Then Lucifer sent several bolts at us, making us separate at once. *No problem, but next time you plan to get distracted, no offense, but please do that when we're not in the middle of a huge fight, especially not in a fight where Lucifer is the opponent.* I projected the words as we threw our own bolts at him.

"Sorry, about that, but Zade . . ." she didn't get to finish her sentence because another voice interrupted her. *"Don't worry, he's okay. I told him to stay out of the fight until the hole in his stomach is closed. He's already passed out anyway. I took the bracelet from him so I can release both mine and his when the time comes,"* Ry said in our head.

Vrae mumbled her gratitude to Ry for saving her mate, and then we re-joined the battle.

Finally, the long fight ended. In only one destined second, Lucifer stopped attacking to reach for the All-Seeing Eye pendant that hung loose around his neck. That moment Belphegor managed to land one solid hit on his chest. After that he fell on the water but rolled back to his feet to face us.

But it was too late for him.

Xaemorkahn immediately said one final word of the spell that he'd put on the lake. "Vada'alma!"

Suddenly a vast geometric symbol glowed beneath the lake and jutting out, and in just two seconds its edges had closed around him, making a huge containment cage in the shape of a pyramid that floated just inches above the water.

"What the fuck!" he roared as he kept sending blasts at his cage, but he wasn't able to move a step from the centre of the huge cage he was in.

"Brother," Ry called Xaemorkahn, who was already starting to chant his next set of spells. We all waited in anticipation as we saw Lucifer go wild in his confinement.

Only five seconds later Xaemorkahn firmly said three words, "Givorzakh Rafaniera Pyliari!" Then he nodded at all of us.

We let loose the gold bracelets onto the glowing cage, and all of them flew around the containment in a perfect circle before they started to emit lightning that shot to the tip of the pyramid-shape cage.

The bracelets suddenly moved and went around the cage in a full circle, making a light on their way that engulfed the whole cage. When those bracelets had finished circling the cage, they formed a second cage over the first one in the shape of a massive glowing ball with symbols all over it.

Lucifer was no longer shooting bolts at his containment.

The princes and Xaemorkahn let out a sigh of relief at the sight, and Ry whispered soothingly in my ear, "We made it, baby." I felt his hand wrap around my shoulders.

I nodded slightly and saw Belphegor glare at his father, who shouted all kinds of foul curses at us. The North Prince smiled wickedly, and then he turned at Xaemorkahn. "That was a neat trick. Good job!"

Xaemorkahn was startled at his words, and then he grinned. "Thanks, you did a great job yourself," he replied.

"It's not over yet." Vassago's disgusted gaze fell on our Lord. "Take that thing off his neck!" he said in a low deadly voice as he turned his gaze to Ry's brother.

Hesitantly, Xaemorkahn lowered his gaze at his sworn enemy. "You wanna do it?" he jerked his head at old Lucy.

"I thought neither of us could use our powers against yours?" Vassago had a puzzled expression on his face.

"I've never said that. You guys could use a bit of your powers with the exception of a major type like Avordaen. You still can use bits of your powers to pull that thing off him for instance. And from your threatening tone, no offense, but I figured you too had a history with the guy." Xaemorkahn grinned evilly at the prince.

Vassago laughed out loud at his words. "I like your style, man! And don't worry, no offense taken." And then he turned to look at

Belphegor who was grinning as well. "Belphegor, you wanna do the honours?" Vassago asked.

Belphegor shook his head. "Nah, you do it. You have a bone to pick with him anyway. Let him have it. I already got to shoot him," he chuckled.

"Yeah, you do it," Seere added.

Without asking the rest of us, he raised his hand towards the helpless Lucifer inside the confinement, and the pendant flew straight into his hand, followed by another train of foul curses Lucifer let loose at him.

"That really felt good. I wish I could strip him of his powers once and for all." All of us laughed at his words

"C'mon, let's get outta here." Ry jerked his head towards the Gillian forest.

"Wait a sec," Belphegor said, and all of us looked at him.

"What is it?" Vassago asked.

Suddenly Belphegor snapped his fingers, and Lucifer instantly went mute.

Still not appeased, Belphegor snapped his finger once again as he raked a repugnant glare at his father. The whole cage suddenly shook as it slowly made its way towards the bottom of the lake. A few seconds later it was completely under the lake, and not even a single light could be seen from it.

"Wow, you do hold a grudge against him," Ry said in disbelief as he shook his head.

Belphegor sighed, looking extremely satisfied. "Now we can get the hell outta here. Xaemorkahn, would you mind taking us back to our place where we were before we came here?" Belphegor gave the king a knowing look.

Before Xaemorkahn teleported us, I held up my hand to stop him. "Wait a sec," I said, and together with Vrae, I went to fetch Zade, who lay unconscious on the ground. After that we flew back up with him clinging onto us. Ry and Belphegor flew towards us and took the limping Varkonian. "We got him," Ry said to Vrae who reluctantly let her mate go.

"We're ready," Belphegor said.

Xaemorkahn nodded, "Okay," and our surroundings changed the second that word left his mouth.

Chapter 28

I felt solid ground beneath my feet, and I immediately put Zade, who was clinging onto me and Vrae, carefully onto the grass.

"Cool! Okay, we'll go back inside Vassago's place first since we left the other two seals in his archive." Belphegor jerked his head towards the area where Vassago's turquoise castle was hidden. Vassago had already started the chant to bring forth his castle.

"And not to mention that we also need time to do something first before we locate that Arzia creature," Seere added.

"What something?" I asked as I stood up after putting Zade down. Vrae was holding her mate when Ry came to me.

Seere raked his hair with his long fingers and looked rather frustrated. "While you and Ry were in that fortress to take the ring, we found something annoying about those seals in that Book of Lost fucking Knowledge."

"And?" Ry prompted.

"All seals can function only if none one of them has been tampered with in any way. That means . . ." Belphegor didn't finish his explanation.

Ry cursed. "The tampering your dad successfully added onto Rygavon should be removed first. Any idea how?"

The moment that question left his lips, the castle appeared. "We'll do the rest of the talking later," Vassago said as he indicated the huge sturdy door leading into his castle.

"Uh, guys, shouldn't we be hiding somewhere else, since I'm sure after what we'd done, and with Lilith knowing about it as well, everyone will be hunting for us?" Vrae asked slightly hesitantly.

Ry sighed. "I know what you mean, Vrae, but we don't know anywhere else that has as many protective spell as Vassago's. And we can't possibly go to my brother's. We would be safe from our people, but I can't say for sure if we could be safe from his." He jerked his head towards his brother, who seemed to confirm Ry's words with a helpless gaze.

Xaemorkahn cleared his throat. "He's right. You three"–he looked at me, Vrae, and Zade, who was lying still on the grass with his wings wrapped around him–"my people can tolerate, but you guys"–he tilted his head apologetically at the princes–"no offense, are more than they can tolerate. There would be a riot amongst my people. There's been no riot in the long history of Irgovaen, and I don't have any intention of being the first to start one." He lifted the edge of his beautiful lips.

"We understand, and no offense taken, your spell's the one thing that locked the bastard up, and besides, from what we heard from Ry, we have more records about that stupid empty thing than you do. Come on." Vassago started to head towards the door and opened it.

Vrae and Ry moved to carry Zade, who was still going under. The moment we set foot inside, we brought Zade into his and Vrae's room. Belphegor and Vassago offered to heal the Varkonian since Lucifer's energy had poison in it that could only be countered by royals and, of course, himself.

They were able to heal Zade pretty quickly since his wound wasn't as bad as Vassago's where Lucifer attacked him. After he woke up, we immediately headed to the archive.

Once we were inside, Vassago put the Rygavon he took from Lucifer on the table near the other two seals.

"So much mess just to take three tiny things." Seere shook his head as he stared at those things.

"You don't say. You have no idea what I went through just to get that annoying Herathim," Ry said sarcastically.

Belphegor snorted. "Boy, that was because you looked for trouble yourself, so enjoy the pain." He grinned evilly at him.

Ry sneered. "Yeah, thanks. Oh and by the way, like I asked you back there, do you have any idea how we're gonna remove everything your dad has gloriously added into the damned thing?"

Belphegor nodded. "We do. Fortunately, along with that annoying record, we found something else–how to return any of the seals to its original state in case there's something unnatural infused into it."

"So now we need you guys to scan my records and Belphegor's to find as much information about Arzia as you can–and ASAP." Vassago folded his arms over his chest.

I arched my brow at that. "Belphegor's record?"

How in the hell could we get into his archive while we were here? They couldn't possibly suggest that we separate and then go back and forth between Belphegor's place and here to pass the info, could they?

Instead of answering my question, Belphegor just snapped his fingers.

A mountain of old thick books and scrolls appeared from out of nowhere in the corner of the room.

"There, those should cover everything I found from the old bastard's den," he said with a grin.

I sighed. "Okay, and meanwhile you'll be . . . ?"

Seere cleared his throat. "The three of us and Xaemorkahn will be cleaning up Lucifer's mess on the Rygavon."

Xaemorkahn was surprised at the prince's words, maybe because he was certain that he could no longer help them, except when they were about to face that Avarnakh. "How could I possibly help you with that thing?"

Vassago exhaled heavily. "I don't know if you guys would believe this, and I don't really care if you don't, but we found these words in that book. 'One powerful being of different realm outside the one where the sons of Adam roamed is needed to purify each of the seals.' That to us sounded more like you than, say, Lilith. Well, her brain is from a different realm, and she acts and looks like an alien, but we don't think that's what the book meant."

All of us laughed at his sarcasm. Vassago sobered up instantly and then cast a dreary look at us. "We'll take these to my study chamber. You guys have fun here, oh and, Ry, we'll need a hand taking that Herathim since neither of us can touch it without destroying our hands." He pointed at the seals.

"I can take it," Xaemorkahn said, making the three princes stare at him in disbelief.

"Come again?" Belphegor asked. The king repeated his words, and I saw Belphegor gape for a second and then close his mouth.

Seere cleared his throat. "Okay, let's not waste any time here." Seere and the other princes, along with Xaemorkahn, rose from their seats.

Belphegor took the Ring of Solomon, and Vassago collected Rygavon, while Xaemorkahn seized the Herathim.

"Call us if you find anything." Belphegor jerked his head to us while Vassago opened the door.

"No problem," I said, and the four of them left us. Suddenly I felt Ry's hand on my shoulder. "Come on, let's scour those things." He indicated the records.

I scoffed as a bothering thought came into my mind. "Let's hope we finish everything before Lucifer busts free."

Zade just laughed nervously, and Vrae narrowed her eyes at me. "Such a delight to have you and your downing thoughts around, Yve," she said sarcastically.

I laughed wickedly. "Of course, I wouldn't be called the Queen of Tyranny if I always thought about cheerful things, now would I?"

Ry chuckled at my rhetorical question and walked towards the Book of Lost Knowledge. "What are you doing?" I asked him.

He grinned. "It's not every day I get the chance to scour this thing, is it? I'll help you with those after I'm done."

I sighed. "Okay."

All three of us started to search one record after another, while Ry immediately hid his face in the book. Even Zade didn't say anything. Perhaps he was still recuperating after Vassago and Belphegor healed him.

So we started to dive in the pile of those old books, hoping we'd find everything we needed to face Arzia.

* * *

Vassago led the way to his room, while the rest of his guests followed him silently.

"Uh, can I ask one question?" All three princes turned to Xaemorkahn as they stopped in front of a big sturdy door with carvings all over it.

"Shoot," Vassago said as he averted his gaze from the king and raised his hand to chest height with his palm facing one particular carving on the door.

Xaemorkahn hesitated as he saw the carving that formed something like a keyhole covered with vines. Vassago touched the vines, and then they slowly moved aside, revealing the keyhole beneath them. Vassago manifested a huge gold key and inserted it into the hole. There was a clicking sound and the door was opened.

The room was huge, with ornaments and sculptures. A big oak desk was placed in the corner. There were a few other books and records stacked neatly on top of the desk, and several chairs stood around it.

"What was it you were asking?" Belphegor turned to Xaemorkahn as they entered the room. Seere was the last to step foot inside. He closed the door and looked at Xaemorkahn, while Vassago walked towards his large oaken desk.

"I was just wondering if you guys made a copy or something from that book regarding the part to purify your dad's memento, since you guys left it in that room along with Ry and the others."

"Oh, that." There was a strange note under Belphegor's voice when he responded as he exchanged a quizzical stare with the other two.

"What is it?" Xaemorkahn asked. His gaze fell on each prince.

Seere cleared his throat. "Uh, actually we didn't."

Xaemorkahn arched his brows at that. "And why is that again? You guys may have memorized them, but I don't know squat about that thing."

"We'll project what we saw from that book into your mind, because we couldn't make a copy or anything of the sort." Seere rubbed his brows looking rather frustrated.

"Hell, we couldn't even make a damn note out of it. Every word we wrote on any other thing we could write on was dissolved without a trace." Belphegor expelled a tired breath.

"Yeah, he even tried to rip one page out of the book and ended up burning his own hand," Vassago added as he laughed.

Xaemorkahn cringed at that. "Okay."

"Hey! No need to tell him that part," Belphegor snapped.

All three except the North Prince stifled a laugh and then headed for Vassago's desk. Belphegor, Xaemorkahn, and Vassago put the seals on the desk.

The Ring of Solomon, Herathim, and Rygavon.

"So what do we do now?" Xaemorkahn asked. He looked at Vassago, who started to walk away from the other two.

"Come here," he said. Xaemorkahn followed him quietly. After they made enough distance from Belphegor and Seere, Vassago abruptly turned and put his right index finger on Xaemorkahn's temple.

"What are you . . . ?" Xaemorkahn started to resist, when suddenly Vassago grabbed his shoulder.

"Stay still," Vassago said in a harsh, commanding voice.

From out of nowhere, flashes of images were flowing into his mind, followed by one blue lightning stroke after another in his head.

The king screamed as pages of the Book of Lost Knowledge from Vassago's memory burned their way into his head. All of a sudden, a deep weird voice echoed in his mind. *"This is forbidden knowledge and must not be spread. God's ultimate destroyer is drawing near. Join the seals together and it will be here. Destroy the seals and the judgment day will be your ordeal. Put the seals on the destroyer's tomb and the world's final doom will be undone until the true time has come."*

Right when the voice stopped, the pain ceased tormenting him. Gasping and panting, Xaemorkahn dropped to his knees as Vassago pulled his finger away from the king. "What the fuck was that?" Xaemorkahn growled as he rubbed his head and glared at Vassago, who raised both hands in surrender.

"Whoa, easy, dude. I didn't do it on purpose. But now we know why we couldn't even make a friggin' note from it, huh?" Vassago cringed as he asked the king.

Xaemorkahn narrowed his gaze at Vassago as he tried to get back to his feet. "Give me a damn warning next time if you're gonna screw with my head and make me hear weird voices, got it?" he shook his head as if to clear the annoying fog that was clouding his mind.

The three princes exchanged confused looks with each other and then looked back at the king, who was still trying to steady himself by heading towards the desk and grabbing its edge.

Belphegor placed one hand on Xaemorkahn's shoulder, making him turn to face the North Prince. "What voices are you talking about here?"

Xaemorkahn frowned as he tried to search for lies in the prince's eyes to confirm that they did indeed know nothing. When he didn't detect anything that would contradict the prince's words, he then told them everything the voices had said in his head.

"The voice said that?" Belphegor asked in a wondering tone. He ran his fingers through his hair as he cast a puzzled stare at the other two, who shrugged simultaneously, indicating their cluelessness.

Seere crossed his hands in front of his chest. "At any rate, there's something that might be useful in what that voice told us." He gave the rest of them a meaningful gaze, and they all gave him a subtle nod in return. "You mean the fifth line, right? 'Put the seals on the destroyer's tomb and the world's final doom will be undone until the true time has come, blah blah blah', that one?" Vassago asked quietly.

Seere nodded. "Yeah, that one–without the 'blah blah blah' part, of course." Belphegor snorted at his comment, and then he went on. "At least we know that to restore the thing to its eternal vocation, we should put all the seals on its tomb, wherever that is."

"Wait, wait, there's one thing I don't get." Belphegor interrupted them.

"Which part?" Vassago asked.

"Uh, the one that said, 'Put the seals together and it will be here.' Ring a bell?" he asked sarcastically.

"Oh, that one. Well, from what I figured, there can be only one meaning behind that," Xaemorkahn said quietly.

"We shouldn't make all three seals function before we get to the damned tomb, right?" Vassago asked as he curled his lips.

Belphegor gaped at his words. "Oh, come on! Are you saying if we removed all the tampering that old bastard did with that damned thing now, that moronic empty dirt bag would come here? Here?" he snarled.

Vassago shrugged. "I guess so. Perhaps what the voice meant with 'here' was the location of whoever heard the words. And why it would come here may be because the seals emit a certain type of energy that can be sensed by that thing. They are supposed to be its weapon after all."

"Right," Belphegor said sarcastically. Xaemorkahn winced at what Vassago told them. That only meant that there was nothing they could do to the Rygavon. Raking his hair in frustration, Xaemorkahn cursed under his breath.

"So, we need to get back to helping Ry and the others search for the damned tomb since we can't do anything here, huh?"

"Hold up, cowboy. We should make sure you know what to do when we need to pull those seals together." Vassago inclined his head to the king.

Startled, Xaemorkahn then nodded. "Okay, let's make sure that I did get everything about the seals from your head."

*   *   *

We'd been digging in the scrolls and books and putting piles of them on the long table for the last couple of hours.

While I was reading one of the scrolls belonging to Belphegor, I heard Vrae let out a long tired breath. She stood by the corner of the archive with her back to me, making a huge mess as she sorted through old books. I was still looking at her when she turned around, and I saw half her face was covered with dust.

She brought piles of scrolls to the table across from me. Putting the scrolls on the table, she sighed again and then seated herself. Her gaze accidentally fell on me. I raised a brow at her. "Find anything?" I asked.

She shook her head. "Nope, big fat zero." She rubbed her eyebrow as if she had a headache.

I chuckled as I pointed at her face. "You might want to clean up all that dust on your face before you dive into those old scrolls again."

She started and then closed her eyes. The dust on her face disappeared without a single trace. Then she opened her eyes and grinned at me.

Sighing, I turned to Ry, while Vrae approached her mate, who was also concentrating on causing other catastrophes with Vassago's bookshelf. We chatted as they scoured through rows of old thick books. "Find anything useful in that?" I asked as I peeked at the book from behind his broad shoulder.

He smiled slightly as he glanced at me. "Nothing useful so far, but the writers are really amazing. I mean, we also have seers and so do humans, but not even our seers would be able to see in advance events that would happen millennia later."

I arched my brows at his amazement. "That is a long time to be called 'in advance'. And from what I heard before, this book also recorded about dear old Lucille. It sure is something."

When he didn't say anything, a thought suddenly went through my mind. "Ry?"

"What is it? You notice something?" he asked.

I shook my head. "No, it's not that. It's just that something occurred to me. If those three tiny things were the Arzia seals, don't you think there would be a tomb or something where it was sealed in the first place?"

Ry's expression changed as he seemed to consider my question. "It could be. Belphegor didn't mention anything about any tomb before though."

"You don't think we can seal that thing anywhere we like, now do you?" I asked in a wondering tone.

He scoffed. "No, I don't think we can go dump Big Boss's ultimate destroyer anywhere we like. We might end up ditching it somewhere inappropriate, say, in the sewer." We both were laughing quietly when Vrae and Zade came to us.

"What are you two laughing about?" Vrae asked. Looking at her, the memory of when we wandered around in D'arksin to look for those Levarchons played back in my mind. "Vrae, do you remember when we looked for those missing Levarchons in the D'arksin?"

She was startled at my question. "Yeah, what of it?"

"Do you recall our suspicions that those soldiers and the Alvadors that also went MIA were all running into something that may had been in a deep slumber all this time undetected?"

Ry gasped at my question. "You're saying that the tomb may be . . ." He didn't finish his sentence as his gaze widened.

I nodded. "It's not one hundred per cent positive yet, but the possibility is quite high that the forest was the very first place where that thing made its move." I glanced at Vrae, who narrowed her gaze at us while Zade gaped in cluelessness. "Would you two mind sharing whatever it is you got?" She curled her lips.

I winced at her, and then both Ry and I explained our suspicions about the tomb.

As soon as we were done with the explanation, the archive's door opened and the elders came in. "Hey, you guys got anything?" Vassago asked as he closed the door, while the rest of the elders approached the table.

Belphegor gaped at the mess we had made. There were mountains of books and piles of scrolls scattered on the table and on the immaculate floor that was now covered with dust. "Wow, looks like you guys are having quite a wild party in here." He winced as he moved several of the books off the table.

"Ha ha ha, yeah, we were having fun with your old books and dust. Hell, we even used the dust as makeup on our faces," I said sarcastically.

Belphegor raised his hands in surrender. "Okay, okay, I was just joking. So, you got anything?"

All of us shook our heads in unison.

Vassago laughed. "Completely nada, huh? Well, we couldn't do anything with Lucifer's handicraft either."

"Why is that?" I asked him. Vassago and Xaemorkahn explained everything that happened in Vassago's study.

"You okay, brother?" Ry asked, when they got to the part where Xaemorkahn's head had been brutalized by Vassago projecting his memories into it.

"I'll live, although I was a bit pissed back then." He gave Vassago a meaningful gaze.

Vassago cleared his throat and looked the other way, and then he turned his gaze back to us to continue with their story.

After they were done, Ry and I exchanged looks with each other. Their story confirmed my thought that there was a tomb to begin with.

"What is it, you two?" Belphegor asked.

We then told them everything and also our suspicions that the tomb may be located in the D'arksin forest.

"This is quite a speculation, but it's the best one we've got so far. We just need to find something to confirm this. Let's get it started then. Ry and Belphegor will dig through the book while the rest of us scour the rest." Vassago jerked his head towards the pile of records.

With that we continued our long search to find the location of the tomb. I just hoped we found it before it was all too late.

Chapter 29

All of us were locked in the archive for the next three days looking for the record about the tomb. We found bits of information about Arzia in a few other parchments, but none of them were useful enough.

I personally thought that our only source in this matter was the Book of Lost Knowledge, but I didn't say anything. Instead I hopelessly scoured the mountain of dusty scrolls before me, hoping I might find something in there.

After three full days of search, Zade found something in one of the scrolls Belphegor had brought. It was an old report about an ancient site found in a forest called Tellian. At that site, a symbol that resembled the union of the seals was seen on the entry gate.

Now all of us were standing around Zade, who sat holding the scroll open on the table. We looked at the scroll closely. "Where is this?" Vrae asked as she looked at me.

I shrugged. "Don't ask me. I've never heard of a forest called Tellian, nor have I heard about this site. What about you, Ry? Have you heard about this?"

He shook his head as well. "No, I haven't. What about you guys?" he asked the princes.

Belphegor frowned as he lowered his gaze, seeming to think about something. After a full minute, he turned his gaze to Vassago and Seere. "Hey, I wonder if this was the same site as *that* one." He gave his old friends a meaningful gaze that made both Vassago's turquoise eyes widen and Seere's gaze darken all of a sudden.

"You mean *that* one? But that's . . ." Vassago's voice faded as he stared at the North Prince.

I sighed in vexation. Could they please share whatever it was with the rest of the class?

Ry cleared his throat. "Uhm, gentlemen, could you tell us whatever you got instead of making us going through first round of Guessing Quiz here?"

The three of them abruptly turned to us. "We've never see the site for ourselves, but we did suspect that something foul was in the works. Since we never had clarity on the matter, we let it be forgotten and didn't think about it again," Vassago said with a tic working in his jaw.

I caught a weird note in his voice and frowned. "Something foul was on the works? Why did you think that?"

"Because the whole Machordaen unit that accidentally ran into it went MIA two days later," Seere said bitterly.

"What?" Zade, Vrae, and I asked in unison.

Ry bit his lip. "Do you think it was that thing? If it was, then it's been on the loose since, wait a sec"–he looked down on the scroll—"since two hundred thousand years ago," he exclaimed in disbelief.

"That's Darkan's era," I added in awe.

Vassago shrugged. "Yeah, it was around his time. We can't tell how long ago exactly this thing started to run amok since we never found any corpses belonged to those guys, unlike the recent disappearances."

The North Prince snorted. "Yeah, right, like you didn't know. You checked that place with Seere and me, and we all know the only bastard who'd leave *that* thing as a souvenir."

All of us looked at Belphegor who curled his lips in disgust, while Vassago just stared. "You guys found something? I thought you said there was nothing?" Ry asked.

Belphegor's crimson eyes swirled as his gaze darkened. "We were curious because not only were those Machordaens MIA, but we got the report that the site was also buried soon after they were gone. So we decided to look for those guys secretly."

"We began the search where we heard the unit was last seen, and it was supposedly pretty close to the site. Since they were the ones who found it, naturally they were entrusted to guard the place." Vassago stared blankly at the scroll as he talked. There was a strange note beneath his voice, but I couldn't tell what. He took a deep breath and released it before he went on. "At first, we didn't find anything." Right there he stopped.

"And?" Ry prompted.

"And then we decided to split up. A few yards from the first spot we'd began searching, we found only two things," Belphegor said grudgingly.

"What were they?" I asked carefully.

"One half of a charred Machordaen emblem and a slight scent of Rygavon's Dark Light from it." He clenched his teeth, as if remembering something so repulsive he could hardly bear it.

"Rygavon's Dark Light?" Ry asked sharply.

"You're saying . . ." Vrae didn't finish her sentence and just stared at the royals in disbelief.

"Yeah, dear old daddy bastard wasted a unit of low ranks all by himself. You see, if he wanted to make it less suspicious, he could at least not have wasted those guys using his famous trademark," he said sarcastically.

I swallowed a bit at their story. Gee, the more I learned about our master, the more I found him repulsive.

Glancing at Ry, I saw his expression change and his gaze fall to the table as if he were feeling really uneasy about all this. Abruptly he exhaled as he looked at the prince. "Do you remember where you found that piece of emblem and your dad's leftovers?"

The princes exchanged looks with each other, and then Belphegor nodded at him. "Yeah, and I assure you, it ain't Tellian. I have no idea who called it that in the first place."

"Where?" I asked.

Vassago inclined his head to me. "The very place you suspected, Yve." He looked down at the scroll.

"D'arksin." Seere's low voice was hollow as he stared blankly.

Vrae gaped at their end of the story. "I can't believe it! That tomb was there and has never been bothered this whole time," she said in amazement.

I started as I remembered something that had happened before we heard about those soldiers' disappearance. Could it possibly be the cause?

"You wanna say something, baby?" Ry suddenly asked.

I hesitated as I saw his puzzled gaze at me. I decided to tell him what went through my mind. "There is something. If I recall it correctly, there was a huge earthquake maybe a few months before the first disappearance. I heard it did quite a bit of damage to D'arksin. From what I heard, the earth even cracked from it."

All of them looked at me. "You're saying that earthquake was what opened the buried site?" Belphegor asked sharply.

I shrugged. "Don't know. Just making a wild guess, that's all, and with this ancient site report and everything . . ." I let my words hang there.

Vassago scoffed. "Really, you should have yourself transferred into Intel Division with a hunch as wild as that." He shook his head.

I frowned at him. "Where's the fun in that? I'd end up destroying the entire intel chamber out of boredom if I got stuck in there."

Ry and the princes laughed at my words.

I cleared my throat to get their attention. "Well, it's decided then. We'll try looking around D'arksin. So when will we start looking?"

Ry's brows knitted. "The sooner the better, but do you guys still remember where that piece of emblem was found or the spot where you began your search?"

Vassago put one hand on his chin. "It is reasonable to think the site's location isn't that far from both those places."

"But?" Ry prompted.

"But we can't tell that for sure. Like I said, we didn't see the site ourselves. Say, what if we check if the place where those Machordaens went MIA is indeed around the place that was damaged by the earthquake?" Vassago asked as his gaze fell on the site's picture in the scroll.

"Okay, let's move out in five hours." Belphegor moved away and stretched his lean body.

"We'll go out at once?" Vrae asked, a bit sceptical at the idea of us all going to the D'arksin in one pack.

"Well, the thing we're about to seal is the Big Boss's favourite catastrophe maker. I'd say my pop would look like a kitten in comparison to that thing, and even fighting him didn't feel like a walk in the park." Belphegor shrugged.

Ry snorted. "Kitten, huh? Well, I guess you're right. We'll need all four of you to prepare the seals for that bastard, and you guys can do the job while we face the thing head on."

I startled as I remembered Aleeria. "Great, I wanna make a blood rain out of that thing," I said with coldness I barely noticed.

All of them fell silent, but they didn't say anything. Vassago then took the scroll and folded it. "Okay, let's get back to our rooms to recuperate. We haven't had the chance to recharge since we fought the old bastard. Meet us downstairs in five hours."

After that we went to our rooms. As usual, Ry and I turned to human form. The silly thing was that even though I couldn't believe it at first, I was gradually growing accustomed to this form bit by bit. Wasn't this hilarious, a devil with such a high pride in being one like myself, didn't mind being human? I still felt extremely disgusted whenever I thought about it, but when I looked into Ry's sapphire eyes, I knew I could do this. If he indeed became a human, then there was no way I would hate to become one too. In that situation, to hate humans would only mean to hate him, and there was no way in heaven or hell or the next dimension I would hate him, no matter what his form was.

Besides, I was never one to deny my own existence. If in the end I was meant to be human, then so be it. To deny it only meant one thing–to wipe out my own existence. I might as well kill myself rather than deny who I was.

Both of us realized how tired we were as soon as we lay down in that comfortable bed, as if most of our powers had been drained without us noticing it.

After that, as he always did when we were together, he pulled me into his arms and held me protectively as he drifted into a deep sleep. I could hear his heart beating steadily before I too fell into the depths of dreams.

When I woke up, it was still three hours earlier than the time we agreed to meet. Ry was still asleep, so I silently sneaked out from his hold, transformed into my original form, manifested my armour, and then headed downstairs. When I got to the bottom of the stairs, there was only one man standing there–Xaemorkahn.

His long, black robe flowed freely around his lean body, and his long hair fell all the way to his waist. His aura completed his regal bearing as a king. He still stood there as if he didn't notice my presence. I saw his lonely expression as he spaced out, as if he were longing for something far away from his reach.

"Xaemorkahn," I called him carefully.

Surprised to find me standing there, he abruptly turned around and smiled to greet me. "Hey, I didn't hear you. So have you had enough rest?"

I nodded. "I have. What about you? Didn't all that spell work drain quite a considerable amount of power out of you as well?"

He shrugged. "I've had enough rest. Besides, though it may have looked like it, all those spells didn't really take that much anyway."

I sighed. "I'm glad to hear that. If anything happened to you, I wouldn't be able to face Varisha ever again. Really, thanks a lot, Xaemorkahn," I said sincerely as I smiled in gratitude.

The king was startled at the mention of his beloved wife, and then he grinned. "Yeah, you'd better watch it. I told Risha to kick my brother's butt if I didn't get home in one piece, and I assure you even I would run for cover whenever she gets mad."

I cringed at that. Xaemorkahn then sobered up and that soothing smile broke on his face again. "Just kidding. I've had a better time here than I imagined I would. At least with Ry and you around, I can act casually around those princes like I can around you both. I get to kick my sworn enemy's ass to boot." He grinned again.

"Good to hear you feel quite at ease here. And yes, you really did kick his butt, good and proper." I grinned back.

"By the way, can I ask you something?" he asked.

"What is it?" I looked directly into his eyes.

He bit his lip as if he were hesitating. "I was wondering how you guys could take down your Master without any regrets like that. No offense–it's not as if I like him or anything–I mean he's been my enemy since the Stone Age, but you guys were his soldiers. Don't you revere him? I don't mean to judge you, just asking."

I hesitated a bit and then answered him. "No offense taken. I knew that you'd be thinking about this. Well, first off, we were his soldiers, and those princes are royals who swore their allegiance to him, but even devils can't escape from the possibility of chaos. That's why every now and again there are devils going rogue. Ever since most of the royals started to withdraw into exile and rarely paid any attention to our problems, my Master's Echelons began pushing their rules onto us and even put commanders like Ry under stupid surveillance everywhere they went. And that's one of many reasons why I started to disrespect him. I mean, he could've picked some other bunch to be his representatives, but he picked them, and what's worse, he didn't even try to stop them from tearing us apart." My voice trembled a bit as old memories began to resurface.

Like what they'd done all those thousands of years to Ry.

Biting my lip, I went on. "During the first days they did that, several Cherxanains like Vrae and me were sentenced to death, and not a single one of them knew who turned them in, let alone why they were being punished. Most of us started to suspect each other. There's no longer any trust amongst us. We're anxious that if we trust the wrong person, we'll end up in the death penalty row.

"There were times when a brother turned his own sister in or vice versa. The 'Cain and Abel' scene happened all around. Hell, Vrae and I were so disgusted by what they were doing that we made every brother and sister we ran into swear that they'd never turn each other in and they'd never tell the Echelons that we made them swear that.

"For a while there were brothers and sisters dropping dead every time their siblings were sent to death. Not long after that they stopped out of fear of having to meet Azrael, and no one dropped dead again. But there are other devils who stick their noses into other people's business, so what we were doing didn't do that much to help." I shrugged.

Xaemorkahn's gaze showed sincere sympathy when he looked at my eyes.

I let out a long suffering breath before I went on with my story. "Ever since then, with Alvadors and lapdogs everywhere looking for mistakes and turning everyone in at will, somehow our trust in the few comrades we had left, weird as it sounds, just grew stronger. Perhaps it even reached all the way to the level where we've unconsciously sworn our allegiance to each other, not to our supposed Master."

I glanced at him and saw the strange look he had on his face. I couldn't tell what he was thinking, so I continued. "Around that time, mysterious disappearances also began to happen amongst the soldiers from lower ranks than Vrae and me. I found out from Ry that several of them were caused by our own master.

"At first, Ry kept it secret. He was scared that if he breathed any of that to me or our other comrades, we'd end up disappearing as well, and that made him so damned secretive about everything that

I got a headache each time I tried to figure out what he was up to or what was troubling him. Only a few days ago, he told me some of the things he was trying so badly to keep to himself. What's worse, our own Echelons can't be relied on to give an explanation without drawing their suspicions onto us, and a huge cliff slowly formed between the lines of commanders and the Echelons."

I stopped as I remembered more of the bitter memories of the old days. "We could only do our work as if nothing had happened if we obeyed their orders without question and didn't run into anything funny. After that, Ry started to take me and Vrae to Belphegor and a few other elders, because it turned out they could be trusted more than our own Echelons. And it was from them we found out things about our master that made us barely have any respect towards him.

"But for me, the ultimate reason why I can't respect him any more is the fact that he himself tried to kill Ry." I looked at him seriously as the memory of him telling me that fact played in the back of my mind.

Xaemorkahn's gaze was sad. "There's one thing I don't get. If you guys feared to trust each other, how did you manage to have such an ironclad belief amongst yourselves and also with your Head Intel and the guards you told us about earlier?"

I clenched my fist a bit. "Let's just say that none of us is willing to give such a cheap price and low respect towards ourselves and each other." I felt grief and anger underneath my own calm voice, so I lowered my gaze, careful not to offend him.

Apparently Xaemorkahn noticed, because he didn't ask further. When I lifted my gaze from the floor, I saw him incline his head respectfully towards me. "I see. I'm grateful though. This is the first time you've told me this much about your past and Ry's ever since we swore to be brothers. Risha's right after all."

I cast a puzzled gaze at him. "What do you mean?"

He smiled. "She once told me that Ry needs to be with you to feel completely at ease with himself. Even after all the centuries since we became brothers, he seldom talked about his past unless she asked him. But amongst the few things he shared with us, he mostly talked about you."

I could feel my own heart go wild in my breast. "What did he say? I couldn't guess what he thought about me back then, and it seemed that we were just meant to be comrades, nothing more. It is true that he seemed to trust Vrae and me more than the others, but not even that could make him tell us everything."

He laughed half-heartedly. "He didn't say that much to me either, because I thought I shouldn't force him to talk if he didn't want to, but since Risha tended to ask him, he talked to her once in a while. Sometimes, when he came and I wasn't there, she would accompany him. It was Risha who told me his stories about you. From what I heard, even then you already had a special place in his heart."

My gaze widened in disbelief as I felt a wave of love for Ry wash all over me.

He smiled at me. "You may want to laugh at me for saying that devils like you have hearts, but that's what my wife and I feel when we talk to him, when we saw you a few days ago, when you held my wife, when Ry told me to help you guys. It never ceased to amaze me that Lucifer's commanders could have such an ironclad trust and belief in each other. Even in us who come from an entirely different race."

I returned his smile with my own as he went on. "He's always been calm and composed, that Ry, even when he acts all sarcastic or when he faces dire situations. But whenever he's at our place, sometimes either Risha or I would catch him spacing out, as if he were longing for something. The second he realized we were there, he would quickly act as if he were busy."

I frowned. "He does that? I've never seen him like that. If he gets quiet, that only means he's thinking of something really serious."

He gave me a patient smile. "You remember when I told you that, days before he went up there, he spent days at my place scouring my archive?"

I nodded slowly. "I remember you said he was terrified."

He cast a weird gaze at me. "Yes, that time I accidentally heard him mutter your name each time we found records of catastrophe in my old archive."

I couldn't speak. I felt guilt go through me that I hadn't been there to share that burden with him.

He sighed. "Both Risha and I are grateful to him because he saved my life, and we personally thought that if there was a devil meant for him, it would be best if that devil shared his unrivalled compassion towards the ones he cares for.

"The moment I heard from Rivorgad and the others that you were willing to trust them when the others weren't and that was because they mentioned Ry's name, it told us how much you cared for him, not to mention your attitude when we talked about him for the first time, and we're really happy when we saw him come with you. He looks so at ease around you, and his affectionate demeanour towards you shows how important you are for him."

I offered him a grateful smile. "Thank you, really, that you care that much for him and me. That you came to believe us even though our former Master repeatedly tried to kill you."

He grinned. "Nah, we're adults. Whatever your master did, it doesn't mean it had anything to do with you, right?"

I laughed. "That's right."

He abruptly sobered up as if something were going through his mind. "But Ry's always been afraid of your Master."

I nearly choked at that. "Come again?"

He quickly shook his head. "No, I mean, he's always afraid what your Master would . . . Never mind."

Arching my brow, I wasn't going to let that go without explanation. "Ry's afraid he'd do what, Xaemorkahn?"

The king shrugged. "I heard from Risha, though. She asked him one day why he had yet to tell you that he loved you," he began sheepishly.

I felt heat creeping up my face. "I was wondering about that. He told me he was too afraid I would say no, which is ridiculous. I do feel there's something he didn't tell me on that part, but I don't wanna press him."

He nodded in understanding. "Right, but, uh, don't ever tell him you heard this from me, okay?"

I grinned. "Okay."

Sighing, he then raked his hair. "So the fact is, he was too damn afraid your Master would harm you, especially after he saved my life. But, whatever the reason was, he's always been afraid of losing you."

His words made both pain and love for Ry clench my chest. "He shouldn't be afraid that our Master would go after me," I said sadly, "but, that's just who he is, and now I see it in a whole different light. Whenever we're alone, it feels like he's afraid to let me out of his reach, as if I would disappear or die on him. It's gotten worse since I shielded him from the Valdam when we went to get the ring."

He was aghast at that. "You did?"

I nodded. "Yes, because I made sure I'd protect him, especially after I knew our Master himself tried to fry him and he's been out there alone all this time for fear he'd endanger me. But that incident with the ring's Valdam made him dwell in guilt for several days, maybe even now, though he doesn't show it. Unless the princes summon him, he never lets me out of his sight."

Xaemorkahn bit his lip. When he didn't say anything, I gave him a cheeky grin. "Don't get all sad just yet. To be honest, I also feel the same fear. Now that he's finally returned, I can't bear the thought of losing him again after I thought I had all this time," I said firmly.

His gaze widened. "You two are indeed made for each other. I hope you'll get to be together as long as possible. Really, you both deserve it."

I nodded respectfully at him. "Thanks a lot."

Suddenly I heard Ry's voice calling my name in my head, but it sounded weird. It was more like he was screaming. "Excuse me, I gotta go back. He's calling me." I tilted my head upward and then willed myself back upstairs.

When I got there, I saw Ry's gaze had widened in horror. He shivered all over as if something had frightened him. "Ry, what's wrong?" I asked as I ran to him.

He suddenly pulled me into him. I immediately changed into human form before my horns accidentally hurt him. He then held me tightly. I could feel his entire body shaking. "I thought I lost you. Lucifer said he would . . ." he said over and over, gasping in a broken voice.

Tears stung my eyes as I buried my face in his shoulder. He was recalling that day when our Master ambushed him.

"Don't worry, I'm here, I won't be going anywhere. Lucifer didn't do anything to me," I said as I ran my hand gently on his back.

He brought us down to our bed, and we lay there in silence holding each other.

I hurled curses at myself. How stupid I was to forget about this! That was the worst moment of his life! He had barely survived, and then he was forced not to come back. He was out there by himself for seven hundred years, fearful for his own life, mine, his brother's, and his brother's wife's as well, while I was here with Vrae and the others, ignorant of everything. How could I be so careless?

When he had calmed down, he sighed. "I'm sorry, it's just this stupid nightmare I had, and then I didn't find you when I woke up, so I thought something bad had happened."

I shook my head while I still had my face buried in his shoulder. "No, I'm the one who should be sorry. I wanted to take you along, but when I saw you, you were so deeply asleep that I didn't want to wake you."

He ran my hair down. "Where were you just now?"

"I was downstairs talking with your brother. I found him standing alone and looking lonely, so I decided to have a chat with him."

He raked my hair tenderly. "So that's what you were doing. Thanks. He does seem a bit lonely here." He moved a bit so he could look at me, and then he kissed me passionately before he stood up and changed into his true form.

"Now, I'm going to return to you what you said to me when I helped Vassago heal Seere," he said as he narrowed his gaze at me.

I turned back into my true form and then frowned at him. "Huh? Which words?"

"'Just remember to wake me up next time you have to go anywhere', remember?" he took my chin and angled it up to face him.

Startled, I winced before I smiled widely. "Oh, that! Okay, I will. Sorry about that."

He shook his head as he removed his hand from my chin and touched my cheek with that warm hand of his, and then he kissed me again.

Then he withdrew. "Come on, it's about time to meet the others," he said, and then he pulled his hand from my cheek. Tucking my hand in his, he led me downstairs.

He was right, the others were already there. When Xaemorkahn's gaze fell on me, he gave me a puzzled gaze, silently asking what had happened. I gave him a meaningful gaze in return and was grateful he caught my meaning. I saw him looked worried for a second before he went stoic again.

"All right then, let's head to the D'arksin." Vassago walked towards the door and opened it as soon as both of us joined them. Vassago hid his castle in shadows after all of us were outside, and then Xaemorkahn once again teleported us straight to where that earthquake had done the most damage.

The second we reached the place, I gaped at the sight. There was a big wide hole in the ground a few meters from where we were standing. Big trees had fallen into it. Vrae and I hadn't got to this part of the forest when we were looking for those Levarchons and Alvadors, so I didn't know that there was a gaping hole this massive.

"This is a pretty big hole," Zade said, his eyes widened in surprise.

I looked down into the hole closely. It went all the way down. The hole was so deep that I couldn't even see the bottom. After scanning the side of that recently formed cliff where some of the trees were stuck, I saw something that looked like the tip of a roof ornament of some sort jutting out a bit from beneath the branches of the fallen trees.

"Hey, what's that?" I pointed that ornament-like object that was barely visible because it was covered by the trees.

All of them quickly looked at the object I was pointing at.

"Is that the site?" Vrae asked.

"Come on, let's check it out." Ry jumped into the hole without hesitation. I followed him with the others. We floated above those trees covering the object and threw them away. Once there were no more trees covering our sight, we landed on the soil that still covered that rooftop object.

Belphegor raised his hand, and the earth began to shake tremendously. As the earth started to shatter, I could see parts of that thing which I suspected to be some kind rooftop. It turned out it was an ornament on top of a huge gate . . . in the shape of what the seals might have looked like if they were put together.

I glanced at the North Prince, and weirdly enough, he curled his lips a bit as if something had offended him. When he didn't say anything, I didn't bother to ask.

Vassago scowled. "So this is where that thing's been cowering all this time. This is nice, for a creature whose only job's drooling until the apocalypse game time."

All of us were standing in front of a massive gate made of gold with that seal's shape on top of it–the ring at its base, followed by the curve of the Herathim and a straight shape like a short sword, ending with the triangle with the All-Seeing Eye inside it.

"Let's open it," Ry said. I felt him drawing bits of his powers to move the gate. After a few seconds, he started to frown, and so did I.

The huge golden gate didn't make any movement.

"What's wrong?" Xaemorkahn asked.

"The gate won't open," Ry said with a strained voice as he drew more powers.

Without warning, the gate started to shine brightly. The light was so bright that all of us covered our eyes with our wings. Well, Xaemorkahn used his duster-like robe. Suddenly, there was a light shooting from the gate . . . and it hit Ry.

He was sent flying and hit the rocks across from the gate.

"Ry!" I called him as I flew to him as he started to roll down below. I got to him just before he fell over into that who-knew-how-deep hole. I sat there on the rock holding him. His chest was somewhat burned by that light, and he was bleeding profusely. "Baby, baby, I got you. Talk to me," I said as I rocked him in my arms. I could feel my own voice trembling as I watched him gasping. "I'm okay, just got fried a bit," he panted, cringing at the same time he tried to grin at me.

"How is he?" I heard Xaemorkahn's voice, and I looked up to find him towering over me with Vrae and Zade behind him.

Wariness was written all over his beautiful face, as it was on my sister's and her mate's faces. "I'm fine," he said as he grabbed the soil around us, trying to get up.

"You sure?" I asked him, and his face broke into that beautiful gentle smile he always given me.

"Hey, how's it going over there?" Vassago yelled from the other side.

Ry waved at the princes. "I'm fine! That damned light nearly fried me, but I'm good!"

I saw Belphegor's lips break into a wide grin. "That was pretty close, boy!" he shouted.

Ry scoffed. "How's the gate going? Any sign it would open up any time soon?" He asked as he began to steady his feet. I stood up and looked at him warily.

Was he really okay?

"Nope, not yet! This gate's pretty sturdy!" Vassago yelled. I saw Seere was checking the gate closely.

"Come on," he said as he extended his hand for me to take it. I took his hand and stopped him just before he took off.

"Are you really okay?" I narrowed my gaze at him. He looked at me and nodded as he dissolved the blood from the front part of his body. The blood disappeared, and the burn on his chest was already healed.

I let out a relieved breath, and we all flew to where the princes were standing. "Is there any keyhole of some sort?" I asked.

Seere didn't avert his gaze as he ran his hands over the huge gate. After a while, he couldn't find anything. He started to float as he placed his hands on the golden gate. "I didn't find anything hole-like down there," he said.

"Perhaps the door's connected to those seals. As long as the seal's scattered, it won't open. Maybe it's something like that?" Ry asked wonderingly.

I glanced at Seere, who stared down at him from above. I turned to see the other two royals to find both of them staring at Ry as well.

"It's worth a shot." Vassago pulled out the Rygavon, and Belphegor took the ring from beneath his wings that turned into crimson robes, while Xaemorkahn pulled out the Herathim.

I frowned as I looked at all those seals. Something was off here, but I didn't have a clue as to what it was.

"Okay, here's the deal. Ry, you and Yve go with Vrae and Zade. Guard us up there while we put these seals together," Belphegor said in a commanding tone as he jerked his head up.

"Don't stray too far. The voice Xaemorkahn heard said that if we put the seals together into the Arkhadim, the Arzia will come to get it," Seere added.

"Right, we'll be close by," Ry said. Together, the four of us left them down below.

When we reached topside, that weird hunch became a bad feeling. "Ry," I pulled his hand that was still entwined with mine.

He turned to me. "What is it? You look like you're worried about something." His sapphire gaze was full of concern when he directed it at me.

"If that gate's been sealed for a hundred thousand years, and the earthquake only opened up that top part of the gate, then how did that void-whatever thing get out?"

Ry lowered his gaze for a second, and then he looked at me again. "I also thought about that, and I can only think of two possibilities. First, the earthquake did make a hole all the way down there and entirely exposed the gate, and then it got out. After that it buried the gate before it got out of here."

"And the other possibility?" I asked.

He averted his gaze and suddenly his brows were knitted to form one hard line. "Someone out there, either from upstairs or from our own place, helped it out," he said with a low deadly voice as if he were ready to tear apart whoever had done it.

The air was knocked out of my lungs at his words. "But none of the others knows about this, well, except Lucille maybe and those guys from up there." I shook my head in disbelief.

Ry gave me a sad look. "We can't say for sure if those three are the only the royals who know about this. Hell, from what I gathered, maybe the other princes like Orobas, Stolas, and Sitri know. If princes know, perhaps royals of other ranks know about it too."

"But why would anybody from upstairs or our own do something like this?"

Suddenly, I felt his grip tighten. "I don't know. It's just the worst possibility I could think of." He gave me a half-hearted smile.

I scoffed. "Wow, your thought's even *more* of a downer than mine."

Another thought went through my mind, and it was an outrageous one. I couldn't help but laugh nervously. "I don't know why, but suddenly I have this weird feeling that the one murdering our soldiers and those of your brother wasn't that void dirt bag." Even Vrae and Zade, who were walking few steps from us, stopped dead.

"Why in the hell do you think that?" Vrae asked sharply as she approached us.

I shrugged. "I don't know. I mean, the gate was sealed, unless the thing was already out here and something woke it up or pissed it off. I can't see how it managed to wreak some havoc. Or hell, maybe it could open the gate from inside, but I doubt that was it, because I'd say it'd really be counterproductive to whole the sealing purpose those guys upstairs did with it," I said sarcastically.

All of them fell silent. Ry sighed and then shook his head. "It is a comforting thought, but one we can do nothing about. Come on, let's guard the hole." He jerked his head to indicate the woods around us.

We nodded and then separated into two groups. Walking farther from the hole where those princes and Xaemorkahn were working on the seals, we then stood beside the trees around us waiting for anything that would show.

* * *

"You ready?" Vassago asked Xaemorkahn as he, Belphegor, and Seere gathered around the king.

Xaemorkahn nodded. He and Belphegor put the seals they had back into their robes. Vassago raised the Rygavon and started to chant.

The triangle piece then began to float and emit black light that engulfed all four of them. The All-Seeing Eye glowed as it blinked slowly. It glowed pretty bright so that it was visible despite all the black light around them.

While Vassago was still chanting, Belphegor followed, he raised his hand in the piece's direction and started to mutter another set of spells. After one full minute, Seere also did the same with the other two.

In the next five minutes, Xaemorkahn just focused his gaze on the little piece. The Rygavon's All-Seeing Eye started to blink rapidly as it rolled slowly in the air.

Xaemorkahn began to draw bits of his powers. He closed his eyes to look within his memories for a set of spells that he was supposed to cast. Once he found it, he inhaled deeply and released it. Then he opened his eyes and started to chant. As he uttered the spell, his deep beautiful voice made the chanting sound like a holy song no creature had ever heard.

The black light around them began to dissolve bit by bit. Now the light only glowed around the tiny triangle, and the All-Seeing Eye that had been blinking so fast now started to slow down and blinked only once every few seconds.

The four of them suddenly felt a weird wave of energy coming from the triangle object they were working on. The air around them turned eerily cold, and it became tighter and tighter, suffocating them.

"What the fuck is going on here?" Belphegor cursed in his thoughts.

A few moments later, they finished chanting all the sets of spells. Then the All-Seeing Eye stopped blinking, and the Rygavon also stopped spinning.

The black light was completely gone, but suddenly, a massive explosion of bright white light came out of the Rygavon, and then it stopped just as quickly as it had come.

Unfortunately, that light was too bright for all of them to take in.

"What the hell is this?" Vassago swore under his breath as he desperately tried to clear his sight. The others also let out a low curse and waved their hands randomly, trying to get hold of something.

All of them saw small blue lights like stars in their eyes.

When they were all barely able to see anything, the cold air suddenly became warm again, and whatever made the air tighter was gone. As they all began to breathe normally, they heard a clear thud of something landing on the ground.

"I think that was your dad's favourite toy," Seere said. His swirling ruby eyes started to see clearly everything around him. When his gaze met Belphegor's, he knew the North Prince's eyes had recovered as well, since he rolled his crimson eyes at him.

"Ha ha ha, I'm amused," he said sarcastically.

No sooner had Belphegor let out the sarcastic response than both he and Xaemorkahn yelled in pain. "What is it?" Vassago asked sharply.

Instead of answering Vassago, they frantically reached underneath their robes and pulled out the seals they carried. Once they grabbed the seals, they hastily threw them to the ground. They gasped and panted as they saw the two seals they carried looking helpless lying on the ground near Rygavon. "That was annoying," Belphegor snapped.

"What is it? What happened?" Seere asked sharply.

Belphegor and Xaemorkahn stood up and shook their hands rapidly as if something had bitten them. "That seal's what happened! That thing suddenly turned all hot, and the next thing I knew, my chest was almost burned all crispy! Now my hand's all charred!" Xaemorkahn snapped.

"Yeah, me too," Belphegor interjected.

Seere frowned. "That's odd. Hey, do you think the Core of Rygavon . . ."

" . . . had something to do with that?" Vassago cut him off, and then he indicated the seals lying on the ground. "Yeah, I think it definitely got something to do with that."

They all looked down and saw the seals start to shake tremendously as they floated a few inches above the ground. In the next second, each of the seals suddenly spun so fast that their eyes could barely keep up, and then they abruptly stopped dead in mid-air. The three seals slowly positioned themselves vertically with the Ring of Solomon on the bottom, Herathim in the middle, and the Core of Rygavon on top.

Those seals just floated there for a moment. "What do you think they're doing?" Seere whispered.

Belphegor shrugged. "I don't have a clue. Perhaps they had a sudden desire to dance?"

Xaemorkahn let out a snort. "I don't think that's what those things are doing."

Vassago gave a subtle nod in agreement. "Yeah, I think they started reforming into the Arkhadim," he said. "The Arzia's toy."

As if to confirm Vassago's and Xaemorkahn's thoughts, the seals began to unite. The Ring of Solomon approached what appeared to be the hilt of Herathim, while the Core of Rygavon made a move onto the base.

There was a clicking sound as the ring and the Rygavon fitted onto the small metallic parts jutting out of the Herathim. After they re-joined, they glowed for a few seconds. When the light had stopped, all the royals saw that the seals had united perfectly.

There was no trace of them ever having been separated.

Belphegor curled his lips. "That was nice. Now that the Arkhadim's been reformed, all we have to do is get back up there and wait for whatever it is to come."

"Wait, look over there," Vassago said sharply as he jerked his head to the gate.

Their gaze fell to the gate. There was a light formed in the shape of a triangle, and then in the middle of it there was a carving.

"I don't know about you, but I do think that looks like a place to fit this seal in." Xaemorkahn averted his gaze from the gate to the seals.

"Thank you, Captain Obvious," Belphegor said, his swirling crimson eyes still on the newly formed carving.

Xaemorkahn had to restrain himself from rolling his beautiful eyes as he started to reach for the seal that was still floating above the ground. He took it carefully, and then he slowly moved to the carving.

"Hold up." Vassago grabbed his hand.

Xaemorkahn turned to him. "That thing's not in there. Let's open this up so can we just grab that Arzia creature and push it inside."

Vassago's voice was full of wariness. "In theory, but even though it's not in there, I don't think it's wise to open this gate up just yet. Besides, to open this gate we must leave the Arkhadim on it, and it's that thing's weapon, so if it sensed it . . ."

"It would take it, and we'd be done for," Seere interjected.

Xaemorkahn hesitated, and then he sighed. "Okay, fine, let's bring it with us and get back up there."

Vassago nodded. "You take it. We can't grab the Herathim."

The king hesitated for a second before he put the seal in his robes. Vassago indicated the surface. "Let's go," he said.

They immediately flew back to the topside.

*   *   *

I was standing behind a big oak tree, staring in the hole's direction. It was then I saw a weird light come out from the hole. I heard the royals cursing and then whispering for a few minutes before I heard Belphegor and Xaemorkahn yelping as if something had bitten them. After that more whispers.

Next I felt some peculiar energy coming out of the hole. "Ry, do you feel that?" I looked at him. He was also standing behind a tree a few steps to my left.

He nodded. "Yeah, I saw that light too. Looks like they made it. Now, we just have to wait until they come back up."

Moments later, all of them showed up and hastily split up. Belphegor walked towards me, Xaemorkahn headed to Ry, while Vassago and Seere moved to Vrae and Zade.

"You guys made it," I said as the North Prince approached me.

He nodded. "Yeah, any sign of whatever it is?"

I shook my head. "Nothing showed up."

As if wanting to say "you wish" to me, I felt the air move at an eerie pace that made all the hair on the back of my neck stand up.

"Scratch that," I whispered. All of us steadied ourselves as something alarming moved in the air.

After waiting cautiously for a few seconds, I finally saw something coming out from behind the trees across the big wide hole . . . or rather someone.

To my surprise, it wasn't a creature or anything of the sort. A beautiful young woman in a long watery-silver-coloured gown gracefully approached that gaping hole in the ground.

What the hell?

"Now that is something. The lady is a beaut," Belphegor murmured in amazement.

I rolled my eyes at his response. I'll admit the woman was something, but then again it just wasn't the time to make comments like that.

Suddenly the so-called lady spread out three pairs of transparent wings and manifested a silver staff. On one end, it had something jutting out that looked like it was missing something.

There was only one thing that would fit–the seal.

"Yeah, what a beautiful *lady* that is," I muttered sarcastically as I readied myself to fight.

Belphegor scoffed as he locked his gaze on the woman or whatever it was that stood before us. She suddenly made a strange movement as if she were sniffing something in the air.

The royals silently flew to the top of the trees, while Ry, I, and the others quietly hid ourselves behind the trees. I secretly drew my powers to reach the ether, trying to sense that . . . woman in order to plan my attack on her. A few seconds after I had everything else around me under my senses, I realized that there was one thing I still couldn't get hold of.

Her.

Dammit, she *was* void, I'd give her that.

Unable to sense her, I slowly moved to look at her. That was when she turned and directed her blank gaze at me. A smile that was twisted yet devoid of emotions broke on her face as she levelled her staff at where I stood.

I went rigid for a split second before I snapped back into reality. That hornless woman headed straight at me.

Abruptly I took a wide step to my right and flew further from the tree, making as much distance as possible from where I was hiding a second before, while that woman or whatever chased me really fast.

Throwing my hands out in front, I drew my energy to the maximum as I made a wide turn and headed back to the hole and launched a massive amount of bolts at her. That was when I saw something that made my blood run cold.

She waved her staff, and my bolts disappeared.

My jaw went slack, and she swiftly launched herself at me. In a second, she closed her distance to me. Now she was just a couple of feet away. She made a movement to strike with her staff, but I managed to fly away right before her staff made contact. As I moved with caution, I heard something come rushing from the trees, or rather, some people.

Ry and Belphegor were flying towards me. They shot bolt after bolt at the "woman", who, like before, wiped their attacks with just one wave of her staff.

Belphegor cursed as he and Ry landed beside me. "Shit. You know, she could be really cute if she wasn't such a bitch," he snarled, yelling the last word at the destroyer who didn't respond.

"You okay?" Ry asked. His voice was full of dread.

I nodded at him and then glanced at the North Prince. "What the hell took you guys so damn long?" I snapped as I averted my gaze from him and fixed my eyes on the woman.

"Sorry about that. We were busy improvising an emergency plan back there. Right now they're waiting for the right moment to ambush the bitch," Ry said quietly as he glanced at me.

"We were about to reach the ether to focus her attention on us instead of his brother"–Belphegor tilted his chin at Ry–"since he has the Arkhadim, but you beat us to it. So, here we are."

I exhaled heavily after I heard what he said. "Great, we're the welcoming committee."

Belphegor snorted. "Well, at least this bitch seems more entertaining. She's not just saying wrong words about fucking anybody, or more to the point, fucking me. Oh wait, that's just my sorry-ass dad."

Rubbing my temple, I tried to zero in on the woman. Really, the guy just didn't know when to stop . . .

My gaze fixed on her despite all his stupid jokes. And then, as if she were offended by Belphegor's insults, she stopped dead and slammed her staff to the ground. The upper end of the staff began to glow, and several energy spheres or some things that looked like energy spheres spurted out of it. All of them were transparent like bubbles.

Since we were not sure what would happen if we shot them, we split up and let those things head towards the forest. Luckily, they didn't go to where the others were hidden.

The second those bubble-like energy balls hit the trees, a whole bunch of them were shredded. The limbs of the trees were cut in the same manner as the butchered soldiers.

I cursed under my breath. "No doubt about it now, huh?"

Turning around, I found Ry busy rolling and flying sideways as he traded multiple bolts with her, while Belphegor sneaked around trying to make an opening.

We'd spent quite some time attempting to land even just one solid hit on her. Unfortunately we had yet to succeed.

Belphegor grew impatient and went berserk. Everything around us shattered, the earth crumbled and began to fall into the big hole where the gate was, and the woods were also destroyed by our fight.

Now Vassago and Seere had joined our huge battle.

I rolled in the air to avoid those energy balls she threw at me and then immediately launched several of my own. That was when something beyond my wildest expectation happened.

She threw void energy spheres again, and all of them came in contact with my bolts, but strangely enough, my bolts and her spheres disappeared altogether, as if they just cancelled each other out. Both she and I stared at what just occurred, a bit taken by surprise. But she recovered a tad faster than I did, and she threw more of her spheres.

Wincing as reality snapped me back to earth, I flew aside and managed to avoid one, two, three of her attacks, but the fourth . . . got through my stomach. My entire body went numb, and I couldn't hear anything. It felt like something had turned the volume off as I fell from a height of several feet.

I could see my surroundings as clearly as if time had become slower. When I was sure I'd be crushed, I felt someone grab me as I was falling from the sky. The firm yet gentle hold and the familiar masculine scent made me realize that it was Ry. "Yve, you okay?" his trembling voice told me how worried he was.

"I'm fine," I blurted out.

He brought me safely to the ground quite far from the heated battle where Belphegor and the other two princes were launching a massive attack at the void-woman. Kneeling, he gently laid me down. I coughed hard as I tried to get up. "Easy, babe, that bitch's bolt went right through you. Just stay here for a few," he wrapped his hand around my shoulders.

I was about to shake my head to tell him that I was all right when that numbness wave hit all over me. Looking down, I saw my hands were invaded by that same blue pale color I got when I examined those Levarchons' remains.

Great, like I didn't have enough trouble as it was . . .

"Yve, what is this?" he asked, not sure what to make of the blue thing.

I shook my head. "It's nothing. You get back there, I'll catch up later. I've dealt with this crap before." I smiled at him and indicated the war zone up ahead.

He hesitated, but he let me go. His lips formed a half-hearted smile before he rushed back to where the princes were busy raising all hell and causing nuclear-like destruction among the woods.

I immediately drew out my healing power and spread it throughout my entire body. This would be the biggest risk I ever took. The last time I made contact with the bitch's energy was enough to make me unconscious. I hoped to hell it wouldn't happen again this time because I so didn't have time for that crap.

But then, maybe the risk was worth taking since I wasn't blown to pieces. Perhaps as Ry said, my own power of darkness neutralized hers like my bolts did before, and instead of getting blown to shreds, this stupid numbness that paralyzed me and my body turning the blue color of a corpse were what I got instead.

Well, it was definitely a lot better than being kicked straight to oblivion.

As I cautiously watched Vassago and Seere simultaneously jump to the sky to avoid her attacks and counter them, I slowly directed my healing power to drive out that thing which, I had no doubt now, was the poison infiltrating my system.

It was then I felt a slight tingling down my spine.

I could feel it. Something at Vrae, Zade, and Xaemorkahn's direction was emitting a peculiar energy. Was it their doing?

After a few minutes trying extremely carefully to eradicate the poison, I finally succeeded, and the good thing was, I didn't even feel any dizziness–except for that weird tingle.

The tingling grew stronger now than before.

Curious, I motioned slowly to Vrae. When I found her and the other males who were with her, I saw all of them circling around as they held a small blue orb.

"What's that?" I asked them.

Vrae looked at me with both her hands and Zade's still above Xaemorkahn's with palms faced down to the orb.

It turned black and purple and after that crimson, before it went back to pale deep blue again.

"Xaemorkahn's idea. It turned out he has a few tricks up his sleeve," she said with one edge of her lips twitching.

"A little surprise we made for that void bitch." Xaemorkahn glanced at me and smiled wickedly.

Zade scoffed. "Yeah, we're gonna throw this at her. Xaemorkahn said that it might incapacitate her, or better yet, knock her out. After that, we get to kick her back to her destination and make her continue her long-time vacation."

I arched my brow. "That's the idea?"

"The general idea, yeah," Xaemorkahn answered.

I grimaced. "Any thought of how we can do that, generally?"

Xaemorkahn bit his lip in trepidation. "I've been observing your fight, and she's really fast. Even though she's surrounded, she's never been flawed in all her reactions. And the biggest problem is . . ."

" . . . that damn staff," I interjected, and he nodded. Averting his gaze back to the orb, he frowned. "So, Yve, since you're here, we need you to do one thing."

*   *   *

Ezryan threw himself aside just a split second before that Arzia woman's attack went through him as it had done to Yverna.

As his thoughts drifted to the she-devil he loved, he glanced slightly towards the place where he left her. But the moment his gaze reached her spot, what he saw almost made his heart stop dead.

She was nowhere to be seen.

"Yve, where are you?" he yelled his thoughts out to reach her. His concentration immediately shattered, he didn't even notice when that woman creature launched her attacks at him. Vassago saw him turning around as if bewildered by something, and he rushed to shove Ry out of the way.

After they were both safe from the Arzia's attack, Vassago harshly turned Ry to face him. "What the hell are you doing? Do you have a fucking death wish?" he snarled.

"I'm sorry, Yve was . . ."

"She's safe, dammit. I saw her go to Vrae and the others. You feel the orb, right? She must've felt it too and headed to their place. Since she didn't show, your brother may include her to the plan, so now get your ass up and fight!" Vassago let him go and started to get back to where Belphegor and Seere were making an all-out-attack on their opponent, who was flying around and sending massive bolts at them.

Reaching out to the ether, Ry noticed the tingling down his spine and realized Vassago was right about Yverna's whereabouts.

Bracing himself, Ezryan followed Vassago and put his concentration back into the fight. Letting out a war cry, he drew his powers to the maximum as he flew into the destructive battle and shot bolts at her while executing an aerial manoeuvre at the same time to avoid her attacks.

$$* \quad * \quad *$$

"Yve, where are you?" I heard Ry's voice frantically calling me in my head. From his erratic voice, I realized that he was terrified. I almost answered him before I remembered he was still in the middle of the fight.

Answering him would mean distracting him. I might end up killing him, and that was the last thing I wanted to do.

I caught myself and put my focus back on what Xaemorkahn was trying to explain to me. The moment he finished, I nodded in understanding and peeked from behind the tree where we were hidden to look for the right moment to strike.

When I saw her in the air waving her staff around to wipe out all the bolts launched at her by Ry and the princes who were surrounding her, I flew from behind the tree and drew my powers out.

She saw me coming, and as she spun around her staff to eradicate the others' attacks, she had already readied herself for me.

I waited until my distance to her was close enough and shot her with my bolts. As expected, she waved that damned staff of hers and erased my bolts like child's play. She then immediately directed her long stick towards me. Knowing that was what she would do, I flew sideways to avoid her bolts, but she anticipated it. Throwing her hand up, she shot her void spheres at me and they all hit me point blank.

"No!" Ry's voice reached my ears as chills assailed me. For a split second, I thought those spheres were going to knock me unconscious if not dead, but to my luck, they didn't.

The chills disappeared as fast as they came, and I still stood there feeling nothing.

Newfound strength burst through me as I levelled a cold stare at the bitch and readied myself to attack her. "Looks like you need more tricks," I said disdainfully.

"See that? You're messing with the wrong girl, bitch!" Belphegor shouted. He opened his palms, manifested two dark red spheres, and threw them at her. I could feel his powers sky-rocket from them. Together with him, Vassago sent two spheres of his own.

She blinked, and without even turning in their direction, she waved her staff and the spheres faded into nothing. "Fuck me!" Belphegor cursed.

As if she couldn't believe I hadn't even gotten a scratch, she threw more bolts at me. It was at that point that my darkness power burst out of my hands without me commanding it. It instantly formed a black fog swirling between me and the spheres. All of them went right into it and disappeared, while the black fog remained.

It dispersed a moment later, and I saw the void woman stood there with the strangest look of bafflement on her face. "What, are your brains really that empty that you didn't notice your mojo no longer worked? Now, thanks to your idiocy, my darkness has its bull's eye on your stupid tricks," I taunted her. "That's what you get for screwing with darkness."

Ignoring the princes who zeroed in on her, she suddenly stormed towards me with a sickening wail, her staff aimed at my face. I readied myself and flew straight at her. Just before her staff hit me, I grabbed it and jumped over her head, putting myself behind her while I had her weapon tightly over her neck.

Luckily, we were in the air with her wings spread out.

She let out a deafening scream as I dragged her from the air to the ground. Furious, she turned her head at me, clenching her apparently human teeth.

At that moment, I felt her wings make a slight movement. Glancing at them, my gaze fell on something that made me let out a foul curse. Her wings were bent towards my back, forming six sharp swords.

Dammit, I couldn't go anywhere. If I moved, she'd escape. Realizing I had no other choice but stay where I was, I tightened my grip around her neck and closed my eyes, bracing myself for the inevitable. And then I felt it. Six deadly swords penetrated the back side of my armour, but there was something strange.

The wounds weren't as deep as they were supposed to be.

Staggering back, I felt someone standing behind me. Horrified, I turned around and found . . . Ry.

"You okay, baby? Sorry I wasn't able to completely intercept the attacks," he said as he cringed. Warm blood began to flow from his mouth.

My blood ran cold and felt like it stopped in my veins at his agonized expression. I gave him a wide-eyed stare. "Ry . . . you . . ." I stammered. My voice broke as I tried to hold back the tears that stung my eyes.

He tried to grin, but he looked like he was in incredible pain. "Hey, I managed to shield you this time, although not as completely as I had planned."

"Xaemorkahn, now!" Belphegor barked as the other two princes quickly moved to hold the Arzia's hands, preventing her from directing her staff anywhere.

Barely able to move, I averted my gaze from Ry towards Vrae, Zade, and Xaemorkahn, who were rushing from behind the woods with the orb. The moment they arrived, they hurriedly shoved the orb into her stomach, making her scream even louder than before.

I cringed as that scream began to hurt my eardrums. And then I felt all six tips of her wings that were stuck in my back move. I flinched, and at the same time I heard Ry let out a low groan.

I was trying to look at him, when suddenly those bladed wings left my back and he ground his teeth in agonizing pain. Next thing I knew, all six sharp tips of her wings were buried even deeper into my back. I cringed and heard a pained groan escape Ry's throat. Cold went through me. "Ry . . ." I slowly called him.

Instead a word of answer, he spilled a lot of blood onto my shoulder. "Ry!" I called him sharply. Fright stirred inside me as I looked at his devastatingly handsome face that was slowly turning ghostly pale.

Xaemorkahn went to Ry's back and held him, while Vrae and Zade came to our side. Belphegor walked towards us and stopped in front of the Arzia. He formed the small sphere of light and shoved it down the Arzia's throat.

She instantly went mute.

I glanced at Vrae who gave me an apologetic expression. "Ry, Yve, sorry, we gotta pull these things out. It's gonna really hurt, so we need you to bear with it." She grimaced and put her hands on the first pair of wings, and Zade followed suit.

Bracing myself, I felt two swords slowly come out from my body. Ry and I struggled not to move, all the while holding our breath to bear with the pain. But when the first two were completely out, we exhaled and cringed in pain.

"Still four more," Zade said quietly as he and Vrae each held one wing so that the woman couldn't stab Ry and me with them again.

And then they removed to the second pair of wings. They pulled out the second and the third pair of the Arzia's wings.

Each time they did it, I tightened my grip on that Arzia woman's staff and felt more of Ry's blood fall on my shoulder and heard his ragged breathing.

When they finally pulled out all the wings that were stuck in Ry's and my bodies and had grabbed them, I felt Ry being dragged away from me.

I staggered but managed not to buckle. Turning slightly, I saw Xaemorkahn carry Ry, who had passed out, and lay him down on the ground.

"Xaemorkahn, is he okay?" I asked him in a low broken voice. I felt rage in my trembling voice when I asked him.

Xaemorkahn knelt to check on his brother. I waited as I absently held my breath. It was a few heartbeats later when he stood up and heaved a sigh. "He's torn up pretty badly, but all in all, he's okay," he said.

I nodded as a wave of relief warmed my body. "That's great. That's great. Look, is there any weird blue stuff spreading from his wounds?"

He observed Ry's wounds once more. "No, I don't think so."

"Good, still, don't heal him. Something might still be in there. I'll do it."

"Because of the darkness, right?" he asked.

"Yeah," I said as I directed my healing powers to the holes in my back.

Hey, you sure you wanna do that?" Belphegor tapped my shoulder. "You've got pretty nasty holes yourself, you know."

I scoffed. "No offense, but it's not like you guys can do anything about it. These aren't even half bad compared to what Ry has got in him. Besides," I said. "I've dealt with her cheap tricks more than she knew. I'm getting more and more immune to her stupid shit."

Seere let out a whistle. "You're getting immunity from God's destroyer's attacks?"

The last hole in the back of my shoulder closed up, and I gave the prince a nod as an answer. "I am," I said with regret, and wrath filled my voice. "The bitch is quite an imbecile to try and topple my powers, which she should've noticed are not too different from hers. She thinks she's the baddest thing on the planet because she commands void? Try darkness. It swallows *everything*."

The Arzia turned and stared at me. "I'll rip you limb from limb," I whispered coldly through clenched teeth. All of a sudden I felt Vrae's hand on my back. "I'll help you rip this bitch's heart out," she said with the same coldness that was filling my own voice.

We dragged the bitch into the hole that was mostly buried again because of the destructive force unleashed during the fight.

We left Ry covered with a protective shield on the topside while the rest of us went back to the gate. All of us flew there in a weird position. Vrae and Zade were each holding three wings, while Seere and Vassago held the Arzia's hands. I was still holding her staff in front of her neck, while Belphegor and Xaemorkahn floated cautiously in front of her.

The moment we were above the gate, Belphegor cleared it of the soil that was closing around it and we landed at its side. I looked at the gate, and my gaze fell on the hole in the shape of the seal. "This wasn't here before."

Xaemorkahn walked to the hole and pulled the united seal from under his robe. "Yes, this appeared soon after we put the seals back together." He started to put the seal into the hole. When it completely fitted the hole, the huge gate made a slight movement and pushed outward.

Now that massive gate was finally opened.

It looked like there was nothing in there but a deep dark tunnel that went all the way inside. "Come on," I said as I started to walk backwards dragging her with me. The others followed me, and then we walked for few moments before we stopped and decided it was safe enough for me to let her go . . . or rather, let her staff go.

"Xaemorkahn, get ready to grab her staff," I said as I readied myself to wrap my hands around her neck.

He nodded and approached the Arzia. He grasped the staff and looked directly at me. "I'm ready."

"Now!" I yelled, and he pulled away her staff at the same time I put my claws in front of her neck. Without warning, she managed to pull her hands out from Seere's and Vassago's firm grip and almost clawed my face, but when I placed my own set of claws on her throat, she stopped.

"Try it and so help me, I'll shred your throat," I said coldly. Xaemorkahn brought the staff and pointed the seal tip of the staff at Belphegor. "Here."

Belphegor grinned and moved a hand towards it. Then he began to chant something, as if trying to infuse something into the staff.

True enough, the staff emitted a slight devil energy now. Belphegor smiled evilly, looked really satisfied. "Well, at least old daddy invented something useful." He flashed a wry grin at the Arzia. "Sorry, babe, you won't be able to summon your toy any more, so behave, okay." I felt her stiffen, and then we dragged her deeper into the tunnel.

Once we were deep enough, we released her. Shoving her to the ground, the others except me immediately made their distance from her. Only Vrae stood next to me.

Looked outraged, she spilled the small glowing ball Belphegor had shoved down her throat. Letting out a piercing scream, she bent all her wing-swords and directed them at Vrae and myself while she ran towards us. A tic worked in my jaw as we raised our hands and made cutting movement in the air towards her.

Stopping dead, her eyes widened before all her six wings were cut. She let out another agonized roar that shook the entire cave. But this time, I could feel excruciating pain tormenting her.

My gaze darkened at her as I licked my lips, enjoying every pain I inflicted on her. "That was for Aleeria, her Fierytarians, Xaemorkahn's soldiers, and ours," I said rather calmly as I approached her.

She dropped to her knees with her hands wrapped around her body, touching her slashed wings.

Kneeling before her, I slowly gouged out one of her eyes, and her screaming grew louder.

I revelled in it but didn't want to leave Ry any longer, so I forcefully pulled her hands to expose her front side and buried my claws on her chest. Then I dragged my hands all the way down her navel.

Her watery-coloured gown was pierced, and her flesh and entrails splattered all over. Hot transparent blood rained down on me. She was too weak to even groan, and she dropped to the ground. Spitting on the earth next to her face, I smiled and stood up. "That's for Ry, you wretched old bitch!" I snarled. Leaving her writhing on the ground, I joined the others as I licked the blood on my lips and fingers.

"Nicely put," Xaemorkahn smiled. All of them grinned at me, and I grinned back as I got rid of the warm blood on the rest of my body.

"Girl, remind me to never piss you off," Belphegor laughed evilly as he folded his arms in front of his chest.

"Hey, look, there's another door." Zade pointed far away into the tunnel.

And I saw it too. A gold door covered the entire end of the tunnel.

Vassago snorted. "I've been wondering where exactly the site is, or the tomb, or whatever. I guess she was put in there originally."

"You think we should put her back?" Vrae asked.

I gave that Arzia woman a piercing scornful look and then dissolved the rest of her blood on me. "If you guys want to, go right ahead, I've done the welcoming job, you want to be her escort, be my guest. I'll wait outside." I started walking to the opened gate.

Apparently, none of them interested in touching that 'woman' any more than I was since all of them followed me out of the tunnel. After we were outside the gate, Xaemorkahn pulled the seals on the gate.

The gate slowly moved inward. Right there a thought occurred to me, so I held it open.

"Yve, what are you doing?" Vassago narrowed his swirling turquoise eyes at me.

I looked at the royals. "Could you pull the ring out? If you could, pass it to me. I'll explain later."

All of them traded puzzled looks, and Belphegor nodded to Xaemorkahn.

A bit hesitant, Xaemorkahn pulled the Ring of Solomon. After a while he managed to separate the ring, and then he gave it to me. Looking back into the dark tunnel, I threw the ring inside and then let go of the gate.

The gate immediately closed.

I turned to look at them and saw gaping mouths and widening gazes of disbelief directed at me. Sighing in satisfaction, I glanced at the gate. "Now that thing can never get out before her time comes, and no one out there can try to collect the complete seal. Why the ring? Because I really don't want it to be used against us once and for all."

Vassago let out a relieved breath. "So, that was your intention. Gee, I almost had a heart attack. Good thinking, Yve." He saluted me.

I returned his gesture. "Thank you, Highness. Now let's get the hell out of here." My robes transformed into wings, and I flew intending to head immediately towards Ry. The rest of them followed behind me.

The moment we got ourselves above the hole, I went to Ry as fast as I could, dissolved the shield, and held him.

"Yve, get him out of here," Belphegor said as he drew his energy to shatter the earth.

From, out of nowhere, I felt an unfriendly heading towards us at high speed. I turned around just in time to find an angel from the second level of their highest hierarchy had landed before us. I recognized his face, which would have been beautiful had the irritating aura of an angel not covered his lithe body.

Zachariah.

"What the hell are you doing here? Have a death wish?" Vassago asked calmly, but there was a thick warning underneath his words, as if he were telling the angel that if he made one wrong move, he would never get back up there alive.

The angel's presence obviously had set his ire off.

Zachariah cast a hostile gaze at Ry. I immediately blocked his gaze. "Don't you even fucking *think* about it," I said in a low voice filled with my anger.

He sighed and gave me a weird gaze. "As much as I wanted to, he's not the reason why I'm standing here before all of you right now."

"Good, let's keep it that way before your head accidentally falls off." Belphegor raked a menacing glare at him.

Seere's ruby eyes darkened as he took two steps towards the angel. "Then, why are you here in our presence?" he asked.

He turned to look at the hole. "That destroyer was originally our responsibility."

"Yeah, and you morons just messed things up as usual," Belphegor interjected.

Ignoring his comment, Zachariah flew to where Belphegor was floating. "I will bury this place."

Startled, I narrowed my gaze at him. What could he be planning here?

He waved his hand over the gaping hole, and the earth closed up in an instant. Belphegor let out a disgusted snort. "Guess you guys will never change, huh? Only want to clean up the leftover mess and let others do most of the hard work."

The angel only lowered his gaze without saying anything and moved away from Belphegor. "I will not deny that this incident is indeed our responsibility, but I owe you all gratitude nonetheless," he said quietly.

"No need for your useless gratitude," I snarled.

The angel frowned a bit. "I will never bow down before you, but in return I will tell you this. On the day after tomorrow, we will bring down the wrath of heaven upon you all." After that, he ascended to the sky without another word.

"What the hell was that supposed to mean?" Zade asked.

I bit my lip as I looked up to where Zachariah had disappeared. "I don't know, but whatever it was, I definitely don't like the sound of it." I looked down at Ry, who was still limp in my arms. "Not at all."

Chapter 30

All of us headed back to Vassago's castle after that stupid encounter. I healed Ry there, and we brought him to our room as soon as we arrived and let him rest. I stayed with him while the others except Vassago and Xaemorkahn went to gather information to confirm whether Zachariah's words were true.

I transformed into human form and lay down beside him right after the others had gone, huddling safely next to him.

It was half a day later when he finally awoke.

Smiling, I held his hands in mine and looked into his gorgeous sapphire eyes. "Welcome back." I brushed his hair from his face and gently placed my palm on his cheek. His skin color slowly returned to look livelier than before, when he had passed out and looked as pale as a corpse.

Transforming himself and leaving his upper body bare, he then took my hand and gave me a soothing smile in return. "It's good to see you again," he said. Underneath his calm voice, I could hear his relief.

I averted my gaze and bit my lip before I looked at him again. "I'm so sorry, baby, I . . ."

Before I finished what I wanted to say, he captured my lips with his and rained one sweet kiss after another. I moaned at the taste of him and heard his growl of satisfaction.

Then he withdrew and put his long forefinger on my lips. "Don't say that you're sorry. I'm not. This is what I should do, not the other way round," he said firmly.

I sighed at his obstinacy. "You really wanna keep on arguing about this, it seems. Okay, you win."

He grinned. "That's more like it. By the way, you guys beat that woman-whatever and sealed her?"

"Well, yeah, you do realize we're at Vassago's, right?"

"Right, I mean, how did it end after I passed out?" he started to get up and sit.

I told him the details, including the parts where Vrae and I cut her wings and where I gutted the bitch. I also told him that we left the ring with her.

He was surprised at first when he heard what I did, but as usual, he caught what I was intending to say even before I said it. But, when I mentioned Zachariah and his warning, he stared blankly at me for a second before he lowered his gaze.

"This is it. They finally moved, I just didn't think it would be this soon." His hollow voice was no more than a whisper.

I stared at him. "What do you mean?" I asked him slowly.

He hesitated before he directed his gaze at me. "Not long after I met you again and then we parted, I immediately went to Belphegor and Vassago, as I told you earlier, to tell them what intel I had."

He sounded calm, but I caught a dire tone under his deep voice. "And what intel would that be?"

"The army of upstairs intend to, as Zachariah said, bring down the wrath of heaven upon us all."

I scowled. "What's new in that? They've been trying to do so since the dawn of time, and not even once have they managed to even touch my wings, let alone my hair."

He snorted and shook his head. "I know. That was why I looked into it further and found something. What they want isn't just death match sparring or other things as trivial as that. It's much bigger. They're even willing to risk everything this time."

That really didn't sound good.

"How big would that be?"

His gaze darkened, and yet he looked like he was engulfed in grief at the same time. He fell silent for a moment instead of answering me.

"Ry, how big?" I asked carefully.

He had the strangest look on his face as he spoke. "It's a full-scale war that would destroy the entire world no matter which side wins. This time, they're prepared to even sacrifice the humans in order to bring us down."

*   *   *

Lenora and Ravendy were walking towards the den when Ravendy suddenly gasped and halted to a stop. Her eyes turned backwards, and several muffled choking noises escaped from her throat.

At her companion's situation, Lenora just stood there, waiting for it to pass. She recognized the sign, for she also experienced it on multiple occasions, and for a completely different reason.

Moments later, Ravendy inhaled deeply, and her eyes were back to normal.

"Rave, what is it?" Lenora asked.

Instead of answering her, Ravendy grabbed Lenora's hand and led her towards Amon's den.

"Rave, what is it?" Lenora repeated as they broke into a run.

"Later! We gotta hurry," Ravendy retorted.

They finally reached the den after a minute of running. When Lenora raised a hand to lift the enchantments on the door, two cold melodic voices arguing with Amon's stopped her. Ravendy gave her a look that said that this was what she had seen in her vision.

Lenora nodded in understanding, and then they both concentrated on hearing what the argument was about. Holding their breath, they focused.

"Iverand, give it up. The entire situation has led us to conclude that you also know something about this. Tell us this instant!" Ravathe Kathiera's threatening voice rang in Lenora and Ravendy's ears.

Ravendy's core was hammering, but she forced herself to stay there in spite of all her instincts to scream that told her to get away with Lenora as fast as they could.

The next voice she heard was Amon's, and he sounded quite calm when most would expect him to tremble under the menacing glare of two Echelon members. "With all due respect, Honourable Ravathes, I really have no idea what you are talking about. Both Yverna and Vrathien, whom you had me kill earlier, and in addition Zaderion, were only here to discuss recent disappearances, or rather, the recent slaughters of our soldiers, which I remind you, also involved the Fierytarians and Kivarda Aleeria too. As I said before, since the three of them didn't have any assignment up to that point, they volunteered to look into it. To be honest, I'm grateful they did, because looking at the fact that even Aleeria became one of the victims, I can say that ordinary Alvadors or even Chonars wouldn't be able to handle whoever that is out there." He let his statement hang and the two Echelon members didn't say anything in return.

At least until Kathiera shot a murderous glare at him. "Yes, they may be a great help in this matter, but still, treachery is the one crime that is absolutely unforgivable." Kathiera's cold fury spread a lethal aura that even reached the pair standing right outside the door.

Unwavering but with his senses on to high alert, Amon tensed under her choking aura. "I'm aware of that single fact, but I will never say things they would never do, which was why I, personally, cannot and will not comprehend the reason behind their assassination."

Kathiera let out a curse so foul that Faemirad actually blushed. Seldom had she seen her companion as out of control as this. The cluelessness might have driven her insane.

Wariness washed over her. Ravendy gulped and grabbed Lenora's hand, indicating the way back with a tilt of her chin. They quietly turned and headed back. "We gotta go. Zade may be well on his way here," she said under her breath.

While they were walking further away, Kathiera sauntered towards Amon and stopped right in front of his face. "You seem to believe in them enough to wage your own life, Iverand, so I shall see to it that your words are true. Should we find the contrary, know this. Not even the status of Iverand will save your own existence this time," she said in a voice so low and cold that the Iverand actually bristled from hearing it.

However, her threat didn't affect him that much, not after the deaths of his brothers and the assassination order they gave. However, they were oblivious that he wasn't affected. His gaze darkened as he levelled a blank look at her. "As you wish, Ravathe. So now, what is it exactly you want me to do? Bring Zade in for questioning, which you and the rest of the Echelons had done before without notifying me in advance?"

Faemirad raked a disgusted glare at him. "There will be no need for you to do so. We have other resources to expose this plot and bring death upon everyone in it."

Running his fingers through his hair, Amon then gave his salute. "Assuming there *is* any plot to be exposed, Ravathe Faemirad, you wouldn't risk losing the allegiance of most of our soldiers, would you? Forgive my impudence, but if the word breaks out that you issued a death penalty against powerful Cherxanains like them both before you found any solid proof, I don't think that would bode well for all the Echelons. About Zaderion, I believe I don't need to remind you that each Varkonian holds a unique ability of his or her own, and his ability in particular is one that considered priceless."

"That is not your concern," Faemirad said coldly.

Amon nodded. "Ah, yes, but please forgive me if I overstep my bounds. It is fortunate for you though, that both former Ravaths Bynethar and Xamian have renounced their seats, since the sisters used to be their primary concern."

Kathiera's eyes changed into blood red, and then without warning Amon was strangled by an unseen force. Choking, he tried not to struggle. He just stood there staring blankly at them both.

"You are correct, Iverand, you do overstep your bounds," Kathiera retorted in an even colder voice. "Enough! We should go, Faemirad. We should look into this as quickly as possible," she said, and then both of them left him.

The second they had gone from his chamber, the force that strangled him was no more. Coughing for air, his gaze was saddened with worries.

Both Echelon members walked in long steps, leaving the den as if they were chasing something. "I can't believe there's no plot! I cannot accept this! I will not!" Kathiera growled furiously.

Faemirad winced as she tried to keep up with her pace. "Look, as annoying as it sounds, maybe you should consider the possibility that there is no foul plot. Even though Amon's audacity is more than usual, I don't see anything wrong, well, not yet," she added hastily, after Kathiera cast a deadly glare at her.

"There has to be something! I can feel it in my gut! Nobody, I'll say it again, nobody would pull that kind of audacity unless they're protecting something or someone!" Kathiera snarled between her clenched teeth.

As they walked, their strong steps left black marks on the brick roads that were surrounded by magma. Her robes and Faemirad's flowed freely around their bodies as they walked gracefully to where they were about to meet another person right now.

Cain.

With fury burning her, neither she nor Faemirad noticed that there were three shadows hidden in the corner.

"We're clear," Zaderion whispered. He used his body to hid Ravendy and Lenora from sight. Stepping aside, he took another look to make sure they were safe before his gaze went to the pair. "Mind telling me again what you were doing?"

Ravendy lowered her voice to a whisper. "We were heading to the Iverand's place to talk to him. We saw several things. Things you guys did."

Zaderion inwardly cursed at that. He hoped to hell no one aside from them knew about it as well. Apparently, his worries were apparent on his face.

"Relax, Zade. Nobody knows what you guys have been doing except us."

"Including the fact that they both are still alive," Lenora interjected.

Ravendy nodded. *"Which is a good thing. We're really glad the Iverand could pull that one off."*

Zaderion inhaled a breath deeply and released it. There really was no hiding from these two. Fortunately they were on their side of the fence, not the Echelons'.

"Anyway, while we were heading there, she had another vision," Lenora started. "It was about those crown jewels of the Echelons," she said in disgust.

"Really? What did you see?"

Ravendy swallowed before she answered him. "Well, they were busy threatening him. You can ask him. Now we gotta run."

"Okay, why?"

"Because I saw more than just a threatening party. They're heading to Cain's cell as we speak. We need to keep our eyes on them. We don't know what they'll do once they see that Cain's no longer there."

Zaderion subtly nodded. "All right, thanks. Get word to me if possible, okay?"

"Will do," Ravendy said.

"Say hi to Yve and Vrathien," Lenora added.

He nodded, and they parted ways. The Varkonian immediately headed to the Iverand. Once he arrived, he lifted the incantations and opened the door. He strolled through the doorway and closed the door behind him.

Walking in, he found Amon leaning forward in his seat with his arms on his desk, covering his mouth with his folded hands. He directed his empty gaze at Zaderion as he approached carefully.

"Amon."

The Iverand stared at him in silence for two seconds before he let out a long-suffering sigh and moved his hands away from his face. "What?" he asked.

Amon's hollow voice made him hesitate. "You okay?"

Amon scoffed bitterly. "Define okay," he snapped, and he closed his eyes as he expelled a weary breath. Looking back at him, Amon shook his head apologetically. "Sorry, I didn't mean to snap. I just had a bad fucking day, that's all. What's up?"

Zaderion shook his head. "I'm sorry. We caught you right in the crossfire. We even dragged Gev and Zoran in it."

He smiled sadly. "Thanks, you don't need to apologize though. We asked for this."

"No, thank *you* for bailing the sisters out. We owe you big time."

Amon scoffed. "Glad I did it. By the way, you picked the best time to come here. It seems two brainiacs of the Echelons have zeroed in even closer on us. Even after the stupid order they had me do, it now looks like they weren't satisfied by it."

Zaderion nodded. "I know. Some people were right outside your door when they were here harassing you."

Amon raised his brows. "That was cutting it close. Who were they?"

"Rave and Len. They wanted to meet you, but the happy pair beat them to it."

Amon let out a sigh of relief. "Luckily they were too busy to notice."

Zaderion snorted. "Tell me about it. I was on my way here when I ran into them. They freaked out and dragged me away just in time before Kathiera and Faemirad saw us. I got to say though, I've never seen Faemirad and in particular Kathiera in such a bad mood before. That must be a world record for her to hurl all kinds of curses at us."

Amon rubbed his brow. "Yeah, it's a world record for her to choke me as well. And, there's another thing. I don't know if you guys should be running for cover right about now, but . . ." he hesitated.

"But what?" Zaderion prompted.

"They're heading to Cain to try to squeeze some info out of him. I don't know if we could trust him not to blow it," he said warily.

"Oh, that. Yeah, Rave caught that too. They're both on it. Thing is, Cain's already out. Bynethar and Xamian took him to Duke Dantalion under the princes' orders."

"They what?" Amon gasped at his remark.

Zaderion nodded. "Yeah, they told us. Besides, even if he's not out, I'm quite sure he won't blow us up. He was a human, but he's not that low. He may hate Belial with all his gut but *he* told us he's pretty trustworthy." He cast a meaningful look that said it all. The one he meant was Ezryan. "Especially when it comes to pissing those Echelons off. Furthermore, given what the Echelons have been doing to him for all these thousands of years, I don't think he would willingly help them."

Relieved a bit, Amon nodded. "I see."

"What we don't know is what those females will do once they find out that he's escaped."

"We can think about that later," he said. "So, since you're here, is there anything new you wanna tell me? Oh, wait," he switched to a blocked channel. *"Don't tell me, you guys made it? I mean, you managed to snatch that thing off him?"*

Zaderion nodded to confirm him, and surprisingly he laughed in delight.

"Well, you're surprisingly happy about this," the Varkonian frowned, half confused, half amused.

Amon sobered up and shrugged. *"Why wouldn't I be? This way I could give all of those high and mighty upper ranks a good and proper bitch-slap."* He grinned.

Zaderion shook his head in disbelief. "Now I can see your resemblance to them. All of you are brave in a really funny and bizarre way."

He gave him a salute as if he were flattered by his words. *"So, is there anything else you guys did?"*

Zaderion then described all that happened up to the point where Belphegor drowned his own father and when they locked the Arzia up in the same way they'd agreed with Yverna before. Every now and again Amon would gape in shock or yell in disbelief. Zaderion had to shove his palm over his mouth each time he did that.

"Gee, is he okay?" Amon asked, when Zaderion told him what happened to Ezryan.

Zaderion gave him a subtle nod. *"Yeah, he's hurt pretty bad, but he's okay. Yve was furious because of it. I seldom see her like that. Vrae helped her handle that Arzia. If she'd been left to Yve's mercy, I've no doubt that . . . woman would have suffered a whole lot more."*

Amon frowned at him. *"What did they do?"*

"Both of them, well, they cut that void woman's wings."

The Iverand grimaced. *"That's gotta be hurt, but it ain't so bad, what's the problem?"*

Zaderion gave him a droll stare. *"The problem was that Yve gouged one eye out and then gutted that thing, nice and messy."*

Amon gasped. *"She did that to the Big Boss's ultimate destroyer? I can't believe it, she is the Tyraviafonza."* He shook his head in disbelief.

"That's what happened." Zaderion grinned at him.

"And then what's next?"

He told him Zachariah's words, and that made him fall silent and stare blankly at him for a full minute without a word. "You're serious?" was all he could manage after overcoming his own shock.

"Like the grave," Zaderion said.

"This is it," he muttered.

Not surprised at his comment, Zaderion slowly put his hands on Amon's desk. *"Yes, I'm sure Ravendy told you before I came here. So Amon, we gotta spread the word ASAP. Gather all the commanders. Hell, warn those Ravaths and Ravathes if you must."*

Amon raised his hands to stop his outburst. *"By the way, you are sure it ain't just a bluff like they always do, aren't you?"*

The Varkonian gave him a dry stare. *"And since when did they start having enough guts to throw bullshit when three princes of hell are present? One knight is enough to scare them shitless, let alone a prince, you know that."*

Amon cringed. *"Uh, yeah, just telling you what's in my mind out loud."*

Zaderion scowled. *"Real funny. So any idea who you gonna call first?"*

The Iverand ran his fingers through his hair. *"I have an idea, but rather than wondering who I'm gonna call first, I wanna ask you what the hell am I gonna tell them? From whom did I get this news? Commanders I can lie to, but Ravaths and Ravathes? Not on your best day!"*

Zaderion let out an irritated breath. *"I know, but I'm afraid that will be your problem because I got to go ASAP. You can't be seen with me right after they saw me taking Yve with Vrae out of the interrogation, dude."*

Amon's expression turned bleak all of a sudden as if he didn't like the idea at all. But he decided to agree, knowing that he had no other choice. *"All right, I'll do it on one condition."*

Frowning at the Iverand who usually just got on with things without any conditions, Zaderion folded his arms. *"Okay, name it."*

Sighing, he curled his lips. *"Should anything go wrong, we're outta here and coming with you guys,"* he said firmly. *"They asked me to relay that to you, and I have to say I more than agreed."*

Now that was one condition Zaderion had never thought he'd heard from him. He burst out laughing. *"Man, I was thinking you'd just ask us to cover you up or something. Anyhow, if that's what you want, then it's up to you. But if you could, will you stay here as long as you can? We need someone on the inside, and right now there's no one but you whom we trust. Well, maybe Ravendy and Lenora, but those two are way beyond my reach."*

Letting out an aggravated breath and yet looking flattered by his words, Amon nodded. *"Okay. So now where will you go? Back to those guys?"*

"Yes, besides, with the Echelons' noses heading my way as well as the girls', we must warn them."

Amon nodded without saying anything further.

Zaderion sighed warily and mulled everything in case he'd forgotten anything. After he was sure there was no more, he raked his hair. "All right then, it's time for me to go back. Good luck, dude."

"You too."

Zaderion winced as he remembered one more thing. *"By the way, if the worst happens, go to Gillian, Vassago's castle. We're all staying there."* His respect showed in his eyes as he looked at him.

Amon answered his words only with a subtle nod and a murmur of thanks. Thinking there was nothing more to say, he left the Head Intel immediately.

This time, Zaderion took the southeast gate. Once he was outside, he headed back to Vassago's castle as fast as he could.

* * *

Lucifer struggled to free himself, all the while fighting the pressure of water around him. Eyes bloody, he swore he'd rip apart every single soul who'd confined him in here.

Suddenly, a devil he'd never expected to come to find him appeared.

Lilith.

Smirking, Lilith's ghostly voice echoed in his head. *"Well, well, I've never thought I'd see the day when only a handful of beings could fuck you this badly."*

He cast a repulsive glare at his female creation in return–the only response he could make since Xaemorkahn's spell prevented him from doing anything else, even from sending a signal to her head.

Realizing there was something wrong, Lilith willed her powers to raise the confinement above the water. The moment they were both out of the lake, Lilith removed the water from her body, making her white hair and black gown dry instantly, and then she gave him a smug smile. "You couldn't even talk back? Damn, they *were* determined to piss you off."

Still he just gave her that repugnant glare.

She inclined her head with cluelessness all over her face. And then, as if an idea had struck her, she snapped her fingers.

The ban on him that had been placed on him by his own son was lifted, and the first words he let out were foul curses. "Go fuck yourself, Lilith, or go fuck Samael if you don't have anything better to do than piss me off even more," he said through clenched teeth.

"Ow, such manners! I just helped you with your voice problem and was intending to help you out a bit more, or at least find out the next stupid thing they're up to. A piece of gratitude would be hell sent you know." She smiled wickedly at him–a smile that could have been beautiful had she not had that twisted expression all over her face.

Lucifer was startled at her offer, and then he returned her smile with the same weight of madness on his devastatingly handsome face. "Well, thank you. For once you show me that you have your use after all. Fine, try to find out as much as you can, but none of the Ravaths and Ravathes can ever know about this. If they do find out, the soldiers will too, and that would be the last thing I need."

Lilith blew him a raspberry. "Whatever, oh and by the way, you do realize that four out of six princes are in on this, right?"

His perfectly shaped brows formed one hard line. "What?" he asked in a low dead tone.

The she-devil burst out laughing. "This is fantastic. Are you really that idiotic or are they really such good actors?"

Repulsed by her, he ground his teeth. "Tell me the last name, you fucking bitch." His growl was so feral that Lilith backed down. Even though he was powerless at the moment, the second his seal broke, nothing could save her if he thought she had also pissed him off. There was no guarantee whatsoever that he wouldn't add her to his 'people whose throat I'm gonna rip out today' list.

Clearing her throat, she sobered up. "Okay, you whinnie, the last one's Orobas. You might wanna wipe that moronic horse out properly so his annoying scent will no longer irritate me."

Lucifer's gaze darkened as his lips broke in an evil smile. "Don't worry; I'll shred him so fucking good that not even horses want to shit on him."

Giving him a sarcastic salute, she started to leave. "Good, now if you'll excuse me, I have some eavesdropping to do." And then she vanished.

As his thoughts and the obsession for revenge began to consume him, Lucifer closed his eyes, creating billions of fantasies of every bloody death imaginable–the deaths he'd rain down on all the betrayers.

While his mind was occupied by these fantasies of slaughter and bloodbaths, someone of the holy was floating in the air and watching him from afar. As he muttered something to countermand Lucifer's cage, his beautiful stoic face didn't show any sign that the fact he was about to set free the cruellest being in existence bothered him in the least.

When he had finished uttering the last word of the spell, at long last Lucifer felt it. Oblivious of the presence of his former brethren and the days of being kept underwater inside a solid confinement, he finally felt his powers tingling in his system.

On the other hand, that mysterious angel knew he had finished what he intended to do and immediately ascended to the heavens.

Meanwhile, Lucifer inhaled deeply as the urge to kill washed over him like a deadly sweet drug. In silence, he waited.

*   *   *

Xaemorkahn was pacing in his own room, thinking about Zachariah's words and his brother's condition, when he felt something begin to tear his spine. He let out a piercing scream and dropped to his knees when one reality slammed into him.

Lucifer had started to regain his powers and was breaking the seal–*his* seal–and it was happening a few hours earlier than it should have as well.

Shaking his head in an attempt at denial, he quickly searched through his mind to find what could possibly be the cause of it. When he couldn't think of anything, he began to stand and tried to bring himself to the bed, while his spine was still under vicious attacks. At that moment Vassago appeared.

"What happened?" he asked sharply. He saw the king was on his knees. He quickly ran to him and helped him to the bed.

Gasping, Xaemorkahn cast a look of horror at Vassago. "It's started. He's busting free." His voice was filled with pain as he struggled to breathe.

"What? Who's busting . . . ?" Vassago stopped dead as one name came right to his brain.

Lucifer.

"But how? Although there's only a few hours left, how could he bust free?" Vassago asked with dread all over his face.

Xaemorkahn groaned in agony. "I don't know. Besides the fact he shouldn't be able to be freed by himself or by anybody else out there, I shouldn't be getting this spine torment either."

Vassago bit his lip and tried to think what they could do about this matter. It was then that he sensed four people outside his castle. Willing himself outside, he found the other princes and Vrathien, who had come with her mate. Intending to bring forth his castle and tell them about Lucifer ASAP, he approached them.

Seere suddenly grabbed him. "We gotta hurry!" he said under his breath.

Vassago immediately realized that Seere also knew about the latest problem. The other three, who seemed oblivious to the dire situation, exchanged puzzled looks.

"What's going on?" Belphegor narrowed his gaze.

"Your dad's getting free," Vassago and Seere said in unison.

The North Prince's swirling crimson eyes flashed in fury. "What? How? We should have more time, shouldn't we?"

"Yeah? Tell that to every creature living in the edge of this forest all the way to my castle. All of them were obliterated by his foul aura alone, and I don't think he will be pleased when he seen us." Seere's voice was full of disgust and dread at the same time, while Vassago began to chant.

"Anyhow, let's get inside first." Vrathien indicated the barren field where Vassago's castle now stood.

All of them hastily went inside, and then the castle vanished just in time, because the entire castle shook tremendously, and hollow screams could be heard echoing throughout the place.

"Terrific," Vassago said sarcastically as he rolled his eyes. He didn't expect they would have to face him again this soon.

After a few moments, the castle stopped shaking. Vrathien and Zaderion simultaneously sighed in relief.

All of a sudden, the thick scent of an animal assailed their nostrils.

"What now?" Belphegor cursed under his breath. Orobas's shade appeared out of thin air. Tall and lithe, Orobas had the bearings of a prince, and even in the shape of a shade, Vrathien and Zaderion could feel his lethal aura from where they were standing.

"What? Vassago snapped.

Orobas's face took on a pleading expression. "Vassago, Belphegor, Seere, I need your help, guys. Vassago, dude, I need you to take me to your place!"

The three princes gave each other a confused look at Orobas's dire tone. "Wait, wait, what's wrong?" Belphegor asked.

"Lilith told your fucking dad that I'm helping you, and now that bastard will be coming here any time. That's what!" he shouted.

Without asking for any further explanation, the North Prince turned to Vassago. "Go," Belphegor said to him. He nodded and then was gone through the shadows.

Orobas nodded his gratitude. "Thanks, I'll see you lot in a few." After that, his shade disappeared.

Belphegor curled his lips. "Gee, I know that this place is utterly impenetrable, but with the number of people coming, we might as well turn it into a refugee campsite." He ran his fingers through his hair in frustration.

Seere cleared his throat. "Okay, we can't do anything until they arrive, so we have to wait. I'm off to my room." He started to leave without even waiting for the others to say a word. Vrathien and Zaderion too excused themselves and went to their room.

Only Belphegor remained in the Great Hall.

Cold fury burned him from the inside out, as he felt his old grudge resurface all over again. At the end of his tether, Belphegor let out a crude expletive. "Looks like it will be a fucking long time before I can put you in your place."

* * *

I gaped at Ry's words. "Are you sure? I thought they would never do something like that." I shook my head in disbelief.

His swirling sapphire eyes cast a sad look at me as his brows knitted in grief. "I'm positive about this one, and from what I've gathered, once they have this in motion, not even Lucifer and all of our powers combined can stop them."

This was totally unacceptable!

Wincing, I leaned back as I laughed nervously at him. "No, Ry, no way. What would they do? What *could* they do?" As I whispered those words and looked at his eyes, I realized that this would come to pass.

He bit his lip. "I've only got something known as 'Heaven's most terrifying weapon', and I don't think we can do anything about it. Slow them down, maybe, but we won't be able to prevent whatever they'll use to bring an end unto us. It's one hard line that's been drawn by God Himself. It will be inevitable."

At his words, tangible fear rushed over me like hot boiling water washing my innards. Would my time with him really be over?

All of a sudden, the entire castle shook, making us shiver in our bed. After a few moments, it stopped. "What the hell was that?" I asked as I looked around.

Ry shrugged, and he looked as clueless as I was. "I don't know."

I frowned as I thought about what could shake the castle, when he placed one warm hand on my cheek and held me tight.

"Ry?"

For few seconds, he didn't answer. He just held me in silence before he broke it. "The moment I knew about this, I was scared like hell for the first time in my life. When I was gonna die by Lucifer's hands, I thought that was fear, but when I obtained this piece of intel and now I think about you, this is the very first time I've ever experienced fear.

"And now after I met you again, it seems I won't be able to get over it. The fear I felt when I saw you shield me. The fear that shattered me into pieces when I saw you were attacked by that Arzia and then you suddenly disappeared. Fear has a firm grip on me where you're concerned."

I wrapped my hands around him as I thought the same. But then, I didn't want to burden him even more. Wanting to comfort him, I gently ran one hand through his hair.

Abruptly, I felt his body tremble in my arms. "And now you've told me about Zachariah's words, I'm scared even more."

His hold on me tightened before he went on, "I don't wanna lose you, not now, not yet. But there's nothing I can do." His voice was broken with deep anguish, and the air of helplessness stirred from him.

Closing my eyes as sadness and love for him burned me all the way to my core, I clenched my fist on his back as I couldn't stop my tears from falling. "You're never gonna lose me. We swore, remember?"

I then moved away from his arms so I could look into his eyes. I cupped his face and smiled at him. "No matter what happens, no matter how many lifetimes I must go through, I *will* find you, because my soul will never rest until I do."

He returned my smile, tenderly wiped my tears, and closed his eyes, as if he were savouring each of my words. Then he opened his eyes and repeated my words and pulled me to lie down. Creating a darkness orb, he gathered me in his arms and we cradled there in the comfort of the dark.

Bad feelings went through me like a million stabs all over my body as I tried to figure out one thing.

What were those angels up to?

$$* \quad * \quad *$$

Shadows appeared from out of nowhere approaching Belphegor. He stared at them blankly until they revealed both Vassago and Orobas.

"Gee, this is better." Orobas stretched his body and then looked at Belphegor, who cast a sour look at him. Inclining his head apologetically, he folded his arms. "Good to see you too, Belphegor," he said, pretending not to notice the stare.

Belphegor scowled and folded his arms over his chest. "So tell me, why were you running again?"

Orobas raised his hands in surrender. "Look, I'm sorry, okay? I screwed up, fine, sue me."

Vassago shook his head at his outburst. "Whatever, but you haven't told any of us how in the hell that bitch knew that you're in on this," he demanded.

"Wait," Belphegor raised his hands to stop Orobas. "Seere!" he called to the air.

The last prince in Vassago's domain appeared. "What?" he snapped. When his gaze fell on Orobas, he arched his brow. "You're here! I thought you were joking about Lilith busting you and offering you as meat on a stake." He looked disdainfully at him.

The addressed prince just shrugged off his satire. Vassago then cleared his throat. "Orobas, answer my question."

The prince cursed at his request, as if it reminded him of something repulsive. "Lately she'd been spying on my domain from time to time. I should've known there was something outrageously wrong, but since I only felt a slight tingling, I thought it was some lower punks accidentally crossing over the line that weren't that worthy of being wasted. Not even in a million years would I have thought it was her, because I didn't feel her presence anywhere. How should I know the bitch could pull other tricks for spying on castles that ain't heavily protected like this one?"

Letting out a frustrated breath, Belphegor inclined his head. "So, how did you figure it out? If she was outside your domain, you couldn't possibly know who it was."

Orobas laughed bitterly. "Not too long ago, that weird tingling just started to annoy me, so I set up some new booby traps. Simply put, she tripped a wire. Trust me; you don't wanna know what wire that was."

Belphegor rolled his eyes. "Something looking or stinking like horses no doubt. No we don't wanna know."

Orobas curled his lips. "Yeah, yeah, your turn. What the hell did you do with your daddy bastard? I wasn't even here most of the time, and now thanks to that Lilith bitch, your pop is out for my throat!" he snarled furiously.

Vassago shook his head. "No, he won't be, well, at least not for the next few hours."

Orobas cut them off with an arch stare. "What on my best horse's shit was that supposed to mean? Ain't he already out? The castle shook, as you all know." He narrowed his darkened light-grey eyes.

Vassago scoffed at his weird curse, and then both Belphegor and he explained everything in turn. When they had finished, Orobas just gave them a wide-eyed stare in silence for a full minute.

Belphegor waved his hands towards Orobas. "Get over the theatrics. We have more to think about."

Nodding in agreement, Vassago frowned deeply as a wary look spread all over his face. "Yeah, so now, since you're here, we need to know, what did your forest tell you?"

*   *   *

A gentle touch on my cheek pulled me back from my train of thought. I opened my eyes and moved from Ry's bare chest.

He smiled soothingly and then placed one quick kiss on my lips. "Hey, baby."

I returned his smile and moved away. "Hi, how are you feeling?"

He started to get up. "Better," he said as he raised his hand towards the darkness orb. The orb flew into his grasp and disappeared. After that, lights from the castle were lit everywhere.

"I wanna go see my brother. Is he still here?" he stood up and transformed into his devil form.

I nodded. "I suppose he is, because last time I checked, he said he want to wait for you before he returned home."

"Good, I want to check on him. You coming?" he extended his hand.

Nodding, I transformed as well and took his hand, and then we went out of the chamber and headed to Xaemorkahn's. After minutes of wandering in the dark hallway, we reached the chamber. Ry knocked at the door twice and then stopped.

There was no answer from inside.

His calm expression turned worried as he moved his hand to the doorknob and slowly turned it. Opening the door, he stepped inside with me behind him. "Brother, you here?"

We heard a low groan from the centre of the chamber. Ry hastily pulled me inside and approached the enormous bed.

Xaemorkahn was lying there and looked as if he were in excruciating pain.

"Xaemorkahn, what happened?" Ry asked sharply.

Xaemorkahn cringed and grimaced before he answered. "Lucifer began to break free a bit sooner than he was supposed to."

Now that was something that made my core almost stop working.

Ry was taken aback by his words. "It can't be." He shook his head in utter shock.

My mind drifted to the tremendous shaking earlier. "Back then, when we felt something shake the castle, it must've been him getting out."

Expelling a tired breath, Xaemorkahn closed his eyes and nodded, and then he looked at us. "Yeah that's the one. I know how it sounds, and like I told Vassago, I shouldn't be getting this stupid torment on my spine either," he snarled under his ragged breath.

"You think something might have helped him?" I asked.

He was startled, but then he closed his eyes as if in deep thought. Several heartbeats later, he slowly shook his head. "No creature could or would get him out of there."

I frowned at the one word he said. "'Would'? You're saying there *is* something that 'could' do so?"

Biting his lips, he opened his beautiful dual-coloured eyes. "If there are beings in either world that could do something about it beside God Himself, who most likely wouldn't help him even if the guy started to beg for forgiveness, they would be angels."

I gasped at his words. "No way! Angels?!"

He laughed bitterly and then scowled. "Not just any angels, archangels, the ones directly below Gabriel and Michael's ranks, including, of course, both of them."

I shook my head as I staggered back. "No, they can't be! They won't be! Since when would they play tag team with that guy?"

"My point exactly, but then I couldn't think of anything else. Well, there's that Avarnakh whatever, but she's officially history, since she's practically caged. So even if she could do anything about my seal, I don't think she could get out from her own ban."

I nodded. "That's right." I gave him a smug smile and then turned my gaze to Ry, who fell silent. "Something is seriously wrong here. If it was really them, why would they help the guy out if they planned to wage full scale war against us?" He still directed his gaze towards the floor while Xaemorkahn and I just stared at him.

Suddenly, he lifted his head and stared at me. His face was full of dread. "Unless what they were trying to do wasn't to bust him free."

I arched my brow. "What do you mean?"

He hesitated and then frowned. His brows formed one hard line as he thought about something. "What if they intend to put him into something more permanent and then do something else?"

"Like what, brother?" Xaemorkahn slowly sat on his bed.

Ry then spoke something that seemed to be quoted from somewhere. "The end of the line has been decided the moment Holy

Light fell into the fire of the damned. He shall have his own army and rule the underworld of men with Dark Light in his hand. As his time to be the conqueror draws longer, the ultimate destruction walks towards his door, threatening every being behind him. When he is dethroned by his own son and commanders with the help from a king of the outer realm, and the destruction is being kept from knocking his door, his moment as the Dark King will be no more, and his time in confinement as God's Forbidden Left Hand shall begin, marked by the largest war either world has ever witnessed."

My eyes almost bulged when I heard his words, but he wasn't finished. "The passing of the war will be seen by men, his retainers, and half-breeds of his own kind, and so shall his freedom. By the time he spreads his wings once more, screams of men will rock the heavens and fire of the damned shall cry with joy as tears of blood drown the earth for ever more. In the end, the world will tremble in fear as holy song from heaven resurrects the ultimate destruction from the tomb and annihilates every existence that walks the earth."

Wincing, I stared blankly at him. "That's some poem."

Ry scoffed at my remark. "That isn't a poem, baby." He gave a half-hearted smile and looked at his brother.

Xaemorkahn's wide-eyed stare was stuck on Ry's face. "Would you mind telling me where in the Zihargan realm you got those lines?" he narrowed his gaze suspiciously.

At his question, Ry cringed. "Uh, not exactly in Zihargan. I got it from somewhere else, and it's just occurred to me."

"And did you tell the princes about this?" I asked slowly.

He nodded. "I have. I wasn't sure if I wanted to tell them at first, but I did it anyway." He sighed helplessly.

"So, you decided to ask for my assistance because of that prophecy, didn't you?" Xaemorkahn asked slowly, and Ry nodded as an answer.

"It's a wonder neither one of you bothered to mention any of this in the first place though." I cast a meaningful gaze at him, which he answered with a sorry-we-forgot-about-that face.

His face was partially blushing as he cleared his throat. "I heard that when I went up there." He pointed heavenward.

I gaped at him. "Where was that again?"

He cringed, and then he repeated his words.

"So basically, you didn't just hear Cain's BS up there, but also those words?" I asked him slowly, and he nodded.

I glanced at Xaemorkahn, who lowered his gaze as if he were thinking about something. When he didn't say a thing, I expelled a weary breath. "We meant to stop that thing from having a slaughter party and we ended up doing upstairs' work for them? That's terrific! I'm flattered to be some use to the holy angels from above," I said sarcastically.

Ry scoffed as he shook his head. "Well, we weren't exactly doing it for them, remember. If we didn't do it, not would only Belphegor's pop be in trouble, but so would every being behind him, as in us."

I laughed bitterly. "Yeah, you have a point."

Ry then turned his gaze to his brother, who remained silent. "Is there anything on your mind, brother?"

"Indeed. With this, we can be certain about one thing." Xaemorkahn cast a weird look at us both.

I arched one brow. "And that is?"

The king looked hesitant before he answered. "You guys and a few others will survive this war."

Ry nodded in agreement. "Yes, I thought about that."

I scowled as I caught what he meant. "'The passing of the war will be seen by men, his retainers, and halfling of his own kind'—that bit, huh?"

The king nodded. "'And so shall his freedom.' You guys will see him thrive again after he was contained."

Ry's face turned grim. "Yeah, the part that mentioned his time in confinement shall begin, right?"

Outrageous ideas went through my mind as I felt my chest tighten. "They'll contain him? They're preparing *him* as a destroyer?"

"As one of the destroyers," Ry corrected.

"Yes, yes, one of the destroyers if you like, but at any rate, you're saying that the ones helping him are indeed people from upstairs. They wanna keep him somewhere more permanent, is that it?" I narrowed my eyes at him, and he gave me a subtle nod.

"You think we should tell Belphegor?" Xaemorkahn asked. He was still cringing and clenching his teeth every few seconds because of the pain he felt.

Ry bit his lip. "There's no need. I figured he and Vassago may have thought about it as well. More importantly, brother, you should rest. When you feel well enough, I'll take you home."

Xaemorkahn looked as if he were against the idea. "No, you don't. You will not take me home before I make sure I will see you again." His eyes darkened.

I glanced at Ry whose face was full of dread. "Please, brother, you have done enough, and I will make sure you get back to Varisha safely. You know I will do it, even if it means I have to drag you there myself." Ry smiled wickedly at Xaemorkahn.

Xaemorkahn opened his mouth to argue, but then he closed it and sighed. "You won't take no for an answer, huh?"

"Nope," Ry said firmly, and Xaemorkahn raised his hands in surrender. But his face was still full of doubts.

I patted the king's hand, and he turned to me. "Don't worry," I said. "He'll see you again. You said yourself that we will survive this war. Well, maybe when he meets you again, you'll just have to look at him in a whole new perspective." I winked at him.

He winced at me, and Ry stifled a laugh.

"You really are alike," he said. "You never fail to see jokes in any situation." He shook his head with an amused look on his handsome face.

I grinned at him. "So, will you go? Don't worry, he's safe."

Xaemorkahn sighed. "Okay, but make sure it's not just him. You stay safe yourself, all right? Stay with him, Yve." He stared deeply at me, and I nodded.

Glancing at Ry, I could tell he was relieved that his brother had agreed to go back. "So when will you be ready? No offense, but the clock's ticking here."

Xaemorkahn abruptly started to get up from his bed, and Ry and I hastily helped him. "I guess I'll be going now."

I frowned at him. "Not that I mean to discourage you, but are you sure you'll be okay? Will you be fine after you get back there?"

He nodded. "Indeed things have been off the grid lately, but I'm sure the connection between me and the powers belonging to whatever's tormenting me should be severed once I cross." I sighed in relief, and then both Ry and I helped him to get up.

Ry lifted Xaemorkahn's hand and put it around his shoulder. Shifting his weight to one side, he supported his brother and told me to let him do the helping, so I let go of Xaemorkahn's hand and walked by their side.

We went out of the chamber and headed downstairs. When we'd reached the top of the stairs, we heard three voices that belonged to the princes arguing with one new voice. Stopping dead, we decided to hear what they were arguing about before we made an appearance.

"Are you positive about this?" I heard Vassago's voice ask whoever it was sharply.

The one answering him was the newcomer. "You're the one asking me, and that was what I heard."

"Prince Orobas," Ry whispered.

Aghast, I turned to him. "Prince Orobas? Why is he here?"

He shrugged and gave me a puzzled look as an answer, and then we focused our hearing on their argument again.

"And talk about positive! Are you guys certain that that boy really heard that up there? I mean, I know that they're planning something, but that's outrageous–and with the ETA just a few hours away to boot? I don't know, man." We heard Prince Orobas's grim voice.

We heard Belphegor curse. "You're one to talk. You were the one who told us what your forest elaborated to you."

"Okay, okay, so what now? Your pop could be here any moment." Orobas's stern voice snapped.

"We need to call them. I'm sure Ry's all right by now, right? Boy!" Belphegor shouted. His voice was loud enough for us to hear.

I saw Ry cringe and nod at me, and then he started to drag his brother downstairs. Once we hit the bottom of the stairs, Ry grinned apologetically. "Sorry, we didn't mean to eavesdrop. You guys seemed too absorbed in your argument to be disturbed."

Vassago waved his hand. "No problem."

Ry turned his sapphire eyes to Prince Orobas. "How are you, Highness? I didn't expect to see you here."

The prince inclined his head. "I'm cool. Hell, I didn't expect I'd come here either," he sneered.

I cleared my throat. "So what were you guys arguing about anyway? About Lucifer?"

Belphegor folded his arms over his chest. "Partially. Mostly it was about what those holy craps are planning."

Sighing, Vassago raked his fingers through his wavy long hair. "Yeah, and stupid us! With all the commotion that went down, we forgot about the latest prophecy your man here told us about a few days ago after he returned."

I scoffed. "That makes the three of you. He just told us about that so-called prophecy, and he said he forgot about it. Nice."

Belphegor snorted. "Well, aside from getting short-term amnesia, we were a bit sceptical about it too. We thought that if we'd mentioned it before we faced off with my daddy bastard, some of us might unconsciously have gone off guard–overconfidence perhaps."

Wincing, I nodded slowly. "That makes sense, although I don't know which one of us you were talking about, but that was a good point."

Vassago looked at Xaemorkahn. "Aren't you supposed to be lying down?"

"Who is this?" Orobas asked.

Ry jerked his head at the king. "Prince Orobas, meet my brother, Xaemorkahn." The king inclined his head in greeting.

The addressed prince looked as if he'd been forced to swallow a thousand needles. "You mean Xaemorkahn the Irgovaen?" he asked with doubt thick in his voice.

"The one and only," Xaemorkahn answered.

I saw a strange look on Orobas's face as he averted his gaze towards the other three princes, who returned his weird expression with a meaningful look.

Ry cleared his throat to get their attention. "I'll take him back. There's no need to involve him in further danger. He's done enough."

Vassago started and nodded respectfully. "Yeah, you're right. I'll escort you outside."

Belphegor approached Ry, who was still supporting his brother, and then he did the most unexpected thing of all.

He extended his hand to the king. Eyes wide, Xaemorkahn smiled and shook Belphegor's hand.

"Thanks for your help, dude." Belphegor smiled wickedly and then pulled his hand away.

"No problem." Xaemorkahn lifted the edge of his lips. Turning to Seere, he nodded subtly, and the prince replied with a simple blink.

After that Ry and Xaemorkahn started for the door. I stepped forward and called the king. "Xaemorkahn." He turned his gaze to me. "Say hi to Varisha and the others for me," I said with a smile.

He nodded. "Will do, and Yve?"

"Yeah?"

"Remember what I told you, okay?" He cast a meaningful gaze at me.

I nodded. "Don't worry, I will."

Smiling in relief, he turned to Ry. "That's good to hear. Come, brother, I'm ready."

"Okay, I'll take you two outside, and be quick. We don't know when that old bastard will come around."

Both of them, along with Vassago, went outside, and a few minutes later Vassago came back by himself.

"So, Yve, you've heard about that prophecy, right? The one your man heard up there?" Belphegor asked.

I nodded. "I have. It really is astounding, to tell you the truth." I lowered my gaze as Ry's words repeated in my head.

Suddenly, a large hand was placed on my shoulder. Looking up, I saw Belphegor in front of me. "Don't get frustrated just yet, girl."

I smiled evilly at him. "Not that I get frustrated."

When neither of the princes said anything but just continued to stare at me, I sighed heavily. Raising my hands, I laughed bitterly. "Okay, I admit it sucks to know my time as an actual devil's gonna end in just few hours. But then, I maybe have some time to bring down lots of them with me." I smiled evilly as Belphegor pulled his hand away.

"Well said," Orobas saluted me. I grinned at him and then averted my gaze to the others. "Has anybody seen Vrae and Zade?"

Belphegor started as if he'd suddenly remembered something. "Oh yeah, now that you mention it, both of them were off in their chamber when Vassago went to pick him up." He indicated Orobas.

"Oh, I see. By the way, why did you decide to come here?" I asked Orobas.

He then told me everything, beginning with Lilith spying on him up to the point where Lucifer busted free. Then he and the rest of them started to talk about that prophecy Ry had told me earlier. And they explained to me a lot more that he had let out.

When they finished, I could only stare blankly at them. A couple of seconds later, I winced. "You guys have got to be kidding me . . ."

"Not on your best day, we're not," Belphegor said as he smiled helplessly.

I bit my lip and frowned. "So what are you suggesting?"

"Just follow the prophecy. Fate will not and cannot be denied. You know that. No matter where we run or hide, we won't be able to escape." Vassago smiled sadly, and Seere looked down.

I cursed under my breath. "Yeah, that much I know. So basically, you're saying that Ry, me, Vrae, and Zade need to go out and meet them, while all of you get back into your cosy castles. Is that it?"

Vassago nodded. "As lame as it sounds, yeah, we'll have to go back. It may give us a chance to resurface millennia later rather than run into Michael and the other punks, who most likely would throw whatever tricks they have up their sleeve and then put us into the same solid cage as Lucifer."

I grimaced. "That wouldn't be good."

"No, it would suck. Well, at the very least, we know you've all taken precautions, so we'll see you in few thousand years from now." Belphegor grinned dryly.

Letting out a snort, I shook my head. "Uh, okay. If you're trying to cheer me up, it's quite a bang-up job, but thanks for trying anyway."

Belphegor chuckled. "You're welcome. Well, like you said, at least we tried."

"Wait up, guys." Vassago looked towards the door.

"What is it?" I asked him.

"Ry's back." He vanished.

Moments later they both came through the door. "I told him everything we talked about." Vassago jerked his head at Ry.

"No wonder he ain't looking too happy." Seere grinned.

Ry just sighed wearily as he shook his head. "So we need to go and meet them head on, right? We'd better call Vrae and Zade and tell them everything."

Belphegor then summoned them both and explained everything for the second time.

"Couple hours left until midnight." Zade lowered his gaze nervously after the story-telling was finished.

Ry nodded. "Let's get out then. Thanks for everything. We'll see you again."

"Yeah, yeah, get your asses out of here. We have one last thing to check ourselves." Belphegor lifted the edge of his lips.

I arched my brow. "What's that?"

"Another part of the prophecy before hell begins the party with heaven." Vassago cast a meaningful look at me.

I caught his meaning and gave them a salute. "Say hi to your old man for me."

Belphegor snorted. "I'd do it if he was safely kept in a steel coffin somewhere," he said sarcastically.

I laughed at his words. "Nice imagery. Okay, let's go." Ry nodded and grasped my hand. Vassago led all of us outside and then his castle disappeared after Orobas closed the door.

Suddenly he stopped dead and looked up. We followed his line of sight just as three devils came from out of nowhere.

"Highness, wait!" one of them shouted as they landed. The other two were holding the third one. They laid him down, and his appearance made the blood leave my face.

Amon.

He was passed out and bleeding profusely. His left wing had been viciously ripped off.

"What the . . . ? Amon, wake up, buddy!" Ry rocked the Iverand.

Vassago turned his attention from the writhing devil to the two who were aiding him and motioned towards them. "What happened?" he asked sternly.

Lenora and Ravendy simultaneously firmed their gesture. "Your Highness, may the—"

"Cut the crap," Belphegor snapped. "Explain this instant."

Ravendy swallowed. "The Echelons got him. We had no choice but to wait for them to let their guard down before we went in to help him get out, otherwise we would've been caught as well," she said with hint of remorse in her hollow voice.

"If that happened, we'd be as dead as a stick, and that's not good," Lenora added.

Zade cast a weird look at the pair. "Those two got him?"

Ry looked up. "Wait, wait, what are you talking about?"

At his question, Ravendy told us everything that had gone down between the Iverand, Faemirad, and Kathiera.

"This is so not good." Ry shook his head wearily.

"What the hell are those assholes doing?" Orobas asked indignantly.

Ignoring Orobas's question, Vassago knelt beside Ry. "All of you, get out of here. If you can get back one last time, it'll be good, but if you don't, then good luck," he said as he saluted us. I returned his salute as Ry stood up, and then we prepared to take off.

It was then we heard a low groan escape Amon's mouth. "No, stop, don't go."

All of us turned to look down and saw Amon open his eyes.

"Don't talk, Iverand. I will tell them," Lenora said.

"Tell us what?" I asked.

Vassago suddenly let loose a feral growl. "They wanted to tell us that they're all waiting outside the barrier. All the Echelons aside from Bynethar and Xamian are there, along with a myriad of Chonars and most of the other Cherxanains."

"What?" I narrowed my eyes at him. I could feel the blackness of my eyes spread from both my irises.

Were they out of their minds?

Seere's face turned dark. "Really, it's like they don't have anything more useful to do than chase their own Head Intel all the way here."

Orobas let out a curse. "This is fucking bad timing. We don't even know where the hell that old bastard went."

I looked at Amon's ripped wing and noticed something really familiar about the wound. There was a burn mark on the edge of the wing in the shape of three claws.

Kneeling down, I touched the wing as I sent my own energy into it. In just one second I recognized the energy left in it, and more to the point, who owned it. Rage consumed me almost in a blink of an eye. "The one that attacked him ain't any fucking Echelon. I can't believe this. Would that guy really stoop that low?"

Vrae patted my shoulder. "What are you talking about?"

"Look at that mark," I said grudgingly as I pointed to Amon's torn wing. Vrae knelt to look more closely. Then she gasped and stood up. "No way!"

"Uh, ladies, explanation please?" Orobas asked.

I raised a hand to the prince. "Sorry, please wait a minute, Highness," I said, and I turned to the pair. "Len, the one who attacked him was Yuraborvan, wasn't it?"

She exchanged a look with Ravendy and nodded. "Yes."

Ry was taken aback by their confirmation. "Are you sure? I mean, I've known him for a lot of things, but he's never willingly sided with the Echelons."

Lenora and Ravendy suddenly gasped at the sight of Ry and firmed their gesture. "It's good to see you, Hieldhar," they greeted him in unison.

"Likewise," he replied, and then he gestured to Amon's wound. "Yuraborvan, huh? That explains the energy emanating from it. It has a signature unique to Cherxanains, but it also has a hint of Imirae."

I nodded. "Yes, it's because he's the only Cherxanain that has the Imirae. But despite that, he's never been a part of the Varkonian ranks since his energy type is much more like that of Cherxanains."

"Even some of the other Varkonians thought he was the son of one of the royals, since he emits peculiar energy, but we didn't know who," Zade said wonderingly.

I curled my lips in repugnance. "That's him, all right, but what I don't get is why he did this, much less why he joined those assholes."

Seere knelt and touched the burn mark. A second later he pulled back his hand, and the mark disappeared. "It seems we have no choice but to meet the brainless pricks first." He spoke with a low and lethal voice.

I caught the note under his voice that told me that he was way beyond angry at the Echelons.

"Okay, I'll get these three inside, and we'll meet them with you guys." Vassago lifted Amon easily from the ground and carried him on his shoulders with Lenora and Ravendy behind him. Then they disappeared.

A few moments later he came back, and all of us flew away. True to Lenora's words, we found them lingering around in the air, with DeVarren, Kathiera, and Faemirad in the front line.

At the sight of Ry, Vrae, and myself, they all either gasped in shock or cast a wide-eyed stare at us, but the one sight that really scared the shit out of them was the four Hell princes floating amongst us.

One of the Cherxanain named Sythain gasped, and her big hazel eyes widened. "Hieldhar Ezryan? He's alive?"

"Yverna and Vrathien too! Didn't they fall in the line of duty?" Katrainne, also a fellow Cherxanain, added.

I traded a disgusted look with Vrae. "Well, at least they were kind enough to try to make us look good in our death," I said sarcastically, and she replied with a scoff.

Abruptly, all the soldiers aside from the Echelons made an honour salute. "May the Dark Light of Rygavon be with you, Your Highnesses Prince Belphegor, Prince Vassago, Prince Seere, and Prince Orobas, Hieldhar Ezryan, Yverna, and Vrathien!" they said in unison.

"Stop it! Ezryan is no longer your highest commander!" DeVarren glared at Ry.

I heard Belphegor whisper to Seere, "I don't know if I should be flattered or insulted by their salute." I stifled a laugh and glanced at Orobas who seemed to have heard it too, since he snorted.

My mate scoffed as he responded to their gesture. "Well thanks, you guys. It's good to know I made quite an impression when I was still here before. And yes, it's nice to see you too, Ravath DeVarren. I see that you and your associates knew I was alive but didn't tell the soldiers as usual. Perhaps more to the point, you didn't bother telling them who really tried to kill me seven hundred years ago." Ry cast a meaningful stare at the Echelons.

Whispers could be heard from the crowd of soldiers. "What does that mean, Hieldhar?" a Cherxanain who went by the name of Vedran asked.

Faemirad threw a lethal glare at me and Vrae. "Enough! He's no longer your Hieldhar! Just as Tyraviafonza and Wartiavega no longer belong to the Cherxanain rank! They both are traitors!"

"Tyraviafonza is a traitor?"

"Vrathien would never do such thing!"

"There's no way Yverna would stoop that low!"

"Ravathe, what is the meaning of this?"

The soldiers blurted out all kinds of questions, although there were a few scumbags who shouted "They're traitors! Kill them!" Most of the Cherxanains demanded answers from the merry band, in other words, the Ravathe bitches.

"Silence!" Kathiera's cold voice echoed, and they all went mute. "Your Highnesses, what is the meaning of this?" Kathiera asked sharply.

"Mind your tone with us, Kathiera." Belphegor's crimson eyes darkened at the Ravathe.

"Forgive us, but we're in pursuit of three traitors who came into Prince Vassago's domain. Those two Cherxanains were sentenced to death, whereas the Varkonian is a suspect. They've all committed high treason, Your Highness." Kathiera's face was torn between fear and anger.

"High treason? If by that you mean they conspired against my father, then yeah, they did that," Belphegor said sarcastically.

The rest of the Echelons had the strangest looks of surprise across their faces. "You know about this, Highnesses?"

"Who the hell do you think we are? We need no golems or bugs or tools for our resources," Orobas interjected.

Seere levelled a cold glare at them. "You know that we know a whole lot more than you do, so shut your traps."

Belphegor let out a wry laugh. "Not only do we know more than you do, we did a lot more as well, because we, along with *Yve* . . ." When he said my short name, indicating that he knew me personally, Kathiera looked like she'd been bitch-slapped by the prince. " . . . *Vrae* . . ." Faemirad suddenly looked ill. " . . . *Zade* . . ." Lazoreth blanched as if he were the one who'd been sentenced to death. " . . . along with *Ry* . . ." Gildam, Havok, and Herron flinched, and weirdly enough, they got the exact same stupid look. " . . . managed to seal our Lord Lucifer."

"Highness, they did what?" A tall well-built devil I recognized as Yuraborvan flew forward out of the crowd. Behind him was Baradyn. Damn . . .

His face was empty, but he levelled a sad and disappointed look at me. His eyes went to Ry, whose hands were laced with mine. I caught a glint of anger in there. Great . . .

I ignored him and focused on the bastard in front of him. "We caged our Master. Do you have a problem with that, you fucking ass-wipe bastard?" I clenched my teeth.

He started to move forward in a stance that warned me he was going to attack, but before he could do anything, Belphegor motioned to my side. "And we're all behind them."

Yuraborvan stopped dead in his tracks and looked at Ry, whose face stayed stoic. "You escaped death and threw yourself into a shit pool? It's obvious now that I overestimated you all these thousands of years. You even let yourself be dragged down by that bitch Yverna. I don't even know why you trusted her all that time," he said disdainfully.

"What the fuck did you say?" I began to storm at him, but even faster than I could blink, Ry suddenly flew really swiftly, floated in front of that bastard, and grabbed him by his throat. "No one insults her and lives. Now die painfully, you idiot disgraceful asshole." And then before anyone could react, he sliced through both Yuraborvan's wings. The Cherxanain roared in agony, but Ry didn't stop. He put his palm on the devil's head. Yuraborvan suddenly bled from every pore of his body as he screamed senselessly. Pulling his hand away, Ry let his victim fall from the sky.

No one even breathed as he slowly turned, and his swirling sapphire eyes darkened as his lethal battle aura wrapped his body.

The rest of the Cherxanains staggered back, including Baradyn. No surprise on that part. Aside from Yuraborvan who just died, most of the others couldn't even match me or Vrae, let alone Ry.

"Anyone else wanna bleed?" he asked the crowd. Even the Echelons couldn't find the courage to open their mouths. He was still as intimidating as ever, and his bearing as the Hieldhar hadn't faded even one bit.

Orobas approached him. "All right, Ry, that's enough. You've made your point." Ry bowed slightly and moved to my side.

Seere then turned to face the Echelons and the rest of them. "We did it to seal the creature that's responsible for the slaughter that's been happening recently. We needed the Rygavon, which was why we caged him. Besides, we placed him inside a temporary cage, and he's already out by now if you must know."

Belphegor let out an indignant snort. "Yeah, but he's about to be put in a more permanent type of containment in just a few hours, and just FYI, it won't be by our doing."

"What is that supposed to mean, Prince Belphegor?" Mezarhim motioned forward.

"It means exactly what it sounds like . . ." Before he could explain any more, there was an explosion of light several hundred yards to the north, followed by thousands of smaller lights descended from the black sky.

Angels. There was no doubt about it, they'd started.

"What the heck is that?" Zade asked with a note of bafflement in his voice.

"Ravaths, Ravathes, it's the Aryad!" Katrainne shouted. Her trembling voice indicated her anxiety and fear. "It cannot be! So Iverand Amon didn't mislead us by saying upstairs' army is going to destroy us, and not even our Master has the power to stop them?" Kathiera staggered back in the air.

I rolled my eyes. "So, have we learnt our lesson, Ravathe Kathiera? Next time, check things out first before you go round make people die for no other reason than mocking that deceitful old bastard," I said sarcastically, making everybody aside from my companions glare at me or let out various curses.

"Soldiers, Ravaths, and Ravathes, head back to the Aryad! We will meet those upstairs bastards ourselves." Seere commanded them sharply.

Mezarhim narrowed his eyes. "Forgive me, but because of your act of treachery towards our Master, we don't have to obey you any more."

As soon as those words left his mouth, Belphegor made a little wiping movement towards him and then there was a gaping hole in his throat.

All the soldiers and his fellow members of the Echelons gasped as they hastily backed away. They watched him choke in his own blood. Kathiera approached him and obviously tried to heal him. After a moment, Mezarhim began limping at the same time I sensed his life force slipping away. "I can't heal him! What is this?" Kathiera stubbornly continued to use her energy in a feeble attempt to heal the dying Ravath.

Only seconds later, Mezarhim's life force was entirely gone, and Kathiera stopped sending her energy into his dead body. She pulled her hands away and let the lifeless Ravath fall swiftly to the earth.

"I'll say again what he just told you. Soldiers, Ravaths, and Ravathes, head back to the Aryad. Don't make us say it one more time, or so help me, none of us would even think about nine of you being the Echelons. We will exterminate you all," Belphegor said calmly, but underneath it, we could sense that he meant business. With his dead-pan tone, not even a whisper could be heard from the crowd as they immediately left.

Belphegor shook his head in disgust. "So, we split up from here." His crimson eyes fell on me, Ry, Vrae, and Zade.

Ry nodded. "We'll meet them, while the four of you check on your pop, right?"

The North Prince gave us a subtle nod as an answer. "That's right, and if our luck turns a bit rotten, we might cross paths with that snotty old bitch."

"And if it doesn't give you too much trouble, give her a good bitch-slap for me if you do meet her." I grinned wickedly at them.

Orobas snorted. "Really, with her taste in finding enemies, it's a surprise she's still even alive right now."

I stared drolly at him. "Yeah well, she's been an out-dated hag far too long for her own good. Maybe someday someone will do her a favour and expire her."

"Okay, people, enough Lilith jokes. This is goodbye. Good luck, and have a safe journey, all of you." Vassago tilted his head respectfully to us.

The four of us saluted the princes. "Thanks for everything," Ry said with sincere gratitude in his deep voice.

"It's been fun, guys. We'll see you all, hopefully, in the next few millennia." Belphegor grinned at us.

The edge of my lips twitched at his words. "We will," I said, and we went our separate ways. The princes headed towards Seere's place, while the four of us flew towards the angels. A lot more of them were still coming down from the sky.

"Looks like this is gonna be one hell of a party!" I glanced at Ry, who smiled at me. "We'll hold 'em up 'till the cavalry arrives."

Vrae scowled. "And which cavalry might that be?"

"Oh, right, we *are* the cavalry," I laughed half-heartedly as we grew nearer to the whole enemy herd.

I suddenly felt the dark energy of multiple devils headed towards us. The others seemed to feel it too since they also stopped dead.

We turned around to find about a hundred Levarchons, Machordaens, and Cherxanains flying towards us. Hell, even several Varkonians and Chonars were among them.

"What the hell?" my eyes widened in disbelief.

They stopped before us. "What do you want? The Echelons officially issued death warrants on our heads?" Vrae asked sharply. I could feel her energy go sky high as she took her stand.

All of a sudden, they gave us a salute. Katrainne, the one on the front line, flew forward. "Yverna, Vrathien, Zaderion, the rest of us don't know what you guys have been doing, but some of us who know you three pretty well would never have the slightest doubt that whatever you do, you'll never betray us, soldiers–unlike the Echelons, who seem to have their own goals."

Darvahl moved to her side. "Well, the others decided to be jackasses, but what the hell, we don't need them anyway. We have the best commander on our side." He jerked his head at Ry.

Katrainne nodded in agreement. "Indeed, since Hieldhar Ezryan is also with you, we've decided we will meet them head on with all of you."

And then the commanders of the Levarchons, Chonars, and Machordaens flew forward. "We're all yours to command, Hieldhar."

"This is unexpected," Zade muttered.

I looked at Ry, whose face turned grim and yet grateful for their loyalty towards him. "I'm honoured, really I am," he said quietly.

I moved to his side and then patted his shoulder. "What are you waiting for?" I asked.

He paused and looked at me. I smiled and gave a subtle nod to encourage him. He returned my smile with his and then turned to the crowd.

He divided us into groups. In his group were only four Machordaens, four Levarchons, and myself, whom he kept by his side. He concentrated the rest of them in other groups. A few Chonars and Machordaens, along with Zaderion, were in Vrae's group. The rest were separated. Some were mixed in Katrainne's group, and the others with a few Varkonians were in Darvahl's.

"Okay guys, may the Dark Light be with you. Best of luck to us all." He saluted them and they answered him. After that we separated in different directions towards our enemies.

"I'm surprised you still bother using the Dark Light to salute them all," I chuckled.

His lips twitched with a smile. *"Well, they don't know what's going on, and we're used to that salutation, so it's not really a problem."*

"All right, Hieldhar, so are you ready?" I asked him.

He nodded. "Here we go."

We drew our energy as we passed the destroyed woods below. They had been reduced to ashes by the explosion we saw earlier. Minutes later, we ran into four Valthors just like Gevirash and Zoran. They were surrounded by sixty angels, and all the guards were bleeding profusely.

"Only sixty and no friggin' Arcs? Damn, they sure are quick in the matter of 'run and hide' or 'hide and ambush'." I shook my head in disgust.

The angels noticed us, and then they diverted their attacks towards us. We simultaneously shot our Avordaen at their multiple bolts of light. As they clashed, we immediately launched hundreds more directly at them.

Forty of them instantly dropped dead like flies.

We continued our battle with the rest of the angels. This small battle was finished in no time. For a while, we could take a breather before we continue on to thousands more.

"That's one of hell of a backup, Cherxanain. Thanks." One of the Valthors, whom I recognized as Baraz, nodded at me, and then all of them looked at Ry and looked like they suddenly had a heart attack.

"Hieldhar!" they cried in unison.

"Yes, I'm back." Ry nodded at them. "How are your wounds?"

"W–well, we can cope with them," he answered.

Ry then turned to the rest of our group. "Riertaf, Ko'ergat," he called the two Machordaens. "Stay here and help them with their wounds. Once you're all fine, regroup. We're heading northwest, is that clear?"

"Yes, Hieldhar!" they said in unison and left the group to approach the four who were wounded and descended to the blackened forest underneath . . . or what was left of it.

Ry then indicated to the group to follow him. "Move out!" And with that, we flew to northwest like he said.

"Great! Sixty down, still thousands more to go. I knew I loved to fight those bastards for a reason." I snickered.

Ry sneered. "Because they always send a whole bunch for us to kill?"

"Yep." I glanced at him, and we exchanged a wicked smile.

He chuckled and then turned his head to look at hundreds more of our enemies heading right at us. When they got close enough for us to clearly see them clearly, we stopped dead as I saw two familiar faces.

Amael and Lestiel.

"It's about time we ran into you punks." I drew out my powers and prepared to attack them.

"Silence!" Lestiel roared in fury, and he drew out his powers.

Amael took her stand. "You are supposed to be dead. You know too much about secrets that have been concealed in heaven for millions of years. Now we will kill you and your army to make everything right again," she said quietly as she directed her cold eyes towards Ry.

Ry snorted at her words. "Yeah, it's obviously right by your disgustingly low standards, not by mine."

The rest of our group floated behind our backs as other angels from lower ranks than the Arcs surrounded us.

"Leave their underlings to us, Hieldhar, Cherxanain." Artare, one of two remaining Machordaens spoke.

"Yes, we will deal with them all." Namara nodded vigorously. She was one of the Levarchons Ry included in our group.

Ry glanced at me and then scanned the unfriendly crowd around us. "Okay, we'll leave them to you guys. If you need aid, call for us. Don't wait until your last breath."

I saw their eyes gleam with respect. Letting out a war cry, they stormed the angels, leaving the two of us glaring at Lestiel and Amael.

"Ry, which one will you take?" I asked him.

He scoffed. "I know you've been itching to tear Lestiel to pieces since he told you to shut up."

I grinned wickedly. "Yeah, nobody tells me to shut up without being dead or at least crippled."

"Let's end them then, but try not to waste them. I'll do that. You're still bound to him. I know it sucks," he added hastily, when he saw my face.

"Fine, whatever." I turned to face Lestiel, while Ry prepared to strike Amael. Oblivious to the huge battle around us, we stared at our opponents as we drew our powers. Without warning, Lestiel appeared before me wielding a sword.

"What the fuck!" I cursed under my breath as I jumped backwards to evade the sword that he had manifested from thin air.

"Not that stupid sword again! Don't you have any other toy to play with? That is so not funny!" I snarled, and I conjured a black sword of my own.

He gave me a murderous glare. "I assure you it will be funny after I cut your head off and use it for baseball."

I laughed mockingly at him in return. "Nice imagination. I didn't know you guys play baseball. I thought you all played soccer using your head as the ball. No wonder you don't act like the other Arcs. Did they kick you in the head much lately?"

"Hold your tongue, abomination!" he bellowed as he flew towards me.

Rolling my eyes, I readied myself for his coming attack. "And here I thought you at least might have invented another nickname for me than dear old abomination." I spat and stormed towards him. Our swords collided, making blinding lights and deafening sounds with each contact.

"Gettin' rusty there, kiddo," I said sarcastically as I deflected some of his light attacks with my sword and made a series of aerial manoeuvres to avoid the others. After that, I sent multiple bolts towards him right away.

From out of nowhere, I sensed a bolt headed my way. I turned left just in time to see two of Amael's bolts just a few meters away. I was preparing myself to deflect them, when Ry appeared in front of me. With his back to my face, he quickly punched away the stranded bolts.

"Yve, you okay?" he asked under his breath. I nodded and then hastily turned to face Lestiel. Back to back with Ry, I made my stand to face Lestiel, while Ry was eyeing his own opponent. "I'm okay. What about you?"

He chuckled. "I'm fine. These two have improved since the last time I met them."

I snorted at his comment. "Yeah right, *improved.* Then why do I have this feeling that you were only using Amael as a sparring partner?"

He laughed quietly as he cautiously moved away from me inch by inch and drew out more of his powers. "I won't deny that I was sparring with her, but you were sparring too, weren't you?"

Shaking my head, I smiled wickedly as I felt him move further. "Damn, we really shouldn't be playing around. C'mon, let's finish this so we can head out to the thousands bunch, not these holy craps."

He glanced at the crowd of the Arcs' underlings . . . or at least what remained of them anyway.

Artare and the others definitely didn't need any help with the bunch, since only ten were still standing now out of the original few hundred. And then with a simultaneous attack, our underlings managed to kill the last ones standing.

Scoffing at the sight, I held my hand with my palm facing upward, and black energy ball appeared, floating about a few inches from my palm. Ry did the same with his energy ball, only his was deep sapphire. "Okay, I don't find this fascinating any more. Let's wipe them out."

"Hecykra Araizenia will be brought onto you all. Now die!" Amael and Lestiel said in cold unison as their bodies started to glow in white light.

Hearing that term, I ground my teeth as I felt anger begin to stir inside. "Don't you fucking dare use those words," I said in a cold voice I didn't even feel. I couldn't control my wrath any longer, and instead of my Avordaen, I unknowingly unleashed bits of my core orb, covering the clear night sky with dark clouds which gathered from out of nowhere, releasing crashes of thunder.

Fear flashed in their empty eyes, and uncertainty was written all over their faces, making the light around their bodies start to fade. Not even Amael could do anything other than blink. Lestiel shook his head, as if trying to cast off the fear that was rubbing their souls.

"You will not threaten us. There's no power can save you from judgement!" he roared furiously, and his body glowed once again. His holy powers reached out to the ether, but with the absolute fury that was engulfing me, I was hardly bothered.

The light that was wrapped around him began to focus on his hands, forming a quite massive ball of light, and he aimed it at me.

I spat in disgust. "Give me all you got, you fucking glowing bastard!"

Black aura covered my entire body and then extended itself to cover the sky around us. Everything turned pitch black. It was so dark that not even the warm light of the full moon could be seen. Hell, even Lestiel's energy ball was devoured by the darkness.

"W–what have you done? You can't do this!" There was no mistaking the tone in Amael's voice. She was scared as hell of me.

I sensed no movement from our underlings and was a bit grateful for it. "*I* can't do this?" I growled as wrath seemed to burst out from my every pore. Clenching my opened hands into tight fists, I made the darkness consume their wings . . . slowly. Their screams became louder and louder as the darkness around them slowly munched through their wings, and their holy powers were slipping away with every single cut.

When it was almost over, suddenly Ry held me from behind. "Yve, that's enough. Let me take care of the rest."

"The hell I will," I said calmly. A smile edged on my lips as the brutality continued, and I felt it increasing my powers rapidly.

"You're still banned. I know it made your powers skyrocket, but the after-effects wouldn't do you any good." He was still trying to calm me without using his powers, the only thing around at this moment that had the ability to incapacitate me. But at that very second, I almost couldn't help it. I wanted to tear them to thousands of pieces.

"I don't care! Even if I am–which I'm not–the darkness is already filled with my wrath, and it'll do exactly what I want."

Turning me around, I found him doing something really unexpected. He was smiling.

"Baby, why you didn't say so?" he asked, and suddenly he kissed me. At first, I didn't feel anything aside from his mouth invading mine. The anger didn't even lessen, but as I savoured the taste of him, my darkness power started to fade, and he pulled away. With his eyes on me, he cupped my face. "I'll do the rest. Just sit and watch."

I took a deep breath to calm down and, though disappointed, I nodded in agreement. His smile widened, and then he waved his hand at the two withering Arcs and completed the cutting since the stupid red-tape ban really included those who cut the wings. After they were wingless, he unleashed a pair of deep-sapphire energy balls, and they went straight through Amael's and Lestiel's chests like a hot knife through butter.

They screamed and then exploded, followed with a huge explosion of light. Then there was a rain of silver blood dropping onto the earth.

He turned and threw a devastatingly gorgeous wicked smile at me. "That's better." He moved towards me and took my hand in his.

I grinned and glanced at our joined hands. "Feels good, doesn't it? I wish I could waste at least one of them." I made a face at him and saw the rest of our group begin to gather.

He suddenly made a firm expression. "Well, you can try next time." He gave me a quizzical stare.

I winced at his unexpected comment. "Really? Swell!" I squeezed his fingers that were entwined with mine, but when I saw him stifle a laugh, I narrowed my gaze at him.

"No, not really, baby," he chuckled, and then he grinned apologetically. "As long as the friggin' red-tape is wrapped around you, there's no way I would let you do that. Sorry." He let go of my hands and ran his palm gently on my hair.

I curled my lips and playfully hit his broad shoulder. "That ain't funny, you fun-raider."

He frowned. "Fun-raider? What's that?"

"You raid all the fun till there's nothing left, you worrywart."

He laughed and then immediately sobered up as all the members of our group joined us. Even the four guards from before and the other two whom Ry told to help them had arrived as well.

From their faces I could tell that they were in quite a bit of a shock when they saw Ry's hand grasping mine. He didn't even bother to hide it either. "Good, now that you're all here . . ."

Before he could continue, a Machordaen whom I recalled he'd placed in Darvahl's group flew straight towards us. "Hieldhar! Cherxanain!" he yelled. His body was full of cuts and bleeding wounds he wasn't even bothering to pay attention to.

Ry let my hand go and approached the soldier. "Whoa, easy. You two, help him." Ry jerked his head towards two Machordaens floating to his left. The Machordaen took a deep breath as his fellow soldiers started to heal him.

"Elaborate," Ry said to the writhing soldier.

He nodded. "They used some sort of stealth weapon against us. We didn't even sense anything. All I recall was that I saw some lights come from out of nowhere. In the blink of an eye, many of us dropped dead. After that they ambushed us, five hundred angels at least. Varkonian Darvahl and the others are making valiant efforts to retaliate as we speak."

"Are there any Arcs among them?" I asked him.

He lowered his gaze and then lifted his head to give me grim look. "Last I saw, there were five Arcs fighting with the others."

Whispers spread instantly amongst the group members. Some were disgusted, while the others sounded worried.

I faced Ry, and his expression turned flat as he eyed the soldier. "Where are they?" he asked quietly.

"They're about thirty miles from here." He pointed in the direction from where he came.

Ry was startled and seemed to be thinking for a second. After a moment, he looked at me. "Yve, we need to be a bit cautious on this one. I'll split us into two groups. You take the other one."

I winced at his decision, above all at his eyes. There were glints of both deep wariness and sadness in there for a split second, but he looked determined to stick with his decision. That was enough to make me not question him. "No problem. You be careful, okay?" I smiled soothingly at him, intending to ease his anxiety.

He gave me a subtle nod in return and began dividing our team. When he had done the splitting, we separated and joined our respective teams. His would cover the air, while mine would go below them throughout the remains of the forest.

I turned from him and was about to jump to the ground, when he suddenly placed a hand on my shoulder, making me stop dead. I turned, and he took my left hand that wasn't holding the sword I manifested earlier. He gently squeezed my hand. "Please, be careful," he muttered, casting a gloomy look at me.

Flashing my sword away, I raised my right hand and touched his cheek. "You too," I retorted. When his gaze still shadowed with reluctance to let me go, pain pressed my chest, but I tried not to let its sway affected me. With smile, I grasped his hands and brought them to my lips. "Hey now, don't give me that "this is the end of the world" look. I *will* see you again. We've sworn it, remember? So get your butt out of here, Hieldhar. See ya!" I winked and immediately jumped towards the ground, followed by the rest of my team.

Without turning back, I quickly headed north. I could feel my team members' stares pinned on my back, but I didn't even bother to snap. Really, he was the only one who could make me unconsciously suppress my violent nature. Their staring at me would have made them dead in a blink of an eye if they had done so during the time before his return.

"Cherxanain!" A Levarchon soldier named Havaza called me. "What is it?" I asked him as we ran swiftly through the woods. We moved so fast, we practically didn't touch the ground as we kept our eyes on the surrounding area. I glanced every few seconds at Ry's team that flew several meters up ahead.

"Are you sure both our teams will be enough to fight against them? I don't mean to disrespect your and Hieldhar's abilities but if there are any Arcs . . ." He didn't finish his sentence.

I cut him an arched stare. "You're right, you *are* disrespecting us," I said flatly. I heard a choking sound came from him.

"That's not what I . . . Forgive me." His trembling voice indicated his fear. Good, that would teach him a lesson.

I exhaled heavily. "It's not just you guys are at stake."

Another member of my team gasped. "What do you mean, Cherxanain?"

"You see, we stumbled upon the fact that this war won't bode well for us. *Not* at all." I felt their spirit faltering. "Hey, it's not like this is really the end for all of us. Many will die in this war, of that I have no doubt, but many will survive." I looked up just in time to find Ry also directing his sapphire eyes and smiling at me.

"Will we survive?" Havaza asked fearfully. I saw his and the others' eyes were all gleaming with fear.

Right, no matter how tough we were, if the Man from up there decided to give no freakin' quarter to us, He wouldn't give shit whatsoever . . . and that sucked, to say the least.

"I don't know. I for one know that my companions and I will not survive." More gasps came from my team, and then I went on, "But we swore, even if today's the day we die, we'll take as many sons of bitches with us as we possibly can. Let them know the reason why we are feared as the bringers of evil," I said fiercely.

After I said that, not even breaths came out, just the wind moving silently among us. And then . . .

"We are with you!" they said in loud unison.

"Good." I chuckled at that and hauled myself faster without saying anything more.

All of a sudden, I saw hundreds of small lights flickering up ahead. "What the . . . ?" I muttered, and I readied myself to attack. Those lights were so small, no wonder Darvahl and the others missed them easily.

And there was something that bothered me even more. I couldn't sense any energy belonging to angels. Were those the lights that Machordaen was talking about? Had they managed to conceal it somehow?

"Get ready. Something's not right. Draw your powers out, but not so much as to make them realize we're here." I turned slightly to face Havaza, and he nodded. All of them immediately did what I told them.

I lifted my head up and saw Ry cautiously looking around. It seemed like he hadn't noticed those lights.

"Ry, can you hear me?" I called him.

His answer was immediate. *"Yeah, Yve, what is it?"*

"There are hundreds of small lights flickering up ahead below you. Slow down, be on guard, and warn the others."

"What lights?" He started to move his head down.

"Don't make obvious eye contact with whatever they are. Just glance at them, I don't know whether they'd strike if they saw you looking straight at them," I said hastily, and I signalled the others to stop and hide behind whatever remains of the forest were big enough to cover us.

"I see the lights you mentioned, but I don't sense any angels around here." He sounded a bit bewildered by that small fact.

"I know. I don't either. What did that Machordaen tell you? Have we arrived at their last position yet?"

His voice turned grim. *"According to him, they should be around here."*

I felt sick with dread after hearing the news. *"And there's no sign of them anywhere, hell, not even the slightest friggin' smell of blood! And you put thirty soldiers with him."*

"And a few other Varkonians as well," he reminded me.

"Well, that could be a problem," I said sarcastically. This definitely didn't look good for us.

Without warning, I felt a weird tingle down my spine. The sensation was unmistakable. Angels were here.

In numbers that would ruin our soldiers' day.

"Heads up!" I said sharply. Those lingering lights suddenly grew larger and began to float. "Follow them!" I lifted myself and drew out my powers.

"I see them. Yve, give yourself and your team some distance from them. Get two of your team members to look at the surroundings in case those angels decide to make an appearance. The rest of you will attack on my mark and fire at will." I saw Ry already directing his energy ball downward as well as his entire team.

"Roger that!" I motioned upward, slowly following those lights' movements all the while and creating some distance between us and them. I did what Ry told me and asked two Levarchons to watch the surrounding area.

"Now!" Ry shouted, and he launched his bolts.

"Fire at will!" I yelled, and all of us instantly shot hundreds of bolts towards those tiny lights. A few moments later, the lights disappeared as they clashed with our bolts.

"Cherxanain!"

Turning around as the warning came from a soldier nearby, I saw an angel of a lower rank lift his hand that was holding a sword and direct it at me. I manifested my own sword and blocked his attack at the right moment.

I lost count of how many times our swords collided, but after several attacks, my sword was able to destroy his to pieces, and that gave him a heart attack no doubt. Not giving him time to recover from the shock, I immediately made a wide swiping movement at him and sliced him in two, good and proper I might add.

I hurriedly turned around to find hundreds of them appearing and engaging the rest of us. Slicing through every underling I met, I continue making my way towards Ry.

That was when I ran into the three of them –Kanael, Nataniel, and Yniel. More archangels.

I rolled my eyes at their approach. Kanael narrowed his cold eyes at me, while Nataniel and Yniel just manifested their weapons, a spear and a sword. "Prepare to be thrown back to where you belong, abomination." A pair of lights engulfed both his clenched fists, while the others circled around me.

Swinging my sword, I let out an undignified snort. "What is it with you people and abomination? Your Father had an affair with a slut named after it, and you guys have harboured a grudge ever since, or what?" I lifted the edge of my lips in an evil smile, while all of them bellowed in rage.

"Watch your dirty tongue! You will not insult Him!" Nataniel stormed towards me with her long, engraved spear. I lazily blocked her attack with my black sword. Intending to mock her, I opened a small hole in my palm and sprayed her with my blood.

It rained all over her face.

"Taste abomination, you piece of shit! And by the way, you people should watch your brains first. Why the hell should I watch something that, according to you, is dirty. And FYBI, I already *did* insult Him, and I assure you, more will be coming from me." I sneered at her.

She jumped backwards and wiped my blood off her face. Appearing to be completely disgusted by what I'd done, she rushed towards me again. "You can't even get the correct letters that stands for 'for your info', and you dare to insult Him?"

I laughed as I blocked her spear and caught her wrist. "No, brainiac, FYBI stands for 'for your brain info', so I didn't exactly make a mistake here, you did." I shoved her with my sword and clashed swords with her companions.

Our weapons and bolts flew relentlessly, and each time they made contact, deafening sounds of thunder and blinding lights appeared. My group mixed with Ry's, and many were still standing.

I guess there was a difference between fighting fair and getting ambushed.

A few devils dropped from the sky, and explosions of lights coming from the souls of wasted angels could be seen everywhere.

Growing tired of them swearing at me, I made one solid swing of my sword, shoving them all aside, and then threw fifty bolts at once, followed by one swing across their chest.

Screaming, their weapons vanished and they fell swiftly towards the earth below.

I tightened my grip on the sword and licked my lips at the sight of their agonized faces as they fell and the blood that was splashing everywhere. "That's more like it," I muttered. I looked down disgustedly and resumed my search for Ry.

"Ry, where are you?" I kept asking myself that over and over as I slaughtered my way through the combatants while searching for his whereabouts. To help my soldiers, I killed as many as I could while I was looking for him. Following his energy through the ether, I blew my way past fifteen angels that were flying in formation as if they were trying to ambush me.

All of them fell like wingless flies.

"There!" I stopped dead as I saw him floating a few meters up ahead of me. He was surrounded by at least twenty angels. Thirteen of them I recognized as Arcs.

I was about to fly in his direction when another bunch of lower angels let out a war cry and positioned themselves around me. Extremely annoyed, I made one black orb the size of a giant carriage in front of me and sent it directly at them. They split up in anticipation, but they failed, as my orb was reduced to a smaller size and pursued the energy they emitted. In a matter of seconds, none of them was still alive.

When I looked back at Ry's direction, his battle had moved a bit farther. I glanced around at the battle of underlings that still went on. Deciding to give some help, I conjured several giant black orbs like before and unleashed them at the angels who were fighting against the remaining soldiers. Without even looking, I immediately left the crowd, as screams of agony could be heard from the angels, followed by shouts of victory let out by the still-alive devils.

I kept on moving and suddenly, there were multiple blasts of lights and screams. I stopped in my tracks and moved my wings to cover my eyes. When the trains of explosions had ceased, I quickly headed towards Ry.

When I arrived, there were only five Arcs still alive, and even they weren't in good shape. Three of them had suffered burn wounds all over and the remaining two were struggling to keep themselves floating because of cuts and burns on their wings.

"Way to go, Ry!" I whispered under my breath. I then sensed a glimpse of movement behind me and turned.

More angels, no Arcs . . . yet.

I *tsked* at the sight of twenty angels approaching. "Nice! Holy crap's reinforcements."

"Kill him!" one of them yelled.

I shook my head in disgust. "You, crap number one! I know he really is all powerful, but before you can get to him, you have to get past me, and not meaning to play gender here, but I"–shooting several bolts directly at him that made a solid hit on his chest and incapacitated him, I gave him an offended glare–"am a freakin' female!"

The others behind him instantly stopped moving and took their stand. "Hold it right there, Tyraviafonza! We have no business with you. Step aside and do not interfere with heaven's judgement!" One of them with grey misty eyes and a long thin sword in her hand snarled at me.

"What are you? Defective? Not even in your wildest fucking delusions would I step aside and let you putrid dumb-asses lay a hand on him. The Hieldhar has returned, more to the point, *my* Hieldhar. Not that you could, but whatever." I taunted.

"Enough words! Vanquish her!" she commanded the rest of them as she conjured white light on the tip of her sword and shot it at me along with the others who launched their attacks simultaneously.

Letting out a disgusted snort, I manifested a barrier. All their bolts, energy balls, and other sorts of long-range attacks were captured by it.

"This cannot be!" some of them shouted in disbelief.

Spreading my dark energy throughout the barrier, I turned all their holy energy into devil's poisonous energy and released it back to its casters. Each of the bolts made a clear hit, and they all fell without even making a sound.

"Believe me, I, this Tyraviafonza, can do it, more than you know," I said coldly as I stared down at their dead bodies that were obliterated as they fell.

Lifting my head, I quickly looked for Ry. But he was no longer where I had last seen him. Flying directly to where he had stood moments before, I frantically turned my head around as I reached the ether as far and wide as I could.

I cursed under my breath. "Damn it, why does he always have to disappear after making a killing?" Suddenly I felt his energy less than a mile to the east. "Found you!" I immediately headed to his place.

The moment I got there, I saw that he and the five Arcs, who had been still alive when I last saw them, weren't moving. "Ry," I hesitantly called him. Suddenly I felt all the life force belonging to those five Arcs disappear at once, and they all exploded in a blinding light.

Ry turned, and when his eyes met with mine, he smiled widely. "Hey, you're okay?" He hastily flew towards me and placed his hands on my shoulders.

Nodding, I touched his hand. "I'm fine. And by the way, do you have to move every time you kill them? I'm having enough trouble locating you!" I hit his chest playfully, and he laughed.

He pulled his hand away, and we turned to face all the remaining soldiers who were approaching us. "Hieldhar! Cherxanain!" They all stopped before us. "Are you all okay?" he asked sharply. He was right to ask, since most of them had suffered lots of burns and were bleeding all over.

"We're all fine. Please tell us what to do next," they said simultaneously.

Hesitating, he glanced at me and then looked at them again. "The two of us will take it from here. All of you must get back to the Aryad to recuperate and warn the others. More importantly, stay alive! You hear me?"

They started to whisper to each other and looked back at him. There was an obvious glint of respect in their eyes as they saluted us. "We will! May the Dark Light be with you both!"

"And with you," we replied. After that they all left us in the opposite direction.

Ry then indicated northwest and instructed me to follow him. "Why didn't you call me earlier?" he asked as we flew together.

I curled my lips. "Yeah, right. You were dealing with those no-fun Arcs, and lots of them were bugging me as well. When in hell did I have time to call you?"

Laughing again, he took my hand and squeezed gently. "Thank you."

I raised a brow. "Uh, yeah, you're welcome, but what are you thanking me for?"

"For being so concerned that you didn't even want to disturb me in the middle of battle."

I fell silent at his words. *"What do you think? Of course I won't disturb you. What if I did, and you fell off guard like you always do these days?"* I asked sadly in my thoughts.

I cleared my throat and changed the subject. "By the way, where are Vrae and Zade?"

"We're heading their way right now." His voice turned grim all of a sudden.

"Is there something I need to know?" I narrowed my gaze at him. He shook his head slowly. "Nothing, it's just, with Darvahl and the others gone MIA, a bit of caution won't hurt, now will it?" he asked quietly.

I let out a slow breath. "Yeah, that would be a cheery thought as well."

He chuckled at my comment, and we continued flying for half an hour. Not long after, we ran into another huge battle . . . with Vrae and Zade as two of the combatants.

"There!" We joined the battle and slaughtered many of the lower-rank angels. Weird, where were the other Arcs?

The battle ended in no time with us helping them. "Now that's how we end this!" Vrae approached us, while Zade talked with the rest of their group.

"Good to see you guys are still alive." Ry grinned at her and glanced at the remaining soldiers.

"You ran into any Arcs?" I asked her.

She shook her head. "Nope, just hundreds of annoying underlings." Ry and I exchanged a puzzled gaze. "What's going on?" Vrae asked as she eyed us both.

"Nothing. It's just that it's pretty weird that you've encountered none of those holier craps, while we've run into eighteen of them already," he said as he manifested a small deep sapphire ball and playfully let it circle his fingers.

Zade arrived then and greeted us. When he was about to talk more, Vrae stopped him. "Wait, eighteen?" she asked sharply.

We both nodded. "Yep, eighteen, and he wasted fifteen of them, making pretty nice fireworks, I might add. I really wish I could do that." I shook my head and let out a long sigh.

Ry laughed. "She's been complaining like this ever since I stopped her from killing Lestiel and I did him instead."

Zade gaped. "You've ganked fifteen Arcs since our groups separated?" I glanced at Vrae, and she narrowed her gaze at me.

Ry shrugged. "It's not like it's a hard-core job, now is it?" he sneered at the two floating beside me.

"So, you wasted three then?" Vrae turned her gaze at me.

I pouted. "Without fireworks as usual."

"Okay, cut the jest hour. I wanna tell you guys something." Ry's sapphire eyes gleamed with wariness as he began to tell them about Darvahl and his team, up to the point where we got ambushed and those peculiar lights we saw earlier.

"What do you think those lights were?" Zade frowned deeply as he crossed his hands over his chest.

Ry shook his head, indicating his cluelessness. "Dunno. I've never run into anything like this before, but I do have an idea whom we have to meet. I bet they have something that can shed some *light* in this," he said sarcastically as he gave me a knowing look which I caught immediately.

"Who might they be?" Vrae and Zade asked in unison.

I scowled before I answered them. "You know, the famous happy couple, Gabriel and Michael. Isn't that right, Ry?" I turned to look at him.

He grinned. "You always know what I wanna say."

Zade gaped again. "Whoa, if we wanna butt heads and horns with the usual Arcs, I'm game, but them? I don't know guys . . ." he smiled nervously.

Ry nodded. "I know. That's why I need you, Yve, Vrae, and a few others to watch the area while I meet them head on. Oh, and dismiss the soldiers. Bring only those from Cherxanain ranks. At least they will have a better chance to survive. As for the Varkonians, get them back with the others. With so few of them remaining, I don't think it's wise to drag them into this–well, you're an exception." He winced at that last remark to Zade.

I raised a brow at him. "You're awkwardly good to the others these days. Feeling sentimental?"

He shrugged, and the small sapphire ball he was playing with disappeared. "Not really, I just don't feel right wasting that many soldiers. Besides, saving them won't do us any harm. Maybe some of those who present right now could be useful to us, if they're still alive to see us."

I chuckled at his words. "You never fail to think many centuries ahead."

Vrae shook her head in amazement. "That is, assuming any of them survive, of course."

Nodding his agreement, Ry glanced at the soldiers who stayed still in the air a few meters from us. "Of course."

Zade cleared his throat. "So do you have any idea where we will find the princes?" His face turned bleak, and his wariness was tangible.

"I'm betting they're somewhere around Logerrian." Ry turned his head and looked in the direction of the waterfall far away from where we floated.

Vrae clapped her hands. "Yeah, right, I forgot. They're supposed to be messing around with our dear old master, aren't they? Is it safe enough to think they're at least still around?" Vrae cast a meaningful stare.

I shook my head. "Not a chance," I said immediately, making both of them gape. I let out a disgusted breath. "If both the light-heads were there, those three would be running for cover. Not that they are scared, but the stated prophecy most likely would make them take precautions."

"Besides, judging by recent events, it is safe to assume those light-asses keep something up their sleeves," Ry added.

Vrae looked as if she had finally caught where our discussion was headed. "Something dangerous enough to seal our Master, right, we got it."

Exhaling heavily, Zade raised his arms in surrender. "Okay, let's go."

Nodding, Ry then dismissed the rest of the soldiers and brought with him the remaining Cherxanains. He also instructed anyone who ran into Katrainne and her team to tell them to bail. After that, we quickly made our way towards Seere's domain where we had left dear old Lucifer before.

It was a few minutes later when we arrived a few yards from the lake, and Ry asked us to split up. He went ahead and checked around the lake, while the rest of us waited ready to back him up.

When we were close enough for the lake to come into our view, I let out a foul curse.

Lucifer was floating on the surface of the lake, and his cage didn't look as solid as before. It was transparent enough to see him struggling inside it and feel his murderous aura radiating around us. To top it all, there was no sign of those princes or that happy couple.

I saw Ry move cautiously towards Lucifer. Focusing my hearing senses while all the while monitoring the area, I narrowed my eyes at them both.

"You dare to come here?!" Lucifer let out a feral growl.

Ignoring him, Ry stopped a few meters in front of our master and turned his head around. "Save your breath from that 'I'm gonna shred you' crap for a second. Where are your dear old pals?" he asked nonchalantly.

Right then I felt unfriendlies heading our way really fast. Sure enough, two of them positioned themselves between Lucifer and Ry, whereas the others hid themselves behind the surrounding trees.

The Holiest of the Archangels, Gabriel and Michael.

"Yve, stop!" Ry said in my head, when he sensed I was about to launch a full-force attack.

I immediately suppressed my already drawn powers. *"Fine, but if I sense anything funny, I will gut them both,"* I replied to him calmly.

"You dare to appear before us?!" Gabriel asked coldly.

Ry snorted with a full display of disdain. "Really, it's like having *deja vu* and SSDB, as in 'same shit, different bastard'."

Gabriel manifested a big broadsword. "You will insult us no more! How dare you break the order of the universe like your predecessors?! You are indeed abominations, beings with no knowledge of remorse, fit only to be forever subjugated in judgement!" he directed the tip of his sword at Ry.

Ry waved his hand in dismissal. "You're dead wrong. I *will* insult you . . . more. Suck it up, and shove that righteous bullshit up your candle-ass. We seek our survival and we're doing all that for it alone. You and your stupid order can go elsewhere and blow yourselves for all we care. It's not like your Big Boss didn't know everything already. He was the one who decreed this. If you've got any problem with that, go cry to Him all you want. And mark these words to your brain if you have one: we devils never know regret, remorse, or any kind of stupidity that falls under that category. Never did and never will."

I stifled a laugh when I heard him quoting me. Even Lucifer looked smug all of a sudden. Sobering up, I glanced at the rest of the unfriendlies. It seemed that, aside from the two scumbags, none of the others came from the ranks of the Arcs.

Michael, who had stayed still up till this point, suddenly placed his hand on Lucifer's cage. Oblivious of the Devil King's deafening wail of protest, Michael chanted something, and the cage glowed vividly before Lucifer went silent.

The Prince of the Archangels then manifested a long bright gold sword. Slowly swinging it around, he directed his brilliant blue eyes and sword at us. "Very well, since we also know you already used Herathim to reseal Arzia, you serve no more purpose. It's time for you to be thrown from this realm forever!"

Without warning, Gabriel swung his sword towards Ry.

I quickly summoned my own black sword and flew towards them. Placing myself before Ry, I intercepted Gabriel's sword with my own. "It's still too early for you to aim your stinking sword at him, and he's not your servant," I said coldly.

"Who give you permission to interfere?!" Gabriel added more pressure to his sword.

Cursing with inward disgust, I drew a bit more of my powers and shoved him backwards. "Obviously not you bastards." I swung my sword and moved to Ry's side.

"No more talk with you, abominations. Garrison, attack!" Michael's sharp voice echoed throughout the woods, and all the angels whose presence I'd felt appeared, each wielding a weapon. Vrae, Zade, and all Cherxanains following us came out from hiding to engage them.

Hundreds of explosions illuminated the forest and burned all over. Despite all the commotion and complete disaster, Lucifer's cage didn't suffer any damage whatsoever. Not long after the battle started, angels from the lower ranks were already falling one by one, killed by the Cherxanains we had brought, as well as Vrae and Zade.

Meanwhile, oblivious to the huge destruction around us, Ry and I stayed motionless in the air. "Still confident you can outrun us?" I chided after the last of the angels fell with an agonized scream.

Both Michael's and Gabriel's faces stayed stoic as they stared blankly at us and just floated there, ramrod stiff. But beneath the empty look they gave me, I still couldn't shake the feeling that they had brought something else.

As if proving my suspicion, I felt something peculiar move in the air. *"Yve, get behind me,"* I suddenly heard Ry's voice clearly in my head. I glanced at him as I moved slightly, doing what he told me.

"You feel it?" I drew out more of my powers.

He nodded slightly. *"Yeah, I feel it down my spine."*

"You have any idea what's causing this?"

"Not a damn thing. Just stay on guard. I don't know what they're up to." I felt him stiffen as he slightly raised his hand to shield me.

"Got it. And it seems Vrae, Zade, and the others feel it as much as we do." Glancing around, we saw the others lingering in the air, turning their heads around as if they were looking for something.

Ry spoke again, this time to warn Vrae, Zade, and the others to stay put and watch our backs in case they send for reinforcements.

It was then that Gabriel abruptly stormed straight towards Ry with his sword. I blocked him like before. "Do you have no manners, Gabey? Striking without warning? I'd expect no more from people who are so fond of doing cowardly moves like ambushes." My gaze darkened at him as I drove him back with my sword once more.

Michael moved towards me and directed his own sword at me, which was intercepted by Ry, who captured it with one bare hand. Was he insane? That sword could burn his flesh! But when I looked at it more closely, there seemed to be no damage.

"You have to go through me first before you can touch her, asshole." Ry tightened his grasp, and then he shoved Michael away.

"We will exterminate you all!" Michael bellowed furiously, and then he stormed towards Ry. At his scream, Gabriel moved to attack. This time, his target wasn't Ry like before. He aimed his sword directly at me.

"Nice to see you finally realized who your opponent is," I said under my breath as I engaged him in a very fast sword battle. Glancing quickly at Ry every now and again, I saw he was as busy as I was. With his own sapphire sword in his grasp, he met each strike Michael delivered.

Both of us were caught in a devastating sword fight that seemed to go on forever, while the others just stayed cautious around us. From their silence, it was as if they were holding their breath, waiting for the battle to end.

More explosions ignited from our fight, making the remaining devils that weren't even involved swirl around to avoid stray blasts. Some even conjured protective shields.

Hours went by, and the blood-red rays of the sun slowly started to shine through the velvet darkness of the night sky. I cursed under my breath as I avoided yet another strike sent by Gabriel. It barely missed me. *"Great! A stupid blazing ball has come to brighten the dance,"* I thought sarcastically.

A few of the stranded bolts flew to the sky, exploding into waves of light with atomic destructive power. The wind blew viciously, carrying dust and rocks, driving away everyone other than the combatants. As the others tried desperately to hold their position, our battle kept on going as the hot glare of the sun fell on us.

My annoyance grew as the yellow ball licked its hot tongue on my skin. This seriously pissed me off since I wasn't in human form. I clenched my teeth, deflecting, striking, and sending bolts relentlessly at the archangel as I planned how to end the battle. It was pretty hard, considering this glowing guy moved so freakin' fast and I had to keep up with his every attack.

One single mistake and I'd be done for . . .

And since when could he move at this speed anyway?

Jumping over Gabriel's head, I split my sword into two and turned just in time to see his sword only few inches from my face. I raised both swords as he nearly cut me face-on. "Not so fast, lightbulb-face!" I snarled, and I shoved him away.

He stopped in his tracks, and I heard a really loud clang of metal. Glancing at Ry, I saw his battle too had ceased. *"Yve, are you okay?"* Ry asked me rather sharply in my head.

"I'm fine. What about you?" I replied.

He chuckled. *"Don't worry about me, I'm doing just fine."*

"Ry, why are they stopping?" I asked him, closely eyeing Gabriel's every move.

"Don't know, just stay on guard." His voice faltered into a hollow whisper, making me bristle all over.

From out of nowhere, that same eerie sensation of something moving silently in the air came back tenfold. It felt more vicious than before, and it went through me like a hot knife slowly cutting my spine.

Cringing, I tried to ignore the pain by gripping the hilts of my swords. I grasped them so tight, I was half-scared I would break them. What the hell was this?

Two seconds later, my question was answered by multiple hot lights descending from the sky . . . directly onto my comrades.

"I believe there's no question that heaven could outrun abominations like all of you, now is there?" Michael's cold voice reached my ears.

One by one, those lights vanquished my comrades without a trace. Their agonized screams tore through me as I braced myself not to look at them as they were obliterated.

"Zade!" Vrae's tormented voice suddenly echoed. Within that single moment, I unconsciously dropped my guard and quickly glanced at her.

In that very second, Michael decided to strike.

Everything went unbelievably slow, like a hundred times slow. As I felt a violent blow from my foe, I heard Ry's deep voice calling me from afar. I hastily turned to face the archangel I was fighting, but what I saw made my blood leave my core.

Both Michael and Gabriel directed their swords right at me, and from out of nowhere, there was . . . Ry.

He faced me, arms outstretched, with the archangels' blades jutting out from his chest. "Yve . . . you . . . okay?" His voice was broken, and blood started to flow from his gaping wound.

The archangels harshly pulled out their swords, making more blood sputter from the holes on Ry's chest. Coughing up blood, he began to fall. I hurriedly caught him as he fell and brought him to the ground. Lifting my head from him, I saw Michael with Gabriel at his side. Both were headed for us.

"Yve!" I saw Vrae immediately fly towards us both. Turning around, I saw there were only three Cherxanains left in the air, and even they weren't in a state to continue fighting.

It seemed like those lights earlier had missed each of them only by a limb. But that didn't stop them from trying to continue fighting, as I would have expected from those of Cherxanain rank. They, together with Vrae, quickly used all their remaining powers to stop the Highest of the Archangels.

But it was futile.

With one single attack by Michael, all of them fell, like leaves blown away from their trees.

"Vrae, no!" I gasped. A slight touch pulled my attention.

It was Ry. He was awake.

Coughing up more blood, he tried to get up. "Stay here!" I said sharply, and leaving him, I faced the two Arcs. "You will not touch him!" I manifested another sword in my left hand. Swinging both swords, I let out a war cry and stormed them both. But even though I wasn't hurt by any means just yet, they were proven to be extremely powerful adversaries.

I could barely breathe as I deflected their endless rain of attacks with my swords. Was this what they were truly capable of? Well, they sure earned the title of the Highest of Archangels, I'd give them that. Their strikes were merciless–not a single mistake in their every move as they delivered blow after blow in perfect harmony.

Hell, I might've enjoyed our fight more if our entire existence hadn't been on the line or if they hadn't been so annoyingly relentless.

It felt like everything went unbearably slow while our battle kept going at a tremendous speed, until it happened. I had just driven away Michael's sword, which he had directed at my head, with my left sword, when Gabriel followed suit with his.

The blade went through my stomach.

I gasped as I saw him move towards me, plant a hand on my chest, and add another blow. It felt as if the flame of hell had spread instantly from my chest and burned me from inside out. I was sent flying right to Ry's side.

"*Yve, no . . .*" Ry's pained voice whispered in my mind. He dragged himself to me and grasped my hand.

I looked up and gave him a reassuring smile. "I'm fine. I won't let them get to you, Ry," I said fiercely, though I couldn't help but feel the heat of the tears that stung my eyes.

Would this truly be the end?

"Yve, you should go," he said.

Before I could reply, the two archangels landed. "Now it is time for you to perish, Fallen Ones," Michael said coldly.

The two walked towards us, and suddenly Ry made a slight movement that was followed by a loud static noise in my head. It only meant one thing.

He was using a blocked channel.

"Die, abomination!" Gabriel said with disgust as he raised his sword.

Reacting purely on instinct, I levelled my palm to his chest and shot a bolt. But I wasn't the only one. Ry followed and sent a blow to Michael. Just when I had readied myself to launch another attack, I felt a hand roughly pull me away from Ry.

Turning to see who it was, I was surprised to find Vrae.

Expecting her to help us both, I exhaled in relief. "Vrae, c'mon. Help me take him," I said as I moved towards Ry. It was then that I saw him smile at me. The look in his eyes only gave me one word.

"Goodbye."

"Ry?" I called him. He looked away and raised his left hand. Suddenly I felt a massive surge of power from him that spread to the air around us. The wind moved towards the archangels and formed a violent tornado that forced the two to keep their distance.

He then shifted his gaze while maintaining his powers. I didn't know how or where he had that much strength left, considering his wounds. Strangely enough, his eyes didn't turn to me, but to my sister. "Vrae, here, take this," he said, extending his right hand. There was a small, dark-coloured . . . fruit. It was from a Miriam tree that sucked away life force.

What the hell?

I tilted my head nervously at the cherry-like fruit on his hand. "That's–that's from a Miriam tree. What are you doing with that? Ry, what's going on?"

He glanced at me, and I saw pain flash in his eyes. Oh, no, what was he trying to do? His gaze went back to Vrae. "I'm counting on you," he said firmly.

Vrae took the fruit and shoved it under her robes. "Hope you're right about this. You know I have a not-so-good history with that damn tree."

"It's safe. Are we good?"

Vrae nodded. "Yeah, leave it to me. We'll see you again. Good luck," she said with a formal salute.

He saluted back, making me bristle as dread wreaked havoc in me. I turned my attention back and forth frantically between him and her. "Vrae, talk to me. What's he saying?" I asked with a hint of uncertainty.

Staring at him, she then abruptly threw more bolts at the archangels. When my attention was back on the enemies, she used the opportunity to do the unthinkable.

She pulled me away from Ry and made me airborne.

"What the hell? Vrae! Get back! Ry's still there, dammit! Get back! You're leaving him behind!" I screamed as I struggled to go to his side.

"*Yve.*" I stopped as I heard Ry's voice in my head. "*I asked her to take you . . .*"

At his words, I struggled even more. "*Why did you? No way in hell . . .*"

"*Go. We will find each other. I love you,*" he said, and amazingly, he brought himself to his feet with his blood pouring down just like a river of crimson.

"*No! No! If we're gonna die now, at least go with me! Or let me die by your side!*"

"*I can't. If I leave here with you, those two will go after me and get you and Vrae as well. I can't let that happen. I asked her to take care of you after this is over.*"

Ignoring whatever that meant, I kept fighting to get to him. "*I can't do anything with these wounds! I'll just die too! You know that!*"

"*Listen, Yve. I've wasted most of my powers just by hurling that tornado. I won't get too far, so I'll just hold them here. As much as I hate it, we're both gonna die now, but I want you to at least be by Vrae's side, not these bastards'.*"

His words struck me deep. I just floated there with my eyes fixed on him.

"*Please, for me,*" he pressed. "*I will turn back now. I'll see you in another life. I love you so much.*" That was all he said, and then he turned his back to me.

Tears streamed down my cheeks; I felt like my life-force had been ripped out of my body. "Come on, Yve," Vrae said with her hand slipped under mine. My eyes were blank, I could barely hear anything as I absently struggled. "*I love you more than my life. Why won't you let me be by your side?*"

He didn't respond, but I could see him trembling even from where I was floating.

"Yve, stop!" Vrae repeated, almost begging. Despite the anguish in her voice, I ignored her as well as my own blood that flowed freely from my stomach and the pain that clawed my body. In the end, I was able to break free. I flew towards Ry immediately, but I was too late.

Michael's voice echoed throughout the air. "In the name of God, I release you from this abomination. Serve Him in exterminating His unholy enemies!"

His command struck Vrae and myself. We yelped in pain, and the tornado abruptly stopped, while the two Arcs went straight for Ry. Just as I neared him, I saw the one scene that shredded my very existence.

Two burning swords penetrated his armour and went through his chest.

"Ry!" I roared in despair as Michael and Gabriel pulled their swords out. I saw Ry's gaze turn to me one last time with the hint of a smile as he fell to the ground. I could feel his life fading away. I unconsciously brought myself closer to him and suddenly went numb.

My body was moving on its own . . . towards Vrae.

"You!" I gritted my teeth.

"Please, Yve, just go with me," she said in a restrained voice. Her tears rolled down her cheeks, but there was a determined look in her blood-red eyes.

She was determined to take me away from there as fast as she could.

"You're throwing him to those bastards!" I growled. For a split second, I felt Vrae's bounds on me loosen. My words had the expected effect. I stole the chance to fly towards Ry, but by then, it was too late.

I saw those Arcs . . . behead him.

"No!" I screamed. My voice seemed to snap Vrae back into reality, since I felt my body once again move further away from Ry yet again.

I forced my head to turn to her. She didn't say anything and merely stared at me. I could feel her powers all over me as I felt my body being pulled towards her. I started to pull myself away, and in turn, she roughly pulled me back. I groaned in pain as she turned my blood against me, rendering me helpless, and at the same time, she stopped the bleeding in my stomach.

Despite her efforts that resulted in my wound slowly closing, I still mentally snapped at her. Before I could say any of the curses, she pulled me aside in time to dodge multiple bolts the archangels threw.

"Damn you!" I snarled, but then I saw two bolts headed her way. My first instinct was to get to her, and to my own surprise, I was able to break loose from her powers. I planted myself in front of her and deflected the bolts. Unfortunately, that wasn't their only attack.

Five more bolts went through the hole in my stomach right after I'd sent the previous bolts away from her.

"Yve!" Vrae screamed out to me.

It was as if someone had stomped the breath out of my lungs with full force. I gasped as I once again felt that numbness from earlier, and my body moved by itself straight to my sister. She tucked her arms around me and took me further from the archangels.

"Vrae . . ." I whispered as my sight began to dim and blood spurted out of my mouth. "I'm really sorry."

"Don't talk. I'm getting us out of here," she said in a strained voice. At that moment, for the first time in thousands of years, I saw her shed her tears.

I coughed up the blood and glanced askance at Ry's head. *"I love you . . . If only I could say it to you as much as I should."*

With one last breath, I was pulled into eternal darkness.

"Ry . . . Vrae . . . forgive me . . .'

*   *   *

Vrathien kept on flying until she was sure the archangels weren't anywhere near them.

Biting her lip in absolute wrath and helplessness, she pushed aside her inner pain that clawed into her as she brought the two of them further. She realized that her sister was no longer alive, but she still couldn't bring herself to stop or leave her there.

"One day we will have our vengeance. We will reunite once more," she said bitterly in her thoughts as she left the battlefield carrying her sister.

Epilogue

Vrathien fled miles away with her sister in her arms. After a while, she came to a stop in the Gillian forest. She knelt and laid her sister's body on the barren field.

One by one, four princes of Hell appeared.

"Vrae," Vassago said as he placed one hand on her shoulder. Tears of blood began to flow down her eyes as she put her hands over Yverna's body.

Oblivious to the princes around her, she closed her eyes and chanted the spell Ezryan gave her in his last breath. Inhaling deeply, she felt the air stir as the spell began to take effect.

Seconds later, she opened her eyes and saw one pale-blue orb appear from Yverna's body the size of a fist. Smiling sadly, she stood up, and Vassago pulled his hand away. "Your Highnesses, it's been an honour to fight alongside you. Now I shall take my leave," she remarked while her face stayed impassive, determined to embrace the repercussions. She pulled out the fruit Ezryan gave her and ate it.

Belphegor stared as her devoured it. "Vrae," he started, but he paused when he saw her body begin to fade.

Sharply sucking his breath, Belphegor lowered his gaze. "Ry really gave you the spell, didn't he? I didn't believe what I heard at first, when you started to chant, and that fruit too. But this? Are you sure?" he asked her. His deep voice was laden with trepidation.

She scoffed. "There's no turning back now, is there?" she slowly extended her hands towards the glowing orb. "Highnesses," she said, "Can I ask you one last favour?" A glint of despair flashed in her faded eyes as she addressed the princes.

"Just ask it," Seere said with strained voice.

She then looked in the direction of Logerrian from where she had come with her sister's body. "If you don't mind, will you please take care of my sister's body and Ry's? Give them the appropriate send off for devils?"

Belphegor frowned. "We'll do it. But what about Zade?" he asked carefully.

Vrae swallowed as a lump of agonizing pain clenched her chest. "I couldn't ask it for him since he . . . was obliterated." She bit back a wrenching sob as the image of her mate being blasted to oblivion played in the back of her mind again.

Orobas stepped forward. "I'm sorry for what happened. Don't worry. We will take care of them. You're sure the bastards didn't do anything to Ry?"

Vrathien nodded. "When I left with Yve, they, uh, they beheaded him," she said sadly.

At her words, Vassago uttered a curse. "Okay, we'll find him."

Smiling in relief, she gave them a nod of respect and gratitude. "Thank you. If we make it, we might see you again."

In reply to her nod, Belphegor gave her a fierce look. "We *will* see you all. It's too soon for you to be really dead."

She chuckled faintly and reached for the floating orb. Catching it with both hands, she glowed, and in one flash of light she vanished with it.

Sighing, Belphegor shook his head. "That boy, any idea where he got that spell?" He turned to Vassago.

Vassago shrugged as an answer and lifted his head to look at the dark sky. His domain was always dark no matter the time and eerily cold as well because of the defensive spell he put all around. From the outside, nobody would expect that the barren field was the domain of one of princes of Hell.

They'd see it as a common forest.

Orobas knelt beside Yverna's body. She looked so at ease in her death and could be mistaken for a devil that was asleep had it not been for the two gaping holes in her chest.

"I hope Vrae doesn't have to wander too long." The other princes raised their brows at him. "Yeah, I know it's unreasonable to even hope for it," Orobas added helplessly.

Belphegor knelt by the side of Yverna's body and without more words, he slipped his muscular arms beneath her and carried her away.

"Hey, where are you going?" Vassago grabbed the North Prince's shoulder.

Belphegor paused and glanced at Vassago. "I wanna send them both from around my domain," he replied in a voice devoid of emotions while keeping his stoic face.

Seere and Orobas abruptly faced the North Prince, but he didn't say anything further.

When Vassago lifted his hand, he averted his gaze from the prince to the she-devil's empty face in his arms.

He then sauntered away from the other princes and spread his wings. As he began to ascend, the other three followed him into the air. They flew straight to Logerrian waterfall where the battle that ended the lives of their four young companions had taken place moments earlier.

Not that it was the last war. More massive explosions could be heard and seen far away to the south. Ignoring the commotion, the princes headed towards the waterfall.

The second they arrived, they stopped in their tracks because there was something extremely wrong here.

Lucifer was no longer in sight, and they couldn't sense him,

Rolling his eyes in disgust, Belphegor scanned the forest. Moments later, he found what he sought.

Ezryan's dead body. His head had fallen not far from it.

"There he is." Belphegor indicated the body with a jerk of his chin. "At least they didn't do anything revolting to his body," he said.

Taking Ezryan's head, Vassago brought it to the former Hieldhar's body. He fixed the head on the shoulders and used his powers to pull them together. A few seconds later he lifted his hand, and Ezryan's head was back in place. There was no trace on his neck that suggested his head had been separated from his shoulders minutes before.

Vassago then carried him. They immediately left the waterfall and headed towards Belphegor's domain. Once they were there, someone whom they least expected, appeared.

Ezryan's brother, Xaemorkahn.

"Now, how in the hell could you get here?" Orobas asked rather sharply.

The king ignored his question and walked gracefully up to Vassago. "So, he *is* dead," he said. His deep voice was filled with anguish. His gaze then fell on the female devil in Belphegor's arms. "She undoubtedly fell with him, huh?"

Laying Yverna's body on the ground, Belphegor lowered his gaze. "You haven't answered his question."

Letting out a tired breath, the king stared down at his brother. "I just followed your energy to get to you, okay?" He frowned deeply with an uneasy look on his handsome face. "Ry gave me something and told me to retrieve the rest of it after his death. He said that . . ." His voice faltered.

"What? He said what?" Seere prompted.

Biting his lip, Xaemorkahn clenched his fist. "He said that . . . I'd know when he died and where he would be."

They fell silent, and the king knelt beside his brother's dead body and chanted a spell.

Soon after he'd done so, the same pale-blue orb appeared. Taking it into his grasp, he looked at the princes. "I'll take it with me. And my brother asked me to tell you he was grateful, as I am, that you were willing to fight alongside me without us killing each other."

Belphegor waved his hand as if to dismiss the king's words. The king chuckled in amusement, before he turned stoic once more. "I'll take care of this. I'll find you when the time's right for me to bring Ry's soul back here."

Inclining his head in farewell, which was answered by the princes, the king vanished back to his own realm.

Moments later, the four of them burned both bodies with their devil's fire and mourned silently for their young companions as the bodies were slowly reduced to ashes and dust.

Once the bodies were no more, they quietly withdrew into their domain, as they waited in the shadows for the prophecy to be fulfilled.

About the Author

Aya Lancaster is a college student who's currently going through her final year. Ever since senior high school, she's been fascinated by novels from overseas. Before she realized it, she had read many genres, especially conspiracy, supernatural, and thriller.

It was from reading so many books that she found a certain excitement in writing. At first she was doubtful, but inspired by the experience of a lot of authors, she began developing the idea for her first book, an idea that was almost forgotten, which she had when she was still on eighth grade.

This trilogy is her first work as a writer. She lives a quiet life with her family in Jakarta, which will turn one-eighty degrees the moment she meets her friends.

CPSIA information can be obtained at www.ICGtesting.com
Printed in the USA
LVOW110151160512

281893LV00001B/1/P